Praise for
Matthew Woodring Stover's
novel, *Heroes Die*

"*Day of the Jackal* meets *Lord of the Rings* . . . A marvelous conspiracy thriller of worlds within worlds, where no one is necessarily who or what they seem."
—SIMON R. GREEN
Author of the Deathstalker series

"Acid-etched, gut-ripping action, with that rare balance of depth and startling insight."
—JANNY WURTS
Author of the Wars of Light and Shadow series

"A grab-you-by-the-throat, drag-you-through-the-adventure, gritty fantasy. I loved it!"
—DENNIS L. MCKIERNAN
Author of the Hèl's Crucible duology

"Terrific entertainment . . . The wildest sword and sorcery adventuring since Robert E. Howard's mighty Cimmerian laid down his sword. Not to be missed!"
—CHRISTOPHER ROWLEY
Author of the Bazil Broketail series

"Nonstop action . . . If you like a heroic action adventure . . . you have to read this book. It is awesome!"
—*Explorations*

Also by Matthew Stover:

HEROES DIE

Books published by The Ballantine Publishing Group
are available at quantity discounts on bulk purchases
for premium, educational, fund-raising, and special
sales use. For details, please call 1-800-733-3000.

BLADE OF TYSHALLE

Matthew Stover

A Del Rey® Book
THE BALLANTINE PUBLISHING GROUP • NEW YORK

A Del Rey® Book
Published by The Ballantine Publishing Group
Copyright © 2001 by Matthew Woodring Stover

All rights reserved under International and Pan-American Copyright Conventions. Published in the United States by The Ballantine Publishing Group, a division of Random House, Inc., New York, and simultaneously in Canada by Random House of Canada Limited, Toronto.

Del Rey is a registered trademark and the Del Rey colophon is a trademark of Random House, Inc.

www.delreydigital.com

ISBN 0-345-42143-4

Manufactured in the United States of America

First Trade Edition: April 2001
First Mass Market Edition: April 2002

OPM   10   9   8   7   6   5   4   3   2   1

This book is dedicated to the memories of some of the best friends any man could ask for. I only wish you could have lived to read it.

For Evangeline, Aleister, and Friedrich;
for Lev, John, Clive, and Terence;
for Roger and Fritz and both Bobs (Robert A. and Robert E.).

Even today, some still listen.

But we have soothed ourselves into imagining sudden change as something that happens outside the normal order of things. An accident, like a car crash. Or beyond our control, like a fatal illness. We do not conceive of sudden, irrational change as built into the very fabric of existence. Yet it is. And chaos theory teaches us . . . that straight linearity, which we have come to take for granted in everything from physics to fiction, simply does not exist. . . .

Life is actually a series of encounters in which one event may change those that follow in a wholly unpredictable, even devastating way. . . .

That's a deep truth about the structure of our universe. But, for some reason, we insist on behaving as if it were not true.

—"Ian Malcom"
Michael Crichton
Jurassic Park

Do what thou wilt shall be the whole of the Law.

—Aleister Crowley
The Book of the Law

A TALE IS told of twin boys born to different mothers.

One is dark by nature, the other light. One is rich, the other poor. One is harsh, the other gentle. One is forever youthful, the other old before his time.

One is mortal.

They share no bond of blood or sympathy, but they are twins nonetheless.

They each live without ever knowing that they are brothers.

They each die fighting the blind god.

ZERO

THE ONLY WAY I can explain why you'll never see me again is to tell you about Hari.

This is how I visualize the conversation that ended up pushing me into Hari Michaelson's life. I wasn't there—I don't know the details—but the images in my head are vivid as a slap on the mouth; to be a good thaumaturge, your imagination must be powerful and detailed—and I'm the best the Conservatory has ever produced.

This is how I see it:

"It's all here in the telemetry," says Administrator Wilson Chandra, Chairman of the Studio Conservatory. He wipes the sweat from his palms on the hem of his Costanti chlamys and blinks through a stinging cloud of cigar smoke. He licks his lips—they're thick, and always dry—as he looks down at the rows of trainee magicians who meditate with furious concentration below. I'm not in that class, by the way; these are beginners.

Chandra goes on: "He's doing very well on the academics, you know, he has a fine grasp of Westerling and is coming along very well in First Continent cultural mores, but as you can see, he can barely maintain alpha, let alone moving to the beta consciousness required for effective spellcasting, and we, we're working only with Distraction Level Two, approximately what he will find in, say, a private room in a metropolitan inn, and under these circumstances I simply don't believe—"

"Shut up, will you?" says the other man on the techdeck. "Christ, you make me tired."

"I, ahm . . ." Administrator Chandra runs a hand through his thinning hair, sweat-slick despite the climate control. "Yes, Businessman."

Businessman Marc Vilo, the Patron of the student in question, rolls the thick stinking cigar around his mouth as he stumps forward to get a better view through the glass panel.

Businessman Vilo is a short, skinny, bowlegged man with the manners of a dockhand and the jittery energy of a fighting cock. I've seen him in the netfeatures plenty of times; he's an unimpressive figure in his conservative jumpsuit and cloak, until you remember that he'd been born into a Tradesman family; he'd taken over the family business, a three-truck transport firm, and had built it into the Business powerhouse Vilo Intercontinental. Still only in his mid-forties, he had purchased his family's contract from their Business Patron, bought his way into the Business caste, and was now one of the wealthiest men—outside the Leisure Families—in the Western Hemisphere. Netfeatures call him the Happy Billionaire.

This is why Administrator Chandra is here right now; normally the Administrator has much more important duties than entertaining visiting Patrons. But Vilo's protégé—the very first he has ever sponsored into the Conservatory—is failing miserably and is about to wash out, and the Administrator wants to soothe the sting, and perhaps retain a certain degree of goodwill, in hopes that Vilo will sponsor further students in the future. This is a business he's running here, after all. Sponsoring an Actor can be extremely lucrative, if the Actor becomes successful—just ask my father. The Administrator wants to make Vilo see that this is only a single failed investment, and is no reason to believe that further investments of this nature will also fail. "There is also, ehm, a, well, a certain history of disciplinary problems—"

"Thought I told you to shut up." Vilo continues to stare down at his protégé, a slightly built boy named Hari Michaelson, nineteen years old, a Laborer from San Francisco.

The boy kneels on his meter-square mat of scuffed plastic, hands curled in Three Finger technique. Of the thirty students in the room, only he has his eyes closed. The monitors on his temples that feed data into the Conservatory computer tell the whole story: Despite the slow three-per-minute rhythm of his breath, his heart rate has surged over eighty, his adrenal production is 78 percent over optimal, and his EEG spikes like broken glass.

Vilo pulls the butt from his mouth. "Why in hell did you put him in the magick program anyway?"

"Businessman, we went over this when he was admitted. His memory and spatial-visualization test out in the low genius range. There is no question that he has the intellectual equipment to be a fine adept. However, he is emotionally unstable, prone to irrational rages, and is, ah, uncontrollably aggressive. There is a history of mental illness in his family, you know; his father was downcasted from Professional due to a succession of breakdowns."

"Yeah?" Vilo said. "So what? I *know* this kid; he worked for me two years. Sure, he's got a temper. Who doesn't? He's smart, and he's tough as my goddamn boot heel." He smiles, showing his teeth, predatory. "Kind of like me at his age."

"You understand, Businessman, that we take these steps only to protect you from the expense of sponsoring a boy who will almost certainly perish on his first transfer."

"So? That's his problem, not mine. The money is—" He spits a shred of tobacco onto the carpet. "—not an issue."

"He will simply never become an effective spellcaster. I'm sorry, but there are certain restrictions imposed by the Studio. The examinations administered by the Graduation Board are very stringent."

Chandra makes a gesture as though to take the Businessman's arm and lead him away. "Perhaps I can show you our newest pilot program, the priesthood school. This particular spellcasting variant has the advantage that the practitioner need enter the casting trance only under very controlled conditions—that is, under the guise of religious ritual—"

"Cut the crap." Vilo stuffs his cigar back into his mouth. "I got a shitload of money in that kid out there. A *shitload*. I don't give a rat's ass about the Studio's restrictions, or the goddamn examinations. That kid is going to graduate from this toilet, and then he's going to Overworld."

"I'm afraid that's simply impossible—"

"You gonna make a liar out of me?" Vilo's eyes seem to retreat into his face, becoming small and dangerous. He hammers the next word. *"Administrator?"*

"Please, Businessman, you, you must understand, he's been in the magick program fourteen months; we must either, either, ah, graduate him or wash him out in only ten more, and his, and his *progress*—"

Vilo goes back to the window; he's more interested in the cherry on the end of his cigar than in Chandra's stammer. "Your parents live in, what, Chicago, right? That nice old frame house on Fullerton, west of Clark."

Chandra stands very still. Ice water trickles down his spine. "Yes, Businessman . . ."

"You gotta understand that I don't make bad investments. You follow? Hari gets his shot."

"Businessman, I—" Chandra says desperately, then with a massive exercise of will steadies his voice. "There are other options that can be explored . . ."

"I'm listening."

"Please, Businessman, perhaps I was too hasty in suggesting that Michaelson cannot succeed. He is, after all, in Battle Magick, which is the most difficult school, but it is the one place where his, erm, aggressive nature may work to his advantage. My idea—with your permission—is to provide him with a tutor."

"He doesn't have tutors? What the hell am I *paying* for?"

"Tutors, yes, of course, staff tutors. Michaelson doesn't respond well to directed instruction. He, ah—" Chandra decides not to tell him of the brutal beating Michaelson had inflicted on Instructor Pullman. I knew about it, so did most of the students at the Conservatory; it was the best gossip we'd had all year. Chandra believes that issue is settled; and, really, the man had gotten no worse than he deserved. In Chandra's mind, to make advances on a boy with Michaelson's psychosexual dysfunctions had been irresponsible to the point of criminality. Speaking for the students—well, Pullman's a nasty little groper; a lot of us wished we'd done what Michaelson did.

"I'm thinking more in terms of another student, someone who'd have no authority over him, who could, well—he doesn't respond well to authority figures, as you might know—someone who could, well, be his *friend*."

"What, he doesn't have friends enough already?"

"Businessman," Chandra says with a nervous laugh, "he doesn't have any friends at all."

And that's when he decided to send for me.

2

OVERWORLD.

When the Winston Transfer first opened the gate from Earth to Overworld, the Studio had been lurking in the background, waiting to step through. Overworld is a land of dragons and demons, of hippogryphs and mermaids, of hedge wizards and thieves, master enchanters and noble knights.

It is a billion dreams come true.

I burn for it. I lust for Overworld the way a martyr dreams of the arms of God.

My father took me to first-hand one of Raymond Story's early Adventures when I was seven years old, and when Story spoke a Word of Power and the Hammer of Dal'kannith smote an evil ogre and splashed the brains from its leering ten-gallon head, I felt the soaring echo of his joy of battle and the surge of pulling magick and well, you know: there really aren't any words.

For my tenth birthday, my father bought me the cube of Story's epic three-day battle with the mad dragon Sha-Rikkintaer. The very first of the thousand or so times I played it, I knew.

I had to do it. I had to be there.

Ten years intervening have only sharpened my lust.

Everything in my life was perfect. I was at the top of my class, had the highest psych rating the Conservatory had ever measured, my elving surgeries were going perfectly, and I was absolutely on top of the world until Chandra called me into his office and took it all away.

When I went in there and took his offered seat, I had no idea of the preceding imaginary conversation. I expected another stroke-up over my spectacular progress, and so it came as a rude shock to be told that I was to be this antisocial, ill-tempered Laborer's new tutor.

I played it off, though; we of Business are trained to take bad news coolly. "Sorry, Administrator," I told him, tapping my face guard. "I don't think I'll have time. I graduate in four months, and I have six more surgeries."

Chandra had flinched visibly when I called him *Administrator*; he hates to be reminded that I'm upcaste of him. I slip the word in from time to time, when he needs to be reminded of his manners.

But now he shook his head. "You don't understand, Kris. This is not a request. This boy needs a tutor. He needs the *best* tutor, and you are the top magick student. You will take him in hand, and you will teach him what he needs to know to pass the Battle Magick exams. Period."

"I'm not interested, *Administrator*." What does it take to get through to this lump of meat? "Ask someone else."

He rose, and came around the corner of his big rosewood desk. He leaned on it and clasped his hands together. "The independence of the Graduation Board is sacrosanct. I cannot influence them to pass an unqualified student, but I can certainly prevent any student from ever coming before them, if I choose. Without my signature, they'll never see you."

He stared at me as though trying to see the inside of my skull—and there was something in his eyes, something dark and frightening: an eerily impersonal hunger that made my stomach knot.

It looked *familiar*, somehow; but I couldn't guess where I'd seen it before.

"Do you understand, now?" he said. "If Michaelson doesn't graduate, neither do you."

The universe tilted beneath me, and I clutched at the arms of my chair to keep from falling off the Earth and tumbling into interstellar space.

Not *graduate*? Never go to Overworld? Far more than a sentence of death—this was the whisper of the headsman's axe. The room darkened around me; when I could speak again, my first instinct was to bluster. "You can't do that! If you even think about washing me out, my father—"

"Would thank me, and you know it."

That stopped me short; I did know it. "But *me*? Come on, Ad—Chairman. I mean—Jesus, I was supposed to graduate last term, but I stuck it out for my elving—if you wash me out, I'll be stuck with this face for the rest of my life! It's one thing, if I'm an Actor, but—"

Chandra's head wobbled on his scrawny neck; he looked very old and weak, but still capable of a dangerous vindictiveness, like a senile king. "This Michaelson boy," he said. "His Patron is Marc Vilo."

"The gangster?" I asked, startled. My father talked about him once in a while, about how he disgraces our entire caste.

"He was, erm, here today. He's—he's very interested to see Michaelson go on. *Very* interested. He, ah, he—" Chandra looked away, and coughed to cover the crack in his voice. "—he asked about my *family*."

"Uh." I understood now. He'd decided to handle his problem by making it my problem. Foolish—my father would have laughed at him and made some rude comment about the whole of the Administration caste, with its penchant for asscovering and buckpassing.

I couldn't laugh. I remembered overhearing a couple of my father's Laborers once, when one of them supported the other as he staggered out from a correction box: "I guess the best you can hope for is not to be noticed."

I'd been noticed; and the simple fact that he was downcaste from me meant nothing at all. This weak buckpassing bitshuffler held the entire rest of my life in his palsied hands, and all I could do was grin and take it like a Businessman.

"All right, Chairman," I said with as much of a front of confidence as I could muster. "Let me look at his file."

3

I LEANED AGAINST the fluted door-column at the arch that separated the weight room from the main hall of the gym, looking in. I rubbed at the flexible white face guard that protected my most recent surgery; enough sensation leaked through the neural blocks that I had a permanent bone-deep itch. Someday, on Overworld, this surgery would enable me to impersonate one of the First Folk, the elflike aborigines of the northwest continent. They were the greatest magicians of Overworld; I might never match them—but I have a couple talents of my own.

Behind me, the hall was filled with Sorbathane-armored Combat students thwacking each other with swords of weighted rattan.

Michaelson stood out in the crowded weight room. Magick students avoid the weights until the late afternoon, when the Combat neanderthals would be in class or outside on the tourney fields. Michaelson was the only guy in the room under a hundred kilos; even the few women present each had at least ten or eleven kilos on him. He lay on his back under the bench press bar, face contorted with strain.

One of the neanderthals elbowed another in the ribs as I threaded my way across the room. "Lookie." The neanderthal got up and blocked my path, rippling his hypertrophied pectorals. He topped my height by maybe a third of a meter. "What's doing, magick girl? Aren't you supposed to be on your knees somewhere?"

I grinned behind my mask as I sidestepped him. "Nah, you just wish I was a girl. Give you a choice of three holes, 'stead of the two your pal's stuck with." I moved on past while the frowning Combat student tried to figure out what kind of an insult that worked out to be.

Michaelson stared blindly at the ceiling while he labored under the bar, veins standing out on his forehead. I was kind of curious about him, I admit; reading his file, I'd discovered that his father was Duncan Michaelson the anthropologist, the same Duncan Michaelson whose book on Westerling was the Conservatory's standard text on the language.

Duncan Michaelson had already been a big part of my life; I'd read his *Tales of the First Folk*—an oral history of the northwest primals—dozens of times. *Tales of the First Folk* had been what drew me toward the elves in the first place.

I couldn't mention that to Hari, though; I'd also read in his file that he never spoke about his father.

Hari was almost a decimeter taller than I am, but wouldn't outweigh me by much. Dark eyes and swarthy skin, black hair, muscles like knotted rope. He grunted as he powered the bench press bar up through another stroke; his lips twisted into a snarl fringed by a ragged growth of black beard.

I glanced at the bench press readout: 80 keys. I grunted out loud, impressed in spite of myself; I knew from his file that Michaelson weighed in around sixty-five. Then I looked at the repcounter. As Michaelson slowly straightened his arms, the counter clicked over to 15.

Chandra had said Michaelson spent a lot of time in the gym; I wondered if even the Chairman knew just how much.

We'd gone over a hasty plan to get Michaelson's confidence; based on his psych eval, we'd decided that honesty wasn't the best policy. A direct offer of tutoring would meet with, at best, sullen rejection; the plan involved a gradual building of a relationship—becoming friends first, maybe occasional advice on meditative strategies for Michaelson's upcoming Virtual Acting seminar, then a casual offer to help him with his studies. No pressure.

But now, as I watched Michaelson pump the repcounter up toward 20, each slowing stroke pushing four or five explosive, gasping breaths through his clenched teeth, I flashed on him.

For that bare, eyeflick instant, I was Hari Michaelson, straining under the bar. I became a nineteen-year-old Laborer, with a visceral memory of countless upcaste spurns and the helpless humiliation of knowing that any payback was forever beyond my reach—with a nuclear kiln of permanent rage lodged behind my breastbone, fueled by the searing knowledge that I was failing.

This is one of my talents, the flashing. It's not an ESP thing, more like that powerful and detailed imagination working overtime, but it serves me well enough. In that instant, I threw out Chandra's plan. I had a better one.

As Hari's arms hit their limit, half extended and trembling, his face gone purple and his eyes barely open, I stepped beside him, put both hands on the bar, and lifted it with him. It didn't take much strength; I probably could have done it with a finger, lifting only the kilo or two that was beyond Hari's capacity. When his arms reached their full extension, Hari snarled, "End." The bar froze in place.

I said, smiling, "Shouldn't press without a spotter, y'know."

Michaelson sat up slowly. I felt his stare like heat from an open fire. "Nobody asked your opinion, asswipe," he said evenly. "Or your help."

"If I'd waited for you to ask," I said through a smile, "I'd have been standing here till the next Ice Age."

"Yeah, funny." He squinted at my mask. "What're you supposed to be, Boris Karloff?"

"Boris who? My name's Kris—"

"Hansen. Yeah, I know. Everybody in Shitschool knows who you are, we hear about you all day long. What do you want?"

Shitschool: the derisive nickname Combat students give to the College of Battle Magick, from its initials. "A couple minutes of your time," I said with a shrug. "I want to ask for your help."

Michaelson turned away, toward the weight machine's control pad. "Piss off."

"Hey, ladies." One of the Combat neanderthals came up beside us. "You need some help with this machine? You want a *man* to show you how it's done?"

Michaelson didn't even turn his head. "Take a fucking hike, Ballinger."

"Uh-huh, right. Excuse me, ma'am." He casually elbowed Michaelson off the bench and lay down under the bar. Michaelson got up slowly and stood with his back to the machine, very still, except for a muscle that jumped at the corner of his jaw.

The neanderthal—Ballinger—gripped the bar and said, "Weight up. Two-zero-zero. Begin." When the readout had scaled up to 200 kilograms he started pumping the bar smoothly up and down, and said, "See? That's your problem, not enough weight."

"Come on, Hari, let's get out of here," I said. "I really want to talk with you."

"You got nothing to say that I need to hear."

I took a deep breath, held it, then took the plunge. "Typical Labor attitude," I sneered. For an instant I felt like my father.

Michaelson turned like he was mounted on a millstone. "What?"

"You downcasters are all alike. 'Fuck off, Jack. It's not my job.' It's born into you. That's why you Labor scum never get out of the ghetto."

Michaelson took one deliberate step toward me. His eyes burned. "You are just *begging* me to kick your fucking ass."

"Yes, in fact, I am," I told him. "That's exactly right."

He blinked. "Come again?"

"Which part don't you understand?"

He stared at me while his mouth stretched into a slow predatory grin: all teeth and no humor. "I'm into it."

"Fine, then. Let's get a hand-to-hand room."

"Yeah, sure. One thing first, though."

He turned back to the weight machine, where Ballinger's heavy arms, trembling now, forced the bar up through the fourteenth rep. When they reached full extension, Michaelson leaned over him and rapped the insides of both elbows with the edges of his hands. Ballinger's arms gave way, and the bar slammed down into his chest. Eyes bulging, Ballinger tried to gasp *"End! End!"* but he hadn't enough breath for the machine to register his voice.

Michaelson patted his cheek and said, "Shouldn't press without a spotter, y'know." He grinned at me. "After you, ma'am."

I grinned back. "Why, thank you, miss."

The line was good, but I felt a chill. I began to comprehend how dangerous Hari Michaelson might be, and I knew I'd better be bloody damn careful.

4

THE HAND-TO-HAND ROOMS are a level higher and directly over the gym. They vary in size and conformation, but they all have floors and walls of three-centimeter Sorbathane to minimize impact injuries. On one wall the Sorbathane's transparent and laid over a mirror, so you can watch yourself shadowbox or whatever.

Michaelson and I met in one. I was already in the required half-armor: a centimeter of Sorbathane protecting elbows, knees, vitals, head, and neck. Michaelson wore that sweaty cotton shirt and baggy black pants, and nothing else.

"You're not wearing armor," I said.

He sneered at me. "Brilliant, Businessboy. What was your first clue?"

To hold on to my temper, I conjured a vivid image of the night sky of Overworld, a dragon silhouetted against the full moon. If I didn't make this work, that mental image was the closest I'd ever get to seeing it.

I said, "Hey, c'mon, armor's required—" but before I could finish the thought he hit me from twelve directions at once.

It was like being caught in a threshing machine—he slammed his knees into my unprotected thighs, his fists and elbows against my ribs, and his forehead into the pit of my stomach and before I really knew what was happening he had my face guard mashed into the floor and my arms and legs pinned somehow and my whole body *hurt*.

"Tell me again about Labor scum, will you?" His voice in my ear sounded flat and metallic, and I suddenly, stunningly, arrived at the realization that *I could die here*.

If he wanted to, he could kill me. Easily.

And get away with it: an unfortunate training accident, and he goes right on with his life, while mine is snuffed in an instant.

And he sounded like he wanted to.

It's a funny feeling: your bowels turn to water and all the strength goes out of your arms and legs, tears well up in your eyes—it's a baby thing, I guess, a reflex to appear weak and helpless in hopes that you can trigger an answering parental reflex. But somehow I didn't think Michaelson had that particular reflex.

I sneered into the floor. "Aaah, lucky punch."

An instant of stunned silence; then he had to let me up because he was laughing too hard to hold me. I managed a little chuckle, too, as I rolled over, sat up, and tried to make sure all my joints still worked.

"Jesus. I didn't think anyone could do that; not so easily, anyway. You know I'm near the top of my class in hand-to-hand?"

Michaelson gave a derisive snort. "Yeah. You're near the top of your class in everything. Doesn't mean you know shit about it."

"I know, Hari. That's why I came looking for you."

He sat up and laced his fingers around his knees. "I'm listening," he said, but in his eyes swam naked suspicion, the permanent shifty *what do you want from me?* of the downcaster.

"I hear you're barely passing hand-to-hand," I said. "And I hear that the only reason you're not failing is that you—like you Labor guys say—can whip shit on every student in the class. I go to Overworld in four months, and I think there's some things you can teach me that I'm not going to learn from Tallman."

"Tallman's a moron," Michaelson said. "He's more interested in making you do it *his way* than in teaching you something that'll keep you alive."

"That's the part I want to learn. That part about staying alive."

"What's in it for me?"

I shrugged. "The chance to beat the snot out of a Business brat every day for four months."

He measured me with his eyes, coldly, for a long time. I fought the urge to fidget. Finally he uncoiled himself, rising with a smooth motion into a natural stance. "Get up."

"Aren't you going to get armor?"

"You think I need it?"

I sighed. "Never mind." I got up and matched his stance. I knew he wasn't going to give me the *Ready . . . Fight!* of classroom sparring, so I was ready when his gaze flickered down to my groin. I dropped my hands to crossblock the kick and he cracked a left hook into my ear that made my head ring.

"Lesson one. That's an *eye-fake*, Hansen. Every time I see you looking at my eyes, you're gonna get a whack."

I shook the ringing out of my ears and got my hands back up. Michaelson tapped himself on the sternum.

"Look here. Always look here. You can see my whole body— the eyes lie, Hansen, but the chest is always honest. And you don't block a groin-kick with your hands, you take it on the thigh. Every time you drop your hands, you're gonna get a whack. You understand?"

"Yes, I'm starting to—"

He whacked me with a right uppercut below the heart that left me gasping.

"Lesson two. Best time to hit someone is when he's off guard. Best time to catch someone off guard is when he's talking. When you talk, you're thinking about what to say next, not—"

I hit him, a good stiff jab right in the teeth. My knuckles stung like a bastard. He took a couple steps back and touched his lips; his hand came away painted crimson, and he grinned at me.

"Y'know," he said, "there's just the faintest chance I could start to like you."

This is going to work, I thought. *I'm on my way to Overworld.*

5

A WEEK LATER, I was sitting in Chandra's office, so much of my body mottled with green and yellow and purple healing bruises that I looked like somebody'd spiked my shower with a carton of expired skin dye.

"I want permission to use the VA suite."

The Chairman looked at me like I was some new species of cockroach. "Vilo screened this morning. He would like to know what progress Michaelson is making. I lied to him. I said everything is going well."

"Ten days from now," I said patiently, "Hari starts Virtual Acting 102. You want him to pass, don't you? I'd think you'd be a little cooperative, here."

"The clock is running on you, Hansen. I do not think that allowing your student to beat you senseless every day is teaching him very much."

"*Allowing?* Administrator, you've never seen him fight."

"His College is Battle Magick, as is yours. Have you even *begun* work on his visualization deficiencies? Have you begun work on his trancing? You are accomplishing *nothing.*"

"Administrator, I've been meeting with him for at least an hour or two every day—"

"And doing nothing of value to either of you. Did you think I was not serious, when I told you what was at stake?"

My temper flared. "Then find somebody else! I didn't ask for this job, you forced me into it! *I'm doing the bloody best I can!*" My face burned. A true Businessman never loses his temper in front of a downcaster. My father would never have done it. Maybe after spending so much time with Hari, his attitudes had begun to color mine.

"No, no." Chandra shook his head. "You're the top student in Battle Magick. If I have less than the best, Vilo will think I *want* Michaelson to fail."

He squinted at me, and I flashed on him.

I'm Administrator Wilson Chandra; I've spent my entire sixty-odd years of life in service, the last fifteen as Chairman of the Studio Conservatory—a position of great responsibility but very little power. I've had to kiss the crack of every Leisureman,

Investor, and Businessman to ever walk through the front doors; I've had to coddle their whining protégés, handjob the Studio's Board of Governors, soothe the swollen egos of the emotionally crippled ex-Actors who make up the faculty, and somehow in the midst of all this turn out Actors who will not only survive on Overworld but provide the Studio with the income that justifies my existence.

I've done a damned good job of it for a decade and a half, and what do I get? A murderous little gangster telling me who I can and can't graduate, telling me *how to do my job*, and a snotty Business brat whining about having to do something his pampered little butt wasn't *in the mood* for.

I leaned back in my chair, blinking behind the face guard. I understood now. He *did* want Hari to fail: because it would sting Vilo. He wanted to fail *me*, because I was born into Business. It would be a double slap at upcasters, one he thought he could get away with. Petty and vindictive, it was exactly the kind of underhanded knife his caste had always pointed at those above it. Whatever threat Vilo might have made against his family, he didn't take too seriously, and Hari was only a pawn, a counter in his game.

I, too, was no more than a pawn. His malice wasn't personal at all. I remembered that glimpse I'd gotten of eerie, impersonal hunger behind his eyes: he didn't care about me one way or the other. I just had the bad luck to be conveniently placed for his little psychodrama of undercaste revenge.

Outside the Conservatory, things would be different. On the outside, I was Business, and he only Administration. If he so much as sniffed at me I could denounce him to the Social Police for caste violation—but none of that mattered, here. He had his grip upon me, and I could do nothing to loosen his fingers.

I started to understand from where Hari got his rage.

For a moment, I felt Hari behind me, at my shoulder, whispering in my ear the precise angle for the edge of my hand to slice at his throat and shatter his larynx; I shook my head to drive it away, and took a deep breath.

"I want permission to use the VA units," I said again.

"This, I think is too much. Unsupervised use of the VA suite is dangerous, and Instructor Hammet—"

"Y'know," I said casually, fighting down a queasy twinge in

the pit of my stomach, "my father contracts with Vilo Intercontinental." This kind of sleazy Business-club innuendo left a bad taste in my mouth, but I desperately needed some leverage—and Hari's fetch still lurked at my shoulder, whispering violence.

Chandra looked blank, but he knew what I meant.

"You can authorize it. I'll take full responsibility," I said more insistently, because I understood the rules of this game. Chandra had to look like he was doing everything in his power to help me help Hari, so that he can shake his head and purse his lips in virtuous regret when he washes us out.

Reluctantly, he nodded. "All right." He drew a card out of a slot on his desk and swiveled his deskscreen toward me. "This is my duplicate access card. Thumbprint the screen here, and also thumbprint the liability release at the bottom of the screen. Any injury to either one of you is wholly your responsibility."

I nodded. "You won't regret this."

He didn't answer. He looked profoundly skeptical.

6

HARI FACED ME over the angled tip of his *bokken*—a wooden practice sword weighted to three-fourths the mass of an Overworld broadsword. He wore the required minimum armor now, as did I; *bokken* are real weapons, and can kill.

Without warning he lunged at me, forcing down my blade with his; when we came into the corps-a-corps an elbow I didn't even see coming slammed into my face guard and lifted me off my feet. I went down sprawling and my *bokken* spun away. He stood over me, wooden sword against my chest.

"You lose."

I slapped the blade away and climbed angrily to my feet. "Goddammit, Hari! You're not supposed to hit me in the face! You could rip my sutures, and you know it. And we're supposed to be working on *swords*."

He shrugged and tossed his *bokken* aside. "Supposed, supposed. You're supposed to be a pretty good swordsman, for a Shitschooler. Then why do you always lose?"

"Because you always cheat."

To a Businessman, those are fighting words. Hari only shook his head. "Listen, there's no such thing as cheating when you're fighting for your life. A very bright guy once said, 'Winning's not the most important thing. It's the *only* thing.' "

He came up to me, an oddly gentle expression on his face. "Kris, you're pretty good, y'know? You're fast and you learn quick and everything. You're better with a sword than I am. If I play by the rules you're gonna beat me. But on Overworld, you play by the rules, you're gonna get killed."

I thought, *Don't talk down to me, you low-rent Labor prick,* but I said, "Yeah, all right." I went after my *bokken*, picked it up. "Let's go again."

"You never quit, do you?" He looked kind of disgusted, and kind of uncomfortable. "I'll hand it to you, you sure can take a beating. But I don't think this is doing you much good. And I think I'm going to need my free period to work on trancing for a while."

That was almost good news—he'd finally recognized that he'd have to put in extra magickal practice if he wanted to graduate. But practice alone doesn't make perfect—you only get perfect through perfect practice. And I knew exactly what he needed. The only way either of us'd ever get to Overworld was if I could convince him to let me help him.

"You're quitting? Just when I'm starting to catch up?"

"Kris, man, I'm sorry. You don't have it, you know?" He started stripping off his armor, every *zzzip* of parting Velcro driving a needle into my chest.

"What do you mean, I don't have it? Who made *you* the expert? I took the same classes you did—I may not be as good at it, but I *know* as much about it as you do."

His penetrating black eyes took on an empty gaze, like he looked through my head to the wall at my back, and his mouth twisted into the kind of half smile you get when you suck on a sore tooth. "You'll never know as much about it. You're too old. And you don't love it."

"Don't give me that crap, Hari. I know—"

"You don't know shit."

I thought about what I'd read in his file, about his father's insanity and downcaste slide from Professional—a professor of social anthropology—to a Temp in San Francisco's Labor slums, and about the physical abuse he'd almost certainly suffered at his father's hands, and for a moment I thought I knew him. "Hey, so you had a rough childhood—"

He laughed in my face, an ugly grunting sound that had no humor in it. "I had a great childhood. Where do you think I learned how to fight? By the time I was eight, I knew: Every fight is a fight to the death. That's what makes it *fun*. You still don't get it, and you probably won't. You won't live long enough. And I'm sorry about that, because I kind of started to like you."

"All right, fine." I felt the singing surge of my temper as I stripped off my armor. "You've a fine taste for melodrama, Hari. It's a pity you're so full of shit."

"Eh?"

"This I'm-so-worldly-wise-and-you're-just-a-babe-in-the-woods act. Give me a break. I've seen it done better; my father has it down to a science."

"Yeah, whatever." He gathered up the pieces of his armor and bundled them together. "Been all right working out with you, Hansen, but now I gotta go."

"Why don't you try coming over to play in *my* yard?" I put a sneering edge of contempt in my voice that stopped him in his tracks. Maybe I didn't understand him completely, but I knew there was no way he'd take that tone from some upcaste boy of questionable masculinity. He looked at me over his shoulder.

"Your yard?"

My heart pounded, and I fought to keep the tremors out of my voice. "Yeah, tough guy." I flipped Chandra's access card between my fingers like a stage magician. "You're so damn tough in your specialty, come try *mine*."

"What's that you've got there?"

"It's an access card that'll get me into the Virtual Acting suite after hours."

A flame of interest kindled within his eyes. "Y'know, I start Virtual Acting a week from Friday . . ."

I shrugged. "Here's the difference between us. This Conservatory is loaded with Combat students who can stomp you without raising a sweat—"

"You think so?"

I ignored him and went on. "—but there is no one, *no one,* who can beat me in a VA suit. I'm the best there is. Check the records, if you want: I'm the best there has ever been. You dish it easily enough, Michaelson. Can you take it?"

Hari, I hoped, was that one kid in every neighborhood who'll take any dare, no matter how dangerous, the one who never runs from a fight, especially when the odds are against him. And I really thought that with my coaching, he might pace through Virtual Acting with high enough marks to push him over the top for graduation. I gave him a grin that lied: it said I didn't really care one way or the other. It was a grin that dared him to take me up on it, and it was a grin that dared him to back down. It was a grin that kept him from noticing I was holding my breath.

My future teetered on his answer.

He squinted at me like he could read my mind. Then he said, "After hours, huh? Like when would that be?"

"Say, 2200?"

"I'll be there."

He walked out of the hand-to-hand room without a backward glance, so he didn't see me fall to my knees and thank the gods for my deliverance.

7

I RUBBED MY stinging eyes as I threaded through the departing Combat students toward the VA suite. I'd been pushing a ragged edge of exhaustion; in addition to healing from my surgeries, recovering from the workouts I'd had with Hari, and constant worry over my future, I had course work of my own to complete. My extra term consisted of studies in the history and culture of the First Folk, not to mention their hideously elliptical, metaphoric, and inflected language. To make it worse, they had no written histories, since all First Folk have flawless eidetic memories and no Actor had successfully infiltrated their society; all I had to study from was second- and thirdhand accounts full of cultural references that I didn't understand and couldn't look up. Like the Actors who had gone before me, I'd be playing an elf who has—for one reason or another—chosen to move through the human world, but still it frustrated me until my head spun.

So I was in no mood for neanderthal crap. The departing Combat students laughed and joked among themselves as they lumbered along the hall like elephants, but less gracefully; I did my best to dodge between the swinging elbows of these two-meter behemoths.

They were all heading for their dorms, or for the venerable rathskeller—except for one, an enormous one with shoulders like wrecking balls. His back was to me, and he seemed to be shaking his fist at someone I couldn't see around his titanic chest. A sinking feeling in the pit of my stomach told me it was probably Hari.

The enmity between the Conservatory's Combat and Magick students is, I think, part of a long historical tradition, stretching all the way back to at least the nineteenth century's rivalry between student athletes and student scholars. They see us as effeminate bookworms, and we regard them as meatheaded apes who think with their pectorals. The situation here is a bit different, though. Most of what we study here prepares us, in one way or another, to kill people.

This colors your thinking—to put it mildly—and raises the stakes in any confrontation far beyond a little humiliation. From time to time, people get hurt—usually, the Magick students. We trainee adepts are mostly helpless without the differing laws of physics on the far side of the Winston Transfer. The Combat students train here in skills that work exactly the same on Earth as on Overworld.

And they're all *huge*.

So my heart stuttered a little as I approached. The crowd had thinned to emptiness, and the last of their voices faded down the hallway. Now I could hear what the neanderthal said.

It was that guy from the weight room, Ballinger. He hulked over Hari and jabbed at him with a finger the size of a sausage. "We'll see how funny you are, you little bastard. One of these days, when I catch you on the grounds. We'll see."

A strange, manic light shone in Hari's eyes that looked nothing like fear. "Fuck off, Ballinger. I'm busy. I'll kill you later."

Ballinger's ham-sized fist tangled itself in Hari's shirt and pinned him to the wall. "You want to say that *again*?"

I've seen this kind of confrontation before; a Magick student gets tired of the constant harassment and finally decides to fight back. This is the one where he gets hurt. Other times, I've hung back, to help the poor guy to the infirmary. Or if I saw the chance, sometimes I'd step between and try to defuse the situation. But this time—

I caught Hari's eye and tipped him a wink . . . then I got down on my hands and knees right behind Ballinger's ankles.

I don't know. Maybe it was from spending a week with Hari,

fighting with him, breathing his air. Maybe he had infected me, somehow; maybe I was coming down with a bad case of Michaelson.

Hari got the biggest, most honestly happy grin I'd ever seen on his face. "What's the best season for a vacation, Ballinger?"

"Huh?"

"Fall, I think. Have a nice trip."

He rapped the inside of Ballinger's elbow to bend his arm, then pushed off from the wall. Ballinger went down over my back with the slow majesty of a toppling redwood. He hit whack-on his upper spine with a thunderous crash that shook the floor, and he lay there, stunned. Before I could get up, Hari skipped around me and kicked him with shocking force in the side of his head; Ballinger groaned and tried to cover, rolling weakly into a fetal position.

I got to Hari and shoved him off balance as he clambered for a kick at the back of Ballinger's neck. "Stop it, Hari! You'll kill him!"

He batted me aside. "Fucking *right* I will—"

Professional Hammet—the Virtual Acting instructor—came limping out the door on his mechanized legs just then and saved Ballinger's life. All he did was put himself in Hari's way until Hari got control of himself again; not even Hari would risk the consequences of striking an instructor.

Hammet was a retired Actor, an ex-swordsman who was far too bitter and generally too crusty to tolerate any bullshit from anybody, especially not Ballinger when he tried to whine about Hari beating him up. Any Combat student who couldn't handle a couple Magick pussies wasn't worth his time. He wasn't interested in writing us up for fighting—too much goddamn trouble, filling out reports—but he also wasn't about to allow any crap to go on in the vicinity of his VA suite. He sent Ballinger one way and us the other. Ballinger stumbled off, muttering under his breath and giving us murderous looks over his shoulder. I, on the other hand, flashed Chandra's access card.

Hammet didn't like the idea of letting anyone into the VA suite unsupervised, but he couldn't argue with Chandra. A quick screencall to the Chairman confirmed that I hadn't stolen the card, and Hammet reluctantly let us in. We slipped inside, and I closed the door behind us.

"Jesus, Hari," I said, leaning against the door. "That was too close. That was too scary. You could have *killed* him! Hari, your temper—that was frightening, seeing you that angry."

Hari sighed; his shoulders slumped and he sank into a cross-legged tailor's seat on the floor. "What makes you think I was angry?"

"Well, Jesus—"

"You should have let me kill him. It was my best chance. Next time I won't be able to catch him alone."

I stared, openmouthed.

He shrugged at me. "This thing between Ballinger and me, it's been building for a while."

"You provoked it," I said breathlessly. "You *wanted* that fight."

"Kris, it's him or me. If it'd been me on that floor, we wouldn't be having this little talk. Or any talk."

"Drop the melodrama, Hari. So you've bumped chests with the guy once or twice, so what?"

He made a chopping motion with his hand. "You're Business, Kris. This is a Labor thing." He curled his fingers into a fist and stared at his knuckles like they were an unpaid invoice he couldn't cover. "Ballinger, he's from Philly's inner city. Him and me, we understand each other."

"I don't accept that. I can't accept that." But even as I said it, I found myself staring at his knuckles, too, which were mostly just knots of scar tissue like wads of old chewing gum.

"You don't have to. You're from a whole different world, Kris. That's why, once we get out of this toilet, I'm gonna be a famous Actor, and you're gonna be an elf-looking corpse."

He pushed himself to his feet. "I thought you were going to show me how you can whip shit on me in a VA suit."

8

I SPENT A few minutes in the claustrophobic cubicle with Hari, helping him calibrate the inducers. The feedback suit is simple enough; it's mostly mechanical—it squeezes and pokes and shakes you or whatever. But the induction helmet takes some getting used to.

This is based on the same technology that allows first-handers in the Studio Adventure Rooms to share an Actor's sense/experience in real time. Calibration is really a pretty simple process, a

matter of tuning the helmet to make a black dot coalesce on a
white field, then stretch to a line, and spread into a well-focused
version of the Studio logo; an analogous process takes white
noise down to a pure tone, et cetera. It's easier in the VA suite
than in the Studio, in fact—the inducers here don't have to deal
with scent, and the touch/pain data and kinesthesia is all handled
by the feedback suit.

This kind of calibration is easy once you've done it a few
times; it's practically second nature for anyone of a reasonable
level of birth, but Hari was a Laborer, and so of course he'd never
been inside a Studio and had never in his life adjusted an induction helmet. It made him edgy and snappish; he ended by slapping blindly at my hands—the induction helmets have eye
shields to prevent actual vision from interfering with the neural
stimulation—and telling me to get the fuck off him.

After I left his cubicle I went to the instructor's station, three
broad curving banks of keys stacked like a steam organ. Four
screens loomed over my head, where the VA computer would
display multiple points of view for the benefit of the rows of
empty seats in the Aud behind me.

I sank onto the bench, lowered my head onto arms folded
across the lowest bank of keys, and gave myself over entirely to
shaking.

I read once, somewhere, that the way you know you've grown
up is when your future death becomes a stone in your shoe: when
you feel it with every step. I kept seeing the corridor ceiling, as
though I had lain where Ballinger did; I couldn't stop thinking
about how easily, almost carelessly, Hari could have taken his
life. I saw myself on Overworld, walking along a city street: in
the vision a man stepped out of an alley and drove a knife into
my throat without a word—no demand for money, no snarl of
threat, no chance to prepare myself.

No chance.

I've heard that your heels kick, that you convulse and shit on
yourself when you die by violence. I *felt* it, again and again,
feeling my own heels kick helplessly, far deeper than imagination, feeling it with the astonishing vividness of my flashes.

When I first started working with Hari, I'd felt like a lion
tamer working with new cats. If I showed no fear, did nothing to
trigger those predatory reflexes, I'd be safe. I'd felt even moderately heroic, kind of proud of myself, because I thought that by

sheer force of character I could shove my life into shape. I could help Hari, I could beat Chandra, and I would sally forth into my vague and misty though certainly glorious Acting career.

But I sat there shaking because *there is no safety*.

Someday, you say the wrong thing to some random Hari Michaelson and an instant later you're on the floor choking out the last of your breath.

And it wasn't Hari that frightened me, even now; it was the world he lived in, the way I'd begun to see my life through his eyes. It was his intimate understanding of the fragility of my life, of his life, of anyone's—and that he just didn't care.

And he wasn't unique; he wasn't even rare. Our Labor undercastes spawn endless Hari Michaelsons. Now, I began to understand what Hari meant when he said I "don't have it."

But did it matter? Without Overworld, did I *want* to live?

I keyed the default setting, then entered my own cubicle and quickly dressed. I needed no calibration; the computer recognized my neural field as soon as I keyed my helmet, and it automatically loaded my file.

The Meadow took shape around me, gently rolling grassy waves that stretched to the horizon in all directions. The sky above was cloudless and startlingly blue, and the sun hung motionless. This is the most basic level, often used for "duels" and magickal practice of all sorts. I had spent a lot of hours in this meadow. The soft ground is forgiving to knees bent in meditation, and no cloud ever passes before the sun.

The generic-featured manikin that represented Hari stood about four meters away. He stepped toward me, then stopped and looked around; suddenly he knelt and ran his fingers through the grass. "Wow."

"Yes, I know. Impressive, huh?"

"Wild. Hard-core wild." His planar features showed no expression, but I could hear the grin in his voice. "You look kind of faggy."

I shrugged with a sigh. I'd programmed my file to bring up features that looked more or less the way I would after my surgeries were completed: thick, close-cropped hair of platinum, elegantly delicate bone structure around large golden eyes, extravagantly pointed ears like a lynx. Maybe I'd overdone it a little.

He came closer. "You know, I've never seen you without that white mask on. Is this what you look like?"

"I might, eventually," I told him. "I'm not sure. I won't find out for another ten weeks."

He nodded. Suddenly I wished I could see his expression. "All right," he said. "What now?"

I took a deep breath. I'd been working for a solid week to bring him to this point; now that we were here, I had butterflies, a twinge of . . . I don't know. Stage fright, maybe.

Maybe I was afraid he could beat me at this, too.

"No spells for this one," I said. "I'm going to take it easy on you. I should be able to whip you just fine using only Flow. Bring yourself to mindview. The computer will sense the pattern in your neural field and start to show you simulated Flow currents. You should also see my Shell."

His manikin closed its eyes, and its thumbs and first two fingers of each hand came together. I, of course, no longer needed the Three Finger technique to shift to mindview—breath control and a simple act of will tuned my consciousness to the proper level. It worried me that Hari, ten days from his VA seminar, still needed physical cues.

The worry vanished in mindview; while working magick, it's impossible to worry. The function of the advanced meditative techniques taught at the Conservatory is to focus the whole mind, even beyond the surface of consciousness, fully and without distraction upon the desired magickal effect. After two years of practice I could tune my mind like a surgical laser.

I've heard it said that every mage sees the Flow in terms of his or her own personal metaphor: as streams of light or a ghostly river, as long glowing strings coiling and uncoiling as they twist through the air, as floating globes of energy like ball lightning; I won't find out what mine will look like until I get to Overworld. The VA suite simulates Flow as shimmering lattices of force, over which scroll pulses of greater brightness or differing colors in the direction of the current.

His Shell looked pretty standard: an auralike netting of lines. It pulsed subtly in time with his heart and flickered like heat lightning around his hands and feet. I watched the Flow, waiting for him to start pulling.

His eyes opened, and he murmured reverentially, "I see it."

I let out a slow, whistling breath that I hadn't realized I'd been holding. "All right. I know this is new to you. I'll give you ten seconds to pull enough current to defend yourself."

He stretched out his hand, upward toward the thickest part of the current, and his Shell extended a slow-moving pseudopod that touched the shimmering net and opened itself to power. The Flow swirled toward him, its stream deepening as it whirlpooled energy into Hari's Shell. His gesture indicated a future problem: an adept who needs his hands to pull is easily disabled—but this could be ignored today.

I counted a slow ten to myself, then another five, while I watched Hari's Shell spin up into ever-higher levels, brighter and brighter and scaling up the spectrum toward violet. He'd feed energy into his Shell until he could hold no more, then lash out at me with undifferentiated power. This is the crudest and least dangerous form of magickal combat, rather like fencing with foam-rubber paddles, but it's a pretty good place to start.

I didn't trouble to pull; he couldn't hurt me.

I said, "Begin whenever you're—"

He fired on me, as I'd known he would. More than ready for his clumsy stream of power, my Shell not only deflected it but spun it swirling around my chest to slingshot back at him. What had approached me as a ragged head-sized stream returned as a focused javelin that punched through his Shell into the pit of his stomach and doubled him over.

"You'll have to do better than that." I hadn't even moved.

He tried again, and again, with similar results, but with each attempt he closed the gap between our virtual selves by a step or two. From this perspective, in the detached calm of mindview, his intentions were transparent. He intended to step outside the rules once again: these clumsy Flow bolts were only cover, to get him close enough to rush me.

I opened my Shell and pulled.

Hari had tapped into a Flow current, diverted some of it for his use; I *created* Flow currents—those shining lattices of force swirled into my Shell like the funnel of a tornado reaching down from a thunderhead. From where I stood to the visible horizon, all Flow drained toward me. My skin sang with power.

When Hari leaped at me, I let him have it.

Flow doesn't interact directly with the material world until it is patterned by the mind of a spellcaster; in its basic state, it only affects the Shell, altering the matrices of energy that surround material objects, especially living ones. About the worst you can do with raw Flow is give somebody a bad charley horse. I gave Hari seven of them.

His arms and legs, his chest and belly and back all cramped convulsively in midleap. He gave out a strangled croak and collapsed at my feet.

I stepped a prudent distance away from him before I let him up.

"That was too easy," I told him. "I'm a better fighter than you are a spellcaster. First off, if you ever want to be good at this, you'll have to improve your reach. Right now, your Shell stops at your hands and feet. But your Shell can have any size and shape that you wish, if you properly visualize it. Start by reaching for Flow without using your hands."

Hari's manikin still sat in the soft virtual grass, arms wrapping knees. He looked up at me, and I wished I could read an expression on those blank features. "This's been fun, Kris. I've been a good sport, and I let you whip me. Now I gotta go." He stood up and his hands went to his head, feeling for the cutoff.

"*Let* me?" I sneered. "Like you could have stopped me."

He sounded tired. "Yeah, you're right. I'm not good at this. But I will be."

"I'd say so. Shit, Hari, with my help, you could be great."

He stopped. His head swiveled toward me, and he neither moved nor spoke for a long time. I began to sweat inside the VA suit, wondering what was going on inside his head.

Finally, he spoke. "You think I'm a fucking idiot, don't you?"

My mouth worked, speechless. I forced out, "Hari, I—"

"You think that because you're Business, and I'm Labor, you can think rings around me, you can manipulate me and push me around and I'll never even know it."

Suddenly I became acutely glad that Hari's real, physical body was two doors away in the VA suite. "That's not true—"

"Drop it. I've bought too much of your shit already." His manikin stepped up to mine. "I don't much mind you thinking you're smarter than me. It might even be true."

It's unquestionably true, I thought.

"What bothers me," he went on, "is that you think you're smarter than me *because* you're upcaste. Like, if I had any brains at all, I would have known enough to be born into a better family."

"It's all about caste to you, isn't it?" I said, turning to the attack.

You couldn't deal with Hari by going defensive; it brought out his killer instinct like a guard dog that smells fear. "That's your answer to everything."

"I don't need answers," he said, rising and turning as if to leave. "I don't need to know why you've been all over me this past week or two; I don't care if it's some upcaste liberal befriend-the-Labor-punk project, or an anthro experiment, or you've developed a taste for my butthole. It doesn't matter. You're trying to con me, and I'm tired of it. Shit, mostly I'm tired of you thinking you're getting away with it."

"Y'know," I said slowly, "your street-butch act goes only so far."

"Hah?"

"Why are you still here? No matter how good your exit line is, it only works if you actually exit."

"Yeah," he said, reaching up for the cutoff switch on his sleeve, but I was ready for him: the instant I finished speaking I drew the slow, controlled breath and summoned mindview, and I gave him a cramp in that arm that would stun a horse.

He grunted.

"I'm not ready for you to go, yet," I said.

He dropped his hand and fixed his manikin's blank stare on me, and I could imagine all too well the homicidal gleam that would be in his black eyes right now. "Don't jump in this shitpool, Hansen. You don't swim well enough."

"Cut it out, will you? I'm not Ballinger—you don't have to intimidate me to prove you're a man."

"Don't pretend you understand."

"I'll tell you what I understand. I understand that *you are going to fail*. Do *you* understand that? You're going to fail. You will never see Overworld. You will never be an Actor. You will be some meaningless shit-shoveling Laborer for the rest of your life. You will always have to suckass the upcasters—and *everybody* is upcaste of you, Hari."

He shrugged and looked away; he knew, or at least suspected, that I was telling the truth, and he couldn't face it. "Why do you care? What's it to you if I live or die?"

"Nothing. I don't give a rat's ass what happens to you," I said. "What I care about is getting there myself. You get it? Yeah, you're a project. Chandra assigned me here. I've got the word of

Chandra himself that if you don't graduate, I'll never even get to take the examinations!"

"Then I guess you got a problem," he said, and flicked his cutoff switch before I could react.

His manikin vanished; I was left alone in the virtual world, staring at the vacancy where my hope had been.

9

I DON'T REMEMBER much of that night.

Lurking somewhere in the back of my brain are vague recollections of coming back to myself again and again out of daydreams of Overworld, sitting at my desk in my dorm room or wandering vaguely on the darkened campus lawns, through tangled native scrub the color of corpse flesh in the moonlight.

I couldn't get a handle on what had happened, not really; whenever I wasn't actively reminding myself that my life was over, I stopped believing it. I couldn't make myself understand that I'd really blown it this time, that some fundamental incapacity in my nature had thrown a wall into my path and I'd dashed out my brains against it.

It was as though I'd spent so many dreaming hours on visions of Overworld that my mind automatically turned to them, despite the cold fact that I'd never see those skies, never breathe that air, never come closer to the surge of true magick through my nerves than the pale tingle of a VA suit's tawdry replication.

And every time I did remember, each time I forced that knowledge back through the muddy strata of my rebellious mind, I had to wade through each level of muck again, one at a time: cursing Chandra, cursing Hari, cursing my father, the Conservatory, the Studio itself, until I finally slogged through to the truth.

It was my fault.

It's crushing, when you've made it through twenty years or so of your life, when you first find yourself against a wall you can't climb. Gifted in caste as well as genetics, I had wealth and status and looks and brains and athleticism, and I could always find a way to get what I wanted: grades, girls, friends, whatever. Until I found the one thing I couldn't live without.

It was a hell of a time for my first failure.

I'd made a fatal error with Hari, and the worst of it was, I still couldn't figure out what I should have done to make things work out any better. I mean, sure, thousands of plans and ideas poured into my mind that night, limitless and swirling, funneled from the stars by a quiet maelstrom of the chill Aegean air, all equally futile—I should have done *this*, I could have tried *that*, why didn't I think of *this*—until finally it was morning and I hadn't slept at all. I stopped by my room just long enough to dry-swallow a couple of caffeine pills, then I stumbled off to class, to spend the next few hours, the next few days, pretending that my life wasn't over.

At least I didn't have any trouble staying awake. I couldn't have slept if you hit me with a rock.

Sometime during that hopeless blur of days, Chandra called me into his office again. I don't remember what he said or what I replied; I think, at that point, all I could do was bluff. With my father's voice whispering advice and scorn alternately in my ear, I sneered at my executioner. *Show no weakness to the undercastes,* I thought. *Fuck him. If he had any brains at all, he'd have known enough to be born into a better family.* That phrase kept ringing inside my head, again and again.

On top of everything else, I had to live with the knowledge that Hari despised me.

In some strange and inexplicable way, that hurt nearly as much as the rest put together. His harsh judgment gnawed at me like a hungry dog worrying a bone. Maybe it was because I was accustomed to the affection of my peers and the respect of those below me; maybe I was appalled that a Labor thug would presume to judge me at all.

Maybe it was because I felt like he was more *real* than I was.

Something about his Labor life, his street life, gave him what looked to me like a mystic connection to some level of existence at which I could only peer from the outside, through streaked and darkened glass. He was right: I'd never understand, not really. I wasn't sure I wanted to.

I *was* sure that I wanted his respect more than I'd ever wanted anything; short of a Transfer ticket to Overworld.

A few days passed in this fog of mingled self-pity and self-loathing. I checked my messages obsessively, hoping for any word that he'd relented; all I got were nagging whines from girls who wondered why I hadn't called them back. I didn't try to call him, or catch up with him at any of his classes; that would have been too pathetic, even for me.

One morning I woke with something resembling my old resolve, and without even stopping for breakfast or a shower I jogged across campus to the gym, foggily wondering if I might find Hari there.

I had no idea what I would say to him if I found him. I suppose I was half planning to fall to my knees and hope the pathetic blankness of my postsurgical mask might soften his clockwork Labor heart.

It was a stupid thing to do; if I'd been thinking clearly, I wouldn't have come within a klick of the gym in the morning. Before noon, that's where the neanderthals gather to flex their muscles and sniff each other's assholes.

Hari wasn't there, of course. He was too wise for this, too experienced to be caught out like a young rabbit upwind of a wolf pack. I strolled into the weight room like I belonged there, and it wasn't until I met Ballinger's eyes, small and red and hungry like a bear's, that I understood how stupid I had been.

Then I made my second mistake of the morning: I turned and tried to walk out of there coolly, with a show of calm confidence. Even though my heart roared in my ears, I would not show fear before these hyperthyroid pinheads. Hari would have been smarter; he would have understood how much trouble he was in.

He would have bolted like a scalded cat, and got away.

I made it through the fluted arch, and past the door from the gym's main hall, and was congratulating myself on my narrow escape when a huge hand grabbed my hair and slammed me against the wall.

The corridor spun around me; grey patches floated raggedly through my vision. Ballinger towered over me like a giant, like a dinosaur, incomprehensibly powerful. Half his face was still swollen and purplish yellow from Hari's kick, and there was nothing human in his eyes.

I sagged against the wall, trying to catch my breath, and Ballinger's mouth split in what he probably thought looked like a smile. "Hey, aren't you Kris Hansen?" he said, his voice rough with mock awe. "Pleased to meet you, you little *faggot*."

Then he hit me, casually, a kind of paternal slap, just to establish our relationship. His open palm struck the side of my neck and clubbed me spinning to the floor. I skidded a little ways, and

I curled up into a ball and lay there, gasping at the shower of stars inside my head.

"Have a nice trip," he said. "Bet you thought that was pretty funny, didn't you? I know *I* did. Shit, I'm *still* laughing."

He tangled his fist in the front of my tunic and hauled me up dangling above the floor. He set my back against the wall and leaned on his fist to pin me there, driving the breath from my guts. He put his other hand up under my chin and started to force my head back, and up, against the slicing pressure of my collar at the back of my neck, the numbing yoke of the tunic tearing down on my shoulders. I pulled at his arm, which felt like stone under my useless fingers, and I punched weakly at his face with nothing but the meager strength of my scrawny arm behind it, and all I could think of was that Tallman's hand-to-hand combat classes, and Hari's training, and my wit and good humor and brains and my record as the top Battle Magick student in the history of the Conservatory, everything I am, everything I will ever be, all came down to the tensile strength of my cervical ligaments. Nothing in the universe was as important right now as whether or not my neck was stronger than Ballinger's arms—and I knew it wasn't. I could hear the creaking and popping of my neck giving way. Stretching wires of pain sang all the way down into my toes.

And I was wrong about his eyes: they weren't hungry like a bear's. What I could see from point-blank was an *impersonal* hunger, an abstract and dispassionate lust.

They were hungry like Chandra's.

This wasn't about *me* at all; it was about him. He was going to kill me just to make a point. To prove something to Hari, and to himself.

I'd done one foolish thing—one thoughtless, fatal act. When I'd dropped to my knees behind him, I'd mixed into a situation I didn't understand. Now I was going to die for it. I couldn't even plead for my life; the pressure of his hand held my jaw shut and cut off my wind.

Then suddenly, blessedly, the pressure slacked and I could breathe again, and I found myself staggering under my own weight as he let me go.

It took a few seconds for me to understand what had happened. There were people around us, and an instructor—I think it was Tallman, but I don't remember for sure—and Ballinger was laughing and joking with them and cheerfully pretending that he and I had just been horsing around. The instructor and his group of students must have come into sight in the corridor just in time to save my life.

Somebody asked me if I was all right, and I choked out some kind of lie. "Yeah, yeah, Ballinger just plays kind of rough, that's all."

I could have filed a complaint against him, sure, but the corridors don't have the same kind of security camera coverage that the rooms do; we were in a blind spot, and probably the worst trouble I could have gotten him in was a reprimand and a few days of push-ups and extra laps.

As they moved past us toward the gym, Ballinger leaned over to me and spoke softly. "I'm gonna find you, Hansen. Nobody does me like you did, you hear me? And you tell that faggot Michaelson that I'm gonna find him, too. And then I'm gonna show both you pussies how we do shit over here in Combat School."

And that's what gave me the idea, right there; it came like a sudden rent in a storm cloud, a shaft of brilliant sunlight straight into my brain, and I thought, *All right, why not?*

"Sure, I'll tell him," I said, grinning behind my mask, the surge of adrenaline making me forget how scared I was. "I'll tell him all you really want is a chance to suck his cock."

And in the half second while what I'd said percolated through twelve layers of solid bone to reach his walnut-sized brain, I kicked him in the balls.

His eyes bulged out, and his mouth twisted open to release a strangled hiss. He reached for me as he doubled over, but I ducked under his hand and ran like hell. He might have come after me for a few steps, but I'm quick and he was hurt. He didn't have a chance.

From behind me as I ran, I clearly heard derisive laughter from the other Combat students. Even through his pain, I'm sure Ballinger heard it, too.

10

I DIDN'T MAKE the mistake of assuming Ballinger was stupid just because he was big. I didn't know whether or not he was popular with the other Combat students; I assumed he was. I assumed that any Combat student who spotted me anywhere on campus would take the news back to him.

Only five students in the Conservatory were undergoing elving surgeries that term; it wasn't like I could wear a disguise. For nearly a week I was extremely careful about where I went and when I went there: I cut some classes, stayed late at others, kept my movements meticulously erratic, and kept in sight of crowds whenever possible.

Another mistake I didn't make was to try dealing with Ballinger rationally, to tell him I thought he was overreacting to what was, essentially, nothing but a schoolboy prank. I understood that the next time he caught me alone, he was going to kill me. I understood that no amount of logical argument, or threat of legal reprisal, would change this fact.

Besides, I didn't think he *was* overreacting. Hari and I, we'd challenged his manhood. A Labor kid like Ballinger, manhood was all he had. He'd defend it to the death.

Even his own.

I didn't need to wonder from where this understanding came; I knew it clearly. I was starting to think like Hari.

I left messages for Hari every day of that week, but he was still ducking me. The few times I spotted him around campus, he'd go the other way, heading places I didn't dare to follow—lonely places, like the windswept crags above the beaches. I had to get to him, though; I needed a place I could corner him, and I needed a way to convince him to listen.

On the morning of his first Virtual Acting seminar, I was waiting outside the door of the VA suite when Hari came walking up. He walked in the midst of a steady stream of Battle Magick students, but as usual, the tangled darkness of his demeanor made him look like he was alone. He stopped when he saw me down the hall, but I knew he'd chew off his own arm before he'd skip VA. He shook his head disgustedly and came toward me.

I could read his walk well enough to know that he was planning to brush past me without a word, counting on the other Battle Magick students to keep us apart. I stepped out to meet him and stiff-armed him in the middle of his chest.

He looked down at my hand as though he could wither it with a glance, then he met my eyes. "You don't want to be touching me, Hansen."

I matched his tone as best I could. "I have news for you, Hari."

"Fuck your news. Move your hand or I'll break your arm."

The last of the BM students filed into the VA suite; we were alone now in the corridor.

"Hari, just listen for one second, will you?"

"You're the one who's not lis—"

I popped him across the mouth, a good smooth right hook with my open palm, not too hard but with my hip behind it to drive the follow-through, just the way Tallman teaches it. He staggered across the corridor, off balance, and caught himself on the wall.

He bared his teeth. "Do you have any idea how dead you are?"

He delivered the line pretty well, but I knew his heart wasn't really in it; if he'd meant it, we wouldn't be talking.

"You want to kill me?" I said with a shrug. "Get in line."

"Yeah, I heard about you and Ballinger." He spat on the floor, then scowled at the pink trace of blood in his saliva. "That 'enemy of my enemy' shit doesn't fly with me, so don't bother. It was a stupid thing to do."

"No, it wasn't," I told him. "It was the smartest thing I've done so far. It's so smart it's going to get us both graduated with honors, and on our way to Overworld."

"Yeah, swell. I'm late for class."

"Can't have that," I said. "Hammet's going to call you for the first solo simulation."

Now I finally had his full attention. His gaze sharpened. "Bullshit."

I just smiled.

He stepped closer to me. "How do you know?"

"I bribed him for it." I chuckled right into his astonished face. "What's the point of being rich, if you don't use money to get what you want?"

He took another step, now close enough that I could smell coffee on his breath. His eyes glittered like the edge of a knife. "Why?"

"It's because of this idea I have. To solve our problem."

Faintly, through the door at my back, I heard Hammet launch into his classic Risk Lecture: *"You, as Actors, have a precisely defined role, irrespective of whether you swing a blade or throw a lightning bolt, joust or heal the sick. It is purely and simply this: Your function in society is to risk your life in interesting ways.*"

Hari heard it, too, and he glanced past my shoulder with thinly veiled longing. I didn't need to flash on him to know that he was wondering if he'd ever get the chance to do exactly that.

"All right," he said grimly. "All right, I'm listening."

"No time to explain right now. When he calls you, he'll put you into the Waterfront. I've been through this sim, and it's a tough one. Don't use any magick."

No surprise, no incomprehension showed on his face; he watched me with transcendent concentration. "Why not?"

"Because you're not good enough, Hari. Hammet will make you look like a fool. He's a sadist; humiliating his students is the only real pleasure he takes in life."

"But if I don't use magick—"

"Just don't, you hear me? Magick is exactly what they're *expecting*. You're a shitty thaumaturge. Stick with what you know."

I studied him, trying to see if I was making any impression, but he was as blank as stone. I shook my head. "Get in there. Hammet will be calling you any second."

"Kris—"

"No time, Hari. You want to talk about it, I'll be at my usual table over lunch. Now go."

11

I SAT IN the back of the Aud, behind the other BM students, and watched Hari on three of the four big screens in front of the banked keyboards of the instructor's station. The three views showed him from behind, before, and above; the fourth didn't show him, but instead was Hari's POV.

He moved with some assurance through the Waterfront; he, like the other students, had had two dry runs the week before, to become accustomed to moving in the feedback suits and to get the feel of pulling the simulated Flow. On the screen, he looked again the generic-featured manikin I'd fought in the Meadow, dressed in loose, nondescript tunic and pants.

The Waterfront was another standardized encounter environment, modeled on the Terana docks on the west coast of the Ankhanan Empire. A tangled maze of clapboard shops, taverns,

and brothels crowded what once were broad rights-of-way between massive stone-built warehouses. The streets teemed with
people of all descriptions as well as a liberal sprinkling of the
subhuman races of Overworld, but these were only for atmosphere. Hari could actually interact only with Hammet's TAs,
five retired Actors who waited in feedback suits of their own, in
other cubicles of the VA suite. They would take on the roles of
the other characters in this encounter.

The first Waterfront encounter is pretty simple. As he's walking along, the student hears feminine screams from a nearby
alley; when he investigates—which he will, as avoiding the encounter is not an option if he wants to pass VA—he sees a man
using a stout stick to beat a woman. The student has three spells
to call upon: a Minor Shield, a fairly powerful Telekinesis, and,
of course, the basic Flow bolt that any spellcaster can use.

What most students do—what I did, in fact—is self-righteously
order the man to lay off, and when he refuses, to enforce the order
with magick, either Shielding the woman or attacking the man
with the TK or a Flow bolt.

This is where your average student gets stomped, because
there isn't just one man, there are four: one behind him, and two
more lying low on the one-story rooftops to either side of the
alley. As soon as the student enters the trancelike state of mindview, all three of them jump him.

Now, don't get me wrong: You *can* fight them. The street and
alleyway are even designed with a number of features that can be
improvised into weapons by a resourceful student, like some
broken jugs and splintered timbers, loose cobblestones as big as
your fist that can be thrown by TK, and a couple of nooks you
can back into and seal with a Shield.

In the end, though, they'll get you. Even if you manage to fight
off all four—which, as far as I know, no one has ever done successfully, except me—the woman herself is part of the plan, and
she'll knife you at her first opportunity. That's where I lost.

The whole purpose of this encounter, it seems to me, is to humiliate the student who goes through it—and to impress upon all
the BM kids how vulnerable they are when they enter mindview.
You can't win the fight; what Hammet does, afterward, is talk
about how you could have made losing more entertaining.

Hammet's first clue that Hari's encounter wasn't going to go
entirely according to plan probably came when Hari peered

around the corner of the alley and saw the man beating the woman with the stick. His manikin's face was, of course, expressionless, but Hari's distinctive mutter came over the Aud's PA rich with scorn.

"Oh, that's original," he snorted. "Give me a break."

He shook his head and shuffled his feet a little; I thought he was searching for a balanced stance to enter mindview, and my heart sank. But he had other things on his mind: his shuffling feet had found one of those loose cobbles, and he bent and picked it up.

This is where the student steps forward and utters some fatuous variation on the time-honored *"Stop, you fiend! Unhand that woman!"* but Hari just stood there for a moment and watched him beat her, holding the cobblestone thoughtfully.

Hammet keyed his mike. "Michaelson, what are you doing?"

"I'm intervening," came Hari's muttered reply. "That's what I'm supposed to do, right?"

"Get on with it, then."

"All right."

He took one step forward and fired the cobble overhand. As the stone left his hand he shouted, *"Hey, asshole!"* The man with the stick turned to look, just in time to catch about half a kilo of stone full in the mouth. The impact lifted him off his feet and dumped him to the ground like he'd been hit with a bat.

Every student of Battle Magick in the Aud gasped like an affronted Leisurewoman.

"All right, I've intervened," Hari said to the air, sounding bored. "Now what?"

Some of the gasps gave way to snickers.

Hammet snarled something unintelligible, and the two men who had waited atop the single-story buildings leaped down toward Hari as though they wanted to land on him. Somehow, he'd been expecting this; he darted toward and past one of them, his arm extended to hook the falling man's legs out from under him. The poor guy tumbled in the air and landed hard on the back of his neck.

The other rolled with the fall and came up with a knife in his hand, but Hari had kept moving to the alley wall, where the pile of timbers stood. By the time the knife guy rolled to his feet, all he had a chance to see was a long section of two-by-four swinging down at his head. He got his arm up in time to take the blow, but it drove him back down to his knees, and Hari kicked him in the face.

By the time the fourth TA arrived, sword in hand, three men were down. Hari faced the fourth with his two-by-four angled before him like a bastard sword at garde. He hesitated, and through Hari's POV I clearly saw his gaze shift over Hari's shoulder; on the front view I saw the woman lunge toward Hari's back.

But again he was somehow ready for this; with uncanny, almost prescient assurance he slipped to one side and backhanded the two-by-four across her chest. It stopped her cold, and in that one second of stunned stillness, he dropped the board, took the knife from her opening fingers, and yanked her around in front of him as a shield, the knife against her throat.

"Drop the sword or she dies," he rasped, and I don't know if the TA believed him or not, but I did.

There was a moment of shocked silence in the Aud, then a scattering of applause, which turned to shouts of useless warning as the man Hari had felled with the rock rose up behind him and clubbed him across the back of the head.

Even then, Hari didn't fall immediately. Half stunned, he still managed to slash the woman's throat and cast her aside to turn on his attacker, but now the man he'd kicked in the face had risen as well, and the one who'd fallen on his head, and they all waded in on him with knives and clubs. He fought with desperate ferocity, but he couldn't handle them all at once.

They beat the crap out of him.

The feedback suits in the VA suite are loaded with failsafes; they can't do much worse than raise a welt or give you a minor bruise and a lump or two. On the other hand, the simulation programs were supposed to shut down a feedback suit when its sim takes what should be a killing or incapacitating blow.

From his keyboard at the instructor's station, Hammet had altered the simulation's parameters, to let his TAs get up after they should have been eliminated—even the woman whose throat was supposed to be cut.

They spent longer than they really needed to take Hari out, battering him from one side of the virtual alley to the other and back again. They punished him as much as the feedback suit would allow, and he never made a sound. When his manikin lay stretched out and bleeding on the cobbles, Hammet ended the simulation.

He rose and keyed his throat mike. "Michaelson? You want to tell me what that was supposed to be about?"

Hari's response, muffled perhaps by the simulated unconsciousness of his manikin, sounded something like, *"Cheating bastard . . ."*

And a faint rustle of assent came from the BM kids in the seats of the Aud.

Hammet's tone went icy, and I could see the man was livid, as though he'd received a deadly insult. "Are you some kind of a joker, Michaelson? Why didn't you use any magick?"

Hari's reply was an open sneer. "What for?"

"Because that's what you *do*, you dumb shit. You're supposed to be a thaumaturge, aren't you?"

"What I *am*," Hari said, "is an Actor. What I *do*, is risk my life in interesting ways, right?"

"Don't mock me, you Temp sack of shit. How do you expect to graduate from the College of Battle Magick if you can't throw a fucking *spell*?"

I rose quietly in the back of the Aud; I had a feeling this argument was going to escalate in an unpleasant way, and I had already seen everything I needed to see.

This was going to work.

12

I SAT ALONE in the dining hall. For self-protection, I chose to be in public view as much as possible, so I'd begun a habit of lingering there at mealtimes.

My friends often sat with me; I was still as popular as ever, and it was considered something of a coup in Shitschool to be seen eating at my table. None of them really understood what was happening; they all thought I was very brave, for the way I'd faced down Ballinger, and they all joked and laughed and told each other, *See? Those Combat jerks aren't as tough as they think they are. Most of them are only Labor trash, after all. Hollow men,* they said smugly, congratulating themselves for their superior breeding, *covered in muscle but empty inside.*

I could have told them how tough those Combat jerks are. I could have told these scions of European Business houses, these social-climbing Professionals and self-conscious Tradesmen, that those hollow Labor men are filled with a terrifying solidity.

But what's the point? They wouldn't believe me, not really; I had no way to bring them to the understanding that Hari had given me. They'd only think I was putting on airs, that I was being melodramatic, the same way I'd thought Hari was. I ached to find a way to lock each of these smug creeps that I used to think were my friends in a room alone with Ballinger for ten minutes.

Let them look into the eyes of that hollow man as he looms over them like a thunderhead. It'd change their fucking lives.

That noontide, after Hari's VA debut, these creeps and hangers-on had left early, and I sat alone at my table, going over Hardanger's *Primal Culture*, barely seeing the words on the screen, wondering if Hari was going to find me here.

I was slogging through the third of Hardanger's five alternate translations of the heroic epic *Dannellarii T'ffar* when Hari came through the door. Two weeks ago, maybe, I would have kept reading, to pretend to be cool and nonchalant; I had neither time nor patience for that now. I flipped the screen closed and waited for Hari to reach my table.

He had a couple lumps coming up on his face, and he approached me cautiously. "All right," he said, eyeing me with a kind of animal wariness. "I'm listening."

"Sit." I waved an offering hand to the chair opposite, and waited while he thought it over.

Slowly, watching me, he slid into the chair. "So. What was that about? Hammet hates my guts, now."

I shrugged. "Hammet hates everybody. Don't worry about it."

"They beat the shit out of me."

"Only because Hammet reset the sim parameters, and everybody in that room knew it. The story will be all over campus by tonight. Nobody beats that encounter. Nobody. Not even me. You're going to be a legend in the College of Battle Magick, Hari."

"Like you? Big fucking deal. Am I supposed to thank you for it?"

"It'll make your career," I told him. "It'll get you graduated with honors and off to Overworld."

"How am I gonna graduate when I can barely throw a fucking spell?"

"Hari, Hari, Hari," I said, shaking my head in mock pity. "I think you're the only guy who was in the Aud today who didn't get it. You don't *need* magick, Hari. Leave the spells to upcaste pussies like me, huh? You're going to graduate from the College of *Combat*."

Give him credit as a flexible thinker: he didn't scoff. He leaned back in his chair and stared through me with narrowed eyes, thinking hard. I went on, "Did you get a recording? You proved today that you can fight—and win—even when you're completely overmatched. Hari, that was *five to one*! You weren't even *armed*. I've never seen anything like it, and neither has anybody else around here."

He shook his head, and his eyes went cold; I could see him talk himself out of it. "Proves nothing. That's why they call it a *simulation*, Kris."

"Yeah, I know. Chandra won't even consider it—unless we force him to."

"How do you plan to do that?"

I took a deep breath and sighed it out; for a moment I had a fleeting fancy of being on Overworld, of summoning mindview and slipping a Suggestion into Hari's unconscious mind. It was a pleasant fancy, and it gave me a warm little smile.

"The whole thing revolves around proving that you, Hari Michaelson, skinny little Labor trash Shitschool student, can take on a highly trained warrior three times your size in the real world, straight up, no rules," I began. I would have gone on, but Hari was right with me.

"You're talking about Ballinger."

I nodded. "You can bump chests with him all you want, but me?" I spread my hands. "I need this settled before he kills me. I have it worked out so we can tie the whole thing up with a ribbon, and everybody's happy."

"How do you figure?"

I held up my hand. "First, you tell me: What do you think?"

"Going over to Combat? Shit, Kris, it'll never happen. Even the *girls* over there outmass me by ten kilos. You ever been hit by somebody who is, like, double your mass?"

"Just once," I said grimly. "I didn't care for it. But we're talking about you. Forget whether you think it's possible. Do you *want* to?"

He sat there and stared through me, and didn't answer.

I leaned forward. "I *know*," I told him. "I know why you're in Battle Magick. Why you want to be an Actor. It's because, deep down, what you really like is to hurt people."

He didn't deny it. I grinned. "Do it on Earth, you're in prison, or cyborged. Do it on Overworld, you're a star."

He squinted at me.

"Sure," I went on, "BM was your best chance to get to Overworld—but not anymore. You don't have it, Hari. You're not going to make it."

His lips compressed, and his face darkened.

"But, you know *why* you don't have it?" I said. "Why you'll never be an adept? I saw it all when we fought in the Meadow. Your Shell? It stops at your fists. It's because when you think about hurting people, when you really let your passion run, you don't care about magick. You want to do it by *hand*."

He picked up my notescreen and fiddled with the lid; he lowered his face, underlit by the screen's sporadic flicker as he flipped it back and forth.

"Today, in the simulation, after you threw the rock, when they all started coming at you—you never even thought about pulling magick, did you? It had nothing to do with what I told you; it never occurred to you to throw a spell. You forgot, didn't you?"

"No," he said, so softly that I could barely hear him, and his eyes were hooded. "No, I didn't forget. I was just . . ."

"Just what?"

He met my eyes, and his face shone. He had the steady, concentrated stare of a stalking lion.

"I was having too much fun."

13

IT ONLY TOOK three days to set up.

At the end of that time, I slipped into the men's washroom in the Language Arts building after my midterm on the western dialects of Primal—my first test of that day—and Ballinger was waiting for me.

The Language Arts shitter isn't much: four stalls, six urinals, a pair of sinks, a small supply closet. Hari and I chose it because it has only one security camera, which covers pretty much the whole space.

I stood at a urinal with my dry dick in my hand, skin crawling up my back; I was too scared to pee. When I had told him my plan, Hari had measured me with that squint he got whenever he was surprised, and murmured, "Y'know, you're betting your *life* that I can take Ballinger."

"Yeah, I am," I had told him easily enough at the time. "Or at least slow him down enough for Security to get there."

Now, though, as I stood at the urinal, the doors of all four stalls behind me opened at once, and a hand like the claw of a steam shovel took the back of my neck and forced my face into the cold tile wall, and Ballinger said, "Tone, hold the door," and suddenly I didn't have any trouble peeing at all.

He wasn't alone.

We were *sure* he'd do this by himself; why wouldn't he? We were sure he didn't think he'd need help, not against me. We were sure he wouldn't want any witnesses, damned sure.

Dead sure.

I'd been expecting, too, some of his brutal, predatory playfulness, some mock-cheerful one-liners to draw things out for a minute or two before he got down to the serious business of killing me. Instead, he bounced my face off the wall.

Stars showered behind my eyes, and my knees went slack. The washroom wobbled around me as his irresistibly powerful hands turned me to face him. He held me pinned against the wall, and his tiny bearish eyes swept contemptuously down my front to my shriveling penis. "Nah, leave your pants down," he said. "That suits."

"Ballinger," I gasped, "don't—"

He slammed me against the wall again, and the lights in the washroom went reddish brown in my eyes, and I couldn't tell if he had two friends in here, or four, or six, because I'd forgotten how to count, or even what numbers might mean.

"You shouldna made a pass at me, Hansen," Ballinger said thickly. "I coulda let that go, but then you jumped me. I hadda defend myself. It was an *accident*, that's all. I dint even really mean to hurt you."

"Ballin—"

"Shut up." His massive fist hit my short ribs like a freightliner, and something broke inside me. Blood bubbled up my throat.

"Here, you little fuck," he said, his thick fingers clawing under the edge of my plastic mask. "Let's have a look." He ripped it off my face. Some of my flesh went with it.

"Jesus," he said, eyes full of revolted surprise. "Dint you used to be good-looking?"

My hands went to my violated face, and he threw me to the ground. I caught myself, just barely, and my palms left bloody streaks as they skidded along the tile; gasping, I stared at these twin parallel scarlet smears as though they had some arcane meaning that could save my life.

Ballinger kicked me in the guts hard enough to lift me off the floor. When I bounced back down, he stepped back for his friends to take a turn.

I heard a wet splintering rip, like a rotting door being kicked in, but at the same instant a boot hit me in the head and darkened the world.

The last sight I clearly remember was the security camera, high up in a corner above me; its little indicator diode, which shines red to let you know it's working, was as black as a seagull's eye.

14

THE THING THAT strikes you the most, watching the recording of the fight in the bathroom, is how *fast* Hari is, all speed and preternatural assurance, like a ballet dancer executing well-rehearsed choreography.

Even as I'm hitting the ground after Ballinger's kick, you see him fly from outside the frame, already in the air, having thrown himself into a vicious cut-block that brings his hip against the side of the nearest Combat student's knee. The knee bends sideways, making the ripping, splintering sound that I thought was the door, and the Combat student—Jan Colon, from Madrid, I found out later—falls hard, too stunned to even guess how bad he's hurt.

One down.

Ballinger kicks me again then; he doesn't yet realize what's happening. The recording shows me still semiconscious, curled around my broken ribs. Another of Ballinger's three buddies, Pat Connor from a suburb of Dublin called Dun Laoghaire, has a weapon, a half-meter length of pipe; but even as he's turning and starting to lift it, Hari leaps into his arms, locking his legs around Connor's chest and his arm around Connor's throat. His back's to the camera; you can't see what he's doing there, but Connor hits him across the back two or three times with the pipe and Hari doesn't seem to notice.

Then Connor drops the pipe and Hari lets him go, and Connor staggers away, howling, his hands to his face, blood leaking through his fingers. By the time we reviewed this recording, I had learned that Hari had stuck his thumb into Connor's left eye hard enough to rip the socket muscles.

Two down.

Actually, three: Anthony Jefferson, the one guarding the door, had come into this expecting a cheerful afternoon outing, a nice, safe beating; he claimed, later, that Ballinger had told him he only planned to rough me up a little. Whatever the truth may be, he certainly hadn't planned on sticking his hand into this particular meat grinder. When two of his friends went down screaming in less than ten seconds, his nerve broke and he ran out the door, yelling for Security.

Ballinger, on the other hand—

The shrieks of his friends seem to make him happy, somehow—to fill him with some inexplicable confidence and joy. He turns on Hari like a bear facing a wolverine, his huge shoulders hulking forward into a graceless wrestler's crouch; there's something of the bear as well in his loose-jointed shambling step, a slow and powerful clumsiness as though he's not used to walking on his hind legs.

Hari strikes like a rattlesnake, an unhumanly swift uncoiling that swings his shinbone toward Ballinger's knee faster than the eye can follow, a kick that will cripple him. That's when you learn that Ballinger's clumsy shamble is an act, a con, a sucker play to draw Hari in. There's a reason why Ballinger's at the top of his class.

He picks up his foot—not high, a few centimeters, just enough that the kick lands harmlessly on his shin—and then falls on Hari like an undermined wall.

His weight bears them both to the ground. Ballinger's on top, and once again you can't really see what they're doing. Part of the training of Combat students is jujitsu matwork; that grunting and those liquid crunches you can hear are the sounds of bad things happening to Hari's joints.

In the background, you can see me, rolling over, trying to rise. I remember knowing that Hari was in trouble, and that I had to move; I'd like to think that I was getting up to help him, but I don't know, that may be wishful thinking.

I was probably getting up to run.

Even as I find my unsteady feet, Hari somehow frees an arm from Ballinger's smothering embrace, and his hand closes around that half-meter length of pipe that Connor had dropped. He bangs Ballinger on the back of the head once, and then again, as though to let him know that the first one wasn't an accident. Ballinger, though, he's no amateur; instead of rolling off and giving Hari an opening for a full swing with the pipe, he snuggles his head down closer to Hari's and reaches out to gather in that free arm. But then you see him twitch, then convulse, and rear up, reaching his feet in a powerful surge that ignores the weight of Hari, who is hanging from Ballinger's face by his *teeth*—

Ballinger roars and shoves him away, and blood sprays; Hari slams off a wall and caroms from a stall divider, but bounces upright like a pop-up punching bag. One of his arms hangs limp from a dislocated shoulder, and one of his legs doesn't seem able to bear much weight, and he's still *smiling* as he spits out a mouthful of Ballinger's cheek.

Ballinger lunges for him again, but now Hari has room and leverage for a full-armed swing of that pipe. The pipe hits the outside of Ballinger's forearm with a wet crunch, neatly breaking the bone, and instead of trying to recover for another swing, Hari uses the momentum to carry himself into a spin like he's delivering a backfist. Ballinger's wounded arm drops; he has no guard at all as the pipe whistles around—actually *whistles*, like a bottle when you blow across its neck—and splinters his skull just above his right ear.

Ballinger's eyes roll up, and he drops to his knees, his face utterly blank, a doll's face, a corpse's, then he pitches forward to bounce, once, on the cold tile floor.

Hari stands over him, swaying, his face burning like a torch.

By the time Security arrives, I'm in the process of striking my sole blow in this battle: I'm on my knees next to Ballinger's body, puking all over his back.

15

LATER, IT MADE us heroes, of course—especially Hari. The evidence on the Security cube was incontrovertible: he had unquestionably saved my life.

There was a discrepancy or two, though, that interested the Security investigators quite a bit. For one, they couldn't seem to figure out how Hari had gotten in through the bathroom door when it was being held by a Combat student who outmassed him by forty kilos. "I don't know," Hari repeated endlessly. "I didn't even see him. Maybe he was just standing *by* the door, instead of actually holding it."

We certainly weren't going to tell them that Hari had been hiding in the bathroom's supply closet for more than an hour, waiting.

They also couldn't seem to figure out how Ballinger had planned to get away with it, when the whole act was carried out in full view of the bathroom's security camera. They kept after us for a few days on that one, and we steadfastly proclaimed our ignorance until finally Ballinger woke up enough to answer questions in his now-thick, halting, slurred voice.

It seemed that a certain Battle Magick student, Pierson by name, had conceived a rivalry with me. Not understanding the deadliness of Ballinger's intentions, he had offered to help Ballinger get even with me by disabling a security camera in the area of his choice. After tracking my movements for a couple of days, Ballinger's cohorts had established that the Language Arts shitter would be the place to take me—I hit it every day at the same time, between classes.

When questioned, Pierson admitted the whole thing with well-acted sheepishness. Of course, he'd had no way of knowing that Ballinger planned to do more than frighten and humiliate me; how could he? As for the security camera, he gave them a shrugging, "Guess I didn't know as much about it as I thought. All I managed to disable was the indicator diode. Kinda embarrassing, really."

Pierson came from a Professional family; both his parents are electrical engineers. He'd done it exactly the way I'd told him to—he was one of those social-climbing creeps who wanted to sit at my table—and he'd also managed to patch into the camera cable to make our own recording of the incident.

That recording was read into the Conservatory computer from an open terminal in the library and was tracelessly e-mailed to Hari's Patron, Businessman Marc Vilo, along with a note from Hari comprising some specific suggestions on how this recording might be used.

Hari and I and Pierson, we'd had our stories straight well in advance, and they weren't complicated enough to lead us into a tangle of lies; handling the Security investigators didn't even make me nervous.

It was a little different, the day the Social Police came in.

Four of them—a whole enforcement squad—came to see me, blank and anonymous behind their shapeless body armor and their mirrored helmets, to park themselves on either side of my infirmary bed and take turns asking me questions in voices flattened to absolute neutrality by the digitizers in their helmet speakers. Talking to them, I was more frightened than I'd been when Ballinger slammed my head into the wall in that bathroom.

They weren't interested in anything I might have done; they were gathering evidence against Ballinger for capital Forcible Contact Upcaste. My father was pressing charges; he thought our family lawyers might be able to find a loophole in the Conservatory's statutory caste-neutral environment. If so, Ballinger could be executed.

All the Social Police wanted was to establish that Ballinger had known I was upcaste of him. That's all. But I could barely speak to them. They scared the crap out of me.

Through it all, the only face I ever saw was my own, distorted and leering in their silvered masks. They spoke only to ask me questions, never among themselves, and each digitized voice was indistinguishable from every other.

I've always believed, along with the rest of the world, that the masks of the Social Police were designed to protect the identities of their agents, so that these agents' ability to go incognito, to infiltrate the ranks of society's enemies, could never be impaired. No Social Police officer's identity was ever made public; no Social Police officer ever appeared without his or her silver mask, shape-concealing body armor, and vocal digitizer, not even in court.

Kids like to tell each other stories that even the wives and husbands of soapies never learn the profession of their spouses; I was old enough to know that those stories had to be wild exaggerations, but now I felt shifting beneath me some underlying truth, as though the earth moved and carried me to a new way of seeing, a perspective that harshened the light of the infirmary and made the antiseptic odor of my skin and bedclothes into something mephitic and sinister.

I caught myself wondering if there was a room somewhere within the Social Police headquarters where soapies might remove their masks and be simply men and women with each other. Instinctively, I doubted it; even a moment of admitting a personal identity would somehow undermine their power—would weaken the invincible magick armor of their anonymity.

They kept pressing me on Ballinger, from one side and another, as though if they kept asking me the same question long enough they'd eventually get the answer they wanted. And I wanted to give it to them, I really did—but the truth was, I didn't *know* if Ballinger really understood that I was from a Business Family. I told them that again and again, but they kept after me like a pack of dogs harrying a stag. Somehow, down inside, I had a sickening feeling that it wasn't really Ballinger they were after—that their real goal was to drag a lie out of me, a lie they could use to kill him.

They wanted him dead, sure; but more than that, they wanted me to be their *accomplice*.

This didn't come to me in a flash. Once or twice, I kind of had that half-dizzy feeling a flash gives me, but I never got anything from them. And maybe that was it; maybe that was it exactly.

Maybe I did flash on them, and there was nothing there.

16

EARLY THAT EVENING, not long after dinner, Chandra came to see me in the infirmary, and he brought Hari with him.

I was pretty well tubed up in the bed—on a respirator and an IV drip—and a little woozy from anesthetic by-products that still lingered in my bloodstream. I'd had a couple hours of surgery, to repair the lung one of my broken ribs had punctured, and to fix the rupture Ballinger had kicked into my spleen. I'd gone through hours of questions from the Social Police. I was exhausted, dazed, and in a growing amount of pain, but when I saw the look on Chandra's face I felt like dancing.

He looked confused, and frightened, and old. Beaten. More than beaten: *wounded*. He looked like a gutshot deer, getting weaker without understanding the pain.

Hari rode beside him in a motorized chair, one leg splinted straight out before him to immobilize his sprained knee ligaments, and his left arm in a clear plastic shoulder cast. But if he felt any pain, I couldn't see it through the fierce triumph on his face.

"Hansen," Chandra said, his voice stretched thin with tense exhaustion, "I have been in teleconference with your father, and—" His face twisted bitterly. "—with Businessman Vilo."

His eyes met mine, and some kind of spasm passed over his face, leaving emptiness in its wake. "Effective tomorrow, Michaelson will have his academic credits transferred and will be enrolled as a student in the College of Combat. You . . ." his voice faltered, then regathered some vague strength. "You will come before the Graduation Board in July, as scheduled. In exchange for this, your father has agreed not to press charges against poor Ballinger for Forcible Contact Upcaste, and Businessman Vilo will leave me—leave the *Conservatory*—alone."

Poor Ballinger? I thought, but had other things to say; I had prepared for this moment, and I had no intention of being gracious in victory.

"I think that's generous of him," I said. My plastic respirator mask gave my words a muffled, hollow authority. "I think that's generous of them both. I think that there is a tradition of *lax leadership* here, Administrator—and it is this failure of leadership that has fostered a permissive and violent atmosphere, where bullying and beating are more than tolerated; they are *encouraged*. I very nearly lost my life because you failed in your *fundamental responsibility*: to keep order in this institution."

It sounded good coming out, and felt even better: I sounded like my father, and I began to understand the keen pleasure of self-righteously dressing down an undercaste.

But Chandra was far from crushed; his sorrowful expression hardened. "When Vilo threatened to petition the Board of Governors for my ouster, I was tempted to laugh at him. *Let* them investigate. Let them find out the truth. I know, you see, Hansen. I know that you and Michaelson set this whole thing up. I *know*."

Hari didn't so much as blink. My first instinct was to bluster, but I followed Hari's lead and held my expression as neutral as I could.

Chandra looked from me to Hari, then back again, and the hardness in his face melted back into weary despair. "But I don't know *why*. I don't know how this—we—ended up here, in the infirmary. I don't know why we'll have to find a donor eye for Pat Connor, why Jan Colon is undergoing reconstructive knee surgery even now. Ballinger is in a coma in Athens; the best neurosurgeon in Europe has just finished pulling splinters of his skull out of the right lobe of his brain. They say he'll probably survive, but the extent of the permanent damage won't be known for days, or weeks."

A slow, sick weight gathered within my chest.

Chandra's eyes were raw with pain.

"You have what you want. Both of you. I—I cannot stand . . ." His breath hitched, then steadied. "I will have no further bloodshed. One student maimed, another crippled. A third with a fractured skull and permanent brain damage. You did this, Hansen. And you, Michaelson. And for what? To get a transfer into the College of Combat?"

He opened his hands helplessly. "Why did it have to be this way? Was there no other choice?"

I wanted to answer him, but no words came to my lips. The respirator seemed to suck air from my lungs, just as it had sucked all the moisture from my mouth. I glanced at Hari, but his face was as unreadable as a fetish mask.

Chandra shook his head, and his eyes glistened with unshed tears.

"Couldn't you have *asked*?"

17

HOURS BECAME DAYS, and weeks. Hari was released from the infirmary long before I was; by the time I saw him again, he was already established in the Combat school. Though he would never have the size and strength necessary to be competitive in the tank warfare of the lumbering, heavily armored Combat Trials, he liked to point out that no one wears armor all the time, not even on Overworld. He never bothered to train in armor, himself, and there was no man or woman on campus who would care to face him over a pair of *bokken* without it.

He spent much of his time working with Hammet and Tallman on techniques that would allow him to defeat an armored opponent, taking advantage of his superior speed and mobility to knock a man down or to close with him into the infighting range where a sword is useless and a stiletto can enter a visor, or slip beneath a gorget. He got good at it, too, as I knew he would. Never good enough to consistently beat a really gifted Combat student—like Ballinger once was—but good enough that no one, not even the best, was entirely comfortable coming into the ring with him, or facing him in a VA sim.

He was a celebrity on campus, a curiosity, a traveling one-man freak show. There was no one on the island that didn't know who he was, no one that didn't want to be able to say they'd spent time with him; he began to hold court in the cafeteria, just as I once had.

He was the idol of a growing circle of awed magick students, and he became the unofficial mascot of the College of Combat. Connor and Colon took to following him around like bachelor wolves behind their pack leader; far from holding a grudge for their injuries, they would proudly point them out and tell the story of how Hari had gouged out Connor's eye, and why Colon still walked with a slight limp. All his course work improved, especially his academics. By the time the Combat Trials rolled around, the week of my Graduation Boards, it was clear that Hari would graduate near the top of his class.

I didn't grudge him any of this. He deserved it. Setup or not, Hari was a real hero. Fighting four Combat students, single-handed, had never been part of our plan—but Hari hadn't even hesitated. I never forgot that he could have just stayed in that supply closet and let them kill me.

Ballinger, though—the bone splinters had sliced into his brain. He has recovered limited use of the left side of his body, they tell me, enough to walk with a crutch strapped to his shoulder, but his eyes will not focus, and half his mouth is forever frozen in rictus, and he will never be an Actor, never go to

Overworld; he'll live out his days in a Temp house in Philadelphia, on subsistence.

I almost screened him, once. I don't know what I would have told him, what I could possibly have said. There was no way to make him understand that I flashed on him in unguarded moments, every day; that every day I *became* him, in his hospital bed, incontinent, a nurse emptying his diaper into a bedpan. I became him struggling through rehab with a steel strut buckled to my shoulder to take the place of a working leg, dragging the dead half of a body that once had been my greatest pride. Feeling the twisting rivulet of drool that constantly trails from my half open lips.

Maybe I wanted to tell him that I would never forget how expensive my dream had become.

I made up my midterms, took top honors in each, as usual. I went through the rest of my surgeries, took my classes, did my course work, went on with my life.

Stayed away from people.

I took my meals in my rooms, didn't speak on campus. I drifted from class to class like a ghost. Soon enough, no one bothered to speak to me, either. My circle of creeps had a new hero to suck up to, and Hari was welcome to them.

It wasn't Ballinger's face I saw in my nightmares. It was Chandra's. It was Chandra's voice I heard, asking if there had been no other way.

Hari, though, he stuck by me. I don't think he liked me much, either; I think he felt like he owed me something, and that kept him coming around, talking to me, trying to keep me going.

It was Hari who kept telling me not to surrender to Chandra's guilt-laying game, who kept reminding me that it was Chandra who put this whole thing in motion. Chandra's speech in the infirmary, he said, had been nothing more than a weak man's attempt to avoid responsibility for the consequences of his actions. Which may have been true, but it changed the facts not at all.

I *hadn't* tried another way. I hadn't even thought about it.

Maybe, if I had tried, I could have saved my dream without killing Ballinger's. I had slid right into Hari's world. I had turned to violence and slaughter because it was *easier*: simpler, more efficient.

More fun.

I could not pay this price for my dream. I stayed in my classes on pure inertia. Though I had told no one, not even Hari, my mind was made up. I would give up Acting. Give up Overworld. Let my dream of magick die. It wouldn't help Ballinger, of course; but it would let me sleep.

All I had to do was shitcan my Boards, and then I would never have to face this choice again. There is no second chance; if you fail before the Graduation Board, they just go ahead and send you home.

The night before I was to go in front of the Graduation Board, Hari Michaelson saved my life again.

18

WE SAT IN my room, sharing a liter of retsina, talking about our careers. It's traditional, at the Conservatory, for a student's friends to sit up with him the night before his Boards. The night before, you're too nervous to sleep anyway, and you need friends to keep you company.

Hari was the only friend I had left.

When his Boards came, next term, he'd have a crowd of well-wishers in his room, a party so thick you couldn't squeeze from one end to the other; that night, the two of us sat at the edges of a pool of pale yellow light from my desk lamp, drank the bitter pine-flavored wine, and talked in low voices. We talked about him, because the words that would come if we talked about me, I could not bear to hear, or speak.

"C'mon, Kris," he said, a little unsteadily, as he drained the last glass. "You really think I'll make it?"

"Hari," I said seriously, "you're a star already. Look at the way people watch you around here. Everyone knows you're going to be huge. You're like something out of a twentieth-century samurai film—or a pirate movie. This industry lives on novelty . . . and it's more than that, too. You've got it, whatever *it* is. Star quality. I can see it. You can, too—I mean, think about how you, like, came *alive* when everybody started paying attention to you. It's like you're a whole different person, now. Shit, if I didn't know you so well, I'd say you were happy."

He smiled into his empty glass, his eyes fixed on some far-distant future. "Where do you think we'll be, twenty years from now? Big stars, all over the nets? Whole magazines devoted to our sex lives, that kind of shit?"

I shrugged. "You, maybe—if you live. Me? I guess I'll be VP of something in Malmo, in the family industry." I managed to say it like it didn't even hurt.

He blinked owlishly, staring at me in half-potted confusion.

I shook my head at his silent question, and took a deep breath that slid painfully around the knot at the bottom of my throat.

In the end, I guess, I had to tell him. It was vanity, really. I thought I could handle the snickers, and the *I knew he never had it in him* stories, and the false commiseration I would get from the other students when word got out that I'd failed. But I couldn't take it from Hari; I had to let him know I was tanking the Boards on purpose. Of all the people I have ever known, he was the one that I most wanted to understand that I could pass, if I wanted to.

I needed him to understand that this was a failure of nerve, not of ability.

"I can't do it, Hari," I said slowly. "I think about it this way, that way, every way, and I just can't do it. Remember what you told me all those months ago, right when we first met? *I don't have it.* You were right, man. I don't have it."

"Bullshit."

"It's true."

"It fucking *isn't* true," Hari said fiercely. "This is still about Ballinger, right?"

"Yeah."

"He got what was coming to him, that's all. He was *begging* for it."

"It's not that."

"Then what is it? What?" His face flushed red, and he looked like he wanted to hit me, as though he could slap the weakness out of my head.

If only he could. "I'm a coward," I said helplessly.

"What, because you folded when he hit you? Jesus *Christ*, Kris! Ballinger was three times your size, a fucking stone killer. You had *no chance* against him—but you walked into that shitter anyway. There are different kinds of courage, Kris. The hot kind, that's mine. Once the action starts, I'm all into it—but there are lots of people like that. Yours is the cold kind. Cold courage, man. You have to be just about the bravest son of a bitch I ever met."

My eyes went hot, and my tongue went thick, and all I could do was shake my head. How could I explain? But if I didn't start talking, I was going to start crying, and I would have rather died.

So I said, "All I ever wanted was to go to Overworld. My whole life, all I ever wanted was to be an Actor. But you know what being an Actor is, Hari? It's stepping back into that bathroom, every day."

"You can handle it," he insisted. "On Overworld, you're gonna be the toughest kid on the block—like when you tore me up in the Meadow—"

"It's not *that*," I said. "It's not the danger. I don't care about the danger. It's stepping back into that bathroom because I'd have to *hurt somebody*, to *kill* him—just to get another point of market share, a few bloody thousand marks. And what does that mean, to me? I'm rich already. What do I need so badly that it's worth somebody's life?"

"Fucking upcaste liberal," Hari muttered. "There's nothing cheaper than somebody's life. If you were Labor, you'd know it—Laborers are *born* knowing it. Shit, in the Mission District, you can buy a murder for less than the price of a steak dinner."

"But that's you," I said. "That's not me, and I can't pretend it is."

"Then I guess we got a problem."

"We?"

He settled back into his chair and set his wineglass on the floor. "Yeah. We. This isn't just your problem. You're my best friend, Kris."

"Huh? Hari, you don't even *like* me!"

"You saved my life. I don't forget that."

I started to protest, and he cut me off. "No," he said sharply. "You did. You wash out, you go back to the life of a Businessman on the Nordic Peninsula. Hey, that's one thing; it's not so bad. I wash out, I go to the Temp slums of San Francisco. That's something else. You saved my *career*, and that's more important than my life. I'm not going to let you suffer for it."

"Too late," I said bitterly.

"Listen, let's say you graduate after all. What then?"

"The usual. Two years of Overworld freemod for acclimatization and whatever final training I can manage; say, if I can find an adept who'll take me on as an apprentice. Then I come back for the implant—"

The possibility bloomed within my head, and Hari tracked its growth by the birth of my first smile in months. He grinned in reply.

"See, Hansen? You're still too locked into the *rules*, man. You're obsessed with what you're *supposed* to do. What's the real issue here, being an Actor or *going to Overworld*? Who says it's both or nothing?"

"I . . . I . . ." I couldn't think of anything to say; inside my head, my brain rang with Hari's echoes.

Who says it's both or nothing?

19

THE NEXT MORNING, I passed my Graduation Boards with the highest score this decade.

20

I SPENT THE next week or so hanging around the Conservatory, packing, making preparations. It had been my home for three years, and it was hard to believe I'd never see it again.

That week, my surgical mask finally came off for the last time. Now, when I look in the mirror, I see the alien features of a primal mage.

My true face.

It still gives me the shivers, a little.

I'm an elf, I say to myself, over and over again.

I'm an elf.

I also spent some time watching the Combat Trials. I led the wild cheers from the Shitschool students as Hari battled his unconventional way up the ranks. He lost in the finals, but the feral joy that showed through the blood on his face when he congratulated the winner made him look like *he* was the champion, instead.

Then I went home for a week, to see my father and my mother, my older brothers and my little sister, and to walk the fields of our estate, to fish, to wander through the neighborhoods of Malmo, where I grew up.

To say good-bye.

Then I came back to the Conservatory, to write this all down
and tuck it away, so that someday it will be found, and someone—
maybe my father, maybe Hari, maybe even I myself—will read it,
and understand.

Tomorrow, I make the Winston Transfer to Overworld, on
freemod. I'm crossing over into the Promised Land. At the end
of two years, I might present myself at one of the Studio's fixed
transfer points, to return to Earth and an Acting career.

And, I might not.

A lot can happen in those two years of freemod. Many students die. Overworld is a dangerous place—more so for us, who
know of it only secondhand. Some students vanish, and are
never seen or heard from again.

I have a feeling that this is what will happen to me.

It's all about Hari, you see. He's smarter than I ever gave him
credit for. He was right: I never wanted to be an Actor in the first
place.

I want to be a primal mage.

Maybe I'm just pretending. Maybe I'm fooling myself.
Maybe I'll die trying.

So what? I've faced that choice already, and I see no reason to
change my mind now.

I can't stop thinking about the look in Chandra's eyes, the
morning he started all this. I can't stop thinking about seeing that
same blank hunger behind Ballinger's ursine glare. The link, the
common thread between them—I spent days turning it over
slowly in my mind, again and again, looking at it from every
angle, trying to understand, and I couldn't quite put it together . . .
until I saw the same look in my father's eyes, as the Social Police
transport van arrived with a new load of Workers for the factory.

I mean, *precisely* the same: as though the same creature had
worn all three faces like a mask. My nightmares whisper of some
vast, unknowable power, buried in bedrock slumber, whose
dreams reach out and don us like hand puppets. Like masks.
Like one of those mirror masks of the Social Police.

I've been thinking about that creature a lot. At first I thought it
was just a metaphor: a myth I'd invented to solidify the way it
made me feel. Now, I'm not so sure. I think that creature wore
my face, for a while: I have a feeling that Hari saw that same abstract, impersonal hunger in my eyes there in the weight room,

the day we first met. I have a feeling that's why he hated me on sight.

He beat it out of me, literally—but that didn't stop me from using Ballinger as ruthlessly, as coldly and impersonally as Chandra was using me. I used him until he was all used up.

I guess it's a habit. I guess it's the way the world works. That's what keeps the gears of civilization grinding along.

But Hari . . . Well, nothing impersonal there: he hated Ballinger's guts. Maybe that's what it's really all about, in the end. Hari and that blankly hungry creature, maybe they're natural enemies.

With Hari, it's *always* personal.

Me, I'm going to run and hide. Hari won't; I can see it every time I look at him. He's going to wade on in and slug it out.

It feels strange, to write that: to admit, even to myself, that a savage, antisocial Labor thug is a better man than I am. And there I am again: He is not a savage, antisocial Labor thug.

Well, he is, but that's not all he is.

I don't think I even have the vocabulary for this. He's Hari, that's all. That's a lot.

I tried to be his teacher, but I learned more than I taught.

I told Hari that Acting was stepping back into that bathroom, every day; what I didn't tell him is that for me, a Businessman born and bred, I'm stepping into that bathroom every time I get up in the morning. That's the inescapable structure of life on Earth.

Use and be used, until you're used up. It's the way the world works.

This world, anyway.

I can hear, with my enhanced elvish ears, Hari's footfalls on the walk outside, far down in the dormitory's courtyard. I'm saying good-bye to him, too, tonight.

We save the most important good-byes till the last.

Good-bye to my best friend that I never liked.

Strange world.

I go to a stranger one tomorrow.

I'll look for you there, Hari. Maybe someday, twenty years from now, you'll be sitting in an Overworld tavern, and a familiar-looking primal mage will offer to buy you a drink. There really isn't any other way to say thanks, for saving my soul.

I only wish I could save yours.

What the life you've chosen to lead will cost you, I can't begin to imagine.

I guess the best you can hope for is not to be noticed.

SHE WAS ONLY a goddess part-time, but she loved her job, and she was good at it. She went to and fro upon the earth and walked up and down in it, and where she strode bloomed flowers and sprouted grain; when she spread her hand, the winter was mild and the harvest bountiful, a summer storm brought showers warm and sweet as a sunlit pond, and the spring sang of things green and growing.

The First Folk called her Eyyallarann, the Flowmind; the stonebenders called her Thukulg'n, the Drowner; to the tree-toppers she was Ketinnasi, the Riverman; to mankind, she was Chambaraya, the Water Father; but her name was Pallas Ril.

It was said she had a human lover, in some far-off place; that for half the year she took the form of mortal woman and lived in peace with her lover and her human child. Others said her lover was himself a god, her shadow-self, a dark angel of slaughter and destruction, and that the half of each year she spent at his side was the world's ransom: that she paid with her body to keep him beyond the walls of time, and preserve the peace of the good land.

As is common with such tales, both were true; and false; and to the same degree.

The part-time goddess had no church, no religion, no fol-lowers; she could not be propitiated by sacrifice or summoned by invocation. She walked whither she willed, and followed the course of her heart as though its turns were the twists of her riverbed; she loved the land and all things in it, and all prospered under her hand. The only prayer that might sway her was the sob of a mother over her ill or injured child—be that mother human or primal, goshawk or bobcat, elk or rabbit—and this only be-cause the human part of her remembered what it is to be a mother.

This was probably, in the end, the real reason why she and her lover both had to die.

For the scent of her green and growing land troubled the slumber of another god: a blind and nameless god, a god of dust and ashes, whose merest dream can kill.

ONE

THE SEVERED HEAD of a child bounced once on his mattress, then rolled against his ribs, and Hari Michaelson began to wake.

He groped for it, struggling upward through smothering blankets of hungover sleep. His gummed-together eyelids parted with the slow rip of shredding meat. Layers of dream shredded into smoke tatters, leaving behind only wisps of melancholy: He had been dreaming of the old days again. Of his long-dead Acting career. Or even earlier—he could not quite grasp the details, but he might have been dreaming of his student days at the Studio Conservatory, more than twenty-five years ago, when he was young, and strong, and full of hope. When he'd still been riding the upward swing of his life.

He found the foreign object on the bed, his fingers flapping blindly across it. Not a head, of course it wasn't a head; it was a *ball*, that's it, just a kid's ball, like the one he used to play rugger with, centuries ago in those bright and happy days before his mother's death and father's breakdown. With the abstract certainty of the dreams he shed, he knew the ball was Faith's. She'd sneaked into the master suite, and this was her way of encouraging him to get his lazy ass out of bed and take her to Saturday morning soccer practice.

He rolled over and coughed a wad of phlegm out of his cottony lungs. "Abbey: Clear th' windows," he said thickly, in a tone the housecomp would recognize. "Get s'm fucking light in here."

Strange ball, though, he thought fuzzily while he waited for the windows to depolarize. Weird shape, kind of irregular—bumpy and malformed—and the texture was strange, too, smooth and soft over a hard surface within, almost like bone—

And what was this shit here? Hair? This ball has *hair* on it?

At the same moment that he realized that the windows weren't working and no light was entering the room, his hand found the ragged mess of bone and bloody shreds of flesh that remained of the neck, and an oiled voice spoke Westerling from a tall shadow at the foot of his bed.

"So, Caine," it murmured with dark, humid lust, "I hear you're *crippled*, now . . ."

And the head in his hand was his daughter's, and the shadow at the foot of his bed was Berne.

The blade of Kosall flickered like a flame in the moonlight, and Hari Michaelson's legs would not move.

2

HARI LAY SHIVERING beneath his tangled, sweat-soaked sheets, and hoped he hadn't crapped himself again.

A warm hand cupped his shoulder. "Hari, it's okay," Shanna said softly from close by. "I'm here. Just a nightmare, that's all."

He clenched his teeth, biting down on his courage until he could open his eyes. She knelt beside his bed, her hair a tousled halo of deeper shadow in the darkened bedroom, her eyes wide and almost luminous, a faint vertical crease of concern between her brows.

"Was I—" he started thickly, then he coughed his throat clear and tried again. "Was it loud?"

She nodded sadly. "Berne again?"

"Yeah."

"Those always seem to be the worst."

"Tell me about it." He rolled his head to the side, staring across the room at the rumpled covers on her bed; he couldn't bring himself to look down at his own. "Did I—is there a mess?"

"I don't think so," Shanna said gravely. "I can't smell anything. Do you want me to look?" She had that nurselike professional detachment in her voice again. He hated that tone; it made his stomach knot into a sick tangle of bile. That tone had loathing and disgust lurking just beneath the calm *I'll handle it* surface.

"You'd better," he said tightly. It hurt more to say this than it had to take the fucking wound in the first place. "The bypass is down again."

The neural bypass that shunted impulses around the break in his partially regenerated spinal cord was erratic, at best; he hadn't reloaded the software in three days, and some unexplained bugginess in the program made the bypass shut down unexpectedly now and again. That part of the dream had been perfectly accurate: he couldn't move his legs, couldn't feel them, or anything else below his navel. Below the three-inch-wide scar Kosall had left in his belly, he was dead as a butchered cow.

A shutdown always gave him nightmares, and sometimes he woke up in a pool of his own shit and piss that he couldn't feel, and sometimes—if he'd been lying there long enough to numb his nose—couldn't even smell. This was the reason Shanna no longer slept in his bed.

One of the reasons.

"Abbey: Room lights to one quarter," Shanna said calmly. "Execute."

The room lit with a soft decentralized glow, and she peeled back the covers. He made himself look. The sheets were stained only with the sweat that made his nightclothes cling to his clammy skin—that meant the shutdown was not yet complete; he still had control of his bowels and bladder. He gave a sigh of relief that threatened to become a shudder. Maybe he could make it to the bathroom before the goddamn bypass rebooted itself.

The regeneration therapy the Studio physicians had used to treat Hari's severed spinal cord had slightly better than a 90 percent success rate—that's what they kept telling him. Looking at it the other way, though, meant it had a 10 percent *failure* rate, and that's roughly where Hari fell.

So to speak.

Sure, it had partially worked—he had some urinary and rectal sphincter control, and limited sensation. But even those partial gains were sacrificed to the spinal bypass. The bypass worked by neural induction, similar to the Studio's first-hander chairs; when it went down, it played fuckass with everything below his waist.

"Administrator?"

The screen on the night table beside his bed flickered to life, casting a cold electric glow into the bedroom, and the disembodied face of Bradlee Wing, his father's nurse, frowned out of it. *"Administrator Michaelson? Are you all right?"*

Shanna lifted her eyebrows at him, and he nodded reluctantly. She hit the voice recept key for him so he wouldn't have to drag himself across the bed using only his arms.

"Yeah, fine, Brad. I'm fine."

"I heard you shout—"

"I said I'm *fine*. Shanna's here, everything's okay."

"Want something to help you sleep?"

Almost half a liter of Laphroaig remained in the bottle beside the screen; the scotch's acidic, iodine bite still lingered in the back of his throat. He saw the expression on Shanna's face as she caught his look at the bottle, and he turned away, scowling. "Don't bother. Just—check on Dad, will you? Make sure I didn't wake him."

"The sedatives Laborer Michaelson takes—"

"Don't call him *Laborer Michaelson*. How many times do I have to tell you?"

"Sorry, Administrator."

"And don't fucking call me *Administrator*, either."

"Sorry—sorry, ah, Hari. The hour—I forget, that's all."

"Yeah, whatever. Check on him."

"Will do, ah, Hari."

"Yeah."

The screen faded to black.

He couldn't quite make himself meet Shanna's eyes. "I, uh, I better go check on Faith. If I woke up Bradlee all the way down on the first floor, I must have scared the shit out of her."

Shanna rose. "I'll go."

"No, no, no," Hari insisted tiredly. "Go back to bed. My fault, my job. I have to go reboot anyway—I'll use the hall toilet so you can sleep."

He whistled for his wheelchair, and it whirred into his bedroom, weaving around the furniture; the proximity sensors of its self-guidance system gave it an animal smoothness of motion. A simple command, "Rover: Stay," locked its wheels into place once it reached his bedside, but Hari engaged the manual brakes as well. His bypass had taught him a grim distrust of microprocessors.

Shanna slid a hand under his armpit to help him up. He lowered his head and didn't move. "I can do it," he said.

"Oh, Hari . . ." She sounded so tired, so inexpressibly sad, as though one breath of his name could compass each of his failures, and all of her forgiveness. It made him grit his teeth till his ears rang. "Go to bed," he said tightly.

"I wish you'd let me help," she murmured, and for a moment the knots in his heart eased, just a little.

He covered her hand with his own. "You help every day, Shan. You're what keeps me going, you and Faith. But you have to let me handle what I can handle, okay?"

She nodded silently. She leaned down and kissed him lightly on the cheek, then went back to the bed on her side of the room. Hari watched her grimly, waiting until she crawled back under the covers and settled in. "Good night," she said.

"Yeah. Good night."

She rolled onto her side, away from him, and gathered the down-filled pillow beneath her head. "Abbey," he said, "lights out. Execute."

Safe in the darkness, he slowly and carefully levered himself from the bed into Rover's seat. It took both hands to move each dead-meat leg, one at a time, into place on the footrests. He sat there for what felt like a long time, breathing too hard, staring at his hands.

He'd made these hands into weapons, conditioned them until they were as deadly as any blade. In years past, he had been widely considered the finest infighter alive. His sole reminder of those days was the crumple of knuckles broken and rebroken, banded with faintly discolored scars.

He'd thought he was tough, back then. Only later, when the most use he had for his hands was shoving a glycerine suppository up his ass and manually disimpacting his bowels, did he find out how tough he really wasn't. The first time Shanna had heard him sobbing, and found him sitting on the toilet with shit all over his futile fists, splattering it in child's footprints across his dead thighs as he tried to pound some feeling, some *use*, back into them, he realized that he'd been kidding himself all along.

He'd never be tough enough for this.

After unlocking Rover's wheels, he gripped their rims and spun the chair roughly toward the door. He'd had a levichair a few years before, but he'd sold it; he'd told Shanna, and his doctors, that he thought the levichair's magfield wasn't properly shielded, and it might have been the culprit behind his software problems. The truth was, he'd hated the fucking thing, and feared it. Any mechanical failure, even a mild powerdown, could leave him helplessly immobilized. At least Rover had wheels.

Which didn't stop him from hating it, too.

The door slid aside at his approach; he wheeled out into the hallway and turned for Faith's room. He should have stopped by the toilet to reboot first, he knew, but some irrational mulishness wouldn't let him be sensible about it. Even if the worst should happen, he wouldn't make much of a mess: Rover had a urine tube, and chemical toilet under the seat—though Hari privately thought that if he ever let himself get into the habit of using them, he'd kill himself.

The smell . . . More than anything else, that's what he feared; the bare thought of it closed down his throat and stung his eyes. He remembered that smell too well: the chemical reek of illness and incontinence. It was Duncan's smell, after his breakdown and downcaste spiral. The tiny apartment he'd shared with his father, in San Francisco's Mission District Temp ghetto, had enclosed that stench, concentrated it, burned it into him like a brand on the inside of his skull. Not sharp, but thick and somehow *rounded*; not pungent but gooey, filling the back of his throat like he was drowning in snot.

It smelled like madness.

Rover's comfort hookups were not a convenience; they were a threat. If he let himself fall that far, if he surrendered in the way every doctor told him he had to, if he *accepted* his disability and tried to *accommodate* it, that smell would cling to him forever. He was afraid that he might get used to it. He was afraid that someday he wouldn't even notice anymore.

Rover rolled to a stop at Faith's door. Hari touched the door with the tips of three fingers, as gently as a caress on his daughter's cheek, and it swung silently inward a few centimeters. He whispered to the Abbey to raise the lights in the hallway, and the house complied, slowly turning up the intensity until a spill of light crossed Faith's bed and gleamed on her spray of golden hair.

She lay in the boneless sprawl of childhood sleep. Hari's chest burned with a fierce ache, and he could not shift his gaze until the slow rise and fall of the nightshirt that covered her chest unlocked his eyes. He remembered staring at Shanna the same way, as Pallas Ril lay bound to the altar in the Iron Room, high atop the Dusk Tower of the Colhari Palace in Ankhana; he remembered the relief—the flood of sanity and purpose returning to the universe—he'd felt when he saw that she still lived.

No such relief ever came to him in these dark nights, when he would stop by Faith's door to stare at his daughter. The cold terror that coiled behind his eyes, the constant expectation that one of these nights he would look in and *not* see her chest rise and fall, never vanished; it was only postponed. He knew, with a certainty that went beyond religious conviction, that she would be taken from him. It was the most basic weave of his fate: Nothing so precious was allowed to remain in his life.

Her translucent skin—it seemed to glow, lit from within by the warmth of her eyes—her hair the color of sunlight on winter wheat, the classical Nordic regularity of her features, all carried just a hint of Shanna's Anglo heritage, and none at all of his. She favored her real father.

Her biological father, Hari corrected himself. *I'm her real father.*

He thought with longing of the scotch bottle on his nightstand. He should have brought it with him. He could use a little peat-fired comfort tonight; these postmidnight hours were a fertile earth for thoughts darker than the night outside.

Sometimes when he looked at Faith, he couldn't help thinking of Lamorak—of Karl. Karl Shanks: second-rate Actor, a minor star, a good-looking swordsman with a small gift for thaumaturgy, at one time a pretty good friend of Hari's. Shanna's lover. Her betrayer.

The father of her child.

Lamorak had betrayed Shanna, and Hari; Hari had betrayed him in turn. Had given him over to torture.

Had murdered him with his own hand.

He could still feel it, even now, more than six years later, if he closed his eyes and thought for just a moment: lying on the arena sand with Kosall through his guts, Ma'elKoth towering over him and Lamorak at his side. With Shanna's tears trickling across his face like the opening drops of a spring shower. He could feel the buzzing hum of Kosall's magick vibrating up his severed spine to his teeth, when he took its hilt to activate the magick of its irresistible edge.

He could feel Lamorak's head slicing free of his body with the ragged *zzzip* of a page being ripped from a book, as he pulled the traitor's neck against Kosall's blade.

It's better this way, he thought. This thought came to him every time he considered whose child he was raising; every time he reminded himself that Faith shared no Michaelson blood. Duncan liked to observe, with Thomas Paine, that virtue is not hereditary; no more so would be its opposite.

Madness, on the other hand, runs in families.

He briefly considered waking her—one sleepy smile from his daughter would chase off a whole night's worth of shadows inside his head—but he knew he wouldn't. He never did. He wouldn't let himself use Faith as a drug against his black moods.

After one last longing look, to watch the rise of her chest, he wheeled Rover down the hall toward his office. When these black fits took hold of his heart, work was his only answer.

But first—

He turned in at the guest bathroom, next door to his office. Rover's arms folded down, and he was able to swing himself onto the toilet using the wall-mounted rails. His pajama trousers fastened up the back with a Velcro closure, so that he could pull them open instead of having to lower them. A four-digit code on the belt unit slung across Rover's back shut down his bypass software, and a single keystroke began the reboot.

As the software that allowed him to walk reinitialized, making his legs twitch and jerk, as his bowels and bladder spastically voided themselves, Hari Michaelson—who had once been Caine—clenched his jaw and squeezed his eyes shut against the familiar tears of his private humiliation. *Why can't I wake up? Please, God—whoever might be listening. That's what I want. That's all I want.*

I want to wake up.

3

HARI SHUFFLED ALONG the hall, a little unsteady on his feet. Good as the bypass was, it would never be the same as a healthy spine; he would forever totter on secondhand legs, operating them by remote control. For the rest of his life, he'd be waxworks from the waist down: a numb, half-Animatronic replica of Caine.

And how, the cold postmidnight of the empty hallway asked him, was he supposed to live with that?

The way I live with everything else, he gritted to himself for the thousandth time, or the millionth. *I'll deal with it. I'll just fucking deal.*

Rover paced him silently, its proximity sensors keeping it a precise two steps behind and to his left; it remained in the hallway, squatting beside the door, when Hari went into the office. Inside, he lowered himself gratefully into the bodyform gel-filled polypropylene of his most comfortable chair and rested his head on his hands. He felt hollow, but also somehow uncomfortably full, and frighteningly fragile, as though his guts were stuffed with eggshells.

He rubbed grit out of his eyes and checked his deskscreen's time readout: 0340. His stomach twisted slowly, sending sour scotch rasping up the back of his throat. He swallowed it again and grimaced at the lingering acid burn it left behind. Some coffee, maybe? Maybe his life looked like shit from nothing more than fatigue and the opening bars of a familiar hangover theme.

For a moment, he flirted with the idea of calling Tan'elKoth, over at the Curioseum. He could stand to talk, tonight, even with an enemy—and Tan'elKoth was hardly that, not after all these years. They had each done things to the other that could not be forgiven—Hari freely admitted he had done more wrong than he'd taken—but somehow it didn't seem to matter.

It's not like he'd wake the big bastard up; Tan'elKoth hadn't slept in something like twelve or thirteen years.

No, goddamit. No, he told himself. *I'm not doing it. Not this time.*

Calling Tan'elKoth would be only a distraction. That's all it ever was. Whatever peace Hari found in the other man's company was a sham, all smoke and mirrors. It wouldn't last an hour after they parted. There was no mystery here; Hari was not so blind that he did not see the real reason he kept company with the former Emperor of Ankhana: Tan'elKoth was the only man alive who treated him like he was still Caine.

That's something else I just gotta fucking get over.

He swiveled his chair around to the mahogany sideboard behind his desk and keyed the coffeemaker for a twelve-cup Yucatán brew. The machine's whirr was only audible enough to let him know it was working as it measured out the mexiroast beans from its refrigerated hopper, ground them, and dusted them with cinnamon. Thick dark coffee drooled into the pitcher, so strong that the smell alone started his caffeine buzz.

While he waited for the pitcher to fill, he idly played with the keypad of his deskscreen. He didn't decide to call up anything in particular, or so he told himself, but somehow his fingers seemed to know what he needed: they entered a long, detailed, specific code.

The dark rectangle of his deskscreen slowly gathered a foggy greyish light: an overcast sky. A blurred patch of brown and cream resolved into a close-up view of a man with the face of a god. Hum and rumble from concealed speakers pulsed into the rhythm of speech; of words, now, in a voice soft and warm and impossibly deep: a voice that is not heard so much as felt: a subterranean vibration, the precursor shocks to an earthquake. Hari didn't need to listen to know what those words were; he remembered them vividly. Even as he remembered that sky, and that face.

Ma'elKoth, framed against the clouds that he had called above Victory Stadium, rumbled his soothing, comforting hum: *let it go, Caine. It's all right. Shh. Lie quiet, relax, and let it go . . .*

Hari stared at the wall of his office while he listened to Caine's voice whisper from the speakers in the artificial speech of the Actor's Soliloquy.

Fuck letting it go.
Never surrender.
Never.

And he hadn't. He hung on, still, every day. He was still fighting. He owed that much, at least, to the man he used to be.

He sighed and reluctantly instructed his deskscreen to link to Studionet. He spoke the required phrases so that Studionet could verify his voiceprint; a moment later, fully updated hardcopy charts began to scroll out of his printer. He gathered them into his hands and shuffled through them. Hari had an innate distrust of data that existed only electronically, on the net; this probably came from growing up in the shadow of Duncan's lunatic libertarianism.

At one time, Hari had possessed an extensive library of non-virtual books, with real cotton-and-wood-pulp pages, cardstock covers—some that dated from the nineteenth and twentieth centuries, bound in leather-covered fiberboard, pages edged with gold leaf. Whenever possible, Duncan had taught Hari from books, the older the better; Duncan claimed that nothing printed after the Plague Years could be trusted.

"The print on the pages—it's an *object*, do you understand? Once it's printed, there it is, in your hand. It can no longer be altered, or edited, or censored—if it is, you can *see* it, see where it's been blacked out or cut away. Electronic text, though, is at least half *imaginary*; anyone can go in and make whatever changes they like, to suit whatever the politics of the moment happen to be. You don't believe me? Call up anything by John Locke on the nets. Call up anything by Abraham Lincoln. By Friedrich Nietzsche or Aleister Crowley. Compare what you see on the screen with what you find in the old books. You'll learn."

Those books were long gone now, of course; hundreds of thousands of marks' worth had been sold. Some of them, too sensitive to be sold—banned works, by unpersons like Shaw, and Heinlein, and Paine—were in a sealed vault on the Sangre de Cristo estate of Hari's Leisure Patron, Marc Vilo. Hari couldn't keep books like that in the house, not with Duncan here.

The commutation of Duncan's sedition sentence was conditional. At the first hint of subversive behavior—for example, possession of banned works of literature—Soapy would sink his teeth into Duncan's ass and drag him away, and not back into the Mute Facility at the Buchanan Social Camp. This time, he'd be cyborged, and sold as a Worker—and Duncan wouldn't last a week under the yoke; as ill as he was, he wouldn't last a day.

He remembered an argument Duncan had had with Tan'elKoth, four or five years ago—back when Duncan still had enough fine motor control to speak aloud. "We hold these *truths* to be *self-evident*; that *all men* are created *equal*; that they are *endowed* by their *creator* with *certain unalienable rights . . .*"

Hari half smiled, remembering. Duncan had been quoting Jefferson with a high, acid-edged screech; that meant Tan'elKoth had been baiting him again. He often fell back on Jefferson when Tan'elKoth had boxed him into a logical corner.

Hari could see the scene as though it unfolded once more before his eyes: Tan'elKoth at the table in the Abbey's kitchen, his bulk dwarfing it to the size of a child's playset. The coffee mug in his massive hand looked like an espresso cup. He wore an immaculately tailored Professional's suit, single-breasted in a stylish taupe, and his mane of chocolate curls was pulled back in a conservative ponytail. He carried himself with the suave cool of a male model, but his eyes danced with unconcealed glee: he loved tangling with Duncan.

"Self-serving propaganda," he'd rumbled, and lifted a finger, pontificating. "Whatever the intent of this hypothetical creator—whose mind you pretend to know—I can tell you this: The gods have no interest in *rights*. There are no rights. Or wrongs. There is only power, and weakness. I have been a god, and I am acquainted with several more; our concern is with the *structure of survival*. A human life is defined by its relationship with others: by its duty to its species. In the face of this duty, *life, liberty, and the pursuit of happiness* are meaningless. What you call *individual rights* are merely the cultural fantasy of a failed civilization."

"Fascist bastard," Duncan had croaked happily. His eyes rolled like misshapen marbles, but his voice was clear, and stronger than it had been in a month. "Can't trust a fascist—truth is always your first sacrifice to the welfare of the state."

"Hmp. As you say. If you do not wish to take my word, ask your daughter-in-law; though she is a weak god, a flawed and failed god, she is a god nonetheless. Ask Pallas Ril where *individual rights* place in her hierarchy of concern."

"Not gonna argue gods with you, you smug sonofabitch," Duncan had croaked.

Duncan had been sitting up that day, his chest strapped securely to the raised back of his convertible traveling bed, its wheels locked alongside the table where Tan'elKoth sat. Veins bulged and twitched among the translucent scraps of white hair that remained on his scalp; his eyes rolled, his hands trembled uncontrollably, and a line of frothy drool trailed down from one corner of his mouth, but he seemed mostly lucid.

Arguing political philosophy was the only thing that had seemed to hold Duncan's attention, even then. Before the autoimmune disorder that was progressively eating his brain had become symptomatic, Duncan had been a professor of social anthropology, a philologist and an authority on the cultures of Overworld. He had always loved to argue, loved it perhaps more than anything else, including his family.

He had nearly ended his life under a sedition sentence in the Mute Facility of the Buchanan Social Camp for one overpowering reason: He could not learn to shut up.

Hari had never been able to argue with him. He didn't have the right kind of mind to spin political fantasies back and forth across a table. Hari had always been too busy surviving the realities of his existence to waste time dreaming about how things *ought* to be. Sometimes a week or more would pass when he could barely get a coherent sentence out of Duncan, but somehow Tan'elKoth always seemed able to draw Duncan up from whatever nirvana into which his private madness had sealed him.

Duncan had gone on, "Don't care about gods. Gods are irrelevant. What counts is *people*. What counts is having *respect* for each other."

"I respect what is respectable," Tan'elKoth replied. "To ask for respect where none has been earned is childish maundering. And what is respectable, in the end, save service? Even your idol Jefferson is, in the end, measured by how well he served the species. The prize of individualism—its goal—is self-actualization, which is only another name for vanity. We do not admire men for achieving self-actualization; we admire self-actualization when its end result is a boon to humanity."

"Huh," Duncan said, wiping his chin with the back of his hand. "Maybe self-actualization is the only way to *really* serve humanity. Maybe it's people like *you* that harm it. When *you* try to 'serve humanity,' you end up making them into sheep. You serve them, all right: you serve them for *dinner*. People *eat* sheep." He rolled his clouded eyes at Hari, a distinct twinkle within them welcoming him to the table, to the discussion, as if to say, *People like you. My son, the predator.*

Tan'elKoth hummed disagreement. "Sheep are very successful, as a species. Humanity, at least on my world, is not. Your individualism leads, inevitably, to men who place their own desires above the welfare of others—of any others, perhaps *all* others."

"Men like Leonardo, and Mozart. Like Charlemagne and Alexander."

"Hmp. Also," Tan'elKoth said with an air of finality, as though he had cunningly led Duncan into an inescapable rhetorical trap, "men like Caine."

That was when Hari had decided he was done with this conversation. "That's *enough*," he said. He set his mug down too fast and too hard; coffee slopped across the table. "Change the subject."

"I meant no insult—" Tan'elKoth said mildly.

"I don't care. I'm not insulted. I'm just sick of listening to it."

Duncan didn't seem to hear; or perhaps he heard, and chose to ignore. "Caine did a lot of good for a lot of people—"

"Purely by accident," Tan'elKoth interrupted.

"Aren't you the one who doesn't believe in chance?"

"Hey," Hari said, louder. "Cut it out, both of you."

Duncan swung his strengthless head toward his son. "I'm only trying to stick up for you, Killer," he said, a tremor leaking into his voice.

"I don't need you to defend me, Dad," Hari told him. "I just need you to shut up."

Deeper clouds had gathered behind the cataracts in his father's eyes, drawing a veil between his consciousness and the world. "Sorry . . . I'm sorry . . ."

Sitting now at his desk in the black morning, those last three words burned him. How could he have said such a thing? How could he have been so childish?

And though he might pretend otherwise, the answer was all too clear. The wound left by the excision of Caine from his life had been too fresh back then. He hadn't had a chance to adjust to the granite fact that he could never, ever be that man again. Never again would he be that strong. Never that sure.

Never that free.

He hadn't known, then, the source of his pain—he'd kept telling himself *I got everything I wanted. I won, goddammit! What the fuck is my problem?* All he'd really understood was that he *hurt* all the time; all he had was blank animal incomprehension and the social grace of a wolverine with a toothache.

Not long after that, Duncan's voice had gone forever. Right now, he couldn't remember if his father had ever spoken to him again.

Hari spent a long time staring at the hardcopy charts spread across his desk. Gradually, he forced himself to make sense of the numbers. *Christ, that's ugly,* he thought. He rearranged them, gathered them up, shuffled them, and spread them across his desk once again. No matter in what order he stacked them, the brutal truth was unmistakable.

He didn't know what the fuck he was doing.

Of the six fiscal years that he had been Chairman of the San Francisco Studio, his Studio had lost money in four; three in a row, now, and getting worse. He had taken the number one Studio on Earth—the flagship of the entire Adventures Unlimited system—and he had pooched it so badly that now only the freight fees paid by the Overworld Company were keeping it afloat.

This is a mystery? he thought bitterly. *This was supposed to be a surprise?*

He had been given the Chairmanship—and its attendant upcasting to Administration—as a blatant public-relations stunt, a transparent attempt to counter the disastrous aftermath of Caine's final Adventure, *For Love of Pallas Ril.* The fallout of that Adventure had toppled SF's previous Chairman, Arturo Kollberg, and had blackened the reputation of the entire Studio system. At the time, briefly, Hari had been the most famous man on Earth—*For Love of Pallas Ril* was the single most popular Adventure in history, setting records for both viewership and receipts that still stood, nearly seven years later—and he could have done incalculable damage to the industry. So they bought him off.

That's a little too generous, Hari thought. *I wasn't bought off. I was just bought.*

Bought with the chance to live in peace with the woman he loved. Bought with the chance to raise his daughter as an Administrator. Bought with the chance to get to know his father again, as a man. And in return?

All he had to do was sit down and shut up.

One of his new colleagues, the Chairman of the St. Petersburg Studio, had put it cogently when they first met, a couple of weeks after Hari's upcaste: "Perhaps the most significant skill an effective Administrator ever develops is the ability to do nothing. Knowing *when not to act* is vastly more important than knowing *what to do* can ever be."

And there he had it: a philosophical rationale for being a good boy, for sitting quietly and marking days till his pension. *Thus conscience does make cowards of us all,* Hari thought.

He was strong enough to survive any given day. But when he looked down the long bleak tunnel of the rest of his life, he saw far too many nights like this one, sitting at his desk after 0300, staring into the cement-grey certainty that today would be exactly like yesterday, tomorrow and tomorrow and tomorrow creeping in its petty pace from day to day, world without end, amen.

If he was lucky.

Another keystroke or two pulled up an abstract of the latest brief filed in Social Court by lawyers for Avery Shanks. Whenever Hari was in a really shitty mood, like tonight, he could access the growing archive of *Bsn. Shanks v. Adr. Michaelson*, and brood about what would happen if Studio Legal ever dropped the ball.

Businessman Avery Shanks—Karl Shanks' mother, *Lamorak's* mother, the head of the electronic chemicals giant SynTech— had personally filed capital Forcible Contact Upcaste charges against Hari within days of the climax of *For Love of Pallas Ril*—before Hari was even out of the hospital. She had used the SynTech legal department as her personal attack dogs, filing and refiling, contending that her son's caste of Professional had been only pro forma, attendant to his employment as an Actor. Syn-Tech lawyers continued to argue that Karl should be considered a Businessman in the eyes of the court.

Which, without the Studio's protection, would be enough to get Hari cyborged and sold as a Worker.

On his worst nights, Hari suspected that the reason the Studio hadn't quashed this lawsuit altogether is that they planned to drop it on him like a hammer if he ever stepped out of line.

He closed the lawsuit archive, rustled his hardcopy charts again, straightened them with an irritable snap, but his attention circled inevitably back . . .

Legal fees alone could wipe him out. Shanna's income couldn't support the family by itself, even without the costs of a court battle; she still had a fanatically loyal core audience, but her overall receipts had been dropping for years. She didn't even have first-handers anymore. She spent each of her twice-yearly three-month shifts on freemod, her experiences being graved into a microcube: an ironic echo of one of Arturo Kollberg's innovations, the Long Form.

The experience of being a goddess has a certain charm—the seamless serenity of her powerful connection to her entire world, the mind-bending awareness of every living thing within the Great Chambaygen watershed, the uplifting consciousness of boundless power perfectly controlled—but her fans had soon discovered they could get the same effect from her cubes. Even from a single cube. Since each day was much like another for Chambaraya, her rentals were shit. To keep first-handers coming back, for good rentals and cube sales, you need *story*. Story was exactly what Pallas Ril didn't have. She was complete; there was nothing she could need that the river did not provide. For Chambaraya, there is no necessity. Without necessity, all is whim.

He shook his head to rattle his attention back to the charts in his hands. He'd been staring at them sightlessly for he didn't know how long. The figures on the page no longer had any meaning he could comprehend; they had become vaguely threatening hiero-glyphs, an apocalyptic prophecy in Linear A.

With a sigh, he finally surrendered. He folded the charts once, then again, then tucked them neatly into the disposal chute alongside his desk. "Abbey: Call out. AV," he said. "The Studio Curioseum. Private line of Tan'elKoth. Execute."

In a moment, the *Waiting* logo on the screen dissolved to a high-contrast, discolored view of Tan'elKoth's face. *"Caine. Another sleepless night?"*

"Goddammit," Hari said for what seemed like the millionth time, "if I have to call you Tan'elKoth, you can fucking well call me Hari." But this protest had become familiar, reflexive, and he could hear the insincerity that blunted its edge.

Tan'elKoth heard it, too. One majestic eyebrow arched, and the creases at the corners of his eyes deepened a trifle. *"Just so."*

"What's wrong with your screen? You're all orange, and the contrast is so bad it looks like half your face is missing."

Tan'elKoth shrugged and rubbed his eyes. *"The screen is fine. I can no longer abide reading from a monitor, and the incessant flicker of your electric lights gives me a headache."* He turned the screen so that Hari could see the large book open on Tan'elKoth's reading desk, and the tall flame of the oil-burning hurricane lamp that sat beside it. *"But you did not rise in these wee hours to chaff me for poor equipment maintenance."*

"Yeah," Hari sighed. "I guess I was wondering, if you weren't too busy—"

"Busy, Administrator? I, busy? Perish the thought. I am, as I have been for lo, these many years, entirely at your disposal, Mr. Chairman."

"Forget it," Hari muttered. He lacked the strength to shoulder Tan'elKoth's heavy irony tonight. He reached for the cutoff.

"Caine, wait," Tan'elKoth said. His eyes shifted, and he passed a hand over his face as though he wanted to wipe away his features and become a different man. *"Please—ah, Hari— forgive my tone. I have been too long alone with bitter thoughts, and I spoke without thinking. I would be glad of company tonight, should you wish it."*

Hari studied Tan'elKoth's image on the screen: the dark streaks beneath his eyes, the new creases and sags of his once-perfect skin, and the downtwist at the corners of lips that had once known only smiles. *Shit,* Hari thought. *Do I look as bad as he does?*

"I was thinking," Hari said slowly, "that I might brew a jug of coffee and sail over. Feel like walking?"

Tan'elKoth's downtwists flattened toward what might have been a smile, on somebody else. *"Into the District?"*

Hari shrugged like he didn't care, fooling neither himself nor Tan'elKoth. "I guess. Game?"

"Of course. I enjoy your old neighborhood; I find it stimulating. Rather like one of your antique nature films: an ocean of tiny predators, circling each other." He cocked his head at the screen and spoke with the soft cheer of a man telling an off-color joke in a crowded restaurant. *"When was the last time you killed someone?"*

Below the desk, one of Hari's hands found its way to the numb, dead-meat oval of scar tissue at the small of his back. "You should remember. You were there."

"Mmm, just so. But, one never knows: Perhaps tonight, we shall be lucky enough to be attacked."

"Yeah, maybe." *If we run across a wolfpack that's stone fucking blind,* Hari thought. "All right, then. I'm on my way."

"I'll be at the South Gate in half an hour."

"See you there."

"Yes, you shall—" He smiled as he poked the cutoff. *"—Caine."*

Hari shook his head and directed a disgusted snort at the dark rectangle of screen. He hit his own cutoff and found half a smile growing on his face.

"Hari? You never came back to bed."

He looked up, and his smile faded away again. Shanna stood in the doorway, looking at him reproachfully through her pillow-twisted hair. Her face wore the fading ghosts of beatitude, a slowly dimming glow of transcendent peace: she'd been dreaming of the river.

It made him want to throw something at her.

"Yeah, I—" He lowered his head and tried not to look guilty, and gestured at the stacks of hardcopy spread across his desk. "I decided to get some work done."

"Who were you talking to? That was Tan'elKoth, wasn't it?"

He lowered his eyes and stared at the fists he'd made against his legs.

"You know I wish you didn't spend so much time with—"

"Yeah, I *know*," Hari interrupted. This was a familiar argument, and he didn't feel like spinning it up again at this hour of the night. "I'm gonna go out for a little while."

"Now?" These days, it never seemed to take long for that transcendent peace to flush out of her face; it was gone already. "You're going out in the middle of the *night*?"

"Yeah. I do that, sometimes." He left unsaid the *And you'd know it, if you were here with me and your daughter more than six months a goddamn year,* but it hung between them anyway, silently poisoning the air.

She pushed back her hair with the heel of one hand, and her face had that pinched, overcontrolled look he remembered too well, from the bad old days when they couldn't so much as open their mouths without starting a fight.

Bad old days? Who am I kidding? he thought.

These are *the bad old days.*

"Will you be back in time for breakfast?" she asked; then she slipped in the cheap shot like a knife between his ribs. "Or do I need some lie to tell Faith about where you are?"

He started to snarl back at her, but caught himself. Who was he to complain about cheap shots? He let out a long, slow breath and shook his head. "No. No, I'll be back for breakfast. Look, I'm sorry, Shanna. Sometimes, I just need somebody to talk to—"

When he saw the look on her face, he wished he'd bitten his tongue in half before those last words had come out.

Her eyes pinched almost shut, and her mouth set in a painfully thin line. "Sometimes I still let myself hope you might want to talk to me."

"Oh, Shanna, don't—look, I do talk to you." He did: whenever he could stand to hear for the billionth fucking time How Easy It Is to Be Happy, if he just let himself Flow Like the River and shit like that. He looked away so that she wouldn't read this on his face. None of this was her fault, and he'd promised himself over and over again he wouldn't take it out on her. "Ah, forget it. I'm going."

He shuffled the hardcopy into a stack and stood up. She came into the room as if she could stop him. "I wish you'd be more careful with Tan'elKoth. You can't trust him, Hari. He's *dangerous*."

He brushed past her, careful not to touch her on his way to the door. "Yeah, he is," he said. He added under his breath, as he walked away down the hall, "Like I used to be."

And behind him, with endless inanimate patience, paced Rover.

4

SHE LEANED ON the window of his study, cooling her forehead against the glass, and watched him go. The black teardrop of his Daimler Nighthawk followed a long, smooth, computer-directed arc upward toward the cloud deck.

She ached for the river.

Forty days, she thought. *That's really just five weeks—well, six. For six weeks, I can stand anything.*

Forty days from today, at 0900 hours, her next shift as the goddess would begin. At 0830 she would snug the respirator and lower herself into the freemod coffin and lock down its lid; she'd lie motionless on the gelcot for the endless minutes of mass balancing—the freemod transfer requires an extremely precise exchange of mass/energy between the universes—and for those slow-ticking seconds she would hang in delicious anticipation, awaiting the mind-twisting soundless thunderclap of freemod transfer. Awaiting the first notes of Chambaraya's Song: the deep, slow hymn of welcome that would fill her heart and draw forth her answering melody. Twice a year, for three months at a time, she could be part of the river.

Twice a year, she could be whole.

She'd never told Hari how she longed for that music; she'd never told him how empty and stale Earth had become for her. She loved him too much to tell him how painful it was to be alone inside her head. *Can't you see?* her heart cried to the departing arc of his car.

Can't you see how lonely I am?

Slow tears rolled down her cheeks. How could she live, with nothing inside her but memory and hope?

"Mommy?" Faith's voice came tentatively from behind her. "Mommy, are you all right?"

Shanna pushed herself away from the window. She didn't bother to wipe away her tears; the intimate bond she shared with Faith for half of each year made lying impossible. "No," she said. "No, I'm sad today."

"Me, too." Faith knuckled her eyes as she slowly came into the study. Shanna met her and picked her up, straightening Faith's pajamas and brushing the fine-spun golden hair back from her face. Faith sighed and laid her cheek against Shanna's shoulder. "You miss the river, huh?"

Shanna nodded silently. She sat back down on the window seat and held Faith on her lap; she looked out toward the orange-underlit gloom of the cloud deck.

"Me, too," Faith said solemnly. "I miss the music. It's always so quiet when you're home—sometimes I get a little scared."

Shanna hugged her daughter tightly, intimately aware of how small and fragile she was, holding her small head against her shoulder. The physical contact was only a poor echo, though, of the intimacy and love they could share when connected by the river. Faith had been born nine months—almost to the day—after her battle at the Ankhanan docks. The cells that would someday become her daughter had been already riding in her womb, that first time she'd ever touched the river and joined its Song.

Faith had been brushed with power at the apotheosis of Pallas Ril.

"I miss you when you're here," Faith said. "It's pretty lonely, without the music. But Daddy needs you, too."

"Yes," Shanna said. "Yes, I know."

"Is that what happened? Were you and Daddy fighting?"

"No, we weren't fighting. No one fights with your father anymore," Shanna said hopelessly. She looked out toward the swell of cloud where the Nighthawk had disappeared. "I think that's most of the problem."

5

THE TENEMENT SAGGED under the weight of two hundred years' neglect. Its smog-blackened walls gave back almost none of the glow from the single cracked streetlight outside: a vacant, slightly lopsided rectangle, it loomed against the overcast night, a window into oblivion.

Hari stood on the crumbling pavement, staring up into the alley behind, at the spot where he knew his window still was: 3F, third floor in the back, farthest from the stairwell. Three rooms and one walk-in closet barely big enough for an eight-year-old boy to have a cot. That tiny closet had been his room until a month after his sixteenth birthday.

And that window, which could be pried open silently if he worked at it carefully enough: with better light—or younger eyes—he was sure he'd be able to pick out rope scars on the ancient aluminum windowsill.

He could still feel the coil of that rope pressing against his ribs from its hiding place between his thin camp mattress and the steel slats of the cot frame. That coil of rope had saved his life dozens of times; sometimes his only chance to escape Duncan's intermittent homicidal rages had been to lock the door of his room and slip out that window, lower himself to the street. Down here among the whores and the addicts and the prowling sexual predators he had been closer to safe than anywhere within his father's reach.

Closer to safe than breathing that apartment's stink of madness into his lungs.

"I once thought," Tan'elKoth said beside his shoulder, "that I understood why we come here. I believed that you come to remind yourself what an extraordinary journey your life has been. From here, one can see both where you began—" He nodded at the tenement, then turned to regard the spire of San Francisco Studio Central, only three kilometers away. "—and the pinnacle which you have achieved. The contrast is, not to put too fine a point on it, astonishing. Yet it seems to give you no satisfaction."

Hari didn't need to look at Tan'elKoth to know the expression he'd be wearing: a mask of polite interest that half concealed a savage hunger. The ex-Emperor had an interest both intense and abiding in anything that might cause Hari pain. Hari didn't grudge that interest; he'd earned it.

"That's not why I come here," he said heavily.

He looked around at the crumbling buildings that leaned over the broken pavement; at the darkened basement bars on every corner, filled with loud music and restlessly still people; at the food bank, where empty-eyed men and women with silent children were already queuing up for the breakfast that was still two hours away. Not far away, a rumpled mound of tattered clothing moved slightly, revealing a ragface in the final stages of his long descent: his eyes rolled sightlessly, blind with methanol poisoning, his nose and part of his upper lip rotted into oozing open wounds. The ragface opened a plastic bag to pull out his dirty wad of fuel-laced handkerchief and pressed it to his mouth, shuddering deeply as he inhaled.

Hari lifted a hand, dropped it again: a brief hopeless flick that encompassed the entire Mission District. "Sometimes I have to remind myself it's a long fucking way down."

An old, old punchline whispered in the back of his head, bitter and unfunny: *The fall ain't so bad—the problem's that sudden stop at the bottom . . .*

"You are considering a leap?" Tan'elKoth said slowly.

Hari shrugged and started walking again. Rover hummed along in the street behind him, keeping its robotic two-pace distance.

Tan'elKoth swung alongside with the ponderous majesty of a battle cruiser at half speed. "And this is why you bring me here? Do you hope that I hate you enough to convince you to jump?"

"Don't you?" He squinted up at the enormous man beside him. Tan'elKoth wore the cable-knit sweater and chinos of a casually stylish Professional, and his dark mane was pulled back in a conservative ponytail. Middle age was softening his jawline toward a curve of jowl, but he still had the titanic build of the god he had once been. The metallic straps of the ammod harness that he wore over his sweater gleamed like armor under the streetlight. It was easy to imagine that the pavement would tremble beneath his step.

"Of course I do," Tan'elKoth said easily. They ambled along another block, passing from shadow to light to shadow again, sharing a companionable silence.

"I have dreamed your death, Caine," he said finally. "I have lusted for it as the damned in your Christian hell lust for oblivion. Your death would not give me back my Empire, would not return to me the love of my Children, but it would ease—if only for the few seconds that I crush your life between my fingers—the suffering of my exile."

He lowered his head as though to examine the sidewalk. "But: once done, I would be bereft. I would have nothing else of which to dream."

Hari sidestepped a pair of drunks who leaned on each other as they tried to decide whether to go indoors or pass out here on the street; Tan'elKoth shouldered them effortlessly out of the way. They shouted something slurred and angry. Hari and Tan'elKoth kept walking. "And further," Tan'elKoth murmured, "I confess that I would miss you."

"You would?"

"Sadly, yes." He sighed. "I find myself living more and more upon memories of the past. They are the sole comfort of my captivity. You are the only person with whom I share those memories; you are the only man alive who truly remembers—who truly *appreciates*—what I once was." He spread his hand in a gesture of resignation. "Maudlin, isn't it? What a revolting creature I have become."

This cut a little too close to the bone for Hari's comfort; he walked on without speaking for a block or two. "Don't you—" he began slowly, then started again. "You ever think about going back?"

"Of course. My home is never far from my thoughts; Ankhana is the land of my birth, and of my rebirth. The bitterest wound that life has inflicted upon me is the knowledge that I will never taste that wind, never warm my face with that sun, never stand upon that earth, ever again. I could leave this life a happy man, if only my last breath might be of Ankhanan air."

Tan'elKoth lifted his massive shoulders and dropped them again. "But that is an empty fantasy. Even if your masters would allow such a thing, the Beloved Children have no need of me; I am of greater value to the Church as a symbol than I could be as a personal god. And that god still exists: The power of Ma'elKoth is a function of the pooled devotion of my worshipers. Priests of Ma'elKoth still channel the power to perform miracles by praying to my image—I should say, His, for He and I are no longer coextensive."

He released a long, slow sigh, empty of all feeling save loss. "I cannot pretend that the world fails to turn for lack of my hand upon it."

Hari nodded. "Shit just turns out that way sometimes," he said. "You should be used to it by now."

"Should I?" Tan'elKoth came to a halt; he appeared to study the urine-stained wall at his side. "And how is it that I should find my defeat more tolerable than you have your victory?"

Hari snorted. "That's easy: you can blame it on me," he said. "Who do *I* blame?"

Chocolate brows canted upward over his enormous liquid eyes as Tan'elKoth considered this. "Mm, just so," he admitted at last, nodding to himself with a rueful half smile. "It is a curiously consistent characteristic of yours, Caine, that you always seem to be just a bit smarter than I anticipate."

"Yeah, sure. I'm a genius with a capital J."

Tan'elKoth laid one finger alongside the bend in his nose where Caine had broken it: the only flaw in his classically perfect features. "Do you know why I have never had this repaired?" he asked. He opened his hand as though releasing a butterfly. "For the same reason that I changed my name."

Hari squinted at him again, narrowing his eyes to overlay his vision with the memory of this man as he'd been in the days he had ruled the Ankhanan Empire, as Emperor and living god. In those days, he had called himself *Ma'elKoth*, a phrase in Paquli that translates, roughly, as *I Am Limitless. Ma*, in Paquli, is the present nominative case of *to be; tan* is its past tense.

I Was Limitless.

"So that every time I hear my name—every time I see my reflection—" Tan'elKoth continued, "I am reminded of the penalty for underestimating you."

His tone was distantly precise. Well rehearsed. More and more, during these Earthbound years, Tan'elKoth seemed to be talking for someone else's benefit—as though he was playing to an audience that existed only in his mind.

Hari grunted. "Flatterer."

"Mmm. Perhaps."

"Is that why you've never made a try for me?"

Tan'elKoth began walking again. "Revenge is an occupation of inferior minds," he said meditatively. "It is the shibboleth of spiritual poverty."

"That's not an answer."

Tan'elKoth only shrugged and walked on. After a moment, Hari followed him. "Perhaps I have not destroyed you," the ex-Emperor murmured, "because it is more enjoyable to watch you destroy yourself."

"That's about right," Hari said with a snort. "Everything I've done my whole life has been somebody's *entertainment*."

Tan'elKoth hummed a neutral agreement.

Hari rubbed the back of his neck, but his fingers couldn't loosen the knots that had tied themselves there. "Maybe that's part of what's so hard to take, at the end of the day. I've done a lot of shitty things in my life. I've done some pretty good things. But when you come right down to it, none of that matters. Everything I've done, everything that's been done to me—win, lose, love, hate, who gives a fuck?—it all only counts as far as it helps some bastard I've never met while away a couple idle hours."

"We are indeed a pair," Tan'elKoth mused. "Our wars long fought, our glories passed. Is it truly that your life was mere entertainment which troubles you—or is it that your life is no longer so entertaining?"

"Hey, that reminds me," Hari said. "I don't think I've invited you lately to go fuck yourself."

Tan'elKoth smiled indulgently. "I wept because I had no shoes, until I met a man who had no feet." He nodded down the sidewalk, at a ragged legless beggar dozing in his ancient manual wheelchair. "Consider this man: I have no doubt he would give up his very hope of the afterlife to walk—even so badly as you walk—for one single day."

"So?" Hari said. "So he's more crippled than I am. So what?"

Tan'elKoth's smile turned cold. "You have a much nicer wheelchair."

"Oh, sure," Hari said. He grunted a bitter laugh. "Rover's a real treat."

"Rover?" Tan'elKoth said. One eyebrow arched more steeply. "You gave a name to your wheelchair? I hadn't thought you the type."

Hari shrugged irritably. "It's a command code, that's all. It lets the voice-control software know I'm talking to it."

"And Rover is a dog's name, is it not? Like Faithful—mm, Fido?"

"It's not a dog's name," Hari said, disgusted with himself. "It's a joke, that's all. It started as a bad joke, and I just never bothered to change it."

"I don't see the humor."

"Yeah, me neither." He shrugged dismissively. "I know you don't watch a lot of net. You know anything about twentieth-century serial photoplays?"

"Little, save that they tend to be infantile."

"Well, there was one called *The Prisoner*. Ever hear of it?"

Tan'elKoth shook his head.

"It's kind of too complicated to really explain," Hari said. "Rover was . . . a very efficient prison guard. That's all."

"Mmm," Tan'elKoth mused. "I think I see—"

"Don't go wise and philosophical on me—every time you pull that shit, I start to regret I didn't kill you when I had the chance."

"Just so." Tan'elKoth sighed. "Sometimes I do, too."

Hari looked at him, trying to think of something to say; after a moment, he just nodded and started walking again, and Tan'elKoth fell in at his side.

They walked together in silence for some time.

"I suppose . . . the actual question is, What, in the end, does one want?" Tan'elKoth asked finally. "Do we want to become happy with the lives we have, or do we want to *change* our lives—into lives with which we will be happy? After all, to content yourself with your current situation is a simple matter of serotonin balance: it can be accomplished by medication."

"Drugs won't change anything but my attitude." Hari shrugged, dismissing the idea. "And changing? My whole life? This was what I was *fighting* for."

"Was it?"

"I *won*, goddammit. I beat Kollberg. I beat *you*. I got everything I goddamn wanted: fame, wealth, power. Shit, I even got the girl."

"The problem with happy endings," Tan'elKoth said, "is that nothing is ever truly over."

"Fuck that," Hari said. "I am living happily ever goddamn after. I *am*."

"Ah, I see: It is *happiness* which has brought you to these streets, at this hour, with me," Tan'elKoth murmured. "I have always supposed *living happily ever after* at four A.M. would somehow involve lying in bed, asleep, with one's *wife*."

Hari looked at the filthy pavement beneath his feet. "It's just . . . I don't know. Sometimes, y'know, late at night . . ." He shook his head, driving away the thought. He took a slow breath, and shrugged. "I guess I'm not handling getting old so well, that's all. This is . . . Ahh, fuck it. Midlife crisis bullshit."

Tan'elKoth stood silently at Hari's side, motionless, until Hari looked up and found the ex-Emperor staring at him like he'd bitten into something rotten that he couldn't spit out. "Is this the name you give to your despair? Midlife crisis bullshit?"

"Yeah, all right, whatever. Call it whatever the fuck you want—"

"Stop," Tan'elKoth rumbled. He put a hand the size of a cave bear's paw on Hari's shoulder and gave him a squeeze that stopped just short of crushing bone. "You cannot trivialize your pain with *nomenclature*. You forget to whom you speak, Caine."

Tan'elKoth's gaze smoked; it held Hari as tight as his smothering grip did. "In this way, we are brothers; I have felt what you feel, and we both know that no mere word can compass and contain this injury. We are *wounded*, you and I: with a hurt that time cannot heal. Like a cancer, like gangrene, it grows worse with each passing hour. It is *killing* us."

Hari lowered his head. The pain in his chest allowed him no answer; he could only stare, grip-jawed and silent, at the faint bands of soft color across his knuckles.

Drunken voices slurred from behind them, "Hey, you fuckers! Hey, shitheads!"

Hari and Tan'elKoth turned to find two men lurching toward them along the street: the pair of drunks Tan'elKoth had shouldered off the sidewalk. As they wove unsteadily through a pool of mercury-argon lampglow, Hari could see the length of pipe in one's hand. In the hand of the other, two decimeters of blade gleamed steel-bright.

"Who th'fuck y'think y'are?" the one with the knife asked owlishly; he turned his head from side to side as though searching for an angle that might clear his vision. "Who y'think y'r shovin'?"

The knife guy was in the lead; Hari took one step forward to intercept him. He could read this bastard like a street sign. The knife was for show—for intimidation, for self-respect: eight inches of steel penis, bright and hard.

Hari saw three ways he could settle this right down. He could apologize, maybe buy them a drink, cool them off a little, let them feel like they mattered—that's all they really wanted. Or he could pull out his palmpad and key the Social Police, then point out to these guys that he's an Administrator and Tan'elKoth's a Professional, and they were looking at life under the yoke if they didn't back off. Simplest would be just to tell them who he was. Laborers are as celebrity-struck as anybody else, and unexpectedly meeting Caine himself on the street would dazzle them.

Instead, he angled the right side of his body slightly away from the guy, presenting about a three-quarter profile, his hands boneless at his sides, a bright tingle beginning to sizzle along his nerves. "Y'know, you shouldn't pull a knife unless you're gonna use it."

"Who says I'm not planning to—"

Hari leaned into a lunge, his left hand becoming a backfist as it blurred through a short arc from his thigh to the guy's nose. It struck with a wet *whack* like the snap of a soaked towel, and tilted the drunk's head back to the perfect angle for Hari's right cross to take him precisely on the point of the chin.

Hari staggered a little, grimacing—his bypass's secondhand footwork left him off balance, open for a countering slash of the knife—but it didn't matter: the drunk fell backward like a toppling pole and stretched his length on the pavement.

"It's not about what you're *planning*," Hari said.

Both his fists burned and stung.

It was a good pain, and he welcomed it.

"Fuck my *mother*," the other drunk breathed, the pipe hanging forgotten by his side. "You—I know you—you *are*, aren't you? I mean, aren't you *Caine*?"

"I used to be," Hari said.

"I'm a big fan—"

"Thanks. Take a fucking hike."

"No, I mean it, I really am—"

"I believe you. Now get out of here before I kill you."

The drunk stumbled off, muttering to himself, "Shit, holy shit, holy son of a motherfucking shit . . ."

Tan'elKoth nodded down at the man who lay on the street. "Is he dead?"

"Maybe." Hari shrugged. "Probably not."

Hari's combat rush faded as fast as it had risen, leaving him bleak and bitter and slightly sick. His hands throbbed and his mouth tasted of coffee grounds. *So, here I am, thirty years later: still beating up drunks in the Mission District.*

Why not just go ahead and roll him for loose change?

"You asked me what I want. I can tell you . . ." Hari said slowly. "I can tell you exactly what I want."

He nudged the drunk with his toe, not even really seeing the man anymore; in this drunken, bleeding Laborer lying in the street, his face busted up because he was too stupid to back off, he was looking at himself.

"I want to find out who it is that keeps reaching down into my life and turning everything I touch into shit," Hari said. "I want to *meet* him. I'm not asking for much: I want to share a little bit of pain with him, that's all." He pressed his fists against his legs, and said through his teeth, "I want to get my *hands* on the motherfucker."

"Mm. This is a dream I can share with you, Caine." Once again, Tan'elKoth laid his hand across Hari's shoulder like a blanket, and through that physical connection sparked a current of understanding.

Hari pulled away.

Tan'elKoth kept his hand in the air, turning it over as though to read his own palm. He loomed over Hari, blank, impenetrable, inhumanly solid: a sarsen stone outlined against the dawn-lit clouds above.

"Be careful for what you wish," he said softly. "A very wise man of your world has observed that when the gods would punish us, they answer our prayers."

THE GOD OF DUST and ashes had slept for an age, fitful in slow, infinite starvation, restlessly gnawing on the bleak cinder that had been its world.

Though the god slumbered, its merest dream maintained its dominion, for it was attended by priests who never guessed at its existence. It had a church that did not seem to be a church, had a religion that did not know it was a religion, and had followers that prayed to other gods, or to no god at all. Years passed while it awakened—but when it finally roused, men leaped to serve it, though they thought they served only themselves.

For this is the power of the god of dust and ashes: to weave the lives of its followers so that the fabric thus created has a pattern none of them intend.

TWO

AS THE CRISP late-summer afternoon faded to evening, the shadow of the God's Teeth mountains stretched to the east and swallowed first the mines, erasing their billowing towers of smoke, then wiped across the Northwest Road and engulfed Thorncleft, the tiny Transdeian capital city.

The Monastic Ambassador to Transdeia, a young man the world named Raithe of Ankhana, sat in a straight-backed, unadorned, unpadded, and exceptionally uncomfortable chair, staring out at the shadow's grope with blank unseeing eyes.

Most unsettling, those eyes were: the pale blue grey of winter ice, set in a face as dark and leathery as that of a Korish desert tribesman. The startling contrast made his stare a disturbing, almost dangerous thing; few men could bear to match his gaze. Fewer still would care to try, if they knew just how deeply those pale eyes could see.

Late in the afternoon, five elves had come to Thorncleft. Raithe had seen them first from this very window: dusty, in clothing travel-worn and stained, mounted on horses whose ribs showed even under their mantles of green and black. Those mantles had been embroidered with the star-browed raven that was the standard of House Mithondionne.

Raithe had stared at them, memorizing every discernable curve of shoulder and tangle of hair, every faded patch where the sun had bleached color from their linen surcoats, all the details of posture and gesture that made each of them individual, as the elves walked their horses up high-sloping Tor Street. He had stepped from the shadow of the half-built Monastic embassy into the street, shielding his eyes against the lowering sun, had watched them answer the challenge at the vaulted gate of Thornkeep, had watched as the gate swung wide and the elves led their horses within.

Then he went back into the embassy, into his office, and sat in this chair so that he could see them more clearly.

He held himself perfectly erect and controlled his breathing, timing it by the subtle beats of his own heart: six beats in, hold for three, nine beats out, hold for three. As his heart slowed, so did the cycle of his breath. He built their image in the eye of his mind, drawing details of their backs from his trained memory, since their backs were what he had seen most clearly: a spray of platinum hair pricked through by the barest hint of pointed ears, a diagonal leather thong to support a waterskin, the inhuman grace of stance, the way shoulders move when hands swing in small, light gestures.

Slowly, slowly, with infinite patience, he fed details into the image: the dark curls hand-tooled into their belts, the lace of scar tissue across one's forearm, the sideways duck of another's head as he whispered to one of his companions. These were details he had not seen, could not have seen; these were details that he created in his powerful imagination. Yet as he refined them, and brought them more vividly before his mind's eye, they became plastic, shifted, and finally organized into plain, visible truth.

Now ghosts of their surroundings materialized in his mind: the marble floor, deeply worn but highly polished, on which their boots made almost no sound, the long tongue of pale blue carpet that entered the doorway before them. He got a vague sense of huge, high-vaulted space, oaken beams blackened by years of smoldering torches below.

He hummed satisfaction under his breath. This would be the Hall of State.

He had been inside that hall many times in the few months since he'd been posted here from Ankhana; using his recollection of the details of the hall brought the scene inside it into sharper and more brilliant focus than he could have seen with the eyes of his body—from the glittering steel of the ceremonial weapons that bedizened the walls to the precise color of the sunlight that struggled through the smoke-darkened windows. There before the elves was the Gilt Throne, and upon it lounged Transdeia's lazy, spineless puppet lord: Kithin, fourteenth Duke of Thorncleft. Raithe could see even the stitching on Duke Kithin's shirt of maroon and gold; with that as a mental anchor, he swung his perception to see the room as Kithin saw it. Now, for the first time, he could get a good look at the faces of the elves.

He didn't trouble to study these faces too closely; elvish features lack the creases that time and care paint upon human physiognomy, and thus reveal nothing of their character. Elves, in Raithe's experience, looked very much alike.

He was rather more interested in what had brought them to Thorncleft, and so he studied the silent motions of lips and tongue; though he spoke little Primal, they would be conversing in Westerling for the benefit of Duke Kithin, and lipreading is easy, when practiced through the pristine vision of his mindeye.

His mindeye had always been one of his most useful talents.

Raithe had been only a boy when he'd discovered his gift: thirteen years old, barely into adolescence. One golden morning he had lain in bed, in his room above his father's tiny smithy, slowly awakening from a dream. In the dream, he'd kissed Dala, the raven-haired sixteen-year-old girl who sold sticky buns on the corner of Tanner and the Angle; as he lay in bed fingering the erection this dream had given him, he'd imagined her rising for the morning and pulling her nightdress off over her head, imagined her round, swelling breasts bouncing free, her nipples hardening as she splashed herself with water from the pitcher beside her bed. In his mind, he saw her stand naked before the mirror, braiding her hair in a new way, coiling it into a gleaming black helmet instead of the long strands she usually allowed to trail down her back; he imagined that she chose her oldest blouse to wear that day, the one he loved the best, its fabric so worn and supple that it clung to her curves and gave a hint of the dark circles of her nipples.

Sheer fantasy, of course: the vivid daydreams of an imaginative boy in lust.

But when he'd gone that morning to buy buns for his father's dinner, blushing so that he hardly dared even to look at her, he'd found that she was wearing that very blouse, and she had chosen that morning to coil her hair up in a new style, tight and shining around her head—exactly as he had imagined it.

That had been Raithe's first hint that he was destined for greatness.

Mastering his gift had not come easily. In the days and weeks that followed, as he spied on Dala's naked body at every opportunity, he found that his vivid imagination was more hindrance than help. Too often, his mental image of her would lift hands to breasts, to fondle and squeeze them as he wanted to do. Too often, he would fantasize one hand creeping down to the silky nest between her legs . . . and the vision would scatter into the random eyelights of total darkness. He discovered that clear imaging required a certain coldness of mind, a detachment; otherwise, his sight became murky, clouded with his own desires, with ghosts of wish-fulfilling fantasies.

Those wish-fulfilling fantasies had a power of their own, though, as he discovered one day when Dala met his eye with a shy smile, when he gazed at her while he held a perfectly formed mental image of their naked limbs entwined in a tangle of sheets—and she reached out, took his hand, and led him to her room on a clear, hot summer's afternoon, and took his virginity with exactly that same shy smile.

That had been the sweet brush of his destiny's lips, as well.

He'd entered his novitiate at fourteen, using the advanced education available only at the Monastic Embassy to sharpen his powers; the Esoteric training of both body and mind gave him the self-discipline to ruthlessly strangle those desires that crippled his gift. Now he used his mind as another friar might wield a sword: as a weapon, sworn in the service of the Human Future.

At twenty-five, he was the youngest full Ambassador in the Monasteries' six-hundred-year history—and not even the Council of Brothers could guess how much their decision might have been influenced by the subtle power of a young friar's dreams.

Now in Thorncleft a haze began to obscure his vision, as though he peered through a twisty veil of gauze, while the great doors of the hall swung wide and in marched a double column of the Artan Guards, their curious springless pellet bows held at ready aslant their scarlet-armored chests. They spread out into the wide arc of an honor guard.

The elves gazed at them with bald curiosity, not yet aware of their import. Lord Kithin, for his part, sprang hastily from the Gilt Throne and dropped to one knee, inclining his head to welcome the Artan Viceroy, Vinson Garrette. Lord Kithin could be trusted only to handle situations of purely ceremonial nature. No business of import could be conducted in Transdeia without the presence of the representative of this land's true rulers.

Raithe's heart began to pound.

Garrette seemed to speak cordially to the elves as he walked among them. Raithe felt a surge of anger at the mental haze that prevented him from fully experiencing the meeting—if he could only hear what Garrette said, perhaps he could understand the import of these legates. He burned for that understanding.

With a need as sharp and immediate as hunger to a starving man, he ached to understand where, in all this, was the connection to Caine.

But his sudden swell of desire ruptured his concentration and scattered his vision; now he saw only the view from this window in the half-completed embassy. He snarled at himself, then shut his eyes, laid his hand across them, and forced himself to concentrate once more. He slowed his breathing, a measured count of nine to inhale, hold for three, exhale for twelve, and the Hall of State began to coalesce once more inside his skull.

"Headache, Master Ambassador?" asked a greasily solicitous voice nearby. "Would you like a cup of willowbark tea? I'm having one."

Raithe's view of the hall vanished as he opened his eyes and glared at Ptolan, the fledgling embassy's Master Householder, a fat and perpetually befuddled Exoteric who seemed perfectly content to pass his fading years humming tunelessly to himself and tending the last few strands of his unruly steel-spring hair. Ptolan stood in the archway, not too far from the small iron stove he kept lit beside his desk for warmth—his sluggish nature made even this late summer afternoon too chill for his sagging, repellently pale flesh. He smiled at Raithe expectantly as he poured water into a teapot from a small brass carafe.

"Thank you," Raithe said icily, "no."

"It'll put a little color in your cheeks," Ptolan said, in what the fat fool must have imagined was an encouraging tone. His own cheeks sported blotches red as a whore's mouth. "Two brew as easy as one, y'know. It's a, well, a sharing, y'know? Brotherhood and all that. I know you began as an Esoteric, but we in the public services do things a bit differently . . ."

Instead of a reply, Raithe gave him a chilly stare—one of those steady bleached-out gazes that he used to intimidate weaker men. Ptolan swallowed and looked away, chuckling nervously in the back of his throat. "Please yourself, haha, you usually do, I suppose. I'll, ah, I'll just—" He rubbed his hands together, and chuckled some more. "I'll just, ah, go ahead for two, and if you change your mind—"

"Don't bother—" Raithe began.

"Oh, it's no bother—"

"I was *saying*—" He bared his teeth. "—don't bother me."

He set his head against the uncomfortable scrollwork of the chair's high back and shut his eyes. "Go away."

For a brutally long moment, the only image he could summon was of Ptolan standing in the archway, his slack thick-lipped mouth opening and closing with the soundless dismay of a hungry chick. Then hesitant footfalls faded toward the outer chamber, and Raithe regulated his breathing; soon, the interior of the Hall of State took hazy shape once more.

Though Garrette stood beside the Gilt Throne, where Lord Kithin sat, there was no question as to who was the true ruler of Transdeia. The Artan Viceroy projected a calm authority that was unmistakable; Lord Kithin himself never spoke without first glancing to Garrette to search his long gaunt face for any sign of disapproval.

Still Raithe's concentration was too scattered to pick up their words, but his hazy perception of Garrette's face let him read one word from the Viceroy's lips: *Diamondwell.*

Raithe nodded to himself and let his vision dissolve into a random scattering of eyelights. So the Mithondionne legates had come about Diamondwell; he had warned Garrette that Mithondion would respond—all subs stick together, in the end—but the Viceroy had firmly refused to worry about that possibility until it presented itself.

Diamondwell had been a dwarfish reservation in the Transdeian hills that had styled itself, with typical subhuman arrogance, as a "freehold." The trouble had begun nearly a year ago—before Raithe had been posted here as Ambassador—when the dwarfs' children and elderly began to fall ill. Having been born and bred to mining, the dwarfs had soon recognized the symptoms of metals poisoning. Viceroy Garrette himself had generously—*over*generously, in Raithe's considered opinion—ordered an investigation, using Artan resources to find the cause. When this cause turned out to be runoff from Artan smelters leaching into the Diamondwell groundwater, Garrette—again overgenerously—had offered to resettle the dwarfs in a new reservation, higher in the mountains and farther away from the Artan mining operations.

The dwarfs had refused, citing some sentimentalized twaddle about their ancestral lands. They had instead chosen, foolishly, to begin a guerrilla campaign of sabotage against the Artan mining machinery and smelting plants, hoping to make mining and smelting in those hills so expensive that the Artans would move their operations, instead. They had failed in the most basic principle of warfare: *Know your enemy.*

Artan military technology was even more advanced than their mining technology; to march into Diamondwell and arrest the entire population turned out to be much less expensive than moving the mining operations would have been. Those who came peacefully had been rewarded with tasks in the mines, clean food and water, and comfortable cots on which to rest; those who resisted had been slaughtered like the animals they were.

It had been a messy situation, one that Raithe privately believed could have been much more simply resolved: merely adding a more potent poison to the Diamondwell groundwater would have settled the issue with great swiftness and economy. Garrette's pretense of good nature and helpfulness, the facade of concern for the dwarfs' troubles he had presented, had only made the situation worse: it had emboldened the dwarfs, and allowed them to wreak considerable havoc upon the mines before they were finally contained.

Raithe imagined that something similar was going on in the Hall of State even now. Garrette was probably hemming and hawing, trying to allay any suspicions the elvish legates had developed; he couldn't understand how much trouble he was already in. He had no conception of the power that Mithondion still could wield if a war should come—of course, conversely, neither did the Mithondionne elves have any idea of the power of the Artan rulers of Transdeia.

It seemed to Raithe that there was a vast opportunity here—but opportunity for what, and how should he approach grasping it?

Once he understood how all this related to Caine, he would know what to do.

2

ANYONE WHO IS of a thoughtful, philosophical cast of mind will occasionally be struck by the appearance of certain organizing principles of history. The form these principles seem to take inevitably depends upon one's specific obsession. For a monarchist, history might be a story of the clash of great leaders; for a socialist, history is a struggle of classes in economic civil war. An agriculturalist sees the dynamic of populations, land, and availability of food; a philosopher might speak of the will to power or the will to synthesis; a theologian of the will of God. Raithe was not by nature a thoughtful man, but the events of his time had conspired to make him aware of one of these vast organizing principles, one so powerfully obvious that he was consistently amazed that no one but him seemed aware of it.

A lifetime ago—when he had been a young, hopeful, passionately dedicated friar, just entering the Esoteric Service in Ankhana—that governing principle of history had intervened and shattered Raithe like overfired pottery. Piece by piece, he had rebuilt—reforged—himself; but the man who emerged from that crucible was no longer Raithe of Ankhana, though he still answered to that name.

In those days, Creele of Garthan Hold had been the Ambassador to Ankhana. Raithe could still see him as clearly as though he stood before him now: a man of grace and beauty, eyes constantly sparkling with his extraordinary wit, a brilliant thinker, an intellect like fire leaping from root to branch. Ambassador Creele had taken an interest in young Raithe, had made clear that his career was upward bound. Creele had encouraged Raithe in his study of the Esoteric arts of fighting and espionage, and the skills of mind that were now his greatest weapon.

Raithe had watched in helpless horror as Creele had died by Caine's hand.

On that day, Raithe had sworn to Caine's face that there was no place the murderer could hide to escape Monastic vengeance. But after Creele's murder, the Ambassadorial post had been taken by that plodding hypocrite Damon, who had muddied and confused the issue before the Council of Brothers—not that it had mattered, in the end; for by that time, Caine was widely supposed to be dead.

Creele's murder had been the opening tap of Raithe's destruction; like the first rap of a carpenter's hammer, it had seated the nail firmly for a single, final blow. Because Creele had died that day—because the embassy had been in great turmoil—Raithe had been on extra duty on that fateful noon five days later. He had been sitting at a writing table in the scriptorium, surrounded by spineless Exoterics, while he painstakingly lettered the fifth copy of his report on Creele's murder.

If Caine hadn't murdered Creele, Raithe would have been in Victory Stadium: beside his father, the honest, pious blacksmith, who'd been proud of his position as the house farrier at Janner's Livery; beside his mother, the quiet, faithful wife and homemaker whose loving arms had always circled Raithe like a mystic ring against the hurts of the world.

His parents had been early converts to the Church of the Beloved Children; his mother, especially, had been passionately devoted to Ma'elKoth. And so of course they both had stood cheering in the stands, when Ma'elKoth's procession had entered Victory Stadium. Cheering—until the riot had begun, and the cheers had turned to screams.

If Raithe had been there, he would have fought for them. He would have saved them. But he wasn't there. Because of Caine.

His parents died in the riot. Slaughtered like animals.

Because of Caine.

Because of Caine, he had reforged himself into a weapon.

In the years that followed he had devoted himself to the study of Caine and his people, the alien race of *Aktiri*. He became the Monasteries' leading expert not only on Caine, but on the *Aktiri* and their world. It had been Raithe himself who had discovered the origin of the mysterious Artans, the outlanders who ruled Transdeia; shortly thereafter, Raithe had persuaded the Council of Brothers to make him the first Ambassador to the Artan court.

The world believed what the Church told them, that Caine had died on the sand at Victory Stadium. Raithe knew better. Somewhere, somehow, the murderer of his parents lived in the smug enjoyment of his rancid victory; Raithe could see him in his dreams. And in every dream, Raithe renewed his promise.

I will teach you my name.

He would teach the world his name; but the name he would teach it was not Raithe. The name *Raithe* was now a mask, a costume he wore to conceal his true face. *Raithe* had been brittle, fragile enough to shatter under a single sharp blow—a bit of pottery, no more. The man who now wore his face was a weapon, a blade of tempered steel gleaming from the forge. Only in his deepest, most cherished dream of dreams, in the stories he whispered to himself in the darkest midnights, when his ghosts all crowded round his heart, did he dare to call himself by his true name.

He had become the Caineslayer.

Childish? He knew it was—but he had been a child when he'd sworn himself to it. Now, seven years later, he could make his cheeks burn merely by imagining the humiliation of anyone ever learning how much he still cherished this adolescent melodrama . . . but that only made him clutch it ever more tightly to his heart.

In swearing himself to that name, he had made a vow that would never be broken. Now he kept perfect vigilance, waiting.

In comparing Caine's history to those of others in the Monastic Archives, he had discovered what he'd come to think of as Caine's defining characteristic. In each of his recorded endeavors, from the smallest assassination to the epic undertaking that had crushed the Khulan Horde at Ceraeno, there would always come a fulcrum, one defining point of balance, where a mere shift of Caine's weight toppled history in an unexpected direction.

Caine was, somehow, behind every twist of history in Raithe's short lifetime. This lesson had been burned into him like a brand upon the inside of his skull.

How had the Empire come to be? Caine saved Ankhana at Ceraeno, and Ma'elKoth triumphed over the superior forces of Lipke in the Plains War. How had Ma'elKoth come to be? Caine delivered up unto Ma'elKoth the crown of Dal'Kannith. How had Raithe come to be the Caineslayer? How had the Caineslayer come to be the Monastic Ambassador to the Artans?

The answer to every question led back to Caine.

Raithe had made it his personal rule of thumb, as private as his darkest fantasies, never to act until he understood how an event was connected to Caine. This rule had been his guidepost of destiny for nearly seven years. The connection might be distant, tenuous, tortuous—but it had always been there. This was how he maintained his perfect vigilance.

This was no longer a matter of vengeance; oh, certainly, he had started along this path seeking revenge, but revenge was a crippling desire, one of those that he had sloughed away like a snake shedding its skin. Caine need not be punished. He must be *extinguished*.

It wasn't personal, not anymore.

After all, was not Caine as much a pawn of destiny as Raithe himself? Caine had not intended to kill his parents; it had been purely an act of fate: as though all the universe conspired to create the Caineslayer.

Raithe thought of himself, of his mission—of his dream of the Caineslayer—as a metaphor, now; just as Caine had become a metaphor. To the Church of the Beloved Children of Ma'el-Koth, Caine was the Prince of Chaos, the Enemy of God. He had become a symbol for all of humanity's basest instincts of low selfishness, greed, and aggression; a symbol for everything against which stood the Church. He represented that part of human nature that set man against man, woman against woman, the self-destructive bloody-mindedness that was the single greatest threat to the Human Future.

This was the fundamental error of the Church: by elevating

Caine to the status of the Enemy of God, they gave power to his legend. Raithe was a loyal elKothan himself, as his parents had been; he found it astonishing that the Church would admit of anyone or anything that could oppose the power of Ma'elKoth. Though it was Church doctrine that Caine's opposition to God had, against his will, served the greater glory of Ma'elKoth, Raithe sometimes suspected that it might be the other way around.

Caine was slippery that way.

So all this led to a single, simple terminus. To act properly on this matter of the Mithondionne legates, he had to know: *Where was the connection to Caine?*

For one awful, dizzying moment, he wondered if perhaps there might not be any connection to Caine at all; black doubt yawned beneath him, and only a frantic mental scramble brought him back from a lethal fall. There was a connection. There would be. And he would find it. He had to.

It was his destiny.

3

"MMM, MASTER RAITHE?" The greasy voice of Ptolan once again shattered his concentration.

Raithe opened his eyes; full night stared back at him through the open window, spangled with hazy stars. How many hours had he sat here, dozing away his opportunity? He twisted, rising from his chair, suddenly red-faced with fury. "Rot your guts, Ptolan—I *told* you not to bother—"

"Sorry, uh, sorry, Brother, really I am—but Brother Talle has come up saying the lamp on the Artan Mirror glows, and your instructions were that, no matter what you're doing, or what time of day it might be, or—"

"All *right*," Raithe snarled. "Jhantho's *Faith*, can't you shut up? I'm on my way."

4

DAMON OF JHANTHOGEN Bluff, the Acting Monastic Ambassador to the Infinite Court, looked out over the teeming ballroom and allowed himself to feel moderately pleased. The orchestra played with spectacular skill; across the broad expanse of dance floor hundreds of couples swayed, while through the crowded fringe and the smaller side rooms wove dozens of young, white-robed friars bearing trays of cocktails and appetizers. The general light came from no specific source, making the air itself seem to glow and pulse gently in time with the rhythm of the waltz, casting a glamour subtler and more enticing than mere lamp flame—making the men more dashing, the women more beautiful, the setting absolutely flawless.

Over Damon's six-year tenure as Acting Ambassador, the Monastic Ball had become the premier diplomatic event of the Ankhanan social calendar. Damon himself was a stolid, pragmatic man, with little time for social niceties and no liking for parties at all, but the value of an event such as this could not be denied. The Monasteries formed a sovereign nation, but it was a nation without borders, one that spread across every known land. On this most neutral of all neutral ground, representatives of every government across the civilized world could meet and partake of each other's company without the interference of protocols of national precedence and the like.

Here within his view stood two perfect examples: the Lipkan Ambassador traded slightly sodden jokes with his Paqulan counterpart, as they leaned on each other in drunken friendship despite the ongoing privateer raids between Paquli and the Lipkan Empire; and on the dance floor, the jel'Han of Kor in his outlandish gold-embroidered bearskin roared with laughter as Countess Maia of Kaarn lowered him into a very competent dip. Damon's normally expressionless face bent into a small grim smile of satisfaction; he reflected that he would never know how many wars and assassinations and diplomatic conflicts of all descriptions had been averted by parties just like this one.

He had not sought this post, nor did he enjoy it—but the job was his to do, and he could take some satisfaction in having done it well.

Faintly through the music and laughter, Damon heard voices raised in anger. They seemed to be coming from beyond the ballroom, perhaps from the Gate Hall, outside the thrice-manheight doors, and were angry enough that they might signify violence. The friars who served as the embassy's security staff were all blooded veterans and experts in unarmed combat; they could

stop any fight without unnecessary injury or insult to the partici-
pants, and so Damon was not overly concerned—until the orchestra fell silent in a chaotic tangle of flattening notes.

A man in the gold-and-blue dress livery of the Eyes of God
stood beside the conductor, gesturing emphatically. The ballroom poised momentarily in apprehensive silence.

A white-robed junior friar had forced his way through the
press, and now he bowed jerkily to Damon and spoke far too
loudly, his breathless words ringing in the quiet. "Master
Damon—the Patriarch, he—the Eyes, the Grey Cats, they've arrested Hern, and Jento, and, and, and *Vice Ambassador t'Passe*!"

A bitterly cold shock went through Damon, and for a blank instant he could neither move nor speak.

The ballroom burst into uproar as Ambassadors and delegates
and entourages from every nation sought each other, gathering
themselves into self-protective knots. The orchestra struck up
the Imperial anthem, "King of Kings," and as the first strains entered the general roar, the ballroom doors swung back. Through
them flooded hard-faced men in grey leather, swords in hand.
Behind the leather-clad warriors walked a dozen Household
Knights in their full blood-colored battle armor, escorting a
small group of Eyes of God.

In their midst limped the stocky, dark-clad figure of the Patriarch of Ankhana.

Damon's paralysis broke. "Summon Master Dossaign to my
office, boy. Tell him to get on the Artan Mirror to the Council of
Brothers, with the word that we have been attacked, and the embassy has been occupied by Imperial forces."

The young friar hesitated. "But I don't understand! How
could even the Patriarch dare—?"

"You need not *understand*," Damon snapped. "You need only
obey. When the Master Speaker has sent the message, have him
disconnect the Mirror and hide it, so that it is never seen by
unsworn eyes. Now *go!*"

He jumped like a startled rat and scampered away.

The Grey Cats fanned out through the crowd, their ready
blades persuading all and sundry that the wisest course would be
to wait silently, and watch, and hope that the Patriarch had not
come for any of them.

Damon caught the eyes of several nearby friars. They moved
toward him, opening a path through the press. Damon stepped

into the gap and waved to the orchestra, which now fell silent. In the breathless quiet, he met the colorless gaze of the Patriarch of Ankhana.

The Patriarch was a man of somewhat less than average size; his face was pale and heavily scored by the burdens he bore. Damon was personally aware that the Patriarch never spent less than twelve hours a day laboring at the business of the Empire—and those twelve-hour days often extended to twenty. The hair that strayed from beneath his flat cap of soft black velvet was the same neutral, undefinable grey brown as his eyes—eyes that now gazed upon Damon with the same expressionless dispassion they had held in the days when the Patriarch had been the Duke of Public Order.

That had been before the Assumption of Ma'elKoth; in the chaos that followed the Emperor's transfiguration, the Duke of Public Order had seized the reins of power, bullying the nobility into confirming him as the Steward of the Empire. Shortly after solidifying his Stewardship, the former Duke had proclaimed the Doctrine of elKothan Supremacy and had named himself the first Patriarch of the Church of the Beloved Children of Ma'elKoth.

By acting always in the name of the Divine Ma'elKoth, the Patriarch had gathered to himself greater political power than the Emperor Himself had wielded; Damon privately considered that Toa-Sytell, former Duke, now Steward and Patriarch, was the most dangerous man alive.

"Your Radiance," Damon said in a tone of flatly correct courtesy. He did not genuflect, or even offer the slightest incline of his head for a bow; he was the sovereign of this tiny nation bounded by the embassy walls, and he owed no deference to any invader. "I presume there is some explanation for this outrageous conduct. Your armed invasion of these premises, and your detention of Monastic citizens by threat of force, are acts of war."

Toa-Sytell's only response was a slight preliminary compression of the lips.

Damon drew himself up and said with clipped, ominous precision, "You are not the first ruler to delude himself into believing he had the power to violate Monastic sovereignty."

"I apologize," the Patriarch said blandly. "No one has been harmed, and it was not the Empire's intention to give offense.

The Empire does not invade. The Empire does not attack. Those detained will be released, once it can be established that they are Monastic citizens in truth, and not terrorist criminals engaged in high treason against the Empire: offenses against God Himself. The matter will be explained fully in Our formal apology to the Council of Brothers. Perhaps we could continue this discussion in your office, Excellency?"

"Perhaps His Radiance could explain *now*, in the presence of all here," Damon said grimly, "how he could come to believe that one of my *Vice-Ambassadors* might *not* be a Monastic citizen?"

The Patriarch did not so much as glance at the breathless crowd that hung upon his every word. "The woman calling herself t'Passe of Narnen Hill," he said imperturbably, "has associated herself with Cainists, and has herself been heard to espouse political views tantamount to Cainism."

This brought gasps and indignant whispers from the assembly— *the astonishing* effrontery *of this man, Patriarch or no*—and a number of outraged and disbelieving looks directed both at the Patriarch and at his attending Grey Cats.

Damon's face remained impassive, but inwardly he raged at his underling for her foolishly idealistic nature, and at himself for forbearing to beat that out of her. He said calmly, "This would be disturbing, if true—but only disturbing, not *criminal*. To the best of my knowledge, holding Cainist views does not constitute high treason."

"The best of your knowledge," the Patriarch said, with a quiet exactitude that touched on subtle irony, "is sadly out of date."

He let those words fall into the silence for a long, long moment.

"On this, the Eve of Saint Berne, let it be known: There is no safety for the enemies of God. Traitors and terrorist criminals cannot take shelter behind diplomatic convention. When the welfare of the Beloved Children of Ma'elKoth is threatened, even Our well-known respect for Monastic dignity must give way. Monastic sovereignty is temporal; the power of Ma'elKoth eternal. Ma'elKoth is supreme!"

The Patriarch, the Household Knights and every Grey Cat struck their chests with closed fists, as though each drove a dagger into his own heart, and then opened their hands as though offering their hearts' blood to their Lord: the primary gesture of their faith.

Toa-Sytell nodded briskly to Damon and limped beyond him toward the doors that led into the embassy's interior, rocking from side to side on his crippled leg. As he passed, he said softly, "Your office, Damon. Now." Four Household Knights trailed in his wake.

Damon stood motionless for an endless second, his mind boiling; finally he pulled himself together enough to speak.

"This matter," he said, not loudly but with a crisp, penetrating tone so that all could hear, "is between the Empire and the Monasteries, and shall be settled as such. Let it not interfere with your evening's entertainment." He waved to the conductor, and the orchestra struck up a sprightly reel. Without waiting to see if anyone would actually join the dance, Damon turned and followed the Patriarch.

Before he left the ballroom, he signaled to six of the embassy's security staff. All six were Esoterics, each man a specialist in personal combat against an armored opponent. He had no illusions that he or his embassy could survive a violent encounter with the might of the Empire—but he intended to ensure that the Patriarch would not survive it either. If he could not settle this matter peacefully, it would be settled in blood.

5

TOA-SYTELL EASED HIS aching joints in the high-backed chair at Damon's enormous, scarred writing table in the Ambassador's office. One hand massaged his crippled knee, while with the other he held a snifter of fine Tinnaran brandy he'd found in a chest beside the table. He took a long, delightfully aromatic sip and gazed across the snifter's lip at Damon, a slight tilt of his head taking the place of a smile. "Are you certain you won't join me?"

The Acting Ambassador only stared at him stonily.

Toa-Sytell sighed. "Oh, unbend a little, Damon. I'm sorry for the show in the ballroom. That was only to make a point—it's a tale that will spread far beyond the Empire's borders before the week is out, as was intended. Meanwhile, I'll let your people go, and the Church will pay whatever reparations the Council requires. All right? I will exonerate your underlings, and deliver a formal apology for the affront to your office—with the codicil that had your people been found to be Cainists, they would have received the same Imperial justice meted out to all enemies of God. But that's only a detail. Have a drink."

Damon released a long breath, shaking his head, but he stepped over to the liquor cabinet, took a glass, and poured himself three fingers of Korish cactus whiskey. "I cannot say what the Council's response to this will be," he said, "but they have ever been open to reparations; they will want war no more than does the Empire."

Toa-Sytell nodded approval and waved his snifter at the furnishings of the office: an expensive array of delicately carved hardwoods, in the light and airy open style that defined recent Ankhanan craftsmanship. "I see you still have Creele's furniture."

Damon shrugged. "I am only Acting Ambassador. I have no authority to make changes."

"Mmm, yes—no one really trusts you, do they? None of the Council factions has the power to get their own toady in here, and so they leave *you* in place: perhaps the only honest man in the Monastic diplomatic corps." Toa-Sytell found himself chuckling at the thought of an honest ambassador. "I've always admired you, do you know that?"

His friendly tone had its effect: the tension began to drain out of Damon's face, and the Acting Ambassador lowered himself onto a lovely embroidered settee. The wariness was still there, but wariness was acceptable, so long as Damon was relaxed enough not to do something foolish—such as order those friars outside to attack the Household Knights who guarded the doorway. Toa-Sytell wondered in passing if Damon might be feeling as much disappointment as relief; the Ambassador had clearly nerved himself up for a noble martyrdom.

"Honesty is not such a virtue," Damon said tiredly. He took a sip of his whiskey and went on. "I tell the truth because that is my nature. I don't incline to the lie. It's like the color of my hair, or my height: neither good nor bad. It simply is."

"Mm, you just do what you do, is that it?" Toa-Sytell murmured, mildly amused. "That makes you sound like a bit of a Cainist yourself."

Damon grunted, and shook his head. "I'm not political."

"Neither are they, to hear them tell it. They're *philosophical*."

Damon's mouth set into a grim line. "You should tell me why

you've come here. I shouldn't think it's to discuss the finer points of Cainism."

"Well, my friend, there you would be wrong," Toa-Sytell said. He drained his snifter and poured himself another drink before continuing. "Tomorrow is the Feast of Saint Berne. Assumption Day is only three months away, Damon. This will be the seventh Festival of the Assumption, by the will of Ma'elKoth."

He lifted the glass to the small elKothan shrine that occupied one corner of the office and drank to his god. "It will be the single most important day of my Patriarchy. There are those, among the more gullible of Our Beloved Children, who expect Ma'elKoth Himself to return on that day."

Damon nodded. "I've heard this tale."

"It is only a tale," Toa-Sytell said. "The Ascended Ma'elKoth will not return in the body; He is transcendent, immanent, omnipresent. He has no need of a physical form. But the Empire, on the other hand—the Empire has a *great* need for a flawless Festival of the Assumption, do you understand? It is crucial symbolism of the doctrine of elKothan supremacy." Glass in hand, he made a gestural sketch of offering his heart's blood toward the shrine.

"I begin to see," Damon said. "You expect that Cainists will attempt to interfere."

"Of course they will," Toa-Sytell said wearily. "How can they not? The opportunity is too good to resist. To disrupt the Festival seems a small enough matter—but to make the Imperial Church appear weak and foolish threatens the very existence of the Empire."

Once again, he drained his glass. He told himself he should not have another; he was so tired the brandy was already making his head swim. The room seemed to press in more closely around him, and the air became thicker, harder to breathe.

"By the Festival, Cainism will be only a memory; whatever Cainists who survive will be too worried about living out the day to risk embarrassing the Imperial Church. I've been lax, Damon. I've let them go too far, and they have become bold. Now they must be crushed before they do us real harm."

Damon's response was a grim stare. Toa-Sytell often surmised that the Ambassador had personal reservations about the value of the Empire in the pursuit of the Monasteries' overall goal of ensuring the permanent ascendance of humanity; he was consistently silent on the subject. The Council of Brothers openly supported the Empire as humankind's brightest hope. Damon's steadfast devotion to the Monasteries wouldn't let him publicly disagree with the Council, but his fundamental bedrock of honesty wouldn't let him pretend to agree—and so he never said anything at all.

Toa-Sytell sighed and poured himself another brandy. It was unexpectedly relaxing, to sit here with a man who—though not quite a friend—was someone he had no need to manipulate, with whom he was not required to maintain his exhausting facade of Patriarchal infallibility. He decided that once he finished his business here, he would go straight back to the Colhari Palace and sleep until dawn. "Do you know," he said slowly, "that it was in this very room that I first met him? Caine. Right here."

"I recall," Damon said grimly.

"Of course, of course. You were here, weren't you?"

Their eyes met, and they shared a glance that skated across the open expanse of carpet between them. Nearly seven years ago, they had stood in this room and watched Ambassador Creele lie on that carpet as the light slowly faded within his eyes: as his heart failed, after Caine had broken his neck.

Toa-Sytell often wondered how the world might be different today, if he had done the wise thing that night: ordered Caine shot down like the mad dog he so obviously was. "It's because of him that you have this post," he mused. "You took the Acting Ambassadorship after he murdered Creele—"

"Executed him," Damon said firmly.

Toa-Sytell ignored the correction. "In fact, it's because of him that you still have it. When you testified on the murder before the Council, neither Creele's friends nor his enemies liked what you had to say. You ended up in the middle, with both sides against you—a precarious position, but you have proved to possess exceptional balance."

"I told the truth," Damon said with a shrug; then he cocked his head curiously. "How do you know of my testimony? Proceedings of the Council of Brothers are—"

"Secret, yes, yes," Toa-Sytell said, waving the question aside. "I simply find it a subject for curious contemplation, from time to time. Caine himself truly was the precise definition of evil, as he is named by the Church: an indiscriminate slaughterer who cared nothing for the lives he shattered in the pursuit of whatever happened to catch his fancy of the moment. He betrayed Our Lord, yet it was through his betrayal that Ma'elKoth was transfigured. He crippled me—shattered my knee beyond even magickal repair, so that I am reminded of him by the pain that wrenches my every step—yet gave me rulership of the Ankhanan Empire. He sparked riots that nearly burned the city to the ground, civil war—the First Succession War as well as the Second, in fact."

Toa-Sytell's chest clutched with suddenly remembered grief; Tashinel and Jarrothe, his sons whom he had loved beyond all measure, his only children, had died in the First Succession War. He shook this aside—it was an old, familiar pain, flooding back now on a rising tide of alcohol—and went on. "Yet he also saved Ankhana at the Battle of Ceraeno. His murders were countless . . . but one cannot forget that he also did our land the very great favor of killing that madman Berne."

"It's your Church that names Berne a saint," Damon pointed out.

"Not mine. Ma'elKoth's." Toa-Sytell made another sketch of a salute toward the corner shrine. "You forget: I knew Berne. What we celebrate tomorrow is his sacrifice for God, not his character. As a man, he was a rapist and a murderer—worse even than Caine, and I don't mind saying so. Privately."

Damon smiled painfully, as though bending his lips made his face hurt. "You sound a bit like a Cainist, too."

"Ah, it's the brandy," Toa-Sytell said, tilting his glass high to catch the last drops before pouring himself another. "It must be made clear, Damon. Cainism is *treason*. Adherents of Cainism openly declare themselves the enemies of society, and of God. It will not be tolerated within the Empire's bound—not even from Monastic diplomats."

Damon frowned. "You cannot expect to dictate the politics and philosophies of Monastic citizens," he said stiffly.

This, too, Toa-Sytell waved aside with a weary pass of his snifter. "I don't. What I do expect is that the Council of Brothers will find it expedient to post holders of such views elsewhere— to avoid the appearance of deliberate offense to the Empire and the Church. After all," he said reasonably, "the Cainist heresy can't be very popular with the Council, either; if Caine had not died at Victory Stadium, I'm sure you would have found it necessary to kill him."

Damon stared gloomily down into his glass and swirled the

whiskey within it. "There are some who say that Caine survived—that he waits beyond the world, and that when Ma'elKoth returns Caine will as well, for their final battle."

"Primitive superstition," Toa-Sytell snorted. "This kind of 'final conflict' myth will always be popular among the ignorant—and it is the Cainists who spread it, no doubt. I intend to ensure that the Cainists never get the chance to fulfill their false prophecies. This is why I now speak with you privately, here in your office, Damon. I want you to understand that what I do is in the same service of humanity to which you and every friar are sworn; Cainism is our common enemy, and it can only be defeated by our common effort."

The wariness he had earlier seen in Damon's face now returned with redoubled force. "I am not yet convinced that Cainism is our common enemy," he said. "What common effort do you expect? What is it you want from us?"

"From you, specifically, Damon," Toa-Sytell said easily. "Time grows short; I do not have the month or six weeks to spare as couriers travel beyond the Empire's borders and return. I wish to converse with Raithe of Ankhana, the current Ambassador to the Duchy of Transdeia."

"Speak with . . . ?" Damon stiffened. "How do you—"

"You have a device—the Artan Mirror, I believe it's called—that you acquired from these Artans who now rule Transdeia. It's generally used here in this room, your office. I don't know how it is operated; if you would be so kind as to use it to make contact with Ambassador Raithe, I would be most appreciative."

"But, but, it's impossible that you should—"

"Know of this secret device?" Toa-Sytell sighed and drained his snifter one last time. "After a lifetime spent in the gathering of secrets as a profession, I find it has become something of a relaxing pastime in itself—a welcome diversion from the heavy cares of church and state."

He allowed himself a rare, lazy smile as he fisted his chest then spread his hand before him. "The Eyes of God see all, you know. Ma'elKoth is supreme."

6

TOA-SYTELL WATCHED ATTENTIVELY as the Artan Mirror was set up for use. He'd had report of this device, but he had never seen it, nor did he know how it worked.

The Artan Mirror was a valise-sized box that the Master Speaker, Dossaign of Jhanthogen Bluff, situated upon Damon's writing table. The Master Speaker then attached a thin, flexible cord of some kind to another that came unobtrusively in through the office window. It was faced with a very ordinary-looking mirror that appeared to be merely silvered glass, and on its side was a ring-shaped handgrip that seemed to be made of gold. Having joined the cords together in some fashion Toa-Sytell couldn't quite appreciate—he seemed to simply jam the end of one into the end of the other, like a branch grafted onto a fruit tree—the Master Speaker retired. One of his assistants—called a Speaking Brother—took hold of the handgrip and briefly closed his eyes.

A long, long moment passed in silence, then the Speaking Brother opened his eyes and said, "I am received."

Damon took the seat, facing into the Artan Mirror; the Speaking Brother took his hand. "Greetings from Ankhana," Damon said. "Ambassador Damon calls upon Ambassador Raithe."

Toa-Sytell shifted his weight forward, peering at the box-shaped device; to his eye, it seemed that Damon looked solely at his own reflection, and spoke to himself.

Another long moment passed in silence, then Damon said, "Not well, Master Raithe. This is not a personal call. I have with me here His Radiance the Patriarch of Ankhana, who wishes to converse with you."

After a pause, Damon said severely, "But he does know. And it would serve you well, Raithe, to remember that the Patriarch once directed the King's Eyes. I chose not to insult him with disingenuous pretense, and I suggest that you follow my example . . . Very well. Yes, I recall, and you may be certain that the Patriarch does, as well. Bide a moment."

He let go of the Speaking Brother's hand and turned to Toa-Sytell. He said with quiet irony, "Master Raithe bids me remember how *busy* he is, in his duties as Ambassador." He rose, and offered his seat to Toa-Sytell.

The Patriarch sat down and regarded himself in the mirror. The deepening creases that accompanied the developing slackness of jowls along his jawline, and the near-black swipes of exhaustion under his eyes, made him wince and promise himself to take a long-needed vacation once the Festival was safely and successfully complete. He sighed—it seemed that he had been promising himself a vacation for seven years.

He forced his attention back to his purpose. "How is this used?"

The Speaking Brother extended his hand. "Your Radiance need only join grips with me, and speak as though Brother Raithe is here within this room."

Scowling, Toa-Sytell took the Speaking Brother's hand. His scowl deepened further when his face in the mirror blurred and faded into greyish mist, which then coalesced into a new image: a thin, sharp-faced man with a pointed chin and skin like tight-stretched leather, a nose like a knife blade dividing rather close-set eyes as penetrating as an eagle's. His tonsured head sprouted a fringe of lank brown hair, and he wore the rich blood-colored robes of a Monastic Ambassador. And those eyes—they were decidedly disturbing: pale, almost colorless blue grey against his swarthy skin, flat and clouded as chips of ice set into his skull.

He could not have been more than thirty years of age, was perhaps only twenty-five or -six.

Astonishingly, Toa-Sytell *recognized* him; though he could not say when, Toa-Sytell knew that he had seen this intense young man before, perhaps years ago—and for a moment, he could only wonder at the tangled web of lives that touch each other again and again, for no discernable reason.

Ahh, bugger it, Toa-Sytell thought. *I must be getting drunk.*

"Your Radiance?" The title had a slightly testy edge—it was Raithe, speaking to him through this device, from hundreds of miles away. The room where Raithe sat could not be seen; it was as though the Ambassador floated within a dense grey mist. "How may I be of service?"

Toa-Sytell huffed a sigh through his nose. He could think of no reason to waste breath in polite chatter or to speak with less than absolute plainness. "You, as a Monastic citizen, are not an Imperial subject, and so I do not command you. The Council of

Brothers does, however, require that the Empire be given aid and support to the fullest power of each and every friar; therefore, think of my request as proceeding from their lips."

Raithe's pale eyes narrowed. "Please continue, Your Radiance."

"Give this word to your Viceroy Garrette. Today, to expound— or even privately hold—Cainist ideas has been declared to be treason against the Empire, and an insult to God," Toa-Sytell began.

At this, those eyes seemed to catch inexplicable fire, as though a winter sun had burned through their permanent overcast. "This is a great day, Your Radiance—but, to tell the Viceroy? I don't understand."

"Of course you do, Raithe," Toa-Sytell said irritably. "It is known that you are not a fool. It is also known that you received your current post for the sole reason that you are the Monasteries' leading authority on the *Aktiri*."

Raithe's gaze focused like sunlight through a glass; Toa-Sytell would have been unsurprised to find his face blistering under its heat. "You cannot *possibly*—!"

"Spare me." When he continued, Toa-Sytell endeavored to recover his customary dry precision of speech. "Our message to Garrette is simply this: To support the actions of these Cainist traitors will, from this day forward, be considered an act of war."

"His Radiance," the young Ambassador said, "is making a terrible mistake."

"This is not a discussion, Ambassador. Tell Vinson Garrette that he is known to the Infinite Court; from the mortal arm of Ma'elKoth, nothing can be hidden. Tell him, We know that he and his so-called Artans are in truth *Aktiri*. Tell him, We know the *Aktiri* have aided the spread of Cainism. And tell him that if he and his *Aktiri* masters continue their campaign of Cainist terror against the Empire, their tiny foothold upon Our world will be utterly destroyed."

Raithe snorted with open insolence.

"We will cry a *crusade*," Toa-Sytell said. "Do you understand?"

Raithe appeared to swallow, twisting his head as though his throat pained him, then nodded. "Yes, Your Radiance. I understand."

"Make certain that Garrette does, as well. We know that the *Aktiri* wield potent magicks—but We also know that they die as easily as any other men. The Artans and the Empire do not have to be enemies; tell him this, too. The path is for him to choose: friendship, or death."

"Your Radiance, please—" Raithe's young face worked as though he chewed upon broken glass. After a moment, he seemed to master himself, and he said thinly, "Though not of your Empire, Your Radiance, I am of your flock. I am, as I have been since the very birth of the Church, a Beloved Child. I passed through the Womb of Ma'elKoth under His own direction, and my devotion to the Church has never wavered. In the name of that devotion, I ask you to reconsider what you require of me. I know Viceroy Garrette too well—a threat this bald may spark the very war we all would wish to avoid."

Toa-Sytell grunted his unconcern with this possibility. "Should Garrette wish to continue his Cainist games, We may turn to the solution Caine himself would employ, in the hope that Garrette's successor will prove more reasonable."

"Your Radiance, you cannot." The young Ambassador spoke with clinical certainty. "You have no conception of the powers you confront—you would never be safe. There would be nowhere you could hide from Artan vengeance."

The words echoed in Toa-Sytell's mind, and in their echo they subtly altered: *You will never be safe, Caine of Garthan Hold. There is nowhere you can hide from Monastic vengeance. "Ha!"* he barked, snapping his fingers and pointing at Raithe's image in the mirror. "I *know* you now—I remember!"

Raithe's brows drew together. "I'm sorry?"

"You were *here*, in this room!" Toa-Sytell said triumphantly. "That night—that night Caine killed him here on the carpet. You were one of the guards—"

"I was," Raithe confirmed grimly. "But I do not see how this relates to your business with the Artan Viceroy."

"Well, of course it does . . ." Toa-Sytell frowned; of course there was a connection here. Wasn't there? He felt sure that the connection was an important one, a point that must be made, though now he couldn't remember why. He reached for his brandy snifter, but found it to be empty; he felt a bit dizzy, and he decided he had drunk enough for the night. "I, ah, the point is . . . I was only thinking," he said lamely, "about the way lives seem to cross each other, for no reason . . ."

At this, Raithe stiffened as though he'd taken a shock, and a vein bulged, pulsing, around his right eye, but Toa-Sytell was too light-headed to attach any significance to this. He wiped his free hand across his eyes and said, "Give my message to Garrette. Now. Tonight."

Before Raithe could begin another protest, Toa-Sytell released the hand of the Speaking Brother, and Raithe vanished. Toa-Sytell blinked at the mirror, somewhat surprised to find himself staring at the reflection of an aging, exhausted drunk. *Time to go home,* he thought, and pushed himself unsteadily to his feet.

From a seat beside the writing table, Damon stared at him, white faced, appalled by even the half of the conversation that he had heard. Toa-Sytell shrugged and shook his head to indicate there was nothing to worry about, though he could not bring himself to form the words.

"Sorry about the ball, Damon," he said thickly. "Hope the rest of it goes well. I, ah, I'm going home now."

He lurched toward the door, thinking *Well, that should have gotten things rolling*.

7

RAITHE SAT FROZEN before the Artan Mirror, his hand upon the golden grip.

Me, he thought in wonder. *It's me.*

He saw it now: his entire life lay unfolded before him, all its twists and turns laid bare. Here at this crux of history, standing on the nexal node of conflict between the Empire and the Artans and the subhuman House Mithondionne, he had found the connection he had sought. He had found the hand of Caine.

He had found it in the mirror.

Caine had *made* him; Caine had driven the quest for power and knowledge that had ended with Raithe being right *here*, right *now*, where history was so delicately balanced as to topple according to his slightest breath. Caine had put Toa-Sytell upon the Oaken Throne. Caine had inspired the heretic terrorists who had sparked Toa-Sytell's use of the Mirror, to bring those words to him: . . . *the way lives cross each other, for no reason* . . .

But there was a reason. *Caine* was the reason.

He saw it now: saw the possibility, saw the opportunity. He saw what *Caine might do here*—if Caine served the true dream of One Humanity. He saw the opening for a Cainelike stroke: a balance upon which he could throw his own weight. On this whole continent, perhaps the whole world, there was no greater threat to the future of humanity than the elves of House Mithondionne. With one elegant gesture, he could bring against them the unguessable power of the other great threat to the true dream: the *Aktiri*—the people of Caine.

And let the two most powerful enemies of the Human Future destroy each other.

He rose.

"Ptolan," he said calmly, distantly amazed at how serene and *normal* his voice sounded to his ears. "Master Ptolan, attend me."

Only the scuffle of a step or two preceded the voice; Ptolan must have been eavesdropping. "Yes, Master Raithe?"

"Summon the Speaking Brother; wake him, if need be." Raithe had the Mirror skill, to send this message himself, but he had urgent business within the walls of Thorncleft Castle above the town—business that could not wait the minutes such a message would require.

"The Council must be informed," he said. "There exists a state of war between the Artan overlords of Transdeia and the elves of House Mithondionne."

"War?" Ptolan asked breathlessly. "War *now*?"

Raithe's lips thinned; he stared far into the night sky. "Let us say, within the hour."

As Ptolan scurried away, Raithe slowly turned to the corner of his room, to strike his chest and offer his heart's blood to the shrine of Ma'elKoth.

8

THE ELVISH LEGATES stood in Vinson Garrette's drawing room with indifferent poise, as jarringly out of place as ballerinas in a slaughterhouse. Administrator Garrette gritted his teeth and tried to ignore the sweat that trailed down his ribs from his armpits.

He had designed the room's decor himself, modeling it loosely upon the Cedar Room of England's Warwick Castle. Darkly polished, intricately carved, and interlocking wall panels stretched fifteen feet to the elaborate, gold-leafed plaster of the ceiling, which was done in the massive baroque style of Italy's seventeenth century. The fireplace was an astonishing edifice of rose-veined marble, half again Garrette's height; upon the mantel stood an enormous mechanical clock, its bejeweled pendulum scattering multicolored fire. Five enormous crystal chandeliers blazed with the light of three hundred candles. The carpet had been hand woven in a single piece, its design mirroring that of the ceiling above, and everywhere on that carpet rested furniture of unparalleled grace in design.

This potent combination of wealth and taste would give any man pause, would place him in his proper relationship with the Artan Viceroy, starting all dealings off with the proper note of deference to Garrette's power and discernment—which, of course, had much less to do with his own vanity than with his devotion to the Company. As Viceroy, he was the public face of the Overworld Company—of what the natives believed was the Kingdom of Arta—and, as such, it was his duty to present an image that commanded the respect the Company deserved.

These damned elves, though—

They had minced around the room, muttering among themselves, occasionally giving out that tinkling wind-chime laughter of theirs. Now and again one would turn to ask him a courteous question on the origin of this fabric or the history of some particular type of scrollwork upon the furniture—questions of the sort that no one could have answered except some bloody interior designer, certainly not a man engaged in the important business of running this duchy. And they had seemed privately amused by his ignorance.

He had hated them on sight.

Those alien faces sketched in a cartoon of hauteur, the inhuman poise that underlay their polite interest in the furnishings—everything about them made him feel like some bloody yokel, a bumpkin displaying his backwoods sty as though it were a palace. They made this magnificent room feel like something an infant might fingerpaint in his own shit.

He could dismiss the insult to himself, but disrespect to the Company was unforgivable. They made a joke of his entire life.

And it was more than that, as the Administrator was not ashamed to admit. Those overlarge, overslanted cat eyes of theirs, their misshapen skulls, brought to mind the child-stealing

bogymen that had haunted his dreams even through his teens:
they looked like the villains of a thousand childish terror tales.

They looked like Greys.

Garrette cleared his throat. "On the matter of, ahmn, Diamondwell, gentlemen—ah, gentle, mm, gentlefolk . . . ?" Damn this
bloody Westerling! Had he insulted them? The blasted language
was purely clumsy. He was an Administrator, not some damned
diplomat. He was uncertain as to the actual relationship between
Diamondwell and House Mithondionne—weren't dwarfs and
elves supposed to hate each other, or something? He couldn't remember if that idea came from Overworld history, or some
damned fairy tale his mother had made him read as a boy.

And now they were staring at him, all five of them. Garrette's
face began to heat up. The damned elves stared at him like they
could read his mind.

"Ah, yes, Diamondwell," one of them said—Quelliar was
the name Garrette had been given, and he'd taken this elf for
the leader. "It was lovely. I guested there, mmm, perhaps it was
in the second decade of Ravenlock—that would be, oh, nine
hundred–odd years ago, as you humans reckon, Your Highness.
Spectacular, it was. Caverns that gleamed of travertine, and a
jolly, sturdy folk: fine cooks and uproarious dancers."

"Though no ear for music," another put in.

"Ah, but the *rhythm*," Quelliar countered. "For their taste,
rhythm outweighs pitch."

"Hmm, true," a third said. "The stonebenders of those days
did not speak of an ear for music, but rather of a heart for dance."

Garrette's face remained attentively blank, while inwardly he
struggled to keep his frustration from boiling down to fury. This
was some kind of damned *game* for them, he was sure of it.

A lovely place indeed, he sneered inside his head. He had seen
those caverns: dark, dank, airless holes in the rock, their only
real value lying ignored in the stone. Those dwarfs had been no
better than savages, bowing down before their tribal fetish while
the very walls around them gleamed and glittered with untold
mineral wealth. The Company's geological survey still explored
the caves, and each new report was more exciting than the last;
stoping had begun around the first two drill sites, and the ex-
tracted ores had been found to be rich beyond imagining.

What a waste, Garrette thought, as he always did when he
imagined all the centuries those dwarfs had squatted in the

caves. Diamondwell was the latest example of one of Garrette's primary rules: *If you don't know how to use something, you have no call to complain when it's taken by somebody who does.* The stunted little troglodytes didn't even really understand what they had lost.

But—as always—it seemed that the solution had constructed a problem of its own. These damned elves—

One had to respect their power, though. Every report had made that clear. Elves can *reach into your mind*; they can make you hallucinate on command. This was why every door to this room was posted with Overworld Company secmen—the "Artan Guard"—wearing the latest magick-resistant ballistic armor and bearing chemically powered assault rifles. At the very first indication that Garrette saw something in this room that didn't belong, one shout would bring six heavily armed men through those doors, and they would come in shooting. He would not take the slightest chance.

And if the damned elves *could* read his mind, let them read that there. Maybe then they'd give him his due respect.

He forced the thought away. That was nothing but a conflict rehearsal. He did this too often; it was a bad habit that he'd been trying for years to overcome. *Rehearsing a conflict brings that energy into your life,* he repeated to himself. It was another of his primary rules.

Back to business: He took a deep breath and tried again. "The, ah, Diamondwell resettlement camp is not far from Thorncleft. Perhaps in the morning, I might take you to it? You could see for yourselves how well they are cared for."

Quelliar's eyebrows slanted even more. "Like pets?"

"Like partners," Garrette corrected firmly, but Quelliar seemed not to hear.

"Humans and their pets," he said, impenetrably patronizing. His voice chimed with alien laughter. "Who owns whom?"

"*Valued* partners," Garrette insisted. Two could play that I-don't-hear-you game, he told himself. "They have been of such very great assistance in our mining—"

"Perhaps our difficulties arise from language," Quelliar said graciously. "In Mithondion, the sort of partners that must be confined by fences are called cattle. Do you not know that word?"

Garrette pasted on his professionally blank Administrator's

smile while he strove to guess at an appropriate response. He was rescued by the opening of a door. A secman, assault rifle slung, took one uncertain step inside and closed the door behind him; then he came to attention and saluted, his right hand to the brow above the silver-mesh face shield of his antimagick helmet.

"Apologies for interrupting, Administrator," he said in English. "The Monastic Ambassador is in the hall."

"Raithe?" Garrette said, frowning. What on Earth would the Ambassador be doing here at *this* hour?

"Yes, sir. In the hall outside."

"What does he want?"

"He wouldn't say, sir. But he insists that it's extremely urgent."

For that matter, how the devil had the Monastic Ambassador gotten this far into Thornkeep without Garrette having been informed? Garrette gave his head an irritable shake. "Very well," he said crisply. "Tell his Excellency that as soon as I have completed this business . . ."

His voice trailed off as the door swung silently inward to reveal Ambassador Raithe standing patiently in the hallway beyond. The Ambassador stood very straight and very still, his robes of crimson and gold draped like folds of stone. He held his hands clasped before him in an unusual manner, his fingers knotted in a way that Garrette's eyes could not clearly resolve.

"Oh," Garrette said faintly. Relief and gratitude flooded through him. "Oh, thank God . . ." *Raithe* was here! At last! Garrette hadn't realized how much he had *missed* Raithe, how much he had needed the simple reassurance of his friend's presence. "Raithe!" he said, brightening. Now that he was here, Garrette could breathe again. "Please, come in, come in. I can't tell you how happy I am to see you."

The Monastic Ambassador paced into the room. "And I am grateful to have arrived in time. Send your guard back to his post."

"Of course, of course." Garrette gestured to the secman, who went back to join his partner in the hallway. "And shut the door, you idiot!"

"No need," Raithe said quietly. He stared at the door, and the door swung closed.

By itself.

Garrette's mouth dropped open. "What?"

Raithe gazed down at the lock, and his colorless eyes narrowed. The lock gave out a flat *snikt* that echoed in the silence like a rifle being slowly and deliberately cocked.

"What?"

From the door opposite came a similar click; Raithe glanced at the third door, and its lock clicked. One by one the siege shutters banged closed over the windows, and their locks secured as well.

"Raithe?" Garrette ventured uncertainly. "Raithe, what are you doing?"

Raithe compressed his lips slightly and met each pair of eyes in turn. He offered them all a narrow smile. "I am preventing the escape of these assassins."

Quelliar turned with the inhumanly deliberate grace of a cobra seeking the sun. "Human child," he said. The chime of his amusement became the toll of distant bells, ancient and cold. "I am the Eldest of Massall. The petty tricks you display? I *taught* them to ten generations of your ancestors, a thousand years before your birth, when humans were no more than our—" A dark glance at Garrette. "—*partners*. Do not force us to demonstrate that your elders are also your betters."

Though the elf neither moved nor even changed expression, he was somehow the source of a chilling wave of awareness that broke over Garrette and drenched him with dread. It was as though Garrette suddenly awoke from some inexplicable dream: he stared at the Monastic Ambassador in growing horror. Friends? How had he believed they had ever been friends? He barely *knew* the man, and privately considered him a tiresome fanatic, a borderline personality who wavered between earnest dullness and freakish monomania. And the look Raithe gave Quelliar, an unblinking stare of expressionless, psychopathic fixity, began to transform Garrette's sudden dread into actual physical fear.

"I am Raithe of Ankhana," he said, and struck his hands together: a rasping, scraping clap as though he dusted sand from his palms in Quelliar's direction.

Nothing happened.

The elves still stared at him curiously. Garrette barely dared to breathe, praying that this was some ungodly prank. Raithe folded his arms, a tiny smile of grim satisfaction wrinkling the corners of his eyes. Quelliar coughed, once. His companions turned to him.

Garrette flinched, afraid to look, unable to resist.

The elf's feathery brows drew together in astonishment; his head cocked like that of a puzzled puppy. He sank slowly to his knees. Still looking only surprised, not even alarmed—much less in any kind of pain—Quelliar vomited a gout of black blood that splashed across the carpet. "I'm sorry," he said quietly, to Garrette. "I'm very sorry."

Then he pitched face first into the spreading pool of bloody vomit. He convulsed, writhing, gagging up great scarlet-laced chunks that plopped from his lips, as though something had diced his stomach, his liver, and his intestines and now forced pieces of them up his throat. A spray of cherry-black droplets splattered across the delicate embroidery of a Louis XIV couch.

Finally, he made only fading aspirated grunts—*"hghkh . . . gkh . . . gkh . . . ghhss"*—and lay still.

"A pleasure to make your acquaintance," Raithe said serenely. He raised his eyebrows at the other elves, but their leader's sudden death seemed to have astonished them into immobility. Garrette drowned in terror, shaking, unable to breathe, certain that the elves somehow communicated with each other without word or gesture, planning some unimaginable alien vengeance; Raithe, on the other hand, turned aside as though they could be utterly dismissed.

Once again he folded his hands in that unusual way, and Garrette's fear vanished; even the memory of having been afraid shredded like smoke and blew away. "Call your guards," Raithe said. "Have these murderers shot."

And because Raithe was, after all, one of Garrette's oldest friends, that was precisely what he did.

9

THE RAILHEAD ONCE had been a square, a plaza in the midst of Lower Thorncleft; the buildings that faced and surrounded it still stood beneath a ceiling that was a graceful arc of steel beams and armorglass—like a medieval street preserved in an Earthside tourist trap—and armor-glass formed the walls that sealed the streets that once had led into the plaza. Only the steel ribbons of the railways entered unhindered. Massive steam-powered locomotives hauled laden freight trains into the Rail-head five times an hour. Little sunlight could enter through armor-glass blackened by near-constant coal smoke; gas lamps illuminated the Railhead's interior twenty-four hours a day. Even at noon, all within took on a greenish moonlit cast. Now, at night, everything became pale and alien.

The Overworld Company offices occupied a large building that once had been the town home of a prosperous merchant. It stood adjacent to the warehouse that had been converted to hold the Overworld link of the transfer pump, and so a trace of ozone and sulphur always hung in the office air: it smelled like Earth.

In what had been the merchant's basement was the true nerve center of the offices: nestled snugly below ground, within an Earth-normal field powered by the transfer pump next door, was the Data Processing Center. Here, where the EN field protected sensitive electronics from the randomizing effects of Overworld physics, lay the computers and Earthside communications equipment that were the brains of the Company.

Crossing the threshold of the DPC awakened Garrette with a shock like a bucket of ice water had been dumped on his head. He staggered, gasping, reaching blindly around himself for something, anything, to hold on to, to support himself against a shattering surge of panic.

A strong hand took his; then a muscular arm enfolded his shoulders with comforting warmth. He found himself staring into the ice-colored eyes of Ambassador Raithe from close enough to kiss.

Garrette screamed.

But only a muffled moan came out past the hand Raithe clamped over his mouth. "Shhh," Raithe murmured soothingly. "It's all right, Vinse; I won't hurt you. Shh."

Garrette trembled with shock, too frightened to struggle. He tried to swallow, failed, and panted harshly through his nose until Raithe finally took the hand away from his mouth. "What—? How did you—? My God—"

He remembered it all: the death of Quelliar, the roar of assault rifles as the secmen had broken down the doors of his drawing room and shot the elves to rags. He remembered inviting Raithe to accompany him while he made his report on the incident to his superiors—remembered sitting in the carriage beside him, chattering like a schoolgirl, all the way from Thornkeep to the Railhead—

Remembered ordering everyone out of the DPC—

Oh, my God, Garrette moaned inside his head, and his eyes rolled wildly in renewed panic. All that returned his gaze were the mindless patterns of screen savers flickering across the screens in empty cubicles. *Oh my God, I did it, I sent everybody out of here—I'm* alone *with him!*

Raithe gazed into his eyes as though his heart could be read there like a book. "Vinse," he said slowly, cajolingly, "Vinse, Vinse, Vinse. Calm yourself. I'm on your side. We're partners, now."

"But, but, but, what did you *do* to me? How did you make me bring you in *here*? And why? *Why?*"

"We're here, Vinse, because as soon as you left my presence, you would have realized that you had acted under my influence. We came here to speak because I wish you to be persuaded, not controlled. Here—" His gesture took in the cubicles and the glowing deskscreens. "—as you will understand, given only a moment's thought, no power at my command can force your mind against your will. For our partnership to prosper, I must reach your reason."

"My reason—? *Partnership?*" Garrette squirmed and pushed himself away from Raithe's encircling arm and turned to face him, livid with terrified anger. "My *God,* man! Partnership? You've started a *war!*"

"No, Vinse," Raithe said calmly. His lips bent in a smile both warm and sad. "You started the war. All I've done is give you the chance to strike the first blow."

Somehow that smile stifled Garrette's urge to bluster. Instead, he turned away and sank into the nearest chair. He swiveled around so that he could lean on the desk and rest his face on his hands. "You're talking about Diamondwell."

"Of course I am. The Diamondwell stonebenders have been allied with House Mithondionne since before the Liberation. More than a thousand years. If those legates had returned to T'farrell Ravenlock, having seen what they had seen, war would have come whether you willed it or no. The war began when you poisoned the Diamondwell aquifer."

"Oh, my God," Garrette whispered. He dug his thumbs into the corners of his eyes, struggling with a sudden suicidal urge to jam them in, to gouge his eyes right out of his head. "Oh, my *God*. Why didn't you *tell* me? You were here—you knew, you could see what was happening. *Why didn't you tell me?*"

Raithe shrugged. "Why should I?"

Garrette lifted his head to stare at the Ambassador. His face felt raw and numb, as though he'd been scalded by boiling water though the pain had not yet hit.

"Stop a war between the limitless power of Arta and the greatest enemy of Humanity?" Raithe said reasonably. "I would be mad to do so. Why should the Monasteries care what losses you take? To rid the world of elves, no price is too high—and war between the two of you costs us nothing at all."

"Then w-why—" he stammered, "what are you doing . . . ? Why . . . ? I mean, you said, partnership . . . ?"

"Oh yes, Vinse. I am not blind to one vital, essential, over-whelming fact: Artan or no, you are as human as I am."

I'm a lot more *human than you are, you crazed savage,* Garrette thought, but he kept his expression perfectly neutral. Right now his situation was so impossibly desperate that he'd take any help, from anyone—even this fanatical psychopath.

"And I know, too," Raithe went on, "that you are not a warlike man. I know that you prefer negotiation to violence, and that is admirable, Vinse; it is truly—so long as there is a chance that negotiation will succeed. But there can be no peace between *species*, Vinse; negotiation would only give the elves more time to mass their forces and organize their campaign. That is why the legates had to die as they did. Now, war is inevitable. It is your sole remaining option. And it may be weeks, even a month, before House Mithondionne learns the fate of its legates. Now, *you* are the one with time as an ally. Use it wisely, Vinse. Prepare your strike."

"But, but you don't understand," Garrette said hopelessly. "I can't just declare a *war*! I don't have the authority . . . I have superiors, to whom I am accountable—and even they are account-able to the, to the, er, the nobility of Arta. Most of the, uh, the *nobility* would never accept a war—I would be ordered to pursue a purely diplomatic solution."

Raithe shrugged. "Can you not merely appear to do so? I may be able to offer you clandestine allies to do the actual fighting."

Garrette squinted at him, calculating. He imagined himself

speaking before the Leisure Congress, cloaked in statesman-ship; he imagined offering the Company's services as a peace-maker, an arbitrator, a go-between seeking *an end to the violence between two of Transdeia's valued neighbors*—

Not only might he be able to protect the Company, his own career might yet be saved.

"Allies?" he said.

"Mm, yes," Raithe replied judiciously. "I should think allies would be very possible. What would . . . your *superiors* . . . say to an alliance with the Ankhanan Empire?"

"Ankhana?" Garrette was dazzled by the sheer boldness of it. "You could arrange an alliance with *Ankhana*?"

"Very likely. Oh, to be sure, it would be informal—even se-cret, at first—but I should think that the common interests of Arta and Ankhana could only serve to bind them together more and more closely as time passes."

"How—how would we go about this?"

"First, as a gesture of good faith," Raithe said crisply, "you and your *Aktiri* brethren can stop supporting Cainism within the Empire."

Garrette gasped and left his mouth hanging open.

Raithe smiled thinly. "Do you forget how I came to be here? I have seen into your mind. I know that Artans and *Aktiri* are one and the same. I know that Caine was an *Aktir*, and that the *Aktiri* fight in the Cainist cause."

"I—I—"

"I also know—I should say, I *believe*—that the ultimate goals of the Empire, the Monasteries, and Arta finally coincide. We all serve the Human Future. Is this not so?"

"I, well, I suppose—"

"Once we've established normal relations between Arta and Ankhana, you can sell Artan military magick to them—those springless repeating pellet bows would be ideal—and I'd imagine they'd be more than happy to use them in the wholesale slaughter of elves."

Garrette bit his lip. It was an attractive idea, audacious, pow-erful, but . . . "It's not that simple," he said. "There's no way we could keep it a secret, and the nobility would resist even that."

"The nobility, the nobility," Raithe spat. "Does your king live in fear of his *nobility*?"

"We have no king," Garrette said. How was he supposed to

explain the Leisure Congress so that Raithe's feudal mind would understand? "We have a . . . a ruling council of nobles. And my ultimate superiors form only a small fraction of that council. Should the majority decide against us, we would be forced to give way. We can't be seen to even *prepare* for war until we've already been attacked."

"You *have* been attacked," Raithe said virtuously, "and treacherously—in your own chambers. Were it not for the alert action of the Artan Guard, you would have been killed."

"Mmm, maybe," Garrette said, "but some will find that a bit too convenient, and a bit less than convincing. No, we can't do it that way."

Raithe gave him a hard smile and reached out to put his hand on Garrette's arm. Garrette met his gaze curiously, and then he realized why Raithe looked so suddenly gratified: Garrette had begun speaking—and thinking—of Raithe and himself as a *we*.

As a partnership, with a common goal.

And he found, too, that he felt gratified as well. He had never realized how lonely he had become, how burdensome had been the weight of protecting the Company's interests day after day, year after year. Raithe didn't seem to be such a bad sort, after all, not really a psychopath, only a hard man—a violent man, certainly, but he came of a violent culture, one not really advanced enough to recognize the sanctity of human life—

Not that elves are actually human, anyway.

Garrette was always careful to remind himself that *an enlightened man does not judge others by his own cultural standards*; this was one of his primary rules.

"We should be looking for some way to win the war before it even starts, but by *accident*," Garrette said. "We have to make it look like we never meant them any harm."

"I know that you—Artans, I mean—are an expansionist people," Raithe said thoughtfully. "You must have found yourselves in conflicts with hostile native populations in the past; I'm sure you've developed some kind of strategy for dealing with them—some way of eliminating the threat that doesn't arouse the resistance of the more fuzzy-minded among your nobility . . . ?"

Garrette stared at him, his mouth slowly opening as he remembered another story from his childhood, one of those whispered legends that Administrator kids tell each other. It had to do with an Amerindian tribe . . . the Su? Something like that. It didn't matter.

Suddenly he was electrified by a jolt of possibility.

He could do it. Right now. Right here. The master stroke that would save the Company, and save himself.

My God, he thought. He rose, his hands fluttering with jittery energy. "Raithe, I'm *brilliant*—I'm a genius, by God, I've *got* it!"

He clapped the Ambassador on the arm, and shook his hand, and barely managed to stop himself from maiming his dignity by doing a little dance. He couldn't make himself sit down; he swiveled the nearest deskscreen to an upward angle and stroked it to life. As the screen saver vanished, he accessed the telecom program and gave his identity code.

English, he reminded himself. *Have to speak English with these people.*

The screen cleared to the cheerfully pretty face of a young man in Artisan dress. "San Francisco Studio Central," he said happily. "How may I help you?"

"I am Administrator Vinson Garrette of the Overworld Company. This is a Priority One Confidential call to your Chief of Biocontainment. Prepare for encoding."

The young Artisan's eyes widened sharply. He swallowed hard and said, "Yes sir, Administrator! Preparing . . ." Through the speaker came the sound of fingers flitting over a keypad. "Prepared."

"Engage."

My God, Garrette thought as he waited for the Biocontainment chief to answer. *My God, you must love me after all.*

THE DARK ANGEL waited in bondage within a prison he had built, shackled by chains of his own making. For a span of years, he had no food but his own body. He fed upon himself: gnawed his own bones, sucked out his own marrow.

He did not know for what he waited, but wait he did, nonetheless.

On one black day, there came the faintest whisper of distant trumpets, and the dark angel stirred within his prison.

THREE

HARI SLID A hand inside the back of his toga, reaching for the ripple of scar at his lumbar vertebrae. He massaged it fiercely through his chiton, trying to rub away the ache; his back felt as if he were lying on a rock the size of his fist. That dull pressure was as dim and rounded as painkillers could make it without knocking him out altogether. He had work to do.

His scar always hurt when he was at work these days; maybe it was this goddamn new chair. It had looked good in the catalog, but somehow he couldn't get comfortable. His back usually started to ache while he rode his private lift down to his office— buried in the bedrock below the San Francisco Studio Center— anticipatory twinges shooting up into his shoulders while the lift sank its silent three stories. The ache would grow all day long, most days; usually it was bearable.

Lately it had been brutal.

This goddamn chair . . .

I should have kept Kollberg's, he thought. *He was a sack of fucking maggots, but he knew how to be comfortable.*

One of the first things he'd done, when he'd finally won his struggle to actually direct the operations of the SF Studio, was redecorate his office.

It was something he'd always been—vaguely, more or less—planning to do, ever since the Studio installed him here six years ago. At first, he'd taken a very real malicious pleasure in sitting inside Arturo Kollberg's office suite, in using the disgraced former Chairman's chair, his desk, staring at the ocean through Kollberg's Sony repeater. But that kind of petty shit swiftly pales. Kollberg's office furniture had been rounded, organic, womblike, no sharp corners anywhere—kind of like Kollberg himself. Hari had loathed this office just as he'd loathed its former occupant, but for years it hadn't occurred to him that he could change it just because he didn't like it.

It had, in fact, never occurred to him that Kollberg had chosen his own furnishings; things look different to a man who grew up Labor. This wasn't just the office where the Chairman worked, it was *the Chairman's Office*. It had seemed to him a sort of mythic sanctum, like the throne room of an Overworld king, its trappings dictated by millennial tradition rather than the whim of its occupant.

It was funny, now—looking back on it, he could only shake his head with a rueful smile. He'd always had a guilty suspicion that this office wasn't really his, that he had been installed here as a piece of replaceable equipment, a temporary plug-in until a real Chairman came along to take the job. Like a Fool King in the Kirischan spring carnival, everyone would pretend he was in charge only so long as he didn't try to make any laws.

The Chairman's office was now a place of dark-grained paneling, deep pile carpet, an immense wraparound desk of burled walnut imported from Overworld, walls lined with heavy bookshelves filled with real books. He had a few plays, a few histories, but nearly all fiction in leather-bound editions: fantasies, mysteries, even some socially irresponsible, slightly risky works from the vanished genre of science fiction. Most of them had been brought out from the vault on Marc Vilo's estate. If anyone asked—say, the Board of Governors, or even the Social Police—Hari could claim that he culled the old novels for Adventure ideas; it gave him a perfect excuse to maintain a collection here that he could never have kept at home.

The only problem was, his fucking back still hurt.

The analgesics he used helped a little, but not much. The Studio doctors wouldn't give him anything stronger; they didn't really believe he was in pain. One of them would occasionally remind him that the touch/pain receptors around his wound had been severed when his bypass was installed—which was true; the scar itself was numb as a slice of steak—and that he really couldn't be hurting, not there.

He was willing to allow that the pain might be psychosomatic. So what? It still hurt.

Hari had given up arguing with them. Instead, he carried a small bottle of grey-market meperidine hydrochloride in his purse, which not only took the edge off the pain of his back, but dulled the pain of his life, as well.

And if it was all in his head, why did it hurt *worse* now, when he could sit in a chair that he *liked*? His new chair was an old-fashioned high-backed swivel, upholstered in calfskin over gel-pack stuffing, more expensive and better designed than the one in his study in the Abbey. It should have been more comfortable than his goddamn *bed*, let alone that shapeless blob of a chair he'd inherited from Kollberg.

He forced his attention back to the display of his deskscreen, which was filled with the latest inspection reports from the mining colony in Transdeia. He'd heard some disturbing rumors about shit going on over there; Garrette, the Overworld Company's Viceroy, was ruthless as a child molester, and some people were saying he had been turning a blind eye to Transdeian pogroms against subhumans on the duchy's borders. So Hari could fantasize about a surprise inspection, dream of writing a report that would really stick Garrette's head in the shitpot, and it would keep him happy enough for an hour or two—

The annunciator on his deskscreen bleeped for attention.

He jumped a little, then shook his head and thumbed the acceptor. His itinerary vanished behind an image of his secretary's weasely face. "Yeah, Gayle?"

"It's the soap booth, Administrator. They say it's urgent."

"Put them through."

"Right away, sir."

The view changed to a nervous-looking man in tech whites. *"Uh, Chairman Michaelson, sorry to bother you—"*

"Forget it, technician. What's up?"

"Uh, well, we got Rossi's visuals back. He's awake, and he doesn't seem injured . . ."

"Mm, that's good news."

Francis Rossi was in one of Hari's pet projects, his Interlocking Serial Program. The ISP involved ten different Actors, all doing three-month shifts in Ankhana. Instead of the usual seven- to ten-day Adventure, their first-handers could sign on for any length of time, from a few hours to a month, and they could even switch back and forth between all the different Actors in the ISP. This let the Actors lead something resembling normal lives in their Overworld personae, let them develop significant relationships with natives and with each other, since they didn't have the pressure of maintaining slam-bang action-packed-adventure every minute. It made their experiences deeper and more emotionally powerful, without the endless violence that other Studios used to artificially generate excitement.

The critics loved it; the audiences were somewhat less enthusiastic—they called it by a derisive epithet that dated back to the early twentieth century: *soap opera*—but Hari intended to stick with it as long as he could.

Hari thought of it as a kinder, gentler form of Acting, less repugnant than the wholesale slaughter that had made Caine, for example, so successful—and it was certainly easier on the Actors. He'd been afraid Frank Rossi was going to be the ISP's first fatality in two years.

On Overworld, Rossi was known as J'Than, a freelance bounty hunter loosely affiliated with the Ankhanan private security service Underground Investigations. His story arc was usually the most action-oriented of the entire ISP. J'Than projected a carefully cultivated facade of hardboiled amorality; Hari had personally created the character, and had made Rossi read *The Maltese Falcon*, *The Underground Man*, and *The Last Good Kiss*.

J'Than had been nearing the end of his current three-month story arc, tracing a gang of politically connected slavers. Last night, he'd swung a freelance security gig at the hottest society show in Ankhana: *The Nasty Little Princess* at Alien Games, which in its very first week was already being declared the hit of the decade. He'd bribed his way past the off-duty PatrolFolk who guarded the private boxes.

After that, it had been far too easy.

The whore assigned to that box had been very forthcoming; human, long-legged and beautiful, she had dropped dazzling hints of where she might be able to lead him, and had followed with a truly spectacular blowjob. With her raven hair splayed across his loins and his penis buried deep in her throat, he never heard the box's door open behind him. He didn't even know he was in trouble until a bag went over his head and its drawstring mouth closed around his neck tighter than the whore's lips around his cock.

When his unknown assailant choked him out, the techs in the soap booth switched his audience over to another Actor in a related storyline, also present at the premiere. When Rossi wasn't immediately strangled to death, two impromptu betting pools sprang up, one predicting the time and the other the method of his eventual demise. But by 1000 this morning, he was still alive, and still unconscious.

"Okay, he's awake, great," Hari said. "Switch his audience back." Why were they bothering him with this? They knew what to do—all this was SOP, covered in the ISP guidelines that were posted on each screen in the techbooth. "Thanks for the report, technician."

"Uh, Administrator, wait—that's not, I mean, I think there might be a problem . . ."

Hari sighed. "All right. Go ahead."

The tech explained. They had been casually monitoring Rossi's telemetry, waiting for him to wake up. They had the usual instructions: to switch his audience back to his storyline when he recovered consciousness. When the hero is taken by the bad guys, something interesting usually follows, whether it be a climactic confrontation with the main villain or a simple death by torture.

But Francis Rossi woke up in a forest.

And not in a forest, too. His transponder signature clearly still came from Ankhana—from Alientown, in fact: almost certainly from inside Alien Games.

"You're sure of that?"

"Yes, sir; all diagnostics check out. Uh, you think I could pipe

his POV through to your desk, sir? It's easier to just show you than it is to explain."

"Yeah, sure," Hari said, frowning. "Put him on."

The image on his deskscreen became noontime in a forest, in the midst of a sort of jumbled shantytown, built of woodland scraps—

Populated with elvish corpses.

Rossi's POV rolled smoothly through the shambles, as though he were mounted on wheels and someone pushed him from behind. The bodies lay strewn haphazardly in the clear areas, some fresh as beef in a slaughterhouse, some blackened with decay, bellies swollen to bursting with internal gases. Rossi's involuntary retching echoed in the booth.

Hari's mouth compressed into a grim line, and he reflected that being confined to a desk job had its advantages: Caine had been in places like that more than once, and he had a vivid memory of how they smell.

The belly of one of the corpses burst with a sound like a wet, sloppy fart. Rossi's POV panned right and left, showing the extent of the carnage—bodies everywhere, some hacked to pieces, most just dead—and then dollied forward once again.

It was that motion, that familiar net-feature swing of POV, that gave it away. Hari's fingers began to tingle. With one startling intuitive leap, he understood exactly what was happening. Whoever had Rossi was using him like a video camera.

This was bad; for Rossi, this was about as bad as it could get. *They know he's an Actor.*

Garbled, hissing semiwords came over the techbooth's speakers, the broken half phrases of the mainframe's translation protocol struggling with an unfamiliar language. The telemetry readout of Rossi's heart rate and adrenal production had shot deep into the red end of the scale, dangerously high. "What's that language?" Hari asked. "You have analysis yet?"

"The TP doesn't recognize it, sir. Maybe some kind of elvish dialect, you think?"

Elvish dialect my ass, Hari thought. "Look at his telemetry. I think *Rossi* understands, even if the TP doesn't. He's scared out of his fucking mind—he's not even *monologuing,* for Christ's sake. Frank's a pro; it takes more than some rotting bodies to make him forget his Soliloquy."

Now the view on the POV screen swung to its first image of a living creature: a bald, sickly looking elf with no eyebrows, tall and broad shouldered for his race. He wore a simple, new-looking shift of clean white, belted at the waist over leggings of forest brown. He walked toward Rossi with a peculiar staggering limp, as though his legs didn't work well and he had to throw his weight from side to side to keep his feet under him.

When he spoke, the techbooth speakers muttered gibberish.

"Who's *this* guy?" Hari asked.

"Don't know, sir. We've seen him once already. He seems to be the captor."

Hari stared at the screen. "Close the translator."

"Sir?"

"Shut down the translation protocol."

"But sir, then the computer won't have a chance to analyze the phoneme—"

"Listen to me, you idiot. This whole thing is *staged*, you get it? He's not in a forest, he's in Ankhana. At Alien Games. This is a little play, and *we're the audience*. They're sending us a message, and they damn well sure wouldn't go to this much trouble and then use a language we can't understand. *Close the fucking translator.*"

"Yes, sir."

Closing the program silenced the speakers for two or three seconds; then they came on again with the elf's unfiltered voice, exactly as it fell on Rossi's ears.

". . . no reason to bother showing you what you already know you're doing to us, here on the borders of Transdeia: the murders of our people, and the rape of our land by your mining machines . . ."

The mikes on the techs' screens in the booth were sensitive enough that Hari could hear them both whisper *Holy crap* in perfect unison.

Yeah, he thought. *That about sums it up.*

The mysterious dialect spoken by the bald, sickly looking elf with no eyebrows was easy to understand.

It was English.

THE SOLE DEFENDER of the part-time goddess was the crooked knight. He was the reflection of knighthood in a cracked mirror, and what he did, he did backward.

The crooked knight wore no armor, and he did not care for swords. He was small and thin, ugly and graceless. He could not ride a warhorse, and no squire would serve him. He was a deceiver, a manipulator, his life built upon a lie.

His strength was the strength of ten, because his heart was stained with corruption.

FOUR

ANKHANA SPREAD LIKE a canker across the valley floor, a rank and oozing fester that drained its sewage and manufacturing waste into the river that men called the Great Chambaygen. As the barge lumbered round a river-bend far to the north and east of the Imperial capital, the city coalesced out of the pall of smog that covered it: a ragged blot upon the earth, washed by the haze of intervening miles to the necrotic grey of dead flesh.

At the bow of the riverbarge stood a fey in woolen clothes tattered by time and hard travel. He looked as though the clothes may have fit him once, long ago—he had the frame for it, broad shouldered for one of the First Folk—but now they hung on him as though on a rack. His face had been carved into deep lines:

scars of privation and grief deeper than any a true primal ever shows. His hair stuck straight out from his scalp around his sharply pointed ears: a platinum brush the length of the first joint of his thumb. His boots might have been fine, if they were not so battered; for a belt, he wore a thick-braided hemp throwline, tied around his waist. He bore no purse, and in place of a gentleman's weapons he had only the mop on which he leaned.

He stared downriver at Ankhana, and his knuckles whitened on the mop's handle. His lips pulled back over teeth sharp as a wolf's, and his great golden eyes, their pupils slitted to razored vertical lines in the afternoon sun, burned with barely controlled desperation. Once, not so long ago, he had been a prince.

His name was Deliann.

"You workin', decker?" the foredeck second rasped behind him. "Or you fuckin' off?"

The primal gave no sign that he heard.

"Hey, shitsuck, you think I'm not talkin' to you?"

Thunderheads spread like a hand extended to grasp the towering twin-bladed spire of the Colhari Palace; they grumbled and spat lightning at the earth. He could see, even from this distance, that the threatened rain held off: the black-brown coal smoke of the Industrial Park still hung thickly over the northern quarters of the city. No rain had yet come to drive it down from the autumn sky and wash it into the river.

Another storm, another fishkill: the runoff from Ankhanan streets slew river life wholesale. Deliann shook his head bitterly. *You have to go a week downriver before you can drink the water again. And my brothers like to remind me that I am one of these people.*

But I'm not. I'm not.

What I am is worse.

For more than a thousand years that city had fouled these waters, from its very birth as a river pirates' camp on the island that was now Old Town. Panchasell Mithondionne himself had laid siege to the city, more than nine hundred years ago, leading the Folk Alliance against it when the city was a haven for feral humans during the Rebellion. He had fallen there, killed in his final failed assault, passing the lordship of his house, and all the First Folk, to the Twilight King, T'farrell Ravenlock.

This is where we lost, Deliann thought. The Folk had fought the ferals for decades beyond the Siege of Ankhana, but this had been the turning point of the war. Now, nearly a millennium later, even feys who were themselves veterans of the Feral Rebellion, who had fought the ferals hand-to-hand, no longer called them *ferals*. Everyone called them what they called themselves: *human*—"of the humus."

The Dirt People.

"Hey." Now the voice behind him was accompanied by a rough shove on the shoulder and a short *rrrip* of tearing cloth— the foredeck second's fighting claw had tangled in Deliann's shirt. He turned to face the foredeck second, an aging ogrillo with a rumpled mass of scar where his left eye used to be and a broken ivory stump where his left tusk had once jutted up from his undershot jaw. The foredeck second kept his snout canted slightly to the primal's right so that he could look down at him with his remaining red-gleaming eye.

"You know the only thing I hate worse'n fuckin' lazy-ass deckers tryin' to scam their passage?" The ogrillo leaned close enough to hook out Deliann's eye with one twitch of his tusk. "Fuckin' *elves*, that's what. Now: You moppin'? Or you *swimmin'*?"

The primal barely glanced at the second; he looked up, beyond the ogrillo's shoulder, at the twin teams of ogre poleboys that now jammed their thirty-foot lengths of oiled oak hard into the river's bed. The teams—each made up of six ogres nine or more feet tall, weighing over half a ton apiece—leaned into their poles in slowly counted cadence, pitting their massive muscles against the barge's momentum, their clawed feet digging furrows in the barge's deck cleats.

"Why are we stopping?" he asked tonelessly.

"You stupid, shitsuck? Ankhana's top port on the river—our slip don't come open till afternoon tomorrow." The foredeck second grunted a laugh as ugly as he was. "You think 'cause we a day early, you don' gotta make you full passage-work? Fuck that. You *work*, elf. Or you fuckin' swim."

"All right. I'll swim."

Deliann opened his hands to let the mop handle drop to the deck. Expressionlessly, he turned and gathered himself to leap into the water, but the foredeck second was too quick: his heavy hand closed around the primal's arm, the fighting claw below the thumb digging into the primal's ribs, and hauled him roughly back to the deck. "Not fuckin' likely," the ogrillo snarled. "You owe one more day's *work*, shitsuck. What're you, some kind of Cainist? Think you can do what you fuckin' want?"

"I'm not sure what a Cainist is," Deliann said. "But you should let me go."

"Fuck that. No fuckin' elf scams me."

He yanked Deliann's arm upward, inflicting a little preliminary pain and pulling him off balance. He expected a struggle or even a fight, and was more than ready for either—but instead, the skinny, haggard primal went absolutely still. "You want to take your hand off me."

The ogrillo's hand sprang stiffly open, and his fighting claw flattened back against his forearm. He frowned at his hand in disbelief. "What the fuck?"

"I've endured you for five days," Deliann said distantly, "because I had no swifter course for Ankhana. Now I'm leaving, and you can't stop me."

"My ass," the ogrillo said, lifting his other hand and making a fist to curl his fingers out of the way of his fully extended fighting claw. There was no law on the Great Chambaygen save what the barge crews made for themselves—and no one would task a deck officer for the maiming or death of a mere decker. "I'll gut you like a fuckin' trout."

The creases that hunger and hard travel had etched into the primal's face deepened now, and transformed into something like age—impossible age, as though Deliann looked down into the world from some millennial distance—and the ogrillo's fist dropped limply to his side.

The ogrillo snarled, his vented lips pulling back from his tusks, and wrenched his shoulders as though his arms were held by invisible hands that he could shake off—but they weren't. They swung freely, but not under his command. Both arms hung dead from his shoulders.

"I'm elfshot," he muttered with growing amazement that swiftly became righteous fury. "Fucker *elfshot* me! Yo, *carp*!" Along the entire length of the barge, heads came up at the foredeck second's yell.

Though the river is a lawless bound, there are a few traditions that the barge crews honor above their lives, and none more than this one. In seconds, all twelve ogres had shipped their poles; all the cargoboys had dropped their bottles, set down their cards, and put away their dice. Even the deckers, the poorest of the river scum who worked for nothing more than food and transport, set aside their buckets and their brushes and mops and picked up belaying pins and cargo hooks, and every one of them came running full tilt toward the bow.

Deliann watched them come with only a slight tightening of his feathery brows. The nearest ogre—then another, then a third—pitched forward and slammed thunderously to the deck, howling and clutching thighs knotted in convulsive cramps that crippled them as effectively as a knife to the hamstring.

The rest of the crew had to slow their headlong rush to pick their way around and over the writhing ogres; before they could, a sheet of flame twenty feet high sprang up from the deck to bar their path.

"It's just a Fantasy!" the ogrillo yelled. "It's just fuckin' *elf magick*, you morons! It can't really hurt you!"

Apparently some of the crew knew, as the foredeck second did, that most of the magicks worked by the First Folk operate on the mind of the victim only; braver than their fellows, they leaped through the fire—and staggered screaming across the deck, clothes and hair blazing, trailing smoke and flame as they dived for the river.

The foredeck second's good eye blinked, and squinted, and blinked again. "Elf magick can't really hurt you," he repeated numbly.

"That might be true," Deliann said, "if I were really an elf."

He reached up and grabbed the foredeck second by his one good tusk and hauled the ogrillo's face down to his own with shocking strength. He put his lips against the ogrillo's ear-cavity and said softly but distinctly, "I don't like violence. I don't want to hurt you, or anyone else. But I'm *leaving*. I don't have time to be gentle. If anyone comes after me, I'll kill them. You understand? And then I'll come back here, and I'll kill you. Tell me you understand."

The ogrillo stepped back and tossed his head, trying to rip his tusk free, but this skinny, almost fleshless fey had astonishing power in his hand and arm. He yanked the ogrillo close once more, and now smoke leaked from within his grip, smoke that reeked of burning ivory as the tusk scorched against his palm; the ogrillo gave out a low moan that rose toward a despairing shriek.

"Tell me you *understand*," he repeated.

"I, I, I—I get it," the ogrillo whimpered. "Go—just *go!*"

Deliann opened his hand, and the ogrillo staggered, his tusk blackened where the primal had held it. He nearly fell into the flames, but as he stumbled back the fire died as though smothered by an invisible blanket, leaving only a broad line of smoldering embers across the deck.

Deliann turned to the bow and looked down, to be certain none of the crewmen who'd sought the river were in his way below, then he dived in and swam strongly to the bank. He pulled himself from the water and struck out running along the river without so much as a bare glance back at the barge: running hard for Ankhana.

Manblood, he could hear his brothers sneer. It was their favorite jab. *Always must be doing; never can be being. That manblood—like a human, you throw time away. Like a wastrel who finds a pouch of gold in the street, you have so little that spending what little you have means nothing.*

Maybe so, he answered them inside his head, *but right now, I have more time than you do*. And he wanted so desperately to be wrong about that; the ache of his wish that this was not true burned his heart like the fire he'd set on the barge's deck.

Ankhana's outskirts lay three miles ahead along the flat floodplain, and night lowered upon the city with the rain.

He had an ugly, stumbling run, as though his legs belonged to someone else—as though both were half crippled, and his natural gait was the average of two conflicting limps. Despite this, he ran hard and fast, pulling Flow to power his overworked muscles, and made the shantytown that surrounds Ankhana's Warrens in a quarter of an hour.

The storm swung out to meet him, and soaked him thoroughly in rain that reeked of sulphur. Without slackening his pace, he turned up the road that circled northward around the Warrens and the Industrial Park.

Even the empty-eyed human dregs that crowded these outlying slums had a moment to spare to spit at him as he passed; to hurry past humans as though he had someplace to go was disrespectful. Ankhana was the heart of the human lands, and the only Folk who had ever been welcome here were those who knew their place.

Finally he reached Ankhana's Folk ghetto, Alientown, and he released the swirl of Flow that had given him strength. He needed more attention than mindview could spare him, if he wished to negotiate these narrow, crowded streets, jostling and being jostled by countless shoulders of primal, stonebender, ogrillo, and human alike.

As night fell, even some trolls took to the streets; now and again one would pause to speculatively watch him pass, and to make hungry sucking noises as it inhaled the drool that leaked around its curving tusks. The stench stole breath from his lungs; the noise and sheer restless energy of this place made his head swim. The filth, the waste, the emptiness he saw in the eyes of the Folk here—Ankhana had been the reason he'd left humanity behind for the deepwood.

Alientown had been transformed in the twenty-odd years since he'd last walked these streets. Then, it had been a tiny cramped ghetto, jammed with primals, stonebenders, treetoppers, ogrilloi and their giant cousins—all scraping out bare livings on the fringes of the capital, selling their strength and the use of their bodies to their human masters, losing themselves in narcotics and drink, snarling and snapping at each other like rats in an over-crowded cage.

In the old days, human constables had kept order in five-man patrols, their brutal tactics and free use of their iron-bound clubs earning them the nickname *headpounders*; now, it seemed that the pounders had been replaced by teams of two—one human and one Folk, usually primal or stonebender. The humans wore black and silver, the Folk scarlet and gold. Again and again, Deliann saw these pairs shouldering through the streets, breaking up fights, forestalling arguments, opening the crowds before the carriages of the wealthy. He could only shake his head in wonder.

Twenty years ago, wearing those colors had announced membership in two of the powerful Warrengangs, the Subjects of Cant and the Faces—but neither of those gangs had had territory in Alientown, and the Faces had certainly never extended their membership to include Folk. And those gangs had been *criminals*: the Faces had been peddlers of flesh and illegal narcotics, and the Subjects of Cant had been pickpockets and beggars, with strong sidelines in protection and extortion. How they had been transformed into a public constabulary, he could not imagine.

The ghetto had tripled or even quadrupled in size, bulging outward like a colony of fungus, and now, at night, it bloomed like a pitcher plant, sticky-sweet and dangerously inviting. A riot of colored lights clashed into muddy rainbows on the wetly glistening cobbles: light cast from blazing coronal signs that wreathed hulking hotels and casinos.

These signs proclaimed the entertainment to be found within: games from knucklebones and roulette to cockfighting, bear-baiting and human/Folk/ogrillo cross-species pit-fighting; food from the most exquisite imported tophalmo wings to all-you-can-eat spiced-pork-and-cornmeal buffets; drink ranging from grain alcohol to Tinnaran brandy; narcotics from simple roasted *rith* to exotic powders that make one's darkest fantasy feel as sharply real as a poke in the eye; whores to suit any species, sex, age, experience, and taste, from delicate pederasty to the kind of action where the price includes on-site postcoital medical care.

Twenty years ago, when somebody wanted something special in Alientown, something that he just couldn't find anywhere else—it might be illegal, or seductively dangerous, or simply too repugnant for widespread popularity—he'd go to an establishment called the Exotic Love. The Exotic Love seemed, to all appearances, to be a small, well-appointed, rather exclusive brothel, just off Nobles' Way; but once a man became a regular, once he had shown he could be trusted—that is, once the proprietor had acquired enough blackmailworthy evidence that this fellow dared not take a breath without permission—he would find himself ushered into a sensual world of literally infinite possibility. At the Exotic Love, nothing was out of reach; it was merely expensive.

But now, it seemed that all of Alientown had been transformed into a street-bazaar version of the Exotic Love, and the place itself could not be found. Deliann stood in the street, staring blankly up at the sign of the fungist who had taken over the building just off Nobles' Way. He read mechanically down the list of stimulant, narcotic, and hallucinogenic spores for sale within; this was a futile self-deception, a dodge to briefly postpone the moment when he would realize that he had no guess what to do next.

He had come so far—

Light fingers brushed his flanks, where most Folk carry their purses. Deliann's hand flicked almost too fast to be seen, and he hauled the owner of those fingers around in front of him: a dirty-faced human child. "Sorry, fey, sorry—I just tripped," the boy said hastily.

"This place," Deliann said heavily. "This place was once called the Exotic Love. What happened to it?"

The boy's eyes went wide and round, then closed to streetwise slits. "Hey, I don't whistle *that* tune—but I gotta sister, she's eleven, never done nothing but the once awhile blowjob—"

"That's not what I asked for."

"Right, right—truth: she's thirteen, but I swear—"

Deliann shook him once, hard. "The Exotic Love," he repeated.

The boy's eyes rolled, and suddenly he screamed with shocking, painful volume, *"Short-eyes! Short-eyes! Get this Cainist buttfucker offa me!"*

The boy kicked him in the shin—it hurt less than his shout—and wrenched his arm free. He dashed away and vanished into the crowd, many of whom now stared at Deliann with gathering hostility, muttering darkly among themselves. One took it upon himself to express the general sentiment: "Short-eyes mother-fucker . . . Wanna stick a kid, y'oughta *pay* for it like *decent* folks!"

It might have turned uglier—some in this crowd looked to be the sort to enjoy a casual stomping, and none of these could see any hint in this ragged, exhausted-looking primal of just how lethal the attempt might turn out—but shouldering through the crowd came a tall man in a chainmail byrnie of black and silver, and a thickly muscled stonebender in a scarlet-and-gold cloth kirtle.

"All right, all right, shove it over," the stonebender repeated tiredly, stepping on toes, elbowing ribs, occasionally giving this one or that an encouraging shove. Her short arms were knotted like cypress knees; when she shoved, people moved. "Break it up. Keep it moving—yah, *you,* shit-in-the-head. Get going."

The man came over to Deliann and sized him up with a cold stare. "Got trouble, woodsie? Or looking for some? Either way, we're here for you."

"What I'm looking for," Deliann said slowly, "is the feya who used to run the brothel here."

"Here?" His brow wrinkled. "Don't think so. Ruufie—the fungist, here—he's been here, what? More'n eight years, I'd have to guess—since before I came on Patrol. Hey, Taulkg'n, you know of any brothel here?"

His partner snorted into her beard and muttered something Deliann half heard, that might have been a derisive comment on humanity's short lives and shorter memories. She gave the last of the onlookers a healthy shove down the street and turned back. "Yah, the Exotic Love, useta be."

"The Exotic? No shit." The man's eyes lit up, and a half smile canted his mouth. "Hey, Taulkie, this woodsie's looking for the *Duchess*."

The stonebender approached, her fists on her hips. She looked Deliann up, then down, then up again, and shook her head sadly. "Don't bother, woodsie. She won't see you."

"I don't know any duchesses," Deliann said patiently. "The feya I want went by the name Kierendal."

"That's her," the man said. "They just call her the Duchess because she's fucked better'n half the Cabinet."

The stonebender trod heavily on her partner's toes. "Mind your manners."

"Just tell me where I can find her."

"She runs Alien Games, now—"

"Alien Games? That whole-block complex, back on Khazad-Lun?"

"Yah, but she won't see you, woodsie, I'm tellin' you. She's *busy*, you hear? She's an important—"

Deliann missed the rest of what the stonebender tried to tell him: he was already running.

2

ALIEN GAMES SQUATTED at the center of the swamp that was Alientown like an immense, malignant toad queen, glistening with multicolored slime. Only eight years old, it had already grown until it swallowed every adjacent building; now the size of its footprint exceeded that of the Colhari Palace itself. Three restaurants, seven saloons, four casinos, two theaters, and dozens of performance booths of varying sizes and degrees of privacy—within that complex could be purchased anything from cigars to sudden death, with room charges prorated by the hour. It shone like a beacon that might be seen from the moon, ringed by a gigantic halo. The halo was the rainbow reflection

that scattered from a stupendous bubble of force—a titanic
Shield—that enclosed the entire structure, made faintly visible
by the drizzle that collected on its surface and trailed to the
streets.

Deliann leaned against a wall of rain-slickened limestone,
within the mouth of an alley down the street. The soggy wool of
his tunic dragged at his shoulders. The runoff that dripped onto
his face from the eaves above had a faintly acid, chemical taste,
and he stood just deep enough within the shadows of the alley
mouth that his face picked up only dim highlights from the lurid
scarlet, green, and golden glare.

Alien Games blazed even brighter in mindview than it did to
normal vision. A gigantic vortex of Flow towered above it, impossibly vivid intertangling rivers of crimson and amethyst,
ichor and viridian, azure and argent curling like party streamers
down toward the roof. At the perimeter of the Shield bubble stood
massed crowds of onlookers, peering at the nobles, celebrities,
and society brilliants who alighted from each carriage of the
endless train as it pulled to a stop at the purple velvet carpet that
ascended the broad marble steps. The onlookers leaned on the
Shield as if it were glass, pressing their noses against it as though
they could will themselves from the chill damp darkness outside
to the endless summer noon within.

A marquee the size of a riverbarge burned on the roof of the
immense vaulted portico, proclaiming the Senses-Shattering
World Premiere of some vulgar-sounding show featuring performers of whom Deliann had never heard.

He spent a moment studying the operation of the bubble.
Clearly, it consisted of several overlapping Shields; Alien Games
must employ six or seven thaumaturges, probably human, to maintain it. Whenever a carriage would approach along the street, its
footmen forcing a path through the crowds, a gap would open,
just large enough for the carriage and its attendants to pass; then
the gap would close behind them like a gate to keep the rabble
out. Some of the Shields would be semipermanent, charged in
advance like those that sheltered the entire complex from the
drizzle outside, maintained by stored power instead of the disciplined mind of a thaumaturge, but the ones that opened like
gateways must be the work of men, not crystals. He could slip
through one of the crystaled Shields without too much difficulty

and without raising much of an alarm—but then he'd have to find some other way to attract Kierendal's attention.

He moved out into the street.

He forced his way through the press, ignoring the counter-shoves and curses that pursued him. When he reached the mid-street point where the carriages had been passing through, he wedged his arms between a large human and a small troll. "Excuse me," he said politely.

The human and the troll looked down at the ragged, bone-thin primal between them, then smirked at each other. The human said, "Piss off, elf. Find your own spot."

"I have," Deliann told them, and shoved them violently apart. They stumbled into the people to either side, neither remotely prepared for Deliann's preternatural strength. The troll wisely recognized that this fey had unknown resources, and faded back, muttering darkly to itself in its native speech of grunts and slurps; the human, less intelligent, decided to take exception.

"Hey," the man said, "hey, you little bastard, who you think you're shoving?"

Deliann stood still, waiting, feeling a little sick.

The man raised a heavy fist. "I'm gonna enjoy making—"

Deliann interrupted him with a stiff overhand right that smashed blood from the human's nose. The human's eyes filled with blinding tears, and Deliann kicked him solidly in the balls. While the man folded, Deliann stepped around him, put one hand on the back of the man's head and the foreknuckle of his other hand against the man's upper lip. The knuckle against the man's shattered nose was more than enough to stand him up and bend him over backward until he fell to the ground.

When he had the man arranged on the ground to his satisfaction, Deliann kicked him once more: the toe of his boot stabbed with exceptional precision into the man's solar plexus. The man curled into a fetal knot of pain, his breath coming in ragged, broken gasps.

Deliann straightened. He eyed the surrounding crowd expressionlessly. "Anyone else?"

No one offered themselves.

He bared his exceptionally long, sharp, carnivore's teeth. "Then *back off*."

He turned away, unable to hide the twist of revulsion on his face. To do such things gently would require him to be clever, and he was too tired to be clever; it would require imagination, and that he dared not touch. For two weeks his imagination had given him nothing but the color of screams, the texture of dead children, the smell of genocide.

Inside the endless summer noon of the bubble, the ushers and footmen all wore livery of scarlet and gold; flanking the door were six sleepy ogres, up past their bedtime in full field armor, their steel enameled in the same colors so that it gleamed like glazed pottery. They held their blood-colored halberds extended at parade rest.

Deliann's mindview showed him no swirls of Flow around anyone on the street, except for a tiny whorl that brought a bright glow to the jewelry of the beefy woman who descended from a carriage with the help of two solicitous porters. He nodded to himself. With any luck, all he'd have to deal with out here would be ordinary guards.

In mindview, he tuned his Shell to the shifting pattern of the Shield in front of him and took the measure of the thaumaturge who maintained it. The man was barely third-rate; this Shield was hard-pressed to hold back the rain, much less the crowd that pushed against it. Deliann gathered Flow, focused it into a lance of power, and punched through the Shield with the brisk efficiency of an injection. His Shell was tuned delicately enough to register the scarlet grunt of pain from the thaumaturge; with little effort, he swelled his lance of Flow until it forced open a door-sized hole in the Shield, and he stepped through.

The crowd at his back stared in silent wonder: to normal sight, he had effortlessly walked through the bubble that had resisted their best strength. They surged against it behind him, but he had already released his power, and the Shield was once again solid as a wall. The thaumaturge inside would have no illusions about what had happened, though; he should have already sounded some sort of alarm.

Sure enough, within the space of a single breath an elegant primal in formal evening wear detached himself from the group at the doorway and touched the shoulders of a pair of burly stonebenders in the scarlet footmen's livery; the trio approached him over the dry cobbles of the Shielded street as quickly as they could without appearing to hurry.

They met Deliann twenty yards from the entrance, arrayed in a loose arc that effectively barred his path without being so obvious as to be rude. The fey was tall and graceful, and his dark suit was immaculately tailored; his manicure gleamed like his buttons as he clasped his hands together and leaned politely toward Deliann. "May I help you, sir?"

"Yes, you may," Deliann said, brushing between him and one of the stonebenders as though they were not there. "Announce me."

"Sir?" the fey said delicately, in an eloquently dubious tone that described, in one word, the tatters of Deliann's clothing, the wear of his boots, his hempen belt, and the unnatural creases that marked his face. He followed at Deliann's shoulder, and the stonebenders brought up the rear; Deliann could hear them cracking their knuckles.

Deliann said, "You may announce me as the Changeling Prince, Deliann Mithondionne, Youngest of the Twilight King."

The fey took this without even a blink. "Does the prince have a reservation?"

Deliann kept walking.

"Please, Your Highness," the fey murmured smoothly, well practiced in his technique of handling lunatics, which he clearly presumed Deliann to be, "this is not an insuperable difficulty. We have a section reserved for visiting royalty; if the prince would care to follow me?"

Deliann could guess exactly what awaited him if he did so: a savage beating in a darkened room, his unconscious and bleeding body dumped on the street outside the bubble as a salutary example for any other gate crashers. "That won't be necessary," he said. "I didn't come for the show. I'm here to see Kierendal."

"Please, sir; I'm afraid I must insist."

Hands as hard as the roots of a mountain seized his arms. The pair of stonebenders bent him forward with efficient leverage, making him look as though he'd half fainted and he needed their help to walk; in fact, his boots barely brushed the cobbles. For one moment, his exhaustion dipped him into unresisting comfort, the childhood ease of being carried, even though their grip hurt his arms—but they were taking him the wrong way. He got his feet beneath him, and he opened his mind.

Far above, the arc of the Shield shimmered in the mental light cast by the vortex of Flow. In one second, his Shell extended to fifteen times the height of a man and touched that Shield; in the next second, he had grasped its harmonic and tuned his Shell to it. Resonating perfectly, his Shell slid through the Shield's arc and touched an argent ribbon in the vortex above. In the next second, the lights went out.

Darkness fell like a hammer.

The sudden absence of those myriad colored lights stunned the crowd to an immobile silence, likewise the footmen, even the horses that drew the carriages—it was like being struck blind. For a second that stretched toward infinity, the street was utterly dark, utterly silent, held like the breath of a child looking for the monster under his bed.

Then Deliann burst into flame.

He burned like a torch, like a bonfire, like a thousand magnesium flares struck in a single instant; he burned as though every last foot-candle of the light that had blazed like the sun around Alien Games had become fire that roared from his flesh. The two stonebender footmen howled and staggered back from him, smoke billowing from the seared flesh of their palms. The primal in formal wear covered his face with his arms and screamed like a terrified child.

Deliann's ragged clothes burned to cinders in an instant, a puff of ash that whirled up into the night. His hair sizzled away. His bare flesh bore scars of recent wounds, badly healed: a curving scab crossed his scalp, like a shallow sword cut. One of his thighs was swollen, inflamed half again the size of the other, and the shin of the other leg had a slight bend in the middle; at the bend grew a knot on the bone the size of an apple.

Naked, bald, engulfed in flame, he paced the purple carpet to the entrance, trailing burning footprints.

Everyone gave way before him except one of the ogres, braver or more stupid than the rest: it made a tentative jab at him with its halberd. At the first touch of the flames that howled around Deliann, the blade melted and dripped to a pool of white-hot metal at his feet, and half the shaft flashed to broken coals.

The firelight reflected from their eyes came back the color of fear.

"I'm here to see Kierendal," Deliann said. "I don't have time to be polite."

A beige shimmer gathered in the air before him, and then a tall feya stepped sideways from nowhere, as though an invisible door had opened edge-on in the air.

Taller than Deliann and even thinner, draped in an evening

gown that glittered as though woven of diamond, she was grace-ful as a soaring hawk. Her platinum hair coiled high above her upswept ears in an extravagantly complex coif, and her eyes glinted with flat reflections the color of money, like silver coins set in her skull. The teeth that showed behind her thin bloodless smile were long and needle-sharp, and the nail of the forefinger that she stretched toward him was filed and painted to resemble a raptor's talon made of steel. "You," she said, "really know how to make an entrance. Want a job?"

For a blank moment, Deliann could only stare through the flames; then he began, "Kierendal—"

"I beg your pardon, as an inconsiderate hostess," she inter-rupted him blithely. "How embarrassing; I've overdressed." And without so much as a hitch of her shoulders, her gown slid down her slender form and piled on the carpet. She stepped out of it toward him, as naked as he, perfectly at ease, opening her arms. "Is this better?"

Deliann's mouth dropped open. Her nipples were painted the same color as her eyes, and they looked as hard as the metal they mimicked. In that second of utter astonishment, the fire that sheathed him faded and winked out.

He hadn't even seen a flicker from her Shell, and in one sick-ening second, he realized why: She had never been here in the first place. What he'd seen had been a Fantasy, projected from some place of safety, probably into his mind alone. And while he'd gawked, she'd retuned the Shield overhead and cut him off.

He started to think he might have made a mistake.

Even as he began to extend his Shell, reaching in a new direc-tion, someone threw a heavy net over his head; the weaving was thick and metallic, and as it closed around him, the image of Kierendal and her gown vanished as though wiped from exis-tence by an invisible hand. A heavy fist knocked him to the porch, and he couldn't even pull enough Flow to enhance his strength and rip free of the net—some kind of scarlet counter-force flared over the net, blocking his best attempt. An ogre grabbed him by the ankles and yanked him off the floor, gath-ering the net around him to make a sack.

The ogre lifted him like a bagged kitten. "Guezz you don' really keep up with the latez zztuff from the zity, when you're ou' in the forezz, eh there, woodzie?"

3

THE CHAIR WAS heavy, very sturdily constructed of hard maple, and bolted to the floor. The manacles that attached Deliann's left wrist to his right ankle were threaded through the support bars that connected the chair's legs.

It took the ogre something less than five minutes, after it unbagged Deliann within this tiny room, to demonstrate to him conclusively that he couldn't pull enough Flow in here to light a candle; some unknown quality of the room's construction cut him off as absolutely as had the weave of that net. The ogre had made this point by knotting its great horned fists and beating him into semiconsciousness with swift, passionless efficiency. Then it had affixed the manacles, and left.

The chair faced a blank grey wall that was stippled with faint brownish smears: probably old, haphazardly wiped blood. By twisting uncomfortably in the seat, Deliann could watch the door behind him, but his battered body swiftly stiffened into knots of bruise. He surrendered with a sigh and turned his face back toward the wall. The room was cold; the manacles were like ice against his wrist and ankle, and gooseflesh bunched his bare skin all over his body. For a long time, he did nothing but shiver and listen to himself breathe.

Finally, the door behind him opened. Twisting to watch Kierendal enter the room cost him a stifled groan. She appeared exactly as she had in the Fantasy; the way she moved wasn't quite gliding, but it was decidedly more stylish than an ordinary walk. At her side paced a thick-muscled ogrillo bitch dressed in loose-fitting coveralls, slapping her palm with a sort of flexible club made of tightly braided leather. The club was as long as Deliann's forearm and as thick as his wrist.

Kierendal had something small and roundish in her hand, like a nut, that she pretended to be interested in rolling back and forth between her fingers. "Didn't anyone ever tell you," she murmured distractedly, "what happens to little elves who play with fire?"

"Don't call me *elf*," Deliann said slowly. "I've taken that name from humans, and from ogrilloi. I don't have to take it from you."

"That," Kierendal said, "is not an answer to my question."

An invisible hand with talons of ice reached into his stomach and twisted his guts into a ball of agony. Pain drove a gasp past his lips, and a red haze descended across his vision—but he was not without resources, even here. With an ease that belied the snarl of pain on his face, he tuned his Shell to hers, tapping into the shaft of brilliant green that poured power from her aureate Shell into his guts; he took some of that power for himself and used it to weave a shunt for the energy she threw at him— a mental chute that funneled her power into his Shell instead of his body.

The knots eased, and he prepared to strike back. She could no more pull inside this room than he could; the little nutlike thing in her hand could only be a griffinstone. Deliann tuned his Shell to an octave that Kierendal shouldn't be able to see and reached a tendril toward it—

"Thought you'd try that," she said. She glanced at the ogrillo bitch, who slapped the braided leather club against the side of Deliann's head sharply enough to shower a galaxy of stars across the inside of his eyes. He lost mindview.

Kierendal bared her teeth.

Steel claws hooked under his ribs and wrenched his stomach inside out. He doubled over, heaved between his knees, and vomited convulsively, retching, splashing puke across his bare ankles. Kierendal stepped back crisply to keep it from soiling her spike-heeled formal sandals.

When he could control his head enough to lift it once again, Kierendal looked down at him, and her starkly chiseled face bent into a mask of friendliness. She didn't seem to mind the smell. "Now you understand your position. I want you to understand mine. In just less than one hour, the curtain goes up on a show I have been preparing to mount for more than a year. I have performers from all over the Empire, from Lipke, from fucking *Ch'rranth*; I have seventy-eight *thousand* royals of my own money on the line, and I have partners who put in *more*—the kind of partners who don't believe in taking losses. If they don't turn a profit, they will collectively fuck my ass until I bleed to death."

She pronounced each crudity with a certain satisfied precision, as though she enjoyed being in this place where she could use whatever language pleased her. "And now, I also have some scary freak who claims to be the Changeling Prince throwing around fire magick like a human thaumaturge's worst nightmare, and I *need to know what's going on*. You're a Cainist, aren't you?"

Deliann shook his head. "I don't know what that is."

"Don't shit me, cock. I have two bishops and a pig-fucking *Archdeacon* of the Church of the Beloved Children in the house tonight. I knew it—I *knew* some crazy Cainist bastard would try something stupid."

"I'm no Cainist. I don't know why people keep telling me I am."

Kierendal snorted. "That just makes it worse. It's this simple, cock: I need to know who you really are, who sent you, and what you're really after, and I don't have much time to figure it out. So I'm going to hurt you until I like the answers you give me. Understand?"

Deliann said, "I need your help."

She clenched her fist around the griffinstone until scarlet power leaked between her fingers like smoke. "You have a peculiar way of asking for it," she said through her teeth.

"I didn't come here to ask," he said flatly. "I would not presume on our relationship. I am Deliann Mithondionne, Youngest of the Twilight King, and by the fealty you owe my father, I demand your service."

"Who do you think you're *talking* to, cock?" Kierendal said disbelievingly. She paced around him, staring, as though his bald, scorched nakedness might look different from another side. "You can bluff the woodsies, but you're in the big city now. I have sources all over this fucking *continent*. First: Prince Deliann is *dead*. He probably died years ago. An *Aktir* had taken his place, an imposter—and don't try telling me the *Aktiri* aren't real; I know better. And the *Aktir*, the imposter, was killed two weeks ago, on the far side of the God's Teeth. One of the Mithondion princes figured out what he was, and the *Aktir* attacked him. The prince's retainers killed him."

"Torronell," Deliann supplied, and his scalded features twisted with some pain that was not physical. "It's all true—almost."

"Almost?"

Deliann smiled, just a little. "I'm no imposter, and I'm not dead."

Kierendal snorted. "And here's the nut-cutter, cock: I *knew* the Changeling. He worked for me, doing security over at the Exotic

Love, almost twenty-five years ago, before his Adoption into House Mithondionne. He worked for me for nearly a year, and I got to know him *well*, if you follow my meaning. And you're not him."

"Are you so sure, Kier?" Deliann asked sadly. "Put hair back on me, and eyebrows, and have I really changed so much?"

She looked at him truly closely for the first time, and she frowned. Her lips pulled back over her teeth as though she saw something that frightened her. "There's a resemblance," she admitted, slowly, as though it hurt her. "But you've *aged*—aged like a *human* . . ."

"I am human," Deliann said simply. "I always was. I am also Deliann."

Kierendal straightened, and she shook her head, denying what she saw, denying whatever she might feel. "Even if you were the Changeling, I wouldn't help you. I don't owe that bastard shit. Or his fucking Twilight King. What did they ever do for me?" Colors roiled across her Shell without mixing, like those on a soap bubble in the sun. "I still haven't heard a reason I shouldn't have Tchako here kill you and dump your body in the river."

Deliann knew this was no idle threat. He could see it in her fists, clenched so tightly that her long sharpened fingernails had drawn blood from her wrists. She was not thinking clearly, was not susceptible to reason, and was as dangerous as a wounded bear. He understood her easily, perfectly.

He felt exactly the same way.

He'd always seen himself as one of the good guys, one of the heroes, someone who has a certain moral center that he could hold against the world, someone who had drawn a line that nothing could force him to cross. He would willingly die before doing what he was about to do; that was a choice he could make. But if he chose death before dishonor, he'd be making that choice not only for himself, but for millions: millions who wouldn't get a choice at all.

"If you fail in your duty to my father," he said, "the death of the First Folk will be on your head, Kierendal. Within two years, we will be *extinct*."

But he was only stalling, only delaying the inevitable; he already knew he wouldn't be able to reach her with words.

"I don't have *time* for this *shit*." She gestured to Tchako, and again the leather club slapped across Deliann's skull, blowing a spark shower across his vision.

When he lifted his head again, a warm trickle down the side of his neck told him his scalp had split under the blow. He wondered idly if this was the sword cut reopened, or if the leather had torn a new wound. He said softly, "Nothing you do to me will change the truth."

"I haven't *heard* any truth yet," she snarled, lifting the griffinstone: a threat.

"You've heard nothing but."

Her snarl thinned to a whine of frustration and her fist tightened around the griffinstone. Agony seized Deliann's guts. He doubled over, retching, his stomach afire as though he'd swallowed burning coals, but he made no effort to tap her Shell and defend himself. This was what he'd been waiting for.

He tuned his mind to the link she had created between their Shells. He opened himself to the pain, accepted it, anchored it to the center of his being, even though doing so caused it to swell to a hurricane of anguish that threatened to snuff him like a candle; this was the only penance he could make for what he did next.

At the last instant, some premonition warned her of what he was doing, and the shades of horror bloomed across her Shell. She fought him then, wildly, as an animal fights when backed into the deepest corner of its own den. She screamed—one thin despairing wail—

Through the link that bridged them, he poured himself into her.

4

IMAGES CASCADE IN roiling, fractal turbulence, unpredictable, incomprehensible, inconceivable: dual views, inside and outside, feeling and watching together, vomit splattering over bare ankles, too near spike-heeled sandals, gut-pain and the heartpain of inflicting pain, a burning man-shape outside on a darkened portico, and yet again, peering out with eyes of flame at a halberd's blade as it melts and drips to a puddle that sets an echoing blaze in the carpet—

WHAT ARE YOU DOING TO ME?

Shh, hush now, it's too late to stop it. Ride it out.

The images begin to organize, to sequentialize: walking through a mutated, horribly half-familiar Alientown, words with the Patrol, a kick from a pickpocket. Faster now: a dive from the bow of a riverbarge, the silky stroke of the water parting around their short brush of hair, flames and shouting, the fierce grip of the ogrillo deck officer—

What is this?

This is my life.

Days of deck swabbing, brush cutting, clearing jams of tangled flotsam—the dangerous, backbreaking passage-work of a decker on the Great Chambaygen. More days, limping down out of the God's Teeth alone, each step a new adventure in pain, through the forest, following a stream for water, pulling Flow for energy, mindholding rabbits and squirrels until they can be taken by hands that break their necks. At first, they sear the scraps of flesh with the fire from their mind, but as days pass and their resources dwindle, they need the Flow they gather for other things, and the bloody tang of raw flesh is sharp on their tongue.

This is our lives?

Our life.

We are Deliann.

And hours wasted in agony, weaker and weaker; days lost to mindview, fighting exposure and shock with Flow, layering new calcium across broken ends of bone in his legs, wishing he understood healing more completely, wishing he had the strength to splint the bones straight—botching the job, leaving a pocket of infection in the bone of his left thigh, fusing his right shin crooked—using his disciplined concentration to fight back the despair, the black fist that crushed his heart—

We don't understand.

Patience. This won't take long.

Coming awake on the broken scree at the foot of the cliff, surprised to be alive, feeling the jagged ends of bone grind together within each leg, looking up to see, high above, one last glimpse of his brother's face, haloed for an instant against the translucent blue-white brush strokes of high cirrus cloud. As I watch, the face pulls back from the brink, emptying the cliff's crisp, indifferent skyline—

Leaving me here to die.

We still do not understand.

There is no we.

I understand.

This is my life.
I am Deliann.

5

I STAND ON the high cliff, overlooking the mines, while Kyllanni and Finnall sing the Song of War.

Far, far below, vanishing into the clear afternoon distance, the earth is pocked like the surface of the moon, a wasteland of craters and broken rock; the mountains are scarred, whole chunks missing as though bitten off by a god. Within this moonscape, tiny figurines move and work, black dots moving earth and directing sluice pipes, biting into the ground and belching black smoke until the crystal mountain air seems to come to a halt outside their dominion: a dome of smoke and dust enclosing Hell.

Closer below is the fence that L'jannella described, a wire and steel monstrosity, decorated with the dim silhouettes of corpses, outlined against the dust behind.

This is worse than I'd feared, worse than I could have imagined. In five short days, my world has crumbled, rotted: eaten from within as though injected with acid. Everything I thought was strong and sure has turned to paper and spun glass.

"It's the Blind *God*," Torronell mutters harshly, softly enough that at first only I can hear him; but then he repeats it, louder, and his gesture takes in not only the wrack of Diamondwell and Transdeia, but everything that has happened since we left the Northwest Road. "This is *all* the work of the Blind God. The *dil-T'llann* has been breached, and the Blind God has followed us from the Quiet Land."

Of us all, I'm the only one who realizes that Rroni isn't speaking metaphorically.

Torronell begins to pace in a tight circle, and his face twists with dark thoughts; his scalp is only now showing signs of stubble, only now growing back the hair I burned from him in my effort to save his life. I move with him, keeping between him and our three companions—whether he's well or not, I have to treat him like he's infected.

Even ordering us to come here, to this cliff, shows his judgment is becoming erratic. I'd like to think this is only a sign of the stress we've been through this past week, but I'm losing hope. I think I'm going to have to kill him.

Kyllanni and Finnall chant on, but I can't take any more.

This has to be stopped before it begins, and there is no one else who can stop it. "No," I say hoarsely. "No war. I don't care what they've done. There will be no war."

Kyllanni and Finnall fall silent; they and L'jannella do not respond to me at all. They turn from me, and look at Torronell.

His eyes blaze with feverish triumph. "Don't you understand?" he says. "I can tell you why he will not cry war against these humans. Join the Meld."

"But the curse—" L'jannella protests.

"A lie," Torronell spits. "Another of Deliann's lies. Join the Meld."

Oh god, oh god he's really sick, after all this, he's sick after all and I'm going to have to do this. I slide my hand into my rapier's basket hilt, and wish I could jam this sword into my own heart, instead. The worst of it is, that's not an answer: my death solves nothing.

His death saves the world.

I try to draw but there is no strength in my arm. How have I come to this? How could I have arrived here?

Why does it have to be *me*?

There is no one else. There is no other answer.

I pull the sword, the silver of its blade flashing fire in the afternoon sun. The brilliant life-green of the Meld plays around their mingled Shells, and they all stare at me: L'jannella, Kyllanni, and Finnall with shock and disbelief, Torronell with acid triumph. "You see?" he screeches. "These *Artans* are not of this world—they're *Aktiri*! He's one of them! He's a damned *Aktir*!"

He will have already spoken this mind to mind, in the Meld; there can be no denial. In the Meld, lies are impossible. They have heard the truth of me, and they all know it.

"He wants to kill me! *He wants to kill us all!*"

This he believes, too; it's even half true. The virus destroying his mind supplies more than enough conviction to carry the other half. The only reply I can make is my fencer's lunge, the razor tip of my rapier reaching for his heart.

Finnall is faster, throwing herself in front of her prince. My sword takes her just below the arch of the ribs; it slides easily through muscle and liver until the point grates on the back curve of her ribs. She shudders with the cold discomfort that is still too fresh to be pain and grabs the blade with both hands as she falls, ripping it from my loosening fingers.

Oh *Finnall*, oh god—

But I can't stop now. My people, my world—they have no one else to defend them.

Training more than a quarter century old, from the Studio Conservatory, reminds me how to kill with my empty hands; I leap at Torronell, and he falls back from me, screeching—and he is still Rroni, still my brother, and the one second's hesitation this gives me is too long.

Kyllanni's sword flashes toward me; I see it from the corner of my eye just in time to leap to one side and face him. I can still hear my tutor's voice: *When you're unarmed and the other guy's got a sword, run like a bastard.*

That's not an option.

Move out of the line of attack and disable his arm. Don't fight the sword; fight the man.

Kyllanni lifts his sword and springs at me; I slip aside, but even as I reach for his arm, something strikes me on the head with a humorous metal-on-wood *bonk*. My vision vanishes in a white glare, and my knees turn to cloth. I stagger back, covering my head, trying to keep moving so they can't take my vitals.

Torronell holds a bloodied sword.

He hit me, in the head, with a sword.

I stagger back another step, and my foot touches only air.

Bottomless air, I find as my body follows it—and I'm flying, flying, flying, and of course it's not bottomless, it just feels that way, like I'm never going to land as the cliff face rushes upward past me. I hit an outcrop and bounce, and another one; I hear something break, loud enough that it might be my leg.

My final impact comes as a burst of colorless fire, and then darkness.

6

L'JANNELLA CROUCHES ON the far side of the clearing, away from the embers of last night's fire. She hugs herself, trembling, though the morning is not cold. Denied the Meld by my order— by my lie—she uses mere words to describe her horror. Language was never designed to carry such freight, but her pale shivering hoarseness is eloquent enough. My best memories of L'jannella all see her giggling with joy at some practical joke, even when it was on her; to see her sickened and so very, very frightened is as painful as the story she tells.

The long silence from the Diamondwell stonebenders is now explained, as is the fate of the legates my father sent to enquire of them. I can barely hear her words over the thunder of blood in my ears, but the sense is clear enough.

The tiny, sleepy, sparsely settled human duchy of Transdeia, formerly a peaceful agricultural land—its only other industry being hospitality for travelers on the Northwest Road—has metastasized into a giant land-hungry termite hill of a nation. Now under the control of a mysterious folk who call themselves *Artans*, it has swallowed Diamondwell as though the millennium-old stonebender freehold had never existed; the mountains that the stonebenders once cherished have become a blasted waste-land of open-pit mines and giant hydraulic slurries that chew away cliff sides, taking daily bites measured in hundreds of long tons.

The news gets worse: suffocating déjà vu closes around my throat as L'jannella describes the machines in the mining pits: huge hulking metal scoops that belch black smoke and roar with hunger, plows on wheels connected by linked metal treads. I can see them in my head, more clearly probably than she can. I grew up with these machines.

My father—my first father, my birth father—runs a corporation that builds machines like these, and so I know, instinctively, who the Artans are.

And she tells of the fence that surrounds them, a fence supported on steel posts, built of interlocking vertical zigzags of wire; she traces the shape in the air with her finger and tells of the wire coils that top it, coils with sharp blades sticking out along their curves. This, as well, I can imagine too clearly: chain-link fence, topped with razor wire.

Torronell catches my gaze, and accusation glares through the pale sweat that coats his face; he has guessed the truth. His mouth opens as though he would speak, but then closes; he pretends to look away, sneaking a crafty glance at me from the corner of his bloodshot eye.

Oh, god—all gods, human gods, any who will listen—please

let that sweat be from fear and disgust, and not from fever. Let his crafty glance bespeak mere hatred.

L'jannella continues mercilessly. At intervals along the miles of that fence, bodies hang—corpses, skeletons, some still in scraps of clothing, mostly stonebenders, some primals, even a few tiny treetoppers—their feet off the ground, arms wide, wired to the fence by their wrists. Crucified.

Crucified by the Artans.

I can't face Torronell now; if I even glance at him, so much as glimpse his face, I might start to explain, words might start to tumble from my mouth no matter how hard I try to stop them. *But those aren't my people,* I want to cry. *It's not my people who have done this. It's someone else, someone alien, someone who does not partake of my blood, of my world.* Even now, old enough to know better, I find myself stunned with astonished revulsion at the horrors of which we are capable.

After twenty-seven years as a primal mage, I can still hate myself for being human.

But I must not show any of this before L'jannella. The secret of my heritage belongs to House Mithondionne, to T'farrell Ravenlock himself, as it has since the day of my Adoption; it is not mine to reveal.

My mind has wandered on these matters, but now L'jannella recaptures my full attention. I gather that she is now relating why she returned alone to make this report, why Kyllanni and Finnall remained behind: "They watch, and wait for us to join them. While they watch, they compose a Song of War."

I can feel Torronell's glare burning against the side of my head; I dare not face him. "They can't do that."

Torronell speaks for the first time, a harsh throat-scuffing rasp. "How can they *not?*"

"This Song will not be sung without leave of House Mithondionne," L'jannella says, "but Changeling, Diamondwell has been under the protection of your House for more than a thousand years, since the days of Panchasell Luckless. The Diamondwell stonebenders are our cousins; isn't this rape of their land alone a strong enough theme for a Song of War?"

"That's not the point."

"What *is* the point, then?" Torronell rasps bitterly. "What? Tell us."

L'jannella goes on before I can find the words. "Changeling, the humans of Transdeia make war on us already. The legates your father sent—did you not hear me? *Their bodies hang on that fence!* Finnall's *brother* hangs on that fence: Quelliar. Murdered. Can you recall the sound of his laughter, and *not* burn for war?"

It doesn't matter. A grinding pain in my chest threatens to close my throat and choke off these words, but I get them out anyway. "No war. There will be no war."

Torronell stands. "That is not for you to say. I am Eldest, here. We will go and hear their Song."

"Rroni, *no,* dammit! You don't know what you're getting into."

"And you do? How is this? Do you want to *explain*?"

He knows I can't, not in front of L'jannella; is he really sick? Is that why he's baiting me like this?

Am I going to have to kill him?

He looks at me as though my thoughts are written on my forehead. He's waiting for me to decide.

I know already: I'm going to cave. What choice do I have?

"All right," I say, defeated. "Let's go hear their Song."

7

"I FEEL FINE," Rroni says thinly. He licks his lips and stares into the flames, and I let myself believe that the flush in his face comes from sitting too close to the campfire. "It's been four days. If I have it, I'd be feverish by now, wouldn't I?" His eyes are raw with dread. "Wouldn't I?"

Our clothes are new, spares from the saddlepacks of the two horses that stand hobbled nearby. We squat on fallen logs around our tiny fire. My hair has begun to grow back, a pale stubble that makes my scalp feel like warm sandpaper; Rroni is still bald and scorched.

Rroni's lip is split, his face swollen with purple bruise where I hit him. Ever since he woke up he has resisted, more and more, opening himself to the comfort of the Meld; we've used our voices in conversation more over these four days than we have in the past ten years.

I miss the Meld, miss the closeness I shared with my brother. I wish, pointlessly, that I could use it now, but I don't even bring it up. I can't. A sick pain that pools in the hollow of my stomach tells me that I don't really want to share the feelings that Torronell conceals. So I can only nod uncertainly, trusting to the night and the campfire's flicker to conceal my expression. "Yes, four days, I think so. I'm not sure."

"How can you not be sure?" Rroni hisses.

It's not like I can flick on a wallscreen and look it up.

I can't say that—Rroni's in too much pain.

I have no secrets from my brother. Rroni knew the truth twenty-five years ago, even before my Adoption. These things could not be spoken of, in front of our companions; my true heritage remains a closely guarded secret of House Mithondionne. Everybody—nearly everybody, at least, our companions included—knows I have a secret, but they have never suspected the truth. Everyone thinks I'm a Mule, one of those rare and pitiful creatures born from a human rape of a primal female. It is generally supposed that *Changeling* is a polite euphemism.

The truth is worse.

I have to face it now: with everything that has happened, I can't run from it, can't deny it. I am an *Aktir*.

Not an Actor, no: my sense experiences have never been transmitted to Earth to be sold by the Studio as entertainment. But an *Aktir*, yes: I was born on Earth. Born human. Surgically altered at the Studio Conservatory on Naxos to pass for primal.

My name was Soren Kristiaan Hansen. I lived as a human for twenty-two years, long enough to graduate from the Studio's College of Battle Magick, long enough to make the freemod transfer to Overworld, ostensibly for training—and then I shed my human skin like the dried husk of a butterfly's chrysalis, and spread my elvish wings.

In my first few years as Deliann, I could barely even think my former name, let alone say it; but the conditioning imposed by the Studio fades over time, if it is not renewed. For dozens of years I have been free to speak the truth of myself, but I never have.

I'm not sure what my truth might be.

I barely remember Soren Kristiaan Hansen: he exists solely as a recollection of a boy who passed his childhood pretending to be the bastard son of Frey, Lord of the *lios alfar*—a boy who'd never wanted anything so much as to be a primal mage. I've been Deliann the Changeling for twenty-seven years, more than half

my life—have been Prince Deliann Mithondionne, adopted son
of T'farrell Ravenlock, for nearly twenty-five.

My human family will have given me up for dead long ago,
and shed few tears. There were other Hansen sons, and in a
prominent Business family like the Hansens of Ilmarinen MachineWorks, Soren Kristiaan had been as much a marketable
commodity as he had been a son and brother.

I don't miss them. I didn't *like* being human, being Business. I
am incapable of the kind of nostalgic illusion that would make
me homesick for the shallow, narrow-minded world of privilege
and profit in which my abandoned family lives. I left Earth behind, shook it off like a nightmare, and have lived my dream for
more than half my life. I never expected that quarter-century-old
nightmare to reach out, grab me, and crush my heart.

Ah, my heart, Rroni . . . you can't do this to me. You can't die.

Torronell is the next-youngest prince of House Mithondionne. He was born three hundred and seventy-three years ago,
and from my forty-nine-year-old perspective, anything that old
should be indestructible. For the love of god—he was born the
same year Darwin sailed on the *Beagle*; how can he be dying?

"I told you," I say, "it's not like I learned about it in school;
HRVP was wiped out a hundred years before I was born."

"Supposedly," Rroni supplies bitterly.

I nod. "All I know about it comes from Plague Years novels I
read when I was a boy. Novels are like . . . like epics. You know a
lot about Jereth's Revolt, say, but you can't quote the actual text
of the Covenant of Pirichanthe."

Rroni looks away. "That's a human story."

"So the best I can remember is that HRVP incubates in something like four days. It could be ten, or two weeks, or a month.
I just don't know. Novelists aren't always too careful with
their facts—and this might not even be the same strain. Viruses
mutate—ah, they change characteristics, and symptoms, and effects. That's how they say HRVP happened in the first place."

We've been over this a dozen times in the past four days. Each
time, I repeat what I know, and detail what I don't know, with
identical slow, patient precision. It's become a bitter ritual, but it
seems to help Rroni, to ease his mind somehow, to let him believe that I might be wrong. I have no other comfort to offer.

"How can I die of a human disease?" Rroni has asked, again
and again. "We're not even the same species!"

I have always the same answer. "I don't know."

All I can say is that rabies—the naturally occurring, original baseline of HRVP—was infectious in all mammals. And, once the infection has developed, it's fatal. No percentages, no treatments, no appeals. HRVP is worse: vastly faster, vastly more contagious. HRVP is persistent in the environment; in the absence of a warm-blooded host it sporulates, remaining potentially lethal for months.

And *airborne*.

I can only pray that I acted fast enough.

The primal male I killed in the village haunts the back of my mind, asleep and awake; I can't stop thinking about the dayslong progress of the disease. How much longer would he have lived in agony? Days? A week? I can't imagine a more hideous death. Sometimes, in my head, the male has Rroni's face.

Sometimes he looks like the Twilight King himself.

I remember standing in line, five years old, with a dozen other Business children. I remember the pressure of the airgun against my hip, and the sudden sharp sting of the inoculation. Tears welled in my eyes, but I had blinked them back, and I had not made a sound. It was a solemn occasion, a rite of passage of my Business caste; the inoculation was my passport to the world, and I had accepted it as a Businessman should. I never dreamed that now, after more than forty years have passed, the fate of a world might hinge on that brief pain.

"And so," Rroni mutters, lacing his fingers into white-knuckled knots, "how long must we wait? How long before we decide whether I shall die, or live? The others will be back from their scout at any moment—they should have been back by yesterday's dusk. Then what? What shall we tell them? How shall we prevent their exposure?"

He nods miserably toward the horses. "If I am infected, then even Nylla and Passi must be destroyed, as you destroyed the village."

Rroni and his horses—he often liked to comment that the horse was the perfect expression of T'nallarann: strong, swift, loyal, fierce in defense, faithful beyond the limits of its strength. Now the gaze he turns upon them is freighted with the anticipation of their deaths.

"Any living thing might carry this disease into our villages, and our cities. So we must kill, and kill, and kill. We must make a wasteland of this place, for your HRVP may spread through any creature alive in this land—except you," he finishes bitterly.

I look at the ground. "We'll stick to the curse story."

"They will know we lie."

"They know that already," I remind him. "But they don't know what we're lying about."

In the time crunch after I burned the village, the story I came up with had been embarrassingly weak; I'm not a gifted liar. I shouted to my friends a confused tale of a potent curse laid on the village—a curse that had slain the villagers one and all—a curse that had now fallen upon Rroni and me as soon as we walked in; I told them I was afraid that the magick of the curse might be able to bridge through the magickal link of the Meld, and so I refused all contact, mental or physical.

I ordered them to continue northeast into the mountains and complete the reconnaissance. Remember the mission, I told them; nothing was more important than the mission; we have to find out what happened to Diamondwell. Rroni and I would stay here and investigate the action of the curse, and see what might be done to counter it. They could not argue. Improbable as it sounded, the story *could* have been true, and I am, after all, their prince.

"I don't like it," Rroni says. "They are our friends. They deserve the truth."

I shake my head, still looking at the ground; I can't face him. "This isn't about what they deserve. We tell the truth about HRVP, we'll have to tell them how we know. We'll have to tell them why I'm immune. And once that's out, they'll forget the rest. All they'll be able to think about is how we've betrayed them."

Rroni turns away, offering me only the back of his bare, scorched skull, and his voice is low and hoarse. "Perhaps we have."

I stare into the fire. I don't trust myself to answer, and I'm afraid to meet my brother's eyes.

"It's your people who have done this," Rroni goes on. The words leak out like drops of gall, slow and bitter, as though forced from his lips by pressure that gradually builds inside his head.

"Rroni, don't. *You* are my people—"

"Your people . . . . *made* this horror. The ignorant say that *Aktiri* rape and slaughter and defile everything they touch, for each other's *amusement*; and perhaps they who say such things are not so ignorant, after all. How else can this be explained? Why else have you done this to me?"

My heart thuds painfully once, then again. "Is that what you think, Rroni? Do you really think I did this to you?"

Torronell turns his face silently away from the fire, toward the night; he has no answer that I can bear to hear.

Many, many years ago, when I rejected both my Business heritage and the prospect of an Acting career, I liked to tell myself that I did so from some unexpected nobility of spirit, because I couldn't bear to profit by inflicting harm on others—I was, after all, very young.

I saw the use of cyborged Workers in Ilmarinen's heavy-machinery factories as being morally equivalent to the brutal violence against Overworld natives that drove all successful Acting careers, because both required a certain objectification of the people they exploited. Ilmarinen MachineWorks used its cyborg Assemblers as replaceable, easily programmed robots; Actors, even those usually considered "heroes," had to cultivate a similar disregard toward the native Overworlders they inevitably killed and maimed during their Adventures. Expendable—*replaceable*—"bad guys" were the staple of Studio success.

As years passed, though, I came to understand myself somewhat more precisely, and I realized that my decision had had little to do with morality, and less to do with nobility; that it was really, in the end, a matter of taste.

I hate killing. I cannot bear to inflict pain, or even to know that pain is inflicted on my behalf. Perhaps this comes from the gift I have, the ability to flash into another's life; perhaps my empathy has become so acute that I feel each hurt in advance. The reason, finally, is irrelevant. The fact remains: I am not, have never been, could never be a killer.

The First Folk do not pray. We do not have gods in the human sense. Our spirituality springs from our inextricable, ineradicable place in the interconnected web of life itself. We touch the source of the Flow, and we find that source within ourselves; the fundamental breath of the world breathes through us, as it does through all living things. We do not ask favors of life, we participate in it.

But I was born human, and in ultimate distress I can't help returning to the ways of my childhood.

In the depths of night that follow the dying of the campfire's embers, I find myself praying desperately to T'nallarann that I will not be forced to kill my brother.

8

THE SCENT OF blood hangs in the silver dusk.

I balance on tiptoe at the edge of the dead village, long hair the color of moonlight floating free in a translucent halo around my ears. As T'ffar sinks toward the western horizon and day fades from the sky, my surgically enhanced eyes respond, bringing the sagging, skeletal hulks of the rude shanties before me into relief as bright and sharp as a chromed knife.

This is a bad idea. This is a stupid thing to do.

But I send, in the octave of the Meld, an image of my companions remaining hidden in the forest, and an image of me being very careful as I enter the dead village: *Stay here. I'm going in.*

The backflow from the Meld, in response, is primarily echoes of alarm and disapproval from L'jannella, Kyllanni, and Finnall, strong enough to make the horses uneasy, overlaid with the acerbic vinegar flavor of my brother Torronell's contribution: a dead ape with my face, rotting for a season on a pile of oil-soaked logs: *Don't expect me to light the pyre when your man-blood finally gets you killed, monkey boy.*

I grin sourly. My answering image is of Rroni holding the reins of a horse while I streak from the village like a cat with its tail on fire: *Be ready. I might come out of here a lot faster than I'm going in.*

The faintest of breezes stirs the forest around me, shifting the canopy of branches and making the green aural Shells of the living trees pulse like shadows cast by candlelight. The village swarms with the smaller, brighter Shells of forest animals, many of them fading now with the day, shading to the earth tones of sleep. Small birds flutter to their nests among the branches; ground squirrels and field mice and their numerous cousins burrow snugly into the earth to hide from the silent swoop of awakening owls. The forest is alive, but this village is dead.

In a living village of the First Folk, these shelters, roughly constructed of woodland scraps, would appear to the eye and hand to be shaped of living trees, polished with rich oils, filigreed with delicate spirals of platinum and beaten gold. In a living village, the air would carry the scents of mushrooms simmering in butter, of fine beer foaming as it spills from oaken casks, of rich wood-smoke from hearths alight with mistletoe and ash. In a living village, even the silences would shiver with the almost-heard laughter of children.

The silences in this village have vanished behind the croaks of ravens, squabbling over carrion.

This village reeks of old meat.

I repeat: This is a bad idea. This is a stupid thing to do.

But I am a prince, and these had been my folk. If I don't go in, Rroni will; though Rroni is far more the sarcastic society wit than he is a warrior, he is equally a prince. This is my job. I have vastly greater faith in my own ability to survive the unexpected. And let's face it: I have less to lose.

Poised at the village edge, I set the frog of my recurved bow on the top of my boot, bend the bow and string it. I slide a silver-bladed broadhead from the quiver at my belt and fit its nock to the string. I slip into the village as quietly as a shadow lengthens in the twilight; this is one of the things I do almost as well as a true primal.

The shelters rise around the boles of forest giants in the deep-wood, letting the shade of the towering trees do the work of keeping underbrush clear. Needing no more than primal skill with Fantasy for defense, these villages are as open as the forest itself. I drift from tree to tree, letting my nose gather information that my eyes, enhanced or not, just can't; the shadows within the crude shelters are too dark.

Each window exhales a miasma of rotting blood.

Beyond the splintery gaps in the corner of one collapsing shanty, a squawking pile of black wings and curved beaks shudders in a span of well-trodden earth. I approach, reaching out with a tendril of my Shell to flick the scarlet radiances of theirs. The ravens scatter, some taking wing clumsily, some only waddling away, too fat and gorged with flesh to fly.

What they had fed upon is the corpse of a little feyal, lying carelessly splayed on the earth like a cast-off doll. This feyal had been very young, six or seven years old, and the bright colors of his kirtle have not yet faded in the sun. Loving hands had woven this kirtle, thread by thread, and loving hands had embossed the broad leather belt that girdled it, had made the wooden toy sword and the bow of bundled rushes that lie beside him.

I squat by the corpse, holding my bow and nocked arrow in my left hand, parallel to the earth. I turn the feyal's face delicately up to catch the last of the day's light. Maggots squirm in one empty eye socket, and inside the nose and open mouth, yet the other eye still stares from the skull like a dusty opal. The ravens have torn off only the tongue and parts of the lips; even the tender flesh below the jaw is still unmarked.

My heart kicks into a gallop. From the size of these maggots, this child has been dead at least three days; the ravens should have stripped his face near to the bone by now. They should be working on his liver and lungs, unless some larger scavenger has been driving them off—and his corpse shows no sign that anything other than birds has been at him. Something has been chasing off the ravens.

Something in this village still lives.

Get out of there, Kyllanni sends in words. Of the four that wait outside the village, she's the best hunter, and she understands perfectly what this child's corpse signifies. This feyal had been left in the open deliberately: bait.

Yes: me, too.

I drop one knee to the earth and pretend that my full attention is engaged in examining the corpse. The faint scrape of a stealthy footfall comes from not far behind me, along with a muffled rasp of breath, labored and harsh.

Changeling, come on! Get out of there! Now L'jannella and Finnall weigh in, adding their urgencies to Kyllanni's, imagery of a shadowy, monstrous shape looming behind my shoulder. *Come on!*

I hunch over the child a little more. I can't help it—it's an instinctive urge to present a smaller target.

Let him be, Torronell offers, sending a picture of the Deliann-faced ape industriously tinkering with some impossibly complicated puzzle: *Let the monkey boy play his game. He occasionally knows what he's doing.*

Please, kind gods, let this be one of those times.

I gently shift the feyal's body, but find nothing that resembles a death wound. The earth on which it lies is scuffed and printed with countless raven tracks, and so tells no useful tale. The child's hands have twisted into rictal talons, still stiff as stone though rigor had long passed for the rest of his limp corpse. Fluid has leaked from his partially eaten mouth and soaked into the ground—and has left a crust of its trail on his cheek, rimmed with flaking blood. This crust has a strange, fractal, *bubbled* look, like dried soap scum.

A sudden coat of sand grows on my tongue and a chilly sickness gathers in my stomach. I peer closely at this crusted streak, holding my breath and cursing the growing darkness.

Sweet shivering *fuck*.

Oh, fuck, fuck me, god. Please let me be wrong.

It could be any number of things. It *could*. The kid could have gotten a mouthful of raw *rith* leaves, for example; he could have been chewing soapbark for the tingle, and had a stroke.

But I don't really believe it; some childhood bogymen are fixed too firmly in one's dreams to ever be mistaken. Dried foam on the face, the clawed hands with earth caked under the fingernails, dirt scraped up in the final convulsions—

If the corpse were fresher, I could tell for sure: The tongue would be black, dried and cracked like a mudflat at the end of a summer's drought; the throat would be so swollen that the head could not be turned.

Again a footfall scrapes behind me, and another. I barely hear them; I'm buried in a fantasy of cracking open the feyal's skull, of excising some tissue at the base of the brain, of improvising some kind of magickal lenses to make a microscope powerful enough to search for Negri bodies in the nerve cells—

The stealthy footfalls become a sudden rush, and now the shout that comes through the Meld is my brother's: *DELIANN!*

I throw myself to the right, the edge of my hand striking the ground to begin a shoulder-roll that brings me to a crouch as my attacker blunders past me. The bow in my left stays parallel to the ground; I stroke the arrow's nock to my chest and release it without aiming, allowing my body to target without the intervention of my mind.

The silver broadhead punches through the ribs of a youthful, powerful-looking fey. He twists, snarling and clawing at the shaft like a wounded cougar. The shaft snaps, and its splintered end slashes blood from his hand. He croaks, "Murderer—*murderer!*" in a harsh and rasping whisper, then springs at me, empty hands outstretched, fingers hooked like a raptor's talons.

I drop my bow and slip aside once again, ducking beneath his wide-flung arm. I draw my rapier from the scabbard that rides my left hip; it chimes like a silver bell as it comes free. As he whirls to charge again, I lunge and drive my blade through the side of his thigh just above the knee, twisting it so that the razor edge slashes out through his hamstring.

His leg springs straight, pitching him sideways to the earth; he writhes there, growling wordlessly, and claws the earth with spastic talons, dragging himself toward me a bloody inch at a time.

He might not be alone, Rroni sends. *I'm coming in.*

NO! My roar into the Meld spikes a backflow of startled pain from all four of my companions. *STAY WHERE YOU ARE!*

Don't shout at us, monkey boy. Being loud doesn't make you immortal. You need someone at your back.

How can I possibly explain? *Rroni, I swear by the honor of our House that you can't come in here. Come into this village, and you die. Believe me.*

Is this some manblood thing, little brother?

Ah, yes, that's it . . . I have to force the phrase; the Meld makes untruths difficult to share, impossible to conceal. My friends' sharp orange sting at my lie stabs like a needle into my heart. *Please, Rroni. Now I'm asking you. Stay out.*

I am Eldest here, Deliann. It was my risk to take from the first. This means trouble—Rroni never calls me by my right name unless he's too upset to be insulting, and years have passed since the last time he pulled rank. *Either come out, or I shall come in and get you.*

Don't. Just don't.

This exchange takes only a second. I crouch in the wounded fey's path and extend my Shell to touch the aura, crimson shot through with crackling violet, that pulses around his form like cold flame. As I delicately tune my own Shell to match the bloody hue and the jagged violet discharge of his, my perception of the Meld trickles away. Now, for the first time since the five of us set out from Mithondion, I am truly alone.

Once my Shell harmonizes fully to his, I open myself to the liquid swirl of the Flow. With the energy of the forest around me channeled through my mind, I gently take control of his muscles and hold him shivering in place.

He fights me, but as an animal fights, or a human, pitting the strength of his will against my mindhold; he refuses to believe his limbs will not obey him, and fuels his struggle with his rage. I'm not an accomplished mindwrestler—any of my brothers can beat me—but no one can match my raw power. My brothers like to sneer that I'm as graceful as a mudslide, but like a mudslide, I cannot be overcome by mere strength.

I play him like a puppet, using his own muscles to roll him onto his back and lift his face for examination.

Both his eyes are ringed with swollen, purplish-black flesh, and crusted with pale yellow scurf that clings in chunks to his eyelashes and forms a trail down his cheeks. Pink foam bubbles from his mouth, streaked with deeper scarlet that swells from the gaping cracks in his blackened lips. His tongue is black and cracked and leaking blood thick as mucus, and the flesh beneath his chin is swollen until his skin is tight as melon rind.

The cold sickness that birthed in my stomach as I examined the child now freezes into a solid brick of ice.

This is not supposed to be possible.

I would speak my silent *ah, shit, holy shit,* but my chest squeezes itself until I can't even whisper.

T'ffar sinks into the west, his rosy bloom replaced by the sheen of T'llan rising over the eastern mountains. I get up, and stand over the fey I hold helpless at my feet, watching his blood fade to black. I lift my slim blade, following with my eyes the moonsilver that ripples over it like water, and imagine the slow, raw-meat rip of thrusting this blade into his belly, probing with the point to find the pulse of his heart, to slash that muscle and drain the life from his eyes.

It's the only medicine I can offer.

I wasn't born a primal prince. I could have refused the honor, and the duty. I knew, even on that day when T'farrell Ravenlock spoke the formula of Adoption before the assembled House Mithondionne, that the kind of obligation I face now could become part of my life.

I chose this. It's too late to take it back.

I lower the point of my moonsilvered blade and touch it to the vault of the helpless fey's rib cage. Current surges through that physical connection, deeper and more intimate than the mingling of our attuned Shells; he rolls his crusted eyes to meet mine, and I flash on him.

In that second, I become the wounded fey—

Immobile on the cooling earth, trapped inside a body that will not obey me, feeling the stiff *sccrrt* of my broken rib scraping the arrow shaft that punctures my lung, feeling the hot pool of blood thicken beneath my hamstrung leg. But these are nothing, not even a distraction, behind the agony of my throat.

Someone took a burning log from a bonfire and jammed it into my mouth; now they are pounding it down my throat in time with the erratic thunder of my heart. A thirst is on me, a savage lust for the faintest touch of moisture, that hurts even more than the broken glass that fills my throat. I have dreamed only of water for four nights now, of cool clear forest springs that could ease my throat and quench the blaze of my fever. My face burns with it, roasting slowly in its internal heat, scorching my lips to bloody charcoal, cooking my tongue to blackened leather within the oven of my mouth; water is my only hope of relief. But even the morning dew, sopped from the hanging sheets of moss that drape the trees nearby, seared my throat like boiling acid. It has been two days since I was last able to swallow.

The flash ends a bare instant after it began, but it leaves me shaken and trembling, greasy sweat seeping over my forehead. It could have been worse: I could have sunk fully into his past, experienced the nervous hypersensitivity, the way the faintest whisper stabs like a needle into the eardrum, the dimmest candle becomes a knife in the eye, the unendurable itching, the insatiate hunger and convulsive vomiting, the growing homicidal paranoia that transforms your wife, your children, even your parents into leering monsters that tear at your mind—

I know these symptoms by heart; they form shadow-shapes in the back of my mind, always lurking, sniffing around the fringes of my consciousness, wondering when they might finally match my experience.

Today, I am grateful for the flash that is my gift, because it makes my duty easier: makes it purely mercy.

I hold the fey motionless while I lean on my sword. The blade enters his belly, with a frictive skidding on the muscle that clenches spastically around it. I twist the blade upward until I find his heart, and slash into and through it, the point grating on his spine.

It takes a minute or two for him to die. Even as his heart spasms and blood floods his abdominal cavity, he's still alive, still awake, still staring up at me with maddened, hungry eyes as his body shuts down piecemeal, blood flow cutting off first to his limbs, then to his guts and chest, trying to keep that last spark of consciousness aflame.

I watch it smolder, and wink out.

I wipe my blade, but instead of returning it to its scabbard, I drive its point into the knot of a tree root that sticks up above the earth and leave it there to gently sway in the moonlight. I yank the broken arrow from the corpse's side and do the same with it.

Slowly, I untie the braided leather belt that holds my scabbard and quiver. I take it from around my waist and hang it from the hilt of my rapier. My shirt and breeches come next, and my stockings, and boots. All these I pile on the knotted root beside my sword and the broken arrow. I collect my bow from where it lies on the earth, a few paces away; with solemn, ceremonial care, I place it on the pile.

"What in the world are you *doing*?" Rroni's voice sounds rusty—it's been days since he's spoken aloud—and its accustomed mocking edge is conspicuously absent. "*Clothe* yourself, Deliann! Are you mad?"

He's there, behind me; I turn to face him, and meet his eyes. My brother: my best friend. Rroni stands over the dead child, revulsion and horror twisting his delicate features, and for the wrenching eternity between one heartbeat and the next, I can only stare. I can't move, can't breathe, can't blink. I am entirely consumed by the agonizing wish that my brother had been born a coward.

A coward would never have come into this village; a coward would never have left Mithondion on a dangerous, useless quest with his half-mad, manblood-tainted brother.

A coward would have lived through it.

I settle into myself, compressing somehow, barely perceptibly, as though the world has become a smaller place and I shrink with it.

"What have you done here? Deliann, answer me! What have they done to you?"

I can't get my mind around it, not yet—maybe not ever.

Rroni is probably already dead.

He steps closer, a tendril of his Shell questing out, its shade cycling through the spectrum as he tunes it for a mindhold. In the instant it drops out of the octave of the Meld, I snatch my rapier from the root and lunge at my brother. One advantage of my mortal birth is a strength of body that no primal can hope to equal; when the basket hilt of my rapier hits the side of Rroni's head, he drops like a stone.

I stand over him, breathless at the fierce ache within my chest.

After a moment, I return the rapier to its place on the root's knuckle, then I kneel beside Rroni and swiftly strip him. I bundle Rroni's clothing on top of mine, and place Rroni's boots alongside. Naked, barefoot, and unarmed, I pace the perimeter of the dead village, gathering Flow within a fiery image I hold in my mind, clear as a dream; from my footsteps, the earth sprouts flame.

At the first hint of smoke, our friends call in alarm from the deepwood, using their voices when they find no answers within the Meld. I brush the Meld for one instant: *Patience.*

I turn to the center of the village, fire skipping at my heels like a faithful puppy. At the knotted root, I take my brother into my arms and turn my face to the indifferent stars.

The death of my entire people dances in this ring of flame around me. I swear—T'nallarann, Lifemind, are you listening?—I swear that this death will not work through me.

With a silent shout of power, I draw the cleansing flame in upon us, a thunderclap cautery that flares like the sun upon the forest floor. A toadstool of smoke rolls toward the moon; it grows from a fairy ring of cinders that smolders like countless eyes in the darkness around us.

I stand at the center, Rroni in my arms, both of us now panting harshly in the smoke-thickened air. His platinum hair has become a reeking tangle-melt of char; his flesh is covered with a fine grey ash, the remnants of its outermost layer. I imagine I look even worse.

"Now," I mutter, my voice as bleak and colorless as the ashes of my heart, "all I need is a good lie to tell the others, and everything might still be all right."

9

THE CONNECTION SHATTERED in a blast of white fire across Deliann's vision, from the slap of Tchako's leather club.

"What are you doing?" the ogrillo howled, lifting her braided club for another blow. "You murdering motherfucker, I'll beat you to death! *What did you do to her?"*

Kierendal lay on the floor in front of him, her face white as though painted with ash. The club hissed through the air and banged his skull again; blood sprayed across the brown-spattered wall, and the room darkened.

The entire flash had happened in the time it took the ogrillo to raise her club.

Deliann tried to lift his free hand up to shield his head and neck, but he couldn't make his arm work, couldn't even hold up his head.

"If you've hurt her, you mother—"

"Tchako," Kierendal said from the floor, her voice weak and shaken but strong enough to save Deliann's life. "Don't. Don't hit him. Help me up."

The ogrillo's coarse features twisted in a caricature of puzzlement, but she lowered the club and went to Kierendal's side, extending a scaly hand to help her mistress rise. Kierendal leaned heavily on her for a moment, and passed a hand over her eyes. "Get the keys. Unlock his manacles."

"Kier, you're not well—"

"*Go,* damn you!" the feya snapped, and Tchako could not bear her displeasure. She left, trailing a murderous glare at Deliann.

The door closed behind her.

Kierendal swayed, deprived of the ogrillo's support. She touched her face again, as though assessing a fever, and then she sank to her knees beside Deliann, heedless of the damage to her exquisite gown.

She placed her hands upon his lap in the ancient gesture of fealty. "I—I can't believe . . . Deliann, I—"

"It's all right, Kier," he said kindly. "I know it's overwhelming. I've had two weeks to get used to the idea, and it still makes me want to scream and never stop."

She lowered her eyes, bending her long, graceful neck before him. "I am yours, my prince. What would you have me do?"

Deliann took a deep breath, and let himself believe that between the two of them, some lives might still be saved.

"First," he said slowly, "we need to catch an *Aktir*."

AND EACH HAD his own role to play: the crooked knight defended the part-time goddess; the part-time goddess served the land; the acolytes of dust and ashes fed their master's hunger.

The dark angel made war.

He answered the call of the crooked knight; he used the part-time goddess to work his will; he named the god of dust and ashes his enemy.

On that day, the dark angel broke his chains and went forth to battle.

FIVE

HARI SAT MOTIONLESS in his uncomfortable chair, the pain in his back forgotten, listening so hard he barely breathed around the knot in his guts.

He knew the voice.

This weirdass-looking fey he didn't recognize, but he still had an Actor's ear for voices. This voice stirred old memories, half buried in passing years; he eased back in his chair and closed his eyes, shutting out the unfamiliar face, concentrating on the familiar voice.

"*. . . but this is what you don't know. At least, I hope you don't know. By all I hold sacred, I pray that even the monsters who* *control the Studio are not so evil that you would inflict HRVP on us intentionally . . ."*

HRVP? On Overworld? His eyes jerked open and he jolted upright, staring at his deskscreen. He couldn't seem to get his breath.

"Remember that HRVP once came within an inch of destroying civilization, even with vaccines and quarantines and the finest medical technology that Earth could muster.

"Remember that here, on Overworld, the primary method of healing is the laying on of hands.

"Resist the Blind God. The greed of your worst should not be allowed to triumph over the conscience of your best. Fight it.

"You are our only hope.

"We are at your mercy.

"Save us."

Hari forgot about the voice; a tornado howled inside his head, and its silent roar drowned out every thought, save one nerveless whisper: *HRVP.*

It had to be a mistake. It had to be an accident. He must have heard wrong—he *must* have. On a nontechnological world, HRVP was the perfect weapon. It could wipe out every warm-blooded creature on the planet.

Except for us, Hari thought.

HRVP had been eradicated on Earth, brought to extinction by quarantine and vaccination, more than fifty years ago. The final outbreak had come somewhere in Indonesia, when a strain that had been preserved in an immunological laboratory had escaped. Someone had leaked news of the strain's existence to the local press, and the story sparked riots in which the laboratory had been destroyed, burned to the ground—but not quite thoroughly enough.

Worldwide, more than two million people died, roughly five hundred thousand of HRVP itself; the other million and a half were victims of the victims. The standard ratio, which had held roughly true for this one as it had for each large HRVP outbreak since the beginning of the twenty-first century, was that an HRVP sufferer killed an average of 2.8 people before either succumbing to the disease or being killed himself. The Leisure Congress in Geneva had acted with extraordinary swiftness: less than twelve hours after the outbreak was confirmed, the island had been sterilized by a series of minimum-residue neutron bombs. The deaths of one hundred and twenty-seven thousand islanders were buried in the disaster's total—and they died for nothing.

Before the worldwide network of slavelanes had gone online, it wasn't possible to quarantine any large area, even an island; thousands of people had fled in their cars at the first word of the outbreak. Within hours, the disease had reached every continent. This was why there remained a mandate of universal vaccination, even today.

Hari, like many of his generation, had grown up with occasional nightmares of seeing that neutron fireball blossom over his own head—but that was less terrifying than the disease itself. The bald elf with the weirdly familiar voice had said that HRVP came within an inch of destroying civilization; *My father,* Hari thought mordantly, *would argue with that.*

Duncan would say the inch was imaginary.

Everything Duncan cherished in the history of human thought, from the democratic franchise to those individual "rights" he so often insisted upon, had been marched up the chute in the slaughterhouse of the Plague Years and had taken the hammer square between the eyes.

The regional and national governments, who were the sole guarantors of those rights, had been completely helpless. A few nations adopted rational, progressive HRVP policies, but they could enforce them only within their own borders—what gains were made could be wiped out by an unlucky shift of the wind. The national militaries became a dangerous, unfunny joke; chain of command is a tricky thing, when one slip of an anti-infection protocol could transform a competent commander into a raving homicidal paranoid. Twenty years after the first outbreak of HRVP, there was no longer even the illusion of a sovereign nation left on Earth—but there was still government.

For centuries—dating back to the Dutch traders and the British East India Company—multinational corporations had pursued their interests globally, as opposed to the provincialism that made national governments so vulnerable. Even before the Plague Years, many of the *zaibatsus* and the megacorps had maintained private military forces, to protect their employees and interests in places where the local governments were unwilling or unable to do so; these giant corporations often had more claim on the loyalty of their employees than did the nations in which these employees chanced to live. After all, the corporation provided the employee's education, housing, child care, health care, income, and finally, as nation after nation collapsed during the Plague Years, the corporation also provided police and military defense. They had no choice; corporations that failed in any of these fundamental responsibilities swiftly found themselves unable to attract the high-quality workers they needed to remain competitive in the unregulated, purely Darwinian jungle of international business. When the nations collapsed, the corporations were already in place, holding the gap.

They were able to act with the ruthlessness that the ongoing crisis required, to act in ways that the merely national governments could not. A national government rules, finally, by consent of the governed; a corporation rules by consent of the *stockholders*.

By the time an effective, mass-producible HRVP vaccine was developed, the three pillars of the current society—the caste system, the tech laws, and the Social Police—were solidly in place.

The caste system, the rigidly enforced social code that forbade cross-caste personal contact, ensured that any outbreaks of HRVP would spread laterally instead of reaching up to the really important people: the business directors, the investment managers, and the majority stockholders—later to become Businessmen, Investors, and Leisurefolk.

HRVP was thought to have been a partially developed bioweapon that escaped from a private laboratory; the tech laws, a loosely bound series of intercorporate treaties, were designed to prevent precisely that kind of dangerous research.

The Social Police enforced the caste laws; violation of a caste law was considered prima facie evidence of HRVP infection. Minimum punishment was isolation quarantine; more usually, violators were summarily executed.

Over the years, caste violation penalties had been relaxed, but the scope of the Social Police's mandate had expanded to include the defense of the social order in the broadest terms, from monitoring compliance with the tech laws to enforcing intercorporate contracts. Lower-priority crimes such as robbery, assault, and murder were handled by the understaffed, underpaid, and overworked CID.

Hari wasn't naive enough to long for the vanished pre-HRVP

days; due to his semieducation under Duncan's direction, he was more aware than most that what had seemed to be the convulsive transformation of the Plague Years had, in truth, only codified and rigidified trends that had been evolving for centuries.

It would not be so on Overworld.

The elf had said, *Remember that here, on Overworld, the primary method of healing is the laying on of hands.*

The trends of centuries would be irrelevant; no one would survive to continue them. If HRVP could infect primals, it could probably kill stonebenders, treetoppers, ogrilloi—given HRVP's ability to mutate and adapt to new hosts, it could be a mass extinction on the scale of the Cretaceous die-off. Twenty years from now, there might not be a warm-blooded creature alive on Overworld—and the ripple effect on the ecosystem would destroy reptiles, insects, plants—

The prospect crushed air from his lungs as though stones were piled upon his chest. No more lancers on lumbering destriers with armor shining in the sun; no wizards; no cheery innkeepers and gap-toothed stableboys; no primals or stonebenders; no treetoppers, griffins, trolls; no more Korish shamans raising dust devils in the Grippen Desert; no ogrillo tribals marauding the fringes of the Boedecken Waste; no more lonely wails of *seniiane* calling the faithful to prayer in the dusk of Seven Wells; no Warrengangs . . . And the numberless creatures now extinct on Earth, but surviving in the wilds of Overworld: no more otters playing in sparkling streams, no more wolves pursuing elk on the high plains, no whales singing to each other from oceans on opposite sides of the world, no condors wheeling on mountain thermals, no coughs of stalking cougars.

This can't be happening.

It made him want to stand up and howl.

Suddenly he comprehended Tan'elKoth utterly: he was being smothered. Choked to death. Earth had forced itself down his throat, and he was strangling on it. Overworld was the only place he'd ever been happy. Overworld was freedom. Overworld was life.

It was home.

This had to be some kind of mistake.

Viceroy Garrette was ruthless, a stone motherfucker, but he wasn't a monster—

Hari recalled a story Duncan had pulled from a two-hundred-year-old hardbound book of Western history: a story of European colonists who'd deliberately infected natives on the American continent with a lethal disease called smallpox.

The monsters who control the Studio, the elf had said.

I'm one of the monsters he was talking about.

"Bastards," Hari snarled through his teeth. "Motherfucking *bastards—*"

"Administrator? I'm sorry?"

He leaned toward the pickup beside his screen. "You're sure he's not an Actor?"

Actors can now speak English on Overworld, if they choose; they can even speak of being Actors. The crusade that Toa-Sytell had led to rid the Empire of Actors in the wake of *For Love of Pallas Ril* had turned the Studio conditioning, which once had prevented Actors from betraying themselves or each other, into the very means of that betrayal. Toa-Sytell had discovered that Actors could always be identified by what they were *unable* to say; the Studio's response had been to progressively decondition the Actors. Not a single conditioned Actor was now on Overworld.

And the elf thing—very, very few Actors had ever successfully played an elf, but Hari was pretty sure there were five or six currently active, out of other Studios.

"Pretty, uh, pretty sure he's not an Actor, Administrator," one of the techs answered him hesitantly. *"We're running a transponder autoscan, but so far all we're getting from Rossi's vicinity is Rossi."*

Hari nodded to himself. What the elf was doing was brilliant, in a pathetic sort of way. Somehow this elf understood that Actors are the Overworld eyes and ears of the wealthiest and most influential people on Earth. Faced with a crisis that could not be met by anyone on Overworld, he turned to the soft hearts of Earth's romantics. A few thousand Leisurefolk—a few *hundred*—seeing this, could pressure the Studio, even the Leisure Congress itself, to mount a relief operation, to find a way to distribute vaccine, to save at least some of the billions of lives that would otherwise be lost. Brilliant.

What made it pathetic was that he'd picked the wrong Actor. Rossi had no audience. No one who mattered was watching this—no one at all. *Well, no,* Hari admitted to himself. *That's not quite true.*

Rossi had an audience of one.

And just that simply, Hari knew who it was, the bald and

sickly looking elf with the queerly familiar voice. How does an elf learn English? There's only one answer, curious as it was: he doesn't.

He's not an elf. But he's also not an Actor. A motto percolated up from the depths of some story Duncan had made him read as a boy: *When one eliminates the impossible, whatever remains— however improbable—must be the truth.*

Hari whispered, ". . . *oh, my god . . .*"

He looked through the image on his deskscreen, out through Rossi's eyes, into golden eyes he had not seen in nearly thirty years. He remembered—

He remembered the white plastic surgical mask, worn to protect the progress of the elving. He remembered the gift for intuitive solutions—

He remembered the cold courage—

He remembered the debt he owed.

He murmured, "Kris . . ."

Kris Hansen looked into him now through Frank Rossi's eyes. Kris Hansen asked him, without even knowing it, for his help.

Hari felt something crack inside his chest; something broke and released a nameless flood that surged fiery and humming into his arms, into his head. *You want my help, Kris?*

"You'll fucking well get it," he muttered.

"Administrator? Is something wrong?"

Hari hissed softly through his teeth, gathering scattered thoughts into a semicoherent plan of action. "Don't do anything," he said. "I'm on my way down."

"What about his audience?"

"Fuck his audience, *technician.*" He leaned on the word to remind the tech of their relative ranks. "Keep feeding to my desk until you hear otherwise."

"Acknowledged."

He pitched his voice to the screen's command tone and said: "Iris: initiate telecommunication. Screen-in-screen. Execute." A screen-in-screen box popped up that overlaid Rossi's POV feed. He began to enter the connection code for Businessman Westfield Turner, the Studio President, already rehearsing in his head what he would say. *Listen, Wes, this is urgent. We need to get on this right away, I have an idea—*

He hesitated, fingers hovering above the keypad, one stroke away from completing the call.

The President wasn't known for his decisiveness. He might stall; he might kick the decision upstairs to the Board of Governors in Geneva. Days might pass before Hari got the authority to act as he knew he needed to act. Authority might never be granted at all.

Sometimes it's easier to get forgiveness than permission.

He hit the cancel, then keyed in a new code. Another box popped up in a corner of his deskscreen, overlaying a close-up of maggots crawling from a blackened mouth. Within the box grinned the permanently youthful, professionally cheerful, recorded face of Jed Clearlake, managing producer and star of *Adventure Update*, the "Only Worldwide Twenty-Four-Hour Source for Studio News"—the number one rated news site in the history of the net.

The recording said, "Hi! I'm Jed Clearlake, and this is my personal message site. Begin recording at any time by pressing Return or clicking on the radio button below."

Hari hit the key and said, "Real time AV. Command code *Caine's here*."

The image in the box wiped to a solid black screen. White letters scrolled across it:

PRESENT SAMPLE FOR MATCHING.

"He who lives by the sword shall die by my knife," Hari said softly. "That's prophecy, if you like."

CONFIRMED.

The image that came up now within the box had the grainy 1024 x 780 resolution of palmpad video, but Clearlake's smile was brilliant as ever. *"Yeah, Hari, what's up? I'm in a meeting."*

"I've got a hot one for you, Jed. A full POV from one of my ISP Actors."

"What, too hot to blip to my site? I mean, come on, Hari, there's only so many hours in the day, and I'm with a seven-figure advertiser right now."

"This isn't something I can leave lying around in your message dump. I'm going to load it straight to your palmpad. Don't lose this, Jed. You'll understand when you see it."

"Hari, Jesus Christ, what did I just tell you?"

"And who are you talking to? If it wasn't for me you'd still be working for that Underwood buttrag as the fucking Ankhanan Affairs Correspondent. Whatever happened to 'God bless you, Administrator Michaelson, I owe you my career,' you goddamn weasel? You ever want to get another tip out of this Studio as long as you live?"

Clearlake looked like he had suddenly developed a terrific headache. *"How long is it?"*

"Five minutes, tops. You won't be sorry."

"I hope you're right."

Hari pulled up the call file from his deskscreen's memory core, selected CURRENT and INCOMING: CAVEA, and dragged the icon onto Clearlake's box on the screen. A progress bar popped up, slowly filling as the file began to upload.

It had reached only 7 percent completion when it self-terminated. Hari frowned. "What the fuck?"

"Hari, what is this crap? Some funny-looking bald elf yapping like a monkey, this is your hot story?"

"Give me a second," he muttered, but when he went to reselect INCOMING: CAVEA, a dialog box popped up on his screen.

THE SELECTED FILE CONTAINS MATERIAL THAT IS RATED CLASSIFICATION RED. UPLOAD OF RED-RATED MATERIAL CONSTITUTES FELONY CORPORATE ESPIONAGE. PENALTIES FOR FELONY CORPORATE ESPIONAGE INCLUDE UP TO TEN YEARS IN PRISON, FINES OF UP TO TEN MILLION MARKS, AND/OR PERMANENT DOWNCASTE TO WORKER STATUS. CLICK OK TO ACKNOWLEDGE.

Hari moved the cursor to the radio button marked OK, and clicked it.

Another progress bar popped up, labeled DELETING RED-RATED FILES; it filled swiftly. Before he could even move the cursor to save the current feed to a new file, the feed wiped to black.

"Jed?" Hari said grimly. "I'm gonna have to get back to you on this."

He stabbed the cancel, and the box went blank. He sat very, very still for a long silent moment, thinking hard. Some net-monitor program must have been set for this; it wasn't hard to program a script to capture and respond to specific words or phrases on a netwide basis—that technology was almost two hundred years old. This one must have been set to capture references to HRVP on Overworld. That meant somebody knew this was going to happen.

That also meant he could guess who that somebody had to be.

He was already in the shit. In deep.

He keyed the Security switchboard. "This is Michaelson. Put two guys in riot gear on the door of the Cavea techbooth. No, don't—specials, make them specials. Two specials in full gear. No one goes in or out until I get there."

"Acknowledged."

He punched a new code. The screen swirled into an image of Tan'elKoth's face. "I am otherwise engaged," the image told him. "Leave a message."

Hari entered his override sequence. "Tan'elKoth, acknowledge," he said. "Acknowledge, dammit. One goddamn question, all right?"

The screen cross-faded into a real-time image: Tan'elKoth scowled at him. *"I am teaching,"* he said testily. *"These are the hours that you, Caine, yourself assigned to my seminar. You should know better than to interrupt."*

"Yeah, whatever. What do you know about HRVP?"

His scowl deepened, and he lowered his voice. *"I am no physician,"* he murmured, *"but I have read widely in the history of your civilization. Why?"*

"No time for a long story. Got an Actor here who might've been exposed. What are the chances he could be infectious?"

"Exposed? How could this Actor have been exposed? And when? And to which strain?"

"If I wanted a bunch of useless fucking questions that I don't know the answers to," Hari said, "I would've called a *real* doctor."

"Mm, just so. Well. I would say—based upon my understanding that several strains of HRVP are capable of remaining potent in the environment for weeks—that yes, this Actor could possibly be infectious. He should certainly be isolated and undergo an antiviral regime before being allowed to make a transfer."

"Yeah," Hari said heavily. "It's a little bit late for that."

"What do you mean?" Tan'elKoth's eyes widened. *"Caine? What do you mean, it's too late?"*

"No time. Listen: I'm on my way over right now. Start pulling; I'm gonna need a little of your on-the-net magick."

"Caine, I am teach—"

"Dismiss the class. This is more important. Believe me. Get your shit together, Tan'elKoth. I'll explain everything when we get there."

"We? Caine—"

He hit cancel and rapidly entered one last code: his personal contact code for Shanna.

The look of annoyance fixed on her face when she answered would have stung him at any other time; right now he had bigger problems. "Shanna," he said. "Where are you right now?"

"I'm in the car," she said, in a *if you weren't such an idiot you'd already know it* tone. *"I'm taking Faith to Fancon in Los Angeles this morning, remember? You coded the travel permit yourself."*

"Yeah, yeah, yeah, right. Shit," he said tiredly. Faith loved conventions, loved meeting her parents' devoted fans—loved getting the day off school at the Admacademy. *Too bad,* he thought. "She's with you now?"

Faith leaned into the video pickup's field wearing a sunny smile. *"Hi, Daddy."*

"Hi, honey. Listen, I'm really sorry, but we have to change your plans."

Her face fell; watching disappointment gather in her sky-blue eyes cut Hari like a slow knife. *"But we're going to Fancon—"*

"Change plans?" Shanna said. *"What are you talking about?"*

"Turn the car around. I need you here right away. Right now."

"Hari, is this really important? I have a panel at 1400—"

"Yes, goddammit, this *is* important. People's lives are at stake. How fast can you get here?"

Her brows drew together. *"It's that bad?"*

"You can't even imagine," he said feelingly.

She glanced away from the screen, checking the car's position on the GPS map. *"Fifteen minutes."*

"But," Faith protested, her lower lip threatening tears, *"but Fancon . . ."*

"Yeah, and uh, listen—" Hari scrubbed his face with the palms of his hands, trying to wipe away the sick dread that gathered in his throat. "Don't bring Faith. Drop her at home, and get your Pallas gear, all right?"

He refused to let himself be hurt by the spark of anticipation that danced in Shanna's eyes. *"It's that kind of problem?"* she asked slowly, like she was trying not to sound eager.

Faith, too, suddenly brightened. *"Mommy's going back to the river?"*

"Yeah," Hari said.

"Wow," Faith said happily. *"I thought we had to wait almost another month before we got to be together again. A month is a long time!"*

"Then you're all right about not going to the con?" Hari made himself ask.

"Uh-huh." She nodded brightly. *"I get to have the river in my head instead. And you and Mommy won't be fighting all the time."*

Shanna made a little grimace of apology through the screen; Hari waved it off. "Meet me at the Curioseum," he said. "At Tan'elKoth's place." He gave her a frown that asked her not to press for an explanation.

She nodded, that spark of anticipation now colored by a breath of wariness. *"I'm on my way. Give me an extra fifteen to drop off Faith and get my gear. Take care of the permit."*

"Yeah. See you."

He canceled the call and accessed the San Francisco travel site. It took him only seconds to register her new destination; as Chairman, he had the authority to code and alter travel permits for any Studio contractee.

It took him one more thoughtful moment to accidentally reinitialize his deskscreen's memory core. "Oops," he muttered flatly, as a keystroke erased all traces of his communications.

"Damn," he said. "I hate it when that happens."

He rose, and stretched to force blood into muscles stiff with long inactivity. *Hey, how about that?* he thought.

My fucking back doesn't hurt.

2

ON HIS WAY out, Hari stopped at the desk of his assistant. "Gayle," he said, "there's something wrong with my deskscreen. I think I lost some data. Can you look at it for me?"

Gayle Keller peered up at him and blinked; he had a round

face, close-set eyes, and a long nose that made him look like a nearsighted rat. Keller had been Arturo Kollberg's assistant; Hari had despised him for years, and six years of closer association had only intensified the feeling. He was pretty sure Keller supplemented his Studio paycheck by keeping the Social Police up to date on Hari's activities, and it wasn't even a secret that Keller filed regular confidential reports with the Studio's Board of Governors. Shortly after becoming Chairman, Hari had begun proceedings to have Keller replaced—until he'd received a call from Westfield Turner himself, who'd reminded him heavy-handedly just how *difficult it is to find a quality assistant, after all.* Keller was, in Hari's clinically unbiased opinion, an unctuous lying little fuck.

"Administrator?" he said, looking politely puzzled. "Perhaps I should call a tech?"

"Aw, come on, Gayle." Hari forced a grin, looking as good-natured as he could manage. "You've been working with this system for twenty years. Where are you gonna find a tech who knows it better than you do? Just have a look, huh? If you can't fix it, go ahead and call MIS."

Keller pushed himself back from his desk with an irritated little sigh, got up, and went into Hari's office. As soon as he was out of sight within, Hari started fiddling with the keypad to Keller's deskscreen. "See, all I did was something like this—"

"Don't touch that!" Keller suddenly appeared in the doorway. "I mean, please, Administrator—"

"Oops," Hari said. "Guess I know what *not* to do, huh?"

"Here, let me—"

"No, no problem," Hari said. "Here, all you have to do is—" and another couple of keystrokes reloaded the previous day's backup. Modern lasergel-core memory has none of the flaws of the antique magnetic media that it had replaced. Core data is 100 percent stable, but it's also nonpersistent: reinitialization physically scrambles the gel medium. Once the core was overwritten by the intersecting UV lasers, no data-recovery software on Earth could recreate whatever Keller had recorded of Hari's communications.

Keller glared at him, his piggy little eyes gleaming with suspicion. "You did that on purpose," he said tightly.

Hari shrugged. "I can't seem to get the hang of this new software."

"I don't believe that. I don't believe that for one second. I don't know what you're up to, but I have a duty to the Board—"

"Hey, my fault. I'm sorry," Hari said easily, stepping close to look down into the little man's eyes. "I screwed up. When you make your report, I guess you should remind the Board that the only thing I was ever *really* good at is killing people with my bare hands."

He looked long and deeply into Keller's eyes, until he saw the threat settle there and begin to work its magic on his attitude.

Hari left while Keller was still trying to come up with some kind of reply.

3

ROVER WAITED WITH gleaming patience at the open door of Hari's private lift. It was a five-minute walk from the lift to the Cavea's techbooth. Rover whirred precisely two paces behind his left heel.

He stopped outside the door. The two Security specials stood motionless to either side like a pair of caryatid columns, power rifles held diagonally across their chests at parade rest. Hari stood for a moment, taking a deep breath.

"I am Chairman Administrator Hari Khapur Michaelson," he said.

The specials replied in flat unison, *"You are recognized."*

The back of his neck always tingled when he came close to a special; he remembered too well the time one of these cyborged bastards shot him in the head. He could still feel the hammer of gelslugs against his skull every time he looked at one. The cyborg yokes around their necks overrode their higher cognitive functions, making them incorruptible, robotically faithful in the performance of their duties, and incapable of disobeying an order.

"Allow no one except myself to enter or leave this room without my express authorization."

"Acknowledged."

Walking between them still gave him a twinge.

Inside the booth, the two techs stared at him like nervous puppies, wondering if they were in trouble; they rose as he entered, respectfully silent.

Hari nodded to them. He glanced through the glass reflexively, into the Cavea; the thousand or so empty first-hander
berths out there tied a brief knot in the pit of his stomach; shit,
Caine had sold out the Cavea every Adventure for ten years—
now he had ten Actors at once working out of SF's main hall and
they could only pull four thousand between them. And god only
knew how many of the private boxes that climbed the walls were
empty.

He shook it off. None of that counted right now.

He scanned the curving bank of POV screens until he found
Rossi's. The show was still going on: now each time Rossi's gaze
settled upon a body, shadowy ghost-images of that person's
living days played around it. Translucent mothers cradled half-
seen infants; cloudy children skipped and laughed and threw
apple cores at each other; youths spun of smoke and cobwebs
played plaintive love songs, wrote poetry, and stole away together among the blasted, dying trees.

And through each shape, as through half-melted glass, could
be seen the bloated, raven-picked corpse, blackened with decay,
that was the end of each bright smile and mother's kiss.

*"You've guessed by now that what you are seeing is a Fantasy—
what humans call illusion. There will be those who will try to tell
you that Fantasy is the opposite of reality, that it is the same as
lies, that what you have seen is impossible—that it is a lie* because *it is a Fantasy. I tell you this is not so.*

*"It is the greatest·gift of my people, that we can bring our
dreams to life for other eyes. Fantasy is a·tool; like any tool, it
may be used poorly or well. At its best, Fantasy reveals truths
that cannot be shown any other way."*

*"This is a Fantasy of what I'm asking you to fight. This is a
Fantasy of the Blind God."*

Hari frowned at the screen and made a faint, thoughtful
hissing noise between this teeth. This was the second time
Hansen had mentioned this blind god—or was it the Blind God?
He'd heard about this before, somewhere, or maybe read it . . .
One of his father's books? Maybe. He'd ask Duncan about it
when he got the chance; he might know the reference.

Hari nodded toward the screen. "Get ready to pull him. On my
mark."

"Pull him—?" The techs exchanged worried frowns. "What
for? He doesn't even have an audience."

"Just do it, Technician. That's an order."

"Administrator, we can't do that—not with the native there. It's an exposed transfer—the Kollberg Rule—"

"Fuck the Kollberg Rule," Hari said distinctly. He thought of one of Duncan's dicta: *All authority, political or otherwise, is ultimately a cloak for naked force—and sometimes you have to remind people of that.* "I'll give you a choice. You can pull him because it's a direct order, or—"

"But the *rule*—"

"Or," Hari overrode him, "you can pull him because one of those specials outside has a power rifle jammed against the back of your head. Any questions?"

The tech squinted like a kid flinching away from his father's fist. "No, sir," he said, and turned back to his board.

Hari looked at the other. "And you?"

"Me? I, I, I didn't say *nothing*. Sir."

"All right, then."

He stared expressionlessly into the tech's eyes until this one, too, turned to his board.

Now on the POV screen, the elf was back in view.

"And I, at least, am no Fantasy."

The elf reached toward Rossi's face, his hand vanishing below the Actor's peripheral vision.

"I am real. Feel my touch. I am here. In the name of all that both our peoples hold sacred, I ask for your help."

Hari listened with only half his attention; with the elf's voice to cover any small noises he might make, he thumbed the reject on one of the dual gravers that recorded Rossi's Adventure. When the cube popped up, he palmed it and swiftly replaced it with a blank from the rack below.

His teeth showed through a particular variety of grin he hadn't used in nearly seven years. "Y'know what?" he said. "I think you're right about that exposed transfer."

The techs flicked brief glances at each other, afraid to be caught looking away from their screens.

"Sir?" one of them said.

"Yeah. It's not worth the risk. Pull him at your first opportunity, and then get his ass back into his storyline ASAP. Call Scripting and have them work out the transition; have a faxpack ready for him. Then we can just forget any of this ever happened, huh?"

4

THE SCREEN SHOWED the animated image of the friendly stenographer that indicated an open channel to the automated recording function of the Report Center. With what he imagined to be cool, professional competence, Gayle Keller made his report.

"At 1017 this morning, visual transmission resumed from J'Than aka Francis Allen Rossi," he said, reading from his notes. He pitched his voice toward his best imitation of the smooth tones of a professional broadcaster; he liked to imagine that occasionally the Board of Governors themselves played his recordings, and in his fond imaginings he saw a dozen Leisurefolk, faceless with absolute power, listening intently around a long oval table—they would nod to each other, favorably impressed with the skill of his delivery and his rich, round vocal tones—

"In what was later determined to be an illusion, J'Than aka Rossi appeared to be in an elven village, which had been destroyed by what was claimed to be an outbreak of HRVP on Overworld. This was reported directly to Chairman Michaelson from the techbooth; immediately on learning of the supposed HRVP outbreak, Chairman Michaelson undertook several real-time communications. Following this, he forcibly erased all record of his transactions from his own desk's memory core, and from that of this reporter. He also threatened this reporter with bodily injury or death."

There, Keller thought smugly. The Board would make certain Michaelson couldn't escape the consequences of such behavior.

"Chairman Michaelson then proceeded to the Cavea's techbooth, where—once again under the threat of bodily injury or death—he ordered the duty tech to perform a transfer that may have been exposed, in violation of the Kollberg Rule—"

He was interrupted by an attention chime from the speaker on his deskscreen.

"Artisan Gayle Keller. You are instructed to remain at your current screen. Hold for voice communication from the Adventures Unlimited Board of Governors."

Keller gagged, then coughed convulsively, spraying spit across his deskscreen. In sudden panic, seeing in his head an irrational vision of the Board staring out at him, knowing they had just been spit upon, he wiped frantically at the screen with the sleeve of his jumpsuit and nearly put his elbow right through it. He had imagined this event so many times that even now, he wasn't sure it was actually happening—but he guessed this must be real.

In his daydreams, he was never this frightened.

He placed his hands on the desk in front of him and tried not to notice how they trembled. He breathed deeply, in and out, in and out, until he became quite light-headed—but still, when the Report Center's friendly stenographer dissolved into the armored knight on the back of the winged horse, rampant, that was the official logo of the Studio, he knew that all the deep breathing in the world wouldn't melt the ball of ice that grew in the bottom of his throat.

"Artisan Keller. Expand upon this transfer that Michaelson ordered by threat of force."

That simply, that coldly, with that precise lack of ceremony or preamble, Gayle Keller found himself in the telepresence of the Board of Governors.

Chairman Michaelson had spoken, now and again, of the digitized, electronically neutral voice that represented the Board of Governors, so that one never knows precisely who's talking or whom one is talking to. One never even knows who is on the Board at any given time, only that there are between seven and fifteen of them, drawn always from the Hundred Families, the elite of the elite of the Leisure caste. Their identities are carefully protected, so that the Studio System as a whole maintains its status as an unbreachable public trust—no private pressure can be brought to influence the Board members' decisions if no one knows who they are. It was rumored that even the Board members were unaware of each other's identities, that the entire Board met only in virtual space, each member participating from his own private screen.

To Keller, this had always seemed a sensible, full explanation of the blank anonymity of the Board. Only now, faced with the static logo on the screen and the passionless neutrality of the voice, did he gather a glimmering of some larger truth. The absolute impersonality of the Board had a power of its own.

"The, hrm, the, the transfer?" Keller stammered. "Mmm, yes—" He made the tale as concise as he could manage; rather than becoming more easy as he spoke, he found his fright inching toward blank terror. Without any of the visual cues—no

nods of the head, no smiles, no frowns, no hint of posture or demeanor, none of the encouraging *Mmm-hmm* or *Yes, go on* of ordinary conversation, he couldn't tell if his report was being
received with warm paternal indulgence, lethal fury, or somewhere inbetween.

"Do you have any analysis?"

"Uh, analysis? I, uh—"

*"Do you know, or are you able to guess, why Chairman
Michaelson was determined to make this transfer, to the point of
threatening physical force, and then arbitrarily changed his
mind?"*

He rubbed his palms together below his desk, trying to wipe
away their thick slimy coating of sweat. "I, uh, no, I guess . . . I
mean, I can't guess, I haven't really thought—"

"These real-time communications. With whom did he speak?"

"I don't, I can't, ah—" He stopped himself and forced a deep
breath. "Ordinarily I, ah, copy the Chairman's communications
files from his deskscreen while he's out of the office, but . . .
well, the data cores, you know—"

*"Do you have any evidence, documentary or otherwise, that
the data erasure was an intentional act of sabotage?"*

Did they think he was lying? Or did they want something they
could hold over the Chairman's head? How much trouble was
he in?

"I, uh, I, well—no, not directly. B-but, why would he have
threatened me, if he wasn't trying to hide something?"

His voice trailed off, his face green in the light cast from that
still logo. The motionless knight on the winged horse stared
back at him for an unreasonably long moment.

Then, finally, blessedly, he heard, *"Artisan Keller. You are dismissed. Return to your duties."*

Keller stared at the blank grey rectangle of his deskscreen for
a long time, then jerked as though he'd started from a doze and
jumped to his feet.

He really, really needed to use the toilet.

5

THE LIFT OPENED onto a service hallway of blank white walls,
steel-colored doors, and nondescript carpet. There was age here,

mold tracks on the walls and dust in the semicirculated air, a sharp contrast to the immaculate public areas of the Studio. Hari marched some distance along its wide curve, Rover whirring at his heels. A palmlocked security door let him onto the skywalk.

The skywalk between the Studio and the Curioseum was little more than a transparent tube a half-klick long with all-weather polyester carpeting laid along its narrow floor. A low grey overcast spat drizzle that rippled the view through the armorglass, and the whisper of atmosphere control was barely audible above the patter of raindrops. Hari walked fast over the honeycombed car hive twenty-odd meters below, over the ten-meter-high security fence that ringed it.

He reached the Curioseum's security door and pitched his voice to his chair's command tone. "Rover: Stay." The chair settled in place and locked its brakes; Hari sat down, shifting his weight from side to side, grimacing—it was bad enough, using this thing when he *needed* it; he couldn't get comfortable, couldn't make himself settle into this chair, with a pair of working legs.

He reached up and flattened his hand against the palmlock's screen. The security program's voder replied, *"Access denied. Persons dependent upon bioelectronic implants may not enter this facility pursuant to the Liability Reduction Act of—"*

"Michaelson one override."

"Please present sample for matching."

" 'Then it's Tommy this and Tommy that and "Tommy, 'ow's yer soul?" ' " Hari said with flat dispassion. " ' But it's "Thin red line of 'eroes" when the drums begin to roll.' "

The door hissed aside, revealing a small airlock-type compartment, just large enough for three or four people to stand in comfortably. On the far side was a steel door secured with a large drop-latch instead of a palmlock. *"Welcome to the Curioseum, Administrator Michaelson."*

Hari made a face; he hated this part. The boundary effect was murder.

He took a deep breath and rolled across the threshold. As soon as the skywalk door hissed shut behind him, his legs began to jerk and twist like the galvanic response in a dissected frog muscle. He snarled under his breath as he maneuvered the chair around so he could swing up the bar on the inside door; his legs knotted into cramps that felt like somebody had sunk dry ice meat hooks into his thighs.

Crossing the boundary between Earth physics and the Overworld-normal field of the Curioseum was always a race between his hands and his asshole: he had to get that inner door open before he lost control of his bowels. In the boundary, the ON field sort of mingles with Earth physics, and the goddamn bypass just goes berserk. Once he was all the way into the ON field, the bypass just surrendered.

After what felt like an hour, he managed to lift the drop-latch and push open the door. Instantly all the feeling drained out of his legs. He thumped his thighs a couple of times with his fists to make sure they weren't still cramping. They seemed to be relaxed; the muscle jiggled slackly under his hands.

Just meat, now.

Like having a couple dead dogs strapped to my ass, he thought. *Except I can't eat them.*

He rolled on along the hallway, heading for the balcony that ringed the Hall of Fame. When he rolled out onto the balcony, the immense exhibition hall suddenly blazed with light. Hanging in the center of the hall, suspended from thin, almost invisible guy wires, was a dragon.

Thirty-five meters of sinuous power, her titanic wings spread a translucent pavilion over the entire hall, and her scales shone iridescent diamond. Her long saurian neck arched high, her titanic mouth gaped with hooked teeth as long as Hari's forearm, and from that mouth gouted flame like a solar flare, scarlet and orange and yellow bursting from eye-searing white at its core. At the center of that unimaginable fire, on a small circular dais twenty meters below, a figure in shining armor knelt in an attitude of prayer, hands folded upon the hilt of a broadsword. A Shield of shimmering blue warded the flames that melted the very stone on which he kneeled.

Hari gave the scene just the barest glance. The armor there was real; it had belonged to Jhubbar Tekanal—the Actor Raymond Story. The dragon was real, too, most of her; he'd sent the expedition himself to the site of the battle and salvaged her scales. He wondered briefly if Kris Hansen had ever watched the recording of Story's legendary three-day battle against Sha-Rikkintaer. He had a vague recollection that Story had been Hansen's favorite Actor.

He rolled on, faster, scowling.

He hated this fucking place. He'd fought the whole idea of a Hall of Fame, but he'd been overruled by President Turner with the support of the Board of Governors. Turner had said it would be a valuable tourist attraction, and the Bog had agreed, and Hari had to admit they were right: the Hall of Fame was less than a fifth of the Curioseum, but it was the primary draw for 90 percent of the visitors.

He turned the chair and pumped its wheels, rolling along the balcony toward a long spiral ramp that led down to the ground floor. He had to keep his ass moving: this place would open at noon, and he had a lot to get done before it filled up with tourists. He pushed the wheels harder, gaining speed even before he swung onto the ramp. He coasted all the way down, half braking with his palms against the wheel rims. He rolled off the ramp and bled velocity in a long, slow curve that brought him to a stop in the middle of the gallery that led to the Caine Hall.

Small in the distance, waiting for him at the far end of the gallery, was Berne.

Inside a large case of armorglass in the middle of an archway, he was posed in a fighting crouch. He wore clothes of close-fitting serge, once red but now faded to strawberry—the same clothes he'd had on when Caine killed him. He had a snarl on his face and both hands on the hilt of Kosall, the wide-bladed bastard sword angled before him as though he guarded the arch against a fierce enemy.

Hari forced himself to roll the chair forward. *I always think I can cruise right past here, not even think about it, just roll on by—*

And I am always dead fucking wrong.

The armorglass case was overpressured with some kind of preservative gas—a faint chemical stench always lingered in the air around it. Taxidermy was a very efficient art these days: the Curioseum staff had simply cleaned him up, patched the slices in the clothes, covered the hole in his skull with a wig, posed his corpse, and shot him full of something to rigidify the muscles.

And there he was: the real Berne. The real Kosall.

The most popular single exhibit in the whole Curioseum.

Hari stopped beside the case and forced himself not to read the plaque. He knew it by heart, anyway. He stared up into Berne's glittering eyes.

Sometimes I have trouble remembering that you lost, and I won.

He set his teeth in a silent snarl and pushed on.

6

THE BROAD MISSION door that fronted Tan'elKoth's apartment stood open, and Hari rolled through the arched doorway without knocking, without even slowing.

The apartment was huge and open, converted from one of the Curioseum's exhibition halls. Smaller than the titanic halls devoted to Jhubbar and Caine, it nonetheless towered a full three stories to the thick skylight of armorglass. On the ground floor was an immense entertainment area scattered with furniture custom-designed for Tan'elKoth's enormous body, arranged to create the feeling of separate rooms: a living room, a kitchen, a den. A simple sweep of staircase would take one up through the open light well to the second floor, which held Tan'elKoth's bed and personal spaces; a second sweep would take one to the third floor, where Tan'elKoth maintained his studio. On that third floor, in the full sun that streamed through the skylight, he sculpted the statuary that dotted the apartment—and that also graced the homes of fashionable Leisurefolk around the world; a Tan'elKoth original had become a hallmark of good taste.

At least that's what Tan'elKoth *said* was up there. With no ramps in the apartment, Hari had never been above the ground floor. He'd never had a reason to go up urgent enough to make it worth the humiliation of asking Tan'elKoth to carry him.

Tan'elKoth's kettledrum rumble echoed hollowly through the cavernous space, though he was at the farthest corner of the apartment. "No, Nicholas, green. Not chartreuse. *Green.* The green of young oak leaves in April."

He knelt in *seiza* on the carpet in the den area, at the head of a small oval of two men and three women in similar posture. He wore precisely faded dungarees and a polo shirt that stretched like latex over his enormous chest and shoulders, looking every inch the casually stylish Professional. The other five in the oval wore the short-sleeved white shirts, neckties, and chinos of junior Professionals; none of the five looked very much at ease, and a couple were openly sweating.

This was Tan'elKoth's graduate seminar in Applied Magick. Every year, the top five Battle Magick students from the Conservatory were awarded the opportunity to come here and do advanced study under Tan'elKoth. The Studio was not in the business of giving out free rides, even to political prisoners. In the mornings, he taught; in the afternoons, he did two matinee lecture/demonstrations per day for the crowds in the Curioseum.

He conducted his seminar in his home, because the Overworld-normal field that sustained his phase-match with Earth also allowed the use of Flow. Only the most minuscule amount was available here—generated by the plants in the arboretum and the animals in the bestiary, as well as the tiny energy traces left behind by the Curioseum's innumerable tourists—but it was enough for tiny, basic effects.

"I, I, uh, haven't, I mean, I've seen *pictures* of an oak—" the pale student began.

"Less yellow, then. Can you not see the color your classmates project?"

"But sir, this is the color that I've always—"

"And that is why you are last in this class, Nicholas. Any fool can enchant a bit of herb; to master the molding of life itself, one must use *green*! *This* green. If you cannot summon the hue for yourself, at least try to open your blurred and misty consciousness long enough to perceive mine."

"Why can't I just memorize the spell?"

"Spells are for fools, Nicholas. They are a crutch for adepts who lack the discipline of a true thaumaturge. The true master of magick forms his intention and charges it with Flow by the pure action of his will: make it real within, and the Flow will mirror your reality without. *That* is true—"

"Hey," Hari said flatly. "Didn't I tell you to dismiss your fucking class?"

Tan'elKoth's leonine head turned with ponderous, inhuman deliberation: a temple guardian of stone coming slowly to life. He gathered a cavernous breath and unfolded smoothly to his feet. "Students. Rise for the Chairman."

The students scrambled upright, four of them blinking at being so suddenly roused from their meditation. All five stood at attention, their faces reflecting various degrees of awe and dread. "Class dismissed," Hari said. "Beat it. All of you."

The only movement any of them made was to cast dubious

glances toward Tan'elKoth. Tan'elKoth stood with arms folded across his ogre-sized chest. "This is my home," he said. "These are my students. I fulfill the task that you have given me. Chairman or no, do not presume to give orders here."

"Here's a fucking order," Hari said sharply, leaning forward in his chair. "Sit down and shut up. This is too important for us to waste time on your shit."

Tan'elKoth didn't move. "You cannot comprehend how offensive this is."

"Yeah, maybe not. You've known me how long? And you still expect me to have manners?"

"Manners? Hardly. Thoughtfulness, perhaps; consideration of the few shreds of dignity that you have allowed me to—"

"Drop it," Hari said flatly.

"I can only hope that you bring me glad news: perhaps this HRVP of yours has broken out among the elves, and you have come to help me celebrate."

Fuck it, Hari thought. *He wants it standing up, he'll goddamn well take it standing up.* "That's right," he said. "There's been an HRVP outbreak among the elves. And you know what? That Actor I was asking about, the one who might be exposed? He's in *Ankhana.*"

Tan'elKoth's eyes went wide and blank, and his breath escaped in a fading hiss. He groped for the back of a chair into which he could lower himself, missed it, and stumbled like a drunk.

"I told you," Hari said. "You should have sat down."

He looked at the students. "Last chance. Beat it."

Again they glanced at Tan'elKoth; he covered his eyes with one hand and waved them away. They scattered without a word, gathering up their belongings and hustling out the door.

"Caine . . ." Tan'elKoth said weakly. "Please say this is but a cruel jest."

"Yeah, sure," Hari said. "I'm famous for my sparkling sense of humor. Pull yourself together. We have work to do."

7

THE KEYS TO Tan'elKoth's deskpad felt alien under Hari's fingertips: a strange mechanical resistance, as though the pad itself fought back against his touch. Instead of an electronic pad, Tan'elKoth's was a mechanical rod-and-lever linkage, like an antique typewriter. The rods sank through the well cut in the center of Tan'elKoth's immense rolltop desk, down into the shielded receptacle in the floor where the actual electronics lay, protected from the effect of the Curioseum's ON field.

Hari stared at the angled mirror propped on the desktop by an ornate stand of wrought brass. The mirror reflected a rectified image of a screen that actually sat beneath his feet in the subfloor receptacle.

Tan'elKoth lay flat on the floor beside Hari's sandals, one massive arm stretched downward into the receptacle, his fore-finger lightly brushing the cube in the screen's socket. The cube held the recording of Hansen's performance with J'Than.

The unfamiliar feel screwed up Hari's typing; it took him a couple tries to key in Clearlake's priority access code. And the speaking tube down to the audio pickup altered his voice enough that he had to repeat the Caine quote three times before the secu-rity program recognized him. The mirror finally assembled an image of Clearlake's face.

"Hey, Jed," Hari said with a tight smile. "Ready for this?"

"For that story you were talking about? I did a little analysis on what you sent me already—from some of the bodies, I'm seeing signs—"

"Don't say it," Hari interrupted. "We can't talk about it on an open line. Just tell me if you're ready for an upload."

"Hari, I'm as ready as it gets," Clearlake answered with a smile of his own. *"I'm just wondering what's taking so long."*

"All right. Now listen: this is important. What I'm about to send you? You need to review it *off-line*. There's a security capture keyed to a couple words in here—I've got a counter-measure, but it's ablative. Save it for the broadcast."

"Security captures and countermeasures—just how big is this?"

"As big as it gets, Jed."

"You sure I'll want to broadcast?"

Hari nodded. "I'm thinking special edition; I'm thinking prime-time preempt. I'm thinking license fees for clips from this report should run into eight figures, easy."

"Bring it on then, Hari. You've always been good luck."

Hari leaned over to glance down at Tan'elKoth. "Ready?" he said softly.

Tan'elKoth's reply had the hollow distance of mindview. "I am."

It's going to work, Hari thought. His fingers trembled, just a little bit. Not nerves, though, no: fuck nerves. This was *fun*.

Maybe not a whole lot of fun, but he couldn't remember the last time he'd had any at all.

Hari stroked the final key.

As the file uploaded, Tan'elKoth channeled the tenuous Flow obtained within the Curioseum's Overworld-normal field into the net. A living nervous system is the natural interface between Flow and the material world; Tan'elKoth could gather Flow here and funnel the energy across the boundary by touch. He couldn't do much—the power he could exert in terrestrial physics was just one hair this side of nonexistent—but a surge of a few microvolts in the right place is all it takes to burn out a molecular circuit or randomize a couple lines of code. He didn't even need to know exactly what he was affecting—hardware, software, it didn't matter. Tan'elKoth had put it this way: "A thing is what it does. My power becomes a needle that will prick any hand which attempts to seize the dream within this cube."

Five seconds of burst-feed later, it was done.

"Got it," Clearlake said. *"Confirmed."*

"All right. Signing off, Jed—miles to go before I sleep, that kind of thing."

"You want your finder's percentage? If you're right about that eight figures, it could run into a substantial chunk."

"Put it in escrow," Hari said. "If this gets my ass fired, I'll need it."

"Will do. Later."

"Yeah."

Hari hit the cancel and folded down the screen. Tan'elKoth rose and stretched until his shoulder joints popped with a pair of meaty squelches. "Success."

"You're sure?"

"I am Tan'elKoth." This he said without even a ghost of a smile.

Hari took a deep breath. *So far, so good.*

This was an improved version of what Hansen had been trying to do by capturing Rossi in the first place—he'd been trying to get through to a group of first-handers, in hopes of finding some

Leisurefolk with big enough bleeding hearts to get involved. But that was because he didn't understand first-handers. Hari did. He'd built his life understanding first-handers.

Rossi's first-handers could have experienced everything on that cube and thought it was nothing more than part of the story. For them, it'd be nothing they need to do anything about, except sit back and watch how J'Than and the rest of the ISP cast handle it. Hari's way, it would go onto the net, out of context.

Instead of being part of a story, it *was* the story.

Instead of watching the hero in place do something about it, each Leisureman and Leisurewoman becomes the hero for their own little story: they see the problem, they see they have the power to do something about it, and they make the choice to do it or not, all on their own. *Not too fucking bad,* he thought. *We're off to a running start.*

Tan'elKoth cracked his enormous knuckles. "Now: I have done as you asked, and it is time to move on. There is only one course of action, and we both know it: You must return me to Ankhana without delay."

Hari shook his head. "Not gonna happen."

Tan'elKoth looked as though he might spit on the floor. "You waste all this effort, all this thought, in *persuasion.* It is ultimately futile. Childish. You depend upon your Leisure caste as surrogate parents, to act for you; thus shall you inevitably fail."

Hari's smile tightened. "We use what tools we have."

"Bah. Useless tools produce nothing of use. Call upon me, Caine. I will help your cause."

"You have already."

"Of course. And I will continue to do what you ask of me, *everything* you ask of me—until and including the moment when you realize that all these plans are useless. Your sole remaining choice is to *send me home.*"

Hari sighed. "It's not gonna happen," he repeated.

"Caine, it *must.* Direct action is my world's only hope. Exposing this crime is a worthy stroke, but it will not win the war. My people—my very *world*—is bent beneath the axe. You must let me save it."

"Yeah, sure," Hari said with a bitter smile. "Save the world, my ass."

"Why do you resist the inevitable?"

That's the main question of my life, Hari thought, but he said, "Because I can't fucking trust you."

The ex-Emperor stiffened. "You doubt that I would save my Children?"

"Oh, yeah, sure, your Children," Hari said. "But what about the elves? Shit, Tan'elKoth, how stupid do you think I am? You think I forgot why the Monasteries were supporting your government? Your policy on the other humanoid races wasn't exactly a secret. Once your *Aktir-tokar* consolidated your power over the nobles, you were gonna fire up your own personal genocide. I have a feeling this primal friend of mine wouldn't be too happy to see you back."

"Yet I am his only hope."

"If you were still Emperor, you'd be the number one *suspect.*"

Tan'elKoth came to Hari's side, towering over him, forbidding, unassailable. "The power of a god is required, to avert this disaster. I am that god."

"No, you're not."

"I am. The gods of my world cannot intervene, bound as they are by the Covenant of Pirichanthe. And even if they could—no god of my world has the faintest understanding of virology, let alone the specifics of HRVP: the minds of those gods are merely the sums of the minds of their worshipers. My world's only hope lies in the action of a god who has both comprehension of HRVP and the power to do something about it."

"Okay, sure," Hari allowed, "But you're not the god."

Tan'elKoth's rumble dripped sarcasm. "And which god, then, did you have in mind?"

"You know her," Hari said. "She'll be here in about five minutes."

With his comprehension, Tan'elKoth's expression twisted into one of distaste. "She is unworthy of this task."

"Don't start with me," Hari said through his teeth. "You know better."

"She is unworthy of *you*, Caine."

"Drop it."

"She is weak. Prissy. She holds herself removed from the realities of deity; I have never understood why you tolerate her manifest frailties."

"Not so weak," he said, heating up. "Not so weak she couldn't kick *your* ass—"

"Perhaps not; but so weak that she *didn't*. Not even to *save your life*, Caine."

Hari lowered his eyes and turned his face away, struggling with his temper. Finally he said, "You're not going back. You're never going back. Knowing what you know about the Studio, Actors, what you know about Earth, with the kinds of power you can throw around over there? No chance."

"You would take the side of the Studio against me? Against my *world*? Caine, who do you think has *done* this? Whom do you think you are *fighting*?"

"There's fighting and then there's fighting," Hari said. "Send you back on my own authority? They'd shoot me down like a dog. The Bog would blow up this whole Studio to keep you off Overworld; shit, they'd nuke the *city*."

"And even if your Board of Governors—the Bog, as you say—should be so rash, one city is a small price to pay for an entire world."

"Yeah?" Hari said flatly. "What if it's *your* city?"

Muscle bulged around the corners of Tan'elKoth's jaw. "I am willing to take that risk."

"Yeah, well, I'm not. Once this story hits the nets, people are going to be all over the Studio to *do something* about it; the Bog, all virtuous, will have to point at me and say, 'Through the swift and decisive action of Chairman Hari Michaelson, and the power of the great Pallas Ril, the situation is already under control.' They're gonna have to *thank* me, don't you get it? When Shanna gets back, Wes Turner will probably be giving her a *medal*."

Tan'elKoth took a step back; with a slow breath, he drew himself up to his full height. He seemed to change, somehow, inhaling some new reality along with his breath, transforming his polo shirt and dungarees into a costume, and his tired, aging face into a mask.

"You are a brilliant tactician," he said slowly, remotely, with that quality of performance as though he spoke once more for that audience inside his head, "perhaps the most brilliant I have ever known. But tactics win only battles; one can win every battle and still lose the war. Remember, in your hour of darkness, that you were offered this chance, and you refused it."

Hari squinted at him. "Y'know, I wouldn't swear to it, but that kind of sounded like a threat."

Tan'elKoth looked away, over Hari's head; his eyes drifted closed as though tired with a familiar pain. "Your—" He seemed to search for the proper word. "—*wife* . . . has arrived."

8

IN THE EMPTY silence left behind by the departure of Caine and his pet goddess, minutes passed like days for the man who had once been a god. They had watched their cube-trapped dream, made their plans, and left to save the world; now he sat alone in the tenebrous gloom.

Silence enfolded him, enwrapped his heart, soaked through his pores: silence so deep it screamed with imaginary echoes. Silence was the fertile earth from which sprouts of possibility budded within his far-ranging mind; these sprouts grew to mighty fractal trees of world-paths, blossomed, and died, only to sprout again in new variations for the future. Like a gardener, he sought ways to guide this growth with gentle efficiency; like a gardener, he would use the course of nature to his advantage.

Thus, the thought, finding a branch upon which the weight of his finger could curve the entire tree toward his desire; *and thus,* another spot where his breath upon its bark would color the blooms of this new curve; *and finally, thus*.

And the tree of the future had the shape of his dreams.

He had watched her—the mock-deity, the make-believe avatar of Chambaraya—watched her review the captured dream, had watched the lust of her river sparkling within her eyes. He had read there the joy of leaving behind this sterile hell of concrete and steel; he had read that she had been only waiting for an excuse.

I can get you there right away, Caine had told her, slowly, as though it hurt him to say the words. *We'll do it freemod, just like your regular shift—no audience, so we don't need approval from the Scheduling Board. How long will it take?*

Four days, she had said. *Maybe five. Creating a new life-form is a complicated thing, even for a god; it'll take at least that long to make sure my cure doesn't turn out to be worse than the disease. Four or five days on Overworld, and I should have a safe countervirus.*

And thus did she pronounce her doom. Three days would be the measure of her life.

He must act now; to wait until she had won his battle would cost him his war. Her power would suffice against HRVP; but the true threat to his people came not from the disease itself, but from the forces gathered behind it. Against those, she had no hope; thinking her war won, she would return to Earth, and be destroyed.

If his people were to be saved, Ma'elKoth must live again.

The men within him clamored for his attention; he opened the gates of his mind to release them. He stood before them as a giant, and he regarded them coldly. First among them, as he had ever been, was the fading palimpsestic remnant of the contemptible weakling he'd once been: Hannto the Scythe.

Hannto of Ptreia—Hannto the Scythe, the bent-backed asthmatic necromancer—had been nearsighted, slight, and nervous, the lonely child of a journeyman scribe. Hannto now begged for caution, cringing against the imagined humiliation of failure. To Hannto, he said: *I am more than you were. I am Tan'elKoth. Failure is impossible.*

At Hannto's side stood a more recent tenant of Tan'elKoth's mind: Lamorak—Karl Shanks—whose life had been etched permanently into Tan'elKoth's brain by magick nearly seven years ago. Lamorak—who'd been terrorized by his older, tougher brothers, who'd been beaten and nearly raped by Berne in the Imperial Donjon, who'd lain helpless under Master Arkadeil's knives in the Theater of Truth—haunted the darkest chambers of Tan'elKoth's mind, whispering surrender.

Lamorak feared and hated Caine. His most potent memory was of that brilliant noon on the arena sand, when Caine had drawn his neck against Kosall's irresistible edge and tossed his head like a child's ball into Ma'elKoth's lap. Lamorak regarded Pallas Ril with mingled lust and fury; his deepest desire was to fuck her to death, yet his spirit was bound with chains of helplessness and despair. Lamorak forever whispered that all is random, mere chance, that life is an accident at the mercy of the universe's whim: since all is meaningless, it is better to survive in safety, here as he was, than to engage in the pain and risk of futile struggle. To Lamorak, he said, *Life is mere chance only when one allows it to be. I am more than you were.*

Behind Lamorak crowded ghosts of the many others consumed over his years as Ma'elKoth: faceless, nearly shapeless
shades, lives too small to remain distinct even in this mock afterlife. Their voices blended together into an oceanic murmur, begging that he remember them, that he love them, that he care for
their children. To the crowd, he said, *Fear not, for I am with you.*

He marshaled his strength and pushed them all back within
the gates, and locked the gates against them. One figure alone remained to face him.

Ma'elKoth.

Towering in his strength, majestic in his armor of polished obsidian, his beard long and bristling, his hair a pelagic cascade
past his shoulders, his eyes black diamonds. To Ma'elKoth, he
said, *I am coming. You shall live again.*

And the silent god within his mind lifted an omnipotent hand
in benediction.

Tan'elKoth breached once more the surface of his consciousness, to regard the wider world. He typed a code into his
deskpad. Each keystroke fell with a measured, echoic cadence:
the drumroll of an execution.

The mirror of his screen lit with an animated image of a
cheerful stenographic clerk, sitting at a desk, and a pleasant
voice told him that he could now record a message for the Adventures Unlimited Board of Governors.

"I am the Emperor-in-exile Tan'elKoth," he said with slow
precision. "Tell your Board of Governors this: in exchange for
certain considerations, I shall undertake to solve their Michaelson problem."

He stroked the disconnect, and sighed.

Soon now, he said to the god within. *Soon.*

9

HARI STOOD ON the techdeck. On the laser scale, beyond a transparent wall of armorglass, lay the dull grey ceramic lozenge of
Shanna's freemod coffin. He tried not to imagine how happy she
must be, lying there right now.

The freemod techdeck was a busy place, these days. Formerly,
it had only been used twice a year, to transfer the most recent
graduates of the Studio Conservatory to Overworld for their

two-year freemod tour; this was the oldest Studio in the system, and was the only Earthside freemod site. On Overworld, there were twenty-five scattered freemod sites—not counting the Railhead in Thorncleft—all in remote locations, all disguised as temples to a particularly forbidding spider god.

The Overworld sites did not require extensive equipment; all they needed was a small transfer pump to drive an Earth-normal field—for data storage and communications—and some exceptionally sophisticated mechanical scales. The freemod process is essentially a swap, an even trade of mass-energy between the universes, and thus requires extreme precision in the weighing of materials to be exchanged. The closer the mass-energy ratio to 1:1, the less energy was required. Even the air inside the coffin was controlled to a nicety.

This was the primary factor that had kept the San Francisco Studio afloat these past few years. Once the studio had formed the Overworld Company and gone into full-scale exploitation of Overworld resources, San Francisco had been the only Studio with freemod technology already in place.

On the far side of the techdeck, beyond another, larger window of armorglass, lay the docks: an immense cavern of a room crowded with sealed crates, each labeled in Westerling with their destinations. Off to another side were titanic slag canisters the size of freight cars; when there were no supplies of equipment to be sent, incoming shipments of ore were balanced by returning to Overworld the waste products left after valuable metals had been refined out. The docks were always loud with the rumble of heavy turbines; an endless stream of freightliners landed and lifted off again outside.

But Hari had no eyes for that now; he could only stare at Shanna's coffin, and listen to the tech at his side mutter low-voiced corrections to another tech a universe away.

Yeah, better not fuck with Caine, he thought, helplessly bitter. *If he gets really pissed, he'll tell his wife on you.*

He shook his head sharply. *Fucking cut it out,* he snarled at himself. *I don't have to do everything myself. Don't be such a suckass.* Yet—how was he supposed to stand here and watch her go, and not ache with envy?

She'd promised to look in on Kris. Hari knew Hansen was in for a bad time; a word of hope from the goddess should do him wonders. She wouldn't have any trouble finding him; once

joined with Chambaraya, she became aware of every living creature that partook of its waters. She'd said the recording had given
her a good enough sense of him that she would know his touch,
even among the hundreds of thousands of people in Ankhana,
and she should make contact with him, anyway: if he was carrying HRVP, he'd be her most convenient source for a sample of
the virus.

He could still taste her lips. Just a little kiss, a little *see ya later*
peck; he couldn't have taken more.

For a few minutes there, it had been almost like old times—
he'd almost felt like he could *do* things. For the brief span they'd
spent walking from the Curioseum, planning together, anticipating a little action, he'd almost felt like they were a team again.
Like they'd briefly been, back all those years ago.

Before they were married.

Be careful, he'd told her, trying—really trying—to keep it
light. *You get in trouble over there this time, I can't come and
bail you out.*

It hadn't raised even the faintest of smiles. *Keep your eye on
Tan'elKoth,* she'd said. *Don't ever let yourself forget who he is.*

He'd answered, *He better not forget who I am.*

It had been a pretty good line, but it was only a line.

Her coffin began to shimmer around the edges as it interposed
with the nearly identical one coming through from Overworld.
It took on a faint translucency; the other resolved into a more
solid existence; within a second or so, Shanna's coffin was only
a ghost shape, and the new one—roughly half-full of water—
became solid, fully *here*. Shanna was gone.

Now, somewhere in another universe, there appeared a goddess named Pallas Ril.

Hari thanked the technician and walked out of the techdeck.
Outside, near the elevator that would return him to the public
areas of the Studio, Rover waited with electronic patience. Hari
scowled at it—but after a moment he sighed, shrugged, and sat
down. As he rolled into the elevator, he dug out his palmpad and
keyed the code for the Abbey. When Bradlee answered, Hari
asked him to put Faith on.

Her smile nearly filled the tiny screen. *"Hi, Daddy. Mommy's
with the river now,"* she reported.

"Yeah, I know, honey," Hari told her. "I was just with her.
Listen—"

"She's pretty worried," she said, her smile fading and her golden brows wrinkling. The familiar glazed, eldritch dissociation gathered in her eyes. When Pallas Ril walked the lands of Overworld, half of Faith walked with her.

Hari nodded. "It's a pretty serious thing she's doing over there."

Faith said solemnly, *"She's worried about you."*

"Listen," he said, "since you're off school today anyway, I was thinking I might take the rest of the day off and go down to Fancon. Maybe even a couple of days off. You want to come along?"

"Really? Really for real?"

"Sure, really for real. How about it? Still in your con clothes?"

"Sure. Uh, Mommy's happy I get to go to the con."

"Yeah, I'll bet. Me, too. One other thing, honey: before Mommy left, we were real busy and in a big hurry, and I forgot something I need to tell her, okay?"

"Okay."

"Just tell her I said I love her."

"Uh-huh. She loves you, too," Faith said with simple, serene matter-of-factness. *"But I don't really tell her things. It's not like that. She just knows."*

"I just wanted to make sure," Hari said. "I just wanted to make sure she knows."

THE CROOKED KNIGHT laid himself down to rest. There was no battle left for him to fight. He had fulfilled his mission, succeeded in his quest. His war was won.

But he remained, nonetheless, the crooked knight.

In winning, he had lost.

SIX

"CHANGELING?" THE HIGH, thin voice sounded like a breathy piccolo, and a hand like a coin-sized grapnel tugged at his ear. "Changeling, wake up!"

Deliann rolled over. He didn't want to open his eyes; he couldn't remember exactly, but he was moderately sure that waking up would hurt, somehow—and he was so warm, so comfortable, and the bed was so soft . . .

"Changeling!" Something poked him hard in the neck; he couldn't be sure, but it might have been a kick from a very small bare foot. "Kier says she needs you."

Just as well, he thought, rubbing at his gummy eyelids until he could part them. *If I sleep any longer, I'll probably start to dream.*

The heavy brocade curtains drawn across the windows in Kierendal's bedchamber were outlined by the yellow glare of the afternoon outside. Standing on the mattress next to his shoulder was an extraordinarily beautiful treetopper, her diaphanous wings a transparent shimmer in the gloom. She looked like a twenty-inch human female of extravagantly sensual proportion: long elegant legs, a tiny wasp waist, outrageously high firm breasts. She wore a minuscule shift, belted at the waist, barely long enough to cover the swell of her ass and revealing a dangerous amount of cleavage.

"Tup . . ." he said thickly. "H'long . . . Timezit?"

"It's about four," Tup said. "You've been asleep for five hours or so. You have to get up, now—Kier sent me to get you."

"Yes, all right," he made himself say, and sat up.

He had only a fuzzy recollection of coming into this room; Kierendal had led him here after they'd let the *Aktir* go; at the end of his performance for the people who were watching through that man's eyes, Deliann had nearly collapsed. He had barely kept his head up long enough to eat some of the soup that Kierendal fed him. He remembered being led in here . . . he remembered Kierendal's lips, soft against his ear: *"Do you know, you are the only human who's ever had me for free?"*

He remembered her mouth against his, and that's when he realized he was naked.

He pulled the sheet around his hips. "Urh, Tup? You wouldn't happen to know where my pants are?"

"On the chair. Come on, hurry up."

He felt as if his whole body were turning red. He had some hazy impression that Tup was—or used to be—Kierendal's lover. Had he done something with Kierendal? What had happened between them? He would remember if he'd had sex—

Wouldn't he?

He gathered the sheet higher around his waist. "Tup, please. If you wouldn't mind—?"

Tup put her hands on her hips. "Changeling, I live in a whorehouse. You think I've never seen a dick before? Please. I've seen *yours*; I was here when Kier undressed you."

He closed his eyes, sighed, and opened them again. *Well, at least that means I didn't have sex.* He glanced at Tup, who glared at him impatiently.

Probably.

"All right," he said. "All right, I'm coming—I mean, I'm getting ready." He climbed out of bed and into the pants Kierendal had given him.

"Better hurry," Tup said. "She's pretty upset."

"About what?" Deliann asked dully, pulling the shirt on over his head. "And what does she need me for? She has plenty of security."

"She didn't say, exactly. Some snarl with a roger, up in the suites. He's got a hostage. She said to tell you this roger's sweaty and feverish—he's claiming his dolly was trying to poison him."

Deliann went still, half into the shirt, while a jagged ball of ice congealed in his stomach. *That's it,* he thought. *That's why I didn't want to wake up. That's exactly it.*

A slow weight gathered on his shoulders, crushing him toward the floor, but he just shook his head and slipped on the pair of sandals beside the chair.

"Show me the way," he said.

2

TUP LOOPED THROUGH the stairwell above him, circling and doubling back to maintain airspeed while she led him up toward the Yellow Suites, in the east wing of the fifth floor. Deliann struggled to keep pace, gasping with the pain each step brought his maimed legs.

Kierendal paced back and forth in the corridor, waiting for them. She wore her afternoon business attire—loose pants and shirt of shimmering black silk set off with a single string of gleaming pearls—and her silver hair was drawn back in a bun so tight it brought an extra slant to her eyes. A spot of blood showed at the corner of her mouth, where she'd been chewing her lower lip with her needle-sharp canines. She had a pair of her overt guards with her, ogres each nearly nine feet tall and five feet wide, dressed in heavy calf-length hauberks and carrying morningstars the size of Deliann's head. "Deliann," she said shortly, nodding him toward an open door beside her. "In here."

When Tup started to flutter in with them, Kierendal shook her head. "You stay out of here. Go back down to my chambers, wait for me there."

"Aww, Kier—"

Kierendal bared her sharp and bloody teeth. "Go. Now."

Tup went.

Within the room, a tearstained human girl of about twenty sat on the edge of the bed. A stonebender knelt on the bed beside her, holding a bloody towel against the girl's cheek. As Deliann entered, the stonebender drew back the towel, revealing an ugly gaping wound on the girl's face. Instead of a cheek, the side of her face was a pair of raw-meat flaps that didn't quite join up; she looked like somebody had stuck a knife in her mouth and sliced through her cheek all the way back to the hinge of her jaw.

Deliann winced; his stomach wasn't steady enough for this.

"Bleed's almost stop," the stonebender said kindly. "Good girl, brave girl. Fix you good, no worry."

Deliann could see that she used to be beautiful.

Dully, through the wall, he could hear the sound of someone pacing back and forth, heavily, like he was stomping cockroaches with big boots. "Whaddaya fuckin' think?" someone was saying in the adjoining room. "Whaddaya fuckin' think? What was I s'poza do?"

The stonebender began to stitch the girl up with his blunt, nimble fingers, using a long curved leather-working needle; the stitches would hold the skin and muscle in place while his magick accelerated the natural healing process. Probably wouldn't scar—not much, anyway—but it had to hurt. She whimpered, and tears leaked from her eyes, and Deliann had to look away.

"Her roger's still next door," Kierendal said. "Near as I can tell, he started acting up out of nowhere, and Tessa cried the carp. He only had time to cut her once; she made the door in a scramble when the guards broke in."

"Tup said something about a hostage?"

She shook her head grimly and nodded at a small spy gate set into the adjoining wall. "Have a look, if you want. The bastard knifed one of my boys and coldcocked the other. I don't want to send in anyone else. It's not just that he might kill Endy; I'm a little worried about letting any more of my people get close to him."

Deliann nodded. "Not just him—if he's sick, she has it, too. We shouldn't be in here. Let the healer stay with her."

Might as well; if the whore was infected, the healer was already dead.

He took Kierendal's arm and drew her back out into the corridor. He lowered his voice, leaning close to her to keep his words private. "Did you touch the girl? Has *anyone* else touched her, or been close to her or the, er, the roger?"

"I don't think so."

"All right. Tup said something about poison?"

"Yes. I can't be sure—you can guess that *she's* not talking too well," Kierendal said with a nod toward the wounded girl. "I'm only going on what I've overheard from next door. He's been saying something about poison in her mouth—crazy talking, like her kiss would kill him and he had to cut off her lips to save his life, like that. That's why I thought you should have a look at him. You . . . showed me . . . more than I want to know about this disease of yours, but you're the expert."

"I'm no expert," Deliann told her gloomily.

"You're the closest I have."

"All right. First, it's pretty unlikely that anyone in Ankhana could be infected—this is probably some kind of drug reaction. The disease broke out all the way up beyond Khryl's Saddle—"

"It's not worth taking a chance," Kierendal said grimly. "You give me a yes, I'll burn down this whole fucking wing. You put me through that fey's death. You made me know what it *feels* like. I won't watch my people die like that. I'll kill her myself."

Deliann's golden gaze met Kierendal's silver for a long moment; he saw how much it hurt her even to say such a thing. He also saw that she'd do it, no matter how much it hurt.

But it's not HRVP, he told himself. *It can't be. It's some kind of drug reaction, that's all. Like I said.*

The hall door also had a spy gate in it. Deliann stepped over and slid it open; he'd take a quick look, glance at the guy to set Kierendal's mind at ease, then tell her everything was all right. Simple. Easy.

Through the gate he could see a fey on the floor in an enormous pool of blood, his head twisted awkwardly, one side of his neck slashed into a ragged mockery of lips. A fly settled onto his face and walked across his open eye.

Scarlet bootprints stained the floor, where someone had tracked through the blood and walked off out of sight.

On the bed was a thick-muscled stonebender, wrists and ankles tied together with a twisted bedsheet, a wadded pillowcase stuffed in his mouth. With small, slow movements, the stonebender rotated his wrists and worked his ankles against each other, surreptitiously loosening the knots that held him.

"Whaddameye s'poza do? Huh? She'da *kilt* me. Whaddaya fuckin' *think* I'm gonna do?" The voice came more clearly through the spy gate; no longer muffled by the intervening wall, it sounded sickeningly familiar.

Then the speaker stomped into view: a huge, broad-shouldered ogrillo, his grey-leather face dripping sweat and one eye glaring feverishly. He wore gaudy, new-looking clothes of garishly dyed linen, now drenched with blood down his right side. He carried no weapon, but the razor-sharp fighting claw on his right wrist was fully extended and bright with blood.

One of his undershot tusks was a broken stump; the ivory of the other was blackened and scorched.

Deliann sagged against the wall.

Better I had died in the mountains, he thought. The pain in his chest wouldn't let him speak, wouldn't let him even breathe. *Oh, Rroni, why couldn't you have been a better swordsman? Why couldn't you have opened my skull right then?*

Oh, god, god, I would give anything, if only I had died . . .

The murderous ogrillo in the suite was the foredeck second.

"What is it?" Kierendal said. "It's bad, isn't it? I can see it on your face."

"It's bad," Deliann echoed.

Kierendal turned to her ogre guards, her face bleak with harsh necessity. "Evacuate this wing. I want everybody out of here within five minutes. Get all the available security and sweep every room. Anybody still in here, five minutes from now? They'll die in the fire."

One of the ogres twitched his enormous morningstar at the door where Deliann stood. "Whad aboud thhem? Whad aboud Endy? How you gonna ged him oud?"

"We're not," Kier said. "Endy, Tessa, Parkk—they're all staying."

The ogres exchanged dimly dismayed glances. "Bud you said—"

"You don't have to understand," Kierendal said. "Just do what I tell you."

"You're the one who doesn't understand," Deliann said.

He pushed himself away from the wall, wondering numbly that he still moved. How could he stand, under this weight? How could he speak? How could he still live, with his heart rotting inside him? "You don't understand," he repeated slowly, painfully. "I know that 'rillo."

"You do?" Kierendal blinked. "Small world. But that doesn't change anything—"

"Yes, it does. It changes everything. He's infected. There's only one way he could have been infected, to be showing symptoms right now."

Deliann spread his hands in absolute surrender; agony like this could not be fought, and could not possibly be endured. "I'm immune. I don't get sick. But he must have somehow caught it from me."

Kierendal's eyes went wide and blank.

Slowly, numbly, she lifted a nerveless hand to her face, staring sightlessly past him. She pressed her lips with her fingers, as though remembering her mouth against his—as though trying to calculate the infinite cost of that one kiss.

3

DELIANN LAY IN the darkness, twisted into a fetal knot of pain. Pain paralyzed him, left him helpless, shuddering on the cold, hard floor. He was only one stride from a couch, half a room away from a bed where he could lie, but the only motion his limbs would make was an intermittent nerveless twitch, a racking convulsion halfway between a lung-rotted cough and a dry sob.

He had never imagined there was this much pain in the world.

Lying at the bottom of the cliff in the God's Teeth with both legs broken had been nothing; it was as though his legs had some kind of a circuit breaker, a transformer that stepped down the pain. His heart, though—

Eaten by acid, it left a smoking hole in his chest, a sucking emptiness that screamed regret. This pain only grew. Long ago it had passed unendurable; he would howl, but the hole in his chest had eaten too much of his strength. He could not even whimper. He could only lie on the cold floor, and suffer.

He had brought madness and death to this whole city.

His stupidity—his simple thoughtless foolishness—had murdered Kierendal, and Tup, and her houseboy Zakke, and the pretty human whore with the slashed face, and the stonebender healer Parkk, and the ogre guards—

and—

and—

and . . .

Kierendal's first thought had been to seal the building—to save the city by burning down Alien Games with herself and everyone else inside it. She knew what she was in for; he'd made her feel every inch of the death of the young fey at the village outside Diamondwell. A shrieking death in fire, going down to darkness with the smell of your own roasting flesh in your nostrils, was far kinder than what that young fey had endured.

But even that would be useless; she'd given up any hope of slowing the infection. She could save nothing.

Alien Games was a brothel, a casino, an attraction for tourists from all corners of the Empire. The infection that he had carried here would have spread already into the city, and would be creeping outward into the Empire along the arteries of the Great Chambaygen like blood poisoning up a wounded leg.

How could he have been so *blind*?

In a minute or two, he'd get up. He'd go into the bedchamber next door, where Kierendal sat in darkness with Tup and Zakke and Pischu, her floor boss. He'd take a cup, and fill it with the wine that they were drinking even now.

He thought of Socrates, taking the hemlock and pacing his prison, walking back and forth to bring it on the quicker; he doubted he could do that. He wasn't entirely sure he could stand at all. Kierendal, she was stronger: she had marched into the bedchamber as though she'd left doubt and fear behind on another world.

On the other hand, only her brief future weighed down on her. Deliann had been crushed by the past.

He hoped that all he would find, on the far side of the cup of wine that waited for him next door, was darkness and an end to pain—but if not, if he was to face some judgment for his crimes, he did not fear it. Even the most brutal hell could not hurt him worse than this.

A small cool hand laid itself along his cheek, fingertips brushing his neck as though feeling for his pulse. Just that simple touch was so comforting, so calming, that he could not pull away from it. That cool touch seemed to draw some of his hurt as a moist towel draws fever. He shuddered as it went out from him, as though something inside him clung involuntarily to the pain, the way muscle clamps tight around a wounding arrow shaft if it's pulled too slowly.

"Shh, it's all right," a woman's voice told him softly. "It's all right, I'm here." Her breath smelled of green leaves turning toward the sun, of grain ripening in fields freshly swept by rain.

"No," Deliann said. She had taken enough of his pain that he now found he could move, could speak. He pulled away from her hand. "No, it's not all right. You've touched me. Now you're going to die."

"I am not so easily slain," the woman's voice told him gently. "Open your eyes, Kris Hansen. I bring glad tidings."

"What?" Deliann said. "What did you call me?"

When he did open his eyes, her face stole his voice.

She glowed in the darkened room with a light of her own, as though a single sunbeam framed itself precisely to her form: a small, slight human woman in ordinary clothing, a spray of dark hair framing an oval face rather ordinarily pretty, features unremarkable save for the serene power that shone forth from them: a shimmering halo of life so refined and concentrated that the sight of her burned away Deliann's previous experience of beauty like ice in a furnace. Looking on her, he could not even imagine another woman's face.

Awe compressed his chest. "Who . . ." he gasped breathlessly. "Who *are* you?"

"I am called Pallas Ril."

"The *Aktir* Queen?" he said involuntarily; Pallas Ril was the name of the ruler of demons in the elKothan pantheon, the bride of the evil Prince of Chaos—but none of the elKothan woodcuts or story windows had shown a woman such as this.

"If you wish," she said.

Electrified, Deliann scrambled to his feet; he made a warding gesture and breathed himself into mindview. "I want nothing to do with the human gods," he said warily.

Slowly, sadly, she straightened, and on her face was a small quiet smile. Her Shell filled the room, and more; he could not see its limit, and it blazed like the midsummer sun. "I am human, and a god—but I am not a human god. Know this: I am your friend, Kris Hansen—"

"Why do you keep *calling* me that?"

"—and I am the answer to your cry for help."

Deliann stopped, stunned, swaying in place, helpless against

the flood of pain and need that thundered back into his chest—
forgotten for one moment, it returned with overpowering force.

"How—? Who—?"

"I am called by many names. The First Folk call Me
Eyyallarann."

Her Shell surrounded him, enveloped him, enwrapped him in
effortless comfort; for half a single second, he relaxed—

And flashed on her.

She roared into him; in an instant he was filled to bursting,
filled beyond pain, but there was more, infinitely more, as
though some cruel giant poured the ocean down his throat. From
the scream of an eagle wheeling above Khryl's Saddle to the
slow squirm of a newt spawning in the mud of the Teranese
Delta, from the creak of ancient branches in the wind of the Lar-
rikaal Deepwood to the hush of a rivulet washing a mossy stone
below Ankhana's Commons' Beach, she entered him with power
that would burst his skull and scatter smoking gobbets of brain
throughout the room—

"That's enough," she said, and the flood cut off as though a
door had been slammed within his brain. "Be careful what you
touch, Kris; there are dangers here for such as you."

Deliann stepped back from her, gasping, his hands pressing
against his face until the room halted its dizzy whirl; then he
lowered himself slowly and reverently to his knees.

"Your pardon, My Lady," he said formally in Primal, his head
bent before her. "I did not know Thee."

"Your reverence betrays your human birth," she replied
gravely in the same tongue. "The First Folk do not kneel to Me; I
am properly greeted with a kiss, for I am your mother, and your
sister, and your child."

Deliann rose and embraced her; he was, astonishingly, taller
than she, and she felt frail in his arms. "What would you have me
do?" he asked.

"Hold on to hope," she said. "Within days, a new disease will
strike this city, and the entire land. Whoever it touches need
never fear HRVP."

"I don't understand."

"It is how I will defeat this plague. A new plague, that confers
immunity to the other."

"You can do this?"

"I can. That is why you must hold on to hope."

"Hope?" he repeated. "Immunity—oh, my heart! *Kierendal!* Kierendal, *stop!*"

He dashed from the room into the bedchamber next door.

What he found there might have been the aftermath of a cheerful party: bodies sprawled across a wide bed and settled at seeming ease into comfortable chairs, all in the boneless relaxation that might have been sleep—

Zakke reclined in a broad sitting chair, his beard spilling down his chest. Pischu lay on the bed, his hands folded peacefully across his chest. Tup was curled up on a pillow on the vanity table.

Kierendal had crumpled to the floor like a broken doll. She lay on the rug at the foot of the bed, and Deliann dropped to his knees beside her. Her long, almost fleshless legs were twisted beneath her; they looked like they would hurt, if she woke up.

He touched her splash of silver hair. "If only you could have waited," he whispered.

The room brightened to the gentle glow of a forest moonset. The goddess stood at his back.

"She was afraid," Deliann said, absently stroking Kierendal's hair. His voice was empty as a raided tomb. "They all were. She knew what it was going to be like. She couldn't face that kind of death—she couldn't watch *them* face it . . ."

"Do you think she would want to live, if she could?"

"Do I—? Would—?" Deliann turned, wide-eyed, gasping with sudden hope. "Are you *asking* me?"

"Those who still live need not die of this poison," the goddess said. "Can you bear the burden of having called them back?"

"I—*yes!* Yes, anything—*anything*—"

"This is not a fairy tale, Kris," the goddess said severely. "I do not take you at your word, when you do not know what you are saying. Any who survive this poison will be infected still. I cannot cure them directly."

"You—you can't? Why not?"

"HRVP is not, exactly, alive. My powers of healing are great, but they are no different in kind than any other: I can only spur the body's natural processes. HRVP is not a natural disease; it is a *genengineered bioweapon*—" She used, astonishingly, the English words. "—and the body's natural resistance system is no defense. To spur the body's processes would bring only a swifter death."

"But I—"

The goddess lifted a restraining hand. "The *vaccine* you received as a child is another *genengineered virus*." She continued to sprinkle English into her Westerling. "This is how I will stop the infection, in the end: I will create a *countervirus* that will block the *receptor sites* to which HRVP binds. If your friends are exposed to it soon enough, it may save their sanity and their lives."

"May?"

The goddess nodded. "They will have a chance, but only that. You might call them back from this gentle death to an unbearable one."

"How . . . how long? How long before—"

"I believe I will have the *countervirus* prepared within four days."

"So they would have a chance. That's a chance I can take," Deliann said, rising. "So? What's the catch?"

The goddess shook her head sadly. "This is the catch, Kris." She gestured toward the bodies. "Two of these four have yet enough strength to be saved; if I strengthen their hearts, and speed the work of their livers to break down the poison, it will wash from them before it can kill them."

"Two?" Deliann said. "Only two?"

She nodded. "That man—" Pischu, on the bed. "—had a weak heart. He is already dead. And this treetopper—"

Tup . . . Oh, Kierendal, how will you stand it?

"—her metabolism was too fast; she died only a moment after she drank. So, Kris Hansen: your friend may not thank you for calling her back from death. Can you help her live with what she has done?"

Deliann looked down at Kierendal.

If I'm wrong, there's plenty of poison left. Once she understands what's going on, she can make her own choice.

He nodded: to the goddess, and to himself. "Yes," he said. "Yes, I can."

"Then it is done," the goddess said.

That simply: without a gesture, without even the faintest flicker of the light around them. Kierendal's shallow hitching breath deepened toward the slow rhythm of sleep.

Now he found that he had recovered the strength to cry.

"My father . . ." he murmured painfully. "My family—

Mithondion ... When you have the countervirus—all of Mithondion will be infected by now ..."

"Mithondion is beyond my reach," the goddess said. "My power is that of the river—beyond the bound of my watershed, I am blind and deaf, and largely powerless. If they are to be saved, the cure must be carried to them, even as was the disease."

"How did you—I mean, when did—" *Torronell,* his heart whispered, breaking. *If she had come two weeks ago, even a week*... "I mean, where have you been?" His heart cried his real question: *Why did you wait so long?*

"I was on Earth," she said simply. "As you named me, I am also the *Aktir* Queen. You called, and I came."

"I . . . *called?* You mean, with J'Than? The *Aktir*?"

Her luminous, liquid eyes gazed deeply into his. "Hari Michaelson asked to be remembered to you," she said.

She stepped sideways, and reality warped around her: in the barest blink of an eye, perspective distorted so that it seemed she had moved half a mile away while still remaining within the room; with another step, she was gone.

Deliann stood rooted to the carpet, shaken, gasping.

Hari . . . *Michaelson?*

At his feet Kierendal stirred, whimpering; Deliann instantly knelt beside her and cradled her head on his knees. "Shh," he whispered. "Shh. It's all right. I'm here. It's all right."

And for a time, he believed he might be telling the truth.

THERE WAS, IN those days, a man who had been a god. Though a god no longer, he still saw with a more than mortal eye, shaped with a more than mortal hand, and thought with a more than mortal mind. He saw the war made by the dark angel, and he saw the acolytes of dust and ashes, but he did not see the god who lay behind them both. To save his onetime children from this war, he shaped himself a new destiny.

But he was a god no longer; even his more than mortal mind could not guess the limits of his vision, his strength, and his wisdom. Thus did he open the tale of his own destruction.

Others had brought war against the god of dust and ashes, many others, more than can be counted on worlds beyond number. Among its enemies on this world had been Jereth Godslaughterer, Panchasell the Luckless, and Kiel Burchardt. Among its enemies on the other had been Friedrich Nietzsche, John Brown, and Crazy Horse.

Each had fallen to its patient, infinite hunger. It had killed them in its sleep.

On the day the dark angel went forth to war, the man who had been a god took counsel with the acolytes of dust and ashes—

And persuaded them to wake it up.

SEVEN

TAN'ELKOTH SAT ALONE in the stony gloom of the Curioseum. Motionless, his eyes glittered in the flickering glow from the mirror that served him as a deskscreen. His fingers were steepled before his impassive face. The ground floor of his apartment had no windows; though it was late afternoon outside the Curioseum, black shadows crowded close around him. He was consumed with the task of waiting.

He had been waiting for this moment for nearly seven years.

The mirror on his desk glowed with a special edition of *Adventure Update*. Tan'elKoth had watched the recording that Clearlake played for a worldwide audience. With his usual canny political touch for self-preservation, Clearlake had seamlessly edited the recording to eliminate every suggestion that the Studio itself might be somehow responsible for the outbreak, thus protecting himself from any charge of corporate slander; other than that, the recording ran uncensored, and unrelievedly gruesome. Tan'elKoth stabbed the cutoff. He'd seen enough.

"One supposes the Bog has, as well," he murmured.

He composed himself to wait.

Seconds ticked by more swiftly than the beating of his heart.

He waited.

Then he waited longer.

And longer.

Still no chime from his annunciator.

Those fractal tree branch world-paths replayed within his mind. No new flowering, no unexpected crook or twist presented itself: this sprouting future was precisely as it had been, in the moment he laid his will upon it.

But still they did not call.

That he had miscalculated was impossible. Even an idiot could now see how easily they had been outmaneuvered; even an idiot could now see that they had only one choice. Even the stupidest fish can feel the hook when it's lodged in its throat.

He thrust himself to his feet and prowled the limits of his cage. He paced up the broad curve of stairs that led through the light trap to his personal quarters, humming distractedly to himself. The voices of the men within him murmured that there was something he'd overlooked.

He climbed the final flight, up to his studio. The skylight showed only the low bloodlit gloom of night clouds over the city. This was where he'd spent most of the past six years—now nearly seven—molding in clay and casting in bronze the interior shapes of his private reality.

It had been a brutal, bitter, soul-searing struggle, teaching his hands to bring forth the shapes within his heart; every time a casting cooled unevenly and cracked, every time he scraped thin grey curls of clay from beneath his fingernails, every time he so much as touched a knife or a trowel, he was forced to confront memories of being Ma'elKoth, of constructing His Great Work: memories of ordering reality with nothing more than the power of his mind. Memories of how far he had fallen—

And yet, working with his hands had taught him things that working only with his mind could never have: had taught him that materials are not infinitely malleable, nor should they be— that to overwork a piece is to destroy it. Materials have shapes of their own. True art is a negotiation, a struggle, even a dance, between the will of the artist and the intrinsic form—the physical properties of strength and balance, the fundamental *possibility*— that defines his chosen medium.

He passed a study for his most famous sculpture, *The Passion of Lovers. Passion* was not his best work; it was merely the most accessible to the limited tastes of his audience. Cast in monumental bronze, two men stand tangled in an intimate embrace, their forms stylized, abstracted into the essence of their desire for each other until they flow together and join as one. One holds a sword that pierces the other through the groin, its blade emerging from that one's back; the sword-pierced figure holds smaller blades in each hand, one seeking his lover's heart, the other buried in the top of his lover's skull.

Obvious. Even trite.

He turned aside from *Passion* and pulled the shroud from his current work, his *David*. He had finally allowed himself to at-

tempt a full figure in marble, a material far more exacting than
bronze. Larger than life-size, to the same scale as Michelangelo's, the half-completed sculpture rested on a large reinforced
dolly with swivel-mounted wheels—locked now—so that he
could at need shift the tons of stone to examine it in differing angles of sunlight.

The figure had begun to emerge from its prison of creamy
stone. Tan'elKoth surveyed it critically, walking around it,
sighing; he struggled to live through his eyes, to forget his tension, his frustration. Even to pick up a chisel in his current emotional turmoil would be an invitation to disaster. He was not
unmindful of what historians termed Michelangelo's *Struggle*
series—each tortured and twisted figure abandoned after a
single flawed stroke.

Tan'elKoth's *David* would be greater than Buonarroti's; instead of the perfection of masculine beauty sought by the Earth
artist, Tan'elKoth had taken for his model an older, more sea-
soned man, a man on the descending curve of his life—a man
whose face and form would show in every line the soul-crushing
burden of being the Beloved of God, and yet would also show
pride, tempered strength, unbendable will. One would see the
beauty of the youth he had been, and see that the scars etched by
time's acid had made him more beautiful still.

But now, as he examined the emerging figure, he could see
that it would develop not precisely as he had envisioned it.
Already the gestural line of its stance had diverged from his intention, as though its form was becoming a vector of two conver-
gent images. *As though there is already at work here a will that
is not my own.*

Tan'elKoth's eyes went wide and round, and he lost a moment
in sheer marvel. Somewhere, somewhere within this revelation
was the fault line that had shifted beneath his certainty—

He had always been a composite entity. Any memories of
having but a single mind had been relegated to the ghost-forms
that peopled his inner world. From the moment of Ma'elKoth's
self-creation in a flare of power from the crown of Dal'kannith,
he had been the master of a choir of interior voices. Through the
years that choir had swelled to a symphony, of which he was the
conductor: many voices, many minds, many lives, but a single
organizing will.

He was Ma'elKoth no longer; his latest act of self-creation

had reduced the god he had once been to merely the greatest of the shades in his internal Tartarus. Despite the self-deprecation of his new name, Tan'elKoth knew that he was more than even Ma'elKoth had been: more human, more connected to the currents of time and flesh that rule the lives of mortals. And a better artist—which may, in the end, have been the most important difference.

Art had always been his ruling passion.

Hannto the Scythe had been an obsessive collector from his earliest years; he had in truth become a necromancer in service to this obsession. The skill of necromancy consists primarily in coaxing forth the remnants of the patterns that consciousness imprints upon the Shells of corpses—capturing the fading echoes of the mind that had once been expressed by the meat. A skilled necromancer can temporarily tune his own mind, his own Shell, closely enough to these residual vibrations that he can access the occasional tatter of the memories they represent.

Many artists conceal works that they do not feel are up to their personal standards; many of these works may be lost forever if the artist leaves behind no record. Hannto had used his power to summon forth memories from the very bones of the great, and eventually his personal collection had swelled with uncataloged works by major artists. He could provide no provenance for any of them, and thus could never receive the full value of a painting or sculpture in a sale, but what mattered that?

He had never intended to sell them.

Hannto had his own feelings about art. Art was not merely the creation of beauty, for him; neither was it merely a reflection of reality. It was not even the depiction of truth.

Art was the *creation* of truth.

It is a truism that when one is a hammer, everything looks like a nail. The glory of art is that it can show this proverbial hammer how everything looks to a screwdriver—and to a plowshare, and to an earthenware pot. If reality is the sum of our perceptions, to acquire more varying points of view is to acquire, *literally,* more reality.

Hannto had wanted to own the universe.

The precise point where he had passed from collector to creator was a mystery. Perhaps truly passionate collectors are always *artistes manqués*: perhaps they choose to buy what they have not the gifts to create. Perhaps touching the minds of all those countless artists had molded him in some way; perhaps seeing the world through the dream-eyes of artists had given him, over time, some vision of his own.

Tan'elKoth was more than the sum of his experiences; he was the grand total of the sums that were the men who lived within his mind. For fifteen years and more he had lived by his absolute control of these self-created shades. What will could possibly have touched this sculpture, other than his own? What will could have altered the curve of his *David*'s stance, could have angled the line of his *David*'s jaw down toward resignation and defeat? What will could possibly drive his mallet to his chisel without his consent—without even his *awareness*?

Faintly, distantly, muffled in the depths of his apartment below, the annunciator on his deskscreen chimed.

2

TAN'ELKOTH FAIRLY FLEW down both flights of stairs into the darkness of the ground floor; he skidded to a halt in front of the desk, then spent a bare moment to order the lights on and straighten his clothing.

The Adventures Unlimited logo flashed in the message box of his screen.

With ponderous dignity, he lowered himself into his chair. "Iris: Acknowledge," he murmured. "Audiovisual."

"Professional Tan'elKoth. You are instructed to remain at your current screen. Hold for voice communication from the Adventures Unlimited Board of Governors."

The screen wiped to the Adventures Unlimited logo: the armored knight upon the winged horse, rampant.

"Professional Tan'elKoth." A subtle change in the voice: where before it had been purely mechanical, now it had the faintest hint of self-awareness, the consciousness of power.

There came next from the speakers deep in the floor beneath his desk a recording of Tan'elKoth's own voice. *"Tell your Board of Governors this: in exchange for certain considerations, I shall undertake to solve their Michaelson problem."*

Tan'elKoth smiled.

The voice of the Board of Governors said, *"What considerations?"*

So: no preamble, no throat-clearing. Clean and direct without a wasted word. Tan'elKoth nodded to himself. He could do business with men such as these. "An alliance, gentlefolk. Return me to my land. Leave the Empire and my people to me; you may use the rest of my world as you desire. Within the Imperial bound, your interests will be better served by the power of Ma'elKoth than by the weak minds and wills of your Earth-bred satraps. We have a common goal, do we not? To ensure the future of humanity, both here and on my world."

"And in exchange?"

Tan'elKoth shrugged. "As I said: I shall undertake to solve your Michaelson problem."

"Our Michaelson problem is hardly worth such a price."

He snorted. "Come, gentlefolk. This protest is fatuous; were the problem in question so insignificant, we would not be having this conversation."

"Michaelson is no one. We created him. He is exactly what we made him: nothing. A cripple, wholly owned by the Studio."

Tan'elKoth let a smile creep into his voice. "And yet, within a handful of hours, this wholly owned cripple has ripped your plans asunder and cast their shreds to the winds of the Abyss."

"You are overdramatizing. This is no more than a public-relations gaffe."

"You," Tan'elKoth replied with clinical exactitude, "are *fools.*"

Only silence greeted this pronouncement; apparently, the Board of Governors was unused to hearing the truth. "Caine is *against* you, now," Tan'elKoth said. "Without my help, you are lost."

"You fear Michaelson so much?"

"Bah." How do men of vision so limited come to wield power so vast? "I fear Michaelson not at all. Michaelson is a *fiction,* you fools. The truth of him is Caine. You do not comprehend the distinction; and so he will destroy you."

"We are gratified by your concern for our welfare."

"I care nothing for your welfare," he said through his teeth. "I want my Empire back."

"This seems a steep price for so small a service: to crush a powerless cripple."

"Doubly fools," Tan'elKoth said. They were repeating themselves; redundancy is the hallmark of muddy thinking. "He does

have power. *One* power: the power to devote himself absolutely
to a single goal, to be ruthless with himself and all else in its pursuit. It is the only power he needs—because, unlike the great
mass of men, he is aware of this power, and he is willing, even
happy, to use it."

Tan'elKoth leaned back in his chair and steepled his fingers
before his face; he had been a professor for enough years that he
fell into his lecture mode without thinking. "Men like Caine—
and, if I may say so, myself—exert a certain pressure upon history; when we set ourselves a goal and extend our energies to
achieve it, the force of history itself organizes into a current at
our backs. You might call it destiny, though that is an inadequate
word for a power of this magnitude. On Overworld, one can even
see it: a dark stream in the Flow that organizes the interplay
of historical necessities—the interplay which the ignorant call
chance."

*"Then we need do nothing at all; he is one, we are . . . several;
if what you say is true, we can think him to death."*

Tan'elKoth clenched his jaw. Could they possibly guess how
this sophistic jabber wore on his nerves? "Will without action is
mere daydreaming; it is as useless as the blind spastic twitching
that is action without will—which, I might add, accurately sums
up your efforts so far."

He leaned toward the screen and lowered his voice as though
sharing a friendly confidence. "You are helpless before him. He
demonstrates this even as we speak. You would have stopped that
broadcast if you could; I know that your machines monitor the
net, and intercept even private messages that might so much as
hint at what that recording explicitly spells out. How, then, did
you come to fail? Do you think that recording reached a worldwide audience by *chance*?"

"Coincidence. A meaningless blip of probability."

Tan'elKoth forebore to point out that *coincidence* is only another name for *bad luck*: the eternal excuse of the loser. "You
may scoff at the power of Caine," he said, "but there is one
whose power demands your respect: one who can stop you with
a mere gesture. I speak, of course, of Pallas Ril."

*"Pallas Ril—Shanna Michaelson—is merely a woman, while
here on Earth. She can be easily dealt with."*

"Mmm, true," Tan'elKoth said slowly. "And you could have

done so, had you not awakened Caine. Pray, tell me now: Where is this *mere woman* at this moment, as we speak?"

"She is appearing at a convention in Los Angeles."

"Is she? Are you certain?"

"What are you saying?" For the first time, Tan'elKoth thought he might even be able to detect a hint of expression in the digitized voice—and the emotion thus expressed warmed him inside. *"She is on Overworld? Impossible. Her next shift isn't until September twenty-first."*

In answer, Tan'elKoth gave them only a tiny smug smile.

"She must be found. She must be stopped."

"And how, precisely, will you do this? She is already beyond your reach; there, she is a goddess, and as near to omnipotent as any living creature has ever been, including myself. You have been completely outfought," Tan'elKoth said. "Caine is too fast for you; your corporate groupthink is slow and innately predictable. But your difficulty is by no means insoluble."

"What solution do you propose?"

He straightened again, and let a gleam of his passion flash into his eye. "You must submit yourselves to a single organizing will—give over the direction of your campaign to one lightning mind. To put it bluntly: Your only hope is to call upon me."

"Why you?"

"I am, false modesty aside, Earth's leading expert on Caine and Pallas Ril. I have in my library every cube either of them has ever recorded; the primary use of my ammod harness is to allow me to leave the Curioseum long enough to review their Adventures. I daresay I know more about their abilities—and their psychologies—than they do themselves."

"Knowledge is meaningless without power."

Tan'elKoth sat silently for a long moment, staring fixedly at the mirror as though some message could be read between the reflected pixels. Finally he said, "Indeed."

He shifted his weight and allowed some of the fire in his heart to reach his eyes. "To amend my previous statement: Pallas Ril is beyond your reach—but not yet beyond mine. I can stop her for you, gentlefolk. Give me the opportunity, and I shall."

"At what price?"

"Her I would kill for free; I despise her. Breaking Caine, however—that will be expensive. Caine's innate ruthlessness makes him extremely dangerous. In his limited fashion, he is frighteningly resourceful, and an exceptionally flexible thinker. In any situation that he can frame in terms of combat, he will not lose."

"A substantial claim."

"Is it? Let me provide a salutory example: one that is—I think pardonably—still fresh in my heart. Once, not so long ago, he set his will upon the life of Pallas Ril. Though a living god stood against him on one side—" He modestly placed his palm against his chest, then opened it toward the screen. "—and the most powerful bureaucracy this world has ever known stood against him on the other, he—one single, solitary man—overcame us both."

"There were special circumstances—"

"Puffery. Mere details. When saving the life he willed to save required that he defeat *in single combat* the greatest warrior of his time, he did so. Forget that this man was Caine's master in every form of battle; forget that Berne, even unarmed, could have killed him in his sleep without breaking the rhythm of his snoring. Remember that Berne wielded a weapon that was *legendary*: Kosall, the unstoppable blade. Remember that Berne was Gifted with Strength far beyond human, and defenses that could make his skin impervious as steel. Remember that when Caine faced him he was bruised, and battered, half crippled—and *poisoned*—and still . . ." Tan'elKoth let his voice trail away significantly.

"Luck."

"Luck." Tan'elKoth spat the word with vehemence surprising even to himself. "*Luck* is a word the ignorant use to define their ignorance. They are blind to the patterns of force that drive the universe, and they name their blindness *science*, or *clearheadedness*, or *pragmatism*; when they stumble into walls or fall off cliffs, they name their clumsiness *luck*."

"We can settle for removing Pallas Ril; perhaps a median price can be negotiated."

Tan'elKoth snorted. "Clearly, you surmise that killing her will save you and your plans—but the truth is precisely opposite. I stand before you as a testament to this. You wish to interfere with Pallas Ril? Destroy Caine *first*."

"And again, why do we need you for this?"

Surely even men as dense as these should see a simple truth, when it is painted before their eyes. "Because," he said patiently, "there is no one else who truly understands *what Caine is*. Without me, you will learn, but too late. He himself will teach you—but it is knowledge you will carry to your graves. You will die cursing your own foolishness, should you reject my offer. Hmp. You wish to understand the fate of those who set themselves against Caine? Ask Arturo Kollberg."

"Arturo Kollberg?" There came a long, long considering pause—far too long in response to a rhetorical question.

"The perfect choice," his interlocutor said. *"We will."*

3

ARTURO KOLLBERG CLUTCHED the melamine surface of his work space, sweat trickling from the scars that pitted the remains of his hairline. His skin had gone to paper these past years: age-yellowed pulp, dry and crumpled over the bones of his face. Only his spoiled-liver lips retained their rubbery thickness, and the teeth around which they tightened were traced with carious brown.

I am dreaming, he thought. *This can only be a dream.*

A shining disk blinked in the mailbox corner of his screen. Within the disk, an armored knight rode a winged horse, rampant. A message from the Studio.

This must be a dream.

But it didn't seem like a dream. The cubicles here—in Patient Processing—were crystal clear, and bitterly familiar. The moaning of patients in the examining rooms came thinly through the walls, and someone sobbed with endless psychotic monotony in the lobby. A pair of enormous houseflies, grown fat and clumsy on a diet of blood, buzzed lazily across the fluorescent bands of ceiling lights.

He risked a glance to either side, after first checking that his supervisor wouldn't catch him looking away from his work. At their adjoining cubicles, the clerks beside him hunched over their keyboards, ticking frantically away. Here in the Mission District Labor Clinic, the data entrars were paid by piecework: one-tenth of a mark for each completed form. They stared with manic fixity at their screens, and the room reeked with their acid, frightened sweat.

His years in the Temp ghetto had sucked the meat from his dead-stick arms and twisted his once-nimble fingers into arthritic claws; he barely recognized the hand that he moved to shift the cursor into his mailbox, because for this single, long, achingly sweet moment, he remembered what he had once been.

What he had once been—

He remembered sitting in Corporate Court, watching the evidence mount against him, watching the parade of Actors and technicians, Social Police and rival Administrators as they each came to throw their handful of earth into his living grave. He remembered watching Ma'elKoth testify against him; he remembered the imperious disdain, the impenetrable dignity, the thundering moral righteousness of the ex-Emperor's denunciation.

During those endless hours of humiliation, Kollberg had been able to do nothing save sit at the defense table, numb and hopeless. He'd known full well he would be destroyed: the Studio— the power that could have saved him, that could have stood by his side, could have rewarded his devotion and selfless service— had turned against him. To save itself, it had savaged him. Raped him. Gutted his life. It had stripped away everything that gave his existence meaning, and had cast him into the gutters of a Temp slum.

He keyed the icon, and a dialog box unfolded in the center of his screen.

LABORER ARTURO KOLLBERG: YOU ARE INSTRUCTED TO REMAIN AT YOUR CURRENT SCREEN. HOLD FOR COMMUNICATION FROM THE ADVENTURES UNLIMITED BOARD OF GOVERNORS.

Kollberg could no longer breathe.

They remember. They've come for me, after all these years. A progress bar flicked into existence in the center of his deskscreen, filling slowly from left to right as something large downloaded from the net. *They've come for me at last.*

Six years—nearly seven—on the Temp boards. Six *years*.

Six years of standing in line at a public access terminal, begging for work, lucky to get four or five days a month; six years of standing in line at slop kitchens, to act grateful as his bowl was filled with his daily share of the befouled swill that he must choke down quickly or gag on the taste of rot; six years of being shoved and jostled and pawed by people who *stank*, whose breaths reeked of cheap liquor and tooth decay, whose clothes had the barnyard odor of days-old sweat and imperfectly wiped assholes; six years of hot-bunking at a Temp flophouse, time-sharing a single bed in eight-hour shifts with two other Laborers, sleeping on sheets damp with their polluted sweat and the stains of their diseased bodily fluids.

Kollberg's ragged fingernails *scritch*ed across his work space, and his lips curled into knots against his teeth.

The progress bar was nearly full.

If this is a dream, Kollberg decided, *it will end when the progress bar fills. That's how I'll know.*

Soon—too soon, bitterly soon—he would be jerked or slapped awake, to find himself in his tiny cubicle at the Labor Clinic, facing his flickering, blurred deskscreen. He'd have to look at one of the Labor trash who were his coworkers and shrug apologetically, would have to smile sheepishly and mumble something about insomnia last night. Or, worse yet, he might wake up to find his office manager leaning over him, that stuck-up Artisan bitch with the plastic tits, the cracks in her face spackled with the makeup she troweled on every morning. That vicious cunt would dock his pay an hour for sleeping, even if he'd only nodded off ten minutes ago.

For this was his life.

After five years of enduring the soul-killing humiliation of the Temp boards, Kollberg had found a job, a real job. It paid less per hour than Temping, but it was steady; over the course of the sixty hours he spent each week inside his cubicle entering patients' data into the Labor Clinic's main core, he made enough to rent himself a room at an SRO only three blocks from the clinic, to rent a netscreen, and even to buy private food three or four times a week. He was, in the brutally limited way only another Temp would really understand, making something of himself.

But now, he somehow knew, he was entering a new world: a world of dream, where all his hopes and his childhood imaginings might still come to pass.

He remembered getting stiffly out of his bed, throwing the bedclothes on the floor, dressing leadenly in yesterday's shirt and pants. No shower: freshwater showers at the SRO cost three marks for ten minutes, and he could only afford two each week. Salt water was cheaper, but it came untreated straight from the Bay; it made him itch and stink worse than he would if he didn't bother to wash at all. He'd used a cream depilatory to smooth his stubbled cheeks, and only then had he realized he'd overslept by half an hour. He'd raced to the clinic without breakfast, and had been able to slide into his cubicle and log on with a full minute to spare; this had allowed him the luxury of answering the Artisan cunt's fisheye with a slightly smug smile.

"Arthur," she'd begun sternly.

Kollberg had hunched over his keyboard, drawing breath for his automatic correction, but he saw the lift of her eyebrow and the compression at one corner of her mouth that said she was waiting for his correction, *hoping* he would remind her that his name was Arturo, purely so that she could call him *Arthur* again: another demonstration of how easily she could trample on whatever little dignity he thought to retain. He'd refused to give her the satisfaction. Instead, he had closed his eyes for a moment, gathered his composure, and said politely, "Yes, Artisan?"

"Arthur," she repeated heavily, "I *know* you're aware that Clinic policy requires data entrars to be on the premises fifteen minutes before log-on. Don't think that you'll be able to sneak away for coffee or to use the bathroom before your 0930 break. You should have arrived early enough to take care of that before you sat down."

"Yes, Artisan."

"I'll be watching you."

His cheeks flamed; he could feel the sneaking stares of the other clerks even through the cubicle walls; he could picture them paused, holding breath, leaning slightly, fingers silently poised above keypads, heads cocked as they listened raptly to his humiliation. "Yes, Artisan."

Kollberg suffered in the ringing silence.

Finally, the Artisan cunt had swept her eyes around at the other clerks, and the muffled thuttering of keystrokes had begun to spread throughout the terminal suite, and he had been able to breathe again. It was at that point, Kollberg decided, that he must have fallen asleep; up to then, it had been a perfectly unexceptional day.

The progress bar filled, and vanished.

For an instant the screen flashed pure white, as though its crystals were breaking down. The flash *hurt*—hurt his face, his temples, hurt his ears, hurt like it had reached inside his skull and squeezed his eyeballs together.

Kollberg gasped, for from the pain blossomed a vision, unfolding as though it downloaded directly into his brain: he saw himself recast as an Administrator, returned to the arms of the Studio in triumph, carried through the iron gates on the shoulders of cheering undercastes.

Flash—

Not only recast, but *up*cast: *Businessman* Kollberg, at the podium in One World Center in New York, accepting the Studio Presidency from Westfield Turner.

Flash—

Leisureman Kollberg, retiring from the Studio to his private island in the Ionian Sea, to finish his alloted span in a life of sybaritic comfort and satyric pleasures unimaginable to the undercastes . . .

And that was when he knew. This was more than a vision: it was an *offer*.

And it was a test.

He had been seven years in the desert, and now he was being offered dominion over all the kingdoms of the Earth. There was more here than any burst-feed from the net into his brain. This was an offer of power unimaginable: the power of a god.

He muttered, through teeth clenched hard enough to make his gums bleed, *"Get thee behind me, Satan."*

Where the progress bar had vanished, in the middle of his screen, now stood a menu box with two radio buttons:

○ SERVICE ○ SELF

Kollberg set his jaw and straightened his spine. With pride in himself and in his calling, with pure, unshakable determination, he moved the cursor to SERVICE, and hit RETURN.

His annunciator chimed, and the menu box disappeared. His screen wiped to brilliant, eye-piercing white that cast black shadows behind him and fogged his vision as though he stared into the sun.

His breath caught and his stomach twisted: something huge and foul forced its way into his mouth, into his throat—tears swam in his eyes, and his face burned with agony as the light charred his flesh. But still, somehow, through the blinding light and the unbearable pain, he could read one last message, written in stark black upon the blazing white.

THOU ART MY OWN SON, WHOM I LOVE.
WITH THEE I AM WELL PLEASED.

Then it entered him with power: into his eyes, down his throat, in through his nose, his ears, ripping open his rectum and jamming up the length of his shriveled penis, forcing into him with howling lust; it filled him to bursting, swelling him from within, stretching him thinner and thinner like a weather balloon expanding toward destruction, while it dissolved and digested his guts, his heart, lungs and bones, everything within the stretching membrane of his skin. His eyeballs expanded, threatening to burst from his face, to explode from the pressure that built within them.

He screamed in pain as he squeezed his eyelids shut, trying to keep his eyes in their sockets by sheer strength—and as though that sudden shriek had broken the spell, the pain vanished without even the faintest twinge to mark its passing.

He opened his eyes again. Everyone was staring at him, leaning out of their carrels or peering meekly over the dividers, showing nothing but greasy hair and curious eyes. The Artisan cunt looked distinctly alarmed.

"Arthur," she said severely. "I hope there is some explanation for this . . . for this *breach* of *discipline*. If you're ill, you should have reported to the Physician before your scheduled log-on. If not . . ." She let the sentence trail off into unspecified threat.

His screen was dark. It gave back a faint reflection of his face, and he could see that nothing of this ordeal had marked him: he looked exactly the same as he had one minute before. But now he felt suspended, floating at equilibrium, airy and filled with light. He understood now: yes, he was dreaming.

This *was* a dream, all of it.

It would always be a dream.

He would never have to wake up.

"Marie . . . ?" He murmured languidly. *Marie* was the Artisan cunt's name. "I think I'm going to fuck you."

One side of her mouth spasmed down toward her hard jaw as though she'd suffered a paralytic stroke. She backed away from him, making guttural *uhm, mm, erm* noises deep in her throat; then she said something unspecific about a breakdown, and something else about calling a Physician.

Kollberg slid the tip of his tongue in a slow meaty circuit

around his slack lips. He became aware, looking at her, that she and he were not truly distinct individuals; that, in fact, he was a more potent expression of an energy that they both shared. She was a leaf, but he was the tree . . . No, that wasn't right. The concept continued to organize itself within him—or, perhaps, he around it. More like: she was a building, and he was the city.

She was human, and he was humanity.

He saw where she fit into him, and he into her, and now he could feel the lives of the Laborers around him: their cool firefly sparkles fed his landscape of light. He knew them thoroughly, inside and out, their petty hungers and their pale lusts, their tiny pathetic hopes and their private niggard fears. The wave front of his expanding consciousness outrippled with geometric acceleration, swelling the more with each mind that he swallowed: through the building, through the block, reaching out into the city. Here and there he tasted lives that were familiar: the fetid swamps of the useless on the streets of the District; the ugly fantasies of his SRO roommate, masturbating at a public urinal; the smug self-righteous timidity of his onetime secretary Gayle Keller; the blank wirehead dedication of Studio techs and the delicious devotion of Worker secmen.

And perhaps this wasn't a dream, after all; perhaps the life of Arturo Kollberg had been a dream, from his childhood disgraced by the miscegenation of his mixed-caste parents, through his spectacular rise to the Studio Chairmanship and his still-more-spectacular fall.

Perhaps he was only now waking up.

He touched the scattered sparks that were the individual lives of the Board of Governors. He gifted them all with a small portion of his gratitude and gave them each the interior warmth and satisfaction of seeing a well-done job come to its fruition. They, in turn, gladly gave up the devotion that he required of them. His loyal priesthood had brought him forth in the body; he loved them for it, and they him.

With echoes of power ringing in his head, Kollberg wondered what he should do now—and the answer was obvious.

Whatever I want.

Joined with that vast sea of human minds, the choice of service and self vanished: there could be no difference between them. His gaze fell once more upon Marie, and sharpened its focus, and he offered his carious teeth to her in a shit-colored smile.

"You stay right there," she ordered, pale as milk. "Take one step out of your cubicle, and I'll call the Social Police."

"No need," Kollberg said, drawing out the word into a drawl of happy lust. "They're already here."

The office door slammed open as though kicked, and Social Police flooded the room, a riot platoon in full combat gear: twenty-five mirror-masked officers in ballistic armor, power rifles slanted across their chests, shock batons dangling from their belts. Everyone but Kollberg froze in place at their desks; in a sudden accession to their ancestral herd instincts, the data clerks understood that to move was to set oneself out from the crowd. To set oneself out from the crowd was to be marked.

They knew: the Artisan supervisor, she had been marked.

Kollberg moved to the center of the room, seeing his own face reflected in every single one of the mirror masks. Those reflections smiled upon him, and he upon them. The nearest officer inclined his head, just a trifle. "At your will," his digitized voice confirmed flatly.

"Seal the room," Kollberg murmured. Then a better idea floated up from the hollow core of what had once been his brain. "No—seal the *building*."

The officer crossed his arms to tap out orders on his suit's forearm keypads.

Kollberg turned, his movement graceful and effortless, a weightless ballet. He met the eyes of the Artisan cunt, and his penis stiffened so suddenly that his breath came thick and hot. His testicles burned. "Her," he said, pointing.

She made a gagging noise, deep in her throat, and turned as though to bolt toward the inner offices. Two soapies sprang after her and tackled her to the floor. She moaned, and cried, and begged. Kollberg stepped over and stood above the three of them.

"Her clothes."

One of the officers held her pinned, grinding her face into the filthy polyester shag of the carpet, while the other unfolded a pocket knife and sliced away her clothes. Her flesh was pale and slack, pockets of fat bulging across her ass, down the sides of her thighs. Kollberg opened the fly of his dungarees, and his penis sprang out. "Turn her over. She has to kiss me when I come."

The officers rolled her onto her back, and one of them forced her legs apart. Her breasts spread huge and limp along her ribs, her nipples like used condoms pointing toward her elbows. *Hmp,* Kollberg thought. *Not plastic, after all.* He lowered himself between her knees.

He had to spit on her crotch for lubrication.

His penis slid into her, and he humped her thoughtfullly, dispassionately, regarding her anguished sobbing struggle with a detached interest as she thrashed under him, held by the relentless grip of the Social Police. Fucking her was interesting, in an abstract sort of way; because they were one, he was also fucking himself—and he was watching himself fuck her through the eyes of his stunned coworkers. Like masturbating while looking in a mirror.

This, he felt, was the ideal way to get up in the morning.

"And, you know what?" he said. "I woke up hungry."

He lowered his head and sank his teeth into her breast. Her flesh was tough, stringy and old, and she struggled harder and screamed more, but after a bit of work he managed to tear a chunk free. He chewed it slowly, interested in its delicate flavor and rubbery texture, but in the end it meant no more to him than if he'd bitten off a hangnail. He licked her blood from his lips, nodded to himself, smiled, then bent his head for another bite.

3

THE LIVE SPECIAL report of *Adventure Update* gleamed and flickered in the mirror on Tan'elKoth's desk. Jed Clearlake had caught up with Hari Michaelson at a convention in Los Angeles and was now conducting a live interview from the convention floor—giving Michaelson a worldwide audience to make his case about the "HRVP crisis on Overworld"—while in the background hundreds of bizarrely dressed fans capered and cavorted for the video pickups.

Though the spectrum of costumes reflected admiration for hundreds of Actors active, retired, and dead, the majority of those picked out by the cameras advertised Caine's continuing popularity. Dozens were costumed as Caine himself, many as Pallas Ril, some as Berne or Purthin Khlaylock or the Khulan g'Thar; some few—generally poorly groomed and enormously fat—had costumed themselves as Ma'elKoth.

Tan'elKoth gave only a fraction of his attention to the report; mostly, he studied his visitors.

Arturo Kollberg sat at the ex-Emperor's side, staring at the screen with monomaniac fixity; his rubbery piscine mouth hung open, and he made half-audible panting noises like a tomcat in rut. He had arrived in the company of a four-man enforcement squad of the Social Police. The four officers boxed Kollberg and Tan'elKoth, standing at riot-ready around them, hands on shock batons and power pistols. The mirrored face shields of their helmets glinted with the reflections of the *Adventure Update* report, and with pinpoint distortions of Kollberg's and Tan'elKoth's screen-lit faces.

So far, Tan'elKoth had been unable to determine if they were Kollberg's jailers, or his bodyguards.

The call from the Board of Governors had come only minutes before Kollberg's arrival. *You are acquainted with Laborer Arturo Kollberg. Laborer Kollberg has our full confidence in this matter. Treat with him as you would with us.*

He knew that dangerous forces interacted here below his level of perception, like predatory sharks jockeying for position around a sinking boat. The Social Police officers did not defer to Kollberg, nor did they seem to direct him; in fact, Kollberg had spoken only to Tan'elKoth since their arrival, and the soapies had remained facelessly silent. He also couldn't guess if any of them realized that their powered weapons were perfectly useless in the Curioseum's ON field; without its nerve-tangling discharge, a shock baton was no more lethal than a whiffle bat.

As Tan'elKoth studied them, he flicked his vision into mindview now and again; this he could do as effortlessly as an ordinary man blinks. When he did so quickly enough, cycling back and forth with ordinary vision, he could sometimes catch glimpses of some strange energy that surrounded all five of them. Not their Shells—they didn't even seem to *have* Shells in the ordinary sense—but rather a strange colorless distortion. This odd energy or distortion would vanish as soon as he fixed his gaze upon it; he saw it only as fleeting twists of reality in his peripheral vision.

Kollberg had changed beyond recognition in the six years since his trial. Had Tan'elKoth not been told to expect him, he would have had no idea who this thin, somnolent, ill-looking man might be. Their arrival had brought with it a smell: blood and more than blood, thick and meaty and sweetly rank: the fermenting shit of a carnivore. In the near darkness of the apartment it was difficult to tell, but Tan'elKoth thought the bloody stench might emanate from Kollberg himself—what remained of the man's hair seemed to be caked with something, and his face bore either some kind of birthmark or a smear of filth.

"The ultimate goal of your masters has never been a mystery to me," Tan'elKoth said by way of a preamble. "It was instantly clear that this release of HRVP was a ploy to increase the Earth presence on Overworld."

"Was it?" Kollberg said tonelessly. His voice was thick and meaty, inhuman, as though the choking stench that cloaked him had itself somehow spoken aloud. "Clear?"

"Of course. That's why you target the elves: They're *cute*. Cute creatures dying horrible deaths are ideal tools to mobilize public opinion. Once a few thousand elves die, the entire Leisure caste will clamor for a massive relief effort; the staunchest rock-ribbed Hands Off advocates on the Leisure Congress will be the first to insist that hundreds of thousands of your people should be shipped to Overworld to combat the disease. Within days, weeks at most, your people are fully in place across the entire continent. It is easy enough to invent excuses to remain, once there—and suddenly, Earth is no longer restricted to a tiny mining colony in the mountains. Suddenly there is cropland, forests for timber, uncontaminated fisheries, billions of tons of coal, crude oil, and *space*—simple space, to relieve the pressure of fourteen billion lives on Earth. This is how I know that HRVP is merely a dodge; in fact, I anticipate that your epidemic will mysteriously blow itself out, not long after your relief effort reaches its peak. It's clear that your Bog must have some method for controlling the infection—uncontrolled, it would destroy too many profitable ecosystems. The Board of Governors would not damage something as valuable as the Studio System, did they not anticipate decades and centuries of ever-increasing returns."

"You're very perceptive," Kollberg murmured.

"I am Tan'elKoth." *And yet*—a niggling worm of doubt slithered through the back of his mind—*he did not say I was correct.*

"What do you propose?"

"An alliance. As I told your masters," Tan'elKoth said, "we have a common goal. Humanity has been locked in a struggle against extinction on my world for a thousand years; we vie with elves, dwarfs, krr'x, and ogrilloi for living space; we struggle against dragons in the mountains and leviathans at sea. In the midst of all this, we continue to war upon each other, giving aid to our enemies. With the power of Earth, we could overwhelm our enemies and ensure our survival—ha, I would not even need your technology: send me ten percent of your Labor caste and I could drown our foes with sheer number."

"So," Kollberg said flatly. "It's clear what we can do for you. Make me understand what you have to offer us."

That worm of doubt began to wriggle through the gates of Tan'elKoth's mind, as though Hannto were trying to gain his attention; there was something about the way Kollberg spoke, something eerily familiar about his affectless voice and academic diction. Tan'elKoth stepped on that worm and ground it beneath his mental heel; he had no leisure for second thoughts.

He spread his hands. "In my role as the rightful ruler of Ankhana—*who is also a citizen of Earth*—I can petition the Leisure Congress for the aid of the Overworld Company. I can invite you into the Empire. I can ensure that your *bleeding hearts*, as you call them, support your occupation, instead of oppose it."

"You may perhaps be useful, after all."

"I am more than useful. I am necessary. Without me, your plans cannot even be initiated." Tan'elKoth gestured to the mirror that flickered upon his desktop. "Have you forgotten Caine?"

Michaelson was saying, *"Of course, that recording was never intended for public release. We didn't want a panic. I've directed Studio Security to open an investigation into the source of the leak. There's been a lot of outcry already, but it's important for your viewers to understand that—thanks to an immediate, aggressive response by the Studio itself—the crisis is already under control."*

"And what was the Studio's response, Administrator?"

"Well, I guess I can take some of the credit for that myself. When you're married to a goddess—" He gave a brief, self-deprecating, professionally charming chuckle. *"—a lot of problems just aren't as impossible as they might look."*

Kollberg grunted wordlessly at the screen.

"Do you understand yet how thoroughly your masters have been outfought?" Tan'elKoth asked. "You cannot even *retaliate*;

not only is he once again a public hero, he is surrounded by thousands of his most devoted admirers—anything that happens to him will be witnessed by all Earth. By the time this convention has ended, it will be too late. Pallas Ril will have utterly destroyed your plan."

Kollberg only grunted again. His shoulders flexed, and his hands worked back and forth across the front of his pants. Tan'elKoth noted with swift distaste that the man had an erection—and he was *rubbing* it through his dungarees.

Clearlake continued to lob Michaelson his lines with cleancut good nature. *"Did you ever consider that this might have been nothing but a hoax?"*

"Sure. Sitting here, on Earth, we can't possibly know the truth. It could be a hoax—or it could be a catastrophe. *Sending Pallas to Overworld is a measured response—if this is a hoax, it hasn't cost anybody much. If this is a real crisis, she can handle it. Speaking strictly for myself, I believe that elf was telling the truth. Look at him. Listen to his voice. You'll believe him, too. You know my philosophy: hope for the best, but plan for the worst."*

"There's been some public speculation that this outbreak might not have been an accident," Clearlake said, *"that it was deliberately inflicted on Overworld by a terrorist group, or some kind of psychopathic personality within the Overworld Company, or even the Studio itself."*

"I'm inclined to doubt it," Michaelson said seriously, *"but the possibility must be investigated. I'm told the Overworld Company's Internal Security unit is already looking into this, but I believe that a situation as potentially grave as this one requires a response by the Studio itself. I've already spoken with Studio President Businessman Turner and offered my own services as a special envoy for a fact-finding mission to Transdeia. I've, ah, offered to go over on ammod. As you know, my thoughtmitter is still in place; on ammod, everything I see will be transmitted and recorded instantly on Earth. There'd be no possibility of mistake, or question of concealment—I'd be like a Registered Witness. The whole world would see how committed the Studio—and the Overworld Company—is to the welfare of the natives of Overworld."*

Clearlake had given one of his familiar suave, knowing chuckles. *"Ever the man of action, eh, Hari? Showing a little of that old Caine spirit?"*

"Well, Jed—" An answering chuckle. *"—sometimes a little of that old Caine spirit is exactly what we need."*

Another chuckle from Clearlake, this time less knowing, more openly appreciative. *"Well, I for one would certainly pay a mark or two to see Caine back on-line. How can the Studio resist?"*

Tan'elKoth allowed himself a grim smile.

Michaelson went on, *"And an investigation should be opened here on Earth, as well. We need to know how this happened. We need to make sure it can never happen again."*

"Do you see?" Tan'elKoth said to Kollberg. "Do you see the avalanche as it descends upon you?"

Kollberg nodded. "He must be stopped."

"You must understand that you cannot simply kill him. Not now. His energies have already been directed against you and your masters; his sudden death—even by accident or 'natural causes'—will result in an explosively destructive release of those energies."

Kollberg's head swiveled as though mounted on gimbals, and his gaze met Tan'elKoth's with the blank incuriosity of a lizard's. "Expand on this."

Tan'elKoth compressed his lips. "Consider only the most obvious, surface level of the effect: Anything that happens to Michaelson will be taken by Caine's admirers as hard evidence of a sinister conspiracy—and there are many admirers of Caine sitting on the Leisure Congress itself. The best you could hope for would be a public investigation into the practices of the Studio and the Overworld Company. You would bring about precisely the events that you hope to avert."

"I do not see how this is related to Michaelson's so-called *energies*."

"I am not responsible for the limitations of your vision," Tan'elKoth said sourly. "Those energies have little to do with Michaelson. They are Caine's. It is not Michaelson who is beloved by a billion fans and more. And even that love is the merest iceberg tip—but how can you comprehend the enormity that lies below the surface, when you are blind to the decimus in plain view?"

"What solution do you propose?"

That worm of doubt wriggled beneath Tan'elKoth's mental heel, and suddenly grew into an icy serpent: he realized why

Kollberg's manner was so eerily familiar. He spoke exactly like a meat-and-bone version of the Board of Governors.

A premonition of disaster rose up in his throat like vomit.

"The key to the successful solution of your Michaelson problem is analysis," he said briskly, to cover his momentary lapse. "Reduce the problem to its components, so that the necessities involved in successful resolution become clear. The Michaelson problem breaks down neatly into two components: dealing with Pallas Ril, and dealing with Caine. Dealing with Caine also breaks down into two components: the public and the personal.

"The public side of the Caine component is his popularity: the attention—and even love—he commands worldwide. This is more susceptible to resolution than it may at first appear; one must simply be conscious of what it is, after all, that Caine's fans love. It is *not* Caine himself, despite what they may claim, and even believe. What they value so highly is the *myth* of Caine: the drama and adventure he has brought into their dull workaday lives. Thus: the necessary resolution of the public component must have a certain high drama—a sort of poetic thunder that will satisfy his fans."

Kollberg said flatly, "They won't mind that he dies, so long as he dies well."

"Precisely. It must have every necessary element of a Caine tale: villains and heroes, a struggle against hopeless odds, and an apocalyptic denouement."

"This can be done?"

Tan'elKoth met his blank gaze without hesitation. "It can. Most of these elements are already in place; success is only a matter of the proper orchestration. It requires, if I may extend the metaphor, the proper conductor."

"This being you."

"This being me." He nodded to himself; he liked the way this was going, now—despite Tan'elKoth's misgivings, Kollberg seemed eminently pragmatic and accessible to reason. "Caine's public energies are not the only energies at his command. The private component deals with his will itself—one might call it his rapier, by contrast with the more public bludgeon."

Tan'elKoth rose restlessly and began to pace: a tiger prowling the limits of a cage marked by the silent, motionless Social Police officers. "The successful resolution of the private component—blunting, as it were, Caine's rapier—involves diverting him, scattering his energies, overwhelming him with multiple problems until he cannot focus on any single one. It is insufficient to defeat him objectively—we must beat him *subjectively*. We must demonstrate to him beyond any shadow of dispute that he is helpless. We must teach him to think of himself as a defeated man."

A hint of a smile began to twitch the corners of Kollberg's thick, dead-meat lips. "You want to break him before you kill him."

Tan'elKoth halted his pacing and met Kollberg's empty eyes. "Yes."

"Is this a true necessity? Or is this revenge?"

"Does it matter?" Tan'elKoth shrugged. "In this case, the concatenation of necessity and pleasure is fortuitous—which is to say: yes, we must do this . . . and yes, I shall enjoy it."

The liver-colored tip of Kollberg's tongue circled his lips. "I approve," he said.

Tan'elKoth gave him a slim smile. "Now, we turn to the Pallas Ril component. This breaks down neatly into another pair, as well: the mystic and the physical. The physical difficulties are obvious, I think. Pallas Ril is a creature of nearly unlimited power, able to sense—and theoretically to affect—every living thing in the entire Great Chambaygen watershed; she can act at nearly any distance. She can stride the length of the Empire in a single hour; even granting the ability to defeat her, she cannot even be *located* unless she wishes to be found."

"You make her sound invincible."

"No one is invincible," Tan'elKoth said darkly, "as I have learned to my eternal shame. It is a matter of selecting the proper weapon."

Kollberg's eyes were flat and dull as chips of slate. "Go on."

"The mystic component is still more parlous. To simply slay her is not enough; she has imposed her will upon Chambaraya to the extent that the death of her body would do far more harm than good, insofar as the success of your plans is concerned."

His great hands knotted behind his back, but his tone remained dry, precise, clinical: the clipped delivery of the professional lecturer. "Consciousness is a patterning of energy; infused with the power of Chambaraya, her consciousness cannot be overcome by a merely physical death. Will is expressed through a body, and is to some extent limited by the body that expresses it. To merely destroy Pallas Ril's body would release her consciousness—and that consciousness could pattern the river itself, the entire Great Chambaygen watershed, as its body. We would have made of our enemy a god in truth, instead of a part-time Actress playing with unearned power."

He turned and regarded Kollberg with a trace of a smile. "On the other hand, she is the only part of Chambaraya that cares a whit whether the races of Overworld live or die. To Chambaraya, life is life: the maggots that would feed upon their corpses are every bit as precious as elves and dwarfs and even human beings slain by your disease. So the solution is obvious: we must *separate her from the river*. In this fashion—*only* in this fashion—can the Pallas Ril component be successfully resolved."

Kollberg's reptilian gaze never wavered. "How will this be accomplished?"

"Not by me personally, you may be assured," Tan'elKoth said. "She would become aware of me with my first breath of Home air, and would be on her guard. No more must Caine be aware that my hand is against him—to give him a clear vision of his enemy is to hand him victory."

Tan'elKoth allowed his smile to sharpen to a razor edge. "The components have been analyzed; the true measure of success shall be the elegance of their solution. We have regarded them individually. We must resolve them simultaneously."

"You say you can do this," Kollberg murmured tonelessly.

"I can."

"Then do it."

Tan'elKoth leaned comfortably back in his chair, taking a deep, slow, easeful breath. He glanced at the four distorted reflections of his face in the mirror masks of the Social Police, then let his gaze slide back to Kollberg.

"First—as Caine would say—let's talk deal."

4

VINSON GARRETTE, VICEROY of Transdeia, leaned forward onto the table, holding his cut-crystal wineglass before his eyes, examining the way the rich cabernet shaded to rusty earth tones at the intersection of wine and glass. "*What if* we—the Artan rulers—as a gesture of good faith," he said slowly, meditatively, "to cement our . . . *relationship* . . . with the Monasteries, were to give you something that you want? Hypothetically. Something of small value to us, but substantial value to the Monasteries. To you *personally*, Your Excellency."

Raithe folded his skeletal hands and stared past his own wineglass, untouched on the table. "What—hypothetically—would we be talking about, Your Highness?"

"What would it be worth to you, for example—" Garrette leaned back into his ornately carved chair at the head of the table. "—to get your hands on Caine?"

Raithe sat motionless as a lizard for a very long time; he did not even blink.

Then he reached out and grasped his wineglass, and raised it slowly to his lips.

5

As His Radiance Toa-Sytell, Patriarch of the Ankhanan Empire, stared at the image of Ambassador Raithe in his Mirror, he wondered if the young Ambassador had any idea how much the Empire was already learning of the inner secrets of the Monasteries.

In only a month, the Artan Mirror had revolutionized communication in the Empire. Now there were at least one or two Artan Mirrors in every major city and not a few of the minor ones; each major military outpost had its own. Only three days ago, a young thaumaturge in the service of the Eyes of God had reported that he had discovered a way to eavesdrop on Mirrored conversations without the knowledge of the speakers at either end.

Toa-Sytell used his free hand to mop faint beads of sweat from his upper lip; he'd been feeling a bit under the weather for a day or two, and now it seemed he might be developing a fever. His discomfort made it difficult to fix his attention on the young Ambassador's words.

"*—as you know,*" the Ambassador was saying, "*the Council of Brothers supports fully the Empire and the elKothan Church. The gesture we are prepared to make, we offer without any expectation of return.*"

Toa-Sytell flicked a glance at the Eye Mirror-speaker, whose hand he held. The Eye nodded, indicating that the Ambassador was telling the truth as he knew it. This was another of the innovations from the Eyes of God researchers: the Eye would have heard the untruth of any lie. "All very heartwarming," the Patriarch responded with his characteristic dry irony, "but I was told this is some sort of emergency?"

"What is urgent, Your Holiness, is our need for reassurance that our gift will be put to its proper use."

"And that use would be?"

"It is a gift for the Festival of the Assumption, Your Holiness. A very, very special gift, to honor the Empire, and the Church."

Again, the Mirror-speaker nodded.

"Yes, yes," Toà-Sytell said testily. "Go on; what is it?"

"What, if you had the power," Raithe said with a secretive smile, as though he already knew the answer, *"would you do with Caine?"*

Toa-Sytell jumped, and his eyes took fire. "Caine . . ."

"Caine was never officially sentenced for his murder of the late Ambassador Creele. He is, insofar as the Monasteries are concerned, a free man, innocent of any crime," Raithe said. *"However, I believe his status with the Empire is rather different."*

Toa-Sytell barely heard the words; he found himself on his feet, trembling, crushing the Mirror-speaker's hand until the poor man blanched. "You can give me *Caine*?"

Within his head roared the flames of a Festival auto-da-fé; in his nostrils the scent of Caine's burning flesh; in his ears the cheers of Beloved Children around the world; around his heart coiled the old, cold serpent that whispered sweet revenge.

Raithe smiled. *"If I can?"*

"I swear—*We* swear, I and God Himself—" Toa-Sytell said, forcing the words from his breathless chest, "you will not be disappointed."

6

THE FACE OF the woman on the screen was attractive, even without makeup, even puffy with interrupted sleep, even though past seventy without ever indulging in the vanity of cosmetic surgery. A long straight nose, planar cheeks, strong jaw, eyes the crystal blue of a Nordic winter sky; her hair was cut to a uniform half inch, a skullcap the color of steel. Only her mouth marred her classic beauty: it was a thin, lipless gash like a hatchet wound in her face.

Tan'elKoth allowed himself to study her. His video was refused; on her end, she glared with sleepy antagonism into a blank screen. Past her shoulder he could see a wrought-iron bedstead, and he could glimpse the curve of a young man's back half buried in tangled bedcovers at her side.

Tan'elKoth glanced up at the Social Police; they stood in an arc behind him. Kollberg pressed close to his side, his breath bloody and rank.

"I don't know who you are or how you got this code," Businessman Avery Shanks said, her voice thick and clumsy, the way it always was when she was unexpectedly awakened—the sedatives she'd been using intermittently for forty years always left her a bit dazed. *"You should know I have no tolerance for pranks. SynTech security is tracing this call."*

There it was: that tone of generalized threat he remembered so well. He let the sound of her voice call forth Lamorak.

Overpowering love swelled within his captured memory, leaving him breathless; one enormous hand came up to touch the unfamiliar curve of his face, as he remembered being smaller, blond and graceful, a master swordsman—and smaller yet, coming in tears with scraped elbows and knees to this woman's hard, unforgiving lap. She had never been comfortable—but she had always been protective, and vengeful as a dragon.

Her hand came up, reaching for the cutoff, and Tan'elKoth whispered, *"Mother . . . ?"*

Her hand froze, suspended weightless in midreach, and her face went utterly blank.

"Mother?" Tan'elKoth said softly, gently, lovingly, in Lamorak's voice. "Mother, it's me. Don't you know me?"

The hard, cold lines of her face crumbled like a glacier breaking up into the sea. *"Karl . . . ?"* she whispered, sounding suddenly sixty years younger. *"Karl, is that you . . . ? Am I dreaming?"*

"Mother, I need you. Please. Help me."

Astonishment glistened in the corners of her ice-blue eyes. *"Help you? Karl . . . oh Karl, oh my god, Karl . . ."*

A single keystroke uploaded the file from Tan'elKoth's personal datacore: a digigraph of a snapshot he'd downloaded from the Studio security-video archives, when he'd been considering using Faith as a model for a sculpture he'd been planning. He'd never done the sculpture—but he'd also never erased the digigraph. The frame-in-frame showed him a small version of what Avery would be seeing on her screen right now: a beautiful golden-haired child with a sunny smile and pale blue eyes.

"Do you know who this is, Mother? It's Faith Michaelson."

"Michaelson?" Avery's face iced over, and her voice congealed. "The *Michaelson? That's his daughter?"*

"No, Mother," Tan'elKoth whispered. "That's Pallas Ril's daughter."

Her eyes widened.

Tan'elKoth said, "That's *my* daughter."

"Your . . . Karl, what—?"

"Mother, please," he whispered, letting his voice fade. "Please help me . . ."

"Karl—"

He stroked the cutoff.

He looked up. Lit by the cool glow of the blank screen, Kollberg leered at him, wiping something from his chin with the back of his hand.

Tan'elKoth said, "It has begun."

AND THERE CAME a day when the god of dust and ashes raised up its hammer against the dark angel.

The hammer was lifted piecemeal, and each piece was a person, and to each person the god of dust and ashes whispered: *This do for me, and receive in payment your fondest desire.*

Each person, each piece said *yes*, and in so saying became the hammer of the blind god.

EIGHT

A PERFECTLY ANONYMOUS digitized voice cut through the dully roaring babble on the convention floor.

"Administrator Michaelson."

Hari looked up from the autograph book he was signing and saw his own face, fisheye distorted and reflected four times over in the mirror masks of a Social Police enforcement squad.

He couldn't breathe.

That instant stripped away Caine's success and fame; stripped away the thousands of fans who crowded around him in this immense overheated room; stripped the power of the Administrator caste and the status of the Studio Chairmanship; stripped every part of him that lay over his most fundamental baseline. The baseline of his soul was Labor.

Every Laborer knows that trouble with Soapy is the last trouble you ever have.

"Administrator Hari Khapur Michaelson. You are under arrest."

The crowd of fans drew back, muttering to each other and exchanging awed glances. He couldn't even tell which one of the soapies had spoken.

The exhibition hall flattened around him, ironing the stalls and the booths and every fan into painted images of themselves, as two-dimensional as cheap cover art; only the soapies still had solidity. The rumble of voices and music and the blare of PA announcements all settled into an insectile buzz that sounded like he had a housefly trapped inside his skull.

He coughed once, harshly. He wanted to ask *On what charge?* but the words stuck in his throat like a chunk of half-chewed meat. He stood nervelessly, unresisting, as one of the soapies turned him and bound his wrists behind his back with plastic stripcuffs. Two held his arms; another kept a shock baton at the ready.

The last of them extended a palmpad. *"Where is this child?"*

The screen of the palmpad showed a bright, cheerful image that he recognized: it was a souvenir photo, a couple of years old, from a visit to the Studio Curioseum. "Faith?" he said stupidly. "She's right over—"

He shut his mouth and clenched his teeth till his ears rang.

He had met with his fans right next to the KidZone, the huge complex of intertwined climbing tubes and game pods that dominated an entire corner of the exhibition hall. The KidZone swarmed with children; supervised by a double handful of Artisan au pairs, it was the place where offspring were deposited so their parents could visit the convention unencumbered. Faith was in a Leisure Call pod with a dozen or so other kids—Faith was the Caller, and half of them were already out, having either failed to follow an order or taken an order that wasn't preceded by "Leisure Calls." Two more were counted out even as Hari glanced up there. No surprise; Faith was lethal at Leisure Call.

What stopped Hari's mouth was a tall, slim woman with an iron-grey crewcut and a jaw like a fire axe. She stood at the chest-high fence surrounding the KidZone, her teeth bared in what might, on a human, have looked like a smile. She scanned the children inside with eyes cold as security cameras. She wore full Business dress, and four bodyguards with SynTech logos on their shirts kept the crowd from pressing too close to her.

Avery Shanks.

The soapy shoved the palmpad at him again. *"Where is this child?"*

Hari said through his teeth, "Ask my fucking lawyer."

But even as he spoke, Shanks lifted her hand and pointed right at Faith up high in the game pod, and three of the SynTech guards moved through the gate of the KidZone.

"Shanks," Hari snarled. The ice that had lodged in his chest became instant flame. *"Shanks!* Leave her alone! *You leave her the fuck alone!"*

He lunged for her, but the soapies yanked his arms back painfully. The one with the shock baton moved its business end closer to his ribs, and he made himself stop; if he didn't, Faith would see the soapies beat him—maybe beat him to death. He couldn't do that to her.

At his shout, Shanks turned and gave him a good view of her shark-toothed grin. She came over, her bodyguard a muscle-bound shadow at her shoulder. "Hello, Hari," she said in a soft mockery of cheer. "Enjoying the convention?"

"If you touch my daughter, Shanks, I swear to you—"

The false cheer vanished instantly, revealing furious black triumph inside her gem-blue eyes. "She's *not* your daughter," Shanks spat. "That's exactly the *point.*"

Hari went numb. He couldn't feel his legs—either his bypass had shut down, or he was about to faint; he couldn't tell which.

"You see, I *can* touch her," Shanks said. "It's you that can't. A simple DNA test will show she's a Shanks. She's *Business.* You understand what that means, Michaelson? Do you?"

Hari couldn't answer; he couldn't draw breath enough to speak.

"She's too young to give consent. That means *every single time you have ever touched her*, you have committed Forcible Contact Upcaste." She bared her teeth, savage as a panther. "If I'd known about this six years ago, I could have had you broken and sent to a social camp for so much as changing her *diaper.*"

He found his legs worked, after all. He lunged at her. But the soapies held him tight and the shock baton triggered against his ribs. They were almost gentle with him; instead of throwing him twitching to the floor, the charge from the baton only shot fire up his spine and made him sag. "Good, good," Shanks said. "Try again. I will enjoy watching these officers kill you."

"You can't hope this'll stand up," Hari said desperately. "I'm married to her mother—her mother can give consent—"

She looked at the soapies. "You heard."

"We heard."

"You've just established foreknowledge, Michaelson. You knew she's a Shanks. You've always known it. I'll see you under the yoke for this."

"My wife—"

"Yes, where is your wife? Is she available to testify?"

"She's on Overworld," Hari ground out between his teeth. "You *know* she's on Overworld. That's why you're pulling this shit now."

"Mind your tone, Michaelson. Unless you liked that tap from the shock baton?"

"Where did you get the image?" There was only one copy of that shot: it was framed on his office desk at the Abbey. "Who gave you that picture?"

Shanks' eyes went distant and soft, and for a moment she did not speak. "It was sent to my message dump . . . ah, *anonymously,*" she said finally. "Yes, anonymously."

Hari was coldly calculating whether he could yank free and get his teeth into her throat before the soapies could pull him down when he heard Faith say, "Daddy? What's going on? Where's Gramma?"

One of the SynTech bodyguards led her by the hand. She looked up at the Social Police with wide eyes that slowly filled with puzzlement and hurt. "He said Gramma was here," Faith said, a little petulantly. *Gramma,* to Faith, was Mara Leighton, Shanna's mother. She looked up at the bodyguard who held her hand. "You shouldn't lie to a kid, Art'san. That's really, really bad."

Avery Shanks turned, six full feet of regal calm. "He didn't lie, child. I am your grandmother."

And seeing them together—the shape of their faces, even the way they both stood, looking at each other—even to Hari, the family resemblance was unmistakable. It went through him like another shot from the baton.

Faith frowned, and bit her lip. "Mommy's really upset." She

looked up into Hari's eyes and said gravely, "She's coming home. She's really, really, really upset."

For one slack second, Hari was grateful—*Oh, thank god, she'll straighten this shit out in a second*—but then he realized what was at stake. He realized what would be lost if Pallas Ril left Overworld with her job unfinished. She would never get the chance to go back.

"No," he said. "No, Faith, *no*—she can't come home. Tell her I can handle it. *I can handle it.* Tell her to stay and finish her work. Stay there until I send for her."

Faith shook her head. "She's really upset." She turned and looked up into Shanks' cold blue eyes. "Mommy thinks you're a bad person."

Shanks pursed her bloodless lips. "What kind of sick fantasy have you spawned in this child's head?" She met his gaze for a full second of undisguised loathing, then nodded to the body-guard. "Take her to the car."

"Faith—Faith, don't be afraid," Hari said. "I'll make it right—no matter what it takes, I'll make things come out right. I promise."

"Make things come out right?" Shanks said. "They already have."

"Shanks," Hari said, just above a whisper. "Shanks, don't do this."

"*Businessman* Shanks."

Cords in his neck winched Hari's head down. "Businessman Shanks."

She smiled. "And that is how you will address this child, should you ever see her again." She waved to the SynTech goons. "Go on."

"Daddy?" Faith's puzzlement turned to flat-out fear as the bodyguard picked her up. "Daddy, make him put me *down*!"

"Businessman . . ." Hari ground out, *"Please."*

"Much *better*, Michaelson," Shanks said delightedly. "Let's have it again, a little louder. I want all your fans to hear you beg."

"Daddy, *please—Daddy!*"

The soapies parted the crowd, and the goon carried her toward the door. Shanks said, "Don't be shy, Michaelson. At least you have the *chance* to beg—which is more than you gave Karl."

The words forced their way out through his locked jaw. "You

will suffer for this, you hatchet-faced cunt. You hear me? You got no fucking clue how deep this shitpool is. I will fucking *drown* you in it—"

"A threat?" Shanks interrupted, smiling. "Am I dreaming? Did you actually just threaten a Businessman in front of an entire Social Police enforcement squad?"

Faith began to struggle, but the bodyguard only held her tighter as he walked away. "Daddy, ow! He's hurting me! Daddy! Daddy, *help!*"

Hari threw himself blindly against the grip of the soapies. For one instant their hands loosened and he thought he might pull free, but the one with the shock baton gave him a shot right over his heart, and this time it wasn't gentle at all. Hari collapsed to the floor, twitching spastically. Faith didn't call to him anymore; now she just screamed like her world was ending.

Shanks knelt beside Hari's head, and he had never thought a human voice could carry so much hatred. "Every night for seven years, Hari Michaelson, I have cried myself to sleep. I've worn out three different cubes of *For Love of Pallas Ril*; I have watched you murder my son two thousand times. I want to quote you, now."

She leaned down as though to kiss him; her lips brushed his ear as she whispered, *"Did you really think I'd let you live?"*

2

AVERY SHANKS FELT warm all over; she felt a satisfaction that another sort of woman would have called sexual. A kind of benignity rose within her as she looked down upon the lovely blond hair of Karl's daughter. If she wasn't careful, she might begin to smile.

Faith sat calmly and quietly beside Avery in the passenger cabin of her Cadillac limousine. Her initial fussing about being separated from Michaelson had stilled almost immediately upon liftoff; Avery had looked upon this display of self-control so extraordinary in a child of six and thought that blood will tell, after all. This girl was unquestionably a Shanks.

"I will call you Faith," Avery instructed her, "and you shall call me *Grandmaman*. We are going to Boston together, where you shall live in a proper home, with proper servants, and shall attend a school proper to a young Businessman. Do you understand?"

Faith's eyes met hers, huge but level and unafraid. "Yes, Grandmaman."

She'd even captured the nasal whine of the antiquated French pronunciation. This child was so astonishingly *apt*—but she maintained her regal sternness with the ease of a lifetime's habit. It would not do to show any sign of warmth or weakness.

"You," she said, "are very well behaved."

"Thank you, Grandmaman."

Avery turned away to the window, muttering her surprise that a downcaste thug like Michaelson had managed to rear an even half-civilized child.

An interval passed in silence.

"Grandmaman?"

"Yes?"

"What is a *hatchet-faced cunt*?"

Avery's left eyelid drooped as though she'd bitten into an impossibly sour pastille, and for one long moment her mouth clamped shut like a locked ledger—but then her thin, almost invisible lips bent into something close to a smile. "I suppose: *I* am," she said. "Give me your hand."

Faith dutifully offered her hand, and Avery took it. "That is not a proper word for young ladies of the Business caste," she said, and gave the back of the child's hand a brisk, stinging slap with two of her fingers, producing a sharp *smack* and a glitter of shocked moisture in Faith's eyes.

Faith bit her lip and took one deep, shuddering breath that threatened tears, but that was all. After a moment, she said, "You shouldn't hit me."

"It is also improper for a young lady of the Business caste to lecture her Grandmaman on propriety."

"You better not hit me again," Faith told her seriously. "Mommy wants me to behave while I'm with you. She told me to always mind you until Daddy comes for me. I'm s'posed to do whatever you say. But if you hurt me, she'll hurt you worse."

So. Here it was: the first clear evidence of the possibly irreparable harm done to this child by her degraded upbringing. Avery allowed a sigh to trickle from her long, straight nose, and nodded to herself. "First," Avery said precisely, "the man you call *Daddy* is not your father; he is—if he has any legal standing whatsoever, which is questionable—your *step*father."

"I *know* that," Faith said dismissively. "Did you think that was a secret? I know all about that."

"Do you?" That sour taste was back in her mouth; she had been entertaining fantasies of instructing this child on her true parentage, and on Michaelson's murder of her real father.

"Course. Mommy doesn't do *secrets* with me. She *can't*."

"Well. In any case, the man you call Daddy will not be coming for you," Avery continued. "In fact, you will never see him again, except in court, and perhaps on the net. Do not expect him, and you will not be disappointed. Your mother engaged in criminal conspiracy with that man to deny you your birthright. Thus, her wishes and intentions are irrelevant; she has surrendered her parental rights. Do you understand this? They wanted to *hurt* you. They do not love you."

Faith's only response was a patient silent stare.

Avery sighed again. "I understand how cruel these truths must seem, but truth is *usually* painful, Faith. Understanding this is the first part of growing up."

"You're the one that doesn't understand," Faith said serenely. "Mommy's with me right now. I can *feel* how much she loves me. And Daddy will come for me. If you do anything to hurt me, Daddy will hurt you worse than Mommy would. He's a *mean bastard*, that way."

She said this in a dry, childishly innocent way—clearly quoting her foul-mouthed stepfather without any real understanding of the words. "He will *fuck you up*."

Avery's eye got that sour-pastille droop again, and she went on. "Finally, threats of this nature are *declassé*. I know that you are . . . disadvantaged . . . by having been forced to live in a household with Actors, but be aware that in *real* life there is nothing that either of your parents can do to cause me the slightest discomfort. Insisting that your Grandmaman must beware of these undercaste creatures is indulging in *fantasy*—which is not only *declassé*, but dangerous, in a Businessman. You will never again repeat these ridiculous threats, nor will you make any mention of this pernicious fantasy that you have some—" Her mouth twisted distastefully. "—*mental connection* with your mother. You must put such childish notions behind you, and prepare to enter the full bright day of Business life. Do you understand, Faith?"

"Yes, Grandmaman."

"Good. Give me your hand."

Faith offered up her hand with such unhesitating readiness that Avery—impulsively, on the spot—decided to hold it, and give it a squeeze, rather than strike it.

Blood will tell, after all.

3

HARI SAT ON the edge of the expanded foam mattress, its ragged edge making the steel struts of the cot frame almost comfortable beneath the numb half-ache that always lurked inside his legs. He stared at the featureless white plastic of the opposite wall.

The Social Police had him in their jaws, and they were gonna chew him up good before they spat him out.

They had taken his clothes, his watch, his palmpad, his boots. They had given him a disposable cellophane dressing gown and stuck him in a cell. Every time he saw a soapy, he asked for a chance to call his lawyer. None of them ever responded. They spoke only to give him orders.

Every once in a while, an enforcement squad came by his cell and marched him out at baton-point. The first time was just a standard identity check by DNA sampling. The next time was a high-pressure wash from a cold-water hose, leaving him bruised and chilled till he couldn't stop shivering. The third time was a manual body-cavity search; gloved fingers forcing themselves into his mouth, his nose, his rectum. And through it all, the only face he ever saw was his own, distorted and leering in their silvered masks.

He'd begun to fantasize that he could detect some kind of expression in the masks, as though some unknown cue of body language—maybe the subliminal angle of a shoulder, or the turn of a head, or even just the slow pace of a gesture—was letting him see into them a little bit: was letting him *feel* something from them.

The specifics? He couldn't get there, and they never said anything to give him a clue, but he was sure they wanted something—

the feel he got from them was kind of like lust, almost. Or maybe hunger.

It was giving him the fucking creeps.

He kept seeing the look on Shanks' face as her goon had carried Faith off: that bleak triumph. Maybe there had been something there, too—she had wanted something from him, too, and he didn't know if she'd gotten it. Was taking Faith enough for her, or was she really going to try this bullshit legal maneuvering with the criminal Forcible Contact charges? No way to know where Shanks would stop. She seemed almost like one of Ma'elKoth's Outside Powers from the old days: like she wanted to feed on his pain.

Just get me out of this cell, he thought. She might be out of his reach, but Businessmen don't rule the world. One screencall to Marc Vilo—*Leisureman* Marc Vilo: his upcaste had been sponsored by the late Shermaya Dole five years ago—and Shanks would have some fucking pain of her own.

She probably wouldn't actually do anything to harm Faith. It was him she wanted to hurt. Taking Faith away from him was the worst damage she could do without breaking the law herself. People that high up the caste ladder don't have to break the law; they can use the law to break you.

We'll see who breaks who. We will goddamn well see.

But fantasies of beating Shanks to death quickly dissipated in the blank white plastic silence of his cell. Sitting hour after hour in that box of featureless petrochemical, he kept thinking about Kris Hansen, and what he'd said about the blind god.

Some of what he'd read came back to him, slowly, in little dribs and drabs over the slow-ticking minutes of his confinement. He was pretty sure that this blind god was something specific, a title in capital letters: the Blind God. He seemed to recall that Duncan's book referred to it as some kind of elvish cultural bogyman, like the Devil, sort of. The Blind God was supposed to be the most powerful god of humanity, but somehow kinda invisible; even though nobody knows about it, everybody does what it says anyway. You could only see it by looking at the things people do—

Like put on silver masks and shove their fingers up your ass, Hari found himself thinking.

Something about those masks—he couldn't quite pin it down, because he couldn't quite remember exactly what this Blind God thing was supposed to be all about—but whenever he thought about the Blind God, he found himself picturing the Social Police. And whenever he thought about the Social Police, he found himself picturing the Blind God. Like Soapy was the Blind God's face. And Soapy's face is a mirror.

He didn't want to think about that one too closely.

Eventually, his lawyer arrived. He'd never had to call him at all; Hari's arrest had been the lead story on the newsnets worldwide. His lawyer had been trying to get in to see him for hours, and the news he brought was not good.

Because of the caste-weighted rules of testimony in legal actions, Avery Shanks' affidavit that Faith was her granddaughter became presumptive evidence, unless Hari could establish otherwise. In addition to the Forcible Contact Upcaste charges against him, she had filed kidnapping charges that named Shanna as co-defendant. The court had already awarded her temporary custody of Faith until the case could be brought to trial.

And there was more bad news: Hari's bail was set at ten million marks.

"Ten . . . *million?*" Hari repeated, stunned.

His lawyer shrugged unhappily. "It's a punitive bail. Businessman Shanks knows you can't afford that much, so she's expecting you to pay a bondsman."

"Ten percent, straight out of pocket," Hari said grimly. "One million marks to get out of jail."

"It's the threat, Administrator. You threatened her in front of the Social Police; all four of them recorded it."

Hari nodded to himself. "All right. Do this for me: Make them let me use a screen. Or get my palmpad back. I need to make a call. Right now."

His lawyer shrugged. "I'll see what I can do."

Whatever the lawyer did, worked: within a few minutes, he'd been led out to a screen, allowed to dial a private priority code, and was on the line with his Patron, Leisureman Marc Vilo.

"Hari!" Vilo said, bluffly cheerful around the thick butt-end of a smoldering cigar. "What news, kid?"

Hari scowled. "I guess you haven't been watching the nets."

"No, I saw it. You've dug yourself a deep one." There was something disturbing in Vilo's expression: a kind of cold distance that had settled in around his eyes, a patient reserve as though he was hiding: waiting in ambush behind a screen of cigar smoke.

"Yeah," Hari said. "It's time to start digging back out."

"Sure, okay," Vilo said. "But what do you want *me* to do about it?"

"What do I *want*?" Hari said, incredulous. "I want you to step on her like a fucking cockroach. What do you *think* I want?"

"It's not that simple," Vilo said, frowning regretfully. "Her legal position sounds pretty strong. Y'know, I warned you years ago that concealing Faith's real identity was a bad idea—"

"The hell you did." What the fuck was going on, here?

"—I always said it'd come back and bite your ass someday."

"Bullshit," Hari said. "Marc, that's a load of shit—you never said a goddamn—"

"Hey," Vilo said warningly. "I know you're upset, but watch your mouth."

"What's wrong with you, Marc? Why are you doing this?"

"Sorry, kid. I just don't think there's much I can do."

"All right, fine, whatever," Hari said desperately. "I'll handle Shanks myself. How about my bail? Can you put up my bail?"

"I don't think so. As serious as these charges are? I don't think so."

"Marc—"

"I said *no*, kid." Vilo stuck his cigar back into his mouth. "Sorry."

"Yeah?" Hari said. Tendons stood out in his neck. "You don't *look* sorry."

Vilo frowned, squinting through the smoke.

That high insectile whine was back in Hari's ears, thickening toward thunder. "What did they give you, Marc?"

"What are you—"

"You've been my Patron for *thirty years*. How much did you get for me, Marc? What was my price?"

"I didn't want to hit you with this when you're already down, kid, but I'm not your Patron anymore," Vilo said coldly. "This afternoon I submitted an Order of Severance. We have no relationship, you and me."

"What did they give you? Money? Christ, Marc, you're richer than God already."

"Nobody gave me any money," Vilo said, waving his cigar impatiently. "I don't give a shit about money. I don't know what you're talking about."

"What was it then, stock? *Voting* stock."

For one second, Vilo didn't move. "That's it, isn't it?" Hari said grimly. "Let me guess: you sold me for goddamn voting stock in SynTech."

"That's ridiculous. What would I want with SynTech?"

"Yeah, you're right," Hari said slowly. "That's not real power. You'd go for the *real* power. Voting stock in the Overworld Company. In the *Studio*."

Vilo didn't say anything, but he didn't have to; Hari could read the truth in his eyes. The real enormity of what was happening to him roared within his head like a funnel cloud dipping toward his life. Numb, stunned, Hari said, "No, I got it: They gave you a seat on the Board. You're on the Board of fucking Governors."

"Hari, these paranoid fantasies—"

"I hope it's worth it, Marc. I hope you think it's worth it. I hope you *still* think it's worth it on the day when you and me, we meet somewhere dark and quiet. When I show you exactly what it is you just bought."

"Hari—"

Hari hit the cutoff, and the screen went dead.

Look on the bright side, he told himself. *Shit can't get much worse.*

4

HARI STEPPED OUT of the cab at the Abbey's front lawn. He moved away, to be out of the cab's backblast as it lifted off, and the unfamiliar weight of the Microsoft Mantrak bracelet around his ankle made him limp a little more than usual. The Mantrak was designed with similar circuitry to a palmpad: as long as he wore the bracelet, the Micronet satellites could track his position to within a meter anywhere on Earth. As the soapy had dispassionately explained to him when it was locked around his ankle, to deactivate or attempt to remove the Mantrak would automatically register a forfeit of his bail and make him liable to further charges of flight from justice. The cab lifted off in a stinging cloud of sand, and Hari stood for a moment, looking at his bail.

The Abbey loomed over him, a black hulk against the stars, every window dark except for the kitchen's.

By pledging every asset he had—all his savings, his investments, Faith's education fund, the cars, all his Caine memorabilia, the royalties from all of Caine's Adventures, and the Abbey itself—he had covered the ten million marks. Barely.

He looked up at his house—this house he had built twenty years ago, just after Caine had cracked the Top Ten. He remembered standing in this very spot and watching its timber skeleton rise from the knoll; real wood in the Abbey's walls had cost an extra million, but he'd never regretted it.

He remembered walking through its empty rooms, remembered the echoes its bare walls had reflected, remembered how it had seemed like a palace, a fairy-tale dream castle of happy endings. He remembered the satisfaction of registering its name with the San Francisco Entertainment Commission, so it would be listed on their star maps. He remembered the day Shanna moved in—and the day she moved out—and all the laughter, the sullen sulks, shouting matches, and sweaty sex in between.

He remembered coming home after *For Love of Pallas Ril*, before his bypass, floating across the threshold in his levichair, finding the moving company there to load all of Shanna's possessions back into the house once more. He remembered the day his father's sentence had been officially commuted, and Duncan had been released from the Mute Facility at the Buchanan Social Camp—the day his father came home to the home he'd never seen.

He remembered thinking that he'd finally found his happy ending.

He shook his head and walked toward the spill of yellow light across the side lawn. His stomach was a little shaky, and he felt unsteady in his balance, as though a mild temblor shifted the ground beneath his feet. *Psychosomatic,* he told himself, just a reaction to walking without Rover whirring at his heels. The Social Police couldn't be bothered to transport his wheelchair; it was still down in L.A. Funny—much as he'd always hated the goddamn thing, he really missed it right now.

It'd be nice to have something waiting to catch him as he fell.

Bradlee, Duncan's nurse, was waiting for him at the kitchen door. Before Hari could even get inside, Bradlee started yammering about the Social Police and SynTech security and how they'd barged in and taken all of Faith's clothes, and her toys, and impounded all the photoprints and vacation cubes, and rifled the office, and pulled all the books off the shelves and taken backups of all the memory cores and this and that and every other god-damn thing until Hari wanted to smack him one just to shut him up for half a second. When he finally stopped for breath, Hari said, "How's Dad?"

Bradlee blinked. "He's fine," he said reflexively. "Well, you know, not *fine*, but about usual—"

"How'd he take it? You kept him away from the soapies, didn't you? You didn't let him talk in front of them?"

"Please, Admin—uh, Hari," Bradlee said. "They searched his room, but I took away his digivoder until they left. I'm not a fool."

"Yeah, I know. That's why I hired you."

"I think he's still angry with me," Bradlee offered confidentially. "He really wanted to give the Social Police a piece of his mind."

"Yeah, no shit. And they would have taken it. All of it. His fucking body, too," Hari said grimly. "Thanks, Brad."

Bradlee accepted this with a nod, as if to say he'd only been doing his job. "Are you hungry? I've put Duncan on his drip, and I was about to have a snack; it's no trouble to make extra."

Hari shook his head. "Is he lucid?"

Bradlee shrugged noncommittally. "He's been in and out all day. The drip should help. You'll look in on him?"

Hari nodded.

"Good. He's a little shaken up." Bradlee coughed apologetically into his hand. "We both are."

"Yeah."

Duncan's room was just off the kitchen, small and dark like a cave, with the flickering screen on his traveling bed's armtable for a campfire. Hari stopped in the hall. Going into Duncan's room was never easy—that powerful back-of-the-throat scorch of antiseptic couldn't quite cover the fermenting shit in his relief bag, or the dark rot that seemed to ooze out of his pores.

The only light in Duncan's room was the screen's cold shifting glow. He lay in his traveling bed like a broken puppet, head lolling bonelessly, veins twisting across his hairless scalp. One arm lay limp on the rumpled sheet; the other was strapped along the armtable to keep his hand in the digivoder. The convertible bed was raised, and he was strapped into it to hold him up in roughly a sitting position. An IV bag hung from a rack over his head, its line plugged into the socket that had been surgically installed in the hollow of his collarbone. The only indication that he was alive was the slow roll of his eyeballs, back and forth like lopsided marbles.

Hari couldn't make himself go in. He couldn't make himself speak. What could he say? What could he tell his father that wouldn't come out of his mouth as a raw scream of pain?

Oh, Faith . . . Hari sagged against the wall and covered his eyes with his hand. Something rose in his throat that felt dangerously like a sob; at the last second he forced it to become a cough. *Ah, gods,* he thought helplessly. *How am I gonna live through this?*

In the same instant, he hated himself for a selfish bastard; here he was, whining about how much *he* hurt, while Faith was trapped by people who thought of her only as a weapon against him—

He gritted his teeth and clenched his burning eyes shut, determined that no tear should leak through to his face. *Shit, Faith's probably handling this better than I am,* he told himself. *She's not alone.* As long as Pallas Ril walked the fields of Overworld, Faith was never alone.

The mechanized voice from Duncan's digivoder croaked, *"Hari. You. All right?"*

Hari took a deep, shuddering breath and rubbed his eyes. Duncan's face had rolled toward him, and his glazed eyes held a hint of sanity. Funny how much more human Duncan's digivoder sounded, once he'd had a chance to compare it to the voices of the Social Police.

"Yeah, Dad, I'm okay," he said slowly. "I'm just kind of tired, that's all."

A thin line of drool trailed from Duncan's slack lips. The muscles in his strapped-down forearm rippled; the digivoder glove that enclosed his hand translated the nerve impulses into digitized speech. *"Tough. Day. Remember. Keep. Your head. Down. Inch. Toward daylight."*

Hari smiled with a sort of nostalgic melancholy; this was the best advice he'd ever gotten. "Yeah. You should make that a macro."

"I. Will. Come in. Sit. Talk."

Hari sighed. He wished he could confide in his father; wished he could tell him everything that seemed to be happening; wished he could ask him for advice more pointed and specific than *keep your head down and inch toward daylight*.

But Hari couldn't say what was on his mind. Those SynTech goons had probably seeded the entire fucking house with microrecorders, and even if they hadn't, there would be a lot of Social Police traffic through here in the next few weeks. And Duncan had nearly ended his life under a sedition sentence in the Mute Facility of the Buchanan Social Camp for one overpowering reason: he had never learned to shut up.

But there was something Hari had wanted to ask his father about, he reminded himself. It should be a safe enough subject.

"Yeah, y'know?" Hari said, forcing himself to walk into the room, breathing shallowly as though that might keep the stink of madness at bay. "Somebody was talking about the Blind God today—you know, that elvish bogyman? Didn't you write something about it, once? It's in *Tales*, isn't it?"

"Chapter. Twelve. Or thirteen. Why?"

"It's kinda hard to explain. It stuck with me, that's all. I couldn't stop thinking about it."

Duncan's gaze twisted out of focus, and his mouth twitched spastically, releasing another foamy wad of drool. Hari pulled a tissue from the nightstand box and gently mopped his father's chin. At his touch, the focus in Duncan's eyes returned. *"Was this. While. Soapies. Had you?"*

Hari jerked like he'd been stabbed with a straight pin. "How—how—" he stammered incredulously. "How did you *know*?"

Duncan looked up at him past his hairless eyebrows. *"Crazy,"* his digivoder rasped. *"Not. Stupid."*

"Yeah, Dad, I know, but—"

"Nets. All day. Been. Watching. Overworld. Shanna. HRVP. Social. Police." He snorted as though his nose might be dripping. *"Makes. Sense."*

"Not to me."

"Get. Tales. Read. Know. Your. Enemy."

Hari leaned over the bed to turn the screen toward him. "Here, I'll just call it up."

Duncan lifted his strengthless free hand and let his arm fall across Hari's. *"Not. Netbook,"* the digivoder rasped. *"Book book book. Netbook. Edited. Stupid. Kid."*

He waved his twisted hand toward a small bookshelf under

the window seat, pointing with the back of his wrist. *"Book book book."*

"All right, all right, I get the picture." Hari circled the bed, sat, and pulled the hardbound *Tales of the First Folk* off the shelf.

He skimmed through the chapter, through all the different stories about the Quiet Land and the Blind God; with just a phrase here and there to spark his memory, he found the stories came back to him more powerfully than he'd expected. He hadn't read the book in probably thirty years—not since school. Who'd have guessed this crap would stick with him?

The Quiet Land read like a version of an Eden myth: a land of peace, where the elves could live without fear of dragons, where there were no savage ogrilloi or krr'x hives, no vampires or demons. All the creatures of the Quiet Land were without speech or magick; the elves used it as a sort of nursery school, a playland for their children, since even the most rudimentary command of magick rendered them godlike by comparison.

The elves could go to the Quiet Land from Home—*T'nnalldion,* the "Living Place," the elvish name for Overworld—through *dillin,* which roughly translates as *gates*. The *dillin* apparently were certain hills, certain ponds, some caves, occasionally grottoes or even forest glades where the physical terrain of the two lands was precisely identical; no matter how different the surrounding topography, the *dillin* matched. The *dillin* were said to be part of both places at the same time, and in the vicinity of a *dil,* an elf could still draw upon the Flow of Home.

In the Quiet Land, the elves found a coarse, brutish race of "wild elves"—short-lived creatures who had no skill with magick, who could not even see the Flow. These ferals, as they were called, became popular pets and work animals; they were very strong, and clever, and could even learn to speak. Though they could become dangerous if badly handled, they were extremely loyal to masters who treated them well. Many were brought back to Home, and inevitably some ran away and formed packs in the wilderness. Because of their brief lives, they were exceptionally fecund, breeding by the million in just a few short centuries; soon the ferals had become powerful in their own right.

Hari nodded to himself. This was all familiar territory: the elvish myth of how humans came to Overworld.

He began to come across the references to the Blind God. It

was never represented directly; there was never a description of its appearance, or its powers, or its motives. As near as Hari could make out, it seemed to be some kind of shadow force driving everything the ferals did that elves didn't like, from clearing land for farms to building roads, from raising cities to waging war. All this kind of stuff was called "feeding the Blind God."

It was the Blind God that had chased the elves out of the Quiet Land a millennium ago; as the feral population burgeoned, the Blind God had become a power the elves could not counter. They fled the Quiet Land and closed the *dillin*. Hari came to the end of the chapter and shrugged. "I don't get it," he said. "This's got nothing to do with HRVP and the Social Police."

"Yes. It does. If. Quiet Land. Is. Earth."

Hari sighed. "Are you gonna start that shit again?"

He knew from public records on the net that Duncan had published a monograph just over forty years ago claiming that Overworld was in fact the place that human legends call Faerie, and that the humans of Overworld are descended from changelings. The monograph claimed that Westerling was an Indo-European language derived from Frankish, Middle English, and Old High German; it claimed that the human culture of Overworld so closely mirrors late medieval Europe because it was created by men and women who'd been born there, or who were descended from people who had. That monograph was regarded in academic circles as having been the first overt sign of Duncan's fast-approaching breakdown.

"Not. Shit. Read. Commentary. Read."

"Dad—"

"Read. Stupid. Kid."

Hari sighed again, and opened the book to Duncan's end-of-chapter commentary.

Clearly, the "Blind God" is a conscious, deliberately anthropomorphic metaphor for the most threatening facet of human nature: our self-destroying lust to *use*, to conquer, to enslave every tiniest bit of existence and turn it to our own profit, amplified and synergized by our herd-animal instinct—our perverse greed for tribal homogeneity.

It is a good metaphor, a powerful metaphor, one that for me makes a certain sense not only of Overworld's history, but of

Earth's. It provides a potent symbolic context for the industrial wasteland of modern Europe, for the foul air and toxic deserts that are North America: they are table scraps left behind after the Blind God has fed.

Structured by the organizing metaprinciple of the "Blind God," the Manifest Destiny madness of humanity makes a kind of sense—it has a certain inevitability, instead of being the pointless, inexplicable waste it has always appeared.

Hari gave a low whistle. "You published this? I'm surprised Soapy didn't bust you on the spot."

"Before. Your. Birth. Things. Were. Looser." He sagged for a moment, and his eyes drifted closed, as though the effort had exhausted him, but the digivoder's impersonal tone never changed. *"Keep. Reading."*

Hari reopened the book.

The "Blind God" is not a personal god, not a god like Yahweh or Zeus, stomping out the grapes of wrath, hurling thunderbolts at the infidel. The Blind God is a force: like hunger, like ambition.

It is a mindless groping toward the slightest increase in comfort. It is the *greatest good for the greatest number*, when the only number that counts is the number of human beings living right now. I think of the Blind God as a tropism, an autonomic response that turns humanity toward destructive expansion the way a plant's leaves turn toward the sun.

It is the shared will of the human race.

You can see it everywhere. On the one hand, it creates empires, dams rivers, builds cities—on the other, it clear-cuts forests, sets fires, poisons wetlands. It gives us vandalism: the quintessentially human joy of *breaking things*.

Some will say that this is only human nature.

To which I respond: Yes, it is. But we must wonder *why* it is.

Consider: From where does this behavior arise? What is the evolutionary advantage conferred by this instinct? Why is it *instinctive* for human beings to treat the world like an object?

We treat our planet as an enemy, to be crushed, slaughtered, plundered. Raped. Everything is opposition—survival of the fittest on the Darwinian battlefield. Whatever isn't our slave is our potential destroyer. We kill and kill and kill and tell ourselves it is self-defense, or even less: that we need the money, we need the *jobs* that ruthless destruction temporarily provides.

We even treat each other that way.

"Holy crap, Dad," Hari said incredulously. "How did I miss this? How did *Soapy* miss this?"

"Edited. Out. Not. In netbook. Never. Trust. Electronic. Text."

"You got that right."

The magickal races of Overworld—the primals, the stone-benders, and treetoppers—they can *feel* their connection to the living structure of their world. This is why they have never developed organized religions in the human sense; their gods are not objects of worship, but only of respect, of kinship. An Overworld god isn't an individual, a unitary Power to be appeased or conjured; it is a limb of the living planet, a knot of consciousness within the Lifemind, just as is each primal or stonebender or treetopper—each sparrow or blade of grass. They are all part of the same Life, and they know it.

They cannot avoid knowing it; Flow is as essential to their metabolism as is oxygen.

The tragedy of humanity is that we are as much a part of our living planet as any primal mage is of his. We just don't know it. We can't feel it. The First Folk have a name for our incapacity—for our tragic blindness.

They call it the Veil of the Blind God, and they pity us.

Hari closed the book and weighed it in his hand. He felt a little breathless, as though the world pressed in upon his chest. He thought of one of Duncan's sayings, one Duncan must have repeated to him a hundred times when he was a kid:

A religion that teaches you God is something outside *the world—something separate from everything you see, smell, taste, touch, and hear—is nothing but a cheap hustle.*

Now, for the first time, he thought he had some clue what Duncan had been talking about. The elves had a different way of looking at things, no question about it—"But all this, it's just a metaphor, right?" Hari said. "I mean, you wrote it yourself: the Blind God is a metaphor."

Duncan's eyes rolled madly, but the digivoder's voice was

relentlessly steady. *"Maybe. A powerful. Enough. Metaphor. Grows. Its own. Truth."*

"Huh," Hari grunted skeptically. "So where do the Social Police fit in?"

Duncan made a dry hacking sound that might have been laughter. *"Inquisition."*

"You mean, like the *Spanish* Inquisition?"

Duncan didn't answer. He didn't have to. After what Hari had been through this afternoon, he didn't need much convincing. "So, you're saying this Blind God has like, polished off Earth, and now it's hungry for Overworld?"

"Studio. Like. Sense organ. Find out. If Overworld. Tastes good."

"That's another metaphor, right?" Hari asked. "Right?"

"Probably."

Hari sat in that chair by his father's side, weighing the book in his hand, for a long, long time.

Finally, he said, "But why HRVP? It's kind of a blunt instrument, huh? Why do something that . . . catastrophic?"

Duncan grunted wordlessly, and the digivoder chanted, *"Because. It worked. So well. On Earth."*

Hari rubbed his stinging eyes. Any other day, he would have laughed this off and gone to bed. Duncan was crazy; he'd been getting progressively crazier for forty years. Here's crazy for you: he sounded like he really believed this shit. *I'd ask him if he does,* Hari thought, *but what difference would the answer make? He's either crazy and he doesn't believe it, or he's crazy and he does.*

Either way, he's crazy.

His internal debate was interrupted by the low murmur of the Abbey's house computer, its hidden speakers digitally phased to sound like it spoke from just behind his left shoulder. "Hari: perimeter alert. An unauthorized vehicle is landing on the front lawn."

Hari's stomach dropped like his whole life had gone into freefall. "Abbey: identify unauthorized vehicle. Execute."

"Hari: the unauthorized vehicle self-identifies as a Social Police detention van."

Hari looked at the book in his hand, and flinched like it had burned him. He stuck it back into the bookcase spine-first.

On the other hand, he thought numbly, *being crazy doesn't necessarily make him wrong.*

<h1 style="text-align:center">5</h1>

HARI LEANED NERVELESSLY against the jamb of the Abbey's front door, staring blankly out into the sky while the Social Police prepared to load Duncan, traveling bed and all, into the back of the detention van. Bradlee said something from beside him, but Hari couldn't hear him over the roar in his ears: the sound of his life going down in flames. His hand opened, and the crumpled hardcopy of the warrant fluttered to the marble-slab floor.

He should have seen this coming.

Fucking Vilo—

The bastard had ratted him out.

He'd turned over Hari's books to the Social Police, the sensitive ones he'd kept in his vault on his Sangre de Cristo estate. As a Leisureman, his affidavit certifying that he'd received the sealed boxes from Hari with no knowledge of their content was weighted heavily enough to be accepted prima facie by a Social Court judge. So Hari now had an added charge of possession of Banned material.

The secondary effect of this, Vilo probably hadn't even anticipated: it had only taken the Social Police a couple hours to find a judge who would reinstate Duncan's sentence for sedition. Hari couldn't blame Vilo for that; it was no one's fault but his own. He should have burned those fucking books. Duncan wouldn't go to the Buke this time.

He would go under the yoke.

The Buchanan Social Camp required upkeep payments for its inmates, with a hefty deposit. They wouldn't accept Hari's pledge, and he had no credit, no asset he could offer; every goddamn mark he had was tied up in his bail. "How long?" he murmured. "How long do you think he has?"

Bradlee shook his head. "He probably won't even survive the cyborg conversion."

"Yeah."

"If he survives the operation, though, who knows? He can't do anything physical; they'll probably hardwire him for data processing. He might live for years." Bradlee coughed apologetically. "Not that you'd, uh, *want* him to, y'know. Not like that . . ."

"Yeah," Hari said. "Yeah, I know."

He leaned on the doorjamb, paralyzed. He couldn't decide who to kill first: Shanks, or Vilo, or himself.

Out on the lawn, Duncan rolled his head toward Hari. He couldn't speak—his digivoder lay in splinters on the floor of his room, crushed under a soapy's boot heel—but he could wave his twisted, crippled hand. He touched it to his head, made a weak patting motion, then he walked his fingers arthritically along the gleaming chrome bedrail. Hari got the message: *Keep your head down, and inch toward daylight.*

His vision swam with tears.

The van's doors closed around Duncan like jaws. The soapies sealed the doors and climbed into the cabin, and the van lifted off; Hari watched it shrink to a rippling liquid dot in the night sky. "Good-bye, Dad," he whispered.

I guess I'm kind of invulnerable, now, he thought numbly. *There just isn't anything left for them to take from me, except my life.*

My life? They can have it.

"I, uh . . ." Bradlee began uncomfortably. "Can you give me a few days, a week, to find a place?"

Hari frowned at him, and Bradlee dropped his gaze uncertainly. "I mean," he said slowly, "I guess I'm kind of out of a job, huh?"

"Yeah," Hari said. He had no room left in his heart for Bradlee's problems. "I guess you are."

Head down, Bradlee walked slowly back toward the kitchen.

Hari hissed at himself, softly through his teeth. No reason to take this out on the nurse; Bradlee had looked after Duncan for years, had really cared for him. Hari called after him, "Brad—stay as long as you need. I mean, shit, I'd hire you to look after the house, but—" He spread his hands helplessly, and shrugged. "—I just realized I can't pay your salary."

"Thanks," he said softly. "Thanks, Hari. You sure you don't want something to eat?"

Hari closed his eyes; the thought of putting food into his mouth clenched his stomach like somebody had reached into his guts and made a fist. "Not tonight. I'm gonna go upstairs and get friendly with a bottle of scotch."

Bradlee nodded silently and disappeared into the kitchen.

Hari stood in the Abbey's front hall for a long time, listening to the silence. Bradlee might as well have been already gone; everyone else was.

Faith. Duncan. Shanna.

Caine.

Cold marble-slab floor, classically austere sweep of stair to the second-floor balcony, rich burgundy runner—everything here he knew so well; he'd dreamed this place for so many years before he'd built it that it was forever engraved into his brain. He'd never dreamed it would be so empty.

It hasn't even been twenty-four hours, he thought in blank awe. A day ago, his worst problems had been a cranky bypass, creaky legs, and a bad attitude.

My god—

He wondered if his chest would implode into the stark unforgiving lack inside.

My god, what have I done?

From behind his left shoulder the Abbey murmured, "Hari: priority screen call."

Hari walked reflexively to the nearest wallscreen and hit the acknowledge. He never considered refusing the call; he felt a strange, abstract gratitude to whomever this might be, for distracting him from the wreckage of his life.

It was Tan'elKoth.

Probably calling to gloat, Hari thought dully.

The ex-Emperor wore a black sweater, over which gleamed the metalized straps of his ammod harness. "Caine," he said darkly, "you must come to me immediately, here at the Curioseum."

"This isn't a good time for me."

"There will be no better time for you. There will be no time at all. Come. Now."

"I'm telling you . . ." Hari let his voice trail off, and he frowned. "Did you say, at the *Curioseum*? If you're at the Curioseum, why are you wearing the ammod harness?"

"For the same reason that you must come here *now*. You conscripted me for your war, Caine. I must speak with you before I become its latest casualty—and I have little time."

"What . . . ? I mean, I don't get it," Hari said. His brain felt like an old rusty engine, groaning as it tried to turn over.

Tan'elKoth's eyes smoldered darkly. "How much do you want me to say over an open line *into your home*?"

Hari thought of the crowd of Social Police and SynTech security that had tramped through here this afternoon, and he nodded. "I understand," he said, "but—"

"No," Tan'elKoth rumbled. "Come *now*. It is a matter of life and death. Mine—and Pallas Ril's."

Hari squeezed his eyes shut and took a long, slow, painful breath. "I'm on my way," he said. "I'll be at the South Gate in ten minutes."

6

STARKLY SIDELIT BY the emergency lights, the exhibition halls of the Curioseum had become eerie, alien caverns of moon-black shadows and bleaching glare. Tan'elKoth paced ahead of him with the ponderous threat of a hovertank, his thick-soled athletic shoes silent on the polished floor tiles. The only sound was the click of Hari's boot heels, echoing crisply from distant walls of cement and stone. His arms prickled with gooseflesh.

This shit was creeping him out.

It gnawed at the pit of his stomach: everything looked so *wrong*, here. And it wasn't just the stippled wash of emergency lighting through the dirty armorglass panels; it wasn't just that none of the displays activated when they passed through the halls; it wasn't even the blank silence, deeper than you could ever really hear on Earth, left behind by the absence of the venti-lation system's constant whisper.

He'd never seen the inside of the Curioseum from the eye-level of a standing man.

The simple fact that he could, for the first time in his life, *walk* through these rooms left him breathless with irrational dread.

At the South Gate, he hadn't been able to make himself come in. He'd stood in the doorway, shaking his head. Sure, Tan'el-Koth *said* the ON field was off—he said his mindview showed not even the trace amounts of Flow that should have been visible—but Rover was still down in fucking Los Angeles. Shit, the Fancon people had probably already auctioned it off. "Why would the field be off?" Hari had asked. "And what's wrong with the power?"

Tan'elKoth's reply had been an exasperated glower. "*You* are the damned *Chairman*," he'd rumbled savagely. "If you don't know, how should I? Follow me."

Hari had a lot of trouble convincing himself to step into the gate. He knew, he *just knew*, that when he took one more step into the Curioseum he would collapse, crippled and helpless, at Tan'elKoth's feet. Tan'elKoth had been as sympathetic as Hari had come to expect. "Fine, then. Let her die," he'd said coldly, then had turned and walked away.

A second later, Hari had followed him. But still he could not get comfortable with walking where he had always rolled.

Ahead, Tan'elKoth turned down the gallery that led toward the Caine Hall and his own apartment. Hari paced in his wake, listening to the echoes and rubbing his forearms to make the hairs on them lie down again. "Are you ever—" he began, whispering instinctively. He caught himself and coughed—some bitter, chemical tang tickled his throat—then repeated loudly, "Are you ever gonna tell me what this is about?"

Tan'elkoth stopped, his back a wide black wall that seemed to half close off the gallery. "Can you not smell it?"

That chemical smell, the one that coated the inside of his nose, his mouth, his throat—he recognized it. It was the preservative gas from Berne's display case . . . but thicker, stronger, far more dense. Until now, he'd never smelled it until he was right up next to the case. The back of his neck prickled.

He leaned out so he could peer around Tan'elKoth's broad back; he dreaded what he knew he would see, but he had to look.

Berne's case was empty. It stood on its pedestal in the archway of the exhibition hall, vacant as a corpse's eyes.

Hari's bowels dissolved into ice water that drained into his legs. He couldn't move, couldn't speak—he was afraid to turn his head, because he knew with irrational certainty that as soon as he looked, he'd find Berne waiting for him, standing in the shadows with Kosall poised to strike, and he'd collapse and start to scream like a stolen baby.

Dead is dead, Hari told himself. He'd jammed a knife through the top of Berne's skull and scrambled the bastard's brains. *You don't get any deader than that.*

After repeating this to himself a few times, he found that he could breathe again. When he finally decided he could trust his voice, he said, "All right. I've seen it. Now tell me what it means. Who would steal Berne's body?"

Tan'elKoth turned, half his face bleached white in the emergency lights, the other half lost in shadow. "Studio security. Your own secmen, Caine."

Hari winced. He didn't like this already, and he knew it was going to get worse.

Tan'elKoth went on. "I was engaged in my usual research this evening after closing, developing a new lesson for my Applied Magick seminar, when I heard the noise of what turned out to be five secmen opening this case. I enquired what they were doing—perfectly innocently, I might add, I had assumed they were acting upon your orders. Their response was to place me under arrest and hold me incommunicado in the security office detention center until perhaps half an hour ago."

"When you called me."

"Yes."

Tan'elKoth moved slowly, almost meditatively, down the long gallery and stopped in front of the empty case. He pressed one enormous hand against the armorglass, like a lover waving good-bye through a car window, and bent his head for a moment as though weary, or in pain. As Hari joined him there, Tan'elKoth turned and seated himself on the case's pedestal, leaned his forearms on his knees, and folded his hands.

"My first thought," Tan'elKoth said, "was that this was some stroke of yours—some plot to wound me by a further desecration of the corpse of my most faithful servant. As if what you had done to him already were not enough."

"Hey, don't try to splash me with that shit," Hari said. "Putting his body on display was Wes Turner's idea."

"A puerile evasion," he said darkly. "This crime was an act of the company that employs you. You cannot exculpate yourself by claiming *the boss made me do it*. The nature of your masters has never been a mystery to you, yet you have continued to take their money and enjoy the borrowed status they lend to you. You are as guilty as they."

"You're gonna debate *morality* with me? You? You're the only sonofabitch I ever met who's murdered more people than I have," Hari said through his teeth. "What about the *body*?"

"Yes." He met Hari's gaze with a level stare. "No long interval passed before I realized this could not be your doing. You are a walking catastrophe of Biblical proportion; this type of petty, emotionally wounding revenge has never been your style."

"I don't give a rat's ass how you knew it wasn't me. I *already* know it wasn't *me*, goddammit. Who *was* it?"

"This is not the central question; the thieves were Studio secmen, acting upon orders from above. Who gave those orders is peripheral—a mere detail. The central question is *for what would they want it?*"

Hari ground his teeth together and resisted the impulse to break the bastard's nose again. "Tan'elKoth," he said tightly, "on my best days, I'm not a patient man. This is not one of my best days. Drop the fucking games."

"Just so." He rose, towering over Hari, starkly outlined against the emergency floodlight. "I can tell you precisely why the Studio would take Berne's body."

"Christ, I *hope* so."

"They intend to use him to kill Pallas Ril."

Looking up into Tan'elKoth's black-shadowed face, Hari could feel the strength leaving his knees as though it trickled out a pair of spigots on his heels. "I don't understand," he said numbly.

"I found it obvious." Tan'elKoth walked away again, into the Caine Hall, heading for his apartment door. "Berne was stolen by the Studio. Pallas Ril is the only obstacle to the success of the Studio's plans for my world."

His voice boomed off the walls of stone. "Berne was the finest swordsman of his age—perhaps of any age. Combat skill—like any other physical skill, even walking and talking—is a matter of reflex conditioning. An animated corpse of Berne would still have the skills of a superior swordsman, even without the higher cognitive functions that govern tactics. And, of course, they also took Kosall."

Hari, following, had to stop suddenly: his back ached fiercely at that name.

The scene, the wax-figure diorama in the middle of this hall, was of that moment on the sand of Victory Stadium, on that hot Ankhanan noon seven years ago. High above, figures of Ma'elKoth and Pallas Ril were locked in deific combat. In the center of the display, Caine brandished a pair of knives while he leaped onto the unstoppable point of the sword in Berne's hand.

If the Curioseum had had power, the scene would have been lit by the white blaze that would radiate from the figure of Pallas Ril. Here in black-shadowed semidarkness, the scene had an eerie, nightmarish life. Darkness hid the wires; for a disorienting, hallucinatory second, Hari wasn't sure whether he was the one standing out here looking at the display or if he was the leaping figure within it.

—and for a moment he could feel again that harsh buzzing in his teeth from Kosall's vibrating edge when the blade had slid, smooth as butter, through his spine—

He rubbed his head as though he could massage meaning in through his skull, and he snarled at himself to pull it together. "An animated *corpse*—?"

Tan'elKoth stopped at his doorway and sighed like an exasperated professor. "Must I forge every single link in this chain of reasoning? Here then, simply: Pallas Ril—Chambaraya—is a god of life. No living thing can approach her undetected, however it may be concealed. If, on the other hand, a potent magickal weapon is borne by, shall we say, an *unliving* thing . . . ? Need I say more?"

The face of the wax Berne above him seemed to shift in the black wash of shadow. The glass eyes glittered with malice; they seemed to turn from the figure of the wax Caine before it and fix upon Pallas Ril high above. In that final instant—the most famous sequence of the most famous Studio Adventure of all time—Caine had thrown himself upon Berne's sword, for that was his only hope of saving Pallas Ril.

Hari's chest ached with helpless rage.

Sure, he thought. *Sure, that makes sense.*

The people behind this could have chosen any random corpse for their weapon; they wouldn't even need to dig one up—they could *lease* one from the Working Dead in Ankhana's Warrens. But instead, they took Berne. So Hari would know it was coming.

So he'd know there was nothing he could do to stop it.

Back in the bad old days, when he and Shanna hadn't been able to open their mouths to each other without sparking a shouting match, she had constantly accused him of being obsessively self-absorbed; she liked to tell him that something or other *isn't about you. Not everything in the bloody world is about you!*

Yeah, maybe not, he thought. *But this is. I don't know why, or how, but you can't get away from it. This is about me.*

He'd been told: the greatest skill of the successful Administrator is to know when to do nothing.

Just like Dad: I can't fucking learn to shut up.

"I am no great admirer of Pallas Ril, as you know," Tan'elKoth said as he fished out his keys—the ON field disabled palmlocks as efficiently as it did Hari's bypass; all the Curioseum's interior doors had Overworld-style manual locks with physical keys. "Nonetheless, she is the sole shield between my Children and the masters of this . . . this death cult you call a Studio. Is there anything you can do?"

Hari shook his head, mouth twisted against a taste of metal and bitter ash. "If I can get a message to her, somehow . . . She can handle pretty much anything if she knows it's coming." He turned up his palms helplessly. "But the Studio is gonna be ahead of me on this, too."

He could taste defeat already. He had been hit too hard, from too many directions at once. He'd lost already.

She would die.

Standing at the freemod dock: *You get in trouble over there this time, I can't come and bail you out.*

How had he ended up so useless, and so guilty?

His head hammered; he pressed the heel of his hand to his temple and squeezed shut his eyes. It felt like a steel band ratcheted tighter and tighter around his skull: at any second the bone would crack and his brains would squirt out his eye sockets.

"I shall do what I can, but first—" Tan'elKoth circled a hand at the particolored light and shadow of the power-dead Curioseum. "—I must find a place to stay. The power cells in these harnesses of yours are not inexhaustible. Amplitude decay is—as you have reminded me many times—an ugly way to die."

"Where will you go?"

Tan'elKoth shrugged. "My art has garnered admirers among the Leisurefolk—some few of them have ON vaults not unlike the one you maintain at the Abbey, only larger, to hold collections of artifacts brought to Earth by Actors that they sponsor. I am certain one or more can be persuaded to accommodate me until this—" Again, the circular gesture. "—situation can be resolved."

He turned to the door to his apartment. "Once I have my spare harness, I will be off."

He pushed the door open—and every light in the Curioseum burst to life.

Hari jumped as though the sudden glare was a stroke of nearby lightning. Overhead, the figure of Pallas Ril blazed like a fusion torch, and the simulated power of the simulated Ma'elKoth became a jet of fire that joined them breast to breast. Hari clenched his teeth until the stuttering of his heart settled into a steady rhythm. "Looks like you won't have to move after all," he said.

"Don't be an idiot," Tan'elKoth said as he disappeared within his apartment.

Hari went to the door. "But with the power back on—"

Tan'elKoth stood at his desk, his back to Hari. "You're still *walking*." His voice was rich with dark-roasted contempt.

"Huh." Hari scowled thoughtfully as he paced through the door. "That doesn't make any goddamn sense."

The Curioseum's ON field generator was hardwired into the Studio grid—which was energized by the Studio's transfer pump. It should have been impossible for the power to be on down here without the field returning as well.

In fact, there was no reason why the damn power should have been off in the first place. There were backup generators, and as a third failsafe the Curioseum would self-connect to San Francisco's civic grid—the Curioseum's collection was irreplaceable, and much of it would vanish into amplitude decay in goddamn short order if the field didn't come back up. If he hadn't been distracted by all the shit that had hit him today, he would have seen it already: the only reason to turn off the power was to turn off the ON field.

But why would somebody want to do that? Was he just being paranoid, or did this smell of enemy action? *It's not whether I'm paranoid,* he thought. *It's whether I'm paranoid enough.*

Now, with the power back on, but still no field—

Hari frowned down at the floor. "What's *this* crap?"

Tan'elKoth's athletic shoes had left tracks, faint but definite, even across the area rug that defined his "living room"—slipper shapes where his tread had disturbed some kind of fine silvery dust that was spread all over the floor and the furniture, like pesticide left behind by a careless exterminator. "What the hell is this dust?" Hari asked Tan'elKoth's back. "You working in marble these days?"

"Mmm," Tan'elKoth agreed distractedly, while he thumbed through an old-fashioned bound-paper address book he'd pulled from a drawer of his desk. "But this is not marble dust—my pneumatic chisel has a vacuum hose that's vented to the outside. There are several fairly serious varieties of lung damage, as well as systemic disturbances, that are caused by the inhalation of marble dust; even with the hose, I wear a self-contained breathing apparatus while I work. Ah, there he is," he said smugly, holding his place in the address book with one sausage-sized finger. "Rentzi Dole. He has several of my pieces, and has invited me to Kauai on any number of occasions. And—most important—he is no friend of this Studio."

Hari's answering nod was equally distracted. He knew all about Leisureman Dole—his late aunt had been Shanna's Patron for many years. Rentzi Dole was one of Hari's least favorite people; the Leisureman had defied the explicit terms of his aunt's will and terminated Shanna's patronage.

Hari had something else on his mind: a thought that was beginning to take shape, still misty around the edges, kind of foggily inchoate as it organized itself—his brain wasn't accustomed to doing this kind of work anymore. "Uh, Tan'elKoth?" Hari began uncertainly. *Why would someone have the power on but the ON field off?*

Clearly, they wanted to run some kind of equipment that requires both power and Earth-normal physics. Something electronic. Like a deskscreen. "Tan'elKoth," Hari said, "don't make that call."

"Don't be ridiculous. What choice do I have?"

No electronics work in the ON field—not even, say, the voice-recognition chips built into palmlocks.

"I'm telling you," Hari said, stronger, more urgently, "don't do it. You have to *listen* to me." He started toward the ex-Emperor, his hand out as though to grab the bigger man and haul him away from the desk by force.

Voice-recognition chips aren't restricted to operating palmlocks or controlling access to netsites; they can be used to trigger almost any kind of device—

"Nonsense," the ex-Emperor said, thumbing the mike key next to the speaking tube.

—like a detonator.

"Don't *do* it—"

Tan'elKoth continued, "Iris: initiate telecommunications. Exec—"

A shattering roar obliterated the rest of the word.

7

THE BLAST HURLED Tan'elKoth backward into Hari, flattening them both like they'd been hit by a freightliner. Hari might have lost consciousness for a second or two; he found himself on his hands and knees, shaking his head, thunder rolling on and on in his ears, joined by a high, singing whine that made his teeth ache. Some kind of thick greyish chemical smoke burned the back of his throat and punched hacking coughs out of his lungs. All that was left of Tan'elKoth's beautiful rolltop desk was a knee-high bonfire—the oil- and varnish-impregnated wood pumped out black smoke of its own, but that didn't worry him.

What worried him was how *bright* it was in here.

White as lightning, the glare *hurt*—and it grew brighter and brighter until he felt like somebody was driving nails into his eyeballs. With the light came heat: searing radiance like a sun-lamp strapped onto his face.

The whole apartment was on fire.

Even the stone of the floor burned: outspreading rings of white flame hissed sparks at the ceiling. In the center of each widening ring was a smoldering splinter of wood—pieces of the desk, flaming, blown everywhere by the bomb. And the hissing, spark-showering rings of fire grew slowly, spreading like ripples in a pond of molasses, and the stone in their wake glowed red-white like slag from a blast furnace.

That fucking *dust*—

Somebody'd sprayed it all over the goddamn place. Thermite, maybe a magnesium compound, maybe something new he'd never heard of—it didn't matter. What mattered was getting out of here.

Holding a fold of his tunic across his mouth and nose against the smoke, he snaked over to Tan'elKoth. The big man lay on his back, limbs splayed bonelessly, out cold. His black sweater had been blown to rags, and the chestplate of the ammod harness looked like the front end of a car after a disagreement with the pylon of a suspension bridge. His face was scorched, his eyebrows burned off; embers still crawled through his hair, making it crinkle and spit smoke.

Hari spent an eternal five seconds feeling for a pulse between the windpipe and the massive cords of Tan'elKoth's neck; he wasn't sentimental enough to get his ass cooked trying to rescue a corpse.

One, two, three, four—son of a bitch if the big bastard wasn't still alive after all. Now all Hari had to do was figure out how a 170-pound middle-aged man who was not in the best shape of his life was gonna get out of here hauling this fucking behemoth who was way too goddamn close to three times his weight. *This,* Hari thought concisely, *is gonna suck.*

He grasped Tan'elKoth's ankles and started dragging him toward the door, but as soon as he stood the smoke blinded and choked him; he had to sit down and push himself across the floor crabwise, and his soft boots could get little purchase—slow going, at best.

That high, singing whine began to overpower the rolling thunder in his ears, and he recognized it now: muffled by his stunned eardrums, he was hearing the blare of the Curioseum's alarm—but it wasn't the rising wail of the fire alarm.

It was the tooth-grinding screech of the *intruder* alarm.

"Mother*fucker*!" Hari threw himself backward into a shoulder-roll that brought him up in a low crouch facing the door—

Just in time to see the security gate ratchet down the last few inches and lock in place.

The intruder alarm kept on screeching, and no fire alarm sounded at all—which meant he couldn't expect any help from the Curioseum's fire-suppression system. Or from San Francisco Fire and Rescue. The security gate was a flex-linked grid of half-inch hardened steel bars: no getting past that without a cutting torch or a hydraulic jack, and the second-floor windows would be gated by now as well. "Okay, I was wrong," he muttered, hacking on the smoke and wiping at tears that streamed from his stinging eyes. "This *already* sucks."

Though the rings of flame grew wider, growing toward intersection, the smoke didn't seem to be thickening at all—in fact, now that he'd noticed, he could see that the smoke was being drawn upward along the broad sweep of stairs, as though the light traps in the middle of the second floor and the third formed an accidental chimney.

Yeah—there'd be ventilators up there, to clear the area of solvent fumes and marble dust. They would be useless for escaping: the Curioseum's outside vents were less than a foot in diameter and heavily baffled—something to do with maintaining the ON field—

The skylight, Hari thought. No need for a security gate: the armorglass skylight was fused with the stone of the roof. It'd take tools to cut it open—but the third floor was Tan'elKoth's sculpture studio. Full of tools.

It was also two goddamn tall floors straight up through a column of toxic smoke, and Hari's sonofabitching legs only half worked.

A new swirl of that smoke choked him, and when he coughed he tasted blood. Tan'elKoth had said something about a self-contained breathing apparatus; that was all he needed to make up his mind.

He grabbed Tan'elKoth's ankles again, took a deep breath and a glance to orient himself, then squeezed his eyes shut and held his breath as he stood up and leaned against Tan'elKoth's weight, dragging the huge man toward the stairs. Heat knocked the strength out of him like a blow from a club. He could barely pull the ex-Emperor along the floor; how in the name of Christ was he supposed to haul this 400-pound gorilla up three fucking floors?

Hari left him half on the stairs, head at the bottom to keep him below the worst of the smoke, and sprinted upward empty-handed. The smoke scalded his eyeballs, blinding him with tears before he'd made it halfway to the second floor. He sagged against the railing—gagging, spitting blood—but shook himself and kept on, driving his failing legs up the steps, hauling himself hand over hand along the rail. When he reached the second floor, he fell outward into the clearer air of Tan'elKoth's bedchamber and lay there, gasping, just long enough to catch a breath that didn't make him convulse, then pulled himself back to his feet.

He shut his eyes again and pounded up the last flight of stairs, holding his breath. He staggered into the sculpture studio; hypoxia made his head swim and turned his knees to jelly, but right next to the wheeled hydraulic scaffolding that surrounded a sculpture in progress, he found Tan'elKoth's respirator mask and slapped it over his face.

He spent a grateful ten seconds just breathing; air came hard and slow through the regulator, but it was clean enough to taste like wine. The faceplate cleared, and now he could see, as well.

A quick glance around the smoke-filled studio gave him half a solution: a crane was mounted on a pivot so that it would swing out over the light trap, bearing a pulley and cable attached to a hand-winch, for lifting Tan'elKoth's raw materials—steel, bronze, and enormous blocks of marble—up to here from the ground floor.

It was *half* a solution because there was only one respirator. Hauling Tan'elKoth slowly up through the ascending column of smoke would suffocate him; if Hari left the respirator on Tan'elKoth, he didn't think he could make it up the stairs a second time to crank the damn winch—and the growing heat that blasted up through the light traps might roast Tan'elKoth anyway. *What I really need is speed,* Hari told himself. *Speed is what I really need.*

That thought rang in his head like a mantra by Dr. Seuss, and then he had it. The enormous half-finished marble statue within the hydraulic scaffolding . . .

The idea came to him whole, perfectly formed, audacious enough to make him laugh out loud: because the marble statue stood on a low, square dolly with swivel-mounted wheels.

He swung the crane arm out over the light trap and knocked loose the winch's ratchet gear so that the cable twisted downward. He let the cable spool out—he couldn't see the first floor through the smoke, and he didn't want to get down there and find out he hadn't left himself enough slack. Tan'elKoth—Mr. Efficient—had marked the cable with a big piece of colored duct tape; when that reached the pulley, Hari figured he'd let out enough.

Tan'elKoth's pneumatic chisel, pressure tank fully charged, rested on one of the scaffolds; Hari ripped the vacuum hose off the chisel and pulled the scaffold over to the winch. A couple of chisel strokes neatly parted the cable strands a few meters back around the spool. Hari hauled the free end over to the statue; then he looped the cable under the marble arms and tied it off to itself with a simple loop knot. He skirted the statue once around, unlocking each of the dolly's wheels, and everything was ready to go. He stood back for one moment to look it over and reassure himself that this was gonna work—and found himself staring, mouth hanging open within the respirator mask.

The figure that struggled free from the block of marble was that of a middle-aged, rather ordinary, conservative-looking man. Something in the texture of the sculpted hair suggested a scatter of grey, and jowls were beginning to soften his jawline. But what held Hari was the look on its face: the sad knowledge within its eyes, a sort of settled melancholy that wasn't even potent enough to be dignified as despair. The statue looked like a man who knows too well he has lost the promise and possibility of youth, who has found nothing with which to replace them— and who doesn't seem to mind all that much. It was the image of a man who'd settled into a comfortable failure.

Holy crap, Hari thought. *It's me.*

The block of marble was labeled in black wax pencil on the side, in Tan'elKoth's bowl scrawl: *David the King.*

I don't get it.

Was he wrong? Was it an accidental resemblance?

No—on the scaffolding that surrounded it were dozens of black-and-white printouts of digigraphs, everything from Caine's first publicity headshots to stills from Studio security cameras showing Hari from every conceivable angle and in every possible posture. *What the fuck is going on here?*

And with that mental question, another tendril of smoke drifted before his eyes and reminded him of the immediate answer. He'd worry about Tan'elKoth's goddamn art after he'd saved the bastard's life.

He sprinted to the stairwell and threw himself into it, sliding down the railing with exhilirating speed. He hit the second floor and sprang to the next flight—the flames below crept closer and closer to Tan'elKoth's side as he stirred now, dazedly—and Hari swung himself onto the rail again and skidded down to stop beside him. Tan'elKoth couldn't even look at him; he was too busy coughing blood and trying to wipe smoke from his eyes.

The cable hung down the middle of the light traps; a few meters of it were coiled within one of the spreading rings of flame—some of it had melted from contact with the white-hot floor near the rim. Hari sprang high over the spitting flame, hooked the cable with his elbow and sprang back again, letting the cable slide through the crook of his arm so he wouldn't take up any slack.

Even that brief instant in contact with the heated stone was too much for his boots: they burst into flame. He kicked them off, but they had already ignited the dust that impregnated the fabric of his pants; an instant later his shirt had caught as well. He swore and held the cable with his teeth while he wildly ripped away his burning clothes; they shredded in his hands and he threw them aside, but not before they'd seared his skin. Smoke rose from his flesh like overdone barbecue. *That's okay,* he told himself. *So long as I get out of here before I go into shock.*

Naked now, he brought the cable's hot end to Tan'elKoth. The ex-Emperor was trying to sit up, mumbling something about all this being wrong, that this wasn't what was supposed to happen. "If we start worrying about what's *supposed* to happen," Hari shouted through the mask above the fire's roar, "we're both gonna *die* in here? Hold *still!*"

"Your clothes . . ." Tan'elKoth said blankly. "You're naked."

"Now I know why everybody says you're a genius," Hari told him. "Don't move." Working swiftly, he looped the cable under Tan'elKoth's armpits.

"What . . . ? What are you *doing*? This fire—what? This hurts . . ."

Hari grinned as he tightened the knot. "Yeah."

The ex-Emperor coughed, spraying blood; tears streamed down his face. "What are you doing?"

"Saving your life. You ever hear of a guy who called himself Batman?"

"Batman?" Tan'elKoth frowned dazedly, as though he couldn't quite make his eyes focus. "I don't understand."

"You will," Hari said, and leaped into the air. Past the top of his leap, already coming down, he doubled his legs up under him and grabbed onto the cable.

High, high above, through the pulley on the crane, the cable pulled *David the King* rolling on its dolly toward the light trap.

It reached the railing at the rim, and tipped. For one awful moment, Hari feared he'd mis-estimated the statue's center of gravity—but then it tipped farther, and farther, leaning over like a toppling drunk. For half a second it hung there, balanced on the rail . . . then it slid out into space.

Hari said: "Going *up!*"

The statue came down like a boulder off a cliff.

Hari and Tan'elKoth shot upward.

The statue swung wide, jerking and bouncing, raking across the light trap and threatening to tangle the cable upon itself. Hari swore as he watched the statue hurtle down at his head like a giant's flyswatter. *Okay, so I didn't really think this through—*

He swung his legs high, like a pole vaulter, and met the rim of the descending statue's dolly with the soles of his feet, kicking himself and Tan'elKoth wide—and it gave him a twinge, it really did, seeing his middle-aged self in marble sail into the depths of the column of smoke below.

Then they were past, yanked up onto the studio—Hari let go of the cable to catch the crane arm—and the statue slammed into the ground floor far below and shattered. One arm hooked over the crane, Hari grabbed frantically for the cable, expecting Tan'elKoth to drop like a stone, gritting his teeth against the anticipated pain of having the cable slice to the bone of his hand as Tan'elKoth's weight pulled it through—

But Hari's kick off the statue had set the two of them swinging like a pendulum; as the statue pulled the moment-arm of their pendulum short, the angle of their swing increased—like a yo-yo going Over the Falls—and swung Tan'elKoth just barely wide enough that he could latch onto the rail of the light trap with one massive hand. He slammed hard into the cutaway floor, but managed to hang on while Hari scrambled down off the crane and got there to help him over the rail.

Coughing convulsively, tears streaming down his face, smoke still spitting from the embers that crawled through his hair, Tan'elKoth roared furiously, "You are . . . *incapable* . . . of doing *anything* . . . the *easy way*!"

"Shut up and haul in that fucking cable!" Hari shouted back. "We're not out of here yet!"

He rolled the hydraulic scaffold—the one that held the pneumatic chisel—over so that it spanned one corner of the light trap, then locked its wheels and cranked it up to its full extension, which took it nearly to the ceiling. He swarmed up the side ladder, picked up the chisel, and jammed its cutting edge against the armorglass on one side of the arched skylight. When he squeezed the trigger handle, the chisel roared to life like a jackhammer.

Working as fast as he could, he scored a manhole-sized circle in the armorglass—the pressure in the chisel's tank was dropping rapidly. Tan'elKoth coughed his way up beside him, carrying the cable coiled in his fist, as the chisel slowed. Its strokes weakened and finally stopped.

Hari put his shoulder against the scored circle of armorglass and shoved, but he might as well have been pushing a mountain. Tan'elKoth caught his elbow and pulled him aside; then the big man lifted the chisel's pressure tank like a Social Police battering ram and slammed its curved end against the scoring. A tracery of cracks bloomed from the point of impact like lightning crawling the face of a thunderhead.

Tan'elKoth slammed it again, a quarter of the way around the circle, and again, and again. His face had gone from bright red to purple, and he hit the circle one more time, in the middle, and the disk of armorglass popped out like the lid of a vacuum pack.

Hari made Tan'elKoth go out first, and Tan'elKoth turned back to help him through the hole so he didn't cut himself on its razor-sharp edges.

Once out in the cool darkness of the roof, Hari stripped off the respirator mask and crouched next to Tan'elKoth, who lay on the roof, still coughing, wiping his eyes. Smoke boiled out the skylight behind him, a long column twisting up toward the gibbous moon.

Hari's hands were shaking, and the inside of the respirator mask was spattered with blood. "Goddamn," he said softly, to himself. "Goddamn if I didn't pull it off."

8

HE LAY DOWN on the roof beside Tan'elKoth and let the heat of his burns drain into the night-cool stone. The pain was only beginning, and he knew it would be bad. Still, though, for this one moment, he was content to lie here under the stars and luxuriate in the sensation of being alive.

"Why?" Tan'elKoth said; his voice was thick, as though he held back a sob. "Why? I am your enemy. Why did you do this?"

"I don't know," Hari answered. "I guess it seemed like a good idea at the time." He rolled his face toward Tan'elKoth, smiling with his bloody lips. "Maybe I just wanted to hear you say thanks."

Tan'elKoth turned away. "My David," he murmured. "Oh, my David—"

"What, is this about the fucking statue?" Hari made himself

sit up. "Your life or the statue," he said. "Which would you rather save?"

Tan'elKoth buried his face in his hands. "This is a choice no artist should ever have to make."

"You didn't," Hari reminded him. "Nobody asked you."

"No more did I ask for your help," Tan'elKoth said bitterly. "No more shall I give you my thanks."

And while Hari sat there, staring at the ex-Emperor, he realized he wasn't interested in gratitude.

Old, tired, whipped by life, one leg tied behind his back—

I've still got it.

He showed his teeth to the moon.

I've still fucking got it.

That feeling was worth every one of his burns.

"Come on, get moving," he said abruptly. "Tie the damn cable to something up here so we can get off this roof."

While Tan'elKoth slid a loop over one merlon of the Curioseum's crenellated roof and walked himself backward down the wall, hand over hand along the cable, Hari Michaelson triaged the casualties of his life.

Duncan was beyond help; the bulldog jaws of the Social Police had locked upon him, and his life bled out through their teeth. Faith would keep; bad as her situation was, alone and probably frightened among strangers, she was in no immediate danger. Shanks wasn't the type to torture and kill a helpless child just for fun; she only tortured and killed helpless children when she had something to gain from it. Tan'elKoth didn't need any more help; warned now, aware of the danger he faced, he could go to his Leisure friends for protection.

And Hari himself—

To save himself would cost more than his life was worth.

Tan'elKoth called up to him from the sidewalk below. "I'm down!"

Instead of answering, Hari walked past the smoking skylight to another one a few yards away; he leaned on it, pressing his palms against the armorglass, and looked down past the actinic blaze from the Pallas Ril figure, down to where the wax Caine leaped upon the blade of the wax Berne. He'd relived that instant so many times in the past seven years that he no longer knew if he remembered it for itself, or if he only remembered remembering; he'd never quite had the courage to play the second-hander cube, to check his recollection.

He did know this, though, beyond a dream of doubt: on that day, on that sand, knowing he was about to die, he had been as close to happy as he'd ever come.

All right, he thought, staring down at the wax Caine. *All right. I understand now.*

Caine *had* died, on the arena sand that hot autumn noon. For seven long years, Hari had been no more than Caine's rotting corpse.

Fuck it. If dying were anything special, they wouldn't let everybody do it.

Tan'elKoth called from below. "I'm down! Are you coming?"

Hari went to the edge of the Curioseum's roof. Out across the carhive between the Curioseum and the Studio, security vans roared toward them, and high against the stars wailed approaching fire and emergency rescue vehicles. He looked down at Tan'elKoth. "You haven't seen me," he said as he pulled the cable up, coiling it around his arm. "I was never here. You got out on your own. You hear me?"

"What are you talking about?"

"No time to explain. I gotta go save the world."

He pulled the last of the cable up and slipped the loop off the merlon. From below, Tan'elKoth said, "Caine?"

He almost answered with his reflexive *Call me Hari, god-dammit,* but he changed his mind. He stood absolutely still for one long second, savoring the feeling.

Then he leaned out over the battlement. "Yeah?" he said. "What?"

"It's my world, too, Caine," Tan'elKoth said. "Good luck."

"Thanks." Looking down, he touched his brow in a sketch of a salute. "Same to you," he said, then turned and ran like hell, streaking across the roof, heading for the skywalk that connected to the Studio.

9

THE RESCUE SQUAD paramedic piled out of the emergency services vehicle before the turbines had even spun down; he staggered through the backblast to reach the side of Tan'elKoth.

"Are you hurt, sir?" he shouted over the declining roar of the turbines. *"Do you need medical attention?"*

"Yes, I do," Tan'elKoth said grimly. "But more than that, I need your palmpad."

"What?"

Tan'elKoth seized the paramedic's shoulder in one titanic hand, his grip so sudden and powerful that it short-circuited the startled man's will; he didn't even try to move while the ex-Emperor yanked the palmpad from his belt holster. Tan'elKoth shoved the man stumbling backward and gave him a volcanic glare that told him to keep his distance. "Initiate telecommunications," he spat into the device's microphone. "Studio two five X-ray zulu four. Execute."

A moment later, the tiny screen shimmered with a view of Kollberg's wasted, leering face. *"Well?"*

"Not at all well," Tan'elKoth growled. "To what manner of fool did you assign this task? I was nearly killed, as was he—mortal danger to us both was never part of the plan."

"Mortal danger makes it convincing," Kollberg said. *"Don't presume to lecture me on the mechanics of entertainment."*

"This is *not* entertainment—"

"Of course it is."

"Your incompetence nearly destroyed the entire—"

"Did it work?" Kollberg interrupted hungrily.

"Are you *listening* to me?"

"Only cowards and weaklings whine about what almost happened," Kollberg said. *"Is he coming?"*

Rising fury swelled the flesh around Tan'elKoth's eyes; he had made similar pronouncements himself in the past, and he discovered that he disliked them profoundly from this side.

"Yes," he said slowly. "Caine is on his way."

10

INSIDE THE STUDIO, Hari discovered that his priority override codes still operated the palmlocks. He slipped into the deserted infirmary and treated his burns to a liberal dosing of anesthetic salve and himself to a couple of potent analgesic caps; after a moment's thought, he picked up the whole bottle, two extra squeeze tubes of the burn ointment, and a bottle of broad-spectrum antibiotics.

They think they have me, he thought. *They think I'm trapped.*

He piled his loot onto the seat of a wheelchair and pushed it out into the hall, jogging along briskly toward the elevator. Inside the elevator, he swiftly tucked the stuff into the magazine pockets alongside the wheelchair's arms, because he was gonna need to sit in this thing in a minute or two.

His next stop was the Studio ON vault.

The vault's armored door swung open with a barely audible whirr of actuators. Hari sat down before he rolled inside. The twitching and jerking of his legs as the boundary effect shut down his bypass didn't matter a damn; he had more important things on his mind.

He picked out a sturdy leather tunic and pants, a pair of boots that didn't fit him too well—which, after all, wasn't really important; you don't get blisters when you can't walk. He found a knapsack full of jerky, hard biscuits, and dried fruit belonging to a swordsman called Masric, and took his canteen as well. A broad belt with a couple of large sheath-knives strapped to it turned out to have five gold royals in the concealed coin pouch sewn inside it. A quick rifling of the rest of the costumes produced three more royals, seventeen silver nobles, and a double handful of copper peasants.

I'm rich, he thought.

He held all this in his hands a moment, grimly reflecting how Caine had once taken pride in the fact that though he might be a killer, he'd never been a thief. *Things change, I guess.*

He rolled back out of the vault, closed it behind him, then went to the greenroom lavatory to reboot. It was a little bit complicated, with Rover still in L.A.—he had to access Rover's controls over the net through his palmpad, and route the return commands through the appropriate subdirectory—but it only took him about three minutes, all told, before he could walk out of the bathroom and dress in his stolen clothes. He filled the canteen and put it in the knapsack along with the medicines, and all the coins that wouldn't fit in the belt's concealed pouch.

When he went to pull on the boots, he was slowed for a moment by the sight of the Mantrak bracelet around his ankle. Designed for durability, the Mantrak had come through the fire with only a little surface blackening. Its diode winked at him like an eye, reminding him of everything he had posted for his bail.

Everything he was about to throw away.

Wink: there goes the job you paid for with your legs and your self-respect, Chairman Michaelson. *Wink:* there goes the caste you clawed your way up to, Administrator Michaelson. *Wink:* there goes every goddamn mark Caine's blood and pain and sweat and courage and rage and joy and victory and defeat ever gave you. *Wink:* there goes the Abbey, built from your dreams, the perfect symbol of everything you have achieved in your life, the only home your daughter has ever known.

Hari thought it over, just for a second; then he shrugged.

None of that shit ever made me happy, anyway.

He pulled the knives from their sheaths. He examined the gleam that ran like water along their edges—fresh and keen, no nicks—and spun them through his fingers, leather-wrapped hilts cool and soft against his skin. He checked their balance, decided they were throwable, if less than ideal; he swung his arms back and forth, loosening his shoulders, then turned the motion into a liquid *kali* flurry that transformed the blades into arcs of barely visible silvery flickers. He resheathed the knives, warm now from the heat of his palms, and rested his hands upon their pommels for just a moment, allowing himself half a smile. Like a chance meeting with an old friend, it was bittersweet: memories of better days.

He saw in his mind Tan'elKoth's statue *David the King*. He saw again that middle-aged jowliness, the bags of defeat below the tired eyes, the aura of comfortable failure. *You,* he said to the image in his mind—the image of Administrator Hari Michaelson, Chairman of the San Francisco Studio—*can fuck off.*

He walked out of the greenroom, strong and sure, but they were waiting for him in the corridor.

11

BY THE TIME the first shock baton swung at his ribs, Hari was already beaten. He never had a chance, but that didn't stop him. It didn't even slow him down.

The baton sparked, whistling toward him just as he cleared the greenroom door. The instincts of a lifetime moved him faster

than thought: his hand slashed down, striking the gauntleted
wrist, bending its arc below his ribs to miss his thigh and trigger
harmlessly against the doorjamb. His hand stayed with the wrist
as though it was glued there, turning it over so that he could lever
his other forearm against the elbow in an arm bar. He yanked
back on the wrist as he shoved with the forearm, and the elbow
snapped with a splintery crunch—muffled by the blue body
armor even as the grunt of shock and pain was muffled by the
mirror-masked helmet.

That's when Hari figured out he'd just broken the arm of a Social Police officer—and there were five more of them bracketing
him in the corridor. Assaulting an officer of the Social Police is a
capital crime.

If I wasn't already fucked, he thought, *I'd be pretty upset
about this.*

He lunged back for the greenroom door, where they could
only come at him one at a time, but the soapy whose arm he'd
broken sagged against him, clawing with his good arm and letting the rest of his body go limp so that Hari had to shove him
off. In that half second when his hands were busy a shock baton
triggered against his lumbar vertebrae.

Right over his bypass.

His legs went dead, and he dropped like a sack of fish, flopping and twitching uncontrollably. Only his left arm still worked
a little; he snarled a wordless wolverine growl and dragged one
of the knives from his belt, but the officer that stood over him
slapped it away with another stroke from a shock baton. Enough
charge was conducted through the blade to make his arm flail
wildly and send the knife skittering down the corridor.

"Hit him again." This was a human voice, not the digitized
soapy drone. The sound of it scorched Hari's throat with vomit;
the voice *hurt* him, burned him like acid poured into his ear.

He had spent too many years listening to it tell him what to do.

The soapy gave him another shot with the baton, and Hari
bucked and thrashed like a depressive taking ECT. Darkness
closed in around his vision, narrowing the lights of the corridor
to a shrinking pool of fluorescent white. A wasted scarecrow
caricature of Arturo Kollberg stepped into the pool.

Hari moaned. Kollberg licked his lips like a bum at a Dump-
ster. "Give him another."

Hari could no longer feel the shock of the baton; he was

barely even aware of his own convulsions. As the light of the world slipped away from his eyes, Arturo Kollberg bent low and kissed him on the mouth.

"You know what?" Kollberg said, making a face. "You don't taste good. I'm not even getting hard."

12

Much of the Curioseum's menagerie was devoted to species that once had roamed the land and sky and seas of Earth. Shuffled among the wyverns and draconymphs, the griffins and the unicorns were creatures now nearly as exotic, nearly as much the stuff of legend: otters and seals, frogs and salamanders, wolves and foxes and hawks, cougars and lions, elephants, an eagle, even two small inbred whales and a pod of dolphins. The menagerie occupied the central rotunda within the Curioseum's arboretum, beneath an immense dome of armorglass that allowed a pale filtering of moonlight to trickle wanly over the cages. But that greasy light was the limit of the menagerie's contact with the environment of Earth; even those creatures capable of surviving without the trace Flow available within the Overworld-normal field would not have found healthful what passed for air outside.

A scent hung in the recirculated, chemically scrubbed atmosphere, even through the acidic back-of-the-throat sizzle remaining from last night's fire: a trace of musk and dung and urine that interlaced the perfumes of chokeweed and marsh poppy and complemented the constant chuckle of living voices, from the chirps of otters and belches of frogs to the whistle of the songtrees and the hissing snarl of a wyvern in rut.

To Tan'elKoth, it smelled almost like home.

He stood in the center of it all, his mighty arms spread wide, his Shell agape like the mouth of a hungry chick, drinking every flutter of wings and rustle of leaves and splash of fins or tail, for in this place was the greatest concentration of the life of his world—and the life of his world breathed out Flow. He was battered and burned, bruised and bandaged; though he had cut away his long chocolate curls that had been scorched to black crinkles, the smell of smoke clung to him. His mighty chest was wrapped tightly to keep his sprung ribs in place, and his fashionable, freshly dry-cleaned clothes bulged oddly here and there with the bulk of burn dressings beneath. An ordinary man would have required potent narcotics to dull the pain of his burns; Tan'elKoth did not. All he needed to salve his wounds, he could draw from the Flow.

Though the Flow here was but a trickle, he was Tan'elKoth. For Tan'elKoth, a trickle would suffice.

At his feet knelt Gregor Hale Prohovtsi, twenty years old, the finest student ever to participate in Tan'elKoth's Applied Magick seminar, a slim intense youth with long dark hair and penetrating hazel eyes. His Shell shimmered bright with the saturated spring green of transcendent concentration, and it grew larger, brighter, and more vivid as Tan'elKoth fed it power. Gregor knelt with his head lowered, his hands folded before him on the inverted hilt of a broad-bladed bastard sword, its tip grounded into the marble tile of the rotunda, staring at the cruciform guard like a Knight Templar at prayer.

This blade was Kosall.

Beside Gregor's knees was a small paintpot of liquid silver—it looked black, in suspension. A small brush of ash and sable lay across the paintpot's open mouth, the end still dark with paint. The liquid silver had been used to paint the gleaming runes that spidered down both flats of the blade, not quite connecting at the tip.

Tan'elKoth stroked an image into shape with the pale fingers of his mind: the last five runes, interlinked and joining the patterns on the two faces of the blade. He affixed this image to his student's Shell and added power to burn it in; Prohovtsi would be able to see this image overlaying the blade as long as he remained in mindview. Slowly, carefully, minding his breathing, Prohovtsi lifted the brush, dipped it into the liquid silver, and began to trace the mental image onto the steel.

"Well done, Gregor," Tan'elKoth murmured, watching. "Well done, indeed. If anything, your hand is more sure even than my own."

Without the Flow of home to energize them, these runes were as silent as was Kosall itself. On Overworld, they would spring to eldritch life when the touch of flesh linked their patterns through the conductive salts of living tissue; with one cut of the irresistible blade, the runes would inescapably trap the consciousness that flees as the body dies—a quite simple variant of the spell that Ma'elKoth had used to capture Lamorak, and so many others.

Even as magick had been scribed in patterns along the blade, so, too, had magick been scribed in Prohovtsi's mind; at the touch of the proper trigger, Prohovtsi would speak the proper words—in a language he does not understand—and his body would perform the proper gestures. Hours had passed in intensive mindwork under the yellow glare of the caged wyvern, as Tan'elKoth had meticulously, painstakingly layered and sequentialized each syllable, each turn of the palm and cant of the head; it was, not to put too fine a point on it, a masterwork. Tan'elKoth was certain that no other man alive could have equaled this feat.

This was an exquisitely satisfying process; infinitely more so than creating sculpture over which the ignorant wealthy might coo could ever be.

He had made of Prohovtsi a puppet—no, more precisely, a waldo: an engine through which his will would work, even at a distance. Submerging his student's will beneath his own had required only the slightest effort; through the months of the Applied Magick seminar, Prohovtsi had been ineluctably conditioned to accept Tan'elKoth's orders without question. By now, he could not even dream of resistance. *Almost as though I have planned for this all along,* Tan'elKoth thought. *Curious.*

This was the fulfillment of his bargain with Kollberg and the Board of Governors: he would gift them with the destruction of Caine and the death of Pallas Ril. Occasionally, he allowed himself the luxury of hoping that the Board would keep their own end of the bargain, but he did not rely upon it. Their perfidy had peeked around the corner of their proclamations last night. Perhaps they would not murder him outright—rather like Caine, ironically enough, he had many admirers among the Leisurefolk, and some few in the Leisure Congress itself—but the Board obviously did not place a high value on his life, or their word.

This distressed him not one whit. He had seen this fork in the fractal branches of the world-tree that he tended with his will, and he had prepared already the graft that would bear the fruit of his desire.

While Prohovtsi brushed the runes onto Kosall, Tan'elKoth turned and walked briskly away. Consumed by the challenging—for him—task of maintaining mindview while painting, Prohovtsi would never notice his teacher's absence. The ubiquitous

Social Police, attached to him like limpets since the fire, had been temporarily banished; Tan'elKoth had been able to claim, entirely truthfully, that their mass of electronic gear and armor and weaponry would interfere with the delicate traceries of Flow in the menagerie. Kollberg had ordered them to stay away from him until the spellcasting—spell *programming*—was complete.

So now, if only for the nonce, Tan'elKoth was free.

He slipped through the arboretum to its twinned field-lock doors of armorglass, then out into the vacant echoic space of the Curioseum's atrium, beyond the ON field. Carbon-fiber bomb shutters were in place across the public accessways, englooming the atrium with artificial twilight; the entire Curioseum was closed during the make-believe "internal arson investigation" of last night's fire. Tan'elKoth paced past the vast empty ring of information and ticket booths to the bank of public screens that filled the wall beside the coat check.

Lamorak's memory provided the Shanks private code: thus this call would be billed to SynTech, and any security captures set to monitor Tan'elKoth's communications would continue their peaceful slumber on the net, undisturbed. He smiled when the personal acknowledgment came back. He had no desire to leave a recorded message. This matter was somewhat too delicate to be committed to a datacore.

Avery Shanks herself answered; her predatory gaze cycled from blankly hostile suspicion through recognition to open hatred. She was really very attractive, he decided. Stark, forbidding, all sharp edges and bleak contrast, yet somehow perfect, as though nature had intended her as precisely this: like a mountain on the Moon. *"You,"* she said flatly.

"Me," Tan'elKoth agreed. "I'm gratified that you know me, Businessman."—*and thus have no need to speak my name,* he thought. The Studio's security captures would certainly register any mention of his name; should the phrase *Tan'elKoth* be spoken, he would instantly close the conversation with the blandest of trivia, and sign off.

"How did you get this code?"

"You know how," Tan'elKoth reminded her gravely. "You must have seen some of Kollberg's trial."

Her gaze lost its needle focus, and for an instant the hard lines of her face softened toward an actual human expression of grief, but for an instant only. *"Yes, I did."* Her eyes iced over. *"What do you want?"*

"Tomorrow morning, within an hour or so of dawn, your granddaughter will suffer a traumatic shock entirely unlike anything you can imagine. It may manifest as schizophrenia, autism, even catatonia—I cannot say precisely. What I can say, however, is that there is no one on Earth who will be able to help her—" Tan'elKoth tilted his head just slightly, a barely perceptible nod to his presumption. "—except me."

"How do you know this?"

"I am who I am, Businessman."

"What kind of trauma?"

Shanks' glare was so direct and levelly hostile that Tan'elKoth felt an absurd desire to apologize for the implausibility of what he was about to say. He set his teeth and spoke with the full conviction of truth. "You have had the child for two days. Surely, by now, you are aware of her connection to the river?"

"I am aware of the ridiculous, pernicious fantasy with which her parents have poisoned her mind, yes. She is forbidden to speak of it."

As though that will make it go away, Tan'elKoth thought. *Typically Business.* "Hardly a fantasy, Businessman," he said smoothly. "Tomorrow morning, her mother will die."

The Businessman's eyes sharpened like a knife, but she said nothing.

"Faith will experience her mother's death in a fashion so intimate as to defy description. I cannot predict with any precision what form her reaction will take. I can say only that it will be extreme, certainly irreparable. Possibly fatal. You will want my help."

Shanks' eyes drifted closed for a moment, as she appeared to think this over, but when they opened again he read nothing but flat rejection. *"Neither I nor my granddaughter have any need of your help,"* Shanks said, crisp as winter's first frost. *"Do not use this code again. It will be canceled within the hour. Do not attempt to make contact with me, her, any member of my clan, or any Shanks affiliate. If you do, I shall file stalking and caste-violation complaints with the Social Police. Do you understand?"*

"As you will," Tan'elKoth said with an expressively liquid shrug. "You know where I can be reached."

The corners of Shanks' mouth drew down, and her voice went

even colder. *"You're not getting this, are you? You will never speak to me or my granddaughter again. You think that I don't know about your . . . prank . . . the other night—the call, the picture. But I do. I'm not a damned idiot. The only reason I haven't had you arrested for impersonating a Businessman is that you handed me a stick I could hit Michaelson with. And this is the limit of my gratitude: I have let you use me to take your own revenge. Because it suits me. I enjoyed it. You gave me the chance to hurt him almost as badly as he hurt me, so I let you get away with it. Don't push your luck."*

"Businessman," Tan'elKoth began, but the screen was already blank.

He shrugged at his dark reflection in the midnight grey of the screen. This particular branch of his fractal world-tree was growing precisely in its predicted curve. He had successfully planted the idea; now it would grow, watered by Faith's coming distress and the ferocious mother-tiger instincts that were the very core of Avery Shanks' being. Lamorak had schooled him well in the art of dealing with his mother; Tan'elKoth had not the slightest doubt of eventual success.

The god within him throbbed with desire. *Soon,* he promised Ma'elKoth for the thousandth time. *Soon you shall live again, and our world shall be saved.*

For Faith could touch the river; through her, he could touch it, too. Once he tapped the river's power, not all the Kollbergs and Governors and Studios in the world could stop him from going home.

He turned away from the bank of screens, and only the massive exercise of a level of self-restraint not accessible to lesser mortals enabled him to suppress what might otherwise have been the leap and snarl of a startled panther when the screen behind him crackled to life, and Kollberg's voice called his name.

His heart thudded like punches against his chest. He strangled a suicidal urge to stammer out a hasty explanation for his presence in the atrium. All this passed in the merest blink; he was, after all, Tan'elKoth. "Yes, Laborer?" he said with magisterial dignity. "How may I be of service to the Board?"

"How goes the work with the blade?"

"It is prepared. Prohovtsi is ready, as well. I will send the blade with him to the docks as soon as I return. All is precisely as I have agreed with the Board."

"I'm not calling for the Board," Kollberg said in a friendly enough tone—though there was something undefinably strange in his voice, as though he spoke words memorized phonetically in a language he could not comprehend. *"The Board doesn't need you right now."*

The Laborer gazed from the screen without expression. Slowly, he tilted his head to one side, as though abstractly curious about how Tan'elKoth might look from a different angle. Kollberg seemed reduced, refined, somehow *less* even than he had on their initial meeting two days ago, as though some inexorable erosion continued to scour away what little humanity had survived his downcasting. His unblinking eyes, with their cold unquenchable hunger, reminded Tan'elKoth of a dragon's. *And yet,* Tan'elKoth thought, *I have faced a true dragon with more ease than I feel right now.*

"In fact," Kollberg said with eerily disconnected cheerfulness, *"I called to* offer *a service. We have a transmission coming through that I think you'll find, ah, entertaining."*

In a single lightning-strike flicker, every screen in the atrium flared, from the public screen banks to the touchscreen infopods to the towering jumbotrons hung like canopies from the ceiling. Every screen showed the same scene—something perhaps from one of those motion picture entertainments of which Caine was so fond—a Western, possibly: the interior of a railcar, low mountains passing outside, beyond a window stained grey-brown with coal smoke.

But none of the five visible passengers wore guns or broad-brimmed hats or any of the other standard appurtenances Tan'elKoth had come to expect from such fare. In fact—Tan'elKoth realized with a mildly disorienting shock—four of them wore the customary dark robes of Monastic ordinaries, while the fifth wore the gold-stitched scarlet of a full Ambassador.

He frowned. "What is this?"

"This," Kollberg replied, *"is what the Studio is currently receiving from Hari Michaelson's thoughtmitter."*

An epithet borrowed from Caine thumped inside Tan'elKoth's skull: *Holy freaking crap . . .* It stole his breath; clutching at his chest as though in pain, he murmured, "Through his eyes—you can show me the death of Pallas Ril through *his* eyes—"

"Oh, yes," Kollberg agreed, and there was an ugly suggestion

of mutual lust in his voice, like a dealer in child pornography warming up a potential customer. *"Wouldn't you like to watch?"*

The prospect stunned him; for a moment, he was closer to speechless than at any time in his entire life. "I, ah, Laborer, perhaps—"

Tan'elKoth told himself that he should be above such things; he told himself that he had done what he had done not for revenge—not to injure the enemies who had destroyed him, not to satisfy any of the myriad such base urges that Ma'elKoth had buried along with the eidolon of Hannto the Scythe—but to save his world.

And yet—

Kollberg might as well have reached into his chest and taken hold of his heart. The force that tugged him toward the nearest screen was far beyond any concept of resistance. He found himself leaning against the glass, staring hungrily, almost panting.

"Laborer," he said thickly, "I wouldn't miss it for the world."

THERE IS A cycle of tales that begins long, long ago, when the human gods decreed that all their mortal children shall know sorrow, loss, and defeat in the course of the lives they were given. Lives of pure joy, of perfect sufficiency and constant victory, the gods reserved for themselves.

Now, it came to pass that one particular man had run nearly his entire alloted span, and he had never known defeat. Sorrows he had, losses he had taken, but reversals that other men would call defeats were to him no more than obstacles; even the worst of his routs was, to him, merely a strategic withdrawal. He could be killed, but never conquered. For him, the only defeat was surrender; and he would never surrender.

And so it soon followed that the king of the human gods undertook to teach this particular man the meaning of defeat.

The king of the gods took away this man's career—took away his gift for the art that he loved and that had made him famous— and this particular man did not surrender.

The king of the gods took away this man's possessions—took away his home, his wealth, and the respect of his people—and still this particular man did not surrender.

The king of the gods took away this man's family, everyone that he loved—and still this particular man did not surrender.

In the final story of this cycle, the king of the gods takes away this man's self-respect, to teach him the meaning of the helplessness that goes with defeat.

And in the end—the common end, for all who contend with gods—this particular man surrenders, and dies.

NINE

THE AUTUMN SHOWER we rattle through leaves the window streaked with diagonal swipes of darker black, bordering swaths almost clear where the rain has washed away some of the collected soot. Now as the tracks curve around another switchback, I press my face against the cool glass and try to get a glimpse of the Saddle through the backbent plume of coal smoke that makes a contrail of soot behind the locomotive.

High, high above us, the twin mountains—Cutter and Chopper, what you might call the incisors of the God's Teeth—soar up through the orange-tinged night clouds, but the gap between them, the pass called Khryl's Saddle, is hidden behind a pall of smoke and rock dust. The sedan chair shifts slightly with the rocking of the railcar, and the steel on steel clicking of wheels over expansion joints has me drowsy as a baby, but I still wish I could see the Saddle.

I've been here before. Twice. Once as Caine—many, many years ago—trekking through the aspens from Jheled-Kaarn to Thorncleft, on my way to Seven Wells, the distant capital of Lipke . . . And once, only about five years ago, back when we still thought I might someday walk again, riding in a sedan chair not quite as nice as this one my best friend gave me. That time, I was with Shanna, and she took me way up Cutter Mountain to show me the tiny spring, high on the western slope above the pass—a little washtub-sized gap through which bubbled hundreds of years of rock-filtered snowmelt—that was the ultimate headwater of the Great Chambaygen.

But the image of Shanna walking beside my chair hurts too much to think about, and I force myself sideways into a different memory.

I can see the Saddle in my head as clearly as I ever saw it with my eyes: a place of beauty so intense it robs breath from the lungs, a broad spine of earth and rock buried in forests of aspen, stark snowbound teeth of stone rising sheer to either side. She stood next to me that morning, holding my hand, while we watched the sun climb out of the distant Lipkan plains. The white-capped peaks above us caught the first direct light and burst into silver flame. Down their slopes the rock shaded from yellow to orange to deep emberous red, which became a loamy brown where it brushed the tops of the shadowed aspens in the pass below.

I put my fist against my mouth through the kerchief, and cough. Like the four bearers of my sedan chair, I've got a kerchief tied across my face against the coal smoke and furnace smut. That cough might be lung damage from the fire last night, I guess. I kind of hope it is. I guess I'd really rather have roasted lungs than find out I'm coughing because of the damn air below Khryl's Saddle.

Things change. Shit, I can see why she went nuts.

We wind upward. All around the railway, the eastern slope of the pass has become an open wound. The aspen forest has been chewed into gaping open-pit mines. Thick fogs of coal smoke and rock dust overhang every valley. Through the dark mist, I can see grimly threatening silhouettes of huge machines at work upon the land, belching smoke and flame as they chop and grind and scoop away the earth. It's the ugliest goddamn thing I've ever seen; it makes my stomach hurt, and brings a bitter acid to my throat that probably isn't just from the sulphur fumes. "Christ," I mutter. "They've turned this place into Mordor."

A warm hand squeezes my shoulder, and the voice of my best friend murmurs in my ear, "Beautiful, isn't it? Magnificent."

And somehow the sound of his voice opens my eyes to the rich red of the flame from the steam shovel's smokestack, deeper and more pure than the sun's—and more special, more beautiful, because it was made by the hand of men. The ruddy gleam it brings to the steel curve of the bucket's sawteeth is no mere accident of nature, but is intentional, deliberate, the result of an act as expressive as the stroke of a painter's brush. As far as the eye can see, men and women work side by side—even now, far into the night—shoulder to shoulder against the inanimate resistance of earth and stone, stamping this entire blank mountain, this random upcrumpling of the insensate earth, with the sigil of Man. Looked at through his eyes, it's a triumph.

"Magnificent . . . Yeah, I guess it is," I say slowly, turning to smile at my best friend. He always seems to do that—adjust my whole world with just a phrase, the touch of his hand. That's why he's my best friend.

That's why he's the best friend I've ever had.

"Yeah, Raithe," I tell him. "I guess I just never looked at it that way before."

Raithe takes my hand, and the glittering smile that sparks the corners of his winter-ice eyes tells me that everything is going to be all right.

2

AS THE TRAIN chugs to a stop at the Palatine Camp station, Raithe pulls an enormous clockworks chronometer from a pocket within his scarlet robes and ostentatiously snaps open the cover. "Eleven oh nine," he announces with the kind of self-important snobbery that you can only get from being a kid in your twenties with the most accurate timepiece in town. "Six minutes late, but we've plenty of time left."

He closes the cover, but he's so obviously reluctant to put it away that I take pity on him, finally, and ask him about it.

"A gift," he says with a distant, slightly grim smile that stays closed over his teeth. "From the Viceroy. He's mad for punctuality."

"Garrette." The name is foul in my mouth; it's all I can do not to spit on the floor. Raithe—sensitive as always—picks up on it instantly. "I thought you and he were friends, Caine. He said he knows you quite well."

"Friends? I guess you could say he's a certain kind of friend," I admit. "He's the kind of friend I'd like to stick in a pit filled to his lower lip with vomit, and toss buckets of shit at his head to see if I can make him duck."

A couple of the chair bearers snort, and one laughs outright—then muffles it to snickering behind his hand when he sees that Raithe doesn't get it. Raithe's eyes go hooded, and his face tightens toward a painful grimace that's probably supposed to be a smile: the look of a kid with no sense of humor, who's not sure if he might be the butt of the joke but wants to look like he's being a good sport about it, just in case. "What if he just moves to one side?" he offers lamely, trying to play along.

"Then I get a bigger bucket," I tell him, smiling, and he finally feels pretty sure that it's okay to laugh, so he does.

He's so eager to be liked—from anybody else, it'd be pathetic, and annoying—but Raithe is such a great kid that I can forgive him anything. "The Viceroy is on our side in this, Caine," he says seriously. "He's the one who decided to bring you here, to see if we can save the elves from Pallas—"

"Don't remind me," I tell him. Something twists inside my guts. "I can do this, but only if I don't think about it too much."

Raithe's lips stretch like he's stuck a pencil in his mouth sideways, and his pale eyes gleam. "You still love her. Even after what she's done—and what she will do, if we don't stop her."

My mouth tastes of ashes. "It's not that easy to stop loving someone, kid. I can do what we have to do. But I can't make myself like it."

He nods. "Let's go see the Viceroy. The ritual must begin at midnight, and he wants you to be there."

"That's another thing I'm not gonna be able to like."

My fingers dig into my numb thighs; I can feel a suggestion of pressure though the leather. With the bypass shut down by the inarguable laws of Overworld physics, I have the faintest ghosts of sensation in my legs—in fact, there's a sudden, surprising *pain*, and when I release my thighs I find dark wet splotches on the leather of my pants, and the palms of my hands are sticky where I touched them. I lift my hands and scowl at them, trying to get a better look at the guck on my palms in the lamplight. "What the fuck is this?"

I'm pretty sure I didn't piss myself—the partial regen on my spine left me with reasonably reliable sphincter control front and back, so long as the goddamn bypass isn't fucking things up—and the guck smells kind of medicinal, like some kind of antibacterial creme. I offer my palms to Raithe. "What is this? Who put this shit on my legs? Some kinda goddamn practical joke, while I was asleep?"

Now pain starts to announce itself from other parts of my body as well: my arms, my back, down my ribs along one flank—a lot of pain, hot crackling pain like deep burns, the kind that feel like you're still roasting inside. And with the pain, seeping in, comes some kind of primitive unreasoning horror . . . feels like somebody's piling red-hot rocks onto my back while an ice-cold anaconda of slime crawls down my throat and curls up in my belly.

I twitch my hands, trying to flick the gunk off them, trying to keep from retching a few yards of that snot-covered snake back up—

And Raithe again rescues me with a touch and a calm word. "No, it's all right, Caine. You have a few little burns, that's all. Nothing serious. When you rescued M—that is, Tan'elKoth, remember? But they've been treated and they don't even hurt anymore. Remember?"

"I, uh . . . yeah, okay, I remember." I put a hand onto my forehead and squeeze my temples between fingertips and thumb. The pain fades as quickly as it rose.

All in my head, I guess.

"It's weird . . . I can't quite get shit straight in my mind," I say slowly, a little thickly. It's hard to make my lips work right. "It's like I couldn't really remember if the fire really happened, or if it was just a dream. I mean, sometimes it seems real, but just now, I couldn't remember . . ."

"Oh, it was real," Raithe says. "It's all been recorded." His voice has a strange edge to it—creepy, almost like lust—but at the same time he sounds a little smug, a little satisfied. Like he's looking forward to something that's gonna get him off in the worst way. I frown at him, but he ignores me.

He flicks his fingers at the bearers—four burly friars from the Thorncleft Embassy—and they hoist my chair onto their shoulders. Raithe opens the double door of the railcar, kicks the extensible stairs so that they unfold to the platform, and all six of us head down into Palatine.

Even now, close to midnight, Palatine is jumping. Two years ago, this place had been only the Palatine Camp, nothing but a cluster of tents and a couple of big-ass corrugated steel sheds—the central camp for the mines that spider out across the eastern approach of the pass. Now, it's turned into an honest-to-shit boomtown, Old West style, with two hotels, a double strip of saloons and whorehouses, stores and stables; even the rail station has tripled in size. Rail spurs web the hills for miles around. Next to the station is a small clapboard building with a huge sign declaring it to be the offices of the Overworld Company newspaper, the *Palatine Tribune*.

I can just imagine tomorrow's headline:

ROGUE GODDESS SLAIN BY CAINE
Returning Hero Helps Artans Save World

It makes me more than a little sick.

The streets blaze with hissing gaslights, painting the faces of the miners and the whores and the general townsfolk all with identically eerie green-white corpse pallor. My bearers slog across the main street, a churn of black mud and horseshit a stone's throw wide; coal smoke and furnace smut coats my skin with greasy brown-black dust before we can get halfway to the hotel. The air tastes of brimstone.

Inside, Raithe leads us past a very old-movie-looking front desk, through a small, cramped saloon where a lonely bartender reads a copy of the *Tribune*, a real old-fashioned newspaper of bleached wood pulp and ink. He doesn't even look up as we pass by. Through one more door is a private party room, with some crude but comfortable-looking sofas covered in leather, and a wooden dining table big enough to seat maybe six.

At the far end, behind a wide arc of papers scattered across the table, sits Vinson Garrette. He looks up as my bearers maneuver my chair through the doorway, and he nods toward Raithe with a grunt of welcome. "Excellent," he says softly, then lifts his head and his voice toward me. "Thank you so much for coming, Hari. As you know, I don't believe we could save this place from your wife without your help. We'll go straight from here to the ritual, if it's all right with you."

I rub my face some more—I have that bad-dream dissociative thing going on again, where I can't seem to make this make sense, although I'm sure it all hangs together in some way I can't quite remember. "This feels kinda strange," I say. "Being here. I don't know why."

"Of course you don't," Garrette says kindly. "I think we'll be able to cut here, and pick up the recording again at the ritual."

"What? Cut? Recording? What are you talking about?"

Garrette nods toward Raithe, and Raithe instructs the bearers to set me down at the foot of the table and wait outside. "Close the door," he says shortly. "You do not want to hear what is said within this room." The four friars touch fingertips to brows in the gesture of Obedience and file out. They shut the door.

Garrette's lips thin to a horizontal slash beneath his long hooked nose, and he rises with the sinister gracelessness of a predatory wading bird. "Restraints, I believe, would be in order," he says, moving around the table with his head cocked as though one eye scans the shallows for fish.

Raithe produces a couple of white plastic stripcuffs. "Sit still a moment, Caine." Moving so slowly and deliberately that it doesn't even occur to me to resist, he uses one to strap my left wrist to the arm of the sedan chair and pulls it tight.

"Hey, c'mon, Raithe," I say, frowning. "Friends are friends, but even my *wife* doesn't get to tie me up . . ." I try to make it sound like a joke, but some of that slime-snake feeling is crawling back down my throat. It's pressing on my lungs now, making my breath come short. I'd like to laugh, but it might come out a kind of nervous bleat—then I'd know that I really am as frightened as I'm afraid I might be, and I'm nowhere near ready for that.

He loops the other stripcuff around my right wrist and chair arm and pulls that one tight as well. Now Garrette picks up a pile of small white cardstock rectangles from the table and consults the one on top. "All right," he murmurs, nodding to himself. He looks at me. "I believe we're ready to begin."

I find myself compulsively testing the strength of the strip-cuffs. "What the fuck is going on here?"

Garrette hefts the stack of cardstock. "I have some very specific instructions here, Hari, which I intend to follow as precisely as possible, as is my way. I confess that I don't see the use of most of them, but I suppose it's not really important that I should. The primary instruction is that I should make you comprehend your position fully and clearly."

"You're off to a goddamn running start."

He exposes a mouthful of teeth that seem too big and square and white for his thin-boned face. "Your Excellency?"

Raithe opens a small knapsack that I don't remember seeing him pick up. From inside it he pulls a shimmery wad of wire that he then shakes out into a net. With a dull shock, I realize it's made of silver mesh, just like the one I used on Ma'elKoth at Victory Stadium, all those years ago. He says, "Do you know what this is, Caine?"

I shrug; it pulls my wrists tight against the cuffs, so I stop.

Raithe's smile looks like the edge of a knife. "Do you know what I'm planning to use it for?"

"Should I care?"

Now it's Raithe's turn to shrug, and it's his breath that's coming a little short. He looks like a virgin getting his first glimpse of nipple.

With a matador flourish, he casts the net over my head.

The net splashes over me like a bucketful of ice water, a stunning shock that hits too fast to be cold or hot or anything other than a spastic convulsion of gasping. I go rigid, making *ukh ukh guh* noises, and the room blazes white like somebody lit a magnesium flare inside my head and now somebody else has more of those flares and he's using them to light the napalm that's spread down my legs and up my back and I'm on fire, all over, burning with fresh crackling agony and the thick reek of roasted flesh and the icy stab of alcohol sluiced over charred skin—

And the stranger who's standing in front of me in the scarlet robes of a Monastic Ambassador, face like suede glued in patches to his skull, he's got a light in his blue-white eyes that looks like it's the reflection of the flames that gave me these burns.

"Who—" I force the words out through a snarl of pain. *"Who are you?"*

"Don't you know me, Caine?" he says through teeth exposed by a predator's smile. He leans toward me like he's gonna take a bite out of my face, then he shoves a hand into my side, eagle-claw style, pinching the flesh through net and leather, scraping the tunic across the burned flesh beneath, making me shudder with fresh pain. His voice is low, and savage, and it smokes like his eyes.

"I'm your *best friend*."

3

"REMEMBER . . . I REMEMBER—" My voice is as ragged as ripping cloth. "I remember waking up . . . on the train, and you . . . and you—"

"A Charm patterns the energy of your Shell. You don't have to be conscious," he says through that knife-edge grin. "Your mind, like your Shell, is a patterning of Flow. In the instant that I remove this net from you, the Charm pattern on your Shell will gather Flow, and you will love me as a son, and trust me as a father."

"Why . . . have you . . . done this to me?"

"I believe I can answer that question," Garrette says. He rounds the corner of the table and leans his butt against its edge, giving me one of those Compassionate Looks that Administrators practice in the mirror and save up to use on somebody they're about to shitcan. "But before I do, I want you to understand something, on my part. I have never liked you, Michaelson. You are a disgrace to our entire caste—you have always pushed our company to serve your ends, instead of properly serving it; you are selfish, egotistical, and rude. You presume to set your own judgment above that of your betters. I know, too, that you dislike me, and always have. That being said, however, I would like to assure you that I take no joy in this task. This is not *personal*, Michaelson."

The pain-sweat beaded on my forehead rolls into one eye, stinging, and for a second that tiny increase of agony nearly drives me over the edge. It's all I can do not to howl like a wounded dog; instead I grit my teeth and pretend to smile. "You're only . . . following orders, right?"

"I try to honorably acquit the duties that are assigned to me," Garrette agrees stiffly. "Nothing personal, yes?"

"Fuck nothing personal . . . *Everything's* personal." I point my chin toward Raithe, at that dark hunger that fills his face as he watches my pain. I don't know why, or where he gets it from, but I can see the hate rolling off him like heatshimmer off sun-baked asphalt. "Ask him. He knows. I can see it."

Raithe's gaze never wavers; he's drinking me in like he's a desert and I'm a storm. He says, "Get on with it."

"Well, then. All right." Garrette clears his throat and consults the top card again. "The first thing you need to know, Michaelson, is that we are going to kill your wife."

I knew it was coming, but it still hits me like a kick in the balls. I keep smiling; what the fuck, why not? I can barely feel my balls anyway. "You're gonna try."

"Mmm, yes. And succeed. And you are going to help us."

"And then you woke up."

"You will be taken to the Cutter Mountain spring, and washed in its water. This will attract the attention of Pallas Ril. When she arrives, she will die."

"She's not that easy to kill."

"You will, I believe, be surprised."

He looks at me for a little bit, like he's expecting an answer, but all I do is stare at the pulse throbbing alongside his windpipe, and show him my teeth.

He coughs delicately into his hand, then goes on. "You will also be interested to know that in dying, she will assume full culpability for the HRVP outbreak. The story is already planted: the outbreak was a terrorist action by Pallas Ril herself, intended to inflame public sentiment against the Overworld Company."

"Bullshit. Nobody's gonna believe that."

"Of course they will. We have documents proving that she had a . . . *prior relationship*—a romantic entanglement, I believe it will be called, with one Administrator Kerry Voorhees—"

"The head of Biocontainment? But Voorhees is a woman—"

"And," Garrette says with a professorial gleam, "a lesbian, yes. This was thought to be a particularly salient twist. Ms. Voorhees will be, shall we say, overcome with guilt? And her suicide note will contain a full confession that implicates Pallas Ril. Ms. Voorhees—with the collusion of some convenient eco-terrorist group which we will credibly create—also set the trap which nearly took the life of Tan'elKoth and yourself. Which you escaped in such a superlatively gripping fashion—I've seen the recording already. It will make arresting entertainment."

"It doesn't make sense," I tell him. "Why would—"

"It doesn't have to make sense," Garrette says clinically. "In fact, it's better if it doesn't make sense, especially if it is sufficiently dramatic—you should understand that as well as anyone, Hari. This way, dozens of conflicting theories will dominate the netshows for weeks, months, or even years. And some of those theories will be more reasonable, more probable—will *make more sense*—than the truth. This is the actual social purpose of conspiracy theories. If someone does happen to uncover the truth, the truth will be relegated to the ranks of the crank conspiracies, no more likely than any of the rest. The perfect camouflage."

"But Pallas' fans will never accept—"

Garrette waves all objections aside. "Pallas Ril has gone *insane*, don't you see? The pressures of her enormous power have driven her over the edge into madness. It is a cultural tradition: Men of great power become gods; women of great power go insane and become destroyers—who must in turn be destroyed by the men who love them. The public is primed already to believe it; this has been a running theme of a certain type of popular entertainment for three hundred years."

"Nobody's gonna believe it," I repeat, but I don't sound so sure anymore.

He turns his palm upward, purses his lips, and sighs with a hint of mild melancholy: a man who's seen it all, and is somewhat saddened by how ordinary it was. "Most people will believe any tale, no matter how silly, unlikely, or outrageous, so long as it agrees with stories they were told as children," he says apologetically.

The sickening truth of this leaves an ugly wormwood taste in my mouth.

"And in the end, they will believe"—Garrette goes on slowly, with a kind of mincing, sadistic *delicatezza*, as though he can hurt me more by breaking it to me gently—"because *you* believe."

I spend a second or two trying to swallow the clot of cold oatmeal that used to be my heart; before I can gag it back down into place, Garrette goes on. "I suppose," he says with the salacious smile of someone about to share a bit of particularly juicy gossip, "you haven't yet realized that you're on-line.".

Another of those mag flares goes off inside my head, and the room begins to white out around the edges again. I *did* know—I *must* have known, somehow; I was monologuing without even thinking about it.

Shit, I still am.

"Don't worry about your audience, Hari. You have no audience. I daresay the Studio has learned its lesson about allowing you a live forum."

He lifts a black valise-sized case from behind the table he's using as a desk. It has a couple of handles that look like they're brass, or maybe gold-plated. He sets it on the table and turns it around so that a black glassy rectangle like a deskscreen faces me. "I don't think you're familiar with the device that this unit is based on," he says. "The locals call it the Artan Mirror. It's remarkably similar in concept to a palmpad, but it's adapted to work on Flow instead of quantum electromagnetism. The point is that this particular unit is powered by a griffinstone; as long as the griffinstone remains, mm . . . charged, I suppose the word would be . . . this unit will record transmissions from your thoughtmitter. This is something of a refinement on the Long Form; since the recording takes place in a separate unit, we won't have to worry about recovering your head after you are executed. In fact, this unit is magickally resonance-locked to a similar one back in Thorncleft, at the Railhead, so that, even though you are on freemod, a certain select group of Earthside—shall we say, auditors?—can follow these events in real time. Including, I believe, your former Patron, Leisureman Vilo."

The flares in my skull get brighter, and their hissing pushes Garrette's voice out to where it sounds thin, metallic, like he's talking from very, very far away, with his head in an aluminum garbage can. "You may say and do whatever you wish; the appropriate material will be spliced with the security video of your rescue of Tan'elKoth—which will open the tale with a bang, as they say. Anything of which the Board doesn't approve will be edited out of the final version."

Edited . . .

The final version—

Garrette and Raithe both lean back, arms identically folded, while they watch me begin to understand. They're gonna use me to bait out Shanna, so that I have to watch her die. They'll make a recording.

And they'll *sell* it.

Both of them disappear into the white blaze behind my eyes, and for a time there is nothing but rage.

4

"THAT MUST HAVE stung a bit, but your burns are feeling better now, aren't they?" Raithe folds up the net and puts it back into the little purse it came from.

I nod. "Yeah, Raithe. Thanks."

My best friend leans toward me and puts his warm hand on my arm, while with the other he cuts away the white plastic stripcuffs that bind my wrists to the arms of my chair. "Now, we wouldn't want to talk about anything that's happened in this room, would we? That would only upset you, and everybody else."

"You're right," I tell him, nodding again. He's really perceptive, that way; he seems to understand things about me even before I do.

"And you don't even want to *think* about that. You'd better just think about the job you have to do; you should forget about everything said here, until I let you know it's all right. I mean, all that thinking—that would only upset you, too. And we don't want you to be upset, do we?"

"No, Raithe. We sure don't want that," I say, giving his shoulder a grateful squeeze with my now-freed hand. "Thanks, kid. You're the best. I sure am lucky to have a friend like you—that's the best luck I've ever had."

A thin smile flickers through his ice-colored eyes.

"Luck? No. Not luck," he says. "It was destiny."

5

THE CRATER IS maybe a hundred yards across, a circular depression near the top of a hill only a quarter mile beyond the lights of Palatine. I'm thinking it might be an impact crater from something like a meteorite; I'm no geologist, but I don't think these mountains are volcanic, and anyway, I don't think a volcanic crater would be this regular—it's shaped like a parabolic reflector.

Stars shine down on the barren crater. All the trees and bushes and grass and shit have been burned to twisted crusty bits of char, scorched down to the bare black dirt—and recently, too, maybe just this afternoon; the whole place still reeks of kerosene.

Down in the center of the bowl is some jointed steel scaffolding a few yards high, supporting two platforms, one under the other. On the lower platform is the guy who's doing the ritual; he's got an altar there, and some chickens and goats and other small cheap bits of living sacrifice: the opening acts. He's naked, but sweating tonight—even in the midnight chill of the mountains—because on the ground underneath him is a broad pit of glowing coals where he tosses the animals once they've been cut and bled.

I can see the grimace on his face. He's new at this, and I think the blood has him a little weirded out. He keeps on chanting, though; the kid has heart. I can barely hear his voice over the nervous clucks and frightened bleating from the animals; and what I hear I cannot understand. This chant is not exactly language—at least, not a human language.

Also beside him on the lower platform is another young man—about the same age—who is only now starting to stir and wake from a drugged sleep to find that he is naked, and that his hands and feet are bound with thin slicing twists of unbreakable wire.

"Greg?" he says, looking up at the young man who kneels before the altar. From fifty yards away, his voice comes faintly. "Greg, what's going on? What are you doing? Why am I tied up?" He's still more puzzled than he is frightened.

That'll change.

He speaks in English. I'm sure that's significant, but right now I can't remember why.

Five tall oil torches blaze around the scaffolding, set on iron poles in a ring about midway between the crater's rim and the pit of glowing coals. Between the poles is strung a network of thick wire cable, bare strands gleaming in the torchlight. The wire crosses from one pole to another, suspended above the barren, blackened earth, and then around the circumference of all five. From where I sit in my sedan chair, at the crater's rim, the wire and the five torch holders that suspend it clearly form a specific design, scaffold at its center.

A pentagram.

Alone on the top platform, naked to the indifferent moon, lies the corpse of Berne. The wig that had covered his naked skull is gone; his chest and groin have been shaved. Intricate swirling designs spider across his bare dead flesh, painted stripes that shimmer like metal in the moonlight.

The guy on the lower platform cuts the throat of a squalling cat, turning its screech into a hacking parody of coughing out a furball—and tosses it, still alive, into the coals below. A couple of the friars who carried my chair here have to turn away; animal lovers, I guess.

All four of the secmen around me—the *Artan Guard*, I mean—face the crater, watching. Their faces are invisible behind their smoked face shields with the silver antimagick inlays—this reminds me with sharp discomfort of the Social Police. I can't say exactly why this bothers me so much.

Something about the Social Police—that's part of what I can't seem to remember.

At my shoulder, Raithe stares down avidly into the crater, licking a thin sheen of sweat off his upper lip. Garrette, on my opposite flank, just looks impatient. He's carrying Berne's sword, Kosall, strapped across his back—probably so much magick bound up in the blade that it would fuck up the ritual if it were down in the crater. The scabbard harness looks ridiculous over his Artan Viceroy getup, and he keeps running his fingers along beneath its straps like it's chafing him pretty badly.

Christ, I hope so.

Down in the crater: "Greg, don't—what are you doing?" the tied-up kid asks. His eyes are so wide I can see the whites of them from here.

Many, many years ago, when I was first starting out in the business, I took a job doing collections for the Working Dead in Ankhana; the job turned a little ugly, and I got the chance to see a couple of my recently deceased accounts settle their debts by having their corpses put out to work. This does not look like any Animate spell I've ever seen, and I say so.

Garrette nods, and he consults his little stack of cards. "This is not, strictly speaking, a spell," he says, in an odd tone that struggles uncomfortably to be clinical. He looks into my eyes briefly, then coughs into his hand and adjusts his cravat like a nervous victim of an ambush interview on the nets.

"The, ah, er, metals content of the rock in this crater acts rather like a Flow reflector," he reads. "An, er, Outside Power is attracted by a combination of the chanting, the magickal resonances of the Flow field within the cable pentagram, and, of course, the, ah, er, emanations of pain and terror that young Prohovtsi elicits from his sacrificial subjects. When it—the Outside Power—comes close to feed, the crater acts to concentrate it, and to direct its concentrated energies at the focal point; that is, er, the young fellow doing the ritual. So Prohovtsi effects the transfer of consciousness—a, mmm, kiss of life, you might say, to the corpse of, ah, Saint Berne on the upper platform."

"A demon . . ." I say slowly, weighing the word in my mouth, feeling its shape. "You're going to feed my wife to a demon. I'm not sure how I feel about this."

"Hush," Raithe murmurs. "You're interrupting his *exposition*." He uses the English term with a small thin smile, as though he's faintly pleased with himself for knowing it.

"Hmp," Garrette grunts, reading ahead. "Interesting."

Down in the crater, Greg Prohovtsi stabs the goat below the ribs, rakes his blade down to part hide and flesh all the way to its pelvic girdle, and tosses it into the coals. Its guts trail behind, looping across the platform, leaving a broad swath of bloody slime. It worries me a little that I know his name—where do I know him from? And the other guy, the kid tied up beside him on the platform, his voice sounds familiar—

Garrette looks up from his cards. "You might find this interesting, Michaelson. It says here that Outside Powers—demons, as you call them—aren't actually strictly sentient. Like Chambaraya itself, they are really rather inchoate; merely, mm, 'energy fields of roughly confluent tropisms, that acquire sentience and will only through interaction with a living nervous system.' Mmm, quite a phrase, that. Berne's corpse will thus be roughly analogous to Pallas Ril herself: an avatar of a greater power—a 'focal node of consciousness,' as it says here. The, er, demon, though, is power of an entirely different order, to which Pallas—Chambaraya, both of them—will be entirely blind."

"Yeah," I tell him heavily. "Interesting. Y'know what? You talk just like fucking Tan'elKoth."

"Do I?" Garrette says with a little smile. He squares the notecards against his palm. "Well, well."

Down on the platform, Prohovtsi chants louder as he drags the other guy toward the edge of the platform. "Greg, *please* . . ." the tied-up kid begs. He's sobbing now, crying his guts out. "*Please,* Greg, Jesus Christ, you can't *do* this! Greg, for God's sake, we went through school together, through the Conservatory, Jesus Christ, you never would have passed Westerling—"

"Students," I mutter. "They're both magick students."

Yeah, that's it: that's Nick Dvorak, out of Tan'elKoth's Applied Magick seminar. The other guy, Greg Prohovtsi, was in the same class—the one I interrupted, just the other day, when I first found out about all this . . .

Is that significant? Why can't I pull shit together in my head? Why do I have this feeling that I'm still *forgetting* something?

Prohovtsi doesn't seem to hear Dvorak's plea; his eyes are rolled backward, up into his head, and he keeps on chanting as he drags Dvorak right to the edge. I wince—this is a little coldblooded, even for me. "Human sacrifice?" I ask.

Raithe nods clinically. "Student thaumaturges are ideal for these operations: their Shells are well developed, powerful enough to attract a greater Outside Power, but they don't yet have the necessary skills to defend themselves."

"Besides," Garrette adds, "it's great theater."

Prohovtsi doesn't stick the kid; he just steps over him and shoves him off the platform with his foot. Dvorak tumbles screaming into the pit of coals. It's only about a ten-foot drop, not even enough to really stun him; it knocks the breath out of his lungs for a few seconds, but pretty soon he gets enough air to start screaming again. He rolls around in the coals, flopping and bucking and trying to throw himself out of the pit, but he doesn't really have a chance, not with wrists and ankles tied together. He's already so badly burned he'd die anyway, even if he could get out.

His skeletal muscles shut down pretty soon, leaving him helplessly twitching. His flesh goes loose and brown as he roasts, the subcutaneous fat boiling out through cracks in his skin, through the wire cuts on his wrists and ankles; the liquids in his abdominal cavity boil to a high enough pressure that his belly finally bursts.

Now Prohovtsi stiffens. Cords stand out in his neck, drawing down the corners of his mouth. Moving slowly, stiffly, kind of jerkily, like a marionette operated by a clumsy child, he begins to climb up to the upper platform to join Berne's naked corpse.

I can't quite shake this frown—it's giving my forehead a cramp. Something's been bugging me ever since I woke up on the train, and finally I decide to just go ahead and ask. "Y'know," I say, casual, noncommittal, "this all feels a little weird to me. Ever have one of those dreams where you're doing things and you just can't remember why? I took a knock or two on the head—I don't know, I could have a little concussion or something—and I can't make things make sense. You think you can help me out?"

"Of course," Raithe says. "That's why I'm here. To put your mind at ease."

"All right, good. Now, just let me go through this. So: Pallas did the HRVP thing herself, right?"

"Yes."

"To embarrass the, ah, the Artans. Make them look bad, so they'll have to stop digging up the mountains and shit like that, right?"

He nods. "Exactly."

"Where do *you* come into this?"

"Me?"

"Yeah. The Monasteries. How does a Monastic Ambassador end up as an Overworld Company—" I avoid saying *flunky*; I don't want to hurt his feelings. "—insider?"

He exchanges a brief glance with Garrette, who is frowning and coming a little closer. "Your company approached us directly, asking for our help," Raithe says smoothly. "You're aware of Monastic expertise in dealing with fractious gods—as you yourself must know, Jhantho the Founder fought in his brother Jereth Godslaughterer's Revolt. The Monasteries were originally founded upon a principle of opposing the willful interference of deities in human affairs, since it is so often to the detriment of the race as a whole."

He spreads his hands, and does his best to look wise and benign—not easy for a twenty-five-year-old with the face of a fanatic mujahedeen warrior, all leather skin and pale sun-bleached eyes. "We of the Monasteries are educated men, Caine. We are not swayed by the superstition of the masses. In the past, we might have resisted the Company, since it is so closely linked with the *Aktiri*—but not because we ever actually believed *Aktiri* to be demons. Demons—" He nods down into the bowl. Prohovtsi now lies on the upper platform, his naked limbs entangled with those of Berne's corpse; he kisses its cold dead lips. "—are something quite different, indeed. And now, the Monasteries and the Company share a common goal, a common interest: to save humanity—and the world—from the depredation of an insane goddess."

"Yeah, okay, I get it," I say. "I guess I'm just having trouble remembering how you talked me into helping you."

Garrette turns wide eyes upon Raithe. "You *swore* there was no way—"

My best friend stops him with a gesture like a bladehand chop to the throat, and smiles down on me. "I'm not sure what you mean, Caine," he says neutrally.

I shrug. "It's kind of embarrassing, really. Can you run down the logic for me, one more time? Why did I decide to help you kill my wife?"

"Logic?" Garrette bleats incredulously. "What logic? What *choice* do you have?"

"Well, y'know," I say, spreading my hands, a little sheepish at being so obvious, "there's always a choice—"

"This is ridiculous! Raithe, make him—"

That chopping bladehand becomes a warning finger pointed at Garrette's eye; Raithe isn't smiling anymore. He stares at me with chilly interest, as though I'm some kind of unusual and possibly dangerous bug. "It's the only way to save the world," he says.

"Save the world from what?"

"From Pallas Ril. From HRVP."

"See, I can't quite figure out what sense that makes."

Raithe's eyes seem to retreat into his face, and his voice becomes blankly cautious. "You can't?"

"Well, it seems to me, if she's threatening the whole world to stop the OC from mining," I say reasonably, "all you have to do is stop mining and she'll stop threatening. Doesn't that make more sense?"

"Stop *mining*?" Garrette is so astonished he can barely even sputter. "Do you have any idea how much that would *cost*?"

"Shut *up*, you idiot!" Raithe snaps, but it's too late.

"You're telling me that I decided your profits are more important than Shanna's life? Don't you think that's a little, mmm—" I say mildly, "—unlikely?"

For a long second or two, the only sounds are the distant lover's moans from the platform in the crater, and the tiny snaps and zips from the Artan Guard—the look on Garrette's face has them checking their weapons. "Uh—" His panicked eyes appeal to Raithe.

"No, no, no, that's not it at all," my best friend says smoothly. "She's *mad*, Caine. Stopping these operations wouldn't have any effect; she's gone completely insane, remember?"

"Yeah. Doesn't seem like a very good reason to kill her."

For a moment, Raithe appears entirely at a loss; he looks at Garrette, Garrette looks at him, and neither of them says anything.

I put out a hand and touch Raithe's arm. "Relax, kid. I'm not saying you did anything wrong. This just might be a little . . . *hasty,* don't you think? Maybe I should try talking to her, first."

"No—no, it's too dangerous, Caine," Raithe says firmly. "*She's* too dangerous. She must be destroyed—now, while we still can. It's the only way to be sure."

"To be sure of what?"

"To be sure," he says with thinly concealed impatience, as though he's tired of explaining the obvious but doesn't want to insult me, "that she never again threatens the Future of Humanity."

The way he pronounces the capitals deepens my frown. "Okay, I get it. You're saying that I agreed to help you kill her, because it was the only way to save the human race. Is that it?"

"Well . . . yes," he says thinly, sounding a little uncertain, but he must like the way it came out, because he says it again; this time, as though he means it. "Yes. The Future of Humanity depends on *you*, Caine."

And for a second or two I can *feel* it: I can feel all those lives piled onto my back. I can feel the weight of the future cracking my spine like the lower rim of a glacier, crumbling under the billion tons above.

But—

I sigh, and shake my head, and my shoulders straighten, and then they twitch in a tiny involuntary shrug. "The Future of Humanity," I say to Raithe apologetically, "is gonna have to fuck off."

Together, in perfectly blank unison, Raithe and Garrette say, "What?"

"It's too abstract," I say uncomfortably. My hands turn over, supplicating comprehension, if not sympathy. "It's . . . impersonal, y'know? The 'generations yet unborn' shit doesn't swing any weight with me. I'm supposed to murder my wife for the sake of people I probably wouldn't even *like*?"

"But—but—"

I wiggle a thumb at the Viceroy. "What if I save these people, and most of them turn out to be just like Garrette?" I say, and shudder. "Eeugh. Better we all die."

"You can't do this," Raithe says.

"That's exactly what I'm saying: I can't do this. I won't."

"No—no, I mean you *can't*—"

"Sure I can. Why can't I?"

"Because—because . . ." He struggles with the words, as though he's trying to find a way around something that he knows he shouldn't say. "Because you *promised*," he says finally. "You *swore* it to me, Caine."

"Sorry," I say simply, and mean it. "I hate to disappoint you, kid, but you're gonna have to find a way to do it without me."

Garrette snorts. "So much for your damned magick powers," he says to Raithe.

"This is *impossible*," Raithe says, his brow furrowed. He leans over me, staring fixedly, as though he can compel me with his bleached eyes. "I'm *asking* you, Caine. Me, Raithe. Do this for *me*."

"Hey, kid, friend or not, you don't really want to push me on this."

Raithe's mouth works speechlessly, then he simply shakes his head. "Amazing," he says, sighing a surrender that seems to be inexplicably mixed with some sort of reluctant admiration. And now, as I look at him, I feel like I'm awakening from a dream—my burns are starting to howl, and some vague recollections of a conversation back in a hotel in Palatine begin to organize themselves behind my eyes.

My heart smokes, but I smile.

No reason to give them any more warning than I have already.

6

"THIS IS USELESS, Raithe," Garrette says. "Now we do it my way."

"Your way?" I ask him.

"Your cooperation," Garrette says thinly, "would be appreciated, but it is not precisely necessary. We'll simply tie you up and throw you into the stream. I'm sure your wife will arrive in time to save your life."

Raithe looks grim. "Perhaps not directly in the stream, but on its bank. Should he drown before she arrives, she may not come at all. His value as bait is tied to his life; dead, he's useless."

"On the bank, then." Garrette adjusts the straps of Kosall's harness yet again and looks down into the crater impatiently. "What's taking them so damned long? This harness is killing me."

Dead, I'm useless?

The decision doesn't even take a full second. I don't mind dying. I've had a long time to get used to the idea. Coming up with a plan takes even less time.

It's not that hard to make someone kill you.

I turn a gentle smile up toward Garrette. "Did you ever follow my Acting career, Vinse?" I ask in a friendly sort of way.

"I . . . am familiar with your work," Garrette says stiffly, looking a bit puzzled. "Never a fan; I don't care for violence."

"Maybe you can answer a trivia question anyway. What do you say? A little Caine trivia, to pass the time while you're waiting for your demon."

"I hardly—"

"What," I ask, finger lifted pedantically, "is the average lifespan of assholes who threaten Pallas Ril?"

"Are you threatening me?" Garrette says, taking a step closer to my right side. "You? The cripple? Are you mad? You can't even stand up!"

"Okay, I admit it: trick question," I tell him as I lean toward him, twisting to take his wrist with my left hand. Before he quite realizes how much trouble he's in, I yank his wrist to straighten his elbow into an arm bar and pull him across me, levering his face down toward my lap, then I snake my left around his throat and grab hold of the strap of Kosall's harness; the blade of my left wrist makes a judo choke across his larynx, levering against the pressure of my right elbow on the back of his shoulder. "Tell you one thing, though. You're gonna lower the curve."

The Artan Guards all yell things about stopping and letting him go and shit like that, and I hear a bunch of ratcheting clicks as they prime their assault rifles and point them at me. For one second I tense, expecting the world to vanish in a blaze of muzzle flashes and hammering slugs.

But instead Raithe shouts, *"Stop! Don't shoot!"*

Garrette scrabbles at my legs with clawed fingers, but I don't have much feeling there anyway. His throat works desperately against my choke; the back of his neck is bright red and he's starting to convulse, and *still* the bastards aren't shooting—

"Don't you see it's a trick?" Raithe says calmly. "It's a complicated form of suicide: *he wants you to shoot him*." He compresses his mouth like a disappointed schoolmaster. "We need Caine alive more than we do Garrette."

He shrugs, and sighs. "Sorry, Vinse."

Well, crap.

On the other hand, that's no reason to let him live.

A friar says something that I don't catch, and Raithe answers, "Certainly. But Caine must not be slain. You're welcome to hurt him all you like."

A burly arm comes over my shoulder; I tuck my chin and squeeze my arms against my sides to keep him from getting a choke on me like the one I'm using on Garrette; his forearm clamps across my face just below the cheekbone in a thoroughly professional neck crank that hurts like a sonofabitch and is gonna separate my cervical vertebrae if he doesn't slack up. "Let him go," he growls into my ear in Westerling, tightening the neck crank gradually, to give me plenty of time to think about what my life would be like if my arms were as dead as my legs are.

"Yeah, sure, what the fuck," I grunt through the pain.

One sharp twist levers my wrist against Garrette's throat hard enough to crack his voice box. I release him and he jerks backward, gagging on his own blood, and as he straightens I get both hands on Kosall's hilt in the scabbard behind his shoulder.

The enchanted blade buzzes to unstoppable life.

It slices out through the scabbard, parting it like soft cheese, and deep into Garrette's shoulder. He staggers away, spurting blood, clutching his throat, making sounds like *khk . . . khk . . . khk*. The friar at my back curses sharply when he sees the blade humming around toward his head; the arm that had clamped my face slips away. He must have dropped to the ground, because I don't feel the blade meet any resistance as I wave it around behind my chair.

Garrette looks at me, blood jetting from the gaping wound in his shoulder, his voice strangled by his broken larynx, his eyes wide with horror. I shrug. "Nothing personal, Vinse."

For a moment, we're at a standoff. Everyone stays back; the Artan Guards have their rifles leveled, but they don't want to shoot me, and nobody is willing to get within reach of Kosall.

And I sure as hell can't go anywhere.

Garrette teeters on the crater's rim. He's still standing, but his knees tremble, going rubbery—he doesn't have long to live. Nobody but me pays any attention to him at all.

"Caine, put the sword down," Raithe orders, and he must be enforcing that order with some kind of power; invisible fingers pluck at my will. "Put it *down*," he repeats, and my hand loosens. His eyes reflect starfire, and he steps closer. "That's it. Drop the sword."

"One more step—" I tell him, raising the blade. It's covered with some kind of unfamiliar design: runes painted in silver. "—and I'll drop it right down your fucking throat."

The runes on the blade seem to take the fire out of his eyes, and he retreats.

What the fuck do I do now?

Before I can decide—

Like a maggot crawling from the mouth of a dead man, Berne's corpse climbs over the lip of the crater.

7

THE CORPSE RISES: a slow unfolding like cereus opening toward the stars. Painted designs like Celtic knots of metal spiral across its naked flesh and catch the moonlight in golden shimmers. The stitching that closes its belly where my knife had opened him up looks like a steel zipper; lacking the wig that had topped it when it was on display, the crown of its head is all exposed bone, skin fixed to skull with aluminum staples around the vanished hairline. In the center of the top of its skull is the jagged gap where my little leafblade went in—no reason to patch it on a dead man—and within I can see something glassy and black, as though the preservative gas turned what's left of Berne's brain to obsidian. When it finally lifts its head, its dead eyes quest blankly, fastening on nothing, wheeling with the generalized slow threat of a snapping turtle waving open jaws through water impenetrable with murk.

Somehow it holds us, all of us, even the secmen: we can only watch, breathless. Down on the platform, Prohovtsi lies motionless: unconscious or dead, no way to tell from here. The corpse of Berne stretches out its arms, fingers waving like the tentacles of anemones clutching at half-sensed prey.

Garrette, dying, twists away from it, spraying blood from the deep gash that opens his shoulder. Blood splashes the corpse's face, and a dark meaty tongue darts out, lizardlike, to lap it away. Something in the taste brings light into its eyes.

I don't even see its hand move—somehow, instantly, it has Garrette by the unwounded shoulder in an unbreakable grip. Garrette's grunting turns to a long splintery *hkkkkkkkk*—which I can only guess is his attempt to scream—as it pulls him into a lover's embrace. The demon-ridden corpse latches onto Garrette's face with teeth opened to a jaw-cracking yawn, covering the Viceroy's mouth with its own: a rapist doing CPR.

Demons feed on pure Flow, but the only kind they like is Flow tuned to the specific frequencies of anguish, terror, and despair by the Shell of a living creature. Usually, they lurk around in their incorporeal way, kind of like vultures, circling and waiting for something to suffer, unable to do much more than nudge a depressive's Shell toward a darker mood, that kind of thing. The chance to actually *inflict* pain and death—which goes along with inhabiting a physical form—must be quite a treat.

The demon that animates Berne looks like it's having a good time, anyway: the corpse has a hard-on like a raw bratwurst the size of my forearm.

Garrette is screaming into the corpse's open mouth.

The corpse's free hand shreds Garrette's clothing, stripping him naked while he still lives—then keeps on clawing at him, ripping away jagged scraps of flesh, tearing into his belly to yank whole handfuls of muscle out of his guts. Garrette's bowels let go, flooding their intertwined legs with shit, but the corpse doesn't seem to notice. It drives its hand through the Viceroy's ravaged abdominal wall, blood gushing over its forearm as the fingers go in, and then the wrist, and then it slides the arm in like a penis, reaching up toward Garrette's heart.

And somehow I know what it's doing. I know I'm right.

Cardiac massage.

It's manually pumping Garrette's heart, to keep the brain alive, to keep it sending out those frequencies of pain and terror and despair. I can't imagine what it must feel like to Garrette—the inconceivable intensity of such violation—and I sure as hell never want to find out.

Finally Garrette's struggles fade into nerveless spastic twitching, and the demon casts his body down into the crater, one-handed: a kid tossing away a licked-clean popsicle stick. Berne's corpse stretches like a sleepy cat, and its eyes now fix upon me with impersonal malice.

From its open mouth comes a mineral clacking like rocks knocking together. The clacking stops for a moment as the dead chest fills with air—lacking the breathing reflex, it hadn't inhaled before trying to speak. Now the clacking returns, gets faster and faster, becoming a stutter, gradually developing into a dry, inhumanly passionless voice. *"You havvvve my sworrrrd."*

It's not Berne. It's not him inside that body at all—I can keep telling myself that, but the look in its eyes and the sound of its voice sucks at my strength in a way that Raithe's commands could not. I can't even hold Kosall up anymore, and when Raithe steps close, one hand taking the pommel and the other levering between my forearms to twist my wrists in a very efficient aikido-style disarm, I don't even try to resist.

The demon turns to Raithe. *"It waszzz dyinnnnng."* It must be talking about Garrette. *"I hungerrrr. Not-t-t-t a violationnnnn?"*

Raithe shrugs, and mumbles what sounds like the Westerling version of *Waste not, want not.* He goes fearlessly to face the demon, reverses Kosall, and offers the hilt to its dead hand. "You understand your task?"

Idiot fucking moron motherfucking *idiot*—!

I could have killed *myself* with the fucking sword. I could have swung it at my *own* head—

But I didn't think of it in time.

The corpse takes Kosall by the hilt—and its blade does not buzz, without the grip of a living hand to trigger its enchantment. The demon lifts it, examining the gleam of moonlight along its edge and the liquid shimmer of the runes painted on the blade from quillons to razor point. *"Pallasss Rilllll,"* the demon clicks, and some abstract image of remembered lust around its eyes makes me wonder if there might not be some of Berne in there after all. And suddenly, without transition, the demon's *right in front of me.* Its eyes glitter like marbles—which I guess they might be—and from its throat comes a slow, low groan like an old, tired lover on the verge of a blood-spurting orgasm.

It says, *"Heyyy, Cainnne."*

Déjà vu claws at my throat, twists my guts toward vomiting.

This isn't happening. This has to be some kind of dream.

"Whyyy donn't youuu runnn? Youuu alllwayszzz used-d-d to runnn," it says, the blade of Kosall rising to exactly the same angle as its stiffened penis. It leans close enough that I can smell the remnants of Garrette's blood and the preservative gas on its breath. *"Whazzza mat-terr? Sssommmethinnnng wronnnng with yourrr legszzz?"*

Small sick noises come out of my throat. I try to push myself down into the chair.

Raithe touches its shoulder. "Pallas Ril," he reminds it firmly.

"Hunngerrrr. Ssshe mussst . . . die fasst-t-t-?"

"Yes," Raithe says firmly. "Swiftly. Instantly. And precisely as you were instructed; otherwise, she will destroy you herself, without effort."

"Nnnhh. Hunnnngerrrrrr . . ." Its voice trails into a mechanical growl like an idling turbine.

"Yes, I suppose you are," Raithe says thoughtfully, and then his colorless eyes swing round to me, and he stretches his lips into what he probably thinks looks like a smile. "And, I think, I have in mind the perfect snack."

8

I DON'T KNOW how long it takes the demon to haul me up the mountain. Hours, probably—an endless nightmare of bouncing facedown over its rock-hard shoulder. I fade in and out of consciousness, blacking out from pain and fatigue and a fucking incredible migraine from hanging upside down: like I'm birthing wasps inside my skull. I puked out the last of whatever was in my guts a long time ago; now, whenever I wake up I retch and dry-heave until my eyes uncross. When I cough, I can taste blood.

And the goddamn sword keeps knocking me in the eye. They found another scabbard from somewhere and tied Kosall into it before they strapped its harness across the corpse's back. I twist my wrists against the thin unbreakable strap of the stripcuffs that bind them together behind my back; it slices through the flesh, and blood trails down my inverted arms to the elbow, then trickles up my back and around my neck to drip along my jaw.

If I can just get one hand loose, and get hold of Kosall's hilt—

The demon jogs upward at a steady lope. There is no such thing as fatigue for its dead muscles, which do not rely on chemical reaction for their energy. It skirts the pass, avoiding the easy road, clambering high up the facing slope of Cutter Mountain, inhumanly agile among the crags, even with bare toes and a single free hand.

Hanging down over its shoulder, I can see nearly all of Khryl's Saddle below me. The crest of the pass has become a rat's nest of rail spurs sprawling around the stark skeletons of a half-completed depot; a customs office roughly marks the official border between Transdeia and the Ankhanan Empire. There are tents everywhere, from small two-man wall tents to enormous canopies: a mess hall, a corrugated machine shed large enough that you could dismantle a pair of steam locomotives inside it and not get the parts mixed up, latrines, a Company store, and god knows what all.

An Overworld Company base camp: they're laying rail down the western slope of the Saddle. Into the Empire. That goddamn rail line looks like a tongue, lapping out to get a taste of Ankhana.

The top curve of the sun lifts out of the eastern foothills, sparking a gold shimmer in my eyelashes. I guess that having this demon burst into flame or something at the first touch of sunrise was too much to hope for.

High on the western face of Cutter Mountain—not far below me, now, where I should have been able to spot the spring—all I can see is a low brick cylinder out of which runs a long, twisting sluice pipe, new enough that the leaking joints haven't yet begun to rust. The pipe empties into a slats-and-pitch watertank on stilts, which in turn sprouts a number of smaller pipes that spider down into the rising skeleton of the depot.

Down in the tangle of rails, a shifting crowd of workmen form a long, disorganized queue—too tired and bleary from a night spent at this elevation even to bother looking up, where they might see us. Now, at dawn, the construction people have come stumbling and scratching out of their tents to line up for water from a spigot-fed trough, churning the soppy earth around it into ankle-deep muck.

That ankle-deep muck is now the headwaters of the Great Chambaygen.

Raithe stayed behind, keeping out of the watershed with his secmen—*fake* secmen, I realize now. They had to be Social Police in drag, because no secman ever born—let alone *four* of them—would have stayed cool through what happened down there at the crater. Soapy, though, he never gets nervy; the fucking Apocalypse wouldn't make a soapy blink.

They have to stay on the far side of the crest of the pass, because Shanna will be able to feel their hostile intention if they come into her watershed. They'll be around, though. I don't know what it is about that Raithe fucker—I don't know why he hates me the way he does—but real hate, bone hate, is something I understand. He'll be watching.

The demon carries me northwest, paralleling the wash of wastewater that trails from the trough to join the overflow from the tank above it. A few minutes' hike takes us down a quarter mile west of the camp, where the sewage and overflow reenters the original streambed: a small, shallow wash that leads to a tiny waterfall, tumbling maybe fifteen feet to a rocky pool in a crevice. The demon carries me carefully around the folds of rock, out of sight of the camp, moving into the wash beside the stream. The surface of the stream is flattened, its ripples rounded and smoothed and thick with grease, and the water smells of urine and sulphur.

The demon clambers down the rocks beside the falls, then tosses me onto the jagged stone like a sack of dead cats. Hands cuffed behind me, useless legs, there's nothing I can do to break the fall except tuck my head and hope I don't fracture my skull. My head bounces off the rock, showering stars through my vision and actually driving off the migraine for about five seconds before it comes roaring back hard enough to kill a bull.

The corpse dips one hand into the stream, and tilts it above my face, drizzling the filthy water across my lips. Then it cups water into its hand again and lifts it to my brow, letting the slime drip down through my hair, baptizing me with the foulness the Overworld Company has made of the headwaters of the Great Chambaygen.

In seconds, my nerves begin to tingle with a warm *here-ness*, an odd and undefinable sensation of being hugged and held and comforted by something inside me. Scabs peel from my burns as my flesh begins to renew itself.

This is her way of telling me she's on her way.

Oh, Christ, if only I could die before she gets here—

If only—

And as scalding tears etch my face like acid, the demon crouches beside me and begins to feed.

9

OUTSIDE THE WORLD Mommy sang with the river; when Faith got too scared, she could snuggle her head a little deeper into these amazing silky sheets and pull the covers up over her head and close her eyes and let the music carry her away. She had been *really* scared at first, when the man had grabbed her and Daddy got so angry, but you couldn't stay really scared very long, not with the river singing in your head.

Cause the river was always gonna be the river, so there was nothing to be scared of.

Besides, this was a really amazing house, bigger than home even, and it was in the middle of Boston, which Faith had never been to before and she hadn't seen very much of it except from the window of Grandmaman's big car, but she was still pretty sure that Boston was amazing, too. She didn't mind too much staying here for a while, because there were all these people who were really really nice to her all the time, and she didn't have to put away her own clothes or make her bed or anything. There was an old lady whose name was Laborer Dobson who didn't seem to have anything to do except follow Faith around and pick up after her. Laborer Dobson was a pretty nice old lady, though she didn't say much, but she smiled all the time and didn't seem mean and once already had slipped Faith a piece of the most amazing candy that was called a *chocolate truffle*.

Mommy had been working really really hard on the Overworld sick people, and she'd been singing the whole time, a new kind of song that Faith didn't recognize but that she loved all the same. Mommy was content, she was happy, and so Faith was happy too, even when Laborer Dobson came in and made her get out of bed and get all dressed up for Sabbath Breakfast. Faith knew it was supposed to be capitals from the kind of serious way everybody looked when they said it, and from the dress she was supposed to wear, which was a big white fluffy dress that went all the way down to the floor, with puffy sleeves and a really amazing satin shirty kind of thing.

A couple of Laborers, whose names she didn't know yet, neatened up her room while Laborer Dobson fixed her hair, and pretty soon she was ready for Sabbath Breakfast. Laborer Dobson held her hand all the way down the three flights of really really big curvy stairs, through the front hall to the dining room.

The dining room was really big, with wood paneling up higher than her head, and satiny-looking wallpaper above that. The table was really big, too, with candles on it and everything. Her uncles—whose names she had forgotten already—and Grandmaman were already sitting down, and there were more Laborers standing behind each chair with fancy uniforms on and real serious looks on their faces. Laborer Dobson showed Faith to a place that was set for her with a special chair, so that when she climbed up into it she was sitting all the way up at the big table just like a grown-up. She clambered up onto the chair and suddenly started to giggle.

"Faith," Grandmaman said in a mean voice. "Stop that snickering at once."

"Sorry, Grandmaman," she said, and she put both hands over her mouth to try and keep her delighted laughter inside.

"What on Earth has you tickled, child? Share your joke with your uncles. I'm certain they will enjoy it."

"There isn't any joke, Grandmaman. I'm just happy."

"Happy? Of course you are. Coming here to a proper household must be a terrific relief—"

"Not your *house*," Faith said, giggling. "I'm happy because *Daddy's* here."

"What?"

"Not *here* here," Faith explained. "*There* here. He's with Mommy, now." Her golden eyebrows drew together in a puzzled frown. "But *Mommy* doesn't seem very happy about it . . ."

10

THE TOUCH OF Hari's lips brought the goddess back to her own individual thread of melody within the Song of Chambaraya.

Since the instant she had stepped forth from Ankhana, she had buried herself in Chambaraya's supernal harmonies, finding within them the infinite mathematical iteration of her theme: an endless Bach invention upon the semilife of her countervirus. Her sole distraction had been Faith's distress—her own moment of maternal weakness—when she had become once again merely Shanna Michaelson, when she had cast aside her task and stridden at speed toward the nearest transfer point. But Hari had sworn, through Faith, that he would handle Earth; he had reminded the goddess that she had her own job to complete. She trusted him.

She had to.

And so she had surrendered to the Song, and watched a billion generations of her creation wheel across her consciousness like a galaxy in which each star is life itself. She had found her HRVP sample in Kris Hansen, and had cultured it in her own bloodstream; here as well did she create and culture its cure. At the close of a billion generations, its chorus still sang sweet and true: without a single discordant mutation.

But when Hari touched her now—sharp as a needle in the swollen chancre that her headwater had become—she felt his pain and his distress. Across the leagues she touched him with power; she knit his skin and eased his heart, while a pang of pure dread struck her own. This sensation was so alien to her nature that for a time she could not identify it, nor could she guess at its source.

Her daughter's distant counterpoint still chimed within her melody, happy to be part of her even in the alien place to which her grandmother had confined her. Faith was not afraid; her father had promised he would come, had promised to make everything right—yet he had come here, alone, wounded and in pain, leaving Faith in the hands of his enemies.

And perhaps, in this, she had found what poisoned her serenity with dread.

The grace note within Chambaraya's Song that was the physical form of Pallas Ril arose from its place of contemplation—a sun-dappled glade amidst oak and walnut, above a willow-lined stream some three days' ride to the south and east of Ankhana—and sought within the Song a hint of remembered phrase, the echoed theme of a rocky splashing rapids seven leagues away. She caught that phrase within herself, and Sang it as the river did; in joining those notes to the slumberous rhythm of the sunlit glade, she brought them together in space and time.

One single stride carried her from the glade to the rapids.

Another seven leagues away, she found the low susurration of a marsh, rustling with the laughter of cattails and the subterranean rumble of solemn trees; again, she melded the disparate melodies into her Song that she might step from the rapids to the marsh.

In this manner, she strode the length of the river.

As she approached, she felt within him pain far beyond any mere insult of the flesh: terror and cold rage. Horror. Despair.

And yet around him there was no threat, no danger. She could taste the camp at the crest of the pass as though its sewage drained into her mouth; she could faintly hear the cacophony of a thousand lives at the very verge of her watershed. None within the range of her perception meant him ill—their lives were merely the baseline of humanity, the all-too-human blind stumble toward vague dreams of food, sex, and comfort.

What had he to fear?

Thirteen steps brought her to a dawn-shadowed slope below the pass men called Khryl's Saddle: a curve of earth that joined sawtoothed peaks soot-stained to the color of steel. Within the

Song, she found the fundamental trickling chime that was a small waterfall tumbling into a rocky cleft, its music now driven by the allegro hammer of Hari's heart. One final reality-warping step brought her to his side, into the rocky cleft with the waterfall tumbling above her head.

He lay on his back at the waterfall's foot, half wedged into a crack in the stone with the spray in his face, his arms bound behind him and a rag tied through his teeth. He moaned thickly through the rag, and his eyes spoke to hers with numb, unreasoning horror.

She knelt beside him, the waterfall's spray cool and welcome across the back of her neck; even its savor of human waste was not unpleasant, because the grasses and algaes downstream fed upon it and burgeoned as they never had before. She laid her hand upon his cheek.

"It's all right, Hari," she said. "I'm here." She could have built a voice of birdsong and tinkling water, of the skitter of marmots and the creak of stones forced open by the roots of grasses and scrub brush, but she spoke instead with the mouth and throat of Pallas Ril, for the same reason that she pulled at the knot of the rag tied into his mouth with her fingers, instead of calling upon her power. Sometimes, even a goddess must use a human touch.

She understood now his distress: someone had dumped him here to die, and he had feared that she would not arrive in time to save him. Within herself, she allowed a gentle, melancholy undernote to enter the harmonies of her Song. After all these years together, she had never been able to make him understand that a human life is only an eddy in the current; when that eddy, beautiful but transitory, unknots itself into the river, nothing is lost. There is nothing that *can* be lost.

The river is eternal.

Tears streamed down his face, mixing with the greasy film from the waterfall's spray. She twisted the knot open in the dirty rag that bound his mouth, and he shook his head aside from her touch, spitting the rag away into the stream with a convulsive gasp. "Shanna—*run*," he rasped, his voice jagged as broken glass. "It's a trap. *Run!*"

She smiled. How could he still understand so little? "There is no threat here, Hari—"

Hari screamed: a wordless shriek of raw overpowering panic. It shocked her, stopped her mouth like a punch. Suddenly, inconceivably, the vague dread that had troubled her shifted beneath her with a tectonic infrasound rumble. The planet, of which she was a part, was no longer solid. She discovered, awe breaking over her like the growing light of the dawn in the mountains, that she was actually *frightened*.

Hari thrashed. His shout came out ripped and bloody as though he vomited barbed wire: *"Shanna goddamn your eyes for once in your fucking life just do what I say and FUCKING RUN!"*

She stood, and started to turn, and she felt a shock at her shoulder, as though she'd been struck on the collarbone, sharply but not hard—a slap from a child, a lick from a switch, nothing more, no real impact, just a cold wave that passed through her almost too swiftly to be felt, icy wire drawing itself from that shoulder down at an angle to her ribs on the opposite side. She tried to finish the turn, to see what had struck her, but now she was falling, sliding sideways and down and she couldn't feel her legs, she couldn't feel her left arm, she reached out for the ground with her right and struck hard on the stone, and flopped faceup—

And standing over her was a woman wearing her clothes, except it wasn't a woman, not all of one—it was only a torso with the left arm attached; where the head and right arm should be was only a gaping wound the size of the whole world, and as the legs buckled and the headless one-armed torso twisted and crumpled toward the ground, the jet of heart's blood from the severed aorta fountained like cabernet spraying from a spinning wine bottle, glittering in the rising sun, a rainbow that took her breath away with its beauty.

She thought: *That's me. That's my blood.*

She tried to speak, to say *Hari—Hari, I'm hurt, you have to help me,* but most of her lungs had been left behind within her collapsing torso. She could do no more than move her lips and make faint, desperate smacking noises with her tongue.

Hari, she tried to say, *Hari, please—*

Then a man-shaped shadow loomed over her, a huge, powerfully built nude figure in silhouette against the lacy white clouds of the dawnlit sky. The silhouette lifted a long broad-bladed sword and reversed its grip upon it, to drive it downward like a fencepost to be set in hard clay.

Its point came toward her eyes, and then she saw no more.

11

IN THE MIDST of the customary Shanks family Sabbath Breakfast, with the morning sun bright through the sheers from the garden outside and the plates still steaming in the liveried servants' hands, Faith leaped upright from her chair, pounded the polished mahogany tabletop with her tiny fists—ripping her antique ivory linen place setting—and shrieked as though rats gnawed her toes.

An instant later, before anyone in the astonished family could so much as enquire what might be wrong, she collapsed. In the shocked silence that followed, Avery clearly, unmistakably heard a plaintive childish whisper from her granddaughter's lips: *"Hari—Hari, I'm hurt. You have to help me. Hari, Hari, please—"*

The servants sprang to her side, and Avery's voice cracked like a whip over their heads. *"Back!* Don't touch her. Dobson, get Professional Lieberman up here instantly."

Faith was neither choking nor convulsing; while everyone waited for the doctor to arrive from his rooms in the coach house, Avery's teeth clenched until her ears rang.

His name—

Bitter, bitter, most impossibly bitter, that in Avery Shanks' own home, her own granddaughter had whispered his name.

12

RIGHT UP TO the bitter, bloody end, I keep on thinking that there must be some way out of this. We've been here so many times—trapped, no way out, no chance to survive—and we've always done it, we've always pulled it off, against all odds, against all reason, against all hope. We've always found a way to live.

Through every second that I've lain here—on this cliff, with the sewage of the construction camp splashing across my face, with the demon inside Berne's corpse drinking my horrible aching dread—I have straight-armed despair by numbering all the times we somehow came through. All the way to the end, I force myself to believe that Shanna will see the trap, that she'll save me, that together we'll rescue our child, that my father will still be alive, that we can all go home again.

That somehow, I can still get my happy ending.

Then when she comes and the demon still doesn't strike, I try to speak to her with my eyes, to reach her with the language of my horror; I try to bite through the dirty rag that fills my mouth with the taste of dust and human shit.

She could crumble the rag to its component atoms with the merest gesture; instead she fumbles at the knot with her too human, too fallible fingertips, and when I can spit the rag aside and tell her, she still does not believe me, she still tries to soothe me, and all the furious dread explodes from my throat in a scream that shuts her down, shuts her up, and I see in her eyes that she's starting to understand—but she's never been fast, that way; it's always taken her time to adjust her paradigm, to see the unexpected, and this is time that no wealth at my command can buy her. I rage at her, howling, cursing, goading her with savage words, anything to get her *up*, to get her *moving*, to get her *away*: and so she stands, and starts to turn—

And dies, with my curses as her only farewell.

With a lifeless hand upon its hilt, Kosall gives no rattlesnake buzz of warning. The corpse appears behind her with that invisible speed, and the blade, too, moves too fast for the eye: I see the beginning of the stroke, and the end—the arc of the blade is visible only as a lick of silver flame that tears out her front in a one-blink flash from collarbone to rib, bisecting one breast—

And half of her falls away from the other half, and I have no breath left to scream.

The pieces of my wife fall, and her guts splash out across the rock with the wet slaps of handfuls of mud hitting a sidewalk. The demon Berne steps over her headless, one-armed torso, stands over her—her hazel eyes pick up the blue of the dawn sky, and her perfect lips writhe soundlessly, and her hair gleams with burnished-walnut flame, and oh my god how am I gonna live, now?

But, of course, I'm not gonna live for long.

The corpse lifts the sword high over its head and lets the blade swing down to vertical. He drives it down like he's staking a vampire, except her heart's over there somewhere, and the blade with its painted-on runes of silver chops through her eyes, through her skull, through her brain, and into the stone beneath her.

The blade buzzes for one scant second, as though registering the passing of her life. It slides a handbreadth down into the stone below her riven skull and sticks fast; the demon releases it, and its hilt waves a slow good-bye in the breeze alongside the waterfall.

"*Yessss,*" the demon murmurs in its cracked-quartz voice. "*Yesss, that'sss it-t-t-t.*"

It does that fast thing to reach my side before I really see it move, and those glass marble eyes open to swallow me whole.

"*Yesss, Cainnnnnne. It'sss allll true.*"

And I know what it's talking about. I know what is true.

Other men, they might ask, *Why?*

I know why.

All this—losing my career, the Abbey, Faith, Dad, and now . . . now . . . this unspeakable thing—all this happened for a reason. For one simple, inarguable, inexcusably self-absorbed reason. Because I couldn't sit down and shut up. Because I'm too fucking stupid to know better. Because I had to *do* something, to feel like a man.

Which are all different ways of saying—

I did this, to everyone and everything that I love, because I had to pretend I can still be Caine, one last time.

13

THE DEMON BERNE clasps its enormous erection and swings its leg across me, straddling my chest like a nightmare goblin, and its other hand strokes my face.

"*I lovvvve youuuu, Cainnnne.*"

It leans toward me like it might bite. Like it might want a kiss. "*I lovvvve youuuuuu.*"

And, you know? I think it's telling the truth.

An odd, distracted peace settles over me, a hollow sort of *oh never mind*edness. The astonishing thing is that in an absent, unexpected way, I'm kind of okay with this. I can guess what's happening; I've seen it dozens of times, in people who take terrible—even mortal—wounds.

The *I'm all right* syndrome.

No matter what happens to you, once the first shock of un-comprehending disbelief is over, the next thing you think is: *Well, it could have been worse.* You're always kind of impressed with how well you're handling it, whatever it might be, from a knife in the guts to the death of a child. I wouldn't be surprised if Shanna died thinking, *This isn't so bad, really . . .*

The demon Berne caresses my face with its cold, unyielding palm, feeding—

And maybe that's where the *I'm all right* thing comes from: a cluster of demons sucking away your despair, your terror, your grief. Maybe that's what people are really saying when they shake their heads sadly and nod at each other and murmur in low tones *It just hasn't hit him yet.*

They're saying: *The demons are still feeding.*

By indulging their own compulsive hunger, demons are doing us a *favor*.

Once they get full, though, you better watch your ass.

That's why I can lie here with jagged stone under my back, with Shanna's blood splashed across my face and her intestines being gently rinsed in the waterfall's mist, with my useless legs and my useless life, and feel nothing but hope that the corpse goes ahead and kills me while it's still hungry.

Because I have an idea what's coming, and I don't want to be here when it arrives.

The demon Berne licks its lips, and a small round hole appears in one cheek with a wet *smack* and splinters of its teeth blow out through the other cheek, then another hole appears in its temple and one of its glass eyes shatters and its head snaps sideways like a horse that's been stung by a wasp and now, from far away up the mountain, I can hear the mechanical chatter of chemical assault rifles.

Sounds just like it does in the movies.

Fucking great shooting—I keep hoping that one of those bullets will go just a hair astray and plow through my skull, but no such luck. Must be the Social Police doing the shooting; everybody knows that Soapy never misses.

More bullets strike with semirhythmic fleshy slaps like a vaudeville hambone guy warming up, dragging the corpse upright and blowing it spinning away, a herkyjerky dance as it wheels its arms and splays its legs, trying to stay with me on the ledge, but more rifle fire sputters above and now a fire hose blast of slugs blows it right the fuck off the cliff.

It drops away, and I can hear a meaty slap or two as it bounces off the rock face on its way down.

And now, I can *feel* that it's gone: I can feel it by the thermonuclear fireball that expands within my chest and burns my heart to ashes and roasts my throat and öh my god oh my god oh my god oh . . . god . . .

. . . god . . .

14

SOME UNIMAGINABLE ETERNITY later: adrift, hopelessly becalmed on my vast bitter ocean, shadows dance before my eyes and voices come to me—faintly, filtering in from the unknowable, irrelevant universe beyond the ache that is all I am.

Our agreement is entirely specific, says a voice that seems both human and synthetic: these are sounds a clockwork doll might make, had it a mouth and throat of flesh. *He will be delivered to the capital for execution. The sword will be secured.*

The voice that answers is exactly the opposite: though the words are dry and precise, it *thrumms* like a plucked bowstring. *Yes, of course. I will see to him. As for the sword, this is a relic of Saint Berne, and is the rightful property of the Church of the Beloved Children of Ma'elKoth. It shall be extremely well cared for.*

I open my eyes and roll my head toward them to tell them both to shut the fuck up, and I see that suede-faced Ambassador motherfucker squared off with one of the fake secmen.

Between them, in the rainbow spray from the waterfall above, Kosall's hilt swings back and forth like the arm of a metronome counting off the measure of all the empty noise the world has become. The spray condenses into a trickle, a tiny rill pale-pink with her blood, channeled by the rocky cleft away from the stream to dry in the sun upon the barren stone.

Her eyes, split by the blade that cleaves her forehead like a horrible Athene-in-reverse, are still bright and clear. The spray has washed away the dust that would settle there, and they still sparkle like gemstones, and I can't understand why I am still breathing.

Raithe turns his own stone-gleaming eyes on me. "What do you say, Caine?" he says with playful mock deference. "Are you ready to go?"

Speech is beyond me.

Raithe shrugs at the fake secman. "You have my thanks. Convey the warm regards of the Monasteries to your superiors in the Overworld Company. Tell them we apologize for Administrator Garrette's death, but you yourself can testify that it was unavoidable."

"Agreed," the fake secman says. "The embassy will be notified of the new Viceroy as circumstances demand."

"We stand ready to welcome him, in the spirit of true brotherhood," Raithe says smugly. "Fare you well."

The fake secmen don't answer; Soapy never says good-bye. They silently about-face and march off along the ledge.

I was hoping they'd kill me. But that would be redundant.

I'm still breathing, but that doesn't mean I'm alive.

So it is when Raithe yanks Kosall free by its quillons, bracing Shanna's face beneath his foot to scrape the blade out of her skull, I feel nothing.

So it is when he leans over me, his blue-white eyes sparking with the same hunger that had been reflected in the glass marbles in the sockets of Berne's dead face, and says—

"I am Raithe of Ankhana. You, Caine, are my prisoner, and you will die."

—I am unsurprised to hear my own hollow voice reply, "I'm not Caine. There is no Caine. Caine is dead."

And somehow this fills him with exaltation. He stands, his brow aflame with glory, and spreads his arms like he wants to hug the whole world. He throws back his head and cries to the limitless sky, *"This is the day! This is the day! I AM!"*

I have the strength to wonder dully what it might be he thinks he is, but I don't have the strength to care about the answer. Right now, I can only think of Faith.

I can't even imagine what this has done to you.

My god, Faith . . . I know you can't hear me, but—

My god, Faith.

I'm sorry.

THE CROOKED KNIGHT, as with all knights errant, had a path to follow and lessons to learn; each turning upon his path was another lesson, and each lesson led to another turning.

The crooked knight slowly, gradually, and painfully discovered some of the truths that his life had undertaken to teach him: what the road to hell is paved with, that there is nothing pure in this world, and that no good deed goes unpunished.

He learned these truths too late, of course; for he was, after all, the crooked knight.

TEN

THE KNOCK SOUNDED friendly enough—not too loud, a brisk double tap like a cheerful hello—but when Deliann opened the door he got only a brief glimpse of a big, square-bodied human with kindly eyes and a face roughly the color and topography of a dishful of overcooked yams. He saw no more than this, because his view was obscured by the human's large fist, which got larger much too fast and hit Deliann's nose so hard that he didn't even remember falling; without a discernable interval, he found himself lying on the carpet, brilliant white sparks curling through his peripheral vision and the taste of blood in his mouth.

"Hiya," the human said cheerfully as he short-stepped to Deliann's side and let him have the reinforced toe of his big square boot in the ribs just above the kidney, hard enough to spring a couple loose with crisp but utterly silent pops.

Deliann doubled up, spitting blood. The human said, "Rugo," as though it was someone's name.

An ogre wearing chainmail painted in the scarlet and brass motif of the guardstaff at Alien Games stepped through the door, shaking out a large silvery net that looked sickeningly familiar. A flick of the ogre's wrist spread the net over Deliann; then he latched one enormous paw around Deliann's upper arm and hauled him up to dangle above the floor. Deliann was bagged and slung over the humps of muscle that rippled across the ogre's broad back by the time he'd managed to convince himself that any of this was really happening.

"Guess what?" the human said. "Kierendal's awake, and she wants to see you."

2

A BOUNCING, JARRING, DISORIENTING ride through the private corridors of Alien Games ended with the ogre unslinging the net like a nine-foot-tall yellow-tusked Santa Claus and dumping Deliann, bag and all, on the floor in Kierendal's bedchamber. He landed hard on his butt in an awkward twist that hurt his ribs worse than the kick had.

Slowly, with patient caution, he tried to untangle enough of the net that he could at least come up to his knees. He made no move that might be interpreted as a struggle to free himself; the ogre's other hand held a morningstar as long as Deliann's leg, with spikes longer than his fingers and about as sharp.

Kierendal lay propped on brightly colored silk cushions piled up on her enormous canopied bed; her steel-colored eyes had black rings beneath them, and her metallic hair splayed in greasy tangles over her shoulders and across the pillows. Her skin was the color of a catfish strangling in a drying mudpool, and her lips hung like raw meat draped over her sharp predator's teeth. The room smelled like a half-filled bedpan that had been topped up with vomit.

"I had an idea," Kierendal said thickly, as though her mouth didn't work very well, "when I sent them for you, that I'd say something witty. You know: about how I wanted to give you my personal thanks for saving my life."

"Kier—"

"Shut up!" she shrieked, ragged and raw, half lifting herself from the pillows; but then she fell back as though the effort of anger had exhausted her. "But I don't want to. I can't. I can't even be bitter about it." She rolled her face away, so that he could not see her expression.

Grief clamped down on his heart, and he could not speak.

"Now they tell me we don't have to die," Kierendal went on, still facing away, looking toward the dark brocade of the curtains that shuttered the bedchamber's window. "They tell me this disease of yours might not kill me. That we might *all* live through it."

"Yes," Deliann said.

"All but Pischu," she said. "All but Tup."

"The goddess—"

"Don't talk to me about your goddess. I know all about her. She's a fucking *Aktir*. Pallas Ril."

Deliann said, "She looked like a goddess to me."

"You know," Kierendal said distantly, as though she had not heard, "there are already rumors. There've been killings, a lot of them. Not all in Alientown. Probably your barge crew. But the story is that it's the Cainists—that it's the start of a terror campaign, reprisals for the mass arrests, trying to fuck with the government's plans for the Seventh Festival. You and me, we know better, though, don't we? Don't we? I thought I did, anyway; but then I got to thinking about it, and now I'm not so sure."

"What are you talking about?"

"I *knew* Caine. Does that surprise you? I was part of it, the whole Assumption of Ma'elKoth—and it didn't go quite the way the Church says it did. I was there. The Church is right about one thing, though: he was an *Aktir*, Caine was. Pallas Ril was his woman. Both *Aktiri*. Like you, Deliann."

"Kierendal—"

"There's this thing about Caine—you can always sort of tell when he's mixed up in something, because everything starts to spin out of control. You can even see it, sometimes: black Flow, a current that comes out of everywhere, and goes nowhere. You'll know when you see it. Nothing ever turns out the way anyone expects it to. Usually for the worse. Just like this."

"All I know about Caine is what everybody knows," Deliann

said, lifting his hands in a helpless shrug that made the net rustle like chainmail. "Mostly just what the Church says. All I know about Pallas Ril is that she promised to help. And that she saved your life."

"Saved my life?" Kierendal rolled her head so that she could face him again, and her eyes were bloody and raw as a half-incubated egg cracked into a cold skillet. "Yes. I should thank her. I should thank her for letting me wake up and find out that . . ." Her voice broke. ". . . Pischu . . . Tup . . . they *died*. And I get to live, knowing I killed them. For *nothing*."

"I'm sorry, Kier," Deliann said with simple honesty. "I wish it could be different."

"Do you? Do you really?" She looked up at the ogre and waved a trembling hand. "Take it off him."

The ogre grabbed a handful of the metal net at the top of Deliann's head and yanked, tumbling him out of the net to the floor. He landed hard on his swollen thigh—the one with the internal infection—and sudden pain made him gasp. Instinctively he sought mindview, to ease his burning leg with Flow; Kierendal gestured, and the human clouted him on the side of the head.

"Don't," she said. "I'm watching you, Changeling. That was just a warning. Reach for the Flow again and he'll kill you. Understand?"

"No," Deliann said thinly through a mouth held tight against a whimper. "No, I don't understand. I don't understand how you can treat me like this. Like an enemy."

"Maybe I can explain," Kierendal said. She lifted a finger-thick rod of polished wood as long as her hand. She turned it this way and that in the pale lamplight; its polish had a distinctive iridescent sheen that made it impossible to tell what color the wood actually was. "You know what this is?"

"Of course I know what it is," Deliann said, frowning. "I've been a Mithondionne prince for twenty-five years. Where did you get a message stick?"

Message sticks were the original records of the First Folk, dating back to the misty millennia before the invention of their alphabet. A trained mind could imprint the semicrystalline structure of the plant itself with a Fantasy; a Fantasy thus encoded into a properly prepared message stick was permanent, so long as the message stick itself remained undamaged. It was a laborious process that had fallen into popular disuse thousands of years ago. Message sticks survived only for the formal matters of state, and even there were rarely used for anything less than a royal wedding or declaration of war. Deliann might never have seen one, save that House Mithondionne was the hereditary tender of the small shrubs that were used to make them; "message stick" was the Westerling translation of *mithondion*.

"It came by bird just a couple hours ago," Kierendal said. "Didn't you ever wonder how I know what's going on halfway across the continent? Have a look." She tossed it to him; he caught it instinctively.

It had an unreasonable solidity, a *weight* to it, as though it were made of gold instead of wood. Deliann turned it over in his fingers, and it awakened in him a dread that chilled his guts.

The message stick could only have come from Mithondion.

From home.

"Go ahead," Kierendal said. "Dream it."

"I, ah . . ." The message stick had become so heavy it made his arm ache with strain; his mouth had gone dry, his tongue a numb lump of muscle.

Torronell would have headed straight to the Living Palace.

Deliann raised his eyes; he could not even look at the stick. "I don't want to, Kier," he said humbly. "Why don't you tell me what's in it? Please."

"That wasn't a request, Changeling. I'll tell you one more time: Dream it. If I have to tell you again, it'll be after Rugo's morningstar makes porridge out of one of your ankles. You got me?" Her eyes were dark, dead flat, lusterless, as though dust had settled upon them.

Deliann looked down again at the message stick in his hand; its iridescence became somehow obscenely repulsive: a growth on the lips of a whore.

But how bad could it be, really? He had seen Mithondion in ruins a thousand times in his dreams already; this couldn't possibly be worse than his dark imaginings. He opened his Shell to caress the faintest breath of Flow into the patterns of the message stick; color swirled around him, joined by forest sound and scent. Soon they organized into a coherent Fantasy, and he discovered just how wrong he was.

He couldn't possibly have imagined anything as bad as this.

3

Deliann knelt on the floor, images screaming inside his head. Kierendal had lain silently upon her bed while the Fantasy had fed unimaginable horror into Deliann's brain.

He saw the Living Palace in flames, fire eating away the very heart of the deepwood. He saw primal corpses by the dozen, the score, the century; he saw feral creatures roaming the forest with blood upon their teeth—feral creatures beneath whose masks of filth and madness could be recognized the features of courtiers and ladies of fashionable society.

He saw the corpse of the King, his father, lying half rotted upon the floor of a closet, where he must have crawled to hide; the corpse had been found there by two starving, maddened feyallin, young males who had torn his uncooked flesh with their own teeth, only to vomit it forth again in great bloody pools across the richly woven clothing the King had pulled from the shelves above to make a rude bed for his dying.

He saw the bird-picked shape of a fey who wore Torronell's favorite vest; he could not know if this was his brother's corpse. It hung high above the forest floor, a broken branch impaling it from crotch to gullet.

"Not easy to watch?" Kierendal finally asked.

Deliann barely heard her.

"So this is how I've got it recked," Kierendal said; without transition, her voice had hardened to a rasp like a knife drawn across a whetstone. "You're an *Aktir*—"

He could only see the image scored into his memory, of an eye—that might have been Torronell's—being gulped by a crow, its head thrown back as though in ecstasy.

"—and Caine was an *Aktir*. Shit's gone completely out of control. Pallas Ril is sniffing around. You're all hooked together somehow, you and Pallas Ril and Caine. I think those rumors are closer to right than they know: somehow, this is all something to do with the Cainists." She pulled her bloodless lips back over her teeth in a pack hunter's fighting grin. "I've been lying here since I woke up, trying to figure what I could have done to make things different, and all I can come up with is this: I should have had you taken out and killed the night you showed up."

Deliann looked at her then, but still had no words.

"Tup," she said harshly, "was the only creature I have ever known who really, truly loved me."

Deliann lowered his head.

Staring fixedly at the cold dark brocade of the curtains, she looked like she was hugging herself under the blankets, trying to suppress a shudder. "Take him to the white room and beat in his skull. Throw his body in the river."

Deliann knelt unmoving as the ogre covered him once again with the silver net, slung him over its massive shoulder, and carried him away.

4

DELIANN TWISTED HIMSELF inside the netting as he bounced against the ogre's back on their way down to the white room; pretty soon his neck uncramped enough for him to speak. "You can't do this," he said.

"Soor I can," the ogre replied cheerfully. "Thass why I got thizz." The ogre underhanded his enormous, blunt-spiked morningstar to give Deliann a little tap with it through the net, just a friendly nudge that punched a couple of spikes into the swollen muscle of his badly healed thigh. "See? Eazzy."

Deliann bit his lip until he tasted fresh blood. The pocket of infection within that thigh made it brutally sensitive; the tap from the morningstar hurt worse than had breaking the leg in the first place. "No, you don't understand," he said, once he was sure he could control his voice. "Kill me if you want. But you can't dump my body in the river. In the river, Eyyallarann alone knows where I'll spread the disease—it could kill thousands before the goddess' cure catches up to it."

"What, you think it's not in the river already?" said the ugly square-bodied human who ambled alongside the ogre, thumbs hooked behind his belt. "I'm no healer, but I hear things, y'know. Always payin' attention, that's me. I figure you already give it to people who's dead by now, and most dead folks hereabouts end up in the river sooner or later."

"Yes," Deliann said softly. The ache in his chest threatened to choke him. "Yes, you're right. I wasn't thinking."

"Don' know nothing about no diseazze," the ogre said. "Kier

sayzz crack your head, I crack your head. She sayzz dump you in the riffer, I dump you in the riffer. Eazzy."

"Yeah, Rugo's got a pretty straightforward outlook, huh?" The human leaned around the ogre's broad back to give Deliann a ruefully companionable smile. "Kinda makes you jealous, don't it? Ever wish your life could be simple?"

Deliann let his eyes drift closed against his grief. "For a long time, I thought it was."

"That's cuz you wasn't payin' attention," the human said sadly.

The white room turned out to be the small chamber with the brown-stained walls in which he'd been chained to a chair upon his arrival. The ogre dumped him rolling out of the net. Deliann lay where he fell, staring at the ceiling that was also spattered with brown splotches—a sort of kinetic record of the backsplash that arcs away from a mace or a morningstar when you reset for another swing. He could see—barely, in his peripheral vision— the faint outline of the Shells of the ogre and the human, but the room was closed to Flow. He would be helpless to resist.

Not that he had any intention of resistance.

There was, in being brought to this particular room for execution, an ironic symmetry that he found poetic.

The ogre let his huge morningstar dangle from his wrist by its leather thong as he carefully shook out and folded the silver net; apparently such devices were expensive enough that he didn't want to risk damaging it when he crushed Deliann's skull. The ogre laid the folded net on the seat of the maple chair that was bolted to the floor in the middle of the room, then flicked the haft of the morningstar up into his hand: killing position.

Deliann wondered, for one stretching instant, if he would see a flash of light when it hit him, or if the flash that goes with being hit on the head was an artifact of memory—something you don't see at the time, just remember seeing when you wake up, a sort of neuronal default to cover the scramble made by impact. He was abstractly curious; since he wasn't going to wake up, he couldn't guess what the actual moment of impact would look like. It seemed important, somehow.

At least as important as anything else you could be thinking about, one second before you die.

The morningstar went up, and up, and up, and the human said,

"Hey, Rugo, hang on a second, will you? I'm not sure I'm all right with this."

The morningstar paused at the top of its arc, and the ogre said, "Huh?"

"Changed my mind," the human said with a shrug. "Let's not kill him."

"But Kier zzaid—"

"You don't have to do everythin' Kier says, do you?"

"But she's the *bozz* . . ." he murmured.

"So?"

The ogre lowered the morningstar, frowning as he chewed over the unfamiliar concept. "I don't get it," he decided.

The human shrugged again, this time uncomfortably. "I dunno if I can explain, exactly. See, I guess I got it figured like this: If this character told Kier and everybody the truth about the goddess, Pallas Ril is gonna be back here in a day or two to fix things up, and everythin'll be all right, y'know? And if he's wrong about the goddess, we're all gonna be dead pretty soon— Kier first, prob'ly. So she won't really care one way or the other, and neither will we. So, I figure, why kill him?"

"Causs Kier *zzaid* zo," the ogre insisted.

The human looked profoundly skeptical, and more than a little troubled.

"You don't understand," Deliann said, licking his lips. "I'm a *carrier*—"

"Yeah, whatever," the human said. "Big deal. If you're givin' it to people, I prob'ly already got it, right?"

"Don't do this for my sake—"

"Who says I'm doin' it for you?"

"I never said I want to live."

"Nobody ast you. You wanna die, you can do it without our help."

"Kier'll get mad," Rugo said dubiously. "Really, really mad."

"She don't have to know." The human spread his hands. "C'mon, Rugo. We'll turn him loose and tell her we dumped him in the river. Whaddaya say?"

Rugo scowled as though all this thinking was giving him an ogre-sized migraine. Finally, he shook his huge head. "Nah. Kier'zz the bozz. We gotta do what she sayzz." He lifted the morningstar again, and the human stepped over Deliann to put himself in the path of the downward swing.

"Don't do it, Rugo."

"Aw, c'*mon*," the ogre said plaintively. "You're gonna get uzz in *trouble . . .*"

"Nope; *you're* gonna get us in trouble, if you yap me out to Kier. What she don't know won't hurt us." The human turned his back on Rugo and offered Deliann his hand. "C'mon, get up. We're outa here."

Deliann bemusedly took the offered hand; it was warm, and dry, and very, very strong. The human lifted him to his feet seemingly without effort.

"Maybe I s'ould crack *you* one, too," the ogre said ominously; he took a step forward, towering over the human, tusks curving up to frame his globular yellow eyes.

The human looked over his shoulder at his partner and cocked his head curiously. "How long we worked together? You really wanna bust my skull? What kinda friend are you, anyway?"

"But . . . but . . . c'*mon*. Let me kill him. Pleazze?"

"Nah. Made up my mind. Sorry, Rugo. Guess you're gonna have to kill me, too." The human gently turned Deliann around and gave him a little shove toward the door, following close behind him.

"I could call more *guardzz*," Rugo said, bright with sudden inspiration.

"And tell 'em what? How y'gonna explain you didn't take care of this yourself?" The human pulled open the door. "We're leavin', Roog. You can come if you want."

Deliann didn't hear a response from the ogre, nor could he see one as the human propelled him out the door. The human led him through the corridors of Alien Games, to a narrow door that opened onto a dark alley that pattered with slow drizzly rain like the piss of old drunk men. The human stepped out and beckoned Deliann to follow with a jerk of his head.

"C'mon. You hungry? Let's go get somethin' to eat."

5

BEHIND THE COUNTER, a fat stonebender in a dirty brown apron spun a plate of greasy eggs, blood pudding, and some kind of unidentifiable meat into place between Deliann's elbows, and a certain color began to return to the world. This was the first time he'd even been outdoors since the night he came to Alien Games; he was as damp as the mud-churned street, cold in his light cotton tunic and pants, and what little sunlight filtered through the grey bruise of overcast was barely enough to show him a hint of yellow in the scrambled eggs.

He perched on a rickety stool next to the human who'd saved his life, and leaned on a splintered wooden counter just a little less greasy than the food before him. The counter made a squared-off ring with a large grill, griddle, and enormous wood-fired kettle fryer in the middle, tended by a pair of stonebenders who acted like husband and wife, but resembled each other enough to be brother and sister. Deliann didn't ask.

An awning kept off the drizzle. Between the counter, stools, and awning, the establishment occupied a good third of the right-of-way of Moriandar Street. Other similar stalls were scattered along the street; the rain kept most of them nearly as deserted as this one. Other than Deliann and the human, the only customer at this stall was a fat treetopper with tattered wings who lay stretched out on the far countertop, face in the crook of his elbow, snoring like an asthmatic bloodhound.

The human shoveled eggs into his mouth and chomped on them noisily. Deliann could only stare and wonder; he could not remember the last time he'd had an appetite.

"You're not eatin'?"

Deliann rotated one shoulder in a diffident shrug.

"Best friggin' eggs in Alientown. *Eat,* dammit. I paid for the goddamn things. Don't make me sorry I saved your life." The human snorted a friendly chuckle around his mouthful of food and gave Deliann a nudge with his elbow as though they shared a joke.

Deliann turned his stool to put his back to the counter and leaned on his elbows, watching the occasional passersby scuttle from shelter to shelter, shoulders hunched and necks turtled against the rain.

"Maybe you should have let the ogre kill me," he murmured. "It's only justice."

"Justice? What's that?" the human said with an amiable smile. He turned his palm upward. "Here. Put some justice in my hand. No? Then just tell me what it tastes like, huh? What's it smell like? What *color* is it?" He shook his head and scooped another forkful of eggs into his mouth. "Don't talk to me about justice. We're both grown-ups here, right?"

Are we? Deliann thought. *I've never been quite sure I am.*

After a moment, he asked, "Aren't you worried about your job?"

His companion shrugged. "Aw, nah. Rugo's maybe dim as hour three of a two-hour candle, but his heart's in the right place."

"He's a killer."

"Shit, so'm I. Just not today."

"This could cost you more than your job," Deliann said.

He shrugged again. "So? My choice." He hit the word *choice* with an odd, subtle emphasis.

"I don't understand why you wanted to help me."

"Well, I guess it wasn't to hear you say thanks."

Deliann looked away.

"Heh," the human said. "That wasn't a shot. Save a guy who's tryin' suicide, you don't *expect* thanks. Guess you learned that one from Kier just now, huh?"

"Yes, I did," Deliann agreed softly. "But I still don't understand."

The human sighed and set down his fork. "It's not real easy to explain. I don't always got a real good reason for the shit I do. Sometimes I just sorta make up my mind, y'know? And once I'm set on somethin' I don't fuzzle around with second thoughts."

"All right. But why?"

"Dunno. I just got thinkin', up in her ladyship's chamber up there, when she was talkin' about Caine and all. She was talkin' about how she knew Caine, and how shit always goes wrong when Caine's around, and all that. And how she figures you're hooked in with Caine, somehow."

"Caine," Deliann murmured. "I don't really know anything about him."

"Well, I do. Knew him pretty good. Wasn't exactly friends ex-actly, but we was—I guess you could say—friendly acquain-tances. He broke my arm once."

"Some friend."

"Hey, it was that or kill me. Shit, I was grateful. Still am. Saved my life, that broken arm, most likely. He broke it the day before the Assumption of Ma'elKoth. See, I useta be a Knight of Cant; not for that arm, I woulda been in Victory Stadium that day, and I probably woulda been killed. Most of my buddies were. Point is, I met my Neela because of that arm; she took care of me for a while—cuz I got a little fever from the break and all—so with the break and the fever, that whack from Caine not only kept me out of the Stadium but out of the Second Succession War. Now I got a home, wife, kid—and a pretty good job—just cuz I knew Caine well enough that he'd rather break my arm than kill me. See?"

"No, I don't see," Deliann said. "What does this have to do with me?"

"The thing is, Kier was wrong. Shit don't go bad because Caine's around. Most of the time, shit goes bad by itself. You can usually find somebody to blame it on, if you look hard enough. Just like she was blamin' shit on you. She don't have the guts to face up to what the world was bringin' her. That's what killed Tup and Pischu, y'know: gutlessness. But she can't face that, so she's gotta hang it on you." He gave half a shrug, a silent apology for his employer's weakness, then took another bite of eggs.

"But I don't have to play along," he went on, chewing with his mouth half open. "*I* say: You never know how shit is gonna play out, not really. So you do the best you can, pay attention, and maybe somethin' happens to make everythin' turn out all right. That's what I did. Why should I kill you for somethin' that wasn't your fault?"

"It *was* my fault," Deliann said.

"Horseshit."

"No, it was. I should have known. I should have let myself die back in the mountains. Now you're infected, for sure; when you die, that'll be my fault, too."

"So what? Why kill somebody over somethin' that's already done? Ast me, only good reason to kill a man is over what he's *gonna* do, you follow?"

"You don't know what HRVP infection is like," Deliann said. "You'll go crazy. You'll start to think everybody hates you, everybody's trying to kill you, even your best friends, your wife, your child—"

"Shit, I get that from a bad hangover."

"So you kill them first. If you live long enough, you will murder everyone who means anything to you. And when you die, you will die in agony."

The human sighed again, picked up his fork, and took another big bite of the eggs. "Yeah, that's gonna suck."

Deliann gaped. "That's it? That's all you have to say?"

"What do you want me to say? The goddess might come back and fix everythin' up. Then, no problem, right? If she don't, well, who knows? Shit might work out. You never know."

"*I* know," Deliann muttered darkly. "I can feel it. Something's gone wrong. The goddess won't come."

"Maybe. But now look at it the other way: she might. If you never came to Ankhana, you can bet this disease of yours would have made it here anyway. We're downriver from where *you* got it, right? So if you'd died up there in the mountains, all this shit could still be happenin' here, except nobody would've got the goddess into it. So friggin' relax, pal. You mighta saved the world after all."

"I still feel like it's my fault."

"Yeah, *fault.*" The human shrugged, chewing a fresh mouthful of blood pudding. "That's another one of those things like justice. Don't talk to me about fault until you can spoon me a mouthful of it and let me chew it up. I don't believe in fault."

"What *do* you believe in?"

"You wanna know what I believe?" The human leaned in and lowered his voice. His kindly eyes took on a conspiratorial twinkle. "This is what I believe: There Are No Rules."

The capitals were clear in his tone, and he searched Deliann's face for a moment, as though this were a recognition code to which he expected some cryptic answer. When he didn't get one, he shrugged and grinned. "Well, there's one rule, maybe. *My* rule: You don't eat those eggs, I kick your skinny elvish ass and stuff 'em down your throat. You better get started."

After a long, slow, considering moment, Deliann couldn't come up with a reason why he shouldn't, so he turned himself around, and took a bite of the eggs. Even lukewarm, they were delicious: buttery and golden and delicately peppered, slightly crisp around the edges. As Deliann chewed and swallowed and took another bite, the knot that had strangled his guts for weeks began to unclench itself like an opening fist.

He said, "My name's Deliann," and held out his hand.

"Yeah, I know," the human said when he took it. "I'm Tommie. Pleased to meetcha."

"Likewise. Uh, Tommie?"

"Yeah?"

"Well . . . I guess—thanks, that's all."

Tommie laughed and gave him another nudge in the ribs with his doubled elbow. "Yeah. Don't mention it. Listen, eat up. It's gettin' dark, and we gotta be goin'."

"Going where?"

Tommie winked at him. "I wanna introduce you to some friends of mine."

6

FIRE SPUTTERED WITHIN a low ring of heat-cracked clay in the center of the room; the chimney hood above it was built of mud brick and stood upon three stout pillars. The room had no windows, and its only furnishings were a crude plank table and a scattering of chairs like the one on which Deliann sat, wrapped in a damp but drying blanket.

He stared into the flames and thought how fire was a living thing.

Fire takes in food—in this case, dried clods of shit, probably bought off one of Lucky Janner's muck carts this afternoon— and processes it with oxygen in a chemical reaction that releases the energy that gives it life. Fire does not evolve, though. There is no mutation, no natural selection of survival traits. Fire has no need of these; it is perfect already. Fire is simply fire: though hotter here, redder there, white or gold or transparent as heat shimmer in the desert, flame is ineradicably a single individual, forever born again whenever conditions favor its existence. Kill it, and it resurrects itself elsewhere; itself immutable, it is the very symbol of change.

Small wonder that fire was humanity's first and most persistent god.

The chair in which Deliann sat was almost comfortable, despite its rude construction. The wool blanket he held around his shoulders prickled his chilled, damp skin like nettles, but he didn't mind. He felt disconnected—floating, drifting away—and nothing really mattered too much right now. He'd put himself entirely in Tommie's hands; drifting along in someone else's wake was surprisingly calming.

Deliann was pretty sure that the room to which Tommie had led him was somewhere in the Warrens. He guessed he should have been paying closer attention, but walking head down through the bone-chilling rain, he had needed all his concentration to maintain mindview; only by continuously pulling Flow could he dull the pain from his legs.

The crooked streets of Alientown had given way at some point to the broad blank facades of Industrial Park manufactories and warehouses, and eventually Tommie and he had threaded twisting alleyways between sagging tenements of moldy plaster framed with rotting, warped timbers. Many of these timbers still showed streaks of blackened char; in the Warrens, little ever went entirely to waste. Even a building that burns to the ground will have a few surviving timbers that can still bear weight.

Tommie squatted by the fire, rubbing his hands together and grimacing against the heat. Deliann watched him blankly while his own shivering gradually subsided. Soon, Tommie dragged a chair over to the fire, reversed it, and straddled it with his back to the flames. "Gotta dry my ass," he said apologetically. "Sittin' around in wet pants'll gimme the piles somethin' fierce."

He settled himself in, squirming as though his rear didn't quite fit on the seat, and rested his chin on the chair's back. "These friends of mine, they're gonna be here before too long. You're gonna tell them your story—heh, I could stand to hear the whole thing, myself. Then we're all gonna talk about what we want to do about it."

"There's nothing to do about it," Deliann said dully. "It's beyond anything you or I or anyone but Eyyallarann herself can do."

"Sure it is, you take the whole thing at once. I don't know all about it, but like I was tellin' you, I pay attention, so I got a pretty good idea. Trick to dealin' with the big problems is to chop them down into bite-size pieces. Like, all right, I can't save the city. If you're right, I can't even save myself, huh? I've got it, and I'm gonna die. But maybe I can save my wife and my boy."

Deliann looked away. "I hope so."

"Yeah, thanks. Savin' my family: this is what I want. Talkin' to you, this is part of what I'm doin' to *get* what I want, you follow? If anybody can give me a clue how to save my family, it's you."

"I, ah . . ." Deliann coughed harshly, to force the tightness out of his throat. "I'll do what I can to help you, Tommie."

"I believe you. And that's why I'm tryin' to help *you*."

The firelight behind him haloed his thinning hair, and a pool of red-rimmed shadow crawled across his face.

Deliann squinted at him, but his eyes were lost in the shadow. "Help me do what?"

Tommie chuckled. "Well, that's the question, huh? Listen, somethin' else I learned from Caine—wanna hear it?"

Deliann shrugged.

"It's this," Tommie said. "There's only really two things about a man that matter: what he wants, and what he'll do to get it. Everythin' else we pretend is important—whether you're tough, or good-lookin', smart, stupid, honorable, whatever—that's just details."

He became very still, and from within that shifting shadow that pulsed in the middle of his face Deliann could feel Tommie's eyes upon him. He brushed the edges of mindview and found Tommie's Shell to be streaked with spirals of brilliant green: tight-wound vortices like the symbols that the First Folk use to mark the *dillin*, the gates between the worlds.

Tommie's voice was low and tight. "So. What do you want?"

Deliann's reply was a blank stare.

"C'mon," Tommie said with an encouraging nod. "Simple enough question, huh? What do you want?"

"I, uh . . . I guess I don't really understand what you're asking me . . ."

"Sure you do."

Deliann shook his head helplessly. "With everything that's happened—everything I've done to . . . to Kier . . . and Alien Games, and the city, to . . . to *you*, even though you saved my life—I've, I guess I've . . . killed everyone . . ."

"Listen, I'm tryin' to teach you somethin' here. Pay attention, huh? What do you want?"

Deliann pulled the prickly wool blanket higher around his neck and hung his head. "What do you want me to say?"

"Not that," Tommie said, chuckling and shaking his head. "Sometimes it's you bright guys that have the hardest time followin' this. All right, look: What I'm askin' is for you to make a decision. Make a choice. Decide *what you want*. Shit, you don't even have to *tell* me, you don't feel like it; just decide. Two hours ago, you were tellin' me you wanted to die. Was that true? Is that what you want?"

Deliann offered a weak smile. "I'd settle for it."

Tommie shook his head again, but this time there was no

amusement in the gesture or his voice. "This ain't about what you'll settle for. It's about what you *want*."

Deliann shut his eyes, took a deep breath, and let it trickle out again. "I suppose what I really want is for none of this to have ever happened. I want to wake up and find out it's all been a bad dream."

"Mm, sorry, man," Tommie said with true regret. "You can't unring the bell. The past is what it is; all you can change is what you think of it. The future, though, that's a story that ain't been written yet, y'know? You were talkin' about justice awhile ago, too. How about that?"

"You said you don't believe in justice."

Tommie shrugged. "Depends. You gotta be a little more specific—gotta get right down to dowels and dovetails, Changeling. Don't say *justice*, say: 'The guy who stole my purse, I want him locked up,' or 'The guy who raped my sister, I want him dead.' *That* I can believe in. You see what I'm sayin'? You gotta be *specific*. Listen, didn't you ever want somethin' so bad you didn't care what it took to get it?"

With sudden, overpowering, inexpressible pain, Deliann thought: *I want to be a primal mage.*

Staring into the pool of shadow on Tommie's face, more than a quarter century of Deliann's life was wiped away. *Hari Michaelson asked to be remembered to you,* the goddess had told him, in the bedchamber where she had brought Kierendal back from the brink of death, and then she had warped reality around her and stepped outside the world . . .

What a strange place his life had become.

"Yes," he murmured in answer to Tommie's question. "Once, a long time ago, I wanted something so much I did some very bad things to get it."

"What happened?"

Deliann lowered his eyes. "I got it. Sort of. It didn't turn out quite the way I was expecting."

"Nothin' ever does, huh? That's no reason to bitch. Listen, dintcha ever do somethin' where shit just went way wilder than you coulda ever guessed? Y'know, somethin' little that turned out huge?"

"Yes," he said, his throat knotted with pain, thinking of a dead primal village in the eastern foothills of the God's Teeth—of stealing in at twilight with his bow in his hand, of a feyal's corpse on the ground with maggots on its tongue. How could he possibly have known where those few short steps from the village edge to its center would lead him?

Tommie shook his head, chuckling. "Nah—I can see that's an ugly story, just from your look. Go the other way. Find a *good* story."

Deliann closed his eyes. "I don't know any good stories."

"Sure you do, ya lyin' bastard. They just don't look so sweet right now. Think about it."

"No. It's . . ." He shook his head helplessly. "Even the best thing that ever happened to me—my Adoption—even that turned hideous. If I wasn't a Mithondionne prince, I would never have been on that expedition. I would never have gone into the village. I wouldn't have carried this disease down the river—"

"You're a prince?" Tommie asked, squinting at him sidelong.

"Sounds unlikely, doesn't it? It's . . . I don't know. It wasn't something I planned on. I just fell into it, I guess."

"*That* sounds like a good story. Got at least a laugh or two, huh?"

"You think so?" Deliann looked down at the blanket; without meaning to, he'd twisted its ends into ropes knotted between his fists. *Torronell . . . ah, gods, Rroni, if only you could be here now . . .*

Torronell would have known how to turn this story into something darkly comic. With his dry, ironic wit, he could spin the most bitter thread into pretty cloth; he had a genius for it. Rroni could take the sting out of a knife wound. Deliann had no such gift. The bitter, aching futility of existence—that's what this story was about, really. Try to raise a laugh with that.

But Tommie's kind eyes never wavered, and after a moment, Deliann cast a sigh into the air between them. "The *finniannàr*," he said. "Have you heard that word before?"

Tommie shrugged. "It's, like, the elvish code of hospitality, right?—er, *primal,* sorry."

Deliann waved this aside. "It's a complex system of obligation, very formal and so ancient that it's almost a natural law. It spells out—specifically and in detail—what the duties are of a guest to his host, and of the host to his guest, and the guest of someone you have hosted in the past, and the host of someone for the second time without a return invitation, and so on and so forth until it's hard to believe that anyone can actually keep them all straight. I became a prince of House Mithondionne because I thought I understood the *finniannàr* well enough to get clever with it."

He remembered entering the Heartwood Hall, that long low cavern of oak that served as the throne room of the Living Palace; he remembered the glittering infinity of the ranked primal nobility—and the hush as they stared at his ragged, travel-stained clothing, and at the hooded figure of Torronell who trembled by his side, who clutched Deliann's hand with both of his own.

He'd reached the small open disk of floor called the Flame, ten paces from the Burning Throne; then he'd raised his head and had met the fierce falcon eyes of T'farrell Ravenlock, the Twilight King. At the age of twenty-three, Deliann had spent more than a quarter of his life preparing for this moment.

He could not possibly have guessed how unready he was.

The voice of the King had seemed to come from the high-sloping walls of the hall, as though the Living Palace itself asked the questions in the Ravenlock's heart. And he'd had his answers ready: his tale of being a weary traveler, asking only hospitality for the night, but bringing one humble gift that he begs the King to accept—

"I gave the King a present," Deliann said, staring past Tommie into the fire. "Something, ah, I was afraid he'd refuse, if it was offered in any ordinary way, so . . . I framed it as a guesting gift, which the *finniannàr* requires him to accept. His response was . . . extravagant."

"I'd say so," Tommie grunted. "He adopted you? Over a *gift*?"

"It was a pretty good gift," Deliann admitted. "I gave him back his youngest son."

Tommie squinted at him silently.

"I met him twenty-five, maybe twenty-six years ago, when I was working at Kierendal's old place, the Exotic Love—I kind of had your job in those days, I guess: I was Kier's best thug. No offense."

Tommie shrugged. "You don't often see primal royalty in the whorehouses around here."

"It was . . . ah, a special circumstance. It doesn't bear explaining."

The special circumstance had been that the Youngest of the

Twilight King had been a *lacrimatis* addict, pale and twitching and semipermanently divorced from reality, and he'd fed his habit by working as one of Kierendal's whores. He'd been with her for half a century, and he'd had a substantial following among the whip-and-branding-iron crowd. He had been famous, legendary; he'd had third-generation clients—men of particular tastes brought to him by their fathers, who had in turn been brought by their own fathers. He had been a bottomless abyss of self-loathing covered by a shield of impenetrably dry, occasionally savage wit, and he'd been entirely successful in erasing his past; no one suspected his true identity—no one suspected he'd ever had any identity other than the whore's face he showed the world.

But he couldn't hide from Deliann's flash.

With scorching grief, Deliann recalled his slow months-long persuasion, the gradual erosion of Torronell's determination never to make contact with his family again. He remembered— with the kind of piercing clarity that seems reserved for bitter hindsight—Torronell sitting on a tangle of bloodstained satin sheets, the floor around him strewn with brightly studded leather straps and boots and collars and harnesses, twisting a black silk hood between his fists.

"I can't go home," Torronell had said, his eyes spilling first one tear, then another, and one single tear more. "I can't ever go home. Don't you understand? This—" A despairing wave of the hood took in this suite of opulent decadence, the Exotic Love, the whole life that Torronell led. "—is what I *like*. This is what I'm good for—*all* that I am good for. How can I live at Mithondion? How can I meet my father's eye? I'm sick, Deliann. That's why I cannot go home. I can *never* go home, because I'm *sick*."

And Deliann had been so reasonable, Deliann had been so rational, so patient and understanding . . . so persuasive . . .

"Sure, I knew the King had to reciprocate," Deliann said to Tommie, in a distant, abstracted tone bleached clean of pain, "but I was half expecting his return gift would be a swift boot in the ass on my way out the door. From what Torronell had told me, he hadn't been welcome at court for something like three hundred years. The whole idea had been to box the Ravenlock into a corner, so that he'd *have* to let Rroni come home whether he wanted to or not. What neither of us could have known was that the scandal that had ruined Rroni's life had blown over centuries ago; the Ravenlock had been looking for an excuse to overturn the banishment for decades."

"So," Tommie said, "that's a pretty good story, huh? Happy endin', anyway."

"Sure," Deliann said. "If you end it there. But the problem is, it's a true story." He closed his eyes. "All true stories end in death."

Though Deliann could see the scene in memory as clearly as if it were a Fantasy of his own creation, he could not hear the voices, the cheers that had arisen from the assembled Court when Torronell had lowered his hood and revealed himself to his father. This memory was as silent as Kierendal's message stick.

That message stick had shown him the end of the road he had followed for twenty-five years, from those very first days on foot out of Ankhana, holding Torronell as he sweated and shivered and vomited through his *lacrimatis* withdrawal. It had shown him the end of the months and years of the pain-filled bond with that profoundly unhappy fey; he had had nothing to offer Torronell save his understanding and his friendship, to which Torronell had responded with loyalty so fierce it had become a byword at court. No one had dared breathe any word against Deliann where the faintest hint of it might reach Torronell's ears. For a quarter of a century they had been inseparable; *Deliann and Torronell* had become a single word.

"Here's the real end of the story," Deliann said slowly. "Because I knew Kierendal all those years ago, I came here. I brought my disease to Alien Games. And because I was his best friend, his brother, Torronell caught my disease from me, and he carried it back to Mithondion. The real end of the story is Tup is dead, and Pischu, and the others." He stared bleakly into the fire. "And my whole family."

"Your family?"

"Yes. Between the two of us, Rroni and I, we have wiped out the entire royal line of the First Folk." He met Tommie's eyes, daring him to answer. "How happy is that?"

Tommie gave him a sidelong look. "No shit? The whole House Mithondionne? You sure about that?"

"That's what Kierendal thought. That's what the message stick seemed to be telling us," Deliann said brokenly. "I can only pray that I'm wrong."

"Well, spank me purple," he said, shaking his head. "Talk about shit goin' bone wild."

"What? What are you talking about?"

He spread his hands. "Maybe I'm wrong," he said. "I'm no friggin' expert on this Folk shit."

"Expert on what shit?"

Tommie started and stopped and started again; he scratched his thinning hair, frowned, and cleared his throat a couple of times. Finally, he managed, "Don't this, well, I mean . . ." He made a face as if to say, *You don't have to tell me how silly this sounds*. "Don't this make *you* the, like, the king of the elves?"

Deliann stared.

Tommie shrugged at him. "Hey, like I said, I'm no expert."

Deliann's voice came out so stunned and tiny that it could barely be heard above the crackle of the brick-ringed fire.

"Oh," he said. "Oh, my god."

7

SOME TIME LATER, people began to join them in that small windowless room. A nondescript knock, a grunt of "Whaddaya want?" from Tommie, a brief reply, and another man or woman would sidle through the half-opened door. Some were large and hard-looking like Tommie; some were smaller, softer, clerkish types; a couple could have been respectable shopkeepers; one might be plump and solemn, the next skinny and full of laughter.

They had in common a certain presence: an air of being profoundly engaged in whatever it was they did, whether talking to each other, or staring at him, or simply warming their hands at the fire. They didn't appear to be thinking about where they would be later tonight, or whatever might have happened this morning, or how their clothes looked, or whether the person to whom they spoke liked them or thought they were witty.

All they were doing was what they were doing.

They reminded Deliann of a saying Hari Michaelson had liked to quote sometimes, all those years ago: *When you eat, eat. When you sleep, sleep. When you fight, fight.*

Slowly, through the dazed whirl of his fever and everything that had happened that day, Deliann pieced together a pattern in the responses to Tommie's growled *Whaddaya want?* at the door. Each answer had been different, which was why Deliann hadn't noticed the pattern at first. One said, *I want to come in;* another simply said, *A choice.* A third had said, *A big fire and a comfortable chair;* a fourth, *A good father for my children.*

What Deliann gradually came to realize was this: Tommie's grunt was more than a rude greeting. It was a question. The same question he had asked Deliann.

It was a recognition code.

"This room," Deliann said wonderingly. "That's why this room has no windows . . ."

Tommie grinned at him. "Well, sure. It's not too healthy for us all to be seen together these days."

"You're *Cainists* . . ." Deliann breathed.

"Like I tolja before," Tommie said, chuckling, "sometimes it's you bright guys that have the hardest time figurin' shit out."

The laughter this brought from the group was warm as a hug. Another knock came, and Tommie growled, "Whaddaya want?" and the reply that came back wasn't an answer.

"It's Caja, Tommie. Let me in."

The room fell deadly silent.

Tommie sighed. "Shit, they broke him," he said, and the door shattered open and shouting men in grey leather flooded the room, firing crossbows in a stuttering drumroll as they came. Quarrels hit chests and faces and heads from so close that they burst out the far sides in sprays of blood and splinters of bone. The impact slammed men and women into each other, going in screaming tangles to the floor, and Deliann could only stare, his mouth shaping a silent *No.*

"Get down get down get down get down!" screamed the men in grey. *"On the floor hands in sight get down!"*

Deliann found his voice, and the voice he found said, "No."

Now more men came through the door, and crossbows swung to cover him. *"On the floor!"*

Deliann rose from his chair, and the fire at his back haloed him with a red-gold gleam. "There's been too much killing."

"There'll be more if you don't lie down," one of them said.

"I suppose you're right," he said sadly, as the fire behind him roared up from its ring of brick and spread phoenix wings that spanned the room: wings that enfolded him, and held him in an embrace of flame.

Quarrels leaped from crossbows, and Deliann did not lie down.

8

THE SLOW, STICKY drizzle was just strong enough to keep the birds off Tup's corpse.

It was an old, tired, swampy kind of rain, warm as spit, dirty and half jellied with the ash and smoke it halfheartedly tried to wash from the sky. It left faint wandering rings of grey like reverse-image sweat stains across the white cotton of Deliann's tunic. The rain sank into the Great Chambaygen with barely a ripple; here at the downstream fringe of Alientown, the river was permanently oiled with industrial sludge and grease and human waste. The Chambaygen's surface looked slick and flexible; it shifted and rolled like a plastic bag full of guts.

Deliann stood on the sand of Commons' Beach, a few steps outside the cordon of PatrolFolk that closed off the ceremony. Their line blocked the whole width of the beach and sealed the mouths of both Ridlin Street and Piper's Alley—a living barrier of alternating scarlet and black bodies, keeping at bay the mass of curious humanity that peered toward the funerary barge. Here and there along the cordon Deliann could see a face he recognized—but he always glanced away before eye could meet eye, and pulled his broad-brimmed hat a touch lower over his brow.

The PatrolFolk—alternating human Knights of Cant with un-human Faces—were armored, and bore staves bound with bright brass rings for crowd control. Each also carried a personal sidearm slung to his or her belt: broadswords, axes, maces, and warhammers were all in evidence, and the gleam in many a coldly suspicious eye was a clear invitation to bloodshed. They looked chilled and wet and miserable, and they were begging each and every unwelcome human gawker to give them any excuse.

Beyond the PatrolFolk, the entire west end of Commons' Beach was scattered with Faces and AG staffers: knots of grieving primals and stonebenders, a few ogres, some humans, ogrilloi, and six or seven sleepy trolls who scowled and rubbed their eyes, uncomfortable with even the dim light leaking through the heavy overcast. The biggest knot clustered around Kierendal's canopied sedan chair.

Beneath the canopy, Kierendal held a handkerchief to her mouth. Her eyes were dry, unblinking, and her face might have been carved from pale grey ice. Each time she moved the hand-kerchief from her mouth to her forehead to mop the fever-sweat from her brow, she revealed sharp predator's teeth through which she panted shallowly, like a cat in pain. Many of the AG staffers wept openly; Kierendal stared at the clouds with black rage, as though she believed eagles might answer the intensity of her need.

With his dirty cloak—already soaked with the ashy drizzle—thrown about his shoulders, and his rumpled broad-brimmed hat drawn low, Deliann looked less like a large, broad-shouldered primal than a small slim human. To come here today, to share even his limited, disconnected sense of Tup's loss, he'd had to pretend to be exactly what he was.

This irony made him feel only a little filthier than the sand be-neath his feet.

He had been on the run ever since that night in the Warrens, hiding, moving, trusting no one, huddling in alleys, crawling under collapsed roofs of fire-gutted buildings, never sleeping, foraging for scraps. He was closer to starvation than he had been even in his first days on the planet, but he didn't really care.

Fever had stolen his appetite.

The pocket of infection within his thigh had swelled, and now sent streaks of red up through his hip, reaching for his heart. He drew Flow constantly, holding down the pain, trying to slow the infection's progress, but it was a losing battle; he needed profes-sional healing, but he had no money. Any who once might have healed him for free worked for Kierendal.

His exhaustion sent his fever flashing and flickering from memory to fantasy and back again; sometimes he could make out a hallucinatory scene, and sometimes all he had were screams and the silhouettes of shapes seen dimly through a cur-tain of flame.

If he so much as closed his eyes—

—the fire bursts out from within its ring of brick and the whole room starts to go up like a torch and the Cats fall back as Deliann and Tommie scramble out a window, but there's more of them outside waiting in the street and both ends of the alley and Deliann's flame springs out an instant too late as a crossbow quarrel goes through Tommie's guts, missing the bone and rip-ping straight through his stomach and out a kidney, and Deliann's answering flame ignites buildings on all sides. "See?" Tommie coughs, palm pressed against the spurting hole in his belly, "guess I don't have to worry about your HRVP after all . . ." and Deliann is carrying him, holding him up with one arm around his shoulders, limping along the alleyway, clearing the Cats from around them with blasts of flame, and Tommie's saying, "Neela . . . gods, Neela, take the money, go . . . at least *try* . . ." when another crossbow bolt that should have hit Deliann in the neck takes Tommie in the back of the head. His skull is strong enough to stop the forged steel vanes so it doesn't go all the way through—its barbed head pokes out through his eye socket with his eyeball punctured and dangling on his cheek—and he starts to convulse and Deliann can't hold him anymore and the last thing he says is ". . . shit goes bad by itself . . . Neela . . ." and he dies in the mud with the fire roaring all around them—

—and he swayed and almost fell, there on the beach, and the sudden motion jerked open his eyes. He swiped his sleeve across his brow, gasping.

The rain on the beach was solidifying now, turning from a misty spray to a thicker drizzle that splashed on the sand. Deliann pulled his cloak up, and snugged his hat lower on his head.

The sand of the Commons' Beach half covered a scatter of greasy food wraps, fish heads, and splintered poultry bones with a dusting of damp shit-brown. Deliann had tried to scuff some of the litter away, to find a relatively clean place to stand, but each swipe of his sandals only revealed a new layer of trash.

Tup's funerary barge was barely the width of Deliann's outstretched arms, and less than twice that long. Built of plaited reeds, it was already softening and pulling apart like a straw hat left in the rain. She should have been suspended high in an oak, but no trees grow on the bank of the Great Chambaygen at Ankhana; the compromise Kierendal had settled upon was to join the treetopper custom with that of the First Folk, and so the corpse that once had housed the life of Tup lay on this disintegrating raft in the river, a fish-oil lamp sizzling at each of its four corners.

The mortal remains of the little treetopper were staked in the center of the barge; thin cords—no more than bits of string—tied her ankles to one stake, and her wrists to another above her head. Her tiny mouth gaped darkness, and her eyes stared unblinking up into the rain. Gaping also was the long slice that opened her belly from the yellow-red bone of her sternum all the way to her brush of feathery pubic hair. The lips of this gash were threaded with coarse black stitching; to these stitches were knotted further threads of black that spread fanlike to either side of the corpse; tied to the reeds of the barge, the fans of black thread held the gash-lips wide, fully exposing their mouthful of intestine, liver, and stomach.

Bits of metal, tiny mirrors, and jewels of glass made a carefully arranged starburst around her, salted with bits of raw meat gone already high. The sparkle and the scent of emergent rot should have drawn crows and vultures, perhaps even an eagle, to feed on the exposed entrails, and so properly begin the body's dissolution into the earth that had borne it, even as the life that had animated it had now dissolved into the Flow—but the tainted rain kept the scavengers away.

Deliann didn't know if Kierendal could survive this.

The slowly twisting knife of Kierendal's pain turned within his guts; he stared from beyond the cordon, suffering with her. The ache in his chest was like the stroke of a lash over salted cuts: more pain than he could stand, but less than he deserved.

There was a sort of current in the knots of Folk gathered on the beach; they seemed to cling together, sharing their grief and their memories of Tup, but every once in a while someone—a primal here, a stonebender there, even the occasional ogrillo or human—would break off from one of the knots and join another; that knot, larger now, would soon spawn offspring of its own, eddies of grief that brought each of them into contact with each other. The contact might be as intimate as a sobbing embrace, or as brief and distant as a nod of the head and a shared grimace of sympathy.

He ached to join those eddies of grief; if he could touch someone and be touched by them, even for an instant, he would not feel so hideously alone. He tried to summon Tup's living face, tried to hold a memory of her, tried at least to feel some real respect for the loss that her friends and lover had suffered, but he couldn't. Standing in the rain, head bent, hating himself, he could only really think about how much he hurt.

And could he be that shallow, after all?

Again he swayed, dizzy, weakening, and his eyes drifted closed—

—he leans his simmering forehead against the cool strap of iron that binds together the door slats of an apartment in the In-

dustrial Park. "No," he says, "no, don't open the door. Get your
mother. I need to talk to your mother," and he sags against the
iron, turning his face to bring his cheek against it, using the chill
to shore up his crumbling courage. When the woman's voice
comes hesitantly through the door, "Tommie? What's going on?
Who are you? Where's Tommie? Has something happened to my
husband?" all he can say is, "Don't open the door. There's a fire,"
he says. "There's a fire, and you have to get out." Her voice goes
shrill, "What do you mean, a fire? Where's *Tommie*?" and finally
he has to say it: "Tommie's dead, Neela. He's dead and you have
to go," and she says "I don't understand! How can he be dead?"
and all he can say is, "There's a fire," and as he says it he makes
it so: curls of smoke leak from the slats of the door beneath
his palms. "Go out the back. Take your clothes and all the
money and go," he tells her, and she shrieks back at him, *"Who
are you? What happened to Tommie? Who are you?"* and he
says, "Nobody. I'm nobody at all," as he thinks *I'm the king of
the elves*—

—and that thought shocked him awake on the sand, staggering, grasping a nearby shoulder for support. The shoulder belonged to a stranger, another of the onlookers, a woman, and she
struck his hand away, then delivered a stinging slap across his
face. She paused one more second, to spit a bigot's epithet, then
shoved away through the crowd.

Deliann shook his head, rubbing his stinging cheek. His wish
had been granted: to touch, and be touched.

How is it that everything I do comes out backward?

At this thought, he glanced over his shoulder involuntarily,
reflexively—

And so was the first of the onlookers at Tup's funeral to see the
massed infantry squares marching toward them, along the beach
from Nobles' Way.

He could not tell if they were real, or phantoms born of his exhaustion and fever, and did it matter?

His only answer was flame.

Fire was so easy, so fast: a reflexive spurt of power that pulsed
down his arms to spray from his fingertips, a kundalini roar from
the base of his spine. With a gesture, he could draw down the arrows of the sun.

With real screams and real blood, the fever dream unfolds—

The infantry marches along Commons' Beach, and there are

archers behind them. The PatrolFolk who had cordoned Tup's funeral unlimber their weapons, and the human onlookers surge against each other in cross-rippling waves, trying all at once both to see what is happening and to get out of its way, and Deliann, crushed among them, thinks *It's just like Tommie, but this time I won't run. I can't run. I am their king, and this is my place,* and with his gesture a sheet of flame roars from the sand toward the grey-leaking clouds, a towering ragged-fringed bastion of fire from the buildings to the river, but the infantry keeps marching and now arrows begin to fly, catching fire as they pass *phffthp* through the flame, and when they strike flesh, clothing burns and now the beach sizzles with screaming burning wounded people scattering: sparks from a kicked-over bonfire.

Deliann clears Piper's Alley with a gout of fire two hundred yards long, sending the troops that had filled it scrambling away coughing blood out of scorched lungs, and the panicked Folk upon the beach flow toward the alley mouth like water toward the breach in a river dam. Deliann swings himself back to the east, to turn his fire upon the advancing infantry in truth now, to roast them within their armor and fill the Ankhanan skies with the smoke of burning corpses, and a hand like the claw of an Ilmarinen MachineWorks steam shovel falls upon his shoulder. He looks back and up into protuberant fist-sized yellow eyes shot through with red, and Rugo the ogre slobbers regretfully around his brass-capped tusks: "Knew I s'oulda kiltya before. Now I'm gonna get in s'it with Kier," and the last Deliann sees is a barrel-sized fist scaled with grey-green horn descending toward his face like a boulder off a cliff.

THE MAN WHO had been a god paused upon the mountaintop, victorious. He had gained these heights by wit and will, and from here he could see before him the promised land.

He could see from where he had come, he could see where he wished to go, but he failed to see where he was; for though he had been a god, he was now a man.

From his very first step down the far side of the mountain, he began to learn what it is to be human.

ELEVEN

THE STORY TRICKLED onto the nets in exactly the kind of dribs and drabs most likely to keep the cauldron of public prurience at a rolling boil. First the fire at the Curioseum, and the suggestion of sabotage and arson by a shadowy group of eco-terrorists, the Green Knights; then came the *Where is Caine?* stories, as a source within MicroNet confirmed that Hari Michaelson's Mantrak anklet had vanished from the satellite position grid and the courts had presumptively seized his house and all his assets.

The investigation of the Green Knights led the CID to one Administrator Kerry Voorhees, the head of Biocontainment for the San Francisco Studio. Professional Voorhees was unavailable for comment—but a few of her associates in Biocontainment were extensively interviewed, and they spoke of certain behav-ioral changes that seemed to have begun with Voorhees' "friend-ship" with Shanna Leighton. When CID searched Administrator Voorhees' Oakland apartment, coded documents relating to the Green Knights were found in her desk's datacore, as was a journal that suggested her relationship with Shanna Leighton went somewhat beyond friendship.

The real fury began when a reliable source within the Studio leaked clips from the security records of the Curioseum fire, when the public learned how close the world had come to losing Caine forever—and when an enterprising reporter uncovered the enlightening fact that the Studio had bought Michaelson's house and the rights to his Adventures back from the civic treasury.

The mystery of Michaelson's disappearance now took on massive conspiratorial overtones, with rumors of secret mis-sions and Studio-sponsored death squads. Had the Studio killed him? There was, for the space of twenty-four hours, a rumor that Michaelson had been seen entering a backstreet cosmetic surgery clinic in Kabul; was he truly on the run, or had the Studio sent him undercover to strike back at the eco-terrorists? And what, in all this, was the connection to the HRVP outbreak on Overworld, and the—by now popularly confirmed—homosexual love affair between Pallas Ril and the terrorist Kerry Voorhees?

After two days, the partially decomposed body of Adminis-trator Voorhees was found floating in the Bay; in the datacore of her palmpad was a full confession. She had dusted supplies waiting for transshipment to the Transdeian mining colony with test samples of several different HRVP strains. This was done, her obviously unbalanced account claimed, to draw public atten-tion to the dangers of Earth exploitation of Overworld resources.

She had made this recording in the depths of guilt and the agony of having been betrayed, when she realized that her lover, Shanna Leighton—her mentor, her idol—had deceived her. En-tertainer Leighton had never intended to halt the outbreak; she instead had sworn to go to Overworld and, as Pallas Ril, carry on the fight against any who would harm the natural world—against any who would till the earth for crops to feed a family, against any who would so much as gather fallen wood for a fire.

Kerry Voorhees could not live with having done the unthink-able. And the unthinkable had been done—as Jed Clearlake himself notably observed with the sort of tragi-ironic bon mot of which most net reporters can only dream—for love of Pallas Ril.

In the furor of the search for Caine, Gayle Keller became an instant celebrity and came off quite well on his many netshow interviews. His somewhat oily facade of unrevealable inside knowledge was nicely balanced by his staunch defense of Chairman Michaelson: loyalty is a primary virtue in an Artisan. He repeatedly insisted that Chairman Michaelson was devoted to his job, to the Studio, and to the world—that he was a real team player. The Chairman had acted hastily, true, in sending Pallas Ril to Overworld without first investigating the source of the outbreak, but you have to remember who he had been, don't you? Caine was a man of action; Chairman Michaelson had seen a chance to end the crisis almost instantly, and at virtually no cost to the Studio. That was responsible Administrating, no matter the unfortunate outcome. He certainly could not have known how unbalanced his wife had become, nor could he have had any idea what she was planning.

"What man, after all," Keller pointed out with a wry shrug, once in each interview, "ever really knows what a woman is thinking?"

When the mystery of Michaelson's disappearance was finally solved, it fell to Studio President Businessman Westfield Turner to break the tragic news to a shocked and saddened public. At a press conference with the Roman facade of the Leisure Centre in Geneva for a backdrop, Businessman Turner spoke to the world.

"Late last week, San Francisco Studio Chairman Administrator Hari Michaelson—courageously, and without consideration for his personal safety—consented to join with the Studio and the Overworld Company in a clandestine effort to combat the most terrible threat that the people of Overworld have ever faced: the cowardly, vicious bio-terrorist who infected that pristine and innocent place—killing hundreds, perhaps thousands, and placing millions at risk—the ruthless Pallas Ril.

"The effort was successful, the danger averted. Pallas Ril and her savage terrorist organization can never again threaten the safety of the innocent millions of Overworld. But this victory has come at a terrible price."

Businessman Turner paused here and could be seen to take a deep, slow breath: clearly moved, and steeling himself for what he must next reveal. *"It is my sad duty to inform you all that Administrator Michaelson—along with Administrator Vinson Garrette, Professionals Gregor Prohovtsi and Nicholas Dvorak—gave his life in this effort."*

Businessman Turner went on to touch briefly upon some of Michaelson's accomplishments, his rise from the Temp slum of San Francisco's Mission District to the Chairmanship of the jewel in the Studio's crown, his services to the Studio and to the world as Caine.

Operations were now under way to recover his body, lost in the cliffs below Khryl's Saddle. According to Chairman Michaelson's expressed wishes, his remains would not be returned to Earth, but would be transported to the city he loved best, Ankhana, for burial. The San Francisco Studio—already shut down for a security review in the wake of the terrorist attack on the Curioseum—would remain shuttered for a month in respect for his memory, and Studios around the world would close for three days of official mourning.

"The job Hari started isn't over; there is work still to be done, to protect Overworld from the scourge of HRVP. Even as I speak, the Adventures Unlimited Biocontainment Administrator is organizing the largest and most comprehensive antiviral relief effort in the history of mankind. As Studio President, I offer my personal word that the Studio is in this to the very end. The job Hari gave his life to begin, I swear that we will finish."

Businessman Turner slicked his snowy hair back with one palm and took another deep breath to steady his voice; his barely restrained tears picked up the glare of the klieg lights and made his eyes sparkle like tiny daggers. *"In closing, I would like to urge Leisurefolk the world over to support the Studio's petition before the Leisure Congress. In the name of the Studio, I ask that Chairman Administrator Hari Khapur Michaelson be posthumously awarded Earth's highest civilian honor: the Medal of Freedom.*

"And finally, on behalf of all the peoples of Overworld, and all the people of Earth—

"Good-bye, Caine. Thank you. You will be missed."

Finally overcome, Businessman Turner waved aside all questions and left the podium, mopping at his eyes; he was seen weeping openly as he was led away by his aides.

The newsworks had obviously been prepared for this announcement: they had an array of recorded reactions from a variety of Michaelson's friends and associates. Of them all, perhaps Leisureman Marc Vilo—in his own rough-hewn way—said it best. *"Hari was always the guy you could count on to do what had to be done. Sure, he loved her; everyone remembers his final Adventure. But she crossed the line. Like he always said: 'A man's gotta shoot his own dog.' When you come down to it, I guess that's what he did."*

2

THERE WERE TOO many loose ends, and the Studio's PR line was too convenient, too neat; competing stories ran wild through the nêt. The Studio fell officially silent, and that silence only fed the flames—if they're not talking, the theory ran, there must be something they're not talking *about*. It was generally agreed that the "something" was most likely the full extent of the HRVP outbreak. Within days, hundreds of netsites were filled with speculation; the first hint of hard news came, unsurprisingly, through *Adventure Update*, when the show broadcast a leaked internal Studio report that HRVP had been identified in the Ankhanan capital. Eventually, the Studio confirmed these reports.

The Ankhanans, on the other hand, seemed to believe that the spasm of random violence that had overtaken the capital was part of a concerted terror effort by Cainists, in response to recent mass arrests and detentions. Patriarch Toa-Sytell had declared a state of martial law, and the army was currently engaged in rounding up the remaining Cainists and their sympathizers and collaborators—and apparently anyone else that someone had taken a particular dislike to—all in preparation for a barbaric auto-da-fé that was planned for the fast-approaching Festival of the Assumption. It hadn't been difficult to locate a suitably large number of victims; this was not so different from the reign of terror in Ma'elKoth's final days. As many of the commentators gleefully pointed out, Ankhanans had developed a certain taste for witch-hunts.

More disturbing were reports that came from Actors in the capital, along with some spectacular recordings. Open warfare had erupted in the subhuman ghetto of Alientown, pitting the

Ankhanan constabulary and some elements of the imperial infantry against a large paramilitary organization of subhumans, most likely members of the transplanted Warrengang known as the Faces. When the mundane Ankhanan constables found themselves overmatched by the potent magicks of the subhumans, they had responded by summoning the Grey Cats and the capital contingent of the Thaumaturgic Corps.

The battle raged for more than a day through the streets of the ghetto, leaving nearly a sixth of the city in rubble and flames, but it had ended with the Imperial forces firmly in control. Mop-up operations were being directed by the Grey Cats, and commentators on the nets spent several days shaking their heads, tsk-tsking the savagery of the conflict, and arguing whether blame for the massacre lay with the "semicivilized fringe elements and squatters" or with the "small faction of irresponsible witch-hunters driving public policy."

Public interest in Studio affairs hit a seven-year high; not since *For Love of Pallas Ril* had a situation on Overworld so captured the public's imagination. The Studio's in-house profit projections were so outrageously positive that representatives of Studio President Turner publicly announced he would be entering binding arbitration on a new contract, expected to nearly double his current salary.

Amid all this furor, it was—perhaps inevitably—Jed Clearlake who scored the journalistic prize of the year: a live interview with the former Emperor of Ankhana himself.

"It is clear," Tan'elKoth said darkly, turning slightly so that the light would properly halo his magnificent profile, *"that the Studio has not told the entire story. Consider: less than seven years ago, Caine destroyed my government—sparking a bloody war of succession—to save the life of Pallas Ril. I do not believe he would act against her, no matter what the provocation.*

"That she was mad, and a threat to every living soul on my world, I do not deny; as you may recall, I fought her hand-to-hand—and mind-to-mind. I knew her better than did even her husband, I believe. But nothing I could say would ever sway him in the least, not when it touched upon Pallas Ril. He claimed once that to save her, he would burn the world.

"This, I believe, is precisely the truth.

"He is that wayward, that selfish, that scornful of the needs of society and civilization.

"And this drivel about his request to be buried in Ankhana? It's ridiculous. Ankhana was not his home; it was where he worked. He loves it no more than a clerk loves his cubicle."

At this point, Clearlake smoothly picked up on something that the viewing public might not have noticed: that Tan'elKoth still spoke of Chairman Michaelson in the present tense.

"Of course I do," Tan'elKoth said with his characteristically suave cool. *"I do not believe that Caine is dead."*

Clearlake sputtered like a faulty datacore; Tan'elKoth only smiled into the video pickup. When Clearlake finally managed to stammer out his question, Tan'elKoth replied without hesitation.

"Certainly President Turner lied. Studio executives always lie; it is for this that they are paid. The question is, What was it, precisely, that he was lying about? If Caine is dead, where is the body? 'Lost in the cliffs below Khryl's Saddle,' indeed," he said scornfully. *"Is it truly Khryl's Saddle—or is it Reichenbach Falls?"*

He turned and faced the entire world through the netcamera pickup. *"Until I see Hari Michaelson's corpse with my own eyes—until I hold his cold, unbeating heart in my own hand—I will never believe that Caine is dead."*

He opened his hands before his face, not an appeal but a conjurer's flourish. *"Show me the body, President Turner. Show the body to us all. Either show us the body, or admit the truth: somewhere, somehow, Caine lives."*

Entertainer Clearlake was no stranger to controversy; some said that he had built his dream home within the eye of a hurricane. There is, however, a clear difference between riding out a storm and twisting a dragon's tail. Wisely, he let that line of questioning drop, favoring instead a neutral wrap-up: *"And what now for you, Professional? Back to work in your own* private *studio?"*

"I think not. My people—my world—are still threatened by the disease this madwoman inflicted upon them. The elimination of Pallas Ril does not save my world. The Studio and the Overworld Company have begun a massive containment operation, putting at risk thousands of lives and costing billions of marks, with every probability of failure, while they ignore an option that is obvious, effective and inexpensive.

"They can send me back.

"Back to my world. Back to my people, who cry out for me in

their anguish. I can do in truth what Pallis Ril only pretended: wipe out HRVP on Overworld—at a cost to the Studio of precisely zero."

He turned to the video pickup, speaking again to the whole world. Some trick of the light made his eyes seem to burn from within, as though a crust of stone had broken to reveal an unexpected flow of lava below. "*This is your choice: Spend billions and fail, or save the world for* free. *If Caine is dead in truth, can you so insult his memory? Let him have died in vain? Do not make his sacrifice go for naught. You know what must be done.*

"*Send me home.*"

3

THE DOORS OF the Social Police riot van opened onto full night on a rooftop landing pad, floodlit a pale frog-belly white. Tan'elKoth shook a fist-sized knot of tension from his massive shoulders and stepped out onto the weather-cracked asphalt.

He breathed slowly and deeply, consciously forcing himself to stay loose, relaxed, ready. Mental preparedness was the key: he must be ready to react smoothly and naturally to any eventuality. Though this would be easier, he reminded himself mordantly, if he had one bloody idea what he might be preparing for.

The riot van had been waiting for him on the landing pad outside the *Adventure Update* soundstage, where he had expected to find a Studio limousine; now, looking back on it, he found ominous the manner in which Entertainer Clearlake had wished him luck before signing off the live interview. That slight squint before he had spoken, that faint glazing of the eye—had a warning come over his earpiece? Had some whispering tech hinted that Tan'elKoth had fallen afoul of Soapy?

A cold suspicion settled onto the back of his neck. He had watched on a security monitor as Kollberg and the Social Police had ambushed Caine.

This landing pad was on the roof of a low building surrounded by looming residential domes. The riot van rested squarely at the crux of a large cross of paint that had once been red, but now had faded to a scuffed and dirty pastel pink, within a wide circle of sooty grey. This was some kind of hospital, then.

Had been some kind of hospital, Tan'elKoth corrected himself. The rooftop was now ringed with Social Police riot vans identical to the one in which he had arrived, turrets bristling with cannon that pointed outward and below, fanned to cover all approaches.

Or, perhaps, all exits.

One of the faceless officers gestured toward an open access door across the rooftop, and Tan'elKoth started toward it, sliding his thumbs beneath the bandolier straps of his ammod harness. It must be binding him up, somehow, or perhaps he had fastened it too tightly over his heavy sweater; he was having a certain difficulty drawing breath.

The access door opened onto an unlit stair: a dark rectangular recession into oblivion. It exhaled a breath of acid sweat, ammoniac urine and bubbling green decay, as though the stairwell were the throat of a scavenger slowly dying of some awful necrosis of the bowels.

Tan'elKoth paused. Hannto the Scythe—Hannto the timid, the weakling, the coward—had somehow struggled to the very gates of Tan'elKoth's mind. Or perhaps not so much the coward: Hannto urged Tan'elKoth to turn upon the Social Police officers beside him, to attack, to crush and kill them, and to be cut down in turn. Better a clean death, up here in this gritty smog-choked simulacrum of open air, than to be swallowed by that unimaginable throat.

Nearly all the lives within him wept with fear; Ma'elKoth, the god himself—even He counseled caution. Lamorak had nothing to say; that dark shade huddled in wordless terror in some black and forgotten corner, for the breath of the stairwell smelled of the Donjon, of the Theater of Truth.

It smelled of the Shaft.

One of the soapies reached toward him, and Tan'elKoth tensed, expecting a stroke from a shock baton; instead, he was astonished to find that the soapy only touched his arm with one gauntleted hand and leaned toward him to speak softly through his digitizer.

"Go on in," the soapy said, with as close to a human tone as Tan'elKoth had ever heard from one of them. *"It's better if you don't keep him waiting."*

The other soapies turned helmets toward each other, nodding infinitesimal agreement; their gauntlets twisted upon their weapons as though their hands ached too much to find a comfortable grip. That transitory brush with the humanity behind those silver masks, so unexpected, turned the twist of nerves in Tan'elKoth's stomach into an icy dread that settled into his bones; it was terrifying to imagine that Social Police might feel some kinship of apprehension.

As though what awaited him below frightened even them.

With a deep, shuddering breath, Tan'elKoth descended the stair, and was swallowed by darkness.

4

BELOW, HE FOUND a nightmare of baffled, terrified Laborers and Adminstrators and Physicians, of blood and sobs and shit and screams, of silver-masked Social Police standing robotic guard. Within, the only light came from the bleached wash of emergency floods. The acid stink of human fear mingled with the mildew that leached from the filthy carpet beneath his feet, nearly overpowering the sweet metallic earth-smell of blood and shit.

He moved through the reeking shadows of a long, narrow corridor, and out into an open space that had been some kind of office; the wreckage of several desks lay among the tumbled carpet-covered panels that Tan'elKoth assumed had once been cubicle walls. Here and there were knots of wretched people in the tattered remnants of Laborer dress—some clutched desperately at each other, some sobbed softly, and some merely stared blankly at the brown stains on the walls.

Also among the wreckage were pieces of what had probably been at least three people: a severed hand here, there a head pulped like a hammered watermelon, a tangled knot of intestine looped over the remains of a water cooler. The ferric slugs from power rifles littered the floor, and one office wall was now only a tattered framework of slug holes. More corpses, here and there, were half buried in the broken ruin of office furniture; something had been chewing on them, gnawing at their flesh—not to feed, but rather out of some restless urge to use its jaws: a dog mindlessly worrying a marrow bone.

An infant, teething.

The shootings had been only the beginning. Someone had been playing among the corpses: someone had braided their guts into tangled ropes, had popped out their eyeballs and disjointed the mangled bodies like a bored child pulling apart its dolls. Tan'el-Koth had no doubt who this bored child was. He could see him.

In the middle of the floor, his dungarees down around his knees, buttocks pulsing between the thighs of a woman with empty eyes and a mouth like a smear of blood. His pitted scalp was unmistakable.

Kollberg.

The woman's only clothing was a brown-crusted bandage that covered the flat wound where her right breast had once been. Even as Tan'elKoth watched, Kollberg lowered his face to her one remaining breast and sank his teeth into her nipple. Blood spurted up across his eyes. The woman only grunted, likely near death from shock. Kollberg dug his face in, chewing deeper and deeper into her, and Tan'elKoth had to lower his eyes.

The other chewed-upon corpses . . . those that were female, the breasts had been torn away. Each corpse that had been male now had only ragged bite wounds in place of its penis. With their equally flat chests and equally empty groins, the corpses bore a gruesome, crudely chopped resemblance to each other: they had been surgically homogenized by a blunt scalpel of rotten teeth.

And this, Tan'elKoth thought emptily, *is what I chose for an ally, against Caine and Pallas Ril.*

O abandoned gods, what have I done?

Kollberg looked up from the shuddering death spasms of the woman and caught Tan'elKoth's eye. He stretched his neck ophidically: a snake basking in warm tropic sun. "Welcome to my home," he said. "Do you like it? I furnished it myself."

Tan'elKoth held his silence.

Kollberg pushed himself up to his knees, off the woman's corpse; he stuffed his penis back inside his dungarees without so much as wiping off the half-clotted blood that caked it. "You," he said thoughtfully, still squatting, "are not a team player."

5

HE ROSE, AND approached Tan'elKoth closely enough that the ex-Emperor had to turn aside from the reek of his breath. "I think your heart's mostly in the right place, you understand, but there are one or two things that you don't seem to understand."

How much does he know? How much does he know about Faith? The myriad that populated the ex-Emperor's mind gibbered and cringed, but he was more than they: he was Tan'elKoth, and he would not flinch. "I understand this: You dare not harm me," he said firmly. "I am no common Laborer, who can be made to disappear without uproar and alarm. Your best hope of life is to release me and pray that I hold my tongue."

Kollberg stretched up onto his toes, until the top of his head nearly reached Tan'elKoth's chin; he swiveled his head and angled his face so that his fetid breath wafted upward as he spoke. "You still don't understand."

Tan'elKoth took a step backward—no amount of fortitude could enable him to stomach that stench—and he would have taken another, but that first step had brought his back into solid contact with one of the soapies who stood immovably behind him. "I have friends and admirers upon the Leisure Congress itself, do you understand? I can no more be detained or harmed than could Caine. Your own Board of Governors oversees my welfare—and I imagine that they would be . . . disturbed . . . by your *lifestyle*."

Kollberg took a step back, still on his toes, his head cocked, squinting at the ex-Emperor so tightly that it pulled up the corners of his rubbery lips into a humorlessly acquisitive smile. "Let me explain."

A sharp stroke from a shock baton across the back of Tan'elKoth's neck: he collapsed into the bloody muck that covered the floor, twitching spastically. One of the Social Police officers kicked him precisely in the groin, another in the ribs, and a third in the kidneys while the fourth went to work on his head. He could do no more to defend himself than writhe; the charge from the shock baton had shut down his peripheral motor nerves, and his limbs would not obey his will.

Tan'elKoth gasped with every kick, and his gasps might have been sobs, if he'd had strength to cry. A shock went through him at each blow, a wave of impact that carried the impersonal malice of the Social Police through his every defense. Helplessness wriggled in through his skin, into his blood, between the cords of his muscle like screwworms digging down to the bone.

The Social Police facelessly inflicted a dispassionate, thoroughly professional stomping. One of these soapies had, only minutes ago, touched him as one man does another; in a way, that made it worse.

6

HE MUST HAVE lost consciousness, perhaps more than once. Some indefinable interval later, the beating had ceased.

Awareness gathered within him, correlating with the surge of sense impressions that grew as though he had reached out and toggled up the volume on the world. A mild discomfort, of the sort he might have suffered while he sat too long motionless in meditation, swelled into a burning, throbbing ache along his ribs, into his kidneys; at his groin it became a spike driven into his testicles—sharp and dull simultaneously, familiar already, but still twisting his guts until he might vomit.

Light now: a dim bloody glow through closed lids. Squinting against it tightened flesh across his raw and swollen face and screwed down a band of pain across his brow. Someone cradled his head on a lap warm and wet; he feared to open his eyes. And the smell—that feculent carnivorous stench—

The smell told him more than he could bear to see.

"Do you understand now?" Kollberg asked, stroking Tan'el-Koth's face like Mary in the *Pieta*. "Are we on the same page?"

Tan'elKoth flinched.

He couldn't help himself.

His face flushed with sudden shame, with the humiliation of discovering himself to be so fragile. Some dispassionate part of his mind considered this, abstractly wondering at the emotional power of a merely physical beating.

Kollberg waited with reptilian patience, but Tan'elKoth could not answer. "Well," Kollberg said vacantly. "You might guess that I didn't find your interview with Entertainer Clearlake very funny. Not funny at all. You think that I might not come through on my half of our bargain. That's insulting. You think that you can use public opinion and political pressure to make me do what you want. That's more insulting."

He bent his neck over Tan'elKoth's immobile face, close enough to kiss. "Don't insult me. I don't like it."

Tan'elKoth tried to speak, but the residue of the shock baton's randomizing pulse allowed only a thick *"Nnnh . . . nnnh . . ."* to pass his lips.

It was as well; he was not yet in sufficient command of himself. He thought of Faith, of her link to the rivergod, and hugged that thought to himself. If he could hold on to that, keep it safely buried behind his eyes, he could still come through this. All he had to do was survive. He would be Ma'elKoth again, and on that day he would have the power to repay abuse a hundredfold.

"But that wasn't what really made me angry." Kollberg didn't sound angry. He didn't sound human. "I got angry when you started that drivel about Michaelson being still alive. Then, when we reveal that he *is* still alive, you have the public's confidence. You thought that was very clever. It *was* very clever. There is another thing you need to understand about me."

He leaned forward and took Tan'elKoth's wrist. "Clever people make me hungry."

He lowered his face as though he might chastely and reverently kiss the ex-Emperor's hand—but instead, he closed his lips upon Tan'elKoth's smallest finger, sucking it fully into his mouth like a five-copper whore warming up for a blowjob. Tan'elKoth tried to speak, but still he could produce only a series of bestial grunts.

Kollberg bit down.

Tan'elKoth said *". . . gunhg . . . guhh . . ."*

Kollberg chewed on the finger, worrying it, cracking the bone like a dog sucking marrow; he turned his head to one side, wedged the finger back between his molars, bit down again, and yanked his head from side to side until the bone splintered at the knuckle and he could rip it free. Blood sprayed, and Kollberg fixed his lips to the wound, sucking greedily.

Tan'elKoth's guts spasmed, and he retched rackingly across Kollberg's knees. Thin, clear vomit came out of the emptiness of his unused stomach, trailed down his legs, and trickled into his shoes. Kollberg shrugged and let Tan'elKoth slide to the floor; one of the officers took his hand and pressed a rag to the spurting stump.

Kollberg chewed on the severed finger for a moment longer, then swallowed it. He smiled at Tan'elKoth with blood-smeared lips. "Now," he said thickly. "Now you understand."

Tan'elKoth trembled, aching for breath, trying to stop the new surge of vomit that forced its way up his throat. *Faith,* he told himself. *He still doesn't know about Faith.*

"Say it. Say you understand."

Tan'elKoth looked away, down, anywhere but at the creature's face.

Clearly outlined through Kollberg's dungarees was his stiffened penis, straining against the fly.

"Say it," Kollberg repeated. "I'm still hungry."

Tan'elKoth struggled to make his numb, slack lips and tongue form the words. "I . . . unners'an' . . ." he mumbled. "I unners'an'."

Kollberg gestured, and gauntleted hands dragged Tan'elKoth's twitching body across the room and balanced him on a tiny swivel chair in front of a child-sized desk. The screen on this desk was already fully lit, showing the Adventures Unlimited logo: the armored knight upon the back of a winged horse, rampant.

Hot breath slid down the back of his neck, and that meaty voice came thick and wet beside his ear. "I believe you wanted to have a word with the Board of Governors, isn't that right?" he murmured warmly, almost lovingly. "You wanted to tell them about me, mmm? Would you be interested to know that they have been watching us, all this time?"

The gradual return of motor function made Tan'elKoth shudder uncontrollably. "T-t-true?" he stammered. "Is-z-z-z it?"

"Professional Tan'elKoth," the digitized voice from the screen replied, *"you were told that Laborer Kollberg has our full confidence in this matter. Are you not wise? Is not a word sufficient?"*

"Th-th-th-this m-m-monster—th-this fiend you employ—"

"Mmm, it seems there has been some . . . misapprehension . . . on your part, Professional. Laborer Kollberg does not work for us."

"N-no? But, but—"

"Not at all. Quite the contrary, in fact; we work for him."

Tan'elKoth, at that moment, wished only that he could use his arms well enough to stuff his fingers in his ears, wished he could use his voice well enough to howl, wished he could do anything at all to shut out the words he knew would come next.

"And so do you."

The logo vanished. The screen was as blank as Tan'elKoth's stare.

He did understand. Finally, fatally, he did. He had thought he was the master of history, that his fractal world-tree had grown according to his will. He had allowed himself to be deceived.

He had let himself believe that the Board of Governors was rational, when in truth it was only hungry.

The Bog, he thought. Caine's joke: the acronym BOG. A word, in English, for *swamp.* A word, in a dead Slavic language, for *God.*

Kollberg sighed. "You're thinking that Pallas is dead, and Caine is destroyed. You're thinking, What other use can he have for me? Why am I still alive?"

Slowly, unwillingly, Tan'elKoth forced himself to meet Kollberg's glassy dead-fish stare. "Yes."

"Well, first, you're still alive because we made a deal, and I don't break my deals—not with my friends. And second, there is still something I need you to do, before we send you back to Overworld."

Tan'elKoth closed his eyes.

"I need you to help me decide," Kollberg said, "how we should use Faith Michaelson."

Tan'elKoth lowered his head. He no longer had even the strength for anguish.

"Talk to me," Kollberg said. "Talk."

Tan'elKoth talked.

THE DARK ANGEL'S spawn was a created thing, a golem, a half-silvered reflection of its sire in a mirror of flesh. In the mind that dreams the world, each was a symbol of the other, and in such dreams, symbol is reality; this is what is called the law of similarity.

Each was the other.

In their mortal struggle, the dark angel and his spawn each fought against himself.

TWELVE

THE CAINESLAYER LEANED on the silvery weather-split rail that surrounded the roof of the barge's deckhouse and stared out over the docks of Ankhana with eyes the bleached blue-grey of a frozen river under a cloudless winter sky. He could have been made of carved oak and knotted rope upholstered with leather; his hair was shaved to an eighth-inch fuzz over his scalp, and muscle jumped at the corners of his knife-edged jawline.

He squinted one eye against the side-glare of the rising sun and thought about destiny.

He wore a simple tunic and pants of brown suede, loose and baggy, a shade or two lighter than his skin. In the case by his cot in the deckhouse cabin were the scarlet robes of a Monastic Ambassador, but he no longer wore them; he planned to resign his diplomatic post as soon as he reached the Ankhanan Embassy.

But after that—?

For the first time in longer than he could remember, he didn't know what to do next.

The city around him now had been his home for more than twenty-four years; he had been born here, had passed his childhood in a neighborhood of the Industrial Park that could be seen from where he now stood. Behind him, across this channel of the Great Chambaygen, rose the massive walls of Ankhana's Old Town, great cliffs built of limestone blocks each near the size of the barge on which he'd ridden the river from the God's Teeth, towering eight times the height of a man, blackened with a thousand years of smoke and weather, dropping sheer to the river's channel.

The smithy built by the man he had called his father still stood, not far from here; if he closed his ice-pale eyes, he could see the small room, off the overhead chamber, where he had slept. With his powers of mind, he could view himself at any age there, could see his parents as if they still lived, or could cast forth his sight to capture the face of someone sleeping in that tiny windowless room even on this bright morning. He could spy upon the tenement where his first love had lived, or the cell beneath the Monastic Embassy where he had spent so many hours kneeling in meditation. The city had been a part of his family, a parent, the older brother he'd never had. And now the city was sick.

Ankhana was coming down with a virus.

The city had been feeling poorly for some days now, feverish fancies invading its collective dreams, but it did not yet comprehend just how ill it was. The city's immune system—the Imperial constabulary and the army—had geared up to fight off a bacterial infection: a growing internal colony called Cainism, a philosophical disease that attacked the citizenry's faith in the Church of the Beloved Children of Ma'elKoth, and in the Empire itself. This particular infection, as it spread, emitted toxins that had caused painful abcesses of disorder at the city's extremities of Alientown and the Warrens, and that had occasionally pocked Old Town itself.

The city's immune system was admirably suited to battle infections of this type; these were swiftly contained, sequestered, and concentrated in only a few places, where each individual bacterium could be sanitized in turn. Yet aches continued to settle into the city's joints, and its fever continued to inch upward every day, for the city's true illness came from a virus.

A virus is a wholly different order of disease.

A black pall of smoke twisted upward from the north-west quadrant of the capital, the Alientown ghetto. All the still-standing buildings that fronted the river were blackened; most others had partially collapsed and still others had burned to the ground. What little he could see of Alientown from here looked like the scorched-earth shell of a castle after a marauding army has slaughtered all within.

All this meant little to the Caineslayer; he merely gazed incuriously at the wreckage. The Caineslayer had been born in the mountains, five days ago. He did not yet know his new life well. He could still be surprised by how the world made him feel, because he did not react to it in the familiar patterns of his former life; he was almost continuously startled by how different he had become.

Now, for example: standing here, he surmised that he was alone, or very nearly so, in the knowledge of the city's illness. Perhaps only one or two of the hundreds and thousands of people around him even understood the concept of viral infection; he himself had not, until it had been explained to him in detail by the late Vinson Garrette. And instead of leaping to the docks to cry the city's doom, instead of racing to the embassy to warn the Acting Ambassador of the danger, instead of taking any action at all upon his knowledge, he simply leaned upon the rail, picking at its splinters with his fingernails, and watched.

On the dock below him was assembled the capital detachment of the Imperial Army Band, two hundred strong, their instruments' brass gleaming gold in the bright noontide sun. They stood at parade rest, horns and pipes slung like weapons, their tall cylindrical caps white as clouds and festooned with braid as iridescent as sun dogs. Within the band's broad arc stood a half century of Household Knights at attention, their long hauberks shining under mantles of maroon and gold, their halberd blades of scarlet steel flashing like torches.

He wondered how many of them were sick: how many already had that boil of madness festering within their brains.

A ribbed gangplank joined the barge's deck to the dockside. At the gangplank's foot waited a pair of stolid, thick-shouldered draft horses harnessed to a large cart. A platform had been built upon the cart, rising perhaps four or five feet above its bed, and on the platform was a sort of rack hastily improvised out of splintery, warped scrap lumber. Waiting at the corners of the cart were four friars, Esoterics despite the dirt-brown robes that proclaimed their Monastic citizenship. Such robes are worn ordinarily only by Exoterics, the public faces of the Monasteries. These robes served admirably to conceal the Artan springless pellet bows that each man bore.

The ice in the Caineslayer's eyes glinted with a new reflection: Down the long ribbed gangplank from the deck to the dock, two friars—real Exoterics, these—bore a litter. On the litter lay a medium-sized, ordinary-looking man of middle age, black hair showing streaks of grey that matched the grey scattered through his untrimmed week's growth of black beard. The man's arms dangled, limp, over the litter's rails, as though he were unconscious; the Caineslayer knew that he was not.

The man did not move because only immobility could hurt more than motion: the man held himself still because to move might lessen his suffering, and that he could not bear. For him, only pain had meaning.

For five days—since the moment of his birth—the Caineslayer had kept company with this man, first on the train down the western slope of Khryl's Saddle to the riverport of Harrakha, then on the barge downriver from Harrakha to the Empire's capital. The Caineslayer had taken his meals in the ugly deck shelter of scrap wood and filth-crusted canvas that had served this man for his cabin, had slept there, read there, had done his daily exercises there; the Caineslayer had knelt beside this man's rude cot for his daily prayers to the Savior, the Ascended Ma'elKoth.

He had never left this man's side, because to leave would be to miss the pain. The Caineslayer ate this man's pain, drank it, breathed it, soaked it in through his pores. It was his reason for existence. This man had many names, of which the Caineslayer knew some few; he numbered them in his head while he watched the friars who had borne the litter lift the crippled man and chain him upright to the rack upon the wagon's platform.

Dominic, this man said he had been called by the slaver from whom he claimed to have escaped, in the days before his arrival at the abbey of Garthan Hold; in Kirisch-Nar, where he had fought in the catpits, he was known as Shade; among the surviving remnants of the Khulan Horde, he had once been k'Thal, and was now known only as the Betrayer, or the Hated One. In the Ankhanan Empire, he had been called the Blade of Tyshalle, and the Prince of Chaos, and the Enemy of God. In the land of Arta, the *Aktiri* world, he had been named Administrator Hari Khapur Michaelson.

But everywhere he was known by one of these names, he was better known by another name, his true name, the name he'd been given by the Abbot of Garthan Hold.

Caine.

It was the Caineslayer's greatest pride that he had taken this name of legend and made of it a mere sound: a monosyllabic grunt of contempt.

2

ON THE COLD dawn of his birth, when he had let himself into the railcar compartment where the cripple who had once been Caine lay, dumb with misery like a wounded dog, the Caineslayer had sat across from him and asked, "How, then, should I call you?"

The cot on which the cripple lay was bolted to the compartment's wall, to the splintered woodwork where seats had been ripped out to make room for it. The cripple was strapped to the cot with leather bands across his knees, hips, and chest, to keep him in his place against the jolting sway of the train. The compartment stank of human waste; the Caineslayer could not tell if perhaps the cripple had fouled himself, or if this stench was only a reminder of the dunking he'd taken in the polluted headwaters of the Great Chambaygen, where it drained away the sewage from the construction camp on the crest of Khryl's Saddle.

The cripple was covered with a filthy blanket, half sodden already with seepage from the oozing burns that splotched his body like patches sewn onto tattered clothing. He did not turn his head or make any indication that he had heard the Caineslayer's question; he stared out the grime-streaked window at the billows of coal smoke that rolled backward from the locomotive, smoke that had stained the leaves of trees that lined the winding railway a uniform necrotic grey.

The Caineslayer settled himself onto the surprisingly comfortable cushion of the opposite bench. For a long, wonderful moment he merely sat, staring, savoring the sight, breathing the smell, letting the cripple's aura of rank despair settle into his bones like the warmth of his home hearth on a winter's night. But there was something missing, something the Caineslayer still needed. He could see a blind lack in the cripple's hollow gaze.

In the face of his pain, the cripple had sunk into some inner circle of animal incomprehension; he had found a state of dreamlike semiconsciousness where his suffering seemed removed, distant, the anguish of a fictional victim in some old half-familiar story. But the Caineslayer had armed himself against even this pathetic defense. He had been forewarned.

The Caineslayer had a device.

The Caine Mirror, he called it privately; a box shaped roughly like a medium-sized valise, filled with tangles of fine cabling and a bank of transparent glass bulbs, powered by a chip of griffinstone smaller than the nail of the Caineslayer's little finger. On its front were a pair of handgrips covered with thin-beaten gold; between the handgrips was a mirror of silvered glass. To hold those handgrips, to direct his disciplined mind into that silvered glass, was to enter an intimacy so extreme that it transcended obscenity: as though he'd gouged out the man's eye and fucked his bloody socket.

It let him inside the man who had been Caine.

The Caineslayer leaned forward and dug his fingers into the blanket that covered the scorched flesh of the cripple's ribs, grabbed, and twisted. "Perhaps you didn't hear me. How should I call you?"

The cripple's response was to roll his head to one side. His face was as empty as his heart.

"Should I call you *Hari*?" the Caineslayer asked pleasantly. "Viceroy Garrette called you *Administrator*"—he pronounced the foreign words with careful precision—"*Michaelson*. Is that what you'd prefer?"

Consciousness swam up to the surface of the man's eyes, and with consciousness came suffering; he stared at the Caineslayer through a haze of pain, and the Caineslayer smiled. "It wouldn't seem right, to call you Caine," he said. "Caine is dead, you told me—and I know this to be true. I killed him."

Those suffering eyes drifted away, back toward the windows, and the cripple spoke in a half whisper still ragged with residual screams. "Whatever."

"Ex-Caine? Perhaps—" The Caineslayer's smile widened into a grimace of happy malice. "—Tan'Caine?"

"It doesn't matter."

"You think not? I say it does. Perhaps I shall use *Hari*, after all. That is how Pallas Ril calls you, isn't it? Mmm, your pardon, Hari: I meant to say, *called* you."

A brief, almost invisible twist flickered over the cripple's features; if the Caineslayer hadn't known better, he might have fooled himself into believing it the trace of a smile. "You're wasting your time," the man he had decided to call Hari said. "I don't know why you think you can hurt me more than I've hurt myself."

"There are many things you don't know," the Caineslayer observed. Hari shrugged and turned once more toward the window.

"Aren't you curious?" The Caineslayer leaned forward to give Hari a theatrically sly sidelong look. "Don't you want to know who I am? Why I have destroyed you?"

"Don't flatter yourself, kid."

The Caineslayer frowned. "You don't care? You don't care why this has happened?"

Hari drew a deep sigh and rolled his head back to meet the younger man's eyes. "You don't know why it happened," he said. "All you know is why you did what *you* did."

The Caineslayer's frown deepened into a scowl; he had not come this far to be lectured like a boy at the abbey school.

"And second? Yeah." Hari shrugged. "I don't care."

The Caineslayer's hands twisted into fists. "How can you not *care*?"

"*Why* is bullshit," Hari said exhaustedly. "*Why* won't bring back my wife. *Why* won't save my father, or return my child, or let me walk again. Fuck why. Reasons are for peasants."

"Perhaps," the Caineslayer said through his teeth. He slid sideways to place himself beside the window out which Hari stared. The trees had closed around the tracks until the train seemed to be rocking through a tunnel of smoke-poisoned leaves. "Perhaps I am a peasant. Then it is a peasant who has brought you low."

"Yeah, whatever."

"I was born to Marte, wife of Terrel the blacksmith. They named me Perrik," he began, speaking with the slow, deliberate cadence of an elKothan priest reciting the daily liturgy.

"You're wasting your time," Hari repeated. "I don't want to know."

The Caineslayer's fist struck like his father's hammer, a long powerful arc of force that exploded against Hari's face, smashing his nose into a splatter of blood and tissue. Hari grunted and his eyes went glassy for a moment. When their focus returned, he expressionlessly licked blood from his mouth and watched the Caineslayer, silently waiting for what he would do next.

The Caineslayer's fist ached with the fierce need to hit him again and again and again; he burned to kill this man, to beat the life from him flesh to flesh and bone to bone—but killing would not answer his need. "This isn't about *what you want*. Nothing is about what you want, not ever again. This is about *me*. About what *I* want."

He clutched his fist with his other hand, trying to massage the bloodlust out of it. "Think of this as a reverse interrogation. There are some things I want you to know. I'm going to tell you. If, at any time, I think you're not listening, I will hurt you. Do you understand?"

Hari's response was a blood-smeared stare, blank as an empty plate.

The Caineslayer once again dug his fingers into a twist of the filthy blanket and scraped the rough fabric of Hari's tunic against the moist scabs of his burns. "I know you've been tortured before, Hari. The, mmm, Black Knife Clan of the Boedecken ogrilloi, wasn't it? And I am not insensible to the fact that only last night you tried to force my men to kill you. I suspect that pain means as little to you as your life—but both your life and your pain are very important to *me*."

He settled into himself and took a deep, slow, patient breath. "Five days from now, we arrive in Ankhana; once there, you will be delivered up unto the civil authorities for execution. In the meantime, I want you to hurt—and I want you to *listen*."

Outside, the trees had fallen away, revealing rugged hills of gorse and bracken rolling toward a blue-misted reach: the unforgiving Kaarnan Wilderlands. Inside, the Caineslayer had begun again.

"I was born to Marte, wife of Terrel the blacksmith. They named me Perrik, and for much of my childhood, I expected to be ordinary—and happy, very much like they themselves seemed to be. My mother was from Kor, and she was older than my father; she had secrets that neither of us understood, but we always knew she loved us . . ."

3

FOR DAYS—THROUGH the whole trip out of the God's Teeth, through the layover in Harrakha while the barge was prepared, on the first days of the maddeningly slow journey down the lazy curves of the Great Chambaygen to Ankhana—the Caineslayer had told the tale of his parents. He rarely spoke of himself at all; instead, he told every incident he could remember of his father and his mother, sparing nothing: from the first belt Terrel had laid across his legs to the honeycakes Marte would bake as the summers faded into autumn rains, from the time Baron Thilliow of Oklian had had Terrel whipped for cutting the frog of his favorite mare's hoof, to the season of savage rows his parents inflicted upon each other when he was ten: when he first learned that Marte had been pregnant when Terrel married her—and pregnant by another man.

Good and bad, dramatic and trivial, he told every faintest detail; he wanted to bring his parents to life for Hari, even as they lived in his own heart.

Strangely, Hari seemed to somehow divine the Caineslayer's purpose; he never enquired why the Caineslayer wanted him to know all this. Only occasionally did he speak through his haze of inner pain; sometimes to offer a comment, or to ask for a clarification of some obscure detail—sometimes a mere grunt of understanding.

Late one afternoon, as the barge drifted through a slow curve that divided low, rolling hills of grassland, Hari said, "I'm guessing, from all this, that I'm never gonna get a chance to meet your folks, huh?"

The Caineslayer met his gaze squarely, and his voice was dry as the desert stone of his mother's homeland. "Both my parents were in Victory Stadium at the Assumption of Ma'elKoth."

"No shit? Died there, huh?"

"Yes."

"How about that." His eyes fixed on some misted reach, miles away and years ago. "Y'know, I can remember thinking, while I was getting ready to go out on the sand—I was hiding in a vent from the gladiator pen, and the wagon with Ma'elKoth and Toa-Sytell and . . . and everybody . . . was just rolling through the gate—I was thinking, that if somebody I loved had died because someone did what I was about to do, I wouldn't rest until I hunted the bastard down and killed him with my bare hands."

"How about that," the Caineslayer echoed expressionlessly.

"So where were you?"

The Caineslayer stared a question at him.

"You weren't there," Hari said. "You weren't at the stadium."

"How do you know this?"

"I know you can fight. If you'd been there, either your parents would be alive, or you'd be dead."

"I was—" The Caineslayer was forced to take a pause, to swallow his old, familiar pain. "—otherwise engaged."

Hari turned his palms toward the canvas tenting overhead. "You're an elKothan, right? A Beloved Child of Ma'elKoth?"

"I am."

"Yeah." For a moment, another of those flickering, bitter almost-smiles passed over his features. "Me, too."

The Caineslayer frowned. "You?"

"Yeah. I went through the very last Ritual of Rebirth before the Assumption. Baptism of blood and fire—signed, sealed, and sanctified, that's me."

"I don't believe it."

"Ma'elKoth did." He shrugged and waved this digression aside. "He summoned his Beloved Children to the stadium that day. How come you weren't there?"

"I—" The Caineslayer had to look away; the pain this memory brought was astonishing, a savage stabbing ache undiminished by the passage of seven years, unassuaged by his sure knowledge that his pain and loss had been the knife that carved his destiny. He could not have changed events then any more than he could reach back through seven long years and change them now.

But the pain—

He had one defense against this pain: he reminded himself that this pain belonged to Raithe of Ankhana. *I am the Caineslayer,* he told himself. *That pain is a revenant of someone else's life.*

"I was in the scriptorium of the Ankhanan Embassy," he said, "copying my report on your murder of Ambassador Creele."

Hari made a grunting noise that could have been a snort of incredulous laughter; after all these days, recognition finally flared within his shadowed eyes. "I remember you . . ." he said wonderingly. "You were one of the kids who frog-marched me up to his office. You had some silly-ass melodramatic shit to say about the Monasteries coming after me; something like that. Yeah, that *was* you—I remember the eyes."

"I would have hunted you for Creele's sake alone," the Caineslayer said softly. "He was a great man."

"He was an asshole. He deserved what he got."

"And I?" the Caineslayer asked. "What did I deserve?"

Hari rolled over far enough to turn his face to the canvas wall of the deck shelter. "Don't come crying to me, kid. You got more out of life than most ever do: when the world hurt you, you got the chance to hit back. Count yourself lucky, and shut up."

"That's it? That's all you have to say?" The Caineslayer found his hands had become convulsive fists once more. "That I'm *lucky*?"

"What do you want from me? An apology?" Hari twisted back to look at him, black rings of bruise around his eyes, his nose still swollen from the blow that had smashed it three days before. "Or forgiveness?"

The Caineslayer's fists trembled, and he could not take his eyes from the bulge of the thyroid cartilage in Hari's throat; he could feel an arc of energy from the hammer edge of his hand to that still target, as though Hari's larynx and the Caineslayer's fist were two pieces of the same lodestone.

Slowly, the Caineslayer forced his fists to open, and he choked back his taste for blood. "So," he murmured. "So."

He rose and folded his hands behind his back, pacing the floor of Hari's deck shelter as though even walking was a wound he could give this man—and perhaps it was. Perhaps the best pain he could offer was the reminder of everything this man would never do again. "So," he said again, "finally, you understand what you have done to me. Now, I wish to understand what I have done to you."

He made himself smile, and he turned that smile upon Hari like a weapon. "Talk to me now. Tell me of Pallas Ril."

4

OF COURSE HE had refused, at first; for hours he refused, while the Caineslayer amused himself with a cheerful alternation of questioning and mild torture. On that day, the Caineslayer had addressed his attention to the nerve cluster in the pad between the thumb and forefinger; even a moderate pinch on it could bring tears to the eyes of a strong man without causing any lasting damage, and the Caineslayer had a grip like his father's furnace tongs. He kept Hari strapped to his cot—he had seen the lethal skill that still inhabited those hands graphically demonstrated upon the late Artan Viceroy. He sat beside him, holding one of Hari's hands in both of his, like a dutiful son. Sometimes he would alternate this with pressure on the radial nerve just above the elbow.

One of the charming features of these excruciations is that—with proper timing and intervals of rest—these particular pressure points become more sensitive as they are abused, rather than less. After an hour or two, the subject feels his whole arm burning from within, as though his blood had turned to acid.

In the end Hari had submitted, as the Caineslayer had known he would. The questions themselves—*How did you meet? Where was your first kiss? What did she wear on your wedding day? What was the scent of her hair?*—would bring the anguish of memory fully to the forefront of Hari's consciousness. It was clear that to speak of these things hurt Hari more than keeping silent could have—yet once he had begun, he seemed disinclined to stop. Nonetheless he did stop from time to time, requiring the Caineslayer to encourage him again with nerve pressure, as though he wanted the pain, as though he *welcomed* it, as though he required both the pain of speaking and the pain of keeping silent; as though to hide from any scrap of his suffering would be a betrayal, a crime, a sin.

The Caineslayer accepted Hari's shattered heart as a sacrament. He had never been so happy.

He kept the Caine Mirror alongside Hari's bed; he could dip into Hari's head at will—immerse himself in Hari's torment. This he did only at intervals; the Caineslayer felt keenly the danger of swimming those deeps. They tugged at him awake and called to him in dreams, whispering of sinking forever from the memory of light.

Hari spoke through two days, and the Caineslayer listened—prompting occasionally with questions, and more rarely with physical coercion. He heard of many faraway and unlikely places, from the depths of the Boedecken Waste to the gleaming brass streets of Lipke's capital Seven Wells, from the jungle kingdom of Yalitrayya to the ice fields of the White Desert. Later, they spoke of places even more exotic and unimaginably distant: places such as *Chicago* and *San Francisco*—and alien names such as *Shermaya Dole* and *Marc Vilo* and *Shanna Leighton* and *Arturo Kollberg*.

We have a very simple, straightforward relationship, the Caineslayer reflected from time to time. He and Hari shared a single need: the need to experience Hari's pain.

That simplicity created a sort of understanding, almost a bond: they cooperated to give each other what each wanted. All the caustic hatred that had corroded his veins for seven years was slowly and surely drained away; his victory had lanced a boil on his soul. Caine was no longer the icon of evil, the Enemy of God, the author of all the world's ills. He had become simply what he was: a ruthless, amoral man, now beaten—crushed by the world, just like any other.

Only human, after all.

And Hari, too, seemed to take some relief; profoundly attuned to his prisoner's moods, the Caineslayer could not help but notice that the needle point of Hari's pain seemed to be slowly blunting. Late on the final night of the journey, the barge lay up along the bank, anchor chains attached to trees that grew beside the Chambaygen's lazy channel, only a few hours upstream from Ankhana. All was quiet as the crew slept—even the two pole-boys on watch drowsed atop the deckhouse—and Hari seemed almost at peace.

The Caineslayer squatted beside him. "You are calm, now."

Hari's sole response was to work the back of his head on his pillow and chafe his wrists against the straps that bound him to his cot.

"You have been calming ever since we began on the river," the Caineslayer said. "Did you love your wife so little that you no longer suffer her loss?"

"Well, y'know . . ." Hari murmured. "It's the river. It's her river."

The Caineslayer said, "Not anymore."

"Are you sure? We drift downstream, and how much has really changed? The leaves still turn, the birds still fly. Fish jump. The river goes on." Hari closed his eyes and gave a sleepy sigh. "Shanna used to tell me that life is a river; a person is like a little eddy that spins in a backflow for a little while, until it uncoils and the river washes it away. Nothing is lost. Maybe a little farther downstream, another eddy spins up, and nothing is gained. Life is just life, like the river is just a river. Other times, she'd say that the river is a song, and a person or a bird or a tree or whatever—an individual—is really just a scatter of notes, a little subtheme, like what they call a motif. That motif might play loud or soft, might be part of the song for a long time or just a little, but in the end, it's all still one song."

"So which is it?" the Caineslayer asked softly. "A song, or a river?"

Hari shrugged. "How the fuck should I know? I'm not sure she really meant either one. She was a goddess, not a philosopher. But she knew a little bit about life and death. She was never afraid to die; she knew that dying was part of the whole cycle—that her little eddy would untangle itself back into the current of the river."

The Caineslayer nodded his understanding. "So: you can bear your loss, because you feel that you haven't really lost her."

"It's her river, kid."

"As I have observed already," the Caineslayer said, "not anymore."

Hari's eyes slitted open; he watched the Caineslayer without turning his head.

"You must have noticed the silver runes painted on the Sword of Saint Berne," the Caineslayer went on. "What do you think they were for?"

Hari didn't answer, didn't move, only watched: a predator become aware of being stalked by something larger and more fierce.

"I confess that I do not know the actual use of these runes," the Caineslayer continued. "It did not seem important enough that I should ask. But consider: If the Viceroy wished merely to destroy her body, would not the bare blade have been sufficient?"

Hari's eyes glittered.

"So: as you go to your death at the hands of your enemies, do not console yourself with vain dreams of Pallas Ril in some misty afterlife where she might be happy, or at least content. The best she might have experienced is an absolute extinction of consciousness. More likely, she screams even now in some unimaginable hell, and will continue to do so. Forever."

They passed a long interval in which the only sound was the soft splash of the river against the barge's hull, and the only motion the gentle rocking of the deck.

"You," Hari said finally, hoarse and slow, "have a gift for hating."

The Caineslayer inclined his head in a grave sketch of a bow. "If so, it is a gift I received from you."

For a moment, he found himself wanting to reach out and grasp Hari's shoulder—to touch him in some way that was not intended to cause pain. In many ways, he was closer to this man than he'd been to the mediocrities with whom he's studied at the abbey school, and to the spineless Exoterics who had staffed the Thorncleft Embassy. He and Hari were joined in ways forever inaccessible, forever incomprehensible, to those grey souls.

He rose and turned away.

"You know," he said distantly, staring out the flap of the shelter at a spray of brilliant stars, "under other circumstances, I shouldn't have been too surprised to find that we had become friends."

"Kid, we *are* friends," Hari told him with a bitter laugh. "You mean you haven't noticed?"

The Caineslayer met his dark glare across the still, pale flame of the lamp between them and thought for a moment of all they had shared in these past five days. "No, I hadn't," he said slowly, frowning and nodding together. "But I suppose you're right."

"Fucking right I'm right. Not that it'll stop me from killing you if I ever get the chance."

"Mmm, of course not," the Caineslayer replied, "any more than it shall stop me from giving you to the Imperial authorities for execution."

"Yeah. Tomorrow morning, right?"

The Caineslayer felt a surprising pang of melancholy as he nodded. "Yes. Tomorrow."

"You sound like you're not looking forward to it."

"Truly, I'm not," he said. "But I am ready for it. You are part of my former life, Hari. I am ready to move on."

"Yeah, whatever. You ready to move to your goddamn bed?"

Another glance at the stars—and at the scant oil remaining in the lamp—reminded him how late the hour had become. "I suppose I am."

"Then shut up and go to sleep."

The Caineslayer smiled almost fondly. "Good night, Hari."

"Fuck off."

5

EARLY THE NEXT morning, as the barge had swung sluggishly out into the Great Chambaygen's current with the first sparkling rays of the rising sun, the Caineslayer had carried a trencher of thick lentil porridge flavored with salt pork into Hari's deck shelter, set it beside his cot, and unstrapped one of Hari's arms so that he could feed himself with the large wooden spoon. Hari took a listless bite or two, then set down the spoon.

"You should eat it," the Caineslayer said. "It's better than you'll get in the Donjon."

"Yeah, whatever. How about the bedpan?"

The Caineslayer shoved the bedpan within Hari's reach, waited patiently while he relieved himself, then carried the pan out and dumped its contents into the river. When he came back, Hari still wasn't eating; he lay on the cot, staring expressionlessly at the canvas overhead. "What's it gonna be today, then?" he said. "You gonna start on my hand again?"

"No," the Caineslayer said. Slowly, he lowered himself into the Warrior's Seat, his legs doubled comfortably beneath him. He rested his hands on his thighs, left cupping his right with thumbs touching: the Quiet Circle meditation posture.

"This is our last time together, Hari; in perhaps two hours I will deliver you to the Household Knights who await us on the Ankhanan docks, and then I shall never see you again—mm, no. I mean to say I'll never *speak* with you again, since I do intend to witness your execution."

"Huh. Don't get all sentimental; you'll make me blush."

The Caineslayer gave his victim a level stare. "I have only one question for you today. I don't even insist on an answer."

Hari eyed him uncertainly; this change in their routine had awakened his animal wariness. "Yeah, all right."

"Was it worth it?"

Hari scowled. "Was what worth what? Is this some of that *If I had my life to do over again* horseshit?"

"Not exactly. I'm not interested in your life, Hari, but in the effect you've had on mine. I want to know: Saving Pallas Ril in Victory Stadium seven years ago—was it worth what you've suffered since?"

"Of course it was," he responded with instant certainty. "I'd do it again in half a fucking second."

"Would you? Would you really? With all you've told me: the destruction of your career, the loss of your legs, of your father, of your home, your daughter . . . and your life. Are you sure?"

"I . . . I mean, I, uh . . ." His voice faltered, and he turned his face away.

"You weren't even happy together, you and she," the Caineslayer said. "You told me so yourself. And so: Your sole accomplishment was to postpone her death for seven years. *If you had known,* then, how that single act would inexorably destroy you, would you have done it?"

Hari's free hand covered his eyes, and he did not respond.

"You need not answer. I merely want you to consider the question."

"Faith," Hari murmured.

"Ah, yes, your daughter," the Caineslayer said. "And have you done her such a kindness, bringing her into your world? Sometimes, in these nights, you cry out in your sleep, do you know that? Do you know that what you say is *Faith, I'm sorry*?"

Something faded then from the man who had been Caine: some spark of the flame that had made him loom so large dwindled and winked out. For the first time, he looked old, and tired, and truly, undeniably, finally: crippled.

After a long, long moment spent savoring this extinction, the Caineslayer rose and moved to leave the tent, but Hari turned toward him once again, his face bleak as winter stone.

"I guess I could ask you the same question."

6

THE CAINESLAYER STOPPED; he looked back past his shoulder. "What do you mean?"

"Ever think about what destroying me is gonna cost *you*?"

"Hari, Hari," the Caineslayer chided, "have we not passed the time when you can expect me to take your threats seriously?"

"It's not a threat, kid. Sure, let's say I took your parents from you. You took my wife from me, and you're gonna watch me die. Whatever," he said with a one-armed shrug. "Fair enough. I don't really give a shit; I'm dead already. But how will you live with what *you've* done?"

"What I have done?" The Caineslayer snorted. "I have saved the world from the Enemy of God."

"Kid, kid." Hari echoed precisely the Caineslayer's chiding tone. "You didn't save shit. When you and Garrette managed to kill Shanna, you wiped out the Ankhanan Empire. And the Monasteries, and Lipke and Kor and Paqula, too. Pretty much everyone on this continent will be dead by this time next year."

"That's ridiculous."

"Sure it is. What do you think Pallas was *doing* here, you fucking idiot?"

A spectral shiver trickled down the Caineslayer's spine, a frictive half-hot *frisson* like the whisk of fingertips across unvarnished wood. "You're talking about Viceroy Garrette's disease— the one he gave to the subs."

"You *knew*?"

The Caineslayer met Hari's blankly astonished gaze and thought, *Well. At last I have succeeded in impressing him.* He wished he could take more pleasure in it; wished he could coolly reply *I know many things*, like a wizard in a campfire tale.

Instead, his stomach dropping, he could say only, "Yes."

"Damn, kid." Hari shook his head, squinting disbelievingly. "Damn, I thought *I* was hard-core. So this all started with Garrette, huh?"

The Caineslayer shook his head. "It all started with you. With Creele."

"What did Garrette tell you?"

"He . . . said it's called *aitcharv . . . aitcharvee . . .*"

"HRVP," Hari supplied. "That's right. How much did ol' Vinse tell you about it?"

The Caineslayer suddenly found the air to have thickened under this canvas tent—thick as water, thick as stew; he could barely force it into his lungs. "Enough," he replied thinly.

"And you still went through with it."

"I don't understand."

"Garrette was dead. You had me. Why did Pallas have to die?"

The Caineslayer allowed himself a thin, chill smile. "Reasons are for peasants."

But Hari's gaze stayed level and steady until the Caineslayer had to look away. "I could say it was because I thought she might rescue you from me," he said. "I could say it was because I had made a bargain in the name of the Monasteries, and that bargain must be kept. But neither would be true. The truth is simpler, and more complex: She was killed because you loved her, and I wanted to watch you watch her die."

Hari nodded at this, frowning, as though he understood and could respect such a desire, but then he squinted upward once more. "You ever wonder why *Garrette* wanted her dead?"

"He said—he said she would have protected the elves from the disease."

"Not just the elves."

That spectral shiver near his spine threatened to become trembling. "The Viceroy assured me that humans aren't in any danger—"

"Humans. Yeah." An echo of Caine's wolf-grin stretched Hari's lips. "You just gotta remember that for Garrette, *human* meant *Artan*."

A sick understanding gathered itself in the Caineslayer's belly.

"Here's a question. Garrette had you inoculated, didn't he? Probably shot up most of the people in Transdeia: they take this black thing and press it against your shoulder and pull a trigger and it makes a sound like *fssst*. You get that?"

"Yes . . . yes, I did. And the embassy staff, and a lot of the miners and rail porters . . ."

"You're today's lucky winner, kid. First prize: a front row seat for the end of the world."

"He said—he said it was just a *precaution*—"

"And just because this stuff came from this world—my

world—and he's got all this fancy technology and shit, you thought he knew what the fuck he was talking about."

"I—" The Caineslayer shut his eyes. "Yes."

"That's the problem with you shitheads who think you're *educated*," Hari said with brutal mockery. "You always think that if somebody talks the same way you do, he's not a moron. But he *was* a moron, and so are you for thinking he wasn't."

The Caineslayer found he could not answer.

"It's loose in Ankhana," Hari said. "That's why Pallas came here. People are sick with it. Human people. Dying already. Killing each other. Locking themselves away with their fevers, because they're already so crazy that they figure everybody's out to kill them. Shanna, Pallas, she was the only hope the people of this continent—probably the whole *world*—had. You killed her. Congratulations. You get to watch everybody die."

The Caineslayer reached blindly to his side and gathered a handful of the tent's canvas wall to steady himself. "Watch . . ." he murmured.

"Sure. That's what that little black fissy thing did for you. You won't get sick. You're immune, just like me. Lucky you, huh?"

"You're lying," the Caineslayer muttered. He liked the sound of that, so he said it again, more strongly: "You're lying. You're making this up."

Of *course* he was lying—was this not the man who had been Caine? The Caineslayer had been hurting him for days, and this was the only way a crippled man could devise to hit back at his tormentor: a silly, vicious lie.

"Yeah, all right, sure. I'm lying," Hari said, maintaining his bleak predator's grin. "You're the one with the mind powers—*use* them, you stupid sack of shit."

"I don't have to," the Caineslayer said firmly. "It's an obvious lie; why would the *Aktir* Queen turn one hair to help the people of Ankhana?"

"Maybe because she wasn't the goddamn *Aktir* Queen. Maybe because the Church has been *lying* about her all these years. Maybe because she cared about every living thing, even useless pinheaded weaseldicks like you."

Hari looked him over then: a long, slow scan from head to toe and back again, as though measuring his every quality, tangible or not. Then he said, "You took an oath when they made you a friar. You took an oath to support and defend the Future of Humanity with every breath of your body from that day forward. And this is how you kept it. You killed them. All of them. Because you wanted to hurt me, you wiped out the fucking human race."

The Caineslayer gripped the canvas with both hands; his stomach heaved, and bile scorched the back of his throat. "You swore that oath, too," he insisted desperately. "And look at all the uncountable lives you have taken, all the suffering you have caused—!"

"Yeah, well, you said it yourself," Hari replied with a shrug. "I'm the Enemy of God."

7

ON THE DOCKSIDE below the Caineslayer's position, the military band struck up "King of Kings" while marching in place, and the first martial strains of the Imperial anthem brought him back to the present. At the refrain following the first verse, the band's diverse elements swung into order like gears interlocking, and sunlight flared golden spikes from polished brass in time with the anthem's ponderous beat. The Household Knights marched themselves into order around the wagon, expressionless as dolls under the gold-filigreed steel of their helmets; their blood-colored halberds swung in identical arcs like the moment arms of fifty perfectly synchronized metronomes. The Exoterics who had borne the cripple's litter took the lead ropes of the horses that drew the wagon and walked alongside.

The man who had been Caine sagged from the harness that bound him to the platform's rack, swinging gently with the wagon's sway, his head down as though unconscious. The band segued smoothly from "King of Kings" into "Justice of God."

The Caineslayer straightened; slowly, thoughtfully, he pulled a splinter of the deckhouse rail out of the flesh of his palm and frowned down at the bead of blood that welled from this tiny wound. How had he been so easily beaten?

He no longer doubted that Hari had told him the truth. Whatever had happened in Alientown was only a prelude. This city was sick, festering with madness. He could feel it, smell it on the air. He could close his eyes and *see* it: see sweat on pale and clammy brows, see eyes parboiled by fever casting hooded glances while trembling hands sharpened carving knives, see the flecks of foam at the corners of dry, cracking lips. He did not need his powers to show him these things. He knew they were there. He knew, because a lie would have been too easy. Too *cheap*.

And he knew, from long years of study, that Caine's victories are never cheap; they always cost, in the end, more than God Himself can afford.

Awe stole over him, a tingling sense of the uncanny, when he numbered the days and nights of their journey down from the mountains. Hari had known this all along. With a single phrase, the man who had been Caine had spiked the Caineslayer's triumph through the heart and burned its corpse to toxic ash. All that time, through all that pain, he'd hugged it to himself, waiting. Waiting until its stroke would kill.

His destiny had betrayed him, had made him a destroyer on a scale that humbled even Caine. Destiny, he understood with bitter certainty, could not be trusted.

He had no idea what he should do now. Without destiny to guide him, he was lost in a vast, whistling darkness. Any direction he might choose was purely arbitrary; it would make no more sense, offer no more hope, than would sitting still. Which offered neither sense nor hope at all.

He swung himself over the rail and dropped, catlike, to the barge's deck. He had a need that burned in him like breath to a drowning man. For this need, there was only one answer, and that answer was within the crude deck shelter that had served Hari as a cabin.

He slipped inside. His possessions were enclosed in three packages: one, the trunk that held his clothes; two, the case that held the Sword of Saint Berne, brought from the mountains to the safety of the Ankhanan Embassy; and three, the valise-sized device with two handgrips covered in beaten gold, with the silvered glass mirror between. It was these handgrips that the Caineslayer now took, and this mirror into which his ice-pale eyes gazed.

This is the last, he told himself—promised himself, like a drunkard lifting yet another glass of whiskey to admire its amber glow in the sunlight. *One last time.*

And he moaned like a lover in passion, low in the back of his throat, as he entered the man who had been Caine.

8

I THINK IT's the roar of the crowd that brings me up from the pit. People everywhere, all around me, staring, shouting, cheering, pointing. There's a band in the neighborhood somewhere . . . There they are, marching up ahead while they play some fucking awful piece of crap that sounds like a Max Reger dirge transcribed by John Philip Sousa.

Chained—they've got me chained as though there were actually some chance I could get away, wrists manacled to my waist, a kind of gallows vest pegged to the block in front of me with about two feet of links thicker than my finger, chains hooked to straps at my shoulders that hold me up to some kind of scrapwood rack so that everybody can get a goddamn good look.

People hang out of windows, waving, throwing stuff—a wad of something wet hits my right arm and splashes across my chest, and the thick retchy stench of it brings a word up out of my raddled memory: *tumbrel*. That's what they used to call the cart, the kind I'm riding in this nightmare parade, a tumbrel. French for *shit wagon*. They've chained me to the shit wagon.

Nice day for a parade. The sun always looks bigger, yellower, hotter here, the rolling cottonball clouds cleaner and more solid as they tumble through a sky so deep and blue it makes you want to cry. Hot for this time of year, Los Angeles hot—in autumn, Ankhana is usually more like London.

Fog and rain, that's what I'd wish for—something to drive the crowds indoors, something that really says *England*. That's what I'd wish for, if I had any wishes left. Instead, I've got Hollywood.

I guess, in a sick way, it's appropriate.

I remember from the old movies that you're supposed to stand upright in the tumbrel; it's traditional. Just one more fucking thing that I can't get right. *Tale of Two Cities . . . Scaramouche . . . The Scarlet Pimpernel* with Leslie Howard . . . That was Shanna's favorite—

Shanna—

Oh, *Christ*—

The weight of it threatens to snap what's left of my spine, and the light of day recedes from me as I spiral back down into the pit.

The pit is a warm and friendly darkness; this is where I have lived, most days since Transdeia, whenever that suede-faced motherfucker Raithe left me alone. What I have for company in the pit are comradely fantasies of having my head blown off by one of those assault rifles that some of Raithe's friars now carry slung beneath their robes, so they resemble mere concealed swords. I can feel it exactly as it would happen, but in two-hundred-frames-a-second slowmo: the initial entry of the slug as it parts my scalp and punches through my skull, goes tumbling and slivering through my brain, trailing a wake of oblivion before a fist-sized splintered hole erupts on the far side.

I can dream of this, and be happy.

The head shot is only one of several friends of mine; sometimes I can cheer myself with the slice of a short blade into my heart, and darkness scaling my carotid artery like blood billowing through seawater; sometimes the billow of blood is literal, as I watch it pulse from opened wrists. Wrists, hell—I've carved enough meat in my day that I could do better, if anyone gives me a chance. I'd only need about an inch of blade to open my femoral artery; that would drop me into my Edenic oblivion almost as fast as one to my heart. It'd be easy. No hesitation cuts: my legs are already dead. Wouldn't even sting.

I don't need the pain. I'm not out to punish myself. Only the oblivion counts.

Everything else is just foreplay.

I'd really kind of like to rest here, drift off in some kind of half nap to close out the ugly truth of myself, but the crowd won't let me. They're chanting a name over and over in the kind of nasty, mockingly petty singsong that reminds me how much people in general are pretty shitty creatures. When I was maybe ten years old, I tried to kill a kid who was singsonging me like that—the only difference was that he knew my name.

These idiots keep calling me Caine.

I'd ignore them, but they insist on getting my attention with the pieces of fruit, and the eggs, with clods of horseshit and the occasional rock that hit me from time to time. Every once in a while, somebody throws a handful of gravel; some of that sticks to the mingled yolk and peach meat and drippy shit, and some of it works its way in under my collar and trickles down my chest and back and ribs and scrapes into the open sores of my burns. The parade passes a little too close to some buildings, and kids in the windows have a contest to see who can spit the biggest hawker into my hair.

You can't rest down in the dark with crap hitting you all the time and the damn band blaring and the sunlight sparking off everybody's iridescent braid and brass horns and halberds polished into scarlet steel mirrors. And the worst thing—the really, deeply, fundamentally loathsome vileness that makes me despise myself beyond any masochistic fantasy of self-hatred—is that I can't stop Acting.

I'm still doing it: still watching, still commenting, still describing what I feel. Even down in the pit, swimming toward the darkness that is my sole desire, I have to tell myself what I'm doing.

I'm telling *myself*.

Seven years ago, when I was last here in Ankhana, as I lay dying on the damp arena sand of Victory Stadium, I thought I understood. I thought I knew who my real enemy was: my audience.

But I'm still performing . . .

Now my only audience is me.

Oh, god, god, what an ugly, ugly creature I am.

Because this is what I did it for. This, right here. What's happening right now. The parade.

This is why Shanna is dead. This is why Faith is gone forever. This is what has killed Dad, and has stolen every joy I'd ever dreamed to have.

And so: Here I am.

The center of attention. The Main Event.

The band plays, the sun shines, the people of Ankhana cheer, and no hell could burn like this.

All this, so that I could be a star.

9

THE CAINESLAYER PULLED himself free of the Caine Mirror with a shuddering gasp, and mopped sweat from his mouth with the back of a trembling hand. *I should heave this damned thing into the river,* he thought. He quieted his shivering and forced his breathing into a regular pattern, but still the weakness in his limbs made him stagger as he stepped back.

Instead of tossing the Caine Mirror into the river where it belonged, the Caineslayer found himself reluctantly offering a silver noble to an ogre who had served as a poleboy on the barge to bear it—and the trunk containing his Ambassadorial robes—to the embassy.

The case containing Kosall he would carry with his own hand. This case was narrow and flat, half again as long as one of his arms, built of light springy slats of wood covered with leather, bound with brass nails.

He held the case cradled like a child, frowning.

Within this case was the most holy relic of the Imperial Church, lost for seven years; a weapon of power that Saint Berne had used not only for the blow that struck down the Prince of Chaos, but now to slay the *Aktir* Queen. He found it wholly curious: Though he knew full well that Caine had been only a man, that Berne had been a rapist and murderer—and lately only a corpse driven by a demon—and that Ma'elKoth himself was no more than a political prisoner in the *Aktiri* lands, carrying this weapon still raised a pious chill along his spine.

Though he now knew the truth behind the faith he'd practiced these many years, the faith remained. Somehow, he was able to see Caine as both an ordinary man and as the Enemy of God at the same time, without contradiction. Within this case was a blade that was only a weapon, but also a mythic symbol of the power of a god—who was only a man, but no less a god.

Curious, indeed.

As a symbol, this sword was too potent for him; he had planned—he *still* planned—to lock it within the embassy's Secure Vault; he'd allow the Council of Brothers to decide its final disposition. But he could not simply sling it over his shoulder and walk, not now; he had borne it down this river, he had kept it safe, he had never even opened the case—

He could not bear to give it up without at least looking at it, one last time.

He could not bring himself to open the case now, though, not here, not in this crude shelter of slats and canvas—not where at any moment he might be interrupted, be *discovered*, peered at by dull uncomprehending eyes. *This is nothing shameful,* he insisted to himself. *There is nothing shameful here; but it is* personal.

He tucked the case under his arm and stepped out into the slanting sunlight on deck. Around him, the deckers and poleboys worked at their own simpleminded tasks, casting only the occasional incurious glance his way. As he stood there in the doorway, a decker shambled up to him sullenly. "Leaving? Done with shelter?"

"With this?" the Caineslayer said distantly, moving away. "Yes. I am done with shelter."

Yet he could not make himself carry the case off the barge. Certainly, the simplest course would have been to slip into the city, to find himself a private room in some random tavern, a room with a lock on its door—the simplest course, but not easy. Not easy at all. Somewhere deep within his bowels lurked a dread of what he was about to do, as though this sword might have a power over him not unlike that of the Caine Mirror. Here on the barge, he still had some control.

Holding the case tight in his armpit, he folded his fingers together in a specifically complex knot, breathed deeply three times, and vanished from the consciousness of the barge crew. Any whose eye fell upon him forgot his existence an instant later; any who thought of him assumed he had left the barge with the triumphal parade. He slipped onto the afterdeck, knelt, and crawled into a narrow tunnel formed by untidily stacked cargo crates bound for the Teranese Delta, where the Great Chambaygen emptied into the sea.

He knelt, and lay the case on the deck before his knees. He shut his eyes reverently, opening the case's latches by feel, then swung back the case's lid. He covered his face with his hands, breathing into his palms until he felt himself to be calm; then slowly he opened his eyes and took his hands away and looked upon the naked blade within its bed of crushed blue velvet. The shadows of the crates that surrounded him were striped with sunlight leaking through their slats: one single shaft shone the length of Kosall, bringing it to golden life.

Long, a handbreadth wide at the quillons, straight grey steel painted with silver runes, now dark with the brown splashes of the *Aktir* Queen's blood—he had not wiped the blade, for fear of disturbing the unknown magick bound into the painted runes, and for the same reason had not returned it to a scabbard.

Kosall.

The blade of Saint Berne.

Its hilt was a span and a half, wrapped with sweat-stained leather, pommel a plain steel knob; his hands trembled, fluttered near and away again like anxious moths. Dare he lift it this one time?

Could he not?

He laid his fingers, delicate as a kiss, upon a quillon. He stroked the chill steel, then took it hard into his hand. As his hand closed around the leather-wrapped hilt, the blade came to life. Warm, humming with power, it left him weak with desire. He pulled the sword up from its bed and raised it before his eyes.

This blade had parted the flesh of Caine.

Holding leather stained with the sweat of Saint Berne, he could *feel* it: could feel the slide of buzzing steel through lips of skin into the hard muscle of Caine's abdominal wall, through the writhe of intestine into the sizzle at the base of his spine.

Breathless, trembling, he reached forth with his mind and touched the steel, searching its energies for memories of Caine's blood and bone. With his power, he looked within the blade—

And something within the blade seized him, gripped his eyes, his heart, his limbs. From his throat came the hope of a scream, strangled to a convulsive gasp; his back arched and his irises rolled up to disappear within his skull.

He pitched backward into darkness. When he hit the deck, he bounced like a doll carved of green wood.

THE DRAGONESS WAS human, but no less a dragoness.

Much has been written elsewhere of the nature of dragonkind. Most of it is wrong. Dragons are not, as a species, creatures of evil bent upon wanton slaughter; nor are they merely great winged lizards asleep upon mounds of treasure. They are neither elemental forces of nature nor repositories of supernatural wisdom.

Mostly, they are individuals. The essential nature of one may vary widely from that of the next.

There are, however, certain assertions that may truthfully be made of dragons as a species. They tend to be acquisitive, vengeful, jealous of their lands and possessions, and surpassingly fierce in their defense. Though slow to anger, they can be extremely dangerous when roused, and none more so than a dragoness defending her young. In these ways, dragonkind is very like humankind.

This is why the dragoness could be human, but no less a dragoness.

The dragoness had lived her life according to the custom of her kind; she patiently oversaw her possessions, slowly extending their borders by gradual effort over many years. She tended her flocks, and added to her wealth by the occasional raid upon an unwary neighbor.

She kept almost entirely to herself; she had little interest in the events of the wider world, and so would likely have never entered this story, save that on one raid—a raid of vengeance, upon her most hated enemy—she had taken the child of the river.

The child of the river was pursued by the god of dust and ashes.

And thus the dragoness became part of this story.

THIRTEEN

AVERY SHANKS DABBED blood from the cut on her lower lip, looked upon her granddaughter, and pondered the fundamental unpredictability of existence.

This was an unaccustomed pastime for her, and she found it both difficult and uncomfortable. She thought of herself as active, rather than contemplative: a doer, a decider. An operative principle. A verb.

Yet now, unexpectedly, reality had jumped her from behind and knocked her over; this verb had become an object, held down and pummeled by a force that was beyond her capacity to resist. This force cared nothing for her self-image of ruthless decisiveness; it permitted only an arbitrarily limited range of decision, rigidly bounded by the fortress walls of her heart. She—who had lived her life in simple declaratives—must now accept a conditional, no matter how it stung.

She might possibly love this child.

Few who knew Avery Shanks would ever guess that she was capable of such an emotion. If asked, she would deny it. For her, love was less an emotion than a pressure: a physical compression that seized her heart, her lungs, every part of her, and punished her mercilessly. In the wilder moments of hallucination occasionally brought on by her overindulgence in sedatives and alcohol, she saw a monster that rode behind her shoulder, its tentacles sliding into her chest through puckered mouths that had opened upon her skin; this monster used its hideous grip to drive her this way and that, to force her into unwise choices and ridiculous actions, and sometimes, simply and purely, maliciously, to inflict pain. This, to Avery Shanks, was love.

She had loved Karl.

Seven years of brutal self-denial had shrunk the monster that had tortured her since his death, carved away its power over her, until it could produce only the odd twinge, here and there. But now, fear pooled in Avery Shanks' belly when she looked at her granddaughter. The monster might be coming back.

And it wore the face of a child she had never seen until just a week ago.

"Faith," she said firmly, though her hand reached out with timid gentleness to the girl's flaxen hair—hair so much like Karl's had been, at this age. "Faith, you must lie still. Lie still for Grandmaman, mm?"

Faith's response was a slow calming, a shuddering release of tension like a bridge cable being unwinched to slack; she had barely spoken for two days now, and her eyes remained empty as a midsummer's sky.

The room was walled, floored, and ceilinged with soft, re-silient, featureless white plastic. SynTech had the contract to produce Social Police holding cells—through Petrocal, the company SynTech had acquired through Avery's marriage to the father of her children, the late Carlton Norwood—and so retro-fitting this room in Avery's Boston mansion had been swift and relatively inexpensive. A screen wider than Faith's outstretched arms dominated one wall, but it remained deliberately detuned so that it showed pulsing electronic snow; oceanic white noise hissed from its concealed speakers.

Since Sunday morning, this room had been the only place in which Faith could open her eyes without screaming.

The technician nodded his thanks to Avery and lifted a gunmetal tiara from which sprouted the fine, nearly invisible hairs of neural probes. "Okay, Businessman. Let's try this again, shall we?"

Avery sighed. "Yes. But for the last time." She stroked Faith's arms and clasped her wrists firmly. "Lie still, now, Faith. This will not hurt, I promise you."

Dozens of tests had been run on the child since Sunday— every single neurological indicator that could be taken while she was under sedation. Not a single abnormality had been found. Professional Lieberman, her staff Physician, had smugly diag-nosed "chronic idiopathic catatonia." When Avery had con-sulted a dictionary and discovered that this clinical diagnosis meant, in plain language, "she won't move and she won't talk, and I don't know why," she had fired the man on the spot.

The next Physician to examine Faith, having failed to find any organic cause for this behavior, suggested that the child might have some sort of emotional disturbance. Avery's reply had been a tight, lipless snarl that she did not need a hundred-mark-an-hour neurospecialist to tell her that a child who alternates catatonia and convulsion might be emotionally disturbed.

Finally, desperately, Avery had decided to have the child fitted with an array of neural probes that function rather like a nonsurgical version of a thoughtmitter; she felt that if she could only see what Faith saw, feel what Faith felt, she might be able to gain some understanding of what it was that caused the child so much suffering.

She feared that she understood already. This neural probe was her last tight-lipped attempt to convince herself that she was wrong.

The process of fitting and adjusting the neural probe distressed Faith to the point of convulsive seizure, despite the use of powerful tranquilizers. They had tried making the preliminary adjustments with the child under sedation, but when she had awakened, the seizures had redoubled. Any attempt to restrain Faith by any means beyond the touch of Avery's hand had shown similar results.

And so: their final attempt would be made with only Avery's touch and voice to keep the child calm. Avery held the child's wrists and murmured alien words in her ear, phrases that came awkwardly from her hard mouth: "Shh, Faith. No one will hurt you. Grandmaman is here, and everything will be all right."

If this didn't work, she would have to call in Tan'elKoth after all.

Her silver crew cut drew down as her face twisted into a scowl that left her mouth hard and sharp as the edge of a scalpel. She had promised herself that she would exhaust every other option first. She had second-handed *For Love of Pallas Ril* far too many times; she knew too well that Tan'elKoth was not to be trusted.

Not one little bit.

Avery's grip tightened upon Faith's wrists as the technician made the attempt to slip the tiara once again around the child's hairline. The previous round of convulsions had been violent enough that Faith had even begun to flail with her left arm—her left arm that, like her legs, she had barely moved since her initial attack. This unexpected use of the left had slipped in the punch that had given Avery her fat lip with its trickle of blood.

Much of Saturday afternoon, on the flight home and after, Avery had busied herself with the necessary arrangements: boarding school; a governess; a court order granting her title to all of Faith's clothing, toys, and other possessions from Michaelson's house; and a stream of outside salesfolk coming by the Shanks mansion with the array of clothing and accessories proper to a young Businessman's first months at school. She had spent more of the day with Faith herself than was, perhaps, absolutely necessary; she found that she took unexpected pleasure in the child's company. Her obedience that was never subservient, her clear and level gaze, her serene acceptance of Avery's every word coupled with fearless boldness and self-assurance—in nearly every way, Avery had thought wistfully, this was the child that she should have had for her own.

Instead she had been saddled with three vicious weaklings: sons that tormented each other—and her—with their backbiting and petty betrayals, their bootlicking and maneuvering for her favor. Even Karl, her precious golden Karl, the youngest and brightest of her sons—even he had not quite lived up to the Shanks name. Oh, he had come closer than his brothers, it was true: in defying her explicit wishes and entering the Studio Conservatory to pursue an Acting career, he was the only one of her children who had shown any spine at all.

It was her own fault: she had married badly. Her husband's company, Petrocal, had concealed its financial weakness until after the ceremony that had brought him and it under the aegis of the Shanks empire. If she had known how weak the company truly was, she never would have married him. The strength of one's corporation is the strength of one's character.

But when she looked upon Faith, she wondered if perhaps she had asked too much of Karl; perhaps the true steel of the Shanks character skips a generation. Perhaps the Shanks for which the world had been waiting was this golden-haired girl.

This was an outrageously romantic fantasy—the sort of smoke-and-moonbeam dream for which one of her children would have received, at the very least, a stern scolding—but it was, by all signs, *possible*; and the possibility alone had been intoxicating. For that one Saturday night, despite the dire tone of her conversation with Tan'elKoth, Avery Shanks came dangerously close to being happy.

But Sunday morning—

Hari—Hari, I'm hurt. You have to help me. Hari, Hari, please . . .

And that innocently romantic dream for which Avery Shanks had allowed herself to hope—however briefly—had, in that moment, burned her heart to ashes. She knew, in the darkness beneath those smoldering embers, that this new wound to the Shanks future was somehow Michaelson's fault, as well.

The child had spent the rest of that day under sedation; whenever she woke up, the screaming and thrashing would begin again. Physician Lieberman had surmised that the convulsions were triggered by sudden stimulus: any kind of noise, or movement, or touch. She was calm enough while left by herself in a lightless, silent room—but Avery could not allow that. She had been through such confinements herself, as a child; the closet had been her father's standard punishment for misbehavior. Avery had thought herself kindhearted, when disciplining her own children, for forgoing the closet in favor of the belt.

Later Sunday night, as Avery had made ready to retire, she'd found herself thinking about the child: a nagging, recurrent image of Faith sobbing in the dark. Two cocktails, a double dose of Teravil, and even extended, athletic sex with Lexi, her current houseboy, while she waited for the Teravil to work its chemical massage upon her jangled nerves, had all failed to erase the imagined quiet hitching sobs.

Even if the child *was* crying, Avery had little reason to care, as she had been reminding herself over and over again through that long and grueling day. Despite being Karl's daughter, the child was of use, primarily, as a weapon against Michaelson. Faith had been damaged, probably irreparably, by her early upbringing in that perverse distortion of a proper household. If the child must pass a truncated existence under permanent sedation, little would be lost.

She refused to allow herself to become attached to the child. She had learned long ago that the sacrifice of sentiment is merely part of the cost of being Business. But the hollow mental echo of a child crying, in the dark, would not let her sleep.

Finally—with a sigh and a mental note to switch to a new brand of sedatives—she had disentangled herself from Lexi's muscular limbs, belted her dressing gown of hand-woven natural silk about her waist, and tramped down the stairs to take a pair of IR goggles from the mansion's first-floor security office. After canceling the lights in the upstairs hallway, she had opened the door to Faith's darkened room—and found the child peacefully asleep. As was the nurse: slumped in a chair with her own goggles pushed up onto her forehead. The room reeked of urine.

The child had wet the bed.

Three rigid steps into the room, Avery had thrown the whole strength of her arm behind a ringing slap that nearly dislocated the jaw of the sleeping nurse. The slap was followed by a clipped, precise stream of invective that had delineated in broad terms the nurse's myriad failures as an Artisan and as a human being, and had finished with a religious admonition: she instructed the nurse to get down on her knees and pray that she would still have a trade in the morning.

And of course all this unseemly commotion had woken the child, who began shrieking again, and when the nurse hurriedly ordered on the lights and tried to remove Faith from the tangle of soiled bedcovers, the child had yowled and clawed and scratched like a panicked cat, tearing away from the nurse and scrambling across the room—

To throw her arms around Avery's legs, and hold on tight.

Avery was too astonished to do more than clutch at the child to keep her own balance. Eyes squeezed shut, face pressed hard against Avery's hip, Faith had quieted her shrieks to gentle sobs, and the thin wires of muscle in her trembling arms and legs had slackened toward some kind of ease, and Faith had spoken her only words since breakfast: a tiny, abject whisper.

"I'm sorry, Grandmaman," she'd murmured, barely audible. "I'm sorry . . ."

"Shh, Faith, shh," Avery had said awkwardly, the words stumbling from her half-numbed lips. Perhaps betrayed by the combination of alcohol and sedatives, she found herself suddenly overwhelmed, close to unexpected, astonishing tears. "It's all right, girl. It's all right."

"It's just so *empty* in here . . ."

Faith's tears had soaked through the silk of Avery's dressing gown and touched her aged skin, warm as a kiss. The gown would be irreparably stained, but Avery had not been able to make herself push the child away; she could only stand, and hold Faith, and gnaw on her lower lip until the pain drove her own tears away.

By the time the sheets were changed, and Faith had been sponged off and dressed in a clean nightgown, it had become clear to Avery that the child was calm only when in her presence. Over the following days—as Avery fed Faith, and bathed her, and changed disposable diapers on her like an infant—Faith would sometimes speak disconnectedly, offering faint, ambiguous clues to the unguessable mental world into which she had retreated, and sometimes she even relaxed into a smile that was in this household more rare, and more precious, than any diamond.

Providing this constant care was a tremendous burden upon Avery—it interfered drastically with the conduct of SynTech business, as she could work only sporadically, over the net—and was one that she resented mightily. But she never took this out on the child; Faith *needed* her, depended on her, in a way no one ever had. Her own children had been reared by their governesses and the masters of their boarding schools—but Faith could not be so lightly shoved aside. There was no one else who could help her.

It was exhausting, physically and emotionally draining, and infuriating. It had even cost her the gratifying sexual gymnastics of Lexi: Last night, when Avery had collapsed into bed, still smelling of the antiseptic soap she'd used to wash Faith after the child's latest round of incontinence, he had made some childish remark about Avery's lack of interest in lovemaking. "It's that child," he'd said petulantly. "That downcaste creature has turned you into an old woman."

She'd looked at her hands, then at the ceiling, then finally at his artfully tanned, synthetically rugged face. "I'm tired of you, Lexi," she had said. "Go home."

His face took on the pinched, almost prim pucker that was how Lexi registered his displeasure. "All right," he said. "I'll be in my room."

"Only to pack." She laid her arm over her eyes to shut out the sight of his extraordinary physique. "You're fired. Severance will be credited to your account."

"You can't—"

"I can."

He had stood in the doorway, posing, and she couldn't help but take one last look. He really was a magnificent animal.

"You'll miss me," he had said. "You'll think of everything we've done together, and you'll be sorry."

She sighed. "I'm never sorry. Go pack."

"But you *love* me—"

"If you're still here when I wake up, I'll have you shot."

And that had been that: it would give her more time to devote to Faith.

She was intellectually honest enough to admit that she would not have so extended herself for one of her own children; she rationalized her effort by insisting privately that this was merely the most temporary thing—some kind of shock brought on by Faith's finding herself in such radically altered circumstances— and the doctors would either cure her, or her difficulty would pass on its own in a day or two.

She needn't have worried.

As the tech fitted the gunmetal circlet around Faith's brow and she began once again her spasms and guttural coughing moans, there came a subtle change in the quality of light. The light of the stark white room had taken on a faint peachy tone: a little warm, a little golden, a little like sunlight. Not at all the usual chilly glow of the overhead tubes.

The white electronic surf from the wallscreen's speakers faded into expectant silence. Avery slowly made herself turn to look at the screen, half flinching; she had somehow become ten years old again, afraid of a sudden slap from her father.

"Businessman Shanks. How pleasant to see you."

The voice was toneless, as mechanical as an antique voder. The face on the screen was desiccated, skeletal, skin of yellowed parchment crumpled over protruding bones, brown-traced teeth exposed by a mouth like a cut in a chunk of raw liver.

Avery swung herself around to face the screen squarely. "Who the devil are you?" she demanded. "How did you get this code?"

"That would be Faith on the table behind you, hm? Excellent."

One quick stride brought Avery to the wallscreen's keypad, and she stabbed the CANCEL sharply.

The face on the screen smiled.

She stabbed the key again, and again, and pounded it with her fist. Faith's moans became louder, more insistent.

"How did you get this *code*?" she snarled. How could *anyone* get this code? The screen had been operational for less than a day—Avery *herself* didn't have its code! How could he override a cancel command? She made a fist once more, and raised it as though to smash the screen itself.

"I am hurt that you don't recognize me, Businessman. Hurt, and dismayed. I am Arturo Kollberg."

Her fist opened nervelessly, as did her mouth. "How—?"

"Thank you for looking after Faith for us. She'll be going now."

"Going . . . ? You *can't*—"

"On the contrary," Kollberg said, and the screen flickered back to its detuned speckling snow.

Faith's moans turned to sobs. The technician stood at the head of the bed, the gunmetal tiara useless in his hands. Avery glared at the white screen, grinding her teeth.

Tentative knocking on the door—"Businessman?" came the hesitant voice of her head butler.

"Go away."

"Businessman, it's the Social Police. They say they've come for the young mistress."

Avery lowered her head.

Behind her, Faith began to scream.

2

AVERY SHANKS WAS not blind to the irony: The Social Police had arrived with a custody order ceding Faith to their control. She was forced to stand, blinking back helpless tears, as the Social Police loaded Faith into the rear of a riot van.

In the days that followed, she found herself thinking of Michaelson with unexpected envy. He, at least, had raged and fought and threatened. He had taken up the gauntlet of his life and cast it at the feet of his enemy, for love of this child.

Avery had done nothing but stand on the landing pad, and try to take her loss like a Businessman.

The image haunted her, awake and asleep: Faith on a psych-ward stretcher, anesthetized, under restraint. She should have been deep into unconsciousness, but instead she struggled in slow spastic motion against the padded sheath that bound her to the stretcher, and she moaned, deep and dark, in the back of her throat. Somehow, even through the blanket layers of drug that enwrapped her, Faith had known she was being taken from her home.

Can't you see what you're doing to her? Avery's heart had cried out, again and again, though the words never touched the bitter silence that sealed her lips. *Can't you see that this child needs me?*

Rising up her throat like vomit was the sickening conviction that a society where such things can happen is in some way fundamentally, ineradicably wrong. There was an old, old saying, going back hundreds of years—she had known of it since before she could remember—but only now did she understand how true it was.

A liberal, the old saying went, *is a conservative who just got arrested.*

The first day passed with no word. SynTech's legal staff could not help her here; Donner Morton, the head of the Leisure clan to which the Shanks were affiliated, promised to look into the matter, but the best even he was likely to be able to do was find out where Faith had been taken.

She didn't understand even the broadest outlines of whatever might be going on, but she was certain it all came back to Tan'elKoth. He had made the call that had given her Faith. He had been in the Curioseum on the night of the fire, and Pallas Ril had apparently died according to his precise prediction.

She knew where Faith must be now.

The second day passed, and the third. She ignored her duties as SynTech CEO; she abused her executives, snarled at her house staff, rejected all contact with her father and her surviving sons; she refused even to dress for dinner, taking meals in her room. She spent these days pestering her Business Tribune, aggravating her Leisure affiliate, filing motions in civil court, and shopping her story around the newsnet sites in hopes some influential reporter might interview her. In that short span she made herself a nuisance to the Leisure Congress, an embarrassment to the Business caste, and a humiliating liability to the Shanks chemical empire.

After three days, she flew to San Francisco personally, thinking to badger and bully her way into the Curioseum, and at least confront that treacherous creature face-to-face—but she found that the streets around the Studio had been blocked by barricades, manned by joint forces of the Social Police and Studio Security; even its airspace was restricted to official security traffic.

Without hesitation, she returned to her campaign.

She knew the damage she was doing, but the monster that rode behind her shoulder had her fully in its slimy grip; she was helpless to resist, and she drove herself even harder than she did anyone else. And so, when she was finally—inevitably—detained by the Social Police, it came as a decided relief to everyone concerned.

Even to her.

Never having had any dealings with the Social Police, Avery had no idea what to expect; arraignment, perhaps, on charges real or fabricated or both, perhaps detention without trial, interrogation, perhaps even torture—the uglier rumors of such things, which Avery had always dismissed as undercaste rubbish, are far more convincing, more threatening, when one is riding in the back of a riot van with one's wrists stripcuffed together behind one's back.

There had been no charges, so far, no warrant—she wasn't even officially under arrest. The officers who had come for her had allowed her to pack an overnight bag before leading her away. She suffered dreadful fantasies of simply disappearing, vanishing into the bowels of the legal system, never to be seen again.

But never in her wildest fantasy did she anticipate being delivered directly to the Studio Curioseum.

3

THE SOCIAL POLICE pulled her swiftly but without violence through the Curioseum, lights blinking on as they entered each room and then blinking off behind them. They drew her through the riot of unfamiliar form and color and odor that was the arboretum: purple-veined chokeweed crashed against its restraining nets, chartreuse and pink-branched songtrees whistled shrilly, marsh-poppy pods jetted soporific pollen across their paths. They skirted the howls and snarls and chatter of the menagerie, and finally brought her into a large, bare rectangular room, its only light what leaked through the broad, bright window at the far end.

Silhouetted against that light was a huge hulking man with hands clasped behind his enormous back, staring down through a broad plate glass window. *I knew it,* she thought. By size alone, this could only be Tan'elKoth.

"I cannot *imagine* what you hope to gain by this," she snapped at the back of his head.

Eyes shifted in his ghostly reflection. "Businessman Shanks," he said in a half-whispered murmur, like a distant turbojet. "Thank you for coming."

"Don't waste your courtesy on me, Professional—"

"Courtesy is never wasted. Please release her, officers—and then please leave us. The Businessman and I must confer in private."

"Confer—?" Avery began, astonished. "This is ridiculous. What have you done with Faith?"

"Officers? If you would be so kind?"

One of the officers buzzed, *"I'm not sure this is a good idea, leaving you two alone."*

"What, precisely, do you fear?" Tan'elKoth's voice sounded eminently reasonable, though still thin and whispery, as though he struggled with laryngitis. "The sole exit from these two rooms is the door through which you came. Or perhaps you think that I and the Businessman will concoct some nefarious conspiracy in your absence?"

"I'm afraid," came the toneless reply, *"that he won't like it."*

"Then go and ask him." Tan'elKoth turned toward them now, and there was something lumpish, disturbingly misshapen, in the curve of his silhouette. "Meanwhile, please do as I request. I believe that you are to comply with my wishes insofar as they do not conflict with your—" Avery got the impression that the ex-Emperor chose this next word with great care. *"—duty."*

One of the officers took a small manual snipper from a belt and clipped the stripcuff apart. Avery shook her hands free and smoothed down the sleeves of her Business suit, then folded her arms and stood, waiting. The four officers seemed to confer in some inaudible fashion, then all turned as one and marched out of the small room. The door closed behind them.

In the first instant that they were alone, Avery snapped, "Why have you brought me here?"

"I did not bring you, Businessman. The Social Police did. They do not, as you may have observed, come and go at my order. Join me here at the window. We must talk."

"I have nothing to say to you."

"Don't be an ass; you've said a great deal already. Come."

Avery reluctantly paced toward him. Tan'elKoth towered over her like some kind of beast that should be extinct in the wild. She did not want to get too close; she could not guess what he might do, but she was frighteningly sure that she could not stop him. When the Social Police had zipped the stripcuffs tight around her wrists, she had been yanked out of the world she knew. Here, her wealth and power and status meant nothing; all that mattered was that she was thin and frail and no longer young, and in the presence of something brutal, massive, and possibly predatory.

But she was still a Shanks. Though society might fail her, pride would endure.

At the window, she placed herself deliberately within the reach of his huge arm, and just as deliberately refused to look at him, gazing instead down into the room beyond—

At a small child with golden hair strapped down to a steel table in a blank white room.

"Faith!" She gasped and pressed her hands against the glass. "Oh, my god, Faith!" An overpowering vision of Faith in convulsion, pounding her skull and spine against this unpadded stainless steel torture rack, nearly paralyzed her; she could hardly speak. "What have you done to her? *What have you done?*"

"Tried to protect her, as best I can," Tan'elKoth replied grimly.

"Protect her?" Avery could not tear her eyes away from the horror of that small sterile room. "This is how you *protect* her?"

"I can do no better," Tan'elKoth said. "Businessman, look at me."

She ignored him, staring through the glass at the only meaning all this had for her: Faith was breathing, she *was* still breathing. "You *must* get her out of here!"

One huge hand caught her shoulder and turned her toward him like a child, so overpowering that she could not even dream of resistance. "*Look* at me," he repeated, his whisper-hoarse voice now a fierce rasp. "My status here is written upon my face."

Avery gaped openly, seventy years of proper Business reserve and decorum wiped away in an instant.

She remembered that he had once been beautiful.

His face looked like a handful of spoiled hamburger, with bulbous growths of moldy yellow and purple and green interpenetrating and overlapping; one eyebrow had been shaved, a vertical wound across it held closed with black insectile stitches, the eye below it swollen shut like a mouth held primly pursed over a tennis ball; a similarly stitched line climbed over the curve of his forehead into a shaved-back hairline; one side of his mouth hung loose and bulbous, two curves of stitches trailing from its corner, one up and one down, giving him a cartoon smile and frown simultaneously.

His left hand still clutched her shoulder; he lifted his right, to show her the bandage that blanketed a stomach-churning absence where his smallest finger should have been. He said, "If you only knew what I have endured, to protect that child."

"Protect her from what?" Avery said, now as hoarse as he. "Tan'elKoth, you *must* tell me what is happening!"

"Do you know where we are? This is the Curioseum *menagerie*, Businessman. This is the *veterinary center*. Specifically, the surgery. If you cannot or do not help me help Faith, this is where the creature who prisons us all will rape her, kill her, and dissect her body." Tan'elKoth's face compressed with pain. "And likely eat the pieces."

"You can't expect me to . . . This isn't *possible*! You cannot possibly be serious!"

"No?" Tan'elKoth lifted his maimed hand and held it out for her inspection.

Avery stared at it, unable to speak, her own hand slowly coming up to cover her mouth. "What—what creature? Who is behind all this? Does this have something to do with Kollberg?"

"It is better that you do not know; you have seen too much already. Some ignorance is a kindness, Businessman—some ignorance may, in this matter, save your life."

"And so you won't tell me."

"You would not believe me if I did."

Slowly, stiffly, feeling now her years, Avery straightened, and she let her hand fall. She looked up into the ex-Emperor's one open eye, and her mouth returned to its customary knife-slash line. "And why?" she asked steadily. "Why should I help you?"

"I am not asking you to help me. I am asking you to help Faith."

"Why should I believe you? I admit that your . . . injuries . . . shocked me, but how am I to know how you got them? You could have been in a car accident. You could have been mugged."

Heat surged up into her face; anger filled every part of her that dread and horror had emptied. She clenched fists tightly against

her thighs, livid. "You are a liar. A murderer. You tied *my son* to a
cross. Did you think I would forget that? Did you think I could
forgive it? Do you think I don't know who *called me that night*?
Do you think I don't know who pretended to be . . ."

Words failed her; the grief that cut her heart would admit no
expression. *Karl . . . oh, Karl,* she thought, and hot needles of
tears pricked at her eyes. "You scum," she whispered. "You vile,
manipulative peasant of a man—"

"Businessman," Tan'elKoth said softly, kindly, his voice
warm as a hug, "there was no pretense. In a way more real than I
fear you can ever understand, I *am* your son."

"I saw," she said through teeth grimly clenched. "I saw your . . .
your *act* . . . at Kollberg's trial. You are *not* Karl."

"Not all of me, no; but all of *him*. Karl is here, within me. He
is frightened, and sad, and he misses you very much."

She lowered her head and tried to stop her tears by pressing
the edge of her hand against her face, as though stanching blood
from open wounds. "How dare you . . ." Her whisper was barely
audible. "How dare you even speak his name?"

"Mother . . ." her son's voice said softly. "Mother, close your
eyes, and I'm here. Maybe just for a little, for a little while—but
I'm here. I need you, Mother . . ."

Grief sawed through her knees, and she sagged against his
chest. "Oh, Karl . . . How can you do this? *How can you do this
to me?*"

Inhumanly powerful arms encircled her, but there was comfort in giving herself over to their unguessable strength. For a
cold moment, she could imagine that she had become once
again a moody, difficult little girl, finally getting an embrace
from a father far kinder than the one with which fate had cursed
her. A maimed hand stroked her brush of steel-colored hair.

"Mother, please—you have to help her. You don't know what
they want to do to her. We—you and all of us—we're her only
hope. She's my *daughter*, Mother. You promised—when I left
for the Conservatory, remember? You promised you'd always be
there for me. Please—you know I'd never ask if we didn't need
you—"

Avery took a deep, shuddering breath and gathered the ragged
remnants of her strength. She straightened, and she pushed herself away from those encircling arms. She had to stare at her fists
for a long moment before she could bear the sight of Faith

strapped to the surgical table of stainless steel. "Swear—swear that you will . . ." she said hoarsely, and stopped, struggling with her self-command.

Cords jumped beside her jaw.

"Swear that you will never do that to me again—" she rasped, staring at her reflected ghost within the glass. "Swear it, and I will do whatever you ask."

4

FAITH COULD BE almost content when she was nothing at all.

Her eyes would go away, and some other little girl would see what was inside them, all the cold lights and bright shiny metal shapes and the big mirror that was part of one wall; her ears could go to some other place, and a second little girl heard the whisper of the vents and the sounds of the door opening and somebody talking that real quiet way Daddy always did around Grandpa; a third little girl felt cold metal beneath her legs and head, and the thin white plastic of her hospital gown; a fourth smelled the hospital smell.

And her remembery had gone to someone else, too—that fifth girl was the unhappiest of them all, because the little fifth girl had to look at the bad thing that made her scream and scream and scream.

But Faith, though, she wasn't any of those little girls. She was pretty much nothing at all. She was here, safe in the big dark hush, and she kept finding ways to make it darker, and even hushier, because she was pretty sure that if she could make it dark enough, and hushy enough, to where none of those other little girls could bother her anymore ever again, she might even be able to hear the river.

Because that was the only trouble; that was how she kept having to be *almost* nothing, instead of really nothing.

If she was really nothing, she wouldn't be so lonely.

Now the rumbly man was coming back. He stomped through her quiet place, shouting at her. He was so *loud*. He couldn't see her, not as long as she didn't move and didn't answer. She knew he didn't mean to be !oud; she could tell from the half-whispery, kind of wheedly voice he was using, the way he kept calling her *honey* and asking her to take his hand.

She didn't like the rumbly man—she remembered him from back when she was something, one time when Daddy had taken her to the Curiemuseum. He'd scared her a little then—with his great big hands and hungry eyes, like the troll under the bridge from *Billy Goats Gruff*—but not too much, because Mommy wasn't afraid of him, and neither was the river.

But now she was all alone in the hushy dark, and he was coming closer and closer. She tried to push him away, to hold him on the outside of the dark, and for a little while it seemed like it was working. She could use the dark to hold him outside; the darker she made it, the farther away he got. She'd done it before, but he kept on coming back, and she was getting so tired—

Tired from pushing him, tired from pushing the five little girls, tired from hanging on to the dark and the hush, and *he* never seemed to get tired at all—

"Faith? Faith, child, can you hear me?"

And she couldn't, not really—it was another little girl, the second one, who heard Grandmaman's voice; the third little girl felt Grandmaman's hand on her hair; the first other little girl could see Grandmaman in the bright hard light, and the fourth could smell her musty Grandpa-smelling breath.

"Faith, you must listen to Grandmaman, now. This is important."

Mommy had told her, way way back ago, that she was to mind Grandmaman until Daddy came for her. No good pretending anymore; Mommy was never fooled by pretending. Faith could pretend so hard that she pretty much believed herself, but Mommy always knew better—and Mommy had told her to mind Grandmaman.

With a little shuddering sigh, Faith let go of the hush, and stopped pretending there was a second little girl who had her ears; she let go of the dark, and stopped pretending about the other little girls who had her eyes, and her nose and her hands and her mouth and practically everything else.

Grandmaman stood over her in the white room, and her hair was sparkly in the bright lights. Faith didn't remember where the white room was, or why it was different from some other white room that she didn't really remember; she didn't remember how she had gotten here, or why Grandmaman should look so upset, because she was still holding on to the last little girl, the fifth one, the little girl who had Faith's remembery. As long as she could hold on to the last little girl, the others didn't really matter.

The last little girl was the one who kept screaming, way off in the hushy dark.

Grandmaman leaned down and kissed her on the forehead. "Faith, you have to—have to—" She looked back at the big rumbly man, who stood over by a little door with his great big troll arms crossed over his great big troll chest.

"Tell her to stop hiding," the big rumbly man said in his big rumbly voice. "Tell her to come to the front of her head."

"Faith, you must stop hiding. Come to the front of your head."

That she could hear Grandmaman and the big rumbly man both meant she was *already* at the front of her head, all alone where it was loud and bright and cold and really scary. Faith blinked and tried to *not*—tried to *be brave*—but a tear leaked out anyway and trickled down into her ear. "It's too empty up here," she told Grandmaman in a little tiny whispery voice. "It's *lonely.*"

"Tell her," said the big rumbly man, "that if she takes my hand, inside her head, she will never be lonely again."

Never be lonely again . . . Faith heard that echo and echo and echo, and it didn't even fade away: *again again again.* She let herself fall back down into the dark, and started to feel around for the rumbly man's hand.

"Faith, did you hear him? I want you to do what he says, do you understand? Take his hand, Faith. Faith?—Tan'elKoth, I feel completely ridiculous. What is this supposed to mean, take your hand inside her head? This is a foolish waste of time."

She couldn't see the big rumbly man, but she could feel him all around her, as though he was made out of really thick fog and she was walking through him, except fog is kind of cold and wet and icky, and the big rumbly man was really warm and dry and kind of, kind of, almost, friendly. Like he liked her. Like he maybe even loved her a little bit.

"You surrender too easily. Not only does she hear you, she struggles to comply. I can see it."

He didn't love her the way Mommy did, of course, it wasn't the same thing, but more like the way she loved her lemon-and-green toga that Daddy had bought her in Chicago: the way you love something that you figure is not really smart enough to love you back.

That was okay with her. She didn't want to have to love him back. When you love them back, you end up like the little fifth girl.

"See? What is there to see?"

"You have first-handed a thaumaturge; Karl himself was somewhat adept. You must remember how the Shell appears to one in mindview—even now, the child crudely and clumsily tunes her Shell to match the frequencies mine generates."

She couldn't find the big rumbly man's hand, but she got herself to just about where it ought to be, and she reached out and sort of *imagined* his hand. Kind of like when you're having a dream and you're lost in a big dark building that you've never seen before, but you decide that it's really your house, and somehow you know it is even though it doesn't look like it at first: she just took hold of the fog and the dark and the big dry warmth and *decided* that this was his hand.

"You're in mindview? Right now? Don't you have to concentrate?"

"I am concentrating."

"Then how can you still talk?"

"I am Tan'elKoth."

And when she kept on imagining—kept on *deciding*—the fog got to be more and more like a hand, got bigger and warmer and drier, until it was sort of really pretty solid.

"She's tuning her Shell? Like an adept?"

"Not like an adept. Like a child. All children have some skill with magick. The primary function of pedagogy, in your society, is the murder of this ability."

She didn't know what any of that was supposed to mean, but that was okay, because she was really mostly paying attention to the hand. So far, it looked kind of like a cartoon hand, you know, the right number of fingers and stuff but it didn't look like it really *belonged* to anybody. It was just real big.

But she hung on and kept on deciding—a real hand would have some wrinkles on the knuckles, and some more on the palm here, and it would have little bulgy things at the bottom of each finger, and of course since the big rumbly man was a grown-up there'd be a little bit of hair on the back—

As the hand got to be really pretty real, the hushy dark wasn't so hushy anymore: She could hear somebody talking, somebody saying in a little tiny squeaky voice *Be careful—oh, please be careful*. Pretty soon she could see him, and the more she listened, the clearer he got. This was somebody she didn't know, some little old man, all wrinkled and bent over, and he looked like he wouldn't smell very good.

There were other people here now, lots of people, all dressed funny—not like real Administrators or Artisans or anybody else—all dressed like they were going to some kind of grown-up costume party, or maybe to a convention, like Fancon. And they all came crowding up around, and they were all talking at once, and it was pretty scary but none of them really looked mean or anything. There was one man who looked kind of like the big rumbly man, except he was a lot bigger, and he had really long wavy hair and a huge bristly beard. And there was another big man with golden hair and beautiful blue eyes, and he came right up close to her and kneeled down and looked like he was going to cry.

Faith? Do you know me, Faith? Do you know who I am?

She really hated when grown-ups asked that kind of question, because usually you didn't, and then they seemed kind of disappointed and sometimes even hurt. So she didn't really want to answer him, even though he had really nice hair and really nice eyes, and he looked pretty upset. He put his hand out and touched her arm and said *Faith: Faith, honey—*

And the big rumbly man shouted inside her head: *BACK! DOWN, YOU JACKALS! BACK WITHIN THE GATES. THIS ONE IS MINE!*

He must have done something to all the people that scared them and maybe even hurt, because they all went away a lot faster than they had come, and the big rumbly man was so loud, and so angry, and kind of mean-sounding that she started to cry, and as soon as she started to cry she wanted Mommy to be here, and as soon as she wanted Mommy to be here she forgot to pretend about the little fifth girl.

Her remembery came back, and she remembered that she was the little fifth girl all along.

She started to scream, and scream, and scream—and the big rumbly man was squeezing her hand, and it *hurt*, and she wanted Mommy or Daddy or anybody to come and make him stop, but then he snatched her other hand, too, and squeezed them both together, *squeezed* them both together, SQUEEZED them both TOGETHER—

Now she didn't even have hands anymore—the big rumbly man had squeezed them until they turned into just one wrist, like her arms were a big wishbone, and her one big wrist just connected right with the big wrist of the rumbly man and she could feel his blood pumping in through her arms and hers pumping out through his.

The big rumbly man bared his big sharp teeth down at her. *Now, child: Where is the river?*

Faith could only shake her head dumbly; she couldn't stop looking at where his big hairy wrist melted into her two little smooth ones. Something seemed to be caught in her throat, like she'd swallowed some kind of little rat and it was climbing back up out of her stomach with its little needly claws scratching little pieces out of her and making her taste blood like that time she fell down and her tooth went through her lip—

The river, child, the big rumbly man—Tan'elKoth, she knew his name now, it flowed into her with his blood—said, louder. *I have not come so far only to be denied.*

He was getting angry, too, really angry, and the anger was *hurting* her, burning her wrists and her arms and scorching her chest and making the rat in her throat struggle harder and harder to get out.

WHERE IS THE DAMNED RIVER? WHY CAN'T I FEEL THE RIVER?

And he was so angry that he made her even more scared, and then the rat finally made it all the way up to her mouth. It pushed out through her teeth and it wasn't really a rat at all.

It was a scream.

Scream and scream and scream and scream.

Because she would never be alone in here again.

5

FAITH'S SCREAM REBOUNDED off the surgery's walls and reflected upon itself until it spiraled up like a feedback shriek. It made Avery want to cover her ears and crumple into a corner; instead she yanked on Tan'elKoth's arm. It felt like a concrete lamp pole. "Stop it!" she shouted. She could barely hear her own voice. "Stop! *You're hurting her!*"

He snarled an incomprehensible reply and made an impatient

shrugging twitch of the arm that shook her off and sent her spinning against a wall with shocking force. Half stunned, she came back at him anyway, snarling, her fingers hooking toward his eye. He caught her arm absently—most of his attention was still on Faith—and held her with irresistible strength.

"Stop it!" Avery shouted again. "Hurt her again and I'll see you dead! You hear me? *I'll see you dead for this!*"

Controlling her effortlessly with his grip on her wrist, he could ignore her. Faith kept screaming, and he bared his teeth as he leaned over her, as if he wanted to bite her face. Avery struggled desperately, uselessly, until she realized that Tan'elKoth had caught her with his maimed hand. She made a fist and slammed it onto the bandaged nub that was all that remained of his little finger.

He gasped, and his hand sprang open. She swung her fist again, overhand like she was serving at tennis, right into the swollen mass of bruise over his eye. *"Leave her alone!"*

He didn't even wince. Before she quite understood what was happening he had her by the throat. He lifted her off the floor and held her at arm's length; she scrabbled uselessly at his iron fingers. His maimed hand became a fist. "I can kill you," he said. "Do you comprehend this?"

His grip on her throat choked off any possible response; she couldn't even nod. "How can you help this child if you are dead?" he asked in a simple and reasonable tone, and he held her there while he waited for some kind of answer.

Avery closed her eyes, and her hands fell to her sides.

If Tan'elKoth killed her now, at least this madness that had overwhelmed her life would end. Instead, he set her down gently and released his grip on her throat.

"Calm the child, Businessman. She may injure herself."

Avery summoned the strength to stay on her feet, to open her eyes and walk unsteadily to the table where Faith convulsed against the restraints. "Hush, Faith," she murmured, stroking the child's face. "Shh, girl. Grandmaman is here. Grandmaman is here, and all is well."

A tear rolled over her sharp cheekbone and dropped into Faith's hair.

Faith's struggles soon quieted, and when Faith slipped back into her silent unconsciousness, Avery's strength deserted her. She sagged against the stainless steel lip of the surgical table, but even with that support she could not hold her feet; she dropped to her knees, covered her face with her hands, and sobbed.

"Businessman," Tan'elKoth said gently, "please . . . Avery, please don't cry."

His huge warm hands took her shoulders and gently lifted her from the floor; he guided her to the surgery's single chair, and when she sank into it, he knelt at her side.

"Please, Avery," he murmured, sliding his arm around her. "There is enough of . . . of Karl in me that I cannot bear your tears . . ."

"What is happening to me?" Avery whispered brokenly through her covering hands. "This is not me. This is not who I am. I don't understand what is happening . . ."

"Where love advances, reason retreats," he said kindly. "It is not unusual to find the corpses of our illusions left to rot on that particular field."

"I won't let you hurt her," Avery said. She took her hands away from her face and met his eyes. "You can kill me. But while I'm alive, I'll do whatever it takes to stop you."

"I understand you. You must understand me." Tan'elKoth rose and went to the surgical table. His hand hovered an inch above Faith's hair, as though he feared to touch her.

"What you feel for this child, I feel for each of my Children," he said. "There are *millions*, Businessman. Each is precious to me in ways that surpass description. My dreams are filled with echoes from their future. Those echoes are of screams."

He turned back to her and spread his hands in appeal. "What would you not do, to protect your grandchild? What should I not do, to protect my Children?"

"I won't let you hurt her," Avery repeated.

His gaze shifted fractionally, as though his eye had been drawn to some movement in the room beyond. His face twisted through a brief, almost invisible spasm: loathing, disgust—and, shockingly, fear.

Avery trembled, suddenly chilled to the bone. What could frighten Tan'elKoth, she didn't ever want to know.

"It's not me," he said slowly, "who will hurt her, Businessman."

Hesitantly, afraid of what she would see, she followed his gaze. Pressed against the surgery's window, face slack with the blankly ravenous desire of a starving Temp outside a butcher shop, was Arturo Kollberg.

6

"How LONG WILL he stand there?" Avery asked softly.

Kollberg had pressed himself silently against the window for hours, now; for how many hours, Avery could not say. She paced back and forth, hugging herself against constant shivering, though the room was not cold.

Tan'elKoth sat on the chair, facing away from the window, leaning over Faith in an attitude of concentration. "It is impossible to predict," he said, his tone distant, bleached free of emotion. "Sometimes he stays for a few minutes. Once for nearly a day. Laborer Kollberg comes and goes at his own pleasure; what may spark this pleasure is not only unknowable, but repellent to speculate upon."

"Are you making any progress?"

He shook his head. "No. I had expected to find the link as soon as I established contact with her mind, but I did not. I presume that the trauma of her mother's murder caused her to wall off that part of her consciousness, not unlike the dissociative reaction that sometimes creates a splinter personality."

"You knew," she said. "You knew about the murder in advance."

"You will recall that I tried to warn you."

"Did you try to warn *her*? Pallas? What did you say to *her*?"

"She and Caine both understood their risk," he said, then added in a bitter undertone, "—better, perhaps, than did I."

"What happens if you can't find this link of yours?"

"As I explained: the sole way we can protect this child is to make her useful to the creature that once was Kollberg. If we fail in that, then we, too, will be superfluous. Death follows hard upon that state, Businessman."

"There are worse things than death," Avery said.

"Indeed," he agreed. "And you will likely become intimately acquainted with several of them. I have recounted how Kollberg passes his leisure time."

Avery looked through the window into those empty, hungry eyes; she began once more to shiver. "Is there anything more we can be doing?"

Tan'elKoth shrugged dispiritedly. "I can only inspect the resonances of mind that might theoretically have produced her link to the river. You might say that I am searching for the link, but you must understand that the mind—even the mind of a child—is, metaphorically speaking, a very large place."

Avery nodded toward Kollberg. "Does he understand that?"

"I cannot say what he does and does not understand."

"He doesn't even seem human anymore," she said.

"He is profoundly human," Tan'elKoth said. "He is humanity concentrated and distilled: refined to its essential core. What you mean to say, I think, is that he is no longer a man."

"You're saying he's more than a man."

"On the contrary. He's quite a bit *less*."

She thought about that for a long time.

Later, she asked, "And what happens once you find the link?"

Tan'elKoth turned his gaze aside from Faith's sleeping face, and he sighed. "That, at least, is no mystery. Life—existence itself—is a pattern of Flow; everything, living or otherwise, is a patterning of the primodial energy of the universe. We see things as discrete individuals only because we are trained so. All that exists is, in the end, knots within the weave that is the universe."

Tan'elKoth's tone remained dry and precise, but his face grew ever more grim. "Chambaraya is, one might say, a smaller knot of mind within the Worldmind: what the elves call *T'nnalldion*. Through Faith, the Bog can get its corporate fingers into that knot, unbind it, and tie it again in their own image."

Avery shook her head blankly, uncomprehending. Tan'elKoth's expression was bleak as an open grave. "They'll make of it a world like this one."

"Is that all?" Avery asked, frowning. "You make it sound like a catastrophe."

"It will be an Armageddon unimaginable; it will be genocide on a scale of which Stalin could not have dreamed."

"Wiping out magick doesn't seem like such a bad thing."

"Businessman," Tan'elKoth said patiently, "you don't understand. Magick has not been *wiped out* on Earth; it is a function of Flow, which is the energy of existence itself. But its state can be altered. And it has been. Once, Earth was home to fully as many magickal creatures as was Overworld: dragons and sea serpents and mermaids, rocs and djann and primals and stonebenders and all. But creatures such as these require higher levels of certain frequencies of Flow than does humanity; as the pattern of Earth degraded, these creatures not only died, but their very bones gave up their integrity. They vanished into the background Flow of your universe."

"You're saying magick works on Earth?" Avery said skeptically.

"Magick *works*, as you say, everywhere. But the *manner* in which magick works on Earth is a local aberration; the physics of this planet and its spatial surrounds have been altered to conditions that favor the ascendance of humanity."

"And what's wrong with that?"

"I did not say it was wrong. I do not debate morality. In my zeal to protect my Children, I once favored such a fate for my own world. But it is *unnatural*. It is both the cause and the result of the ugly twisting of human nature that we see around us, and of the society in which you force yourselves to live."

"Earth's not so bad—"

"How would you know?" Tan'elKoth said acidly. "It is only in these past few days that you have had contact with the actual realities of Earth. Are you having *fun*?" He waved toward the window, where Kollberg now had one hand openly kneading his groin while he leaned one cheek and the side of his open mouth against the glass. Avery flinched and looked away.

She hugged herself more tightly. "I don't understand. If you hate what they're going to do, why are you helping them?"

"I am *not* helping them!" Suddenly he was on his feet, towering over her, shaking an enormous fist. "I am helping *you*. I am helping *Faith*. I am . . ." The passion drained out of him as swiftly as it had arisen. He let his fist open and fall limp against his thigh. "I am trying to go home."

Outside the window, Kollberg panted like an overheated dog.

"Well," Avery said finally. "I'm afraid you're out of luck."

"How do you mean?"

She shook her head. "You're such a *man*, Professional. That's why you can't find this link of yours."

"I do not understand."

"Of course you don't. That's what I mean: You're a man. You think this link is with the river. It wasn't. Faith spoke of it, in the car on our way back to Boston when I first picked her up. She was quite clear about it. Her link was never with the river. It was with her mother."

"Her mother—?"

"Her *dead* mother, now."

Tan'elKoth's eyes narrowed. "I *have* been a fool," he said. He spun and seated himself once again at Faith's side, bending over her with redoubled energy. "Power," he murmured. "All that is required is a usable source of power—"

"What are you doing? She's *dead*, Tan'elKoth. There *is* no link."

"Dead, yes—but the *pattern of her consciousness* persists, even as your son's does within me. It was trapped at the instant of her passing. It is powerless, yes—having no body to inform it with will. It is analogous to a computer program stored on disk, you might say: a structure of information that requires only a computer on which to run, and the necessary power to activate."

"What kind of power?"

From the doorway behind her, the soulless rasp of Arturo Kollberg said, "My kind of power."

DURING HIS YEARS of walking the world, the crooked knight came to find himself bemazed within a dark and trackless wood. In this wood, all paths led equally to death.

The crooked knight did not lose hope; he turned to various guides for help and direction. His first guide was Youthful Dream. Later, he turned to Friendship, then Duty, and finally Reason, but each left him more lost than had the one before.

So the crooked knight gave himself up for dead, and simply sat.

He would be sitting there still, but for a breeze that came upon him then: a breeze that smelled of wide-open spaces, of limitless skies and bright sun, of ice and high mountains.

It was the wind from the dark angel's wings.

FOURTEEN

A FEW DAYS before the Festival of the Assumption, a new report detonated like a suitcase nuke in the heart of the net. Actors in Ankhana had witnessed the riverboat arrival of a Monastic delegation, an entourage of dozens of functionaries, and servants, and heavily armed friars with the sword-edged eyes of combat veterans. The delegation had been met at the Industrial Park docks by an honor guard suitable for vassal kings and the entire capital army band; the assemblage had formed a huge parade, a processional that surrounded a large wheeled cart drawn by four humpbacked oxen.

The band had struck up a solemn hymn, "Justice of God," a standard of the Church of the Beloved Children of Ma'elKoth. The parade marched north up Rogues' Way, through the midst of the Industrial Park on its broadest boulevard, Artisans' Angle, then south along Nobles' Way, past the makeshift barricades that sealed the smoldering ruins of Alientown, across the rebuilt Knights' Bridge into Old Town, and on down Nobles' Way to the South Bank, west the length of Dukes' Street and north along Rogues' Way once again, crossing onto Old Town before turning east along the grand central artery of Gods' Way.

The entire circumference of this rough spiral was lined with cheering, jeering, hooting crowds, drawn by the thundering music and the triumphant proclamations of the heralds that preceded the parade, trumpeting the announcement of the capture of the Enemy of God.

On the cart was a tall platform; on the platform was chained a medium-sized, rather unremarkable-looking man with dark hair and a ragged tenday's growth of black beard. By midnight, nearly everyone on Earth had heard the news.

Caine was alive.

2

HIS RADIANT HOLINESS Toa-Sytell, Patriarch of Ankhana and faithful Steward of the Empire, leaned on the chill stone of the windowsill and stared at the eastward sweep of Gods' Way. With the sun westering toward twilight, the shadowy room had grown cool. Only the lightest brush of autumnal ochre warmed the top of the Sen-Dannalin Wall, but the gold-leafed spires of the neighboring Temple of the Katherisi blazed like bonfires; Toa-Sytell shaded his eyes against the glare.

An occasional wind-shift brought twists of smoke past this window: smoke from buildings that still smoldered in Alientown. The Patriarch hated that smoke. It seemed to fill his head in choking billows that strangled his thoughts. And below the ruins of Alientown, the fighting still continued.

Thinking about it made him queasy. He had been troubled in both stomach and head of late, as though he had become the city that he ruled, and the conflict had given him fever. He was acutely, almost painfully aware of the fighting that might be going on now, in the caverns below the city—below, perhaps, the palace itself. Even after these several days of what the army had begun to call the Caverns War, he couldn't get used to it. It made the earth itself seem unsteady, temporary, dangerously frangible, as though any street where he walked was only a soap bubble, decaying in the sunlight, and at any second it might vanish and he would fall, and fall, and fall.

So he no longer left the palace.

Down on Gods' Way, an avenue so broad it was almost a plaza, the people of Ankhana crowded shoulder to shoulder in bright festival colors, a tightly woven carpet of knobbled heads and hats and hair planed almost smooth by range and elevation. No sign yet of the triumphal procession that brought Caine in public disgrace to the Donjon—but faintly to the Patriarch's ear came the distance-thinned strains of "Justice of God," and he allowed himself a slim smile as chill as the stone on which he leaned.

Three respectful paces behind Toa-Sytell's left shoulder, His Grace the Honorable Toa-M'Jest, Duke of Public Order, coughed into his fist.

"Join me here, M'Jest," Toa-Sytell said informally. "He should be arriving soon. Don't you want to watch?"

"If it's all the same to you, Radiance—"

"It isn't. Join me."

Toa-M'Jest ducked his head and surreptitiously mopped sweat from his brow with his sleeve; the Patriarch pretended that he did not see. When the Duke came to the window, the Patriarch could smell him—a sour, slightly rank sweat smell, with a taint of the outhouse to it that cut through the Duke's expensive perfume. Toa-M'Jest took the Patriarch's casually offered hand; the Duke's fingers were clammy, chill like raw meat off a butcher's iceblock, and they trembled, ever so slightly.

While the Duke lowered dry lips to his master's fingers, the Patriarch stared into the empty distance above Ankhana's towers. "Seven years ago next tenday, I stood at this very window with the Count—shortly thereafter Saint—Berne," he mused. "Then, too, we watched for sight of Caine approaching along Gods' Way. Then, too, we thought he had been taken, chained, rendered harmless."

The Patriarch took the Duke's chin in his hand and raised it so that their eyes could meet. "Then, too," he said, "we did not learn how wrong we were until far too late."

Toa-M'Jest swallowed. "I don't know what you mean, Holiness."

"Of course you do. Don't be an ass." The Patriarch sighed. "I know that you once counted Caine your friend—that you even go so far, privately, as to credit him for your current position. I know that you will be inclined to aid him. I tell you plainly, Toa-M'Jest: This inclination may cost your life."

"Radiance—"

The Patriarch waved the objection aside; Toa-M'Jest could have nothing of interest to say on the subject. "How goes the mopping up?"

The Duke took a breath to gather his wits. "Better, Your Radiance, but still slowly. We hold the Alientown surface from Commons' Beach to the north shanties. I think we'll have everything locked down within a tenday."

"So long?" the Patriarch murmured. "The Festival of the Assumption sprints toward us, Toa-M'Jest. This situation must be resolved."

"It's the caverns—the rock cuts off Flow," the Duke reminded him. "The Thaumaturgics are short of griffinstones. It's bad enough, sending men down there against ogres and trolls without magickal cover, but stonebenders? You can't fight stonebenders in those caverns, Your Radiance. Not without griffinstones. It's suicide."

"You understand, do you not, that your failure to arrest Kierendal is of especial concern now? She was once your lover; sent against her by my order, you failed—"

The Duke bristled. "The kind of magick those fuckers throw around?" he snapped, relapsing into the gutter talk of his former life. "We *had* to fall back. You should have seen the shit they were throwing—like goddamn *Ma'elkoth*, excuse the profanity. How many soldiers did you want to lose?"

"The circumstances of their resistance are irrelevant. Half the Alientown Patrol are Knights of Cant; you should have been better prepared."

"She's not going anywhere. She'll either surrender with the rest or die where she is."

"Nonetheless. Your record against your former . . . *associ-*

ates . . . is less than stellar, M'Jest. We can afford no similar, mm, *errors* . . . in dealing with Caine."

"There won't be any," the Duke promised grimly.

"I understand you have already financed a private cell for him."

Toa-M'Jest settled into himself as though anticipating a blow. "Yeah."

"Perhaps you have an explanation for this which might allay my fears . . . ?"

"Isn't it obvious?"

The Patriarch allowed himself another thin, cold smile. "Several conflicting explanations are, I think, equally obvious. I am curious which you will select."

"He's crippled," the Duke said simply. "Berne put Kosall through his spine. The Pit's full of street scum. He wouldn't last a day down there, maybe not even an hour—everybody'd want to be the Man Who Killed Caine. Not to mention that most all of them are facing execution on charges—mmm, you might say *dubious* charges—of Cainism. I don't think anyone'll care to stand up for him."

"I see," the Patriarch said. "So your sole concern is to ensure that he lives long enough to be executed."

Toa-M'Jest turned his face toward the window, looking out over the broad parade route below. "Yeah," he said slowly. "It's not easy to admit, y'know? But I got a *position*, now; I got responsibilities. I love the guy like my own brother, but every time he comes to town we end up in a fucking war."

The Patriarch's eye was caught by the scarlet flash of the afternoon sun off the halberd blades of the Household Knights as the parade turned the corner from Rogues' Way onto Gods' Way and began its final triumphal leg. Far, far below, he could barely make out the limp figure on the rack above the dungcart's bed.

"Yes," he murmured. He ran his tongue around lips that had become dry and cracked and hot. "Yes, we do."

3

THE IMPERIAL DONJON of Ankhana began its existence as the final line of defense for the river pirates who had founded the city more than a thousand years ago. In those days, what would later become Ankhana was nothing more than a simple fort of stone and a cluster of huts, enclosed by a wooden stockade wall at the west end of the island that would later be called Old Town.

Below the fort lay a natural cleft in the limestone that was the predominant geological formation of the area; this cleft led far below the river itself, into a bewildering three-dimensional tangle of caverns and passages, including one that was a straight vertical chimney down to another river, underground, that paralleled the Great Chambaygen above. This cleft became known satirically as the Donjon, in the sense of *stronghold*, from its use as the escape route when the fort above fell to siege.

The Donjon's actual use as the Ankhanan civic dungeon did not begin until nearly a hundred years after the Liberation, when Ankhana's stand against the armies of Panchasell the Luckless and his Folk allies had assured the city's dominance over the surrounding lands. At that time, the pirate chieftains of Ankhana had taken to calling themselves kings; kings are perpetually in need of secure places in which to deposit those enemies who would be inconvenient to kill.

The Donjon was a place of deep shadow and bad air, rank with fermenting exhalations of decayed lungs filtered through mouthfuls of rotting teeth.

The Pit was an already-large natural cavern that had been enlarged and altered over the years, first crudely—by inexpert human engineers—and later with astonishing skill by teams of convict stonebenders. By the morning on which Hari Michaelson, the man who had once been Caine, was carried down the stairs from the Courthouse, the Pit was fully forty meters across, ringed by an overhanging balcony cut from the stone ten meters above the floor. A single stairbridge, hinged to the balcony, could be lowered on winched chains to deliver new prisoners to the Pit floor. The prisoners' daily rations were lowered by hand in cheaply woven baskets, and eaten without the benefit of utensils.

Newer features included a tic-tac-toe square of plank-floored catwalks crisscrossing the Pit at the same ten-meter height as the balcony, suspended from the arched stone ceiling by heavy chains. On chains as well were five enormous brass lamps—each the size of a washtub, with a wick as thick as a man's arm—that provided the constant light. They burned without interruption, their oil replenished and wicks replaced as necessary by the crossbow-armed Donjon guards who paced the catwalks.

In the Pit, darkness would be a luxury.

In years past, the Pit had been a temporary holding area, a pen of stone for prisoners awaiting trial and convicts awaiting transportation to frontier garrisons, or to the mines of the high desert, or to the galleys of the Ankhanan navy out of the port city of Terana.

Things were different, now.

On Saint Berne's Eve—slightly more than two months ago— the army and the constabulary had begun a systematic program of mass arrests of Cainists and Cainist sympathizers. Holding areas had been prepared to house the detained Cainists outside the Donjon, but soon they had all been filled, many of them with varieties of subhumans who required specially prepared cages: ogres, trolls, treetoppers, and stonebenders, each of whom presented their own particular difficulties as prisoners. Ogres and trolls are predatory carnivores, enormous and incredibly strong, as well as naturally armed with huge hooked tusks and steel-hard talons; treetoppers are tiny, hardly larger than birds, and not only can they fly, but they have the inborn thaumaturgic ability to Cloak themselves, which can render them effectively invisible; stonebenders are able to shift and shape stone, metal, and earth with their bare hands. Not that all or even most of these subhumans were actual Disciples of Caine, of course; but the Empire and the Church found it expedient to pretend that they were, so that they might all be executed in the mass auto-da-fé planned by the Patriarch to celebrate the seventh Festival of the Assumption of Ma'elKoth.

The climax of the festival—the grand finale of the grandest festival, the pinnacle of the celebration of the seventh anniversary of Ma'elKoth's transfiguration from mortal god to Ascended Godhead in truth—would be the burning of the Enemy of God: the Prince of Chaos himself.

The Pit was now filled with the less problematic overflow of the street sweeps: humans, primals, and ogrilloi. Not that all or even most of these were Cainist either; on the contrary, the majority of them were merely the sort of street trash, thugs, and minor criminals that the constables could easily lay hands upon and thus demonstrate to the Church their zealous prosecution of their duties.

The Pit could hold four hundred prisoners in something resembling comfort; perhaps six or seven hundred in what would be called dangerous overcrowding. On the day that the aforementioned Prince of Chaos was carried down the long, straight stairway cut through the living rock below the Courthouse that was the Donjon's sole entrance or exit, nearly fifteen hundred souls were crammed into this overflowing jar of flesh. There was nowhere one could sit or stand or lie without touching another living creature. The flesh-to-flesh contact that could be such a comfort in the harsh chill of the outside world became a positive horror in this damp bowl of rock, where the walls dripped with the endless meaty condensation of living breath; the Pit was as warm and moist as the inside of somebody else's mouth.

The Pit's sole supply of fresh water flowed through three trenches, each a hand-span wide; they curved out across the floor from a single source in one wall and converged again to empty into a single sump in the opposite wall. These trenches also served as the Pit's cloaca.

The politics of the Pit were simple: the healthiest, strongest, most privileged of the prisoners sat or lay nearest to the source. The internal pecking order described a strict geographic descent from that position to the opposite end: to those who through helplessness and timidity were forced to drink the urine-and-shit-fouled wastewater that drained from the happier climes forty meters upstream.

Hari Michaelson was to be secured in a cell along one of the corridors that radiated from the Pit balcony like spokes of a crooked wheel. Strapped to a litter, unable to move, he lay back silently, not even turning his face to see where he was being taken; he had been here before, and he remembered how it looked. The smell told him everything else he could possibly have wanted to know.

The Donjon guards who bore his litter carried it swiftly around the balcony, but his arrival did not go unremarked. The Pit itself fell silent, as hundreds of eyes tracked his passage; no sound could be heard above the low hush of massed breath and the gurgle of water slithering along trenches of stone.

Rumors of the eventual coming of the Enemy of God had whispered themselves from mouth to mouth on twilit street corners, around low fires, and within darkened pubs for months now. The Ascended Ma'elKoth was expected to return as well, and the two were to meet in final battle at noon of the seventh Assumption Day, just as their initial great conflict had occurred on the first. There were competing rumors, too: that Caine had been no more than a man, just as Ma'elKoth had been only a man, and that any "final battle" on Assumption Day would be merely a dumbshow to impress the gullible masses, a parable of Good versus Evil played out by mummers in Church employ; these rumors were popularly dismissed as Cainist propaganda.

Newer tales had been told, too, of the capture of Caine by the heroic friar Raithe of Ankhana. Raithe, it was said, had conjured the spirit of Saint Berne to sustain him in pitched battle against the Prince of Chaos and his whore-consort, the *Aktir* Queen once known as Pallas Ril. The epic battle had been fought from peak to peak in the distant mountains of the God's Teeth: the *Aktiri* legions had attacked with weapons of lightning and flame, against which the small band of friars led by young Raithe could set only their strength of purpose, their purity of heart, and their faith in the justice of Ma'elKoth.

It was told that the *Aktir* Queen had been slain in that battle by Raithe himself, even as Jereth Godslaughterer had been slain by Jhantho the Founder at Pirichanthe; it was told that the touch of Raithe's hand had reopened the wound of the Holy Stroke upon the Enemy of God, and that the Caine who approached Ankhana in chains was no more than a broken cripple. It was told that the Patriarch himself considered already the question of Raithe's possible sainthood.

Among the hundreds of pairs of eyes that tracked the litter's progress around the balcony were those of a former member of the Monastic diplomatic delegation to the Infinite Court: t'Passe of Narnen Hill, onetime Vice Ambassador to Damon of Jhanthogen Bluff. T'Passe was a thick-bodied, plain-faced woman whose eyes held a curiously unchanging expression, both manic and contemplative at once.

She had been among the very first of the Cainists to be arrested, at the embassy itself, on Saint Berne's Eve. Only a few days later, all the Monastics who had been arrested were officially freed; their status as diplomatic delegates of a sovereign nation demanded it. No fuss came from the Church over this; neither the Church nor the Empire had ever intended the detained Monastics to be imprisoned long enough to require a Monastic response.

T'Passe, however, had refused to leave the Donjon. Threatened with forcible ejection by the civil authorities—to avoid a confrontation with the Monasteries—she had resigned her post on the spot. She would have surrendered her Monastic citizenship as well, had not Acting Ambassador Damon assured her that the Monasteries would make no special effort to have her freed, now that she no longer filled a diplomatic position with the embassy.

"If to speak the truth is a crime, then I shall always be a criminal," she'd said. Now, as she watched Caine's progress on his litter, she might have been carved of the same rough stone as the Donjon itself.

The first words to break the silence were a murmur from an unidentifiable mouth. "He looks so *helpless* . . ."

Another soft voice said, "Maybe it's not him," probably a Cainist's, from its hopeful tone. "It's not, huh? It can't really be *him*, can it?"

"It is he," t'Passe said stolidly. "I saw Caine at the Ceremony of Refusal after the Battle of Ceraeno."

"But that was, like, twenty *years* ago—" someone objected, and t'Passe answered the objection with a flat shake of her head.

"I am not mistaken."

A hulking young ogrillo smirked around his tusks. "Kinda shoots yer whole theology in the ass, dun it?" he asked as he coolly examined his wickedly hooked fighting claw. Snickers came from his small circle of toadies.

"Cainism is not theology, Orbek," t'Passe responded with her customary mild courtesy. "It is philosophy."

"And you can call a turd a sandwich, but it still tastes like shit, hey?"

"I bow to your superior experience," t'Passe replied, "regarding the flavor of shit."

The ogrillo took this with a widened grin and a nod of the head. "Yeah, arright," he said in a friendly enough way. "But one of this day, this moutha yours—it gonna get busted, hey?"

"At your convenience." T'Passe stared calmly at him until he finally shrugged, laughed, and turned away, shouldering through the close-packed mass of prisoners with his toadies in his wake.

After he left, t'Passe turned once again to the conversation that Caine's arrival had interrupted. Her interlocutor was a broad-shouldered fey, tall for his folk, who was folded into a sitting position beside one of the water trenches. One of his thighs looked subtly wrong, as though something malign grew within, and the shin of the other leg was knobbed a few inches below the knee, as though it had been broken and never properly healed.

He clasped his knees to his chest and looked up at the former Vice Ambassador with great golden eyes, their vertically slit pupils spread wide in the murk of the Pit. Despite the eyes, despite the thick brush of platinum-colored hair that stood stiffly out from his scalp to the length of the first joint of his finger, he did not look entirely elvish; his face had been scoured into a map of age, a contoured terrain of harsh living, until he looked almost human—almost like a man fast approaching his fiftieth birthday. "Why do you bait him like that?" said the elf who looked like a man. "What do you get out of it?"

"My desires are of no concern to you, unless they either coincide with or conflict with your own," she said severely; then she shrugged and hunkered down beside him. She lowered her voice and kept her face near his, so that they could converse softly through the constant general buzz of voices around them. "That is the dogma, at least. In truth, I enjoy the banter. It's a verbal display of dominance; you may have noticed that I am an intellectual bully."

"There is dogma? Cainist dogma?" the man-elf asked. "How can there be Cainist dogma?"

"Dogma in the sense of a set of shared premises, from which we reason. But you are avoiding the subject, Deliann. We were talking about what *you* want."

"I know," Deliann sighed. "That's just the problem."

"You must want *something . . .*"

"I want a lot of things." He lifted one shoulder, dropped it again. "I want my brother to be alive. I want my father to be alive. I want—"

She raised a hand. "You can't unring the bell, Deliann."

"Yes," he said. "I've heard that."

"The question is not what you hope might happen, or what you wish had happened differently. Tell me what you want to *do*."

He lowered his face to his knees. "What I want doesn't matter," he said, his voice half muffled by his legs. "You're wasting your time with me, t'Passe. Ask a dying man what he wants, he'll tell you he wants to live. You say, 'Oh, sorry. What's your second choice?' " He made a twitching gesture with his head, as though he wiped his eyes against the scraps of his trousers. "I'm just sitting here waiting to die."

"We can each sit and wait to die, from the very day of our births. Those of us who do not do so, choose to ask—and to answer—the two questions that define every conscious creature: *What do I want?* and *What will I do to get it?* Which are, finally, only one question: *What is my will?* Caine teaches us that the answer is always found within our own experience; our lives provide the structure of the question, and a properly phrased question contains its own answer."

"I need you to leave me alone, t'Passe," Deliann said, his mouth pressed to his knees as though he would gnaw his own flesh. "I can't . . . talk about this right now. Please."

She rocked back on her heels, her mouth a thin horizontal line; then she nodded. "Perhaps we can take this up again later, when you're feeling better."

"Yes," Deliann said. "Maybe later."

She could hear in his voice that he did not expect her to live that long.

4

DELIANN LIFTED HIS head as t'Passe delicately stepped from bit to bit of open floor, her broad back stiffly erect, her shoulders square as cut stone. Most of the prisoners in the Pit passed their days sitting or lying down; he could follow her with his eyes until she found a place to squat, among a knot of fellow Cainists beneath one of the hanging lamps.

Deliann had flashed on her when they had first met, shortly after he had been prodded down the stairbridge by the bluntly insistent business end of a Donjon guard's iron-bound club. His flash had shown him more than he wanted to know of her.

He had learned how it felt to have been a girl of plain, square face, a teenager with a sturdy, strictly functional body as graceless as a mallet, but cursed with a nature as sensitive as her mind was sharp. He had learned how it felt to use a bitter tongue to turn men aside before she could even look for any spark of interest in their eyes. Before she could be wounded by its absence.

He had learned how it felt to turn to the Monasteries, because she'd believed they were a different world, a separate reality where mind counted above beauty, scholarship above flattery—and how it felt to age slowly in a minor diplomatic post, while smaller, duller minds, those more facile with hypocrisy, those that chanced to inhabit more attractive bodies, received promotion and honor that should have been hers.

He had seen how it felt to devote one's entire life to the Future of a Humanity one has discovered, too late, that one despises.

Cainism answered needs she'd never even known she had. As a philosophy, it was elitist, radically individualistic; such a brilliant woman, who had taken such bitter disappointment from every form of society, could not possibly resist. Perhaps Cainism *was* purely a philosophy, as she constantly reminded everyone in the Pit—but for her, it was theology, too.

She needed it to be true.

When he had asked her, shortly after she had begun her explication of Cainist philosophy, the most obvious question, "What if everyone behaved that way? What if everyone just made up their own rules as they went along?" she had only shaken her head sadly.

"What if everyone could shoot lightning bolts from their arses?" she'd countered. "It's a specious question; very few people are *capable* of behaving this way. It's like asking, What if everyone had perfect pitch? Or an eidetic memory? The capacity for personal freedom is a rare talent. Talents exist to be used. We do not ask the sheep to be wolves; we, the wolves, do not ask ourselves to be sheep. Sheep can make such rules as happen to suit them—but it's foolishly naive to expect wolves to obey."

And in the name of this gospel of freedom, she had imprisoned herself; in the name of "living life honestly," she would go to her death. It was, he supposed, the only way she could make herself feel special.

Deliann trailed his fingers in the befouled water that trickled along the trench beside him. He could not discuss Cainism with t'Passe; he had known what he wanted, and had done everything he could think of to make it happen. The outcome had been, would be, unimaginably hideous death on a scale this world had never seen.

Whenever Deliann looked up, all he could see was a roomful of corpses.

There's where your whole system breaks down, t'Passe. In this room, we're all dead. Free or slave, hero or victim—dead is still dead.

When he brought his damp fingers to his lips, he could smell the urine and feces that stained the water. He was desperately, bitterly thirsty, but he couldn't summon the energy to come to his feet and struggle through the mass of prisoners toward the cleaner water near the source. When he got there, the group of Serpents—members of a Warrengang who had taken over that prime real estate—would make him beg on his knees for a drink of pure water. Or worse: begging was innocuous enough that most of the prisoners no longer minded, and the Serpents seemed to have gotten bored with such petty, everyday humiliations.

No chance of help from above; the Donjon guards left the Pit entirely alone, so long as nothing reached the point of open riot. Even murder was tolerated—roughly once a day, the stair-bridge would come clanking down and a team of litter-bearing guards would descend, covered by crossbows from above, to clear away the accumulated corpses. Not that most of these died by violence—disease and malnutrition were the prime killers in the Pit—but the guards made no distinction for cause of death. Starved or strangled, a corpse was a corpse.

In the past day or so, the price of water seemed to have risen from begging to the kissing of bared asses; an hour or so ago, a desperate woman had given one of the Serpents oral sex in exchange for a single drink. Deliann had turned away, sickened; he hadn't had the courage to look back since. He couldn't face whatever the current asking price was going to be.

He let his fingers trail in the water beside him once more, as though he could soak enough moisture through his skin to take the edge off his bitter thirst. Those Serpents, it seemed to him, were a clear example of what Cainism really was: they had the power to make their own rules, and look what they did with it.

On the other hand, he seemed to hear t'Passe's voice whisper in his ear, *Cainism also says that you can fight them, if you choose. Might doesn't make right; this isn't a question of right; it's a question of what you want to do.*

And what *did* he want to do? Everyone kept asking him that, just as though it were important.

5

MY CELL IS just down one of the corridors that radiate off the Pit. They keep a lamp in here, but I can't light it; it's on the little writing desk across the room from my cot, and I don't have the energy to drag my dead legs over there. Besides, enough dull orange glow trickles through the window vent in the door—leakover from the big brass lamps that light the Pit—that I can see better than I really want to, anyway.

I am haunted by that statue of me Tan'elKoth made, his *David the King*. I can see every sagging line of its jowl, every defeated droop of the bags under its eyes. A calculated, deliberate insult: he used my image for an icon of comfortable failure. The slow slipping-down life of a finally insignificant man.

If only I could have understood . . .

He knew better than I did, all along.

I would give anything if I could be that insignificant, comfortably failed man one more time.

That image wasn't an insult. It was *advice*.

It was, *You have better than you deserve. Be grateful, and don't rock the fucking boat.*

6

DAY AND NIGHT have no meaning in the Pit. New prisoners were shoved down the bridge now and then; occasionally guards would descend to remove corpses and those who would soon be corpses. For a long time, the only benchmark had been the arrival of Caine. They'd been fed a few times since then, but Deliann found he couldn't remember if the food baskets had been lowered four times, or six . . . or two . . .

His fever worsened. He'd thought he was getting better for his first few days in the Pit, but that was only because the forced inactivity had taken the edge off his exhaustion. Deliann slept when he could no longer keep his eyes open, and he woke when jostled or kicked.

Though he was well downstream of the Pit's midpoint, and he no longer risked the brutally whimsical Serpents who guarded the source of clean water, he'd managed to keep his thirst mostly at bay; he'd found that by sniffing fingers he'd trailed in the water trench, he could tell when the incoming flow was relatively free of the shit of upstream prisoners, and he would then risk a swallow or two. He imagined that he was exposing himself to infections that could range from hepatitis to cholera, but he couldn't make himself care.

During most of his waking hours, he passed the time by listening to t'Passe and her growing band of Cainists proselytize the other prisoners and argue with each other; there were almost as many different interpretations of Cainism as there were Cainists. T'Passe's position seemed to carry a certain authority, though; her fierce intellect was supported by an extremely penetrating voice and an aggressive temper, and few dared to argue with her.

She would from time to time cast a glance in Deliann's direction, implicitly asking permission to approach him once more; he rarely met her eyes. Like right now: someone objected that the goal of Cainism was mere anarchy, and she stared directly at Deliann as she answered. "Cainism is not anarchy, but autarchy," she said. "Not the absence of rule, but *self*-rule."

"It's the same thing."

"It may appear so," t'Passe allowed serenely, "if you think of Cainism as *advocating* autarchy; but we do not. We do not advocate, we merely describe. Autarchy is simple fact. Every day, every thinking creature decides which rules to follow, and which to break. Our *reasons* for following or breaking these rules may be wildly different, but the *fact of choice* is identical. Perhaps the only difference between a Cainist and anyone else is that we make these choices consciously, instead of allowing habit to guide us along with the herd. The elKothan Church says: Obey. Love each other. Serve the good of your neighbor. Do not lie. Do not steal. Do not kill.

"It is certainly possible for a Cainist to be a faithful elKothan, and a 'good person' by the standards of the Church—the only difference being that the Cainist is aware he is making a choice. He does not obey Ma'elKoth or His Church, he obeys himself."

T'Passe spread her hands, and from across the Pit offered Deliann a gently knowing smile. "You might say that the real key to Cainism is nothing more than paying attention."

7

LYING IN THE cell, staring at the rock above my cot—

My legs rotting like week-old hamburger—

Coughing up blood—

And the worst part is that I can still hear that fucker yapping about Cainism.

I can't tell if this particular fucker is a man or a woman or something roughly in between; all I know is, this fucker has a voice that can chip my goddamn teeth. All the fleshy jabber from the Pit, all the muttering and grunting and farting and the occasional scream, this voice slices through like a knife, but I'm the bone.

If there's anything that hurts worse than steel on bone, I don't want to know about it. It's a pain so intense you can't even feel it at first; it's a searing numbness, a shivering empty shock that ripples along your nerves and turns your body to jelly. That's what this fucker is doing to me, every time I hear that goddamn voice remind somebody that Cainism is *not theology, but philosophy*.

I got some philosophy for that fucker, and plenty of it: the trusty hasn't been around to empty my bedpans in two days.

Jesus, it stinks in here.

Isn't your nose supposed to numb out after a while? Mine did before, waking up in bed with the goddamn spinal bypass fritzed out, not being able to smell whether I'd crapped the sheets. But this place smells like a slaughterhouse.

Some of the burns on my legs have gone necrotic, soppy with greyish goo. That's gonna be a pretty good joke on Raithe and the Church, if gangrene kills me before the execution. And it might not be gangrene that kills me, the way I've been coughing; I was bringing up a lot of bloody snot for a few days, but now I just keep coughing and nothing much comes out. I'm guessing it's chemical pneumonia from breathing the smoke from whatever that incendiary dust was.

I don't really mind any of this. It just means that I'm gonna die pretty soon, and I'm all for it. It's the only thing I've been looking forward to since they murdered Shanna.

But for for some reason I keep on living, and I don't know why.

It's not that hard to kill yourself, even for a paraplegic. I've got plenty of strength left in my arms and hands; it'd be easy enough to tear this sheet into strips and braid them into a reasonable facsimile of rope. The inside of the bronze-bound wooden door that seals my cell has a couple of age-warps gapping the timbers that an experienced climber could wedge his fingers into, to pull himself up high enough to slip a rope around one of the bars in the small window vent. Then when I tie the rope around my neck, I can haul myself up, hold my breath long enough to tie off the rope—then I'll strangle fast enough that I probably won't even have time to change my mind.

But I don't do it. I can't.

I can't seem to make myself give up.

Oh, I can come close enough—I can make myself lie here and do nothing but smell the goo from my festering wounds; I can make myself stare emptily at the trusty when he comes to exchange my uneaten dinner for a fresh meal that I will also not eat; I can lie in my own filth and remorselessly enumerate all the multiple uselessnesses of my existence.

I can hate myself, and the world, and everything in it.

But in the end, Shanna's still dead and I'm still alive, still locked alone in this stone box, still lying on this goddamn cot, still listening to that fucker in the Pit yap about the "core of all freedom."

"It's that voice, the quiet inner whisper of intransigence, that anyone can hear if one listens hard enough. It's the voice that whispers *My will, or I won't*. That is the voice of the Caine Within: it is not the Caine's voice, but it is the voice of that small part of each of us that is the Caine."

Does this fucker have any idea what an idiot he is?

Tyshalle, if my prayer swings any weight with you at all, kill that yappy sonofabitch. Hurt him some, first.

But despite my prayers, he keeps talking and I can't stop listening.

You could work a thousand years and never come up with a more perfect hell.

8

DELIANN OPENED HIS eyes when the shouting started, and he managed to lever his aching back far enough off the stone to see that the guards were lowering food baskets from the catwalk again. He had some impression that it had been a long time since the last feeding, and his stomach confirmed this hypothesis with an unhappy snarl.

The healthiest and strongest of the prisoners had already mobbed the baskets. Deliann stayed on the floor; he wasn't at all sure that he'd be able to walk that far. The rock of the Donjon impedes Flow, and his degrading health made mindview difficult. He was no longer able to suppress the infection within the meat of his thigh, and the constant pain wore on him even more than his gnawing hunger did.

The only other prisoners who did not scramble for food were those too weak to do so—and, of course, the Serpents who guarded the water source. This enterprising group had found that there were plenty of prisoners who would enthusiastically serve their every whim in exchange for more frequent drinks of the cleanest water; the Serpents had taken to letting these volunteers compete with each other for this privilege. Those who offered the largest and most appetizing morsels from the food baskets got the longest and deepest drinks of water. A particularly choice hunk of sausage, and the Serpents might even allow the supplicant to wash himself—an almost unimaginable luxury. The Serpents never had any shortage of eager auxiliaries.

Often, now, the only way to get more than just a mouthful of food was to fight for it.

Deliann also feared that if he did manage to struggle over in time to grab a bite or two before everything was gone, he might return to find someone had taken his spot beside the water trench. Reasoning that, on balance, dying of thirst would be swifter and uglier than starvation, he lay back down on the cold damp stone and closed his eyes.

Some undefinable time later, a soft voice at his side spoke his name.

He opened his eyes. T'Passe stood beside him, a fist-sized crust of bread in one hand and a chunk of hard cheese in the other. "Here," she said, offering him both. "Can I *buy* the chance to talk with you?"

Deliann sighed and struggled into a sitting position. He bent his neck to look up at her; she was perceptibly thinner now, as though the Donjon carved away her flesh, but her eyes gleamed even brighter. She had been having more than a little success in her evangelizing of the other prisoners; she had a sizable following now—the Cainists were almost as numerous as the Serpents, and Deliann more than half expected to see a power struggle develop between the two groups for control of the Pit—but she had never given up on her attempts to win him over.

"What is it about me, t'Passe?" he asked slowly. "Why am I so important to you?"

She squatted beside him and placed the bread and cheese in his lap. "I don't know," she said. "You're so profoundly *unhappy* . . . I think there's something wrong with the world, that a person like you should be in so much pain."

"And you want to use food to bribe me to cheer up," he said, smiling wistfully at the recollection of scrambled eggs at the stall on Moriandar Street. "You know what? That's how I got into this place." A strengthless wave of his hand indicated the Pit. "I let somebody cheer me up."

9

AND I SLEEP and wake and sleep again, my bedpan is emptied and I refill it, and still that fucker in the Pit just never seems to shut up. "Consider, for a moment, the lazy blacksmith: In shoeing a horse for a stranger, he finds that he is one nail short. Rather than trouble to make another, he leaves the last shoe without its last nail. Is his laziness good, or is it evil?

"Then follows the rhyme that we all know:

For want of the nail, the shoe was lost,
For want of the shoe, the horse was lost,
For want of the horse, the rider was lost,
For want of the rider, the battle was lost,
For want of the battle, the kingdom was lost.

"His laziness was evil, then, unless—for the sake of argument—the stranger is not a courier of his own king, but a spy of the enemy; so that the kingdom which was lost is the *enemy* kingdom. Then, to have done a 'good' job might have cost this blacksmith and his people all they have, perhaps even their lives.

"The lesson here is this: The consequence of even the simplest action cannot be reliably predicted over any long term. One cannot control how events unfold, and whether any action is 'good' or 'evil' can only be judged in terms of its consequence—and even that judgment will alter, over time. An action initially judged to be 'good' may later be found to have 'evil' effects—which eventually may be seen, in fact, to be 'good.' *Good* and *evil* are, after all, only code words for outcomes we either favor, or of which we disapprove. We all must accept that *anything we do*, however 'good' it seems at the time, might have consequences that will be too horrible to contemplate.

"What then, is the answer? To do nothing? But even inaction has consequences. The essence of Cainism is this: The truly free man chooses his own goals and seeks his own ends, purely for the joy of the choice and the seeking."

And this is the one that I can't get out of my head. I can lie here for hours and argue with my memory of that voice, but I go to sleep hearing it, and I hear it when I wake up, and I guess I'm not really registering it as meaning anymore.

It's soaked in, somewhere. I've sucked it in through my pores, and I can't sweat it out. I stare at the ceiling for a day or two, counting the cracks in the stone by the unchanging glow from the Pit lamps.

I will go to my grave with the vision of her bright eyes staring, washed clean by the spray from that waterfall at the headwaters of the Great Chambaygen, the blade of Kosall driven through her skull down into the stone beneath her head—I did the right thing, and it came out wrong, and I should have known better.

But I didn't.

I once murdered an old man—the Khulan G'thar—and saved maybe a million lives, when the Khulan Horde collapsed at Ceraeno. Later, I murdered another old man—Prince-Regent Toa-Phelathon—and turned a series of minor border skirmishes with Lipke into the First Succession War.

And maybe that fucker down there in the Pit is right. Maybe there's no telling which way shit will break. If I listen hard enough, I can hear that voice: that small quiet whisper in the back of my head that keeps on insisting *My will, or I won't.* But the fucker in the Pit is dead wrong about it: it *is* Caine's voice.

It's my voice.

I keep thinking about the Assumption Day Festival. I keep thinking about how they're gonna wheel me over to the Cathedral of the Assumption in that tumbrel of theirs, then put me up on a pyre and burn me to death to amuse a few thousand Beloved Children.

I am so tired of my life and death being somebody else's *entertainment*.

And, that simply, my mind is made up.

Up there at Khryl's Saddle, it took me too long to realize I should have killed myself. That's a mistake I won't make twice. Suicide isn't my trip—but there are other ways to die.

I get the jitters, waiting. By the time the trusty comes again, swinging wide the door of my cell, shuffling in with lowered head to empty my brimming bedpans into his tumbrel, I have to cough the tremors out of my voice before I can speak to him.

"Tell the sergeant—Habrak, is that his name?—you tell him Caine wants to see the Duke of Public Order."

The trusty's eyes roll at me, wondering just how mad I am.

"You tell him, that's all. Tell him to get a message to Toa-M'Jest that Caine wants to see him. The Duke will make it worth his while. And yours, too."

The trusty's head bobs, once, and he wheels his tumbrel away down the hall.

Fuck being helpless.

There's nothing I can do from the inside of this goddamn cell. But get me out in the Pit, out there among the criminals, malcontents, and troublemakers, and I will show them something I can do.

I will rip the head off their precious Assumption Day, and I will shit down its fucking neck.

10

DELIANN COULD TELL something important was about to happen from the way the Donjon guards were turning up the lamps.

He folded his arms behind his head and watched as a little group of them went from lamp to lamp around the tic-tac-toe square of the overhead catwalks. One of the group had a pole with a little Y-hand on the end; he'd catch the lamp chain in the Y and use the pole to push the lamp over to where another guard could grab it by the big brass handles that were welded in a ring around each lamp's barrel. A third guard would use a snuffer the size of a helmet to douse the flame, then he'd use his knife, inserted flatwise through the grey arm-thick hawser that served as a wick, to pull the wick farther out through the green-scaled brass lamp mouth, to make it burn higher and cast more light.

His fever had surged lately, and he rode its waves, drowsing and waking and drowsing again through dreams of deserts and ovens, summer noons and slow-twisting flame, and he fancied in a vaguely amused way that each time they relit one of the big brass lamps, the Donjon guards were turning up the heat inside his head.

For a time he lay on his back, staring up at the lamps, reflecting upon fire: light and heat, safety and destruction. He'd always had a gift for flame; it was the core of his magickal skill. He could do things with fire that an ordinary mortal could barely imagine. He thought now that perhaps fire was the central metaphor of his existence—like fire itself, he had been a perfectly faithful servant, but once set free of his master's control, he'd burned down the world—

He never did learn what the *something important* was; by the time the balcony and catwalks filled with crossbow-armed guards and the sergeant roared for the prisoners to rise at the entry of His Grace Toa-M'Jest, Duke of Public Order—and had the guards shoot one prisoner who appeared prepared to insult His Grace by remaining seated—Deliann was fast asleep upon the stone, his recumbent form screened from view by the close knot of Cainists that t'Passe had gathered around him.

Deliann never saw the Duke; he was dreaming of fire.

11

MAJESTY COMES THROUGH the door of my cell like a fox with hounds baying inside his head. He shifts inside his clothes like something's crawling on his skin, and he licks sweat from his upper lip. These past few years have been hard on him: He's gained a lot of weight, but his cheeks sag anyway and the flesh under his eyes is dark. His hairline has retreated somewhere north of the White Desert. A couple Eyes of God officers flank him.

"Caine, I have come here out of respect for the fact that you once saved my life," he says, the second finger of his right hand scratching the corner of his mouth. "But we are not friends, and you can expect no consideration from me. When you turned

against Our Lord Ma'elKoth, you sacrificed our friendship
as well."

The finger-scratch at the corner of his mouth is part of the
Quiet Cant, the gestural code of the Warrengang he once ran.
This gesture means *Hostiles present. Play along.* Using the
second finger means two—he's saying both of these Eyes of God
officers are spies, and he has to play nice in front of them.

From his sweats and jitters, it's not too much of a stretch to
figure that he's in the early stages of HRVP—which means this
bit about the officers being against him might be nothing but a
paranoid fantasy. On the other hand, Toa-Sytell used to run the
Eyes; it's also not too much of a stretch to assume that he'd have
informers among the officer corps.

"Fuck friendship," I tell him. A slight motion brings together
the tips of my left thumb and forefinger against the blanket that
covers my legs: *I read you.* "I want to make a deal."

"There is no deal you can make which will save your life," he
replies, scratching the other corner of his mouth with his left
thumb: the signal for *truth*. "You will die on Assumption Day, as
planned."

Yeah, well, to tell *you* the truth, I'm looking forward to it; the
prospect of having years and years to pick through the wreckage
of my life is not a cheerful one.

But I will choose my death.

I will not have my death chosen for me.

"I can tell you lots of things," I offer. "I can tell you why
people are killing each other all over this city, and why it's gonna
get a lot worse. I can tell you what you can do about it."

Now that thumb that had just scratched his mouth taps the
same spot twice: *Truth?*

I just stare at him. Let him fucking wonder.

"And what do you want for this information?"

I take a deep breath and lace my fingers together on the pretext
of cracking my knuckles. "I want to go out the same way I came
in: right past the Pit." My thumbs are touching each other for the
words *I want to go*, then separated for *out the same way I came*,
together for *in*, separate *right past*, together *the Pit*.

Majesty squints at me narrowly while he parses the interaction
of signal with word: *I want to go in the Pit.* His eyes bulge like
overboiled eggs. "Are you *insane*?"

He recovers swiftly and gives me the *I read you* while he

smoothly works his reaction into our little vaudeville. "You are the Enemy of *God*, Caine. It'd take an order from His Radiance himself to set you free. I can't *believe* you would ask such a thing."

I pretend to scratch my chin with my left hand, while I make the *truth* sign. "Maybe you oughta go ask him, then. You got a monster shitstorm spinning up, Majesty, and I'm the only one who can smell it."

"Toa-M'Jest," he corrects me absently, and glances from one Eye officer to the other like he can't figure out what to do. They both stand at a relaxed parade rest, pretending they're not paying attention. "How am I supposed to bring this crap before the Patriarch?" he asks, rubbing his hands together nervously. "You insult me, to even make the suggestion."

His thumbs brush each other on the words *insult me*.

Okay, I get the picture.

"That's it?" I say, blinking disbelief at him. "That's what saving your worthless ungrateful butt buys me? 'Kiss off, see you in your next life?' When did you turn into such a suckass?"

"Mind your tone," he says frostily. "You are speaking to a Duke of the Empire—"

"Duke of the Empire, horseshit. I'm speaking to a fucking ass-bandit. How'd you get Toa-Sytell's shit stains off your nose? With your tongue?"

He turns red. "Caine—" he begins, but I'm all over this.

"I can guess how you got into the Cabinet. You think if I give that zombie-faced cocksmoke a rimmer every night, he'll make me a Duke, too? You ever have to play Guess What the Patriarch Had for Dinner?"

The Eyes of God guys make noises like they're strangling, and they start toward me, but Majesty beats them to it. He leaps forward and gathers my stained tunic in both fists, yanking me up off the cot. "Say what you want about me," he snarls in my face, "but never insult the Patriarch. *Never,* you understand? It is only by his leave that I could give you this cell—otherwise you'd be in the *Pit*. Is that what you want?" He gives me a pretty violent shake, then another. "Is it?"

"Your *hospitality* can suck shit out of my ass—nah, sorry, don't want to ruin your appetite before Vespers, huh?"

He throws me back onto the cot hard enough to bounce my head against the wall and shoot stars across my vision. "You have an unusual way of persuading a friend to do you a favor," he says coldly. "I think I have done you one too many already."

He turns to one of the Eyes. "Tell the sergeant of the guard that I will pay for this man's cell no longer. They can throw him in the Pit with the rest of the scum."

"Hey—" I say uncertainly, "hey, c'mon, Majesty, I was only kidding—"

"My name is *Toa-M'Jest*," he says, "not that you'll have occasion to use it again. I'll see you on Assumption Day, Caine." He does a pretty fair military about-face and stalks out of the cell.

"Hey, come *on*," I call after him pleadingly as the Eyes follow him out. "Can't you take a fucking *joke*?"

They lock the cell door and swing the bar into place.

It's good to have friends.

12

THE ROAR OF the flames on Commons' Beach, in the Warrens, around Alien Games, and on the deck of the riverbarge all converged into the purifying blaze of a village high in the God's Teeth and fused itself with the voice of a mob, of an army, of all the prisoners in the Pit suddenly starting to yell at once, and Deliann discovered that he was awake.

He rubbed at his face, trying to clear eyes that did not focus well; his skin was hot to his touch. The prisoners around him were standing, shouting, but he couldn't understand what they were saying. "What's happening?" he asked thickly of no one in particular. "Why is everyone shouting?"

T'Passe looked down when he spoke, and she squatted beside him so that she could be heard above the shouting. "You might want to see this," she said, waving one hand toward the balcony around the Pit while with the other she took his arm to help him up.

Numbly, he allowed himself to be pulled to his feet, though his legs ached fiercely to be taking his weight once more. Where t'Passe pointed, a pair of guards pumped the rocker arms on the winch, clanking the jointed pawls in and out of ratchet teeth to lower the stairbridge on its long chains. Prisoners pressed aside as its foot settled to the stone floor; at the stairtop stood a pair of grey-robed Donjon trusties, bearing a litter on which lay a dark-

haired man. "That's *Caine*," t'Passe said. Her voice hummed
with astonished reverence. "That's Caine. They're bringing him
down."

Deliann swayed, feverish; the moment oozed, gooey and la-
bile, between the beats of his pulse. Stung, almost blinded, rapt
with a shivering perception of being present at an event of unex-
plainably transcendent significance, as though he had fallen
right out of his life and landed inside an epic that no one had read
for a thousand years, he leaned on t'Passe's arm as the trusties
turned and slowly bore the litter down the stairbridge.

The man on the litter was dark of hair and swarthy of skin, of
athletic build but no longer young: a scatter of grey marbled his
ragged black beard. He lay still, eyes closed, limp as a corpse,
and the grey cotton pants that covered his motionless legs were
stained here and there with crusted blotches of brown and red.
This could not be Caine, not truly: he looked so fragile.

So human.

The surge of the shouting took on an ugly edge.

Deliann swung his head from side to side in blank denial; he
could not speak, could barely think, his breath strangled by
crushing déjà vu. *He had seen this man before—*

As though all the tales he'd heard of Caine had solidified
somehow inside his head, so that he'd somehow known already
that the Enemy of Ma'elKoth was only a slender dark-haired
man in the grip of middle age, of completely unextraordinary
appearance.

But he hadn't . . .

In his heart, had he ever troubled to examine it, he had carried
the same icon of Caine as had everyone else who had listened to
the legend but never seen the man: fists like steel gauntlets that
can break stone with a single blow, shoulders an axe-handle
wide, muscles like boulders, eyes like torches in a cave, the grin
of a predator fed upon human blood—

How was it, then, that he could look at this man and feel that
he somehow *knew* him?

He breathed himself into mindview, searching for that current
of black Flow of which Kierendal had spoken. At first he could
see only scarlet swirls ghosting outward from the shouting prisoners: their mob-anger energy drifting toward the man upon the
litter. The man on the litter, impossibly, seemed to have no Shell
of his own—but those swirls of scarlet found something to latch

on to around him, some shadowy pulse in the air, a vague darkening that deepened as though it fed upon the anger from below.

The shadow didn't look like a Shell at all; instead of the almost gelatinous solidity that Deliann could usually see filling
the air around a living creature, this was smoke and ghost-shade,
shifting and twisting, half imaginary, as though it were a trick
of his fever-hazed eyes. With concentration, his disciplined
mind could struggle through his haze to draw it gradually into
focus . . . But as it came clear—swirls of opalescent grey and
white within the black, like a semisubstantial gemstone—the
Shells of the other prisoners, of the trusties and the guards and
Deliann himself, all faded into only a vivid memory.

Flow is Flow: all the colors and shapes of magick are finally
one single force, even as all the shapes and colors of energy,
from light to steel to the neutron-soup of a collapsar, are finally
and fundamentally energy. But even as energy can have wildly
differing properties according to its state, so, too, do the states of
Flow. The limestone from which the Donjon was carved impedes and reflects the states of Flow used by human and primal
thaumaturges, rendering them powerless; but that rock has a
Flow of its own, its own note within the song of the Worldmind.

This small dark broken man, it seemed, inhabited a Flow state
of a different order than that of those around him.

Deliann stared at the currents of black Flow that surrounded
this man. He had heard of such things—had heard of men whose
Shells showed black—but he had never seen one; and even as
he stared, the small dark broken man stirred and spoke to the
trusties who bore his litter. Halfway down the stairbridge, the
trusties paused.

The angry, ugly shouting welcome of the prisoners turned to
jeers, hoots, and mocking singsong invitations: the baying of
human hounds who believe they smell fear.

Ca-aine! Hey, Ca-aine!

Hungry, Caine? I got something to feedja!

Lookit them pants—wet himself already.

I gotcher Holy Stroke right here!

Come on, bring him down! someone shouted at the trusties.
Bring him down! and more prisoners took up the call, and more,
until their voices washed together into an oceanic roar.

Deliann barely heard it; he was fascinated by the swirl of
black Flow. It darkened visibly around the small dark broken

man until Deliann wondered if he might have been able to see it even with his normal sight. It poured in through the walls of the Pit as though the rock were empty air, and the small dark broken man seemed to draw it into himself, inhaling it as though taking a deep, deep breath of power.

He used one hand against the litter pole at his side to lever himself up into a sitting position, and he looked down into the jeering, hooting mob of the Pit.

And he smiled.

"Oh, my god," Deliann whispered. "Oh, my sweet loving *god*—"

It was the smile that did it: the white teeth wolflike within the fringe of ragged black beard, the eyes that burned with a cold dark flame like obsidian ice.

You are just begging me to kick your fucking ass.

Yes, in fact, I am. That's exactly right.

And the identical grin, the identical cold dark flame within the eyes, undimmed in a memory more than a quarter of a century old: *I'm into it.*

The shock of recognition drove him right out of mindview. The instant staggering pain from his legs unstrung him, and he sagged against t'Passe's arm. "What's wrong, Deliann?" she asked. "What happened? Are you all right?"

The goddess had spoken of this man, and told Deliann that he wanted to be remembered to him—but Deliann had never dreamed of being reminded like this. He couldn't even make himself think the name. "That's not Caine," Deliann gasped. "It's *not* Caine."

"It is," t'Passe assured him stolidly.

The small dark broken man lifted his free hand as a fist and slowly, deliberately, as though savoring the sweetness of one moment's surpassing joy, he turned the back of his fist toward the Pit. He grinned down on the hostile mob.

And then he gave them the finger.

There came a second of silence, as though everyone together had drawn a single breath, and in that silence his voice could be heard clearly: cheerfully brisk, hard as flint and dark as burnt coffee. "Fuck you all, shitheels," he said. "You want some of this? Step up and take a fucking bite."

Deliann barely heard the howls that answered; that voice struck sparks within his mind, and Deliann flashed on him.

13

THE FLASH TOOK him instantly, involuntarily: it crushed his bones between its teeth and sucked out their marrow, shattered his skull like a nutshell, drew out his guts with strokes of a barbed-wire tongue. Kris Hansen had written, *What the life you have chosen to lead will cost you, I can't begin to imagine.*

He no longer had to imagine.

The flash whipped him to a day years before: it crumpled him on arena sand with a cooling corpse beneath his back and a sword through his spine. With one hand he took the hilt of that sword to trigger its magick, while with the other he pulled the neck of a traitor across the blade. The traitor's head came off in his hand, and he flipped the head like a ball into the lap of the god who knelt alongside. The god stammered out the words Hari had died to hear, the words that would save him and the goddess he loved—and as the prismatic haloes of the Winston Transfer limned the edges of the world, to draw him and anyone he touched back into hell, he reached out . . . and took that kneeling god's hand.

Why?

To this day, Hari had never thought to wonder.

In the answer to that simple question might be the central truth of his life.

Deliann remembered, all those years ago, feeling that this man had been more *real* than he, that the murderous, charismatic streetpunk he had known was in touch with some fundamental structure of existence; he recalled dreaming of touching that reality himself. Now he had: a spiral galaxy of pain and loss wheeled within his chest.

The flash ended in the same instant it began. Deliann, breathless, clung to the woman at his side. Above, the small dark broken man waved negligently at the trusties like a noble directing bearers of a sedan chair, and they started down the stairbridge once more.

Deliann put his lips against t'Passe's ear to be heard through the shouts of the prisoners. "Get me to him. Please, t'Passe," he said. "We have to protect him—they'll tear him apart!"

She shook her head and leaned close to shout in his ear in turn. "It's already handled!" she said. "I have men waiting to receive the Caine at the foot of the stairs."

"We should go—we should be there. We have to be there,"
Deliann insisted.

T'Passe cocked her head, giving him a long slow considering
look before answering, more quietly now. "And what is it that
you think you can do for the Caine? Deliann, you can barely
stand."

"All right," Deliann said, sagging. "All right, but—"

He looked at the roof, the floor, the prisoners around them,
anywhere but her. Finally, he said, "It's not what I can do for him;
it's what he can do for me. I need to talk to him, just for a
minute." He hated how desperate—how wounded—this made
him sound, but t'Passe either didn't notice or did not care. He
could not tell her: *Because he once told me I was the bravest son
of a bitch he ever met.* He could not tell her: *Because I deserted
him twenty-seven years ago.* "You keep asking me what I want. I
want . . . I *need* . . . to talk with that man. Maybe just for a
minute; I have to talk to him."

T'Passe squinted at him as though trying to see something
tiny and dark inside his head; then her face cleared into a sudden
smile. "All right," she said. "I wouldn't mind a word with him
myself."

14

WITH T'PASSE TO elbow her ungentle way through the press, the
two of them reached the ring of grimly jubilant Cainists who
held back the other prisoners only a moment after the trusties
had ascended once again. There had been some scuffling—a few
in the crowd were already bleeding, as were a couple of the
Cainists—and the prisoners were giving them a little room, now.
The trusties had already taken the empty litter back up the stairs,
and the guards above began winching the bridge back up into
place.

The ring of Cainists parted to allow t'Passe and Deliann
within.

The small dark broken man sat on the stone, his legs splayed
nervelessly before him. He scanned the ring of Cainists around
him like a wolf in the midst of a herd of caribou; when he looked
up at t'Passe, he scowled and waved irritably at the backs of the

men and women who protected him. "You the head freak of this sideshow?"

"I am t'Passe of Narnen Hill, formerly Vice Ambassador to the Infinite Court," she said stolidly. "I do not know what a sideshow is, but if I take your meaning correctly, then yes, I am the . . . head freak."

"Monastic," he grunted. "I knew from the way you argue: like you're teaching half-witted kids."

"You could hear?"

He pulled his lips back over his teeth. "I've been praying that somebody would kill you."

"At the Festival of the Assumption, your prayer will be answered. Does this please you, to have the power of your faith so amply demonstrated?"

"Ask me then," he said, and leaned to one side, bending his neck so that he could see around her broad body. "And who's your puppy, here? What's his story?"

T'Passe shifted her weight, and his gaze met Deliann's for the first time. Those black eyes widened, then narrowed. "Well," he said. "Fuck me like a goat."

"Hari," Deliann said breathlessly. Even now, he couldn't make himself believe this was happening. "It's you, isn't it? You really are. You're *Hari Michaelson*—"

A melancholy half smile slowly developed under those narrowed eyes. "Been a long time, Kris."

The shouts of the prisoners had already begun to fade toward the usual undertone of grumbling, but the roaring in Deliann's ears made up the difference. Under that roar was a kind of slack-jawed wonder: the meeting of their eyes had peeled back the layers of Deliann's life. It was as though the past twenty-seven years had been only preparation, training, rehearsal, for a part he could only flee then, but now, finally, had the strength to play.

I can do this, he thought. *At last, I'm ready.*

"Yes," he said finally. "Yes, it has been a long time. I'm not Kris Hansen anymore, Hari. You should call me Deliann."

"Yeah? Like the Mithondionne prince, huh?"

"That would be me," Deliann said.

"You're the Changeling Prince?" Hari shook his head, smiling as though at some private joke.

I suppose you could say I'm the Changeling King, Deliann thought, but he said, "Something like that."

"No shit? Well, all right, then."

The small dark broken man leaned to one side, taking the weight off one hand so that he could offer it. "Pleased to meetcha, Deliann," he said. "I guess you can call me Caine."

"And so: you *are*," Deliann murmured. "You really are, after all: you're Caine."

Hari shrugged, and his fingers tangled themselves in the stained cotton breeches covering his motionless legs. He shook himself like a man holding off a nightmare. "Yeah," he said. "I'd love to play catch-up for a couple hours, but I got a move to make while I still have everybody's attention. Tell me one thing."

"What do you need to know?"

He flexed his hands and cracked his knuckles one by one: a series of flat, deliberate clicks of lethal intent, like bullets being loaded into a pistol.

"Who do I have to kill to get a fucking drink around here?"

THERE IS A cycle of tales that begins long, long ago, when the human gods decreed that all their mortal children shall know sorrow, loss, and defeat in the course of the lives they were given.

Now, it came to pass that one particular man had run nearly his entire alloted span, and he had never known defeat; for him, the only defeat was surrender. It soon followed that the king of the human gods undertook to teach this particular man the meaning of defeat. And in the end—the common end, for all who contend with gods—this particular man surrendered, and died.

But among the wise, the tale of this dead man does not end in death.

This dead man lay unquiet in the grave; the earth's embrace could not hold him. His corpse shifted and writhed, and moaned with the memory of life.

One day a wanderer sought a path out from a dark and mazy wood. This wanderer followed a wind from beyond the world, and that wind led him to this unquiet grave. The wanderer looked upon the grave and spoke to the corpse within it, saying: Dig deeper, and find a darker tomb.

For the wanderer was the crooked knight, and he had learned that only by descending can one rise.

Fifteen

THE PATRIARCH'S LEFT hand trembled ever so slightly, as the tip of its middle finger marked a drier line through the sweat that beaded his brow. Then this unsteady hand slid along his cheek to cup the corner of his jaw, feeling for fever; a moment later it massaged the swollen glands in his throat.

"Is His Radiance unwell?" the Eyes of God officer asked somewhat anxiously. "Shall I summon a healer?"

"Not at all," Toa-Sytell murmured. Even if he did feel ill—which he *didn't*, not at all, not one little bit—he certainly wouldn't show it before this officer.

The man could not be trusted.

"Continue your report," he directed absently. He listened with barely half his attention to the officer's tale of the meeting between Duke Toa-M'Jest and Caine in the Donjon cell. A premonition muttered inside his head: a dark echo of calamity's swift approach.

"And the Duke defended the Patriarch's honor quite vigorously," the Eye of God was saying.

"Of course he did," Toa-Sytell murmured. "He always does. It's how he thinks to deceive me."

"Your Radiance?"

"Nothing, Captain. Continue."

"So the cell has been cleared, and Caine is being moved down into the Pit even as we speak. Shall we post additional guards?"

"Mmm? Why?"

"Well, I—" The Eyes captain shifted uneasily. "I had understood that His Radiance was concerned for Caine's safety."

"Me? Oh, no, no. No. That was the *Duke*," Toa-Sytell said. "That was his excuse."

"Your Radiance, that Pit is filled with men and subs that *hate* him. Death will inevitably follow—"

495

"Unquestionably," the Patriarch murmured. "But I very much doubt this death will be Caine's."

2

IT TAKES ALL of a minute for me to get a grip on the way shit works in the Pit.

Dad would have loved this place: a culture in a bottle. They've already cycled through warlordism into a classic water monopoly—a real Lords of the Nile kind of thing, with the Serpents as the ruling civil authority and this t'Passe and her buttlickers as the fundamentalist insurgency out to reform by destabilizing yadda yadda yadda horseshit.

And there's a lotta goddamn Serpents down here, couple hundred at least. No surprise: The Serpents were always the Kingdom of Cant's biggest rival. Figures Majesty would use Toa-Sytell's Cainist-purge shit to pay off old grudges.

I beckon to this t'Passe character. "Who's the hump?" I ask, nodding at an ogrillo—a big bastard with fighting claws the size of *kukhris*—who walks around like all he lives for is fighting and fucking and he's not particular about which he does to who. He's carrying a lot of scars for a 'rillo pup his age, too. Six flunkies orbit him in swaggering arcs, and he's giving me the fisheye: he's got something to say, but he's waiting for me to give him an excuse.

"He is called Orbek," she says. "He's become part of the Serpent organization."

"Perfect. Get him over here for me, will you?"

She stiffens. "Am I your servant?" she asks with a frosty stare.

I give her a quizzical lift of the brow. "You mean you're not?"

"We don't *worship* you, Caine," she says, getting that hectoring schoolmaster tone that makes me want to pop her one. "You are not a god to us, but rather the symbol of a philosophical stance—"

"Yeah, whatever, shut up, huh? You gonna do it, or should I ask somebody else?"

"I, ah . . ." She blinks, frowns while she tries to decide what her doctrinal purity might require, then sighs. "I suppose . . . I'll go get him."

"Hey, thanks."

Hansen—Deliann, whatever—watches her waddle off, and he shakes his head like he'd find this all pretty funny if he wasn't so tired. "I don't think you've changed at all, Hari."

If only that were true.

I look him over, and I have to look away. He's not easy on the eyes; some of it is that I keep expecting to see that white plastic postsurgical mask of his, but most of it is that the last twenty-seven years haven't done him a hell of a lot of good. He's got a dent in his skull that's only half scabbed over—like somebody rapped him a good one with a sword—and his hair's growing out screwy, patchy and ragged like he's got the mange, and every time I get a glimpse of his legs it makes me glad I'm pretty much dead below the waist.

I wonder if it's as hard for him to look at me.

Deliann Mithondionne, the Changeling Prince, whipass-in-residence for T'farrell Ravenlock: a More in Sorrow Than in Anger legbreaker. He still has those sad puppy-eyes, though; probably still tells himself that Violence is the Last Resort.

He lowers his head like he's afraid to look at me. "The Flowmind . . ." he begins hesitantly, ". . . I mean, the goddess—uh, Pallas Ril—she came to me a few days ago."

I manage to get out a word. "Yeah?"

"She told me that she could create a countervirus, one that would give immunity to HRVP . . ." His voice trails off hopefully, and I can't look at him because I don't want to watch that hope go out of his eyes.

"She could have." I bite down on the words hard enough to chip a tooth. "If she'd lived."

"Then it's true," he says in a voice so small he might have squeezed it out his tear ducts.

"It usually is. That's the thing about stories. One way or another."

"There's another story," he murmurs. "About you and she, that the two of you were—"

"Yeah, that's right," I tell him. "Eleven years. Almost."

And I can still taste the hot copper of her blood. I can still smell the steam that swirled up from her severed heart.

In his eyes, now, I can see a brutal comprehension. He whispers, *"How do you stand it?"*

I shake myself, hard. I can't let him drag me back down into my private darkness. "I don't have to stand it," I mutter. "A few days from now, neither of us will have to stand it anymore."

3

NOW T'PASSE'S COMING back, with Orbek and his flunkies saun-tering along behind, kicking prisoners out of their way and gen-erally making assholes of themselves. The circle of guys t'Passe put around me to hold back the crowd parts to let her through. "At your request," she says, nodding toward Orbek.

"Swell." I swing a hand around at the ring of Cainists. "Now tell your lapdogs to stand down."

"Caine," she says with exaggerated patience, "nearly every prisoner in the Pit is facing execution, accused of Cainism. Falsely accused. You are not, as you might imagine, popular here. My *lapdogs*, as you call them, are all that stand between you and an ugly death."

"Nothing stands between any of us and an ugly death," I re-mind her. "Now fuck off, and take your puppies with you."

Her face ices over, and she waves to the Cainists, who reluc-tantly move a few paces away. The other prisoners start to crowd around, and a lot of them are shouting *Down in front!* and shit like that because people farther away want to be able to see. Orbek has his own flunkies clear a little space around us, while he stands there with his gorilla arms folded around his barn-sized chest.

Pretty soon things quiet down; everybody's watching. Over at the head of the water trenches, a bunch of the Serpents stand on the bench ledge that rings the Pit, staring and grinning.

"You got something to say to me?" Orbek growls. He's got a trace of a Boedecken accent, which explains the attitude. He might even be a Black Knife. Could I be that lucky?

"Nah," I tell him. "I just wanted to see you up close. You look stupid enough to be a Limp Dick."

He takes a couple long strides and towers over me; his fighting claws swing out over his closed fists. "I am Black Knife. My dead father is Black Knife, from before. From when the land likes Black Knives," he snarls.

Well, how about that? Happy birthday to me.

I grin up into his smoldering eyes. "Tell you what, nutless: Give me a lift over to where I can get a clean drink, and I won't hurt you."

"Hurt *me*, little human?" He holds one of his fighting claws up alongside one of his tusks, so I can see how sharp they both are. "You?"

"Hey, Deliann," I say loudly, so that everybody in the Pit can hear me, "maybe you don't know this: In the Boedecken ogrillo dialects, the word for knife is the same as the word for fighting claw—which is a, y'know, a euphemism for *penis*. The Black Knife clan lived out in the Waste—up until I had a little fun with them a few years ago. By the time I got done, all the other clans were calling them the *Broken* Knives clan—the Limp Dicks. That's why most of them left the Boedecken and came to the cities. They can't get it up."

"Hari—uh, Caine," he says, rising uncertainly, like he's wondering if he should get between me and Orbek. "Maybe you don't want to go into this right now . . . ?"

"What, because of dangledick here?"

"Uh, well—"

"My father tells me about you," Orbek begins, low and deadly.

"Fuck your father," I suggest, then decide I should apologize. "Oh, shit, sorry—I forgot. You *can't*, can you, softie?"

He reaches down and tangles one fist in my shirt. He hauls me off the ground, my useless legs dangling free, and brandishes his other claw in my face. "How limp is *this*?"

I snake one hand over his arm from the outside and grab the claw he was waving at me. An ogrillo's fighting claw is like an extremely muscular extra thumb that's jointed to the forearm below the wrist; like the thumb itself, it's not so strong against force that vectors outside its normal range of motion. I twist it sideways and down, and Orbek gasps.

"Hey, it's like magick," I tell him, showing my teeth. "I've just turned a Limp Dick into a Jack Ass. Carry me over to where that clean water comes out of the wall, and I'll turn you back into an ogrillo—one who hasn't had his fighting claw torn off at the root. You follow? Play nice, and maybe you'll get the chance to fuck your father after all."

But he's in no mood to be reasonable; maybe hitting the father-fucker line again was over the top. He howls rage and pain and lets go of my shirt because he needs that hand to hit me with. When he releases me, the only thing holding me up is my grip on his fighting claw; my full weight sags onto the joint, forcing it sideways and out, and it snaps with a dull liquid pop. His howl chokes down into astonished gargling.

I hold on, and for half a second I hang there while he supports me with the broken claw—*damn* he's tough—but my weight pulls him off balance, and we both go to the floor. He comes down on top of me, but I still have enough play to bend his arm like a chicken wing; then I can extend my other arm behind his shoulder, grab his wrist and grab my own wrist with my other hand, my forearm levering his elbow up and back. I use the leverage to push his other shoulder into the floor beside us, so he can't get a swing with his unbroken claw. I straighten my arms a bit to take up the slack, and he grunts with pain, since I'm only about ten foot-pounds shy of ripping every goddamn ligament in his shoulder.

His face is right up against the back of my left shoulder; if he was thinking about hurting me instead of thinking about how much I'm hurting him, he could rip the fuck out of my armpit with his tusks. I draw back my chin so he can get a glimpse of my smile.

"Think about what you're doing, Orbek," I say helpfully. "So far, you've got a busted claw; that'll heal. About ten seconds from now I'm gonna break your shoulder, which will chew the shit out of your rotator cuff and fuck you up for life. And if breaking your shoulder doesn't work, I'll kill you and start again with somebody else. You want to negotiate, here?"

His flunkies are all gathered round, shouting along with the other prisoners—a couple of them shove Deliann back out of the way—but Orbek's on top and he's wide as a house. One of them winds up for a kick, and I grin at him. "Even money says I can take that kick, kill him, and kill you, too, before you get in another. Go ahead, tough guy. Take your shot."

The ogrillo decides he should wait and see. It warms my heart, how much mileage I can still get out of my reputation. "So, Orbek, no help there. What's it gonna be?"

Pain-sweat drips off his forehead, and he snarls wordlessly for a couple seconds, then lowers his head by my ear and whispers, "I give, but leave me some face with my boys, hey?"

I give his arm a painful-looking twist, and he snarls again, tossing his head in a pretty good performance of agony. "Think about it," I repeat loudly. "Ten seconds. Then you die."

He gets close to my ear again. "You couldna fuckin' *asked*?" he whispers.

"This way's better," I whisper back. "If they kill me, you're covered."

He snarls and writhes and goes through some decent pro-wrestler thrashing. "Yeah, arright," he whispers, then he hooks one of his tusks into the back of my shoulder joint, just for a second. "But remember. You win this one? You remember I coulda hurtcha. Maybe I be dead, but you be hurt, hey? I want some fuck-me *consideration*."

Reminds me of me at his age. "Deal."

I switch my grip on his arm so that I free up a hand to get a forearm under his chin, take his collar, and lever my wrist against his trachea in a judo choke. His head comes up and his eyes bug out and he gasps, "All right—all right—don't kill me . . ." all nice and hoarselike as if I really were putting pressure on his throat.

Together we negotiate the complicated process of getting up from the floor while making it look like I'm still hurting him, and together we manage to convince his boys of the dubious proposition that I can kill him before they can haul me off. We end up with me riding his shoulder, one arm around his neck like a choke from behind, one hand still on the broken fighting claw to keep his wounded arm bent in a half-assed hammerlock.

"Caine—" Deliann says again, his eyes asking me if I want him to jump in.

"Stay there," I tell him cheerfully. "I'm just going for a drink of water. My jackass and me, we'll be right back."

As Orbek sets out toward the clot of Serpents and their hangers-on, I tip a wink over my shoulder at Deliann. I'm not sure he sees it; he's rubbing his face like he's got a headache.

The water streams out a pipe in the wall and pours into a little round pool with three trenches leading out; the whole Pit floor slopes gently down from there. Everybody will get a good view.

Almost like being onstage.

4

PRISONERS SCOOT BACK out of Orbek's way, clearing a narrow path of bare floor. "Who's in charge up there?" I whisper in his ear.

"The guy with the green rag on his head," he whispers back through a ventriloquist's grimace. "Calls hisself Adder."

One of the lesser luminaries in the Serpent constellation stands in our path. "Hey, Orbek, you all right?" he says, thinking he's being witty. "Don't that hurt? Musta been real painful when he yanked your claw, huh?"

I give him a hard look over Orbek's shoulder. "You want to find out?"

He chuckles. "Where you think y'going, cripple?"

"I'm thirsty. I'm going to get a drink."

The Serpent points back at Orbek's feet. "Water's fine right there."

"Are you kidding? It smells like your mother's ass."

This gets a pretty good laugh from the prisoners, and the Serpent's face goes red. "You got a wise mouth for a cripple, old man," he sneers. "I wonder, will it still feel that smart when it's wrapped around my dick?"

"Hey, all I want is a drink. A clean drink, kid. Is that a problem?"

Here it comes: Adder and his lieutenants are into this now, making their way over, grinning. They can't believe I'm stupid enough to put myself into their hands. "No, no, no, no problem," the Serpent says broadly. "But we got some *rules* around here, crip. Everything's got a price, huh? Right now, going rate for a drink is, you gotta suck me off. Nothing personal. Rules, huh?"

"You think you're gonna get some off me?" I give a horselaugh. "I'm not a child molester, kid. Come back when you grow up."

"I'm growin' plenty right now," he says, rubbing his pants.

"Aw, for shit's sake, Dinnie," Orbek says, thin and hoarse past my elbow around his throat. "Lemme through, hey? He's fuckin' *killin'* me."

"Not my problem," the Serpent answers, but Adder puts a hand on his shoulder from behind.

"No, let them through," he says, playing Lord of the Manor. "Caine's a *celebrity*, Dinnie. We need to bend the rules a little to make him feel welcome." He offers me a slight, ironic bow and sweeps a hand toward the pool of clear water. "And you *are* welcome, Caine. Please, be my guest."

"Hey, thanks. You're a prince," I tell him as Orbek lumbers past. "You want to make me feel really welcome? Keep this shit-eating Limp Dick off me once I get down."

"Orbek takes my orders," Adder says, "and he won't bother you if I tell him not to. Right, Orbek?"

"Like you say, Adder," the ogrillo wheezes.

"There, you see? You're perfectly safe here, Caine. I'm only sorry you weren't properly announced; we would have put out the good silver."

Christ, everybody's a comic. "Yeah, whatever. One knee, jackass." I enforce the order with what looks like an agonizing yank of the claw, and Orbek groans as he kneels. I slide off his back and he rises over me, snarling.

"Bastard," he says. "Fuck *your* father!" He draws back his big clawed foot to bust some of my ribs, but Adder stops him with a sharp word. Wonder what he would have done if Adder had told him to go ahead. Killed me, probably.

Guess I'll never know.

Orbek backs off, cradling his wounded arm and grumbling obscenities under his breath. Adder leans over me, just out of arm's reach, hands on his knees. "You understand, don't you, Caine, that I can only bend the rules so far? Sure, I let you in here. But I *am* gonna have to get over on you." He gives me a winning smile of shit-colored teeth. "Hope you don't mind."

"I don't give a handful of snot what you do, so long as I get some water."

"First things first," he says, his hands going to the waistband of his pants.

"What, you afraid I won't put out? What am I gonna do, run away?" I roll myself over so I can get a taste of the water. It's good: cool, sparkling clear, with the high mineral content that comes of filtering through a hundred feet or so of limestone. I take a nice, long, satisfying draft.

The general quiet in the Pit drops to stone silence.

"You know, Caine," Adder says, grinning like a friendly alligator, "I think in the mouth isn't enough. Not for you. I think I'm gonna have to *do* you. Do your ass. That's like a, a, y'know, a *surcharge*, y'know? For taking the drink on *credit*."

"What is it with you guys?" I ask him. "This whole butt-raping thing, I don't get it. I mean, I don't have any quarrel with rump-humpers—whatever sharpens your sword, you know what I mean?—but what is it about nutballs like you that makes you want to fuck a straight? I mean, I don't go around raping dykes, do I? Where's the fun in that?"

He straightens, still grinning, and starts to unlace his pants. "Maybe it's an acquired taste," he says.

"Berne was like that," I say slowly. "You've heard of Berne? I never could figure out why. I was gonna ask him—" I push myself up onto my hands and show him my teeth. "—but he *died*."

Adder mirrors my look. "Then I guess you're lucky to have me around to *satisfy* your *curiosity*."

Some guys just can't take a fucking hint.

"Yeah, all right, I've heard enough." I pull myself onto the stone bench at the foot of the wall next to where the pipe comes out. It takes a little maneuvering to get turned around so I can look out over the Pit.

Everybody's on their feet now, almost breathless in anticipation—watching Adder get ready to rape me is probably the best entertainment they've had in weeks. Even the guards line up along the catwalks, grinning and nudging each other. Some of them probably can remember the last time I was here, and they don't like me any more than the Serpents do. I can see Deliann, not too far away, at the fringes of the Serpents who surround me. He looks worried, but he's holding it together and keeping his mouth shut. A few shoulders away stands t'Passe and her crowd of buttlickers.

I take a deep breath and shout, "All right, asswipes! Shut up and listen!"

Like I don't have their complete attention already . . .

"People've been telling me how things work down here—telling me the *rules*." I roll my eyes at Adder, inviting him to laugh along with me. "You know what? Your rules suck."

He starts to say something, but I hold up my hand and keep talking. "I've got some new rules. My rules."

I fold down all but my first finger. "Rule One: Fuck with me, you die. No warnings. No second chances."

This causes an astonished rumble to boil up from the mass of prisoners. Adder can only stare at me like I've gone bugnuts.

I pop the next finger. "Rule Two: What I say, goes. It comes out of my mouth, it's law. Break a law, you get hurt. Break it again, you die."

Adder snorts contemptuously. "Done yet? Anything else?"

"One more," I tell him with a shrug. "Rule Three: Fuck with my friends, it's the same as fucking with me. When in doubt, see

Rule One. So—" I lift one hand up above my head and waggle it. "How many of you want to be my friends?"

Adder gives another one of those snorts. Sounds like he's got a turd up his nose.

"C'mon, don't be shy," I call. "Let's see some hands."

The Serpents are holding down the crowd with hard looks. They don't even have to go as far as make a threatening gesture; a simple shift of weight, a coolness in their eyes, makes it goddamn clear what they plan for anybody stupid enough to take my side.

Somewhere in the middle of the Pit, a hand goes up.

Prisoners step away from him.

"You're dead, you stupid shit," Adder says. "You hear me?"

In the middle of a clear space of Pit floor stands Deliann, his hand high. "I would like to be your friend, Caine. I hope I already am."

Well.

I guess that cold courage doesn't wear off.

Adder says, "Put your hand down, dead man."

"Hey, mind your manners, shitbrain."

"What?" Adder looks down at me. "What did you just say to me?"

"I told you to mind your fucking manners. What d'you think I said?"

Out in the clear space, t'Passe joins Deliann, and silently puts up her hand. Now one of her followers goes out there, and another, and another.

"I thought—" Adder says, "I thought I heard you say, 'Adder, tell your boys to kill every one of those dumb cocksuckers.' That's what I thought I heard you say."

I shake my head sadly. "If I were you, I'd be thinking pretty seriously about hiking my stupid butt-raping ass out there and raising my own damn hand."

"And why would I want to do that?"

"Because if you don't," I tell him, "I'm gonna fuck you up."

Adder rotates his shoulders, loosening himself up like a boxer between rounds. "Bold words from a crippled old man."

"Think it over, Adder. It's kinda humiliating. Ask Orbek."

"Worse than being gang-raped in the ass?"

I roll my head around and sneer at him with scalding contempt. "You got a move to make, shitbrain? Bring it on."

He squints at me. "Man, you are asking for it—"

"I'm begging for it. C'mon, what are you, afraid of me? Shit, what a puss."

"Fuck it," he says, and lunges at me. He starts to grab for my shirt, then stops himself—he saw what happened to Orbek, and he's not *that* stupid—and he settles for a hard kick that thumps one of my legs where it hangs over the lip of the bench.

"Yeah, that'd hurt—if I wasn't *crippled*, dumbshit. I can't even feel it." I give him a better horselaugh than the one I used on Dinnie. "How'd a moron like you end up in charge around here, anyway?"

"Feel *this*," he snarls, and grabs one of my ankles, yanking me off the bench. I slap the stone floor in a stinging breakfall. He twists me over facedown, and I let my arms swing high to open my ribs for his kick. The idiot goes for it: his shoe crashes in, but I'm ready for it and I absorb the blow with a *muay Thai* hiss. I wrap his foot with my arm, locking his toes into my armpit. With my other arm I push into a roll toward him; he lets out a startled shout as my leverage on his ankle forces him to the ground.

It takes me a lot less time to adjust my hold than it does for him to adjust to being thrown; before he knows what's going on I've got his ankle and heel in a jujitsu lock that makes him howl.

"You win!" he shrieks. Not so tough after all. "You *win*!"

"Fucking right I win." I bear down on the lock until his ankle shatters with a crunch like somebody stepped on a wet pile of broken glass. "I *always* win."

He screams: a rabbit in the jaws of a wolf. I pull myself up his leg and punch him in the balls.

This chops off his scream and sits him up, gasping; I whip my right arm around his neck into a forward headlock, brace my left hand against his shoulder, and grab my own wrist in a figure-four. He flails at me, raining punches at random up and down my ribs and legs, but he can't get any weight behind them; the only place he can hit me hard enough to hurt is my crotch, and there's no feeling in my balls anyway.

The gassy thing about the figure-four headlock is that it leverages both of my triceps—two-thirds of the total muscle in each arm—and a fair amount of pectoral and lat into the lock, and it twists his head so that the only muscles he can use to resist are those on one side of his neck. From the inside, it's a losing proposition. Even though I'm weak as a kitten with this chemical pneumonia or whatever, he doesn't have a chance. I apply a little pressure, and he squeaks when he feels his cervical vertebrae start to separate.

"That's it, calm down," I tell him gently. "Fight's over, bubba. You lose." The other Serpents are closing in around us, uncertain exactly how to go about hurting me. "Tell your bitches to back off, Adder. Before I break your neck."

I give him some slack in the headlock, and he gasps through his clamped teeth, "Back off—*back off!* For shit's sake, *do what he says!*"

They press away some. "More," I tell them. "Keep going. Little more, that's it, go on." I chivvy them back until we've got a sizable open space in front of us—I want to make sure everybody sees this.

Now, the catechism.

"All right, Adder," I say. "Who's in charge here?"

"Motherfuck—" he starts, but a twitch of my arms cuts him off.

"Let's try that again, huh? Who's in charge here?"

"You are," he growls.

"Very good. Who makes the rules in the Pit?"

"You do."

"Hey, two for two," I tell him encouragingly. "You're doing great. Now, here's the gristle. I hope you were paying attention. What's Rule One?"

"Uh," he begins, and then I kill him.

He keeps talking while he dies, sort of: the only sound he can make is a wet *kh kh kh* noise—reminds me of Garrette—because a sharp push of my arms broke his neck, which used his cervical vertebrae to scissor through his spinal cord, which makes him lie there like a marionette with his strings cut while the light goes out of his eyes.

A shove rolls his corpse off me, and I haul myself back up onto the cut-stone bench. I look out on the silent mass of prisoners.

"Any fucking questions?"

And those couple hundred Serpents gathered around me slowly realize that they're trapped in a stone room with over a thousand people who have their hands in the air and who don't like any of them one little bit, and I watch them each and severally decide—given Rule Three—that maybe they want to be friends of mine, too.

5

FOR A TIME, Deliann contemplated.

He could not have said how long this time might have been; the waves of fever that washed over and through him compressed and expanded time unpredictably. He might think for an hour, and find only seconds had passed; some hours did pass during which he could only shiver and sweat, his mind a nightmare jumble.

As soon as the guards who removed Adder's corpse had trudged back up and the stairs had lifted behind them, Deliann had gone to this strange man who had once been his friend. "I want to help."

Hari gave him a long, darkly measuring stare. "You used to get a little squeamish. This is gonna be ugly for a day or two."

"I'm still squeamish. But it won't stop me."

Hari nodded, remembering. "I guess it never did."

"No," Deliann had said. He'd felt an icy, tingling non-pain, as though someone had slid a thin, very sharp knife between his ribs. "I guess it didn't."

Hari hadn't needed his help to pacify the Pit; between the Serpents on one side and t'Passe's Cainists on the other, order came to the prisoners whether they liked it or not. "It is better to be feared than loved," he observed to Deliann once, in an abstracted undertone, "for men love at their own inclination, but you can make them fear at yours."

This was shortly after the death of Adder. Deliann knelt over Hari's legs, scrubbing dead flesh from his sores with a wad of coarse burlap. If Hari could feel even discomfort from this rough treatment, he gave no sign. "I've read *The Prince*," Deliann had replied in a matching mutter. "I seem to recall that Machiavelli goes on to point out that best of all is to be feared *and* loved."

Hari flashed him a dark grin. "Yeah, that's the trick, huh? Nice work if you can get it." He shrugged dismissively. "Maybe I better stick to what I'm good at."

"Love isn't so hard, Hari."

The grin faded, and his eyes went hooded. "Maybe for you."

"It's a connection, that's all. It's a recognition of the connection that's already there." Deliann shook his head. Fever was scattering his meaning. "Show them the connection, that's all. Let them know it works both ways."

Hari scowled. "Yeah, all right, Confucius. Gimme a fucking hint, huh?"

Deliann cast a significant glance toward Orbek, who sulked on the wall-bench a quarter of the way around the Pit. "He's been taking abuse all day for the way he let you manhandle him. The right word could get him—and the whole ogrillo faction— solidly behind you."

Hari nodded thoughtfully. "Worth a try."

After Deliann finished tying bandages of more burlap over the sores, Hari called a couple Serpents to carry him out into the middle of the Pit, then summoned Orbek. "That was a shitty thing I said about your father, and your clan," he said gravely. "I shouldn't have done that, and I'm sorry for it."

Astonishment prevented the ogrillo's reply.

"You were ready to fight and die for your father's honor," he went on. "I respect that; I respect *you* for that. You are a true Black Knife, Orbek. Your clan should be proud."

He raised his voice and spoke to the entire Pit. "None of you know that when we were fighting, Orbek could have ripped me a new mouth or two with his tusks. The only reason he didn't was that I made him a deal. I didn't beat him, I *bribed* him." He held out his hand. "I'd like to claim you as my friend, Orbek."

"Rule Three, hey?" Orbek said with a smirk around his tusks, but he took Hari's hand. And for a moment, he seemed curiously reluctant to let it go. The ogrillo said, "You, uh, you maybe should have somebody regular to help you get around. Somebody you can trust."

Hari squinted up at him. "You offering?"

Orbek shrugged.

"You want the job, it's yours."

Orbek gravely swung Hari up onto his back and carried him back to where Deliann sat on the bench. Hari had looked down at Deliann and said softly, "You are one smart son of a bitch."

Over the hours or days that followed, Hari had seemed to be everywhere all the time; Deliann didn't know if he ever slept. Orbek carried him wherever he went—he insisted upon it, and that insistence somehow transformed his earlier humiliation into a badge of honor.

The prisoners in general seemed to be actively grateful to

have someone telling them what to do. The rare moments of re-sistance to Hari's rule came mainly from the Cainists them-selves. As t'Passe never tired of explaining, "Cainism is not a religion, it is a philosophical stance. Your personal significance is purely symbolic; we've appropriated your iconography—the Prince of Chaos, the Enemy of God—from the Church of the Beloved Children, as our symbol of resistance to everything that Ma'elKoth stands for."

"If anybody'd asked me," Hari had said to her, "I would have told them to leave my iconography the fuck alone."

"You are free to disapprove," she'd replied. "Your disapproval means only as much to me as I choose to allow it to mean. I am free to resist your will."

"Sure." Hari nodded at her, smiling. "I respect your right to resist. You should respect my right to break your legs for it."

"Perhaps respect is the fundamental issue," t'Passe had an-swered agreeably.

Hari spent most of his time training his army.

He had selected a cadre of the strongest, most aggressive of the Serpents, liberally intermixed with ogrilloi and primals. In exchange for the authority to use force in the Pit, they were charged with the responsibility for maintaining order. They also received organized training in unarmed combat, with t'Passe as a demonstrator. This was a strong drawing point for many of the younger and more impressionable prisoners: the opportunity to learn some of the subtleties of infighting from Caine himself.

The guards, of course, would not have allowed such training if they had understood what was taking place, but the combat prac-tice was carefully stylized so that it looked like a dancing game, conducted in the midst of a ring of prisoners who would sing and clap to keep time. Hari confided to Deliann that he had hooked this idea from an Earth fighting style developed by slaves in Brazil, disguised as dance so that they could practice under the eyes of their Portuguese masters.

The distribution of food had become strictly regimented. Now, when the woven baskets were lowered, a single prisoner stood to receive each, and portions were carefully doled out to an orderly line of prisoners, one at a time. A sort of economy had sprung up, with the primary media of exchange being food and sexual favors. All were allowed to make any trades they could—his "soldiers" only ensured that all deals were ruthlessly enforced. Extortion or coercion of any kind was swiftly—and unerringly—punished. No innocent was ever wronged by Caine's justice in the Pit; his judicial system was the only one in the history of two worlds in which innocence was an absolute defense.

The sole judge of truth or lie in the Pit was Deliann's flash.

Something in his fever had made his flash more frequent. Now, he had only to stare at an individual long enough, and eventually his flash would come; he saw not only the facts of each case, but the character of the claimants. Disputes of any kind became rare, and the Pit's ad hoc police force—despite the criminal propensities of most of its members—became absolutely incorruptible, after an incident of minor extortion by one of Hari's soldiers was punished by a spectacularly brutal execution.

The Pit was *quiet* now, as well. When there was no training, conversations could be carried on in a normal tone of voice, instead of the half shouts that had always been required before. The guards overhead had not known what to make of this sudden change; Hari had forbidden his subjects to reply to the guardsmen's taunts and crude insults. He'd directed them to obey any direct order and answer respectfully any direct query, but they were otherwise to ignore all the guards said and did.

He'd made himself a seat, a roughly padded throne on the bench ledge beside the spillpipe. From there his miniature Peaceable Kingdom spread before him: lions and lambs both too respectful of his uncompromising ruthlessness to even complain, let alone start trouble.

The arc of water channel to his left had now become the Pit's sole sewer. After one killing and several severe beatings, no one dared relieve themselves in either of the other two. The center channel carried the Pit's bathwater, and each prisoner bathed and washed clothing in that water; even lacking soap, by the end of the first bathing rotation the animal stench in the Pit had faded to a faint and not-unpleasant musk. The channel that curved to the right—scrubbed with rags made of prisoners' shirts, all the way from the pool to the drain on the far side of the Pit floor—carried the drinking water, now clean and clear as the stream that sparkled from the spillpipe.

Whenever he was not called upon to be a judge or legal oracle, Deliann passed the span sitting on the Pit floor with his aching legs folded beneath him, living in mindview, studying the swirls of black Flow that enwrapped Hari's shadowy Shell, watching his fever make the stone walls ripple in slow, deep swells like the open ocean.

He spent a lot of time thinking about black Flow. He spent a lot of time thinking about the interplay of chance and will that is misnamed destiny.

He spent a lot of time thinking about Caine.

Twice he tried to tell Hari what he had discovered, but circumstances were against him. Hari was caught up in conquering and administering his tiny demesne; Deliann was able to capture his attention for only moments at a time, and often a surge of fever would half scramble what he was trying to say.

"Your Shell," he'd begun, the first time. "You know what a Shell is?"

"Yeah," Hari had confirmed distractedly. "I was married to a thaumaturge."

"Yours is black. Someone must have told you yours is black."

"So?"

"It's all about Flow. Stone—this stone, Donjon stone—doesn't stop black Flow. Nothing does, I think."

"The point, Kris. Let's have it."

"Your Shell, it's black because of this kind of Flow, don't you understand? *You can't stop it.*"

"It's not that big a deal. Lots of people have black in their Shells."

"Everyone has black in their Shells. Everyone. But usually you can't see it for all the other colors. But a Shell that's solid black? It's rare. *Rare.* I can't tell you how rare that is. The last one, I think—last I know of—might have been Jereth of Tyrnall."

"Ancient history," Hari had muttered. "He's not much more than a myth."

"Not ancient. *Not.* Just history. Only ancient for humans. Hari, the Covenant of Pirichanthe—that ended Jereth's Revolt—that was only five hundred years ago. I know people who were *there.* My father—I mean, the King—T'farrell Ravenlock, he was there, as Witness for the First Folk. Jereth Godslaughterer was as real as you are. Most of what you know of him—most of what the songs and stories tell—is more true than it is false."

"What's it got to do with me?"

"Same energy: you decide, and then you do. That's what made Jereth the Godslaughterer, and that's what makes you Caine."

"You better lie down for a while, huh? You're not making a whole lot of sense."

"Your power is my power: everyone's power. We all have power; we just don't use it. Black Flow, don't you see? It's mostly a *metaphor*. Like throwing a punch. Focus. Directed energy. Concentration. No fear. The release of desire. Presence. *That's* who Caine is."

"I don't follow."

Deliann had laced his fingers together in front of his knee and leaned back against the wall of sweating stone. Some of his fever had seemed to drain into the cool stone, and when he had continued, he'd felt a bit more lucid. "Every once in a while," he'd said slowly, "I think about some of the things you taught me, back at the Conservatory. I remember the time you dressed me up in Sorbathane armor so you could demonstrate a real punch. It's been twenty-seven years, Hari. I've done a lot of fighting— I've been punched by an *ogre*—and no one, *no one*, has *ever* hit me that hard."

"Power doesn't have that much to do with strength," Hari had said. "A good punch is half physics and half attitude."

"So is black Flow. Anyone can use it, just like anyone with arms can throw a punch. You're better at it, that's all. You strip away the nonessentials. How hard can you hit if you worry about breaking your hand? How well can you fight if you worry about losing?"

Hari murmured, " 'Do not be concerned with escaping safely—lay your life before him.' " He flattened his mouth into a grim line. "Bruce Lee."

"A philosopher?"

"Yeah." The grim line stretched a little. "He died young."

Deliann had shrugged. "Caine didn't."

Hari had looked away. "Don't talk to me about Caine," he had said. "Trying to be Caine—that's how I ended up here."

"No, no, no. You ended up here because you were trying to *not* be Caine."

Which was entirely the wrong thing to say; Deliann could see it now, too late. Bringing up Caine had battle-axed the conversation. Hari had told Orbek to carry him to a pair of Serpents whose voices were inching upward toward a quarrel, and had curtly suggested to Deliann that they should talk about this some other time, when he was feeling better.

His second try, some indeterminate hours or days later, had

produced only slightly better results. He had led into it more carefully, this time; once or twice, he'd sat down and talked with Hari at some length, without ever mentioning any of this. They had spoken of the lives they had lived since they had parted at the Conservatory, twenty-seven years ago.

Hari had only briefly sketched some of Caine's adventures, since Deliann knew already the broad outlines of many of these; mostly, he spoke of his wife and his daughter, of his father and of the home that had been taken from them. Deliann had more to tell: from his earliest days on Overworld, when he'd very nearly starved before landing his job as a bouncer at Kierendal's Exotic Love, to meeting Torronell and his Adoption; from his life at the Living Palace and the surrounding lands as the Changeling Prince—the Fist of the Twilight King—to his disastrous journey on the trail of the vanished legation to Transdeia. He had told Hari of Tommie, and was obscurely warmed as well as saddened to learn that Hari remembered Tommie well, with respect and some affection.

"Tommie died a Cainist?" Hari had said softly, shaking his head. "Hard to believe. He was always so, well, so *normal*, you know? Practical."

"T'Passe would tell you that being practical is the essence of Cainism."

"Can we not start that shit?"

"Tommie was not an ordinary man. He may have been, at one time; but the man who saved me was wholly extraordinary. I can't really say what made him so special. Cainism might be as good a name for it as any."

"Names," Hari had grunted. "What's that line Orbek likes? *You can call a turd a sandwich, but it still tastes like shit.*"

"You think there is no power in names, Hari? Tommie wouldn't agree. Tommie gave *me* a name. One that's too powerful for me. I can't make myself use it, though it seems to be mine."

"What kind of name is that?"

Deliann had had to look away, to conceal the tears swelling into his eyes. "He named me as the Mithondionne. What humans would call the king of the elves."

"No shit?"

Deliann had shrugged helplessly. "Torronell brought HRVP back to the Living Palace. My family is dead. Though Adopted, I am Mithondionne." He had lowered his head and swallowed. "The last of my line."

Hari had been silent for a long, long time. Finally Deliann had looked back at him, and had been astonished to see stark new pain in Hari's black eyes. "Christ, Kris," he'd said softly. "I'm sorry. I—" He'd shaken his head, scowling, disgusted with himself, and had looked down at his hands. "I forget, you know? I get so trapped in the wreckage of my own life that I forget other people got destroyed, too. I am such an asshole, sometimes."

Deliann had smiled gently. "That's a name, as well."

"Kris—"

"You have to admit that some names have power, Hari. You must see that."

"Yeah, all right, whatever. Is this important?"

"It's extremely important. It's incredibly important. There is nothing more important. Think about this. Think about the names *you* use. Think about the names others use for you. They call you the Blade of Tyshalle, Hari. Do you ever think about that?"

"They call *Caine* the Blade of Tyshalle."

Deliann had waved this aside; he had no interest in arguing the distinction. "Tyshalle Deathgod is also called the Limiter, and the Divider. Tyshalle himself is the energy of change; he is the outer darkness beyond the edges of organized reality. That's why he's the God of Death: death is the *primary* change. The big one. Change is, itself, the structure of experience. Think about it: The absence of change is stasis—which is also the absence of experience. Experience *is* reality. That's what reality *is* to us; no more, no less. That's why you get the quantum observer effect. Reality is *change*. That's all it is. The Blade of Tyshalle is the leading edge of reality. It's the knife that cuts everything."

"The Blade of Tyshalle," Hari had answered heavily, "is a goddamn *marketing* gimmick. Some Studio flack thought it sounded cool, that's all. It's a good hook for an assassin. It doesn't mean anything; they just made it up."

"Shiva's Dance," Deliann had said, conjuring another name. He'd felt his line of reasoning slipping through his fingers as more and more connections tied themselves within his brain. "Your mother was Hindu, wasn't she?"

"Bengali."

"And your name: Hari. An alias for Vishnu, right? Did she ever talk about any of the other old gods?"

"Maybe some," Hari had said warily. "She died when I was, what, eight? I'm not sure I'd remember."

"Did she ever talk about Shiva?"

"The Destroyer. You don't have to be Hindu to know who Shiva was."

"Is," Deliann had corrected. "*Is* in the sense that the force for which Shiva was a metaphor is entirely real, and still with us. Shiva is power in its purest sense. Absolute motion. Destruction, creation: the same energy informs both. Destructive creation, creative destruction. This isn't a paradox. It *isn't*. It's a breakdown of language. Destruction and creation *are not opposites*. They are both opposites of *stasis*."

He had started to talk faster and faster, trying to get all the words out; his chain of logic smoked under his acid fever. "The old name—the *best* name—is Shiva: the Dancer on the Void. The power that shatters order into primordial chaos is the same power that patterns chaos into a new structure of order— because pure chaos is also a kind of stasis, don't you see? Shiva is the enemy of *everything that does not change*. Shiva's Dance is the play of energy in the cosmos; it's not good, it's not evil, it simply *is*. It's change itself, and it touches everything. Power. Life. Mind."

Hari had squinted. "Life?"

"Power and Life are the same thing. Both of them together are Mind. Mind is a patterning of energy, nothing more, nothing less. The elemental particles that make up this stone, right here—" He had rapped his knuckles on the bench above the spillpipe. "—electrons, the quarks that build the protons and the neutrons, are exactly that: patterns of energy. The *same* energy, Hari. At its most fundamental level, energy is energy. That's why, say, a stonebender rockmagus can shape this stone with her bare hands—she's trained her mind to resonate harmonically with the inherent Mind of the rock. Stonebenders have a saying: 'When you work the rock, the rock also works you.' "

"You're saying everything has a mind."

"No: I'm saying everything *is* Mind."

"Metaphysics," Hari had said, waving a hand disgustedly. "A guy name of Pirsig once wrote that 'Metaphysics is a restaurant with a thirty-thousand-page menu—and no food.' "

Deliann had responded with a faintly whimsical smile. "Chew on this, then. I think the same elemental force of change that an ancient Hindu would have named Shiva is what I've been calling black Flow. It's what a Lipkan priest would call the Breath of Tyshalle. It's the power behind his Blade." He'd said gently, "That's you, Hari."

"You think so?"

"They say that destruction follows Caine the way crows follow an army."

"Yeah, yeah. You know why they say that?"

"Because it's true."

"Because another guy from Marketing came up with a good line. I met him once; he told me they had every Actor out of the whole North American system repeat it every time somebody mentioned my name until it caught on. This is all just coincidence, Kris. It doesn't mean *anything*."

"Everything is coincidence, Hari. It means whatever you decide it means."

"Just coincidence," he'd repeated stubbornly.

"The entire universe is *just coincidence*, Hari. The existence of these particular planets around these particular stars in this particular galaxy, the appearance of life, the interplay of chance that brought you and me together here, now, having done what we've done, and become who we are: coincidence. The universe is a *structure* of coincidence."

"I thought you said the universe is a structure of *mind*."

"Yes," he'd said. "Yes, I did."

And he'd been about to go on and explain why these two statements were not contradictory, but he'd lost Hari again to a sudden scuffle between an ogrillo and two primals, and after that was settled Hari had managed to find business more important than returning to a conversation that hadn't interested him in the first place. Deliann had gone too far afield with this; it was too abstract. Hari was a nuts-and-guts man. No conversation would hold his attention that wasn't about something he could bite, or that could bite him.

Now Deliann watched the dancing game, within its shifting ring of hooting, clapping prisoners. He recognized some of what the dancers were learning from his old HTH classes at the Conservatory, and still more from Hari's own tutorials: the small movements, shifts of weight to alter the point of impact of a blow that cannot be dodged, the sliding footwork that gracefully flanks one's opponent with deceptive speed, the focus on joint destruction—especially of the elbow and knee—and the use of headlocks for more than just control. These headlocks were for throws, for cracking the skull and breaking the neck.

For killing.

Deliann saw clearly what Hari planned. He had always had good eyes. Maybe that was his only real talent: to see, and understand.

All right, time to get up, he thought. *Last chance to save the world.*

6

TOA-SYTELL HAD BEGUN to suspect that the whole world had a fever very much like his own.

From the window of his bedchamber, on the ninth floor of the west wing of the Colhari Palace, the soldiers on the walls of Old Town looked like dolls. They seemed to walk with an unnatural, artificial gait as though they were some badly shapeshifted creatures impersonating men.

Across the river, in the splay of ruins that still smoldered where Alientown had once stood, the antisprite netting that draped over the command posts was clearly designed as an arcane code: Toa-Sytell couldn't read it, but the troops down there were definitely sending some kind of signal. Something to be read by griffins, or dragons passing overhead, or some invisible spirit of the air.

Perhaps the same spirit of the air that had crept in through his nostrils while he slept, and given him this awful fever. How lucky he was to have awakened before the spirit had consumed him entirely!—though he knew the spirit still lurked about, just out of the corners of his vision, slipping into shadows behind his bedcurtains before he could quite make out its shape.

He could defeat it easily: it only had power when he slept.

So he did not sleep.

Behind him, the Eye of God droned on with his interminable report. Exactly as the Patriarch had predicted, Caine had crushed every threat against him—and had finally given Toa-Sytell the proof he required.

Far, far below, figures moved among the troop tents pitched on what once had been the streets of Alientown. One of them was Toa-M'Jest himself. That one, in the scarlet doublet. Or was he the one in the dark cape? Perhaps he was the slimmer, smaller man nearby; as the Patriarch watched, that tiny figure called others to him. They gathered in a knot and whispered together, thinking that they could conceal their treason from him with lowered voices. They didn't know how much he could hear.

He could hear *everything*.

All across the city—across the Empire—his subjects whispered against him. They all thought he didn't know. They all thought they were safe. "Arrest him."

"Your Radiance?"

"Toa-M'Jest. The Duke of Public Order. Draft a warrant. He is hereby relieved of his duties and placed under arrest."

"Your Radiance?" the officer repeated blankly. "On what charge?"

"It doesn't matter. Conspiracy with the Enemies of Humanity."

"But, but, Your Radiance—he's prosecuting the Caverns War with great success against the subs—"

"That's part of his *plan*." Toa-Sytell sighed, exasperated. How could this man have risen to his rank in the Eyes of God, when he was so thick he could not comprehend the plain truth? "He does not conspire with the elves and the dwarfs and the ogrilloi. He conspires with *Caine*."

"I, er, with Your Radiance's pardon, I find that difficult to accept," the officer said. "The Duke had Caine put in the Pit."

Toa-Sytell slicked back his thinning hair with the sweat from his palms. "That's exactly where Caine *wanted to be*, don't you understand?"

"No, Holiness. I don't."

Toa-Sytell waved an irritable hand. He could not be troubled to explain the bleedingly obvious.

The officer ventured, "I'm certain the Duke is loyal, Holiness."

Toa-Sytell turned from the window. His eyes burned, but they were so scratchy that blinking hurt. So he no longer blinked.

The Eye of God looked distinctly uncomfortable.

"Are you?" Toa-Sytell asked. "Certain?"

"I . . . I believe . . ."

"Do you?"

The Eye of God swallowed and did not answer.

"Arrest the Duke," Toa-Sytell said, and this time the officer did not argue.

"The, ah," the officer said hesitantly, "the *official* charge, Your Radiance?"

Toa-Sytell shrugged. "Cainism, I suppose."

Far, far below, the river itself seemed to writhe and boil, as though it had a fever, too.

The officer turned to leave. Toa-Sytell extended a hand. "No, wait. Not yet. We don't know yet what Toa-M'Jest is planning. Watch him. Discover his confederates. Just watch them all, and be ready. When he makes his move, *take* him."

The officer nodded, clearly relieved. "Yes, Your Radiance."

"But Caine . . ." the Patriarch said. "Caine. He is one traitor we know already. Our coddling of the Enemy of God is at an end."

His teeth showed yellow and savage, and his stare was filled with blood.

"Put him in the Shaft."

7

I DON'T EVEN see Deliann coming until he stumbles and almost goes down. One of the prisoners nearby catches him and tries to steady him on his feet, but Deliann shoves the guy off and keeps moving. "Orbek," I say quietly. "Get up close on him. He looks like he needs some help."

That's massively understated: he looks like he needs a couple weeks in a hospital with an IV-drip of broad-spectrum antibiotics. He manages to stagger along one of the walkways the boys keep clear, and he stops in front of me, swaying. "I know what you're doing," he says.

I give Orbek a look, and he nods. He pushes himself to his feet and works his way around behind Deliann, to where he might be able to catch him if the poor bastard collapses. If Deliann sees him move, he doesn't show it.

He's so shiny with sweat that his skin looks like wet porcelain, and his eyes are red-rimmed pools of bruise. His hand shakes when he goes to slick back his hair, and he says, "You're teaching them to kill Donjon guards."

"You think you could say that a little fucking louder?" I ask him. "For shit's sake, Kris."

"I've seen it before," he insists drunkenly. "You angle in under the club; you take the middle of the club on your shoulder instead of the end of the club on your head. Break his arm, because chainmail doesn't have any joint support. I've seen it. I know what you're doing."

"Kris, man, sit down." I pat the stone ledge beside me. "Come on. Sit down before you fall down."

He shakes his head. "No. No, this is hard enough. Standing up helps me think." He clenches his teeth, and makes a fist, and says tightly, "This is a mistake. What you're doing is all wrong. It's all *backward.*"

"I don't need your approval," I remind him.

"It's *wrong*—"

"My whole life has been somebody's *entertainment*," I say through my teeth. "My death won't be. Neither will theirs."

He flinches like he's too close to a fire that scorches his face. "Hari—but—"

"No. We're gonna make them *earn* it. When those bastards come for us, they are gonna get the surprise of their fucking lives."

Orbek folds his arms so that his splinted fighting claw rests in the crook of his other elbow, and I can read stolid approval in his yellow eyes. We splinted his broken claw in full extension. It must hurt like hell, but he'll be able to fight. He doesn't follow the entertainment crap, but the rest makes perfect sense to him: *May you die fighting* is how ogrilloi wish each other luck.

"No no no," Deliann insists. He squeezes his eyes shut like he's afraid they'll pop out of his head, and speaks very slowly and clearly. "You're preparing to *lose*, don't you understand? You're preparing to lose. All this?" He waves a hand over his shoulder, eyes still shut, indicating the whole Pit and my fighters and dismissing them all at the same time. "All you're doing is practicing *dying*."

"Maybe I need the practice," I tell him. "I haven't had a lot of luck with it so far."

Orbek snickers—that's his kind of line—but Deliann's concentrating too hard on what he's trying to say even to acknowledge it. "Ask t'Passe," he says. "My will or I won't: you've got the *I won't*, but you're leaving out the *my will*. Half right is all wrong, Hari."

From where I sit, I've got a clear view of the wide bronze-bound door on the balcony that seals the stairshaft down from the Courthouse. The door swings open; armored men file through from above. They carry crossbows at full cock, and they start to fan out around the balcony. They're looking at me.

I guess half right is all I'm gonna have time for.

"Should've had this talk yesterday, Kris." I meet Orbek's grim stare. "You ready for this?"

Orbek shows me his fighting claws. "Born ready, boss."

"Go get t'Passe."

He nods, and when he swings around to walk away there's a hard-rubber bounce in his step; he prickles fierce anticipation like an electric charge. Prisoners fall silent as he passes. Everybody starts by looking up at the crossbows; after that, they just look at me.

"What do you want, Hari? What do you *want*?" Kris says. "Ask for more, Hari. You don't aim high enough."

"I live a little closer to the ground, these days."

The floor detail forms up on the balcony: six full-armored guards bearing only clubs. Nobody with a bow or an edged weapon ever leaves the balcony. The floor detail guys wear plate mail, instead of the chain hauberks the rest of the guards have on. The crossbows the others carry are underpowered, designed specifically for Donjon work; their X-head quarrels won't penetrate steel.

They made this change after the last time I came through here. I and a dead girl named Talann showed these fuckers what happens when prisoners get their hands on full-powered crossbows.

Deliann weaves close and takes me by the wrist. "What if you could *live*?"

"Why would I want to?"

Orbek comes back with t'Passe. She looks as grim as I feel.

"It seems early. I thought we had more time," she says. "I could use another two or three days."

"Pretty much everybody feels that way on the steps of the gallows, huh?"

She nods.

"When I give the word, mob the floor detail. Three on one or better," I tell her. "Use your weakest guys—all they have to do is draw a flight of quarrels."

The guards overhead won't have to be shy about shooting; that's why the crossbows are underpowered. Those X-heads won't punch through armor, but they'll chop up flesh and bone like an industrial meat grinder. "That's where I need the extra days," t'Passe says. "They're just not ready. If one or two break, the rest might fold as well."

"Then pick some that won't break. You know who they are, t'Passe: the ones who don't want to live long enough to be executed."

"None of us want to live long enough to be executed, Caine."

"Yeah, no shit. Don't even think about jumping in yourself. I need you for floor marshal. Keep people organized once the shit starts flying. Keep them moving up the stairs." Crossbows take time to reload. I've never seen a guy recock and reset a fresh quarrel in under five seconds in perfect conditions; the stress of combat should at least double that time.

The stairbridge is only a gnat's ass over forty meters long.

"Orbek, you take Dinnie, Fletcher, Arken, and Gropaz—" Two of the youngest, meanest ex-Serpents, and two cheerfully savage ogrilloi. "—and hit the stairs as soon as the bowmen let loose on our mobbers. You are third up the stairs, you hear me? *Third*. Serpents in front; we can spare Dinnie and Fletcher easier than your boys. We gotta take that winch—if those stairs go back up, the party's over. You're topside marshal. Don't waste time killing the guys on the winch. Just toss 'em over the rail; we'll take care of them down here."

"Like you say, boss."

"T'Passe, we'll need another screen of mobbers right behind Gropaz; the next flight of quarrels will go toward the winch. After that, it's hand to hand."

"Hari, stop," Deliann says. "Think for a minute—*think*! You can do better than this."

Orbek answers for me, through a wide grin around his tusks. "There is nothing better than this."

The guards on the winch start cranking down the bridge. It drops in arrhythmic clanking jerks. I nod at Orbek. "Get your boys together and get close to the foot of the bridge."

"Like you say, boss." He jogs off.

"T'Passe—" Deliann begins, but the empty focus in her eyes stops him. She's ready to die.

"I'll stall as long as I can," I tell her. "Get your mobbers ready, t'Passe. We don't have much time."

She nods and starts to turn away, but she changes her mind and gives me a level look, her mouth a hard flat line. "It's an honor," she says.

I mirror her. "The honor's mine."

She actually cracks a smile, and then she's gone, moving through the prisoners, taking one and then another by the shoulder and leading them away.

Deliann turns back to me desperately and takes me by the wrist; his hand is blazing hot and slick with sweat. "Hari, you have to aim higher. You have to try for *more*. Dying is *easy*! You've said it yourself. Since when does Caine take the easy way out?"

The foot of the stairbridge is only a couple of meters from the floor, and I just don't have time for this shit. I yank my hand away from him and snarl, "Caine is just a *character*, goddammit. I *made him up*. He's *fictional*. I'm not the Blade of goddamn Tyshalle, I'm just Hari fucking Michaelson. I used to be a pretty good Actor, and now I'm a middle-aged paraplegic with a few minutes to live."

"*If,* Hari! *What if?*"

"What if what?"

"What if everyone's *right* about you? What if the stories about *you* are true? What if you *are* the Blade of Tyshalle?" Deliann asks. "What if you are the Enemy of God?"

"So? What then? You want me to just shrug and grin? Okay, I'm crippled. Okay, Shanna was butchered. Okay, I had to lie in her smoking *blood*? Okay, my father's dead, okay, Faith is gone, and o-fucking-kay, I don't fucking *care*? I'm supposed to just get *over* it?"

"No," he insists, urgently, shaking his head like he's rattled his brain loose and he's trying to roll it back into place. "No no no no no no *no*! No one gets over *anything*, don't you understand? Everything that happens in your life—*every single thing*— leaves a *scar*. A permanent scar. You're not *supposed* to get over it. To get over something—to erase the mark it left on you— erases part of *who you are*."

He leans close and grabs my arm with both hands. He's

shaking with fever; his eyes roll above a twitch in his cheek. "Scars are the key to power," he says. His breath smells of acetone and rotten fruit. "Scars are the map of beauty."

He's close enough to kiss me when he whispers: *"Each of us is the sum of our scars."*

The floor detail starts marching down the stairs.

I shake off his grip and push him back. "They're coming. You better dodge out while you still can."

"What if," he says, "it's *Hari Michaelson* who is the fictional character? What if the middle-aged paraplegic is just a role that *Caine* plays, so that he can get along on *Earth*?"

The floor detail leaves the stairbridge behind. They prod prisoners out of the way with their clubs and breast toward me. The floor detail officer has a swagger that I know too well: he's expecting a fight. He just doesn't have a fucking clue what kind of fight.

"No more talking, Kris. Dodge *out*," I snarl, and enforce my advice with a sharp shove that sends him staggering sideways to collapse on the floor. I have to shut my eyes against the hurt that cascades over his face.

When I open my eyes again, the floor detail is standing in a knot in front of me. Orbek and his boys are ten feet from the foot of the stairbridge. T'Passe stares expectantly at me from a few yards away, her signal hand motionless at chest level, waiting for my nod. The floor detail officer flips up his visor, shakes out a pair of rusty manacles, and says, "We're getting reports that you're a potential problem down here."

Oh. Oh, shit, I get it.

I understand, now.

This isn't about the Festival of the Assumption; that's still days away. This is about me. I'm a potential problem, they say, and to tell you the truth, I can't really argue with them.

Problems from the Pit go into the Shaft.

This is gonna make my life fucking complete.

I look at Deliann.

If, his wounded eyes whisper.

And all around stand people who are ready to die for me—

I hold my arms out and turn my wrists up, and sigh as the floor detail officer locks the manacles around them.

"Yeah, all right, whatever," I say. "Let's go."

8

WITH A GUARD holding each shoulder, their hands jammed hard into my armpits, they haul me up the stairbridge. I can hear my dragging toes slap each step, but I can't feel them.

The Pit watches me go, echoing with stunned silence. Nobody can believe I'm letting them take me away.

I've always been full of surprises.

Up to the balcony: I start talking while everybody can still hear me. "Keep your shit together," I tell the prisoners. The guards drag me along a catwalk, past the long, long file of men cradling crossbows. "Keep working—keep *dancing*. Stay alert. All three rules still go."

I say this generally; to address Orbek or t'Passe directly would mark them for the guards, and they'd end up chained next to me in the Shaft. "When I come back, you all need to be ready to party."

We stop in front of the Shaft door. The crack beneath it exhales madness and corruption and lunatic screams.

The detail officer picks up a lamp from the lightstand by the door and touches its wick to the standlamp's flame, and a couple of his men do the same. The officer smirks at me while he unbars the door. "You're pretty tough, huh?"

I don't bother to answer.

"Y'know what?" he goes on. "Lotsa guys are pretty tough, up here in the light."

He swings the door wide. The air that rises from the Shaft is wet and sloppy and so thick it's like the tongue of a week-dead cow jammed into my mouth. It's not just old meat and bad air down there; it's the breath of people who've gone so crazy they eat their own shit until their teeth rot.

The Shafters chained to walls on either side squirm and hide their faces against the weak light leaking in from the Pit; farther down the dark throat of the Shaft a few still have enough energy to scream. The walls are beaded with the condensation from their breath: the beads themselves are grey with the filth the Shafters exhale. The step-cut floor slopes down into infinite black, and it's wet and slick with human waste.

I remember the last time I was here. I remember the people

who had lined the Shaft as Talann and I picked our way down the treacherously slippery stairs to the sump, carrying Lamorak on my back. Most of them were too far gone even to beg. They had been reduced to objects, not even animal: mere bundles of shattered nerves and dripping gangrene, whose sole remaining function was to experience the slow shit-slickened slide into death.

Just walking by was as much as I could take—and I was younger then, and a hell of a lot tougher.

Now I don't walk anymore.

It's a good thing I don't have to go down here under my own power. I'm not sure I could make it.

As they drag me in, all I can think about are the festering burns on my legs, and what they'll look like after a few days of lying in other people's shit—but when we pass the door there's a dark notch, just about two fingers wide, on its latch edge.

I remember:

The throwing knife from between my shoulder blades will serve perfectly. I pull it out and feel for the crack of the door, slip the blade within it, and pound it home with the pommel of my fighting knife. It's just like pennying shut a door in the apartments where I grew up. It won't stop the guards when they come for us, but it'll slow them down and give us a little warning— we'll hear them pry it open.

I lift a hand over a guard's shoulder and brush that notch with my fingertips as we pass. Seven years soaking up the dank fungal exhalations of the Shaft have darkened it to the same greenish black as the rest of the wood, but that's the mark that Caine put there.

That I put there.

The detail officer scowls. "What are you grinning at, asshole?"

I turn the grin on him. "Fuck off."

He whacks me one: a looping overhand right that splits my lip, loosens a couple teeth, and shoots stars down into the black abyss before me. I keep smiling. Smiling hurts, but so what?

It always did.

"When I come back," I tell him thickly through my smash-numbed lips, "I'm gonna teach you Rule One."

He snorts. "When you come back, shit," he says. "You ain't comin' back. You're gonna die down there."

"All right." I twist my head far enough around to catch Deliann's eye, far below. I remember sitting across a table from him in the cafeteria, more than twenty-five years ago. I remember him saying *Forget whether you think it's possible. What do you want?* Like the monkey's paw, he took my answer and gave me more than I asked for.

I give him a nod: my oldest friend. Like him or not, the best friend I ever had.

"All right," I say again. "*If* I come back."

THE PART-TIME GODDESS thought she was dead. She was right.

She was dead right.

But this was a time of unquiet dead, when spirits and corpses walked the earth, separately and together. Among gods, death and rebirth is a natural cycle. When the man who had been a god called upon her spirit, he was sure she would answer.

He was dead sure.

He commanded the power of legions: at his back stood the myriad that he encompassed, and all the billions of the god of dust and ashes, and the power of the goddess herself.

Against them all stood one solitary man, and he said, "No."

With all their power, the gods could not break him. They could only hope to transform that *No* into *Yes*.

They were deadlocked.

SIXTEEN

TIME.

Long time.

Long, long, long time.

Awareness.

Awareness of a *lack*: something was not there.

Everything.

Everything was not there.

Everything with a name, everything that had a word to describe it, was not there. Not even darkness. Not even nothingness. Not even absence.

Only awareness.

At play upon the field of awareness, one random thought:

When I got there, there wasn't any "there" there.

With that thought came understanding, and with that understanding came memory, and with that memory Pallas Ril wished she had a mouth, because she really, really, really needed to scream.

But a mouth and a scream both have words to describe them, and there were none of such things.

2

OVERNIGHT, A NEW immersion game had sprung up like mushrooms, suddenly appearing on sites all over the net. Called Sim-River™, it was an extension of the classic world-building series, with a couple of original twists. At its heart, it was very straightforward: The player takes on the persona of the overseeing god of an Overworld river valley. The goal was to promote the growth of a high civilization among the tiny simulated farmers and miners that form the valley's population base. The path to that high civilization was fraught with dangers, however, from simple drought and flood cycles to natural disasters such as tornados, earthquakes, and even volcanoes; from crop disease and equipment failure up to marauding dragons and invasions by hostile elves and dwarfs. The player accessed the game through a second-hander sim helmet, the same one used to replay recorded Adventure cubes, and so the immersive experience was very intense, detailed, and realistic. None of that was particularly original, or very different from dozens, if not hundreds, of similar games.

The original twists, however, brought the game to a whole new level of popularity. One was that this game was interactive: Every person logged on worldwide played together in real time, all participating in pursuing their collective goal. The actions of the river god represented the average of their intended moves. Further, the more people who were logged on at any given time, the more powerful the god became—this was the trade-off for the reduction of individual choice in the specific moves.

Finally, the game was based on reconstructed Studio Adventure files, taken from the Adventures of a real Overworld river goddess, Pallas Ril. More than simply watching its effects, a player could *feel* the power of being a god.

It was overwhelmingly addictive. In only a few days, the hardest-core of the hard-core players had adopted a nickname: they called themselves *godheads*.

Everyone played it. Marc Vilo played it while he recovered from the implant surgery that had linked him with the electronic group-identity that was the Board of Governors. Avery Shanks would have played it, even through her Teravil-induced haze, had her Social Police guards allowed her into the Earth-normal areas of the Curioseum. Perhaps even Duncan Michaelson might have played it, save for the cyborg yoke that shorted out his higher brain functions; he now existed only as an organic switching nexus for the net lines hardwired into his brain's sensory cortex.

The creature that had been Arturo Kollberg played it, though he had no need to; it amused him to pretend to be only a peripheral part of a grand mass-consciousness, instead of its focal node. He, alone of all the players on Earth, actually understood the game's true function: to gather and concentrate the attention of billions of people at once. To make them all think about the same thing, in the same terms, at the same time—to align and synchronize the patterns of their consciousness into a single shared intention—and to feed all of that mental energy into the net, structured in a way that made it extremely convenient to use. He, alone of all the players on Earth, could feel the progress of the game without resorting to technological resources.

He had only to close his eyes.

He was not the recipient of that energy, however. The energy of concentrated attention is essentially magickal; use of magickal energy is best left to an expert. The energy was directed precisely, surgically, for a single purpose: to enhance and strengthen a tiny white pinpoint of a star upon the brow of Tan'elKoth's mental image of Faith Michaelson.

Channeling the energy through the boundary effect between Earth-normal and Overworld-normal fields had originally presented something of a problem; Tan'elKoth had to remain in the

Overworld-normal sections of the Curioseum for his personal powers of magick to function, yet to receive the energy coming to him, he must also be linked to the net.

And so, as Tan'elKoth knelt in a meditative posture beside the bed into which Faith Michaelson had been strapped, he would occasionally rub the shaved-bald patch on his skull, just behind and above his left ear, and finger the neat arc of stitching that held the flesh closed. Beneath that stitching was a thoughtmitter: proprietary Studio technology orginally designed as a data and energy link between the differing physics of Earth and Overworld.

For days he sat, motionless in concentration; he would not allow mere mortal exhaustion to limit him. The child, lacking his resources, was kept continuously medicated. A cycle of stimulants and hypnotics maintained her in a dreamlike state of semi-awareness. Periodic injections allowed her to enter REM sleep for half an hour or more—the REM state was close enough to waking consciousness for Tan'elKoth's purposes—but to allow her to fall deeper than that would risk all they had so far gained.

She never achieved real rest, but neither did he.

All would be worthwhile, if he could only touch the river's power. The irony of so extending himself to summon back the shade of Pallas Ril made him occasionally smile; but, in the end, were they not both gods? He had spoken of this to no one; he did not dare even think it too clearly. But he knew, within his heart of hearts, that once he joined with the rivergod, all would be different. There would be no more beatings, no more torture and humiliation at Kollberg's hands.

Kollberg, he told himself with a trace of contempt, *believed Pallas Ril would be trouble.*

That vile little man had no conception of what real trouble was. Once the link to the rivergod had been completed, Tan'elKoth would undertake to teach him.

3

SHE REMEMBERED THE point of Kosall ramming between her eyes, remembered the sound when the frontal bone of her skull splintered around it, remembered the brief instant of humming buzz that made her whole body burn as oblivion swallowed her.

But something had changed. Something had touched her

within the vast lack that was her death; something must have, or she wouldn't have recovered awareness. Perception filtered through her, slow and pure as springwater through limestone: She was not alone.

A body, living breath and blood and bone—a body that was hers, but not hers: hard and lean, tanned suede and knotted rope, a hand that clutched steel wrapped in sweat-damp leather, a shaven skull—

She clutched at that body, poured herself into it, howling. But this was no empty vessel; an ego held this body already, an ego with an identically fierce need to exist—a mind disciplined and directed, that struck back at her with the force of absolute terror: a rejection so utter that her grip upon the body burned her like the heart of the sun.

But she could not let go.

Even agony was welcome, after the lack.

She shrieked pain and rage, and the other shrieked pain and rage, and the battle was joined.

4

A DECKER FINALLY found him there among the cargo crates, two days downriver from Ankhana. This particular decker had been troubled ever since the barge had undocked with a peculiar, intermittent buzzing in his ears. He could hear it only when he chanced to be on watch in the quietest quiet of night; even the faintest breeze would bury the sound, to say nothing of the daylight chatter of deckers and crew, and the sonorous chanteys the poleboys used to keep themselves in step.

Finally, half through his watch in the small hours of moonless morning, the decker reached the end of his patience; he took his lamp, left his post, and began to explore. It was neither a swift nor an easy search, especially since his natural initial assumption was that the humming buzz must be coming from within one of the crates; he spent nearly an hour pressing his ear to the splintered slats of one crate after another.

Finally, his wavering lamp flame picked out the shape in its cramped tunnel, deep within the least tidy of the stacks. One look at the rigid body of the young man lying on the deck, corded tendons standing out from collar to jaw, both hands locked around the hilt of a sword—the edges of whose blade seemed to fade into a shady nonexistence—and he went right back out and woke the afterdeck second.

The afterdeck second was less cautious. He crawled in beside the young man, scowling at him. He sat, and scowled at the way the young man's back was arched, bridging above the deck. He scowled at the rictal terror locked onto the young man's face, and he scowled at the bands of white across the knuckles of the young man's hands. "Maybe I should give him a kick or something," he told the decker. "See if I can wake him up."

The decker shook his head. "What if he don't *wanna* be kicked?"

The afterdeck second's scowl darkened. "What's that friggin' noise?"

He was referring to the peculiar sizzling hum that seemed to come from the young man's vicinity, the same hum that had finally drawn the decker within. "I think," the decker answered hesitantly, "I think it's the *sword* . . ."

The afterdeck second pushed himself back, pressing against the crate behind him. It was an open secret, whom they'd carried from Harrakha down the river to Ankhana. The decker could be right. This could be the Sword of Saint Berne.

"Get a poleboy down here," he said. "Right now. Get a couple of poleboys and shift some of these crates. But *quietly*, for the love of fuck—wake the captain, and you'll be swimming to Terana."

The poleboys were ogres; a pair of them were able to swiftly and quietly enlarge the space where the young man lay. Once done, the afterdeck second instructed one of them to give the young man a poke with his pole—thirty feet of sturdy oak, as big around as a man's knee. The poleboy gave the young man a hesitant nudge on the shoulder.

The young man writhed, and the humming buzz got briefly louder and lower in pitch, and the pole was now twenty-seven and a half feet of stout oak; its terminal thirty inches rolled slowly across the deck and came to rest against the afterdeck second's feet.

The afterdeck second recalled that he had been considering giving the young man a kick, and he imagined what the rest of his life would have been like if thirty inches had come off his leg.

"Go wake the captain," he said grimly. "Tell him we gotta

send somebody back up to Ankhana, to the Monastic Embassy.
Right now."

5

IN SILENCE SO absolute that he had no memory of sound, the
Caineslayer fought for his life.

At its most basic level, this was a battle for the physical territory of his nervous system. From her beachhead in the palm of
his left hand, she scaled his nerves like leprosy: tiny incremental
snippets of death creeping beneath his skin. He fought back with
a fiercely vivid mindview image of his body, but—

He could no longer imagine his left hand.

Intellectually, he could remember details: the curve of a new
hangnail on his little finger, the arc of a scar across one knuckle,
the deep-etched battle cross in the center of his palm—but these
had become mere description, abstract and juiceless. He could
no longer put them together into the image of how his hand had
looked. His self-image ended at his wrist. The hand beyond had
become a clouded shape, mostly undefined . . . but slim and long
and clearly a woman's. Seen with physical eyes, the hand would
appear unchanged; but within, where it counted, the life of that
hand now resonated to a different mind.

She had taken his hand and made it her own.

At its broadest, most metaphysical level, this battle was symbolic. The Caineslayer had made of himself a knot: a gnarl of
memories and intentions, of love and rage, hate and fear and desire. She enclosed the knot, turning it this way and that, teasing
out its raveling ends, patiently untying him. He clenched himself
against her every touch: this knot was the pattern of his identity,
the structure of consciousness maintained by the resonance of
his nervous system. Maintained by the runes painted upon the
blade they both now held. To be untied would be to vanish into
undifferentiated Flow. It would be death.

Absolute death. Consciousness and identity extinguished.

The permanent lack.

Up and down the spectrum between these two extremes their
battle raged, and their primary weapon was the logic of pain:
*This hurts, doesn't it? How about this? Don't you know how easy
it is to stop the pain? Just let go—*

He hit her with his father's fist; she tore his belly with childbirth; he scorched her with the humiliation of Dala's scorn, when the woman who had taken his virginity had laughingly called him a child in the presence of her new man; she smothered him with the drowning grief of knowing she would always come second in her husband's heart. In sharing pain, he learned her, and she him; they became more intimate than husband and wife, or parent and child, and this intimacy made their fight more savage. They fought with the passionate frenzy of betrayed lovers.

And the Caineslayer was losing.

Sucked into the darkness—

Eaten by the *Aktir* Queen.

On one thing, the antagonists were perfectly agreed. When he felt an approach of any kind, he lashed out wildly, and she helped guide his hand. If his concentration were to break, she would eat him whole. If hers faltered, he would cast her back into the outer darkness. Only gradually did he come to realize that his eyes were squeezed shut, that the sense he used to detect intrusions was not his, but hers: some malign perception of the life that animated the meat around him, and made it men.

That was when he knew she had taken too much of him already. If he had seen one slim chance of survival, he might have clawed for it in wild panic, but he had no chance at all. He became calm. Even serene.

In that serenity, he found strength.

He would go down into the darkness, but he would go down fighting.

His own powers of mind gave him unexpected resources: just as she fought to tune his nerves to resonate with the pattern of her mind, he could tune his own mind to hers. He drove his attention into the void that had been his left hand, and he found her perception there. He felt the barge captain and the deckers and the poleboys and the wider sweep of illness and burgeoning insanity that was the city upstream; he felt the fish in the river, and he felt the weeds and algae on which they fed.

Now, he understood her. The theft of his body was not her goal, it was only a stepping-stone, a staging area. She wanted the river, and more than the river: She wanted all that the river touched and all that touched the river. She wanted the Flow of life that sluiced through him. She wanted to hold him under that river until all that they both were had been washed away.

Among the lives he could now feel, he sought one that might capture even a fringe of the *Aktir* Queen's attention: anything that might turn the edge of her scalpel mind. Far, far away— muffled yet painful, a splinter in a frostbitten finger—so distant and faint that he doubted the *Aktir* Queen could have felt it without the focused refinement of his own powers of mind, he detected a tiny wail of absolute terror.

It was a little girl, screaming for her mother.

6

DOSSAIGN OF JHANTHOGEN Bluff, Master Speaker of the Monastic Embassy in Ankhana, had set up the Artan Mirror atop its own brass-bound carrying case within a small shelter on the barge's deck. The shelter was made of crate slats and tar paper, hastily appended to the similar structure the barge crew had constructed to keep the autumn rains off the rigid form of Ambassador Raithe.

Around Raithe circled four Esoterics armed with staves; at intervals, one or more of the Esoterics extended his staff. None ever came closer than arm's length before the humming blade flashed out and sheared away the staff's tip. Raithe's eyes never opened, and his catatonia never altered, save for the instant convulsive slash that met each approach.

The deck was littered with small cylinders of fresh-cut wood. Just inside the door stood two more friars, each bearing an armload of fresh staves. Just outside the door stood another four friars, who grimly barred the shelter's entrance to the curious barge crew and the increasingly belligerent captain.

Dossaign glumly looked askance at his two lieutenants—a Keeping Brother and a Reading Brother—who responded with uncertain shrugs. Dossaign rubbed his eyes exhaustedly; the jarring bouncing coach ride from Ankhana to where the riverbarge had moored had taken more than a day and had left him exhausted and feverish. He suspected that he might be coming down with the same fever that had kept Acting Ambassador Damon in bed in the embassy, despite the Acting Ambassador's express desire to come here personally and see the situation with his own eyes.

Damon had been obsessive in his search for his Transdeian counterpart ever since Ambassador Raithe had failed to present himself at the embassy days before. He had spoken privately to Dossaign of his growing conviction that something was going hideously wrong in Ankhana, in the Empire as a whole, and that Raithe was somehow at the center of it. He had mumbled disjointedly of Caine and the Patriarch and how he felt the surreptitious gathering of enemies around the Monasteries and around himself personally, and Master Dossaign had successfully dismissed all this as fever-induced raving—right up to the point when he'd boarded the barge.

Certainly he'd never suspected the bargeman's wild story might be exactly true. Finding that unlikely truth had made him uneasily worry that some of Damon's mutterings might have more truth to them than a reasonable man would reasonably expect.

Dossaign had already Mirrored the embassy, and had been given assurance that Damon himself would be on hand to receive his next transmission.

Reluctantly now he began the cycle of breath that tuned his Shell to match the power of the griffinstone within this Mirror; a moment more, and his Shell tuned their shared energy to the specific color and shape of the Artan Mirror's Shell in the Ankhanan Embassy. His own image in the Mirror was replaced by that of a Speaking Brother from Ankhana; Dossaign greeted him formally and asked for Acting Ambassador Damon.

Damon's hair was rumpled and his brows slick with sweat; his eyes looked like scalded oysters, and he seemed unwilling to meet Dossaign's gaze squarely.

"We have made our first inspection, Master Ambassador. The circumstance is—" Dossaign shifted uncomfortably. "—exactly as the bargeman described. Ambassador Raithe is locked in some kind of rictus. He does not speak or move, except to lash out with the sword he holds when anyone attempts to approach him. Our antimagick net is useless, and now needs repair; on our attempt to net him, he cut through the net before it could enclose him."

Damon coughed harshly and wiped his mouth. "And the sword?"

Dossaign turned to the Keeping Brother. "The Acting Ambassador wishes your assessment of the sword. Take my hand and look into the Mirror."

As the Keeping Brother complied, Dossaign watched the focus of his eyes shift from seeing his own reflection to the image of Damon. The Keeping Brother twitched with an imperfectly suppressed flinch at what he saw, and spoke uncomfortably. "The Reading Brother and his assistant both agree with my provisional assessment—barring closer, uh, study of this, mmm, situation. This is most probably, almost *certainly*, the enchanted blade Kosall—now known as the Sword of Saint Berne—though there is no record of a possessive or an, er, a convulsive effect in the history of this particular blade, which is, as you might imagine, extensive. This is, in itself, a contraindication; also, the figures on the blade, which appear to be a runic or magickal script of some sort, which we have been, as you might imagine, unable to examine closely—well, Kosall is known to appear as plain steel. Other than that, however—"

"So," Damon said solidly, his voice strong and dark despite his illness. "You don't know what is happening to Brother Raithe, and you don't know what can be done to stop it, or even if such an attempt should properly be made."

"I, ah, well . . ." The Keeping Brother swallowed. "Mm, no. But—" He waved weakly toward where Raithe lay rigid upon the deck. "—Brother Raithe's, er . . . *radius of reaction* . . . continues to increase, as it has ever since we began the examination this morning. We expect his reaction-radius to stabilize at five to six feet, this being the maximum reach he can achieve with the blade, unless he somehow manages to get to his feet."

"And if he does reach his feet?"

"I, ah, well—"

Damon scowled. "You believe this to be a magickal effect?"

The Keeping Brother nodded. "Both of our available mindview-capable friars have confirmed it—although their reports present some difficulties of their own. While he clearly manifests an abnormal Shell pattern—indicating probable magickal causation—there is no discernable current in the Flow-surround; which is to say, if it is a magickal effect, we cannot say from whence the power might be coming."

Damon sighed. "There is only one solution. We must put him, sword and all, into the Secure Vault."

Dossaign understood Damon's thinking. The Secure Vault

was part of the Keeping Brother's domain within the embassy: a basement room built entirely of plated steel, with a door two feet thick. Carefully shielded against Flow, it was the storage vault for dangerous magickal artifacts. The vault itself—and its doorway—were quite large; it might be possible for Raithe to be brought into it without triggering his deadly defensive reflex. Within, Raithe would be entirely sealed off from the general Flow, and he might be able to break the hold of whatever magick gripped him now.

"But, but, but," the Keeping Brother protested, "how are we to get him to the embassy? We can't even move him off the barge!"

"First," Damon said, "we need not move him off the barge— we need only move the barge."

"The captain will be difficult, Damon," Dossaign murmured. "He is fractious already, and muttering of reparations from the Monasteries for the days he's lost. I think if he could have, he would have simply dropped Ambassador Raithe in the river and continued to Terana."

"Buy his cargo," Damon said. "Buy his damned ship, if need be. Get Raithe back here. I don't know what is happening, but I do know that Raithe is at the center of it."

"But—but, the expense—" the Keeping Brother protested.

"Ambassador Raithe is a Monastic citizen in distress," Damon said through clenched teeth. "Do as you are told."

"But," Dossaign said mildly, "assuming the Ambassador's situation is unchanged when we arrive, we still have no way to get him off the barge."

"That's not your concern. Get him here."

The connection was broken.

Dossaign sighed. "Well, then. We're on our way back to Ankhana."

7

IN THE END, it was what They were doing to the little girl that turned Hannto the Scythe against Them.

He had decided, in the vague and foggy muddle that passed for thought among the shades, that he would have melted the damned crown of Dal'kannith down for scrap metal, had he known that transforming himself into Ma'elKoth would bring him here: a ghost within his own skull, and an unwilling participant in the permanent, infinite rape of this innocent child.

Sometimes, Hannto felt as though he were part of a great sticky web of mucus—glassine slime that clung to the naked body of this little girl, dripping on her eyes, forcing itself into her mouth, her nose, her ears, every drop searching for the orifice that would let it leak into the river. At other times, it felt as though the child had been slit open through the belly, and he drew her entrails out one slow length at a time, examining every inch in turn for any hint of her link with the mind of Chambaraya. Sometimes it had been a pure and simple rape, a punishing insertion, inflicting agony to force surrender: *Let us into the river.*

Sometimes it felt as though the child had been skinned, and her living flesh draped around him like a costume, as though he might gain the river by a grotesque imposture.

Hannto was not conscious, exactly; he was a personality, but not a person, in any real sense. Like many of the shades, he was a group of interrelated experiences and memories, attitudes and habits of mind, that Tan'elKoth maintained to attend to particular tasks that might otherwise occupy too much of his attention. Hannto in particular was a specialized subroutine that Tan'elKoth used to access the art- and esthetics-related subset of his stolen memories and skills.

But he was also more than this: he was the baseline, the original, the core of the creature that had become the god Ma'elKoth. Hannto, when he could think, liked to think of himself as Ma'elKoth's soul.

Hannto the Scythe had never been a pursuer of women, or of men; lusts of the body meant little to him. He had never pursued wealth, for wealth was at best only a tool, never a goal. He was not a lover of ease and leisure, not interested in a life of endless play; he did not seek power over others.

His sole passion had been beauty.

Perhaps this had come of being saddled by the circumstance of his birth with a twisted body that inspired only pity, with a face that women compared unfavorably with horse turds; perhaps. He had never cared to analyze the roots of his obsession. It was a simple fact of his existence, like the sun and the wind and his crooked spine. He had never been able to concern himself with right and wrong, good and evil, truth and lie. Beauty was his life's sole meaning.

Not long after he had taken the enormous step from mere acquisition to true creation, he had even created a new self: he had made of himself the icon of beauty and terror that was Ma'elKoth. But even at his most terrible, there had been nothing of ugliness about him. Until now.

It was this that made what had been done to Faith Michaelson so repugnant to Hannto the Scythe. It was ugly.

Overwhelmingly, irredeemably, fatally ugly.

He could not close his eyes, for he had no eyes; he could not turn his head, for he had no head. Due to the peculiar specifics of his existence, there was no way he could avoid a savagely intimate knowledge of the endless rape of this child. Hannto found this unendurable, but he could not in any way affect it; he was only a set of traits, skills, and memories, after all. He had no will of his own. He was a personality, not a person.

All the shades resonated with loathing; poor Lamorak could do nothing but sob. Even Ma'elKoth—formerly a god, now merely the splinter personality charged with securing the link to the river—seemed to hate the whole process, but he, too, had no choice.

It had become so *crowded* in here.

Tan'elKoth's mental world was crammed to bursting with innumerable, almost insignificant lives: the faceless traces of the faceless masses of Earth, tiny bits of virtually will-free mind.

But *virtually* is not the same as *entirely*; their sheer numbers made the power of their aggregate will overwhelming. Hannto felt sure that Tan'elKoth would never have continued to brutalize this child, if not for their ceaseless pressure; but whatever scruple might still have existed within him had drowned in an ocean of people—the ocean of people that Hannto had come to call Them.

Tan'elKoth could no more resist Them than he could turn back the tide.

Every one of Them was hungry for the river, for what it represented: open space, breathing room. Wealth. Land. Clean water, clean air. Fresh food—real fruit right off the tree, real vegetables, real meat. And They didn't care how They got it.

Individually, perhaps, They might have been repulsed by the

thought of harming a child, any child—but each of Them could blame her pain on millions and billions of others as well as themselves, and so each was willing to pour himself into this little girl until their combined pressure ripped her to bloody rags.

One ten-billionth of the guilt for her terror and agony was easy enough to bear.

And so, when the tiny searing pinpoint of the link had opened upon her forehead, like a single star in a vast black sky, Hannto had discovered that one does not need eyes in order to weep. From his rage and despair, from his love of beauty, from somewhere beyond the wall between the worlds, he found an unfamiliar strength. He found, for the first time, the power to say *no*.

Privately, hugging the thought to himself, shielding it from Ma'elKoth and Lamorak and all the other shades and all the countless, countless blank-faced billions of Them, he said: *I won't.*

He was only one against the billions, but he could wait, and he could watch.

If any chance came, he could act.

8

FOR TWO DAYS, the riverbarge had toiled back upriver, pushed by chanting poleboys and pulled by the ox-teams that Master Dossaign had hired along the way. Now it was moored against the foot of the Old Town wall just upstream of Knights' Bridge.

To get the myriad necessary Imperial permissions had taken nearly a day and a half; over the last few hours, a team of Monastic engineers had hurriedly constructed the enormous swivel-mounted crane that towered above the wall's top. A double-sheaf block was lashed to the outer timber of the crane's arm, set up as a luff tackle; from the single-sheaf block at its lower end hung four chains. Each chain attached to a large wooden hook, nailed foursquare around the area on the barge's deck where Raithe still lay, still twisted in unnatural rictus, the sword still clutched in his hands.

The deck shelter had been cleared away, and now a magick-capable friar worked his way from corner to corner, slicing out the section of deck where Raithe lay with one of the embassy's prized relics: a Bladewand, recovered from the river six years before, believed to have once belonged to Pallas Ril.

Damon leaned through a crenel of the wall, the embassy's Master Keeper beside him. Damon picked obsessively at his fingertips, the skin dry, cracked, and oozing blood. He was aware of the sidelong looks from the Master Keeper, but he could not make himself care. The man was an idiot, and he'd always been against Damon—just another of the petty voices who whispered together behind his back. They both silently watched the blue-white plane of energy flicker in and out of existence from the Bladewand's focal crystal.

The stone of the merlon beside him was moist and cool with dew. Damon leaned his face against it to let it draw some of his fever. Since this morning, he had had little to drink; his throat pained him, making swallowing a chore.

The barge captain stood nearby, wringing his hands, muttering under his breath.

"An inelegant solution," the Master Keeper murmured for perhaps the hundredth time.

Damon grunted. Yes, his solution was not elegant; neither was it cheap. But it should get Raithe into the Secure Vault without any loss of life.

"I say just shoot the son of a bitch," the barge captain growled from behind them. Between the damage done to his deck and being pushed around for four damn days by a bunch of Monastics who all acted like they owned the damn world, he had swallowed about as much crap as any one man can. "A couple guys with crossbows could settle that little cock right down. Whyn'tcha just shoot him?"

"Because he is a Monastic citizen in distress," Damon said without turning, "and as such, he is by right entitled to whatever aid I can lawfully offer."

"What about *my* rights?" the captain said. "I got rights, too!"

"Do you?"

The captain looked at the back of Damon's head, then at the several heavily armed friars who stood in various postures of attention around him on the wall. Some of them stared back at him with disturbingly expressionless faces.

Damon said, "Perhaps you would care to enumerate these rights?"

The captain lowered his head and stalked away, grumbling under his breath. "Sure, fine, go ahead and serve your goddamn Human Future, who cares if you're buttfuckin' people along the way."

The friar on deck below stood and stepped back, waving the depowered Bladewand three times over his head. The men who held the ropes hauled away, and the section of deck upon which Raithe lay lifted clear, swinging gently and twisting in the late afternoon sunlight.

They'd raise him, deck and all, up over the wall and lower him on the other side, directly onto the bed of a cart that waited in the alley below, with a team already harnessed. Then a slow, careful journey across the cobbled streets of Old Town to the rear of the Monastic Embassy, where ten more friars waited near the loading dock; they would carry the section of deck on their shoulders, slowly and gently, all the way into the Secure Vault, without ever coming close enough to the stricken Raithe to place themselves in danger from the deadly blade.

This operation had garnered a large crowd of curious on-lookers, both on the docks opposite and lined up along the stone rail of Knights' Bridge. As the section of deck went higher and higher along the tall curve of the Old Town wall, spontaneous applause broke out here and there.

Damon barely heard it. He was mesmerized by Raithe's stillness—even a corpse would have relaxed from rigor long ago.

"He's been like this for *days*," Damon muttered to no one in particular. "How can he keep going? I'm exhausted just looking at him."

The Master Keeper shook his head. They had speculated end-lessly about this, and no one had a reasonable answer. "Effort like that over this length of time—over half this length of time—would kill any ordinary man. I cannot imagine what he's using for strength."

"Whatever it is, he uses it still," Damon said grimly. "He's moving again."

Perhaps it was something in the motion of the piece of deck that had roused him, something in the gentle swing and sway as it rose beside the black stone of the wall; perhaps it was the laughter and applause from the crowd. For all Damon would ever know, it might have been some arcane perception of the plan to move him into the Secure Vault.

Some things are destined to remain mysteries.

All Damon knew was that something made Raithe roll, and brought the edge of Kosall against one of the chains that supported the deck; the chain parted with the bright *schinnng* of sandpaper scraping a silver bell.

"Haul away!" Damon shouted. "*Haul,* rot your eyes!"

The section of deck swung a little farther than it had before. Two more friars leaped to the rope, yanking on it desperately to get him up and over the wall, but Raithe rolled to the next corner and Kosall sheared the next chain. The crowd yelled in alarm as the deck section swung down like the trap door of a gallows and Raithe tumbled insensibly toward the deck of the barge some sixty-odd feet below.

Damon tracked his fall with grim eyes.

When Raithe missed the deckrail by inches and hit the water with a mighty splash, the crowd cheered again. The Master Keeper waved his arms and shouted, "Divers! Divers, go!" Friars on deck started toward the rail until Damon overpowered the uproar with a shockingly loud, *"Hold your posts! That's an order!"*

The Master Keeper turned on him. "Master Ambassador, you cannot—"

"I can. It is you who can't. I am in authority here. Never presume to issue orders in my operation."

"But he might still be *alive*! He can still be saved!"

"Not by us," Damon said. He opened a hand down toward the impenetrably murky waters of the Great Chambaygen. "You would send men into that? And what will happen to those who are unlucky enough to *find* him?"

"I—I . . ." In Damon's eyes, the Master Keeper could see the reflection of severed staff ends clattering across the barge's deck, and the image struck him speechless. "I am sorry, Master Ambassador," he gasped, when he had finally recovered his voice. "I wasn't thinking."

Damon said, "Fortunate for them that I *was*," and turned away. He leaned over the retaining wall and looked down at the roiled murk of the river for any sign that Ambassador Raithe might still be alive.

Minutes passed, and the stricken Ambassador never surfaced. Damon closed his eyes.

Some time later, the Master Keeper asked in a very soft and thoroughly chastened tone, "Do you think we might try divers now? He's surely drowned, and we must recover the sword. We cannot risk that it should fall into unwary hands."

"I am not at all sure he is dead," Damon said. "He should have been dead hours ago, or days. I do not know what sustained him then; I do not know that it does not sustain him still."

"What, then, shall we do?"

"What we would have done from the beginning, had I not been so enamored of my own cleverness," he said stolidly. "We shall wait, and watch, and guard."

"Huh," the barge captain grunted from his place along the wall. "Woulda been simpler, you just shot him like I said, huh?"

"Simpler, yes," Damon agreed. He gave a heavy sigh. "You should go now. I find myself tempted to simplify the problem I have with you."

9

AT THE BOTTOM of the river, he drowned in the *Aktir* Queen.

The river itself could not harm him, for the *Aktir* Queen defended his body with her power; like a child in the womb, breath was unnecessary while the living water flowed around and through him.

He fought as stubbornly and savagely as ever, though he knew he was dying. She continued to hurt him, and he continued to hurt her back. Her endurance was illimitable and her power overwhelming—but he could himself draw upon the power that sustained her, and use it to resist.

So the murder was taking a long, long time.

A day passed, and another; through the goddess' river-born senses, he could feel the slow wheel of the sun. There may have been more days, or less; though he could sense whether day or night clothed the world above, he could no longer remember if it had done so once, or three times, or five, or a dozen.

Slice by onion-skin slice, she cut away his life.

The final turning point came when some disconnected part of his brain wondered why, exactly, he was putting himself through this. What, exactly, did he have to live for?

To watch Caine die? He had taken his revenge. He had wounded Caine as deeply as he himself had been wounded; he had proved to the world that the Enemy of God was no more than a man.

He discovered that he was no longer interested in Caine's death. Now, with the final darkness closing in around his mind, he discovered that he was no longer interested in anyone's death.

Perhaps he was the Caineslayer no longer.

Perhaps he had never been.

He remembered vividly Caine's despair, his fantasies of oblivion, visions of death seductive and sweet. He thought of how Caine had longed for the emptiness, and the end of pain. The billowing clouds of darkness that would fade until light and dark were no longer even memory—

Here, at the final link of his long and tangled chain of destiny, he found, unexpectedly, a choice.

He chose.

It's better this way, he thought, and let himself fall into the infinite lack.

10

LATE IN THE dark of autumn, under stone-grey clouds that bleached sunlight to the color of dust, new grass sprang up from the banks of the Great Chambaygen. Among that ankle-high jungle of brilliant young green, crocuses raised their faces and unfolded like warm snowflakes toward an invisible sun. Trees creaked and shivered as new leaves opened like fists that had been held closed against the approach of winter.

The hills below Khryl's Saddle echoed with the gunshot reports of bighorns clashing in rut, and birds proclaimed their territory with bursts of song; along the river's length, horses kicked and bucked, cats howled, dogs chased one another through the unseasonably warm breeze. Even slower, duller species such as humanity felt a quickening surge in the blood: the intoxicated fizz inside the head that says *It's spring*.

And so it was: all of spring in a single day.

The streets of Ankhana suddenly burgeoned with young corn twisting upward from horse turds; flagstones cracked and split into green-swarmed rubble. Oak and ash, maple and cottonwood splashed out from seeds that should have drowned within the river itself, curling branches up the outer walls of Old Town and twining the piles that supported Ankhana's bridges. Window-boxes became cascading riots of new greenery, and trellises vanished under the sudden spread of climbing vines. In moments Ankhana could have been a city abandoned to jungle decades before: a skeleton giving shape to the verdant explosion that consumed it.

This was no false spring; for, after all, spring is precisely the earth's echo of a goddess, when she shouts *I AM ALIVE*.

DARKNESS IS THE greatest teacher.

A tribe of the Quiet Land once had a rite of passage in which the aspirant was buried alive, deep beneath the earth, where no light could find him and no ear could hear his sobs and his screams. This was the final rite; after a span of days spent in such a coffin the aspirant was released, and numbered among the wise.

They did this because they knew:

Darkness is a knife that peels away the rind of what you think you know about yourself. The shades of your pretenses, the tones of your illusions, the layers of deception that glaze your life into the colors that tint your world—all mean nothing in the darkness. No one can see them, not even you.

Darkness hides everything except who you really are.

SEVENTEEN

THEY CARRY ME down the steps until they find a Shafter who doesn't move when the officer kicks her; good odds she's dead, from the bloat of her belly, but it's hard to be sure. There's so much filth caked on her skin that the lamp can't pick up post-mortem lividity. She might only be catatonic. They unlock her wrist from its wall shackle, and drag her down toward the sump at the foot of the Shaft.

The officer notices my gaze following her. He smirks.

"Yeah, I heard," he says smugly. "That's how you got out last time. That's probably how you'll go out this time, too—it's just that they got iron bars set in the stone down there now. With just about this much space between them." He shows me with one hand, like he's holding a loaf of invisible French bread. "So we got a new piece of equipment, too, right next to the sump: a sausage grinder. One of those bigass ones. We bought it off Milo, the livery guy. Big enough to take a half-ton porker. Plenty big enough for you."

Sooner than I would have liked, the gleam from the guard's lamp picks up the grinder's black-crusted shape: a stone idol, maw open for offerings. The guard shoves the woman in head-first and inches the wheel ahead a few times until the teeth engage in her hair; then he lets go of her torso and cranks for all he's worth. It's geared way down, to be used by one man, so he has to yank that wheel around a few times before the meat paste it makes of her starts to churn out its ass end and drip into the sump.

The hot billow of stench that rolls up the Shaft is actually a little comforting: at least I know she was already dead.

The detail officer unlocks my manacles and says, "Strip down," and then he whacks me one after I again suggest he should fuck off. He cuts away my shirt with a small hooked knife that might have been designed for exactly that use, and then we have a bit of low comedy while they try to strip the breeches off my useless dangling legs, until the officer slaps their hands aside and goes after my pants with the knife. If I had a sense of humor left, I'd get a chuckle out of the look on his face when he discovers another layer under the breeches: those burlap bandages of Deliann's, now dark and stiff with dried pus. He cuts those off as well, then makes one of his flunkies bundle them up and carry them. "Right-handed or left?"

This time, I don't even have to speak: the look on my face is eloquent enough to earn me another whack.

They drop me in a heap in the dead woman's muck, lock the wall shackle around my right wrist, and tramp off up the broad, shallow steps of stone, taking their lamp's paltry glow with them. The last of the light vanishes above, leaving me in the dark with the whimpers and screams and soft hoarse giggling.

And the smell.

I know this smell.

I have drowned in this before.

It's the smell of 3F in the Mission District: third floor in the back, farthest from the stairwell, two rooms and one walk-in closet barely big enough for an eight-year-old boy to have a cot.

It's the smell of the chemical toilet inside Rover's seat.

It's Dad's smell.

The slow shit-slickened slide—

I have been eaten by my nightmare.

The mouth of Hell has yawned beneath my feet, and I will fall forever.

2

I SEE THE darkness of the hours and days before me, identical to whatever hours and days behind: no light to define the world, no silence. Eternal night with staring eyes, straining against the shimmering dark. Sometimes people talk to me, and sometimes I answer.

Not people. Shafters. We're none of us people anymore. The next guy upslope has dysentery, and every time he lets go more acid shit he starts to cry. He keeps telling me how sorry he is.

I tell him we're all sorry.

I don't tell anyone who I am. Who I was.

I mean, how can I?

How do I know?

No sleep. No sleep ever again: the screaming never stops. They will scream until their anguish erodes the last of my sanity. That's what I tell myself, but I know I do sleep . . .

Because every once in a while, I awaken from a memory of light.

I awaken from the touch of my daughter's hand, from the scent of my wife's skin. I awaken to the endless night and stench and screams. Sometimes beside me there is a wooden trencher with broth-soaked bread or a bit of cheese, that I can find by touch over the stone. I eat with shit-caked hand.

Once or twice I'm awake when the trusty slouches down the stairs with his lamp in hand: he's some kind of wetbrain, mismatched drooping eyes and a line of drool trailing from slackly open lips. He looks at us, but I cannot imagine what his semi-functional brain makes of what he sees.

Here in the Shaft, I might slip from life to death seamlessly, never realizing that I have passed; how should death be different? The funny thing is, I'm pretty much okay with this. *More* than okay.

This is no demon-drained numbness. This isn't even a grip-jawed *I can handle it*. It's a feeling warm and chill, a tingling of skin and sweet taste on the tongue, an expansion of heart within my chest so alien to me that some hours or days or years pass before I can really figure out what it is.

It's happiness, I guess.

I can't remember the last time I felt this good.

I am, right now—lying naked in the pool of a dead woman's shit, chained to stone, gangrene eating my rotten-meat legs—as happy as I have ever been.

Maybe it's the smell.

3

Now THAT THE stench of the Shaft—of my life—lives inside my nose and my mouth, now that it's soaked in through my pores and oozed around my cortical folds, I don't really mind it.

It reminds me . . .

I can't draw the memory all at once. I tease it out, bit by bit. After a day or a month, I have it all together. I remember what the smell reminds me of.

It reminds me of the day I came home walking funny.

This is the smell of 3F that day when I slunk through the door, maybe thirteen years old, with a severely bruised rectum and a storm-surge of tears gathering behind my eyes.

Dad was having one of his better days, and he was trying to clean out the room off the kitchen where he slept. He'd been in one of his paranoid delusional phases for a while, saving his shit in plastic bags because he was afraid his "enemies" had been trapping the hall toilet we shared with 3A, B, C, D, E, and G. He thought these imaginary bad guys could separate out his stools and use some kind of whackass SF machine to analyze them until they could tell what he'd been thinking; he was convinced they would steal the ideas of some book he was secretly writing.

That day he was pretty lucid: he'd been trucking the bags down to the storm drain in the alley below the aluminum sill of my window. I guess even his imaginary bad guys would have a hard time figuring out which shit was his, once it was down in the sewer.

Anyway, one of the bags had ripped open and slopped across the kitchen floor, and when I came in he was trying, in his dizzy, blurred, ineffectual way, to scoop up the turds with a dustpan and pour them into another bag. All I wanted that day was to make it to my little closet and curl up on my cot and forget how scared I was for a while, but somehow I'm never that lucky.

Or maybe I'm always luckier than that.

After a few years, it gets hard to tell the difference.

Dad grabbed me when I tried to hustle past and told me I had to help him clean this up. I remember vividly the pain of trying to get down on my hands and knees, and even as crazy as Dad was, my screwed-shut face and old-man moves woke something inside him. He put his arms around me and held me to his chest and asked me what had happened in a real calm, gentle voice like he really cared about the answer, and I burst into tears.

There was this kid named Foley. Toothpick Foley. Big kid, maybe sixteen or seventeen, twice my size. He was a courier for a black-market chit trader named Jurzscak, which made him kind of a big deal on my block. Foley always had a couple of guys hanging around him, trying to pick up the odd food or booze chit by gophering and general stooging.

I thought, in those days, that Foley had a pretty good line of work; I'd been supporting Dad and myself as a burglar, being small and agile and not overly concerned with the niceties of personal property, but it doesn't take too many close calls with big mean drunk Laborers coming through the front door while you go out the back window to make a guy think that there's gotta be an easier way to make a living.

So I went to work for Jurzscak. My whole life, nobody ever called me lazy; I hustled my ass off for that guy, and he was starting to toss some of the perks and goodies my way that used to go toward Toothpick, and Toothpick took exception to this.

He and a couple of his boys cornered me in an alley and got me down on the pavement.

I don't remember Foley's first name. Everybody called him Toothpick—I think it was for his skinny little needledick, but I never knew for sure. When he realized he was never gonna be able to shake the name, he'd decided to attach it to something else: he started carrying around this bigass sheath knife, with a blade something like nine or ten inches long, and started calling *it* his toothpick.

That's what he tried to jam up my ass.

He didn't bother to take down my pants; this was just a warning. While his boys held me down, he took the point of the sheathed blade and stuck it against my asshole and just *leaned* on it. It's a pain that does not bear describing.

He told me in very clear words of one syllable that I should get my ass off Jurzscak's team, or next time he sees me, he sticks it in up to the hilt.

No sheath.

I don't think I ever did manage to explain it to Dad. I couldn't get the whole story out between my sobs, and anyway there were no words for how scared I was. The whole long limping walk home, I couldn't think about anything but the ice-slide of razor-sharp steel up my butt, slicing through me from the inside out—

I've never been so afraid of anything in my life, before or since.

Dad just held me, and rocked me in his crazy stinking shit-smeared arms until I was almost calm again. Then he asked me what I was going to do about it. I told him I was going to quit. What else could I do? I had to quit, because if I didn't, Toothpick would kill me. What Dad said then changed my life.

He said, "He might kill you anyway."

I thought about that for a while, until I started to shake all over again. I had just barely enough control of my voice to ask Dad what I should do.

"Do what you need to do, Hari," he said. "Do what will let you look in the mirror and like what you see. This boy might kill you. He might not. A building might have fallen on him on his way home tonight. Tomorrow, you might get caught in a crossfire, and then you'll never have to worry about Toothpick again. You can't control the future, Killer. All you can control is what *you* do, and the only thing that's important is that you feel good about it. Life's hard enough without going through it ashamed of yourself. Do something you can be proud of, and let the rest go."

The words of a madman.

But he was my father, and I believed him.

The next day I reported in to Jurzscak as usual. It was the

hardest thing I've ever done. And instead of hustling straight out, I hung around for a few minutes until Toothpick showed up.

I'll never forget the look on his face.

He stared at me, blank as the moon. He couldn't comprehend what he was seeing. He was four years older than me, he outweighed me by a hundred pounds, and he'd seen that unmistakable stark terror on my face just the day before. He couldn't bend his mind around a reality in which I wasn't running away from him.

While he stood there trying to figure out what the hell was going on, I pulled two and a half feet of copper pipe out of my pants and played teeball with his kneecap.

He went down screaming; Jurzscak popped up yelling; Jurzscak's boys all jumped at me; I was spinning and swinging my pipe and howling that if anybody wanted some of this, they should step up to the plate. Toothpick managed to get his blade out and lunged at me off his good leg. I let him have another stroke right on the top of his head and he went down hard, writhing and moaning, blood going all over the damn place, and Jurzscak finally managed to get the pipe out of my hand and he hit me in the belly with it hard enough to fold me over gagging.

"Michaelson, you crazy little *fuck*," he said breathlessly, "what in the name of crap is going through that shithouse rat you use for a brain?"

When I got half my own breath back, I told him. "Toothpick said the next time he saw me he'd jam his blade up my butt," I said. "I believed him."

So Jurzscak had a talk with Toothpick, which ended up with Toothpick's shattered kneecap bearing the weight of Jurzscak's shoe and Toothpick finally mumbling out the truth through tears as bitter as mine had been the day before. "But it was just a *joke*," he sobbed. "We was just kidding *around*."

"You were?" I said, thinking *Ask my asshole how funny it was*. "Hey, me, too. Just kidding, Toothpick. No hard fucking feelings, huh?"

Then Jurzscak turned on me, weighing that pipe with his hand. "I won't say you didn't have reason," he told me a little sadly, apologizing in advance for the stomping he was about to inflict, "but that don't mean I can let it go, either. You know the rules, Michaelson: Two of my boys have a problem, they bring it to me."

Nothing Jurzscak could do scared me half as much as what I'd faced to walk in there that day. So I looked him in the eye and said, "Isn't that what I just did?"

He thought about that for a little while; then he nodded. "I guess you coulda snuck him, you wanted. But why the pipe, kid? Why not just *tell* me?"

"My word against his?" I asked. "You would have believed me?"

He didn't answer, but then he didn't have to.

"The pipe," I told him, "was to let you know I was serious."

I worked for Jurzscak for most of the next year, until he pissed off the wrong guy and Soapy broke up his gang and put him under the yoke. Toothpick was, as they say, a dead issue: In the Mission District Labor Clinic—the same one where my mother died—the meditech got so interested trying to reconstruct Toothpick's knee that she missed the slow hemorrhage inside his skull, and Toothpick shuffled off this mortal coil about three the next morning.

Toothpick Foley was the first guy I ever killed. Didn't even mean to; it just happened that way. I knocked him on the head, and a few hours later he died. Like the Cainists say, you can't un-ring the bell. Not that I'd want to.

Christ, I was strong in those days.

What the hell happened to me?

4

THAT STATUE STAYS in my head: that *David*. The more I think about it, the more it makes a creepy kind of sense. David was, after all, the Beloved of God, who fell from grace—

Over a woman.

It's not exactly a secret that Tan'elKoth's always had a little thing for me.

Not sexual—I'm pretty sure that sex was one of those things, like eating and sleep, that he gave up to become Ma'elKoth. But I know he is capable of love; he loved Berne. And he hinted to me, all those years ago, that he'd turned to Berne because he couldn't find me. He hinted that I'd been his first choice, all along. And, Jesus, the way Shanna felt about him, you could say she was jealous. And he despised her; he never even tried to pre-tend he didn't.

Is that what built this whole pile of shit? A goddamn *love* triangle?

It makes a certain amount of sense.

Even in *For Love of Pallas Ril*, you can see it: He was trying to get me to choose him over her—over anyone. And on Earth he moved into that Other Woman position in our lives—

Now that I think about it, he could be behind the whole goddamn thing. The way Garrette was reading off those cards—that stuff sounded like it might have come right out of Tan'elKoth's mouth. He could have done it all out of jealousy and revenge. It hangs together.

But, you know what?

All these stories—the stories that I tell myself, to try and understand why what happened happened; the stories that are all I have of my life—

They *all* hang together.

The longer I think about it, the more different ways I can tell it. It's like what Raithe was talking about: He had found a way to trace everything in his life, good or bad, back to Caine. He could just as easily have turned it sideways, and traced everything back to Ma'elKoth, or to Pallas Ril, or to the goddamn weather twenty-seven years ago Sunday.

Sure, this could have happened because the big bastard was in love with me. I can also swing the same facts around and make it all happen because I wanted to play at being Caine. I can make it all happen because Raithe wanted revenge for his parents. I can make it all happen because a pack of damn fools decided that Caine was really the Devil, or because Kris Hansen wanted to turn himself into a goddamn elf.

Shit, I can make it all happen because Toothpick Foley bruised my butthole.

Like that statue: It's an insult. It's a piece of advice. It's a love letter. What it means is a function of who I am when I look at it.

What anything means depends on how you tell the story.

5

JESUS, I REMEMBER—

I remember crouching in the supply closet inside the Language Arts shitter, waiting for Kris' setup to draw in Ballinger. I remember how dark it was—just a single line of white light under the door from the shitter's fluorescents—and the smell, the opposite smell from the Shaft: harsh chemical tang of cleaning solvents leaching from the ruck of mops and brooms and the rag-draped bucket. I remember having to keep still, so I wouldn't knock anything over or kick something and give the game away; we couldn't clear a space for me in there, because open floor inside that crowded supply closet might look suspicious to an investigator. I remember how hard it was to breathe in there with the smothering walls close around my face, and how I started doing long slow-motion kneebends to keep my legs from cramping up.

I remember the prickly ball of needles that rolled over my whole body when I heard Ballinger's voice, and the hot drop of my stomach when I realized he'd brought backup.

I remember thinking, *So: there's four of them. All right.* Four Combat cavemen against a pair of Shitschool pussies; we were probably both gonna die, and who cares? Nothing they could do to me would be as bad as Toothpick's knife going into my asshole. And I knew that if I stayed in that closet and listened to Kris die, I could never look myself in the mirror and like what I saw.

If I ever get a chance, I should tell him the story of how my father and Toothpick Foley saved his life. Shit. I wish I could tell Dad that story, too.

If any of that other shit hadn't happened to me—if my father hadn't gone crazy, if my mother hadn't died and left me running wild on the District streets, if Dad hadn't beat the snot out of me every other day, if Toothpick hadn't gone for me, basically my whole fucked-up life—I would have stayed in there. All the bad shit that ever happened to me had made me into a nineteen-year-old kid who could jump out against four guys without even thinking about it.

And I *knew* it. In those days, I knew it. I even said it to Kris once: *I had a great childhood.* That's what Kris was talking about—that's *exactly* what Kris was talking about. Scars are the key to power.

Each of us is the sum of our scars.

Because if any of it had been any different, I never would have gotten the chance to be Caine.

Kris had it right. I should have taken my own goddamn advice.

I never wanted to be a fucking Actor, not really. All I ever wanted to be was Caine.

How's this for irony: I can see now that Caine is who I already was.

That scene with Jurzscak and Toothpick Foley? Caine, right down to the dialogue. At the Conservatory, Kris could see it already. *"When you think about hurting people, when you really let your passion run, you want to do it by hand."*

He understood me better than I did.

He probably still does.

I mean, is that fucker ever wrong about *anything*?

"No, no, no. You ended up here because you were trying to not *be Caine.*

"What if it's Hari Michaelson who is the fictional character? What if the middle-aged paraplegic is just a role that Caine *plays, so that he can get along on* Earth?*"*

6

Damn.

God damn.

That Kris, he is one scary son of a bitch.

Because when I think about it that way, I can see it perfectly. I can see the exact moment when Hari Michaelson was born.

I was just out of my freemod debriefing: two weeks of interrogation by Studio brainsuckers going over everything that had happened to me over my almost three years of freemod training at Garthan Hold abbey and elsewhere. I wasn't the first Actor to study with the Monasteries, but I was the first to be sworn to Brotherhood. They made me an Esoteric even though I sucked at mindview. I didn't need magick to be good at stealing stuff and hurting people.

So the Studio decided they wanted me to rise within the Monasteries for a while. They wanted to feature me as an assassin. I wasn't into this shit at all; I've never been good at taking orders. I wanted to do straight Adventures, explore, see strange creatures, and hunt for treasure and all that kind of crap. I was even thinking about maybe going pirate—y'know, the high seas and shiver me timbers and island girls and shit. But the Studio wanted an assassin.

I was more than half ready to tell them to fuck off. Assassins are *boring*. I'd known a couple of contractors when I was little, and met a few more while I worked for Vilo. It's plodding, methodical work. Real killers are not stylish, or dashing, or even imaginative. They're more like accountants with guns. If you do your job right, there's no drama in it at all. Who wants that kind of life?

They and Vilo had a lot of money invested in me, and I figured that gave me enough leverage to get what I wanted. Then Vilo took me for a ride in his Rolls and explained how the world works.

He started off trying to placate me. The Studio didn't want me to be a real assassin, he tells me. They wanted me to be a Hollywood-style assassin: kind of a high-fantasy James Bond. *Sure, they say that now,* I'm thinking, *but five years down the road, when my audience numbers suck wind from all the Monastic scutwork I'm doing, they won't be talking to me about James Bond anymore. They won't be talking to me at all.*

Being generally full of piss in those days, I wasn't gonna do it. Let them shitcan me; who cares? Contract violation would get me busted back to Labor, but that didn't scare me at all. Shit, with the skills I'd learned between the Conservatory and the Garthan Hold abbey, I could drop right back into the District and make a solid living as freelance muscle, maybe end up a neighborhood boss and not have to kiss any Studio ass in the first place.

Vilo, though, didn't get to be the Happy Billionaire by being stupid. He had me tagged and bagged before I even knew I was hurt. The Rolls touched down in a nice, quiet Labor neighborhood, mostly twencen sixflats and courtyard buildings—light-years better than a Temp ghetto like the District—and took me to Dad's apartment.

I hadn't seen Dad in six years, since I blew the District when I was sixteen to go work for Vilo. The last time we'd been in a room together, it was a roach-infested shithole, garbage six inches deep covering the floors, one whole room converted into Dad's personal septic tank and the damn place only had three rooms to begin with. The last time we'd been in a room together, he'd tried to open my skull with a pipe wrench.

Where he lived now was a pristine one bedroom, with cream

walls and honest-to-Christ wooden molding around the doors and windows. Curtains. Furniture. A dining-room table. A refrigerator with real food in it, a kitchen sanitary as a surgical theater. A bathroom—his own private toilet, right inside the apartment, and even a stall that would measure out ten minutes of hot shower every day.

And Dad.

Dad: shaved and dressed in clothes that were clean and whole, if not actually new. With hair gone entirely grey and cut close to his scalp, and the light of reason in his eyes. Dad: who could shake my hand and tell me he hoped we could get to know each other again, now that he was sane. Who could put his arms around me and smell like a man, instead of a slaughterhouse.

I don't even remember what we talked about that day; I was lost in marveling at this man who was simultaneously so Dad and so alien. He almost made me feel like I was five years old again, like he was normal and Mom might just walk into the room and give me a hug.

After we left, Vilo took off his velvet glove.

Vilo, y'see, took real good care of his undercastes. He was famous for it. He'd started looking after my father only a few months after I went to work for him. Turned out that Dad's condition wasn't curable, but it was treatable; with the right combination of drugs and therapy, he was able to hold down a steady job as a net research assistant—could pay for that apartment and even get a decent meal at a diner every once in a while.

Vilo explained to me that Dad's employment was contingent upon mine. If I screwed him on my contract, he'd cut Dad loose. It wouldn't take a week for Dad to be back in 3F, or worse.

So I swallowed my piss and did what I was told. It was the only way I could keep that smell out of my head.

That's who Hari Michaelson is, I guess: he's the guy who will do anything to stay out of 3F.

No, Hari's more than that. He's the good guy, I think.

He's the guy who thinks that if he does what he's told, the people he loves will all be okay. He's that profoundly unhappy man who sits at his desk at 3 A.M., head full of bitter smoke from the ashes of his heart. He's the guy that Shanna wanted me to be.

He's the model for *David the King*.

Funny: Shanna fell in love with Caine, but she couldn't live

with him. She could live with Hari. Did she love him? I really
can't remember.

If only I could ask her.

7

ALL THE DAMAGE we did each other—

Christ, I remember the first time I saw her: at the table in that
conference room at Studio Center. I had just come off back-to-
back megahits, *Retreat from the Boedecken* and *Last Stand at
Ceraeno*; and I had just been approached by Hannto the Scythe
to locate and recover Dal-kannith's crown. Kollberg had decided
to put together a serial Adventure, a multiparter featuring an entire team of Actors with me playing lead. There were six of us,
and Kollberg had even set up a romance for me—he was always
on my back to put more sex into my Adventures. I was supposed
to spend my idle hours dallying with Olga Bergman, a big gor-
geous Nordic blonde who played a Khryllian knight named Ma-
rade. Olga was a good kid, a rising star with a booming laugh
and a spectacular Ms. Olympia physique, and she was more than
willing to play along.

But Shanna was sitting at the end of that table.

She was shy for an Actor, at least in those days. Reserved. Intense. A little spooky.

Luminous.

They all knew me, of course; I was the hottest property in the
whole Studio System. They'd all rented *Last Stand*, and every
one of them had to tell me how great they thought it was. Standard showbiz stroke-up. All through the whole meet-and-greet,
they were laughing and joking and asking each other which was
their favorite part. All but Shanna. She never said a word.

When Kollberg himself finally pushed her on it, she said quietly, "My favorite part isn't on the cube."

She blushed, and dropped her eyes like she was embarrassed.
Kollberg didn't let up. Finally, she revealed her shameful secret:
"My favorite part is thinking about all the people in Ankhana who
get to go to bed at night, who get to get up in the morning, who get
to kiss each other and hug their children. All the people who will
never know what you did to save their lives."

"Ah, grow up," I told her. "I didn't do it for them. I did it for audience share."

She shrugged. "They'll never know *that*, either," she said, and gave me that incendiary little half smile of hers that made my chest go tight and my heart stutter, and I was pretty well done for.

The shitty thing is, we never had a chance. If we'd lived together for a hundred years, she never could have comprehended 3F. I look back on my life with her, and I cannot believe I didn't understand what was happening to me.

I wanted a world where there is no such thing as 3F—where it belonged to the frozen past, entombed in millennial dust, never to rise again. I wanted my world forever purged of that smell.

So I built my own 3F and called it the Abbey, and locked myself in, and tried to pretend I was happy about it. Shit, the Abbey was worse. My old room was something I could run from. I could fight the smell.

The Abbey had me fighting to *stay* there.

Now that I'm down here, now that 3F is my whole reality in the bottomless stench of the Shaft, I'm so much happier it makes me want to laugh out loud. I can't remember the last time I was this happy.

No, wait: Yes, I can.

I remember—

8

A few of the costumed mock revelers see me now, and still themselves, hands drifting toward folds of clothing for the weapons concealed there.

I keep walking toward them, slowly, offering a friendly grin.

The golden sand of the arena crunches as it shifts slightly under my boot heels. The sun is hot, and it strikes a reddish glow onto the upper reaches of my vision, where it glistens in my eyebrows.

All my doubts, all my questions fly away like doves in a conjurer's trick. Adrenaline sings in my veins, a melody as familiar and comforting as a lullaby. The thunder of blood in my ears buries all sound except for the slow, measured crunchch ... crunchch *of my footsteps.*

Toa-Sytell sees me now; his pale eyes widen and his mouth

works. He tugs upon Ma'elKoth's arm, and the Emperor's head swivels toward me with the slow-motion menace of the turret of a tank—

That was the last time I was truly, utterly, completely happy: seven years ago, on the sand at Victory Stadium.

Happy. For the same reason I'm happy now.

I knew I would die there.

It's not death that cheers me, though; it's not death that draws a stinging smile from my battered mouth. It's that I get to die on Overworld. It's that *I don't have to go home.*

I'll never have to go home again.

Shit, y'know what?

I even kinda *like* the smell.

It smells like running the streets on a San Francisco summer night; it smells like stickball and fistfights, like rolling ragfaces for loose change and dodging down blind alleys to skip over a fence one step ahead of the cops.

That's why I'm happy.

Oh, Shanna . . .

If only—

That's one bell I wish I could unring.

I wish I could have gotten to this while Shanna was still alive. I wish I could have shared it with her. She might not have understood—shit, I *know* she wouldn't have understood—but I'd like to think she would have been glad to see me happy.

I'm gonna die a free man. Is anything better than that?

I'm free.

9

I THINK OF Kris, and his stuff about names. I think I understand a little better what he meant. Dad once told me that I am more than Caine, and he was right. But he didn't understand that I am more than Hari Michaelson, as well. Hari was a good guy. He loved his wife, loved his daughter, loved his father and this world. He was in over his head, that's all. This wasn't his fault. He didn't have a talent for it.

He never really had a chance.

I never gave him one.

The corner of the manacle around my right wrist makes an

imperfect tool, and I have no light by which to work. On the other hand, I have nothing but time. The wall of the Shaft is that same porous limestone, much softer than the iron that binds me to it. I work slowly, and do a good job, even though I'm working entirely by feel.

Once in a while the trusty comes by with the soaked bread that passes for dinner, and by the dim flicker from his lamp's flame I can see my handiwork grow.

It reads simply:

HARI MICHAELSON

And a pair of dates.
The first is the day Vilo took me to see my father.
The second is my best guess at today's.
He deserves an epitaph, but I don't scratch one in the stone.
I am his epitaph.

10

THE WORLD WANTS to call me Caine. But that does not encompass me. I must remember that Caine is the name for only part of what I am. Someday, that name will grow to name me more truly. Right now, it names all of me that I need. Caine is an Actor. An actor.

One who acts.

I need something to work on. Something to try to *do*.

To be shackled here in the Shaft, dying—it's a gift: I don't have to waste time trying to make up my mind. There is only one thing I can even try.

Kris said that black Flow comes through even this Donjon stone. That it comes through everyone; that we draw it and direct it without even knowing what we do. That it is energy in its most fundamental form. Energy is energy, he said. No reason why Flow can't go through wires and microcircuits, I guess. It only needs to be properly tuned.

Calling upon skills buried for a quarter of a century, I curl both of my hands into the Three Finger mudra and begin to cycle my breathing in that ancient, ancient rhythm. Mindview won't come right away, but Caine can find it. Years and years ago, he was trained for it. I was trained for it.

I will find it.

That middle-aged paraplegic was just a part I played, so I could get along on Earth. I don't need him anymore.

I will move my fucking legs.

THE PART-TIME GODDESS passed into the lands of the dead, and there she strove with monsters. She brought with her the dark angel's spawn, and the man who had been a god. They fought sometimes beside her, and sometimes against her, for in that land of shadow and illusion one cannot always distinguish friend from foe.

In the lands of the dead, there is only one certainty. It is the certainty of self. This is why tales and legends people those lands with monsters.

It has been written that when one contends with monsters, one risks becoming a monster. This is not true.

The true risk is that one might discover the monster one has always been.

EIGHTEEN

ANKHANA EMBRACED DAMON of Jhanthogen Bluff with a jungle of dreams.

An oak shouldered him aside as it lashed upward from a crack in the flagstone dockside, shoving him stumbling into a head-high corn patch; the stalks crackled and burgeoned with young ears that grew from fingerlings to the size of his hand while he stood and watched with open-mouthed awe. Pumpkin and watermelon vines snaked along the stone and coiled around his

ankles. Intertangled apple and peach and willow leaped from
the Chambaygen so fast that the reeds festooning their upper
branches dripped chill river water onto Damon's feverish brow.
Barges and boats and floating piers were shoved and twisted and
overturned.

In minutes the river had become a marsh, and the great wall of
Old Town had become a vertical forest of leaves and brilliant
blossoms.

I have done this, Damon thought.

The buzzing in his veins—a strange fizzy bubbling up and
down his neck that swirled into his head and out again—had
started as a tiny hiss, but had boiled and burst since the green
had come to devour the city. He walked in a dream, and knew it
was a dream; this could not happen, except in a dream.

The friars Damon had detailed to patrol the dockside and
watch for any sign of Master Raithe and the Sword of Saint
Berne were all Esoterics: veterans, experts in covert operations
skills ranging from hand-to-hand combat to demolitions to
magickal counterespionage. At the first creak and rustle of the
foliage that sprang to life around them, they had scattered and
taken cover like the professionals they were.

He was alone.

Damon couldn't see them anywhere within the riot of waving,
weaving green, and he wasn't sure he wanted to. He wasn't sure
of anything. *I've been sick,* he thought. *I've had a fever.*

I must still have a fever; this must be a fever dream.

He'd been at the dockside for days, he guessed. He couldn't
bear to be away. He'd posted his guards and watchmen, but he
couldn't trust them to watch and guard, not really; whenever he
left the riverside he was tormented by visions of Raithe slipping
away, sneaking, escaping—

And Raithe, he knew, was at the core of what was happening
to Ankhana; let him go, and all hope of answers would be lost
with him. So Damon always came back, to pace and brood and
contemplate the river, because the only man in Ankhana he
could still trust was himself.

Because this is my *dream.*

His stomach had been troubling him, and now in the green
storm his guts twisted, and he retched: a brown-traced milky
fluid spilled from his lips. How long had it been since he'd last
eaten?

What had he last eaten?

The streaks of brown in his vomitus looked like blood.

He wiped his mouth with the back of his hand, and its touch stung him sharply. His lips had cracked and split and smeared his hand with fresher blood. He was thirsty, dreadfully thirsty . . . He knelt and cupped river water to his mouth, but his tongue turned the cool water to nails and broken glass. He could feel it tearing open his throat, shredding him inside—

Maybe what I need isn't water.

He looked back at the pool of his vomit, at the swirls of brown; he looked down at the smear of red across the back of his hand. *Blood,* he thought.

Blood.

He would have to hunt.

A flash of furtive motion caught his eye. He rose to a stalking crouch, parting reeds with his hands, then slipped forward through the stand of corn. There it was again—was it again? Was it the first time? Had he seen this before, or was he remembering an older dream?

The flash of a boot heel, as it vanished behind the trunk of an ash; a startled glimpse of a woman's face, eyes wide and staring for one brief second until screened by rustling corn, the smell of unwashed crotch and armpit, the mouthwatering earthmetal savor of blood—

His dreaming jungle was full of people.

Slowly, his jungle came to life in his ears. Grunts and growls, screeches and screams, all manner of bellows and howls and shrieks echoed near and far: calls not of beasts, but of men. Calls of the beasts that men had always been.

He followed a crackle of motion and was brought up short by a yell that was chopped to a thin moan. Thrashing a clearing in the reeds was a tangle of human flesh: a man and a woman and a knife struggled together near the river, and Damon couldn't make his eyes interpret who was doing what to whom. He could see only limbs, and metal, and blood.

Blood—

The blood pulled him forward, and he followed, thirsting. This was only a dream, after all.

He entered the reeds, and something struck him from behind.

Overborne, crushed to the ground, he tasted the viny resin of the broken reeds that jabbed his face, while what might have been a knee dug painfully into his back and frantic hands scrabbled at his clothing. He lay unresisting, abstractly wondering how this happenstance figured into his dream, until dully ripping teeth latched into the joining of his neck and shoulder and gnawed at his flesh. The pain—real pain, too-real pain—woke him from his daze. *This is no dream of mine.*

Damon reached back and gripped with one hand the head of the man who chewed on him, while his other hand sought the man's eyes with stiffened fingers. The fellow grunted into Damon's trapezius, and his fists flailed ineffectually. Damon's fingers drove slowly deeper into his eyes, and the man stopped punching and started trying only to get away, thrashing and pushing and moaning. Damon let him go, and heard a grunt of impact and a wet gurgle; before he could roll over and sit up, one of his Esoterics had tackled the man, pinned him, and cut his throat.

"Master Damon!" the Esoteric gasped, springing to Damon's side with his bloody knife still in hand. "Master Ambassador, I'm sorry—I couldn't get to you—all this—" He waved his bloody knife at the riot of green around them.

Damon couldn't take his eyes off the knife: rivulets of red trickled from the blade along the friar's wrist. It looked so warm, so . . . *satisfying*—

He had to remind himself that this was not merely a dream. He still had duties here. "I'm hurt," he said distantly. He took his hand away from the bite wound on his shoulder, and more blood spilled down his robe. "This must be washed, and bandaged."

The young friar gasped, reaching for Damon's shoulder to examine the wound, but Damon pulled away. "Your knife," he said, averting his face.

"Master?"

"Clean your weapon, Brother," Damon said thickly. "First, clean your weapon. Always."

The friar flushed. "I, I, I'm sorry, Master—" he stammered. "It's just—" His defeated wave took in the jungle around them, the towering cliffside forest of the wall, the throat-cut corpse two steps away, the man who lay on the riverbank with a knife handle sticking out from his eye socket, the bloody trail of broken reeds that led to where a woman lay pumping out the last of her life a few yards away. "—everything's so *crazy* . . . What's happening—it's driven everyone mad."

"What's happening has driven no one mad." Damon pushed himself exhaustedly to his feet, and the fizzy buzz in his head got louder and louder. "It's merely given us permission."

"It's like a dream," the young friar said helplessly.

"Yes," Damon said. "But not my dream. Or yours." The buzz in his head fizzed louder still, bubbling in his arteries, gurgling through his heart.

"Yes, that's it," the younger man murmured. "That's exactly it. We're not even real. We're trapped in someone else's dream."

"Get up. Gather the others. We still have duty, here."

"Duty? What duty can we have in a dream?"

"This is a dream. It is also real. It is the dream of a god, and the gods dream reality."

The buzz became a growl, then rose to a grinding whine.

"What god?" The young friar grimaced disbelief. "What god would dream this—this *insanity*?"

For answer, Damon pointed out over the river.

The long grey blade snarling in his hand, water streaming from his buckskin tunic and pants, Raithe of Ankhana strode along the surface of the river as though the rippling waters were carved of stone. He walked awkwardly, half stumbling, his legs barely able to support his weight. He headed upstream, and on his face was thunder.

Damon said, "That one."

2

". . . SO BEAUTIFUL . . ."

Avery Shanks rolled over and locked her jaw against a groan. The expanded-foam pallet that had been her bed on the cold tile floor of the veterinary surgery had been comfortable enough to let her sink into occasional periods of exhausted sleep, but every time she awoke she felt as though someone had removed all her cartilage and replaced it with industrial-grade sandpaper.

Her sleep had been plagued by nightmares of being seized and fondled, her elbows and knees and hips grabbed by bony fingers fleshed with rotting meat, her breasts and buttocks and crotch squeezed and rubbed by a mass of Laborers who crowded around her, stealing her air with their horrible breath, and all of their faces had Kollberg's empty leer. She rubbed grit from her eyes and tried to remember what had awakened her.

"I never knew . . ."

It was Tan'elKoth: a reverent whisper. Avery took her hands away from her face, and caught her breath.

A new light had entered the surgery: a light softer, more full, more golden than had been seen on this planet in a thousand years: as though someone had captured the first breaking dawn of a preindustrial May, bottled it like brandy, and decanted it only now, aged and mellowed and purified into a glow that shouldn't exist outside of sonnets and fairy tales: a light that is felt with the heart more than seen with the eye, a light that draws the spirit upward beyond the dull confines of Earth. It was the light that poets write of, when they describe the transfiguring brilliance of a lover's smile; it was the light that painters dimly echo with the secondhand image called the halo.

This light shone from Tan'elKoth's face.

"Is it done, then?" Avery whispered, afraid to speak aloud. "Have you done it? Is she safe?"

Tan'elKoth's gaze was farther away than miles can measure: he looked into a different universe. "How could I have dreamed—?"

Avery's eye, though, was drawn to the slow writhe of Faith, where she lay strapped to the table, an IV drip keeping her in permanent nightmare. "Is it *over*?" she asked, more insistently. "Can she rest now? Tan'elKoth, can she *rest*?"

Slowly Tan'elKoth's gaze returned from that unimaginable distance, and to his lips came a smile of gentle satisfaction that threatened to become triumph.

"Soon, Businessman," he murmured. "Soon."

3

THE ONLY LIGHT in the techbooth that served the Interlocking Serial Program came from the heart of Ankhana itself, translated into the cold electronic glare of eleven POV screens. In the center of the booth sat the creature that had been Arturo Kollberg; its eyes could have been mouths, swallowing the raw uptangling of Ankhana's unnatural spring.

The creature never moved as the techbooth's door opened behind its chair. The Social Police officers who ushered Tan'elKoth inside said nothing, nor did the creature acknowledge this arrival. The door closed again.

Electronic screens gleamed moss green and sky blue and stone brown.

Tan'elKoth said, "It is done."

The creature closed its eyes for a moment, enjoying the fountain of power it could taste flowing into Tan'elKoth and out again.

"It is well," Tan'elKoth said, "that you have sent for me now. We have much of which to speak."

A filth-crusted hand waved at a screen, where a skeletal young man armed with a shimmering sword walked unsteadily upon the surface of a river, between trunks of saplings that twisted out from the water as though in pain. "Have you seen this?"

"Seen it?" Tan'elKoth snorted. "I *created* it."

Eyes closed and opened again: chewing.

"The goddess walks within that body," Tan'elKoth said. "By my will she died; by my will, she lives again." His voice carried subterranean echoes of triumph. "It is time, I believe, to renegotiate our *deal*."

"Oh?"

"I pledged to neutralize both Caine and Pallas Ril. This I did. You pledged to return me to my people. This you did not. Instead, I was kidnapped. Threatened. Beaten. And maimed. Had I known your nature, there would have been no agreement between us. Now, though—*now*!" The triumph rose from the caverns beneath his tone into full dark malice. "Now the goddess walks the fields of home. Forewarned. Forearmed. Unbeatable. Your only hope is to deal with me. Only I can influence her. Only I can counter her power. Only I can save you."

"Where is Avery Shanks?" the creature said tonelessly.

"With the child." Tan'elKoth made a slicing gesture with the edge of his hand, dismissing any possible threat. "Businessman Shanks gives you no leverage. Your sole hope of success is the link I have with the goddess *through the child*. This link depends entirely upon the child's well-being: It is a function of a certain configuration of her nervous system, both physical and chemical. If Faith even falls too deeply asleep, the link will be severed; more convulsions—of the sort that separating her from Avery Shanks seems to cause—may destroy the link altogether.

Permanent brain changes result from even mild emotional trauma; the effect on the link would be entirely unpredictable. You cannot risk harm to any of us."

The creature did not answer.

"Further, you dare not delay. The goddess' connection to the river is also a function of nervous configuration—right now, this connection is tenuous and unreliable, but it will become progressively less so as she reconfigures the body she has possessed. With the power she already has, she can reshape the body she now wears, or duplicate her former one: at that time, she will have regained all of her former power. Even I, perhaps, could no longer resist her."

"Then now is the time to act."

"There will be no better time. With every minute of delay, your task grows more nearly impossible."

"All right. I'm convinced."

Tan'elKoth scowled; it seemed he had not expected to win so easily. "These, then, are my demands—"

"Screw your demands," the creature said, its voice gathering humid lust.

Tan'elKoth shook his head pityingly. "Do you understand *anything* of what I've said?"

The creature rose, and offered the chair to Tan'elKoth. "Sit."

"Don't think that you can continue to bully me," Tan'elKoth began, but the creature walked to one of the techbooth's control boards.

"Stand, then," it said emptily. "Here, look at this."

Tan'elKoth glanced reflexively at the bright bank of screens. The creature touched a control stud, and from each screen lanced a searing blade of light. Tan'elKoth shielded his eyes against the glare, but from inside his skull, just beneath that short arc of stitching that circled behind his left ear, a burst of power slashed his brain to ribbons, and he fell facefirst to the techbooth floor.

The creature looked down at his twitching body as though it wanted to say something, but could not remember what.

4

SHATTERED, SLASHED AND burned, broken, deep in the shadowed retreats of his mind, Tan'elKoth at last began to see the truth.

I have been a fool.

The implanted thoughtmitter was doing something to him—doing something to his mind, to his spirit—calling to him, revealing both itself and him in a way that the limitations of his physical senses would never have allowed him to perceive. The blades of light had sliced away his eyes, but in robbing him of sight they had gifted him with vision.

He saw, vague as a half-remembered dream, the Face in the Lesser Ballroom of the Colhari Palace: the Face that had been the highest, purest expression of the dreams of a sleepless god. That Face had been a jigsaw sculpture, pieced together of the clay-formed shapes of his Beloved Children, layered and built one laboriously perfect figure at a time, into a face. A Face: the Face of Ma'elKoth. His greatest work: *The Future of Humanity.*

Now, as he reached forth his metaphoric hand toward that icon of his vanished godhead, he saw that his art had been instead prophecy. This hand, with which he reached for that ghost of a dream, was no hand of flesh and bone, but was some shifting agglomeration of tiny figures, thousands of them, naked and clothed, birthing and dying, eating, screwing, shitting, killing.

Those tiny shapes had become his flesh and bone.

He had become a hive of humanity, a structural framework that organized and shaped and gave purpose to the millions of tiny lives that fed him their devotion. A dizzy shift of perspective brought him an inch closer to the truth: The jigsaw figures were fully life-sized. He himself was an unimaginable giant, built of a dozen million people, twenty million, more—

Laborers and Leisuremen, Investors and Artisans, all burning for a taste of Home. Their hunger overpowered him, left him shivering, gasping, sweating tears of human blood.

He had been blinded by his eyes: This world of gleaming steel and glass, of toxic sludge and chirping electronic voices, was a fraud. A confidence game. A sucker play. The institutionalized alienation that was the metastructure of modern Earth had deceived him into believing himself an individual—a deception directed not specifically at him, but generally, over each and every one of the millions who together made him what he was.

Each of the millions who organized themselves into his body wore blank white fabric tied across their faces: Magritte's lovers, kissing through eyeless hoods.

They could not even guess that they were each part of one greater form; they had been veiled so that they could not see what they had become. Those sheets were tied about each neck with a hangman's noose. Tan'elKoth felt about his own neck an identical noose, even as he became aware of an identical sheet tied over his own head.

He lifted his agglomerate hands and tore the veil from his eyes.

He found that he, himself, was only a small part of something as much greater than he as he was greater than the man who formed a curl of hangnail upon his thumb: a titanic shapeless mountain of blind humanity, and more than a mountain. Tan'el-Koth was himself a mountain—

This amorphic pulsing mass was the size of a planet.

The size of Earth.

And in its roiling, shifting pseudolife, it shaped itself into a Face of its own, a face with blankly staring eyes like lakes of people, nostrils greater than whole nations, a mouth like the ocean, wide with an idiot's gape.

A face like Kollberg's.

And the hoods that cloaked the uncountable billions comprising this amoebic groping Kollberg-mass covered only their individual eyes: their tens of billions of mouths were open, and every single one of them howled to be fed. This was the shared hunger for Home that burned within him: not homesickness, but starvation indeed. That bright, sweet world on which he'd built his Face, was to this great hungry mass only food.

How bitter, bitter, to be so easily deceived—

He had thought *he* was leading *them*; he had thought he was deceiving them; he had thought he was entering an alliance of convenience . . . But in truth, he had surrendered himself years before he ever came to this world; he was only an expression of this blind god writ small. He was nothing more than a link between this conglomerate creature and its supper: a hand, a tongue—

How has this happened, that I must feed my world to the monster I have become?

He stood upon the blind god's finger, as it lifted toward its slack oceanic mouth. He was finally—inarguably, revoltingly—only a crust of snot that this creature had picked from its nostril and was now about to consume once more. Those gargantuan writhing lips closed around him.

The blind god licked him from its finger, chewed him up, and swallowed him.

The god who had been a man opened the eyes of its new body, where it lay on the techbooth's floor. Kollberg sat on the edge of the control board, swinging his bare feet and holding his hands clasped between the knees of his filth- and bloodstained dungarees.

Tan'elKoth's prophecy had come fully to pass: The god within him lived.

For one long, long suspension of movement, Kollberg stared at Ma'elKoth, and Ma'elKoth returned his gaze: the blind god regarded itself thoughtfully, like a man gazing at his image in a mirror—except that here, the mirror gazed back.

5

PALLAS RAITHE STUMBLED forward, driven by screams.

She—for Pallas Raithe was female in ways more profound than any detail of anatomy—clung for a moment to the branch of a willow that had sprung from the river's bed only minutes ago, and that already suffered the slow murder of drowning. She held the buzzing blade of the sword out away from her stolen body and wrapped her other arm around the branch to keep herself upright on the river's shifting surface. Her halting spray of melody within the Song of Chambaraya limped painfully among the contrapuntal shifts of harmony and rhythm; it lurched from offbeat to discordant and back again, a squeal of random noise that befouled the music, tainted and twisted it.

She pressed her palm against her ear and pushed as though she could squeeze the screaming out of her head.

Her spring had quickened the virus as well.

Because each life within the city was its own motif within the Song of Chambaraya, Pallas Raithe was acutely aware of each cold slide of steel into flesh, of each crunch of bone beneath a hammer, of each panted breath half held behind a barricaded door, each erratic drumbeat of a terrified heart. She ached for every one, and she could help none of them. Those screams were only human.

In the symphony of agony that was the Great Chambaygen, they were barely a whisper.

One can think of an individual mind as a specific radio signal within the broadcast spectrum that is the universe; following the same metaphor, a living nervous system is a receiver, tuned by birth and experience to capture just that signal. In seizing Raithe's body, Pallas had been able to detune his nervous system so that it no longer captured his signal; she had warped it close enough to her own frequency that it could receive hers.

Like a detuned radio, where one signal bleeds over another, it received her badly indeed, through bursts of static and waves of interference that made her blast at shrieking overdriven volume one moment, while in the next she was buried in a white hissing wash. Her feedback shrieks had transformed Chambaraya's Song from stately Bach to a postmodernist screech of pain.

She spun crazily from the willow to a nearby oak, then threw herself into the cattail thicket along the bank. She fell to her knees, clutching the cattail stalks to her hard, breastless chest, and vomit clawed up her throat.

Mommy . . . Mommy, why won't you help?

Something was happening to Faith, something Pallas Raithe had not the power to comprehend. This body limited her perception until she could barely make out her daughter's voice.

Touching the river through Raithe was analogous to broadcasting a live netshow over an antique voice-only radio: information could be exchanged, but only in the most limited way. To reconstruct him for the necessary range of broadband infinite-speed access, she would have to steal everything about him that made him who he was, replace each piece with a new creation, and make everything fit and work together in a viable living creature. Simpler to build herself a whole new transceiver.

Simpler, to build herself.

She knelt with her knees still in the water, and dug a trembling hand into the clay: drawing forth minerals into the crystalline structure of bone. Even as she shaped the bone into vaguely female form, she gathered amino and aliphatic acids from the unnatural plant life around her. The river's water itself would serve for blood and bile and lymph.

Kosall within it contained the perfect template of her mind at the instant of her death. Mind and body are expressions of each other; the pattern stored within the blade was a template for a new body, as well.

A single human body is not such a complex thing, when compared to a full ecosystem.

She built the body from within, beginning with the brain and spinal cord; the more properly tuned nerve tissue she had, the more power she could draw to speed her self-creation. She began to experience a certain doubling of perception: a blurred parallax, like the vision of a person partly blind in one eye.

With the clearer perception of the brain and nerves that lay half complete within their cradle of clay, she felt the blind god enter her.

6

IT FLOWED INTO her like oil. She choked on grease that seeped in through her nostrils, that slid between her lips and poured like poison into her ears, that cupped her breasts and slipped up through her rectum and oozed into her vagina. At the same instant, it seemed a huge abscess had burst within her belly, spilling pus and yellowish corruption; the oil in her mouth and nose and between her legs oozed out from within her, poisoning the world.

There was no mystery for her here: she comprehended instantly what this suppuration truly was. She knew the blind god, and the blind god knew her. The channel that joined them was an inextricable part of what she was; through this channel the blind god poured itself into the Song.

This was what had been making Faith scream.

The blind god flooded into and through her, and Pallas cried out as she opened Raithe's eyes. The blind god looked out upon the jungle Ankhana had become, and within her it murmured in Ma'elKoth's baroque contrabasso. *Mmm, spectacular. We love what you've done with the place.*

For an answer, she lashed back with the scream of the river's agony.

Please, dear girl. The suggestion of a wince: not of pain, but of distaste. *This jungle is merely random; of course it hurts.*

Growing pains, no more. Just imagine what you might do if you act, instead, with purpose.

Images clustered thickly, visions in her mind's eye. Every puddle became a rice paddy. Every field burgeoned with corn and wheat. Fish swarmed the river so thickly that men lined the banks to catch them with their hands. Cattle and swine bore fat healthy young at need, all year round.

Is lumber needed for the building of homes? Acorns scattered in a patch of dirt became mature oaks in days—in an hour, just like this tangled spring of her creation.

Is the air dirty? Overnight, a billion new trees—a rain forest to order.

Your river alone could support BILLIONS.

And you'll kill billions to give it to them, she replied. She summoned sharp-edged images of the primal village filled with bloating corpses, and filled their depths with the onslaught of murder in Ankhana itself.

Ah, yes, the disease. Sorry about that.

Sorry? SORRY?

Quite. You must understand, dear girl, this was an instinctive—ah, shall we say, preconscious?—maneuver on Our part. From the days when the appellation "blind" was more than a metaphor. An image grew within her of a newborn infant, eyes not yet open, groping for the tit. *This is the great advantage of having allowed Ma'elKoth into Our Union: His vision makes things rather dazzlingly clear.*

Think of the disease this way: She saw an oak spring from fertile soil, saw the sapling shoot forth branches and the branches open leaves to the sun—leaves that shaded the ground beneath it, so that by the time the tree was mature, all the other little trees beneath its limbs had died for lack of light. *Purely natural. Nothing malicious in the slightest.*

On the other hand, one cannot argue with success, can one? Rather clears the board at one swipe. Ah, well: We would take it back if We could—but this is a difficulty you have already addressed, is it not?

And you killed me for it!

Not at all. We killed you because you opposed us. We killed you because you are selfish and willful. We killed you because your opposition would kill Us. We killed you, justifiably, in self-defense.

Look at this: Within her consciousness wheeled the globe of

Earth, spinning silently in space: a tiny island in a vast and hostile ocean: an island jammed with fourteen billions already, and more on their way every second. *Earth passed the brink of ecological collapse two hundred years ago. Only an extravagant waste of irreplaceable resources has allowed the human race to continue thus far; only a die-off comparable to the Cretaceous can save it now. Five years from now, ten at the most, the die-off will begin.*

This is why We killed you: because you would deny the human race what it needs to survive. Can you say We were wrong?

She could not even hope that this was a lie. The truth streamed into her. Twelve billion people would die. Possibly more. She could not imagine it, not even with the power of the god: a planet carpeted in human corpses.

Now see Overworld: Imagine a new Earth, untouched. Imagine Earth as if it had always been in the care of a kindly goddess. With you and your power to guide Us, We could make of this world a perpetual garden.

She could not even lift her head to summon a response.

She was drowning in the truth.

She clung to a single strand of resistance: the distant howls of her daughter's anguish.

7

AH, YES, FAITH. A writer of your world—Our world—once posed the problem this way: If you could ensure the future survival and happiness of all humanity by allowing one single wholly innocent, utterly inoffensive being to be tortured to death, would you do it? This is a conundrum only when faced by mortals. For gods, the answer is clear. Obvious. You find the stories wherever you look: Attis, Dionysios, Jesus Christ—the Wicker Man, by any other name.

But Faith— Pallas began to recover some scraps of her outrage. *She's my DAUGHTER.*

But, dear girl, it was you who gave her over to this torture. We merely use the tool you have crafted for Us.

Faith? Shh, Faith, I'm here. It's all right.

But Faith could only sob. She was, after all, just a little girl:

yet another in the endless litany of innocents violated by a god. *By two gods,* Pallas thought. *The blind god, and me.*

She could have sung Faith a human life; instead, she had sung her own dream: complete, perfect union with one she loved.

The cruelty of what she had done had never occurred to her. *How could I have known?*

Now within her she saw Ma'elKoth in all his majesty: the chiseled face, the glorious sweep of hair, chest like a barrel and shoulders like wrecking balls; she saw the limpid purity of his eye, the transcendent nobility of his brow. At his side stood Faith, naked, sobbing; the two of them were joined somehow, in some way that she couldn't make her mind clearly resolve: as though Faith's two hands had melted together within Ma'el-Koth's grip. *She need not suffer so; it is you who prolongs and compounds her suffering. It is you who can release her this very instant.*

I can save her?

The image of Ma'elKoth extended his other hand toward Pallas, in a gesture of peace. Of friendship. Of union. *All you must do,* he told her, *is take Our hand.*

But Pallas Raithe turned away.

She didn't even know why.

8

TAKE IT, THE image of Ma'elKoth insisted. *Does your daughter's suffering mean so little to you? Take Our hand, and We no longer have need of the child. We will have no reason to harm her.*

Perhaps she had lived with Hari for too long; perhaps that was it. *And you'll have no reason not to.*

The image of Ma'elKoth rolled and shifted, rippling from within like a reflection in a water pot gone to boil. For an instant another face showed through Ma'elKoth's classic beauty: a skull stretched with parchment and raddled with mold and rot, tangled teeth stained grey-brown, eyes glaring with an endless, limitless hunger that terrified her. *Yes, a part of Us desires her suffering. The love of cruelty is as human as is the love of a mother for her child. But when you join us, your desires will color Ours. You have learned this from the river; does not your will color its Song? Join Us.*

Pallas wept. *I can't.*

The blind god showed her a girl child, perhaps eight years old, crouched in an alley behind a Manhattan Labor tenement. She smeared snot from her lip with a dirty hand, and coughed thickly into a drizzle of grey rain that raised blisters on her exposed neck. *Can you look at this child and say she has no right to breathe clean air? No right to eat fresh food? Can you tell her she has no right to be free?*

The girl picked listlessly through a mound of garbage, only to cry out in joy at finding a dirt-greyed chicken leg with yet a few scraps of meat upon it.

I serve the river, Pallas answered hesitantly, searching her feelings. *She's not my responsibility—*

But she is. You know of her suffering, and you have the power to save her. What crime has she committed, that you can condemn her to the life you know she must live?

She's living in the world you *made—*

And We have accepted responsibility for that. We are fighting to change it. What are you fighting for?

She summoned an image of the headwaters of the Great Chambaygen before the days of the Khryl's Saddle railway: the pristine crystal trickle over mossy stones among the majesty of the God's Teeth. She summoned the rolling waves of virgin forest below the mountain slopes, the slow curve of an eagle riding a thermal, the splash of a grizzly haggling salmon—

Come now, dear girl. This is fatuous. Consider this bear of yours for a moment: Should this bear threaten the life of that young girl, you would kill it without hesitation.

She insisted, desperately obstinate, *I will not have your faceless billions unleashed upon my world.*

But they are not faceless, not at all. "Faceless billions" is only a phrase. It's a slogan that you invent to dehumanize them: as abstractions, it is easy to condemn them to their hideous fate. But they are not abstract. Each is a human being, who loves and hates, who cries when he is hurt and laughs when she is happy. All of them are right here. Every single one has a face. Would you like to tell them, in your own words, why they must choke to death on the ruined cinder of Earth?

Don't pretend you care!

You know We care. You can feel it. Each of them is a part of Us; how can we not care? We care precisely as much as they do.

She had run out of answers; even in this new aspect, Ma'el-Koth remained remorselessly logical. She could not imagine allowing ten billion people to die for the sake of bears and elk and trees. But still, she resisted, and still, she did not know why. Perhaps because Overworld was so beautiful, and Earth was so . . . *ugly*.

Only because We were too young—too blind—to shape it properly. Overworld need not suffer the same fate. Again, a vision blossomed: a city surpassing Athens of the Golden Age; surpassing Imperial Rome; a city emcompassing the best of London, Paris, St. Petersburg; a city with the grace of Angkor Wat, the majesty of Babylon.

Even those bears for which you seem to care so much, and all the trees—every creature, in fact, that grows in the earth or walks upon it, swims the waters or soars the air—can remain. And everywhere she looked, the city opened itself to parks and woodlands, stretches of prairie and silver curves of rivers.

Overworld need not be a second Earth. Between Us, We can make it a second Eden: where women bring forth young in comfort, and men no longer water their fields with the sweat of their brow. Where all that is, and all that ever shall be, is peace.

And this was the world of which she had always dreamed, wasn't it? Maybe that's why she and Hari couldn't ever quite manage to be happy: that dreamworld of hers wouldn't interest Hari one little bit. He'd hate it.

He'd say, "Eternal peace? That's for dead people."

He'd say, "Sure, to you it's a city. To me, it looks like a hog farm."

Of course, the blind god told her with a hint of irony. *In Our second Eden, there is no place for a Caine.*

9

SHE REMEMBERED SITTING in Shermaya Dole's simichair, running the cube of *For Love of Pallas Ril*. "Fuck the city," Caine had said. "I'd burn the world to save her." And she had never understood how he could say that.

And yet, the answer is so simple. He is evil. From the raddled memory that rode the brain within the body that she now wore rose another memory: Hari again, older now, grey in his hair, no beard, only a smear of time-salted stubble along a jawline threatening to become jowls, shrugging in a sedan chair at the rim of a crater high in the Transdeian mountains, near Khryl's Saddle. "The Future of Humanity," Hari had said, slowly, a little sadly, as though he were recounting an ugly but unavoidable truth, "is gonna have to fuck off."

How could he say that? Could he really believe it?

You see? We are not your enemy. He is. He is evil incarnate. Shall We list some of his crimes?

Oathbreaker. She saw his face through Faith's eyes of memory, as he struggled in the grip of the Social Police and swore that he would save her. As he swore he would make everything turn out right.

Liar. Images cascaded from *For Love of Pallas Ril*, as Caine ruthlessly and repeatedly lied, even manipulating the King of Cant—his closest friend—into risking his own life and the lives of every man he led.

Murderer. She experienced again finding him in a dank back alley of Ankhana, at the end of *Servant of the Empire*. She experienced again holding him in her lap as he bled out his life from a deep belly wound, left by the sword of a guard outside the bedchamber of Prince-Regent Toa-Phelathon. She experienced again the shock and sickness of recognizing that the rag ball on the cobbles nearby was no rag ball, but was the blood and shit-stained head of the Prince-Regent, murdered in his bed.

She could not argue with any of these charges, and yet—

And yet—

Caine—

In the instant she thought his name, she felt his rhythm in the Song: a savage throb of rage and despair masked with dark cheer. She could feel him where he sat at this very instant: chained to a sweating limestone wall, naked in his own shit, gangrene eating his useless, lifeless legs.

She saw the star of absolute white she had glimpsed once before, in the Iron Room, as she had lain bound upon an altar while he bargained with a god for her life. He *burned*: raw surging energy, sizzling, profoundly alive.

That star—

She remembered facing the god Ma'elKoth in the battle that had raged across the skies above Victory Stadium, seven years ago. She could have crushed him—the river had sung power unimaginable—but the cost of that victory would have been the deaths of tens of thousands of his Beloved Children and untold millions of the trees and grasses, fish and otters and lives of all kinds that fed the river's Song. So she had offered up her life, and Hari's, for the sake of those numberless others.

All these years she had blamed him for turning away from her. *But it was I who turned away. He was less important to me than creatures I had never seen, and who had never seen me. How, then, can I claim to have loved him?* With the love of a goddess, perhaps: the love that cherishes all lives equally, but none especially. *Being both goddess and woman has made me a poor goddess, and a worse woman.*

Now the choice she faced was a mirror-reversal of that one: She could take the offered hand—she could cooperate, instead of kill—and in so doing save not only the massed billions of Earth, but save her daughter as well.

And still, she did not.

Could not.

Could not forget what they had done to Faith. Could not *reward* them for it. Could not become an accomplice to her daughter's rape.

Could not, finally, do as she was told.

Because she didn't *like* them.

Illumination dawned within her, and in the new light she saw what had held her back.

It was Raithe.

She had reconfigured his body—and his body had reconfigured her. It shaped the way her will could be expressed; it shaped even her self-image, and the way she thought. She was now something other than she had been, before. She was now a little more human.

More like Caine.

There had burned in Raithe a star of his own.

Now at last she could understand why Hari would get so angry when she would ask him to release his unhappiness and flow with the river. She thought wonderingly, *I suppose that if it's wrong to be unhappy, human beings wouldn't be so good at it.*

But this is only a reflex, dear girl; an artifact of the body you have seized. If you take a different body, your answer may change.

This body is my body. This answer is my answer.

The stakes are too vast to be settled by an accident of biology.

Are they? Then, I suppose you would have to call this— She allowed herself a bitter interior smile. *—bad luck.*

She resummoned the blind god's world-Rome, that Edenic city of peace overspreading the whole of Overworld. She sent their joint vision soaring through its skies and diving among its shining white buildings, through its streets and rivers, into its gardens and parks, among its pools and trees, through bedrooms and dens, searching the whole of the blind god's fond future.

What do you seek?

She found bakers and butchers, scribes and dustmen, farmers and gleaners, teachers, storytellers, playful children, and amorous lovers. She found carters and coopers and masons and millers; she found housekeepers, potters, glaziers, and smiths. She found every sort of human being save one.

What? For what do you search?

I am looking for a white star.

Think not of beauty; beauty is a seducer. There are lives at stake. What of the children?

A wise man once told me, she thought succinctly, *that compassion is admirable, in mortals. In gods, it is a vice.*

You would kill the human race for the sake of one man?

No, I suppose I wouldn't. A slow certainty grew within her heart and swelled until it spread out among the trees in the newborn Ankhanan jungle. *But who says it's one or the other?*

You serve either life, or you serve death.

What kind of life? This fight isn't between life and death. It's between your life and his life. Guess what? I like his better.

He is evil. You have seen his evil, and know its truth.

Another wise man once told me that when somebody starts talking about good and evil, I should keep one hand on my wallet.

She felt a wash of quiet resignation that was almost a shrug, and then a darkening of tone to bleakly impersonal threat. *If you are not with Us, you are against Us.*

She passed one infinite instant examining herself for fears and second thoughts. She found several of the former, but of the latter none at all. *Let it be so.*

There came a long, considering pause.

Then:

We have your daughter.

And she is your only weapon, Pallas answered with all the coldness of Raithe's wintry stare. *You dare not harm her.*

Perhaps so. You, on the other hand—

You, We can hurt.

10

A UNIVERSE AWAY, in the cool green glow of electronic screens that showed a thin young man kneeling on the surface of a river with a sword in his hand, the body that had once contained Ma'elKoth rumbled, "It is better this way."

The body that had once contained Arturo Kollberg replied, "More fun."

"Yes, fun. Like the Labor clinic."

"Yes."

"Yes."

In perfect unison, they murmured, "It's a pity there's no way to tell Caine that we're raping his wife."

11

IN THAT INSTANT, Pallas Raithe began to die.

All across Ankhana, trees and grasses and flowering plants sagged, wilted, softening and decaying, dripping stinking black goo while still on the vine. This black goo had a chemical reek, of acids and metals and burning oil, and where it dribbled over stone and wood it left vividly permanent stains. Ivy that had scaled the heights of the Colhari Palace wilted, sweating the black oil; corn that had sprung from city streets curled and withered and bled across the stones. Where the oil drained into the river, it killed fish and smothered reeds; in the stables where oat bins had become burgeoning gardens, it flowed around the lips of stamping horses, who choked and vomited and fell kicking to the earth.

The black oil burned Pallas Raithe where it oozed across her skin. The burns swelled with blisters that blackened and burst to release oil of their own that burned her burns again, sizzling deeper and deeper into her flesh. She pushed herself out from among the rotting cattails, back into the river, letting the water close over her, but it could not wash away this acid. It wasn't on her skin; it came *through* her skin.

From the inside.

She clutched at the dying willow, shaking. She drew the river's power—her power—to heal this body that she wore, to build it afresh and renew flesh and bone, but that only brought forth a thicker flow of the black oil; the black oil was part of her, part of the river, part of her power, and it ate Pallas Raithe's flesh as fast as she could heal. The river howled her pain in a voice of human screams and bird cries, of cat snarls and the shrieks of wounded rabbits, and only a tiny fraction of this pain was physical.

I might pray for help—but to whom? Whom does the goddess ask for help? What am I supposed to do?

—you can fight—

The remembered voice was Hari's, of course; what other advice did he ever offer? Fighting was his whole life.

—quit whining get off your ass and fucking FIGHT—

She could never make him understand. Some things cannot be fought; some things just *are*. Day and night. The turn of seasons. Life. Death.

Horseshit, she remembered him saying. *What the fuck is a house, then? It's how you fight the seasons. What's a campfire? It's how you fight the night. What's medicine? It's how you fight death. That's what love is, too. Just because you're not gonna win is no fucking reason to give up.*

All right, she exhaustedly told that remembered voice, surrendering. *All right. But you have to help me. Hari, I need your help.*

—I AM helping you, goddammit—

Which was so like him that it made her smile while the river's oil-fouled current washed away her tears.

She pulled herself up from the water, carrying Kosall, climbing one-handed the branches of the dying willow. Muscles shivered with oncoming shock; blister-scarred palms blistered anew, swelling into solid boils of blackened corruption. She turned back to the half-formed body she had built in the cradle of the Great Chambaygen's clay. As she feverishly willed that body into existence, building it of clay and stone and river water, the blind god entered her more fully, more roughly, thrusting itself into her with the overpowering force of billions of desperate lives. It would let her rebuild herself.

It *wanted* her to.

Already she could feel, with the half-formed nerves of the Pallas Ril body in the clay beside her, the searing poison of the black oil up and down the river. The more life she summoned, the more death it produced. The more one they became.

She could see, now, through the eyes of the Kollberg and Tan'elKoth bodies in the techbooth in San Francisco: could feel the avid lust with which they watched her on the POV monitors: could feel the anticipation of victory building like an orgasm, as they breathlessly watched her create a woman's body from the earth. She looked down at the half-shaped clay, at its swell of breast and curve of hip, and then she turned away.

She could not do this to her river.

She could focus her power upon the sword itself, one swift twist of will destroying it and herself together—but that would release her pattern from the blade into the river. Destroying the sword would flood her river with her consciousness, and the blind god would ride that flood forever.

The blind god had her in Chinese handcuffs: every move she made tightened its hold upon her.

She had to retreat: to throw herself into the lack, become nothing in that sea of nonexistence. Unmake herself. Using the partial nervous system she had created in the riverbank, she began to restructure Raithe's nervous system to its original resonance.

The blind god hummed its satisfaction, like a chess player who has caught his opponent in a particularly gratifying fork. Through the two sets of eyes in the Studio's ISP booth, she saw the swing of Actors' POVs and understood the blind god's new pleasure. Actors closed in upon her, crept closer and closer, their breath going short, penises stiffening and labia moistening with the blind god's lust. These Actors were tools of the blind god already; once she was again nothing more than a pattern bound in the magick of the sword, she could not stop any new hand upon its hilt from calling her forth—but she would not come forth the same.

A different hand upon Kosall would bring a different goddess: one bent already to the blind god's will.

The ring of Actors closed around her. She could feel them

with the blind god's perception: she knew precisely where each one was, knew his name, her history, the whole of every one of them. She gathered power in the river: she could destroy them with a gesture—and the blind god laughed. Let her kill them.

It had many, many Actors.

And even this shrug of power had quickened the venom that poured through her. Already the river stank of death for a mile downstream; already trees upstream sweated pinpricks of black oil, pocking their trunks with growing lesions of dead bark.

Please, she begged herself. *A little inspiration, that's all I ask.* She dived deeper into the Song, begging the river itself for any clue it might offer. *Even just a hint.*

And a small, timid voice with the querulousness of nervous exhaustion whispered from the far side of Faith's tears: *Well, if all you're worried about is* Aktiri, *I think I may be able to help you.*

12

THE SHADE OF Hannto the Scythe wasted no time trying to form thoughts and words and explanations: he knew They would come for him, and he knew Their billions were an ocean in which he would drown. Instead, he took his understanding of a technique of Ma'elKoth's and passed it through the link. It was a slight—even minuscule—alteration of local physics, a tiny shift in the resonance of reality itself that could be made self-sustaining.

He felt her puzzlement as though it were a question in reply, but They were closing in, sucking him down, and he had time to offer her only a fading memory of the Colhari Palace, and a reminder that Ma'elKoth had once suffered an *Aktir* problem, too.

And then the sea of lives dragged him under, and swallowed him.

13

HOLDING HER NERVES of clay in mindview, Pallas built the image at the forefront of her mind: a spherical lattice of shimmering violet, as the shade had shown her. It was an elegant variant of a simple Shield, retuned to near-ultraviolet from its usual warm gold. As she channeled the river's power into it, it vanished from her mindview: it had reached frequencies she could no longer perceive.

Its centerpoint hovered an inch behind the forehead of the Pallas Ril of clay that grew upon the riverbank, an inch above the midpoint between her eyes. She sang its melody into the Song, and it expanded like a slow-motion shock wave, enclosing all that it touched: the dockside, the warehouses, the caverns below, Old Town behind her, the Warrens, Alientown, and even the South Bank across the river: a million, two million, ten million times the volume of the field Ma'elKoth had set about the Colhari Palace, and more.

The clay Pallas shifted and bubbled, and smoke rose from its eyes. The unfinished nerves within that body of clay were less than ideally efficient, and to overpower any circuit beyond its efficiency causes energy to be lost as waste heat.

She stripped herself from Raithe's body, and his nerves spasmed with shock and agony. In so doing, she rewrote herself within the sword, overlaid her pattern there with the memories she shared with Raithe; should a mind ever draw her back to consciousness again, she would remember all they had learned.

She could not return him to himself entirely; she could heal neither the burns of his body nor the memories she had scorched into his brain, but what she could do, she did. And she left within him the answer he would require, should he choose to fight on in this war against the blind god: the hiding place of her weapon. It was the only way she could thank him for saving her.

She knit one final command into his brain, hardwired it like an instinct—

Defend the sword.

—then she poured what was left of her will into the clay.

The final burst of power that made her elegant invisible Shield self-sustaining detonated the clay half-body of Pallas Ril in an explosion that left a smoking crater on the dockside and blew Raithe spinning backward through the air all the way across the river.

The sword fell from his hands, splashed into the oil-fouled waters of the Great Chambaygen, and vanished into their oil-sealed murk; Raithe crashed into one of the enormous limestone blocks that formed the base of the Old Town wall, then he, too, fell into the river. He floated facedown, limp as the wilted leaves of the trees that rotted around him.

And the black oil that leaked from those trees burned like gasoline.

14

A HUNDRED YARDS downstream, a man called J'Than—or Francis Rossi, depending on which world he walked—crouched behind the gunwale of a boat canted half-over in the branches of a dying willow. In the narrow brick right-of-way between the Palnar Drygoods warehouse and the steelworks, a likewise dual-named woman—Cholet or Tina Welch—pressed herself against a wall, gasping. On the roof of that same warehouse, a pair of experienced thieves from out of town—from way, *way* out of town—suddenly paused in the act of belaying a rope they had planned to use to rappel down to the dockside.

Each of these—and seven more like them—had been creeping toward the man on the river, had been watching intently the shimmering sword in his hand, had come closer and closer while the eldritch jungle sprang to life unheeded around them, had slid untouched past the weeping black oil to approach their goal.

And all of them had felt a prickling, tingling wave pass over and through them, an instant before the riverside erupted in a gout of power that spread flames over the oil—flames that sped outward, reaching hungrily toward them and the black oil that dripped from the jungle on all sides. Each of them felt as though he or she now awakened from a bad dream, a dream that had carried them toward this moment without volition. Each of them said to himself or herself, with minor variations according to their individual usages, *What the fuck was I THINKING?*

And all of them, finding their wills now their own, ran like hell.

15

IN THE TECHBOOTH of the Interlocking Serial Program, the blind god talked to itself.

It had two mouths here. The voice from one was deep and round and mellow as honey; the voice from the other was a harsh cindery rasp. Which voice spoke mattered not at all, because it was only talking to itself.

"A setback," one murmured, as the POV screen that had shown a view of Ankhana's decaying-jungle dockside in flames flickered to white static. "Only a setback."

"Not even serious," one replied, as another screen that showed the black oil burning on the surface of the river went white, and another.

The booth became brighter and brighter as the POV screens exchanged views of Ankhana in flames for rectangles of featureless electronic snow. The blind god understood what Pallas had done as completely as Pallas had comprehended the blind god, and it was not in the least dismayed. The link to the river shut down only an instant after the last of the screens blanked, and Faith Michaelson sobbed in some remote corner of the blind god's mind.

The city was now sealed against the Winston Transfer.

"Do we need Actors to get the sword?"

"I should say not. We have *troops. Combat* troops. Social Police. Armed men. We can take the city, if we want."

"We want."

"Yes. We need a story. We need a story to keep the people behind us. To keep everyone on board."

"Nothing could be simpler. We can tell them we *have* to invade."

"The city's in flames."

"We don't have any choice."

"Of course we don't have any choice."

"It's the only way to save Caine."

"That's true. It's the only way to save Caine."

The hiss of electronic snow from the techbooth speakers was joined by a wash of rusty, breathless cackles—innumerable MIDI files of canned laughter culled from netshows around the globe—which was the blind god snickering at its own joke.

THERE IS A sense in which the matrix of stories that we call history is itself a living thing. There is a structure to it, a shape, that we call its body; it has certain habitual progressions that we call its movement. We say history advances, or retreats, that it recalls this and forgets that; we look to it as a teacher, as a parent, as an oracle.

We say and do these things, and somehow we still delude ourselves that we are speaking metaphorically.

History is not only alive, it is *aware*.

It meets every test of consciousness. History anticipates. History intends. History *wills*.

Its anticipation, intention, and will are the sums of ours; it vectors our hopes and fears and dreams with the stern logic of the inanimate. And there are times when history lifts the hammer, and times when it bends the bow, and there are times when it draws a long, long breath.

NINETEEN

WITHIN ITS SMOTHERING blanket of sudden jungle, Ankhana writhed.

This was an instant holiday, a festival, a Carnevale: a suspension of the ordinary rules of life and society. How could one go to work or to the market, when the streets were choked with trees? Grain bins had burst across the city as mills vomited sprouts, and shoots sprang from drying seeds. Door planks shot forth branches that burgeoned with leaves; dungheaps transformed instantly into high-mounded gardens.

For some it was a time of joy and release and childlike play, to dance among the waves of new-sprung life; for others, it was a time of profound contemplation, a time to wonder at the irreducible strangeness of the universe. For most, it was a time of terror.

Most people cannot face a world without rules.

Those rules of life and society—rules that are so often railed against as stifling and degrading—serve a profound purpose: they provide patterns of behavior that allow one the comfort of believing one understands the rules of the game. Without rules, there is no game. There is only the jungle.

This particular jungle swarms with tigers.

Humanity is the only species that is its own natural enemy. The virus that had eaten its way into so many brains had digested already most of the inhibitions and repressions that make civilization possible. The instant jungle dissolved the final trace of even the most elemental animal caution, which had been the last restraint.

Now was the time to hunt and feed.

Two types of people best dealt with the sudden jungle. The first were the sort for whom rules never change. To a bishop of the Church of the Beloved Children of Ma'elKoth, for example, the laws of his god transcended any temporal consideration, even such a shattering transformation as this; to the soldiers finally charged with the arrest of Duke Toa-M'Jest, orders were orders, whether issued in a garrison, a tent, or the branches of an oak that had sprung from bare earth ten minutes before.

The second were the type of people for whom there never had been any rules: the ones who had *always* lived in the jungle.

The last few Cainists still at liberty banded together to defend their families at a warehouse in the Industrial Park, waiting grimly with spear and sword and bow, dispatching each human tiger who hunted too near; His Grace the Honorable Toa-M'Jest, Duke of Public Order—who had once been His Majesty the King of Cant, and before that had been Jest, a young pickpocket, petty thief, and aspiring thug—scented the approach of pack hunters with instinctive animal wariness.

He, like the others of the second type, actually felt safer now than he had before, when he'd still had to pretend to be following the rules.

For the rest of Ankhana, there was only the jungle.

2

WHEN HE FIRST glimpsed the line of infantry picking their way through the rubble-choked streets of Alientown toward his improvised stockade, Toa-M'Jest realized that he'd held on too long.

The stockade wall on which he stood rose from the ruins of what once had been a dry goods store at the corner of Moriandar Street and Linnadalinn Alley. It was overspread by a broad canopy of antisprite netting, now burdened with a new growth of spreading hemp leaves sticky with resin; Toa-M'Jest parted the jungle of dangling weighted ropes and squinted at the advancing troops.

In their vanguard strode an officer in the formal dress-blues of the Eyes of God.

Toa-M'Jest clenched his teeth to keep a string of curses behind them. He knew exactly what was going on, and it was bad. Their orders must have come from the Patriarch himself, and he had a pretty damned good idea what those orders were.

The crazy old bastard had fucked him.

The Duke turned to the Grey Cat alpha at his side. The alpha, like the pride he commanded, wore the latest in experimental antimagick combat technology: a full bodysuit of overlapping jointed steel plates, painted with protective runes of silver. It made the usually lithe and nimble Cats lumber like overweight bears, but in the close-quarters combat of the war in the caverns below the city, mobility counted for less than did protection.

"This is what I've been worried about," Toa-M'Jest said grimly. "Looks like the elves have taken control of those officers."

"Your Grace?" the alpha said blankly, his voice muffled within his steel helm.

"Nobody gets in here, you understand? We can't trust anyone but ourselves. Those poor bastards out there probably think we called for reinforcements. They might even think they're acting at the order of the Patriarch himself. But no matter what they say, we can't let them inside the stockade."

"But, Your Grace," the alpha said dubiously, "what if their orders *do* come from the Patriarch?"

"We can sort all that out in a day or two, after things calm down." Toa-M'Jest waved a hand at the jungle that choked the ruined city. "You've seen what the damned elves have done to us. We will take no more chances. No one enters. That's an order."

He turned away and clambered down the ladder before the alpha could reply. He had three more alphas—the commanders at each wall—who needed the same order, and pretty fucking soon, too.

He winced as he scrambled through the rubble that choked what once had been Moriandar Street. He hated that his feet must touch the ground; every step brought a nervous grimace. The fuckers were still *fighting* down there. How could they keep on? His men had taken prisoners—he had interrogated some himself—ragged and malnourished, untreated wounds inflamed and suppurating, most of them sick with the fever and raving. Any second he expected the cobbles to sprout a thicket of clawed hands—for the street to liquefy beneath him and then close over his head like quicksand as those hands drew him down, and down, and down—

But as soon as he moved clear of the canopy of antisprite netting, he worried less about the caverns beneath than what might come at him from above. Damned sprites—

Shit, he hated those little fuckers.

Now and again, treetoppers had slipped out of concealed cavern exits and taken a terrible toll with their yard-long birdlances of needle-pointed steel. The sprite attacks were only occasionally fatal, but this was cold comfort. The damned sprites were naturally Cloaked; you don't even know you're under attack till you feel the lance jam into your eye. Usually your right eye. It was their favorite target.

Toa-M'Jest paused for a moment when he came within sight of the wreckage of Alien Games. This was where Kierendal's Faces had fought their last desperate rearguard action, to cover a retreat into the caverns. For more than an hour, the air around AG had been an inferno of lightning and flame as the Thaumaturgic Corps attacked and elvish mages within answered with power of their own. At the last, the mages had detonated the building itself to seal the cavern entrance below; now, days later, the flattened rubble still smoldered.

The Duke was captured not by memories of the battle, though, but by his wistful recollection of all the happy hours and days he had passed here. *Didn't know how good I had it,* he thought. *Kier, if you're still alive down there, I wish I could tell you how much I miss you.* He shook his head and moved on.

Clinging to the past was not a survival trait.

None of his troops here had understood, when he had put his men to the task of constructing this stockade of stone. Some had questioned the utility; their enemies, after all, had been driven underground. From whom did he expect attack on the surface?

He hadn't bothered to explain; as the Patriarch sometimes liked to say, he did not require their understanding, only their obedience.

He certainly wasn't going to tell them that the whole Empire was tumbling down a giant pissoir. He certainly wasn't going to tell them that Toa-Sytell had gone crazy. He certainly wasn't going to tell them that he planned to hunker down here for a few days, then step out once Toa-Sytell collapsed, and end up in charge. It looked now, though, like he'd been a little too optimistic.

He should have cut his losses and bolted days ago.

Wishful thinking, that's what it was. He'd decided he could stay and make things work out because that's what he *wanted* to happen. He liked being a Duke; he liked being a confidant of the Patriarch, the head of the Eyes of God, wealthy and respected and getting more tail than a man his age has any right to dream of, let alone expect. And he'd really thought he could do some good, too. He had a talent for bringing order out of chaos; he'd shown that during the Second Succession War, when his Knights of Cant had become the capital's unofficial police force. When this shitstorm finally ebbed, he might be the only one left who could put everything back together again.

So he'd hung on, waiting, hoping for a break, while everything slid down the pissoir all around him. He couldn't even count on his own men. There had been fights, with fist and sword; there had been surreptitious knifings in the dark, and even one wild brawl between a pride of Cats and two T-Corps mages that had ended with five Cats and both thaumaturges dead.

Still he had held on. He might be the last sane man in the government. If he ran, who would take care of the Empire?

But the world, he reminded himself as he slipped under the anti-sprite canopy that sheltered the north wall of the stockade, *doesn't give trophies for good intentions.* He had a motto, one that had kept him alive through many a dangerous time: When the prize is survival, second place is dead last.

These words echoed inside his head as he heard a starchy voice from beyond the wall proclaim loudly that it was in possession of an Imperial Warrant for the arrest of Toa-M'Jest, formerly Duke of Public Order, on charges of treason, conspiracy, and crimes against the Empire. "Shit," he muttered. "Time to go."

No point troubling with either of the other walls; this was obviously a coordinated operation. There was only one direction left.

Down.

Without another word to anyone, he ran.

His instincts told him he might be able to bargain with Kierendal and her subs; those same instincts warned him not to bluster or bluff or argue with these soldiers, and so when they met in the center of the stockade, searching for him, he was long, long gone, down into the caverns his erstwhile gang had ruled: a hare down its warren-run, five steps ahead of the hounds.

3

NIGHT FELL ON Ankhana.

It was a night without a moon, and rolling clouds smothered the stars. Some scarce unshuttered windows—even scarcer open doors—sparked yellow lamplight here and there across the city, but the only real light as dusk dissolved to full black night was the bloody snarl of flame on the dockside.

In that hellglow, men and women pounced and fled and fought and died; in that hellglow constables pounded heads and backs and occasionally each other. In that hellglow, soldiers marched out through a dying jungle, and pike brigades became bucket brigades.

The river burned along with the buildings, and water was useless: it only spread the oil so much the faster. Soldiers with shovels scratched for dirt and sand to throw on the flames. Soon officers gave over shouting orders and encouragement, and seized shovels and buckets of their own.

Sixteen kilometers upstream from Ankhana, one hundred meters north of the Great Chambaygen's bank, a cube of twilit air shimmered itself into a prismatic spray. The burst of dusk-darkened color resolved itself into twelve men who wore armor of metalized ballistic cloth over semirigid carbon-fiber ceramic leaves backed with Sorbathane. Their helmets were made of identical carbon-fiber ceramic, and each helmet had a full face shield of smoked armorglass inlaid with hair-fine silver wires.

Instantly they marched toward the river, and the cube of air shimmered once more behind them.

The first man to reach the river laid his microfiber pack on the bank, unzipped its plastic sealer, and pulled a clear nylon lanyard. With a hiss, the pack unfolded itself and inflated to become a large boat, into which the balance of the dozen men began stowing their gear in Velcro-lined pouches along the gas cells. Precisely five meters upstream, the leader of the second dozen began to unzip his own pack. A third dozen marched toward a point five meters farther upstream, while a fourth shimmered into existence.

Of all the men on that riverbank that night, four wore different armor. The design of their armor differed only in that the ballistic cloth was not metalized, and the smoked glass of their visors had no lacing of silver wires. The boats were lashed together in groups of three; one of these four men took his place at the stern of the lead boat of each group and held a staff in the water, trailing behind like a rudder. Each of these four men produced a large piece of polished quartz, held it in his other hand, and concentrated.

The boats slipped silently into the gathering darkness.

In the city that was their destination, friars choked and died in the river as they struggled to retrieve the body of a fallen Ambassador.

Below that city, down in the dark, beneath the sheltering stone—

—A killer chained to a limestone wall stared unseeing, and touched with his mind strands of darkness deeper than the absolute night in which he lay.

—A human who had been a prince of the First Folk lay twisting in mortal fever, hours from death.

—A former duke wandered, lost, in permanent impenetrable black.

And a man named Habrak—who had been Sergeant of the Guard in the Donjon for twelve years with only a single stain upon his record; who was a man of the first type, for whom the rules never change; who had faced the sudden jungle and the surge of black oil and now the flames that threatened to swallow his city with the same stolid, profound, unimaginative devotion to his duty; who had believed, in his heart, that in his thirty-seven years of military service he had done so much and seen so much more that he was no longer surprised by anything—could only stare with mouth agape when His Radiant Holiness, the Patriarch Toa-Sytell himself, limped down the Courthouse stairs to the basement guardroom.

4

THE PATRIARCH'S SKIN had gone slack and corpse-waxy, and his eyes drowned in pools of bruise; his lips were cracked, seeping blood that trailed down his chin. His robe of office was torn, stained with food and blood and vomit, and embers climbed its hem along a patch of the black oil. He had for escort six nervous, sweating, lip-licking Eyes of God officers who wore full hauberks and chain coifs under steel helms, who walked with bared swords in unsteady hands.

Habrak finally remembered himself and sprang from his desk chair to attention. The Patriarch leaned upon the gate between them as though only those steel bars kept him on his feet.

"Sergeant," the Patriarch croaked. "It's time."

He paused, and glared at Habrak expectantly, waiting for a response. "Come *here*, man. Don't make me shout. My throat hurts. Didn't you hear me? It's *time*."

Harbrak swallowed. He moved away from his desk, closer to the gate, stopping a respectful arm's length away. "Time for what, Your Radiance?" he said carefully.

"Time to kill Caine."

"Your Radiance?"

The Patriarch mopped his raddled brow with a shaking hand. "It was the fire, you see? That's how I knew. Foolish. I was so foolish. I thought I could be clever. I thought I could use him, but he has used me. Just like before. The city burns. *Burns*—it burns like before. You remember? You remember before? You remember the city in flames?"

"I do, Radiance," Habrak said grimly.

"Go, then. Handle it yourself." That shaking hand shot forth between the bars of the gate and seized Habrak's shoulder. "You're a good man. I can trust you. I've always known I can trust you."

"Thank you, Radiance."

"What—" The Patriarch's eyes drifted closed, and Habrak thought the man might be about to faint, but even as he lifted a hand to catch his sovereign, those blackened eyes popped open again and fixed him with a glare as sharply inhuman as an eagle's. "What is your name, again?"

"Habrak, Radiance. Sergeant Habrak."

"Habrak, don't try to be clever. Keep it simple. That was my mistake. I thought I was clever enough that I didn't have to keep it simple."

"Keep what simple, Radiance?"

"Killing Caine."

"Sir?"

Toa-Sytell gripped Habrak's other shoulder as well, and drew him close to the bars that kept them apart. His breath stank of corruption. "Do it yourself, Habrak. Do it. Take your club. Go down into the Shaft. Bash in his skull. Do you understand?"

Habrak stiffened. He had never questioned an order in his life. "Yes, sir."

"And when you're done, feed his body to the grinder."

"Yes, sir."

"Bash him. Bash him good. Grind him up. Bash him, and grind him. You will do that? You will bash him and grind him?"

Habrak saluted. "Yes, sir. But, sir—?"

"Yes?"

"What about Assumption Day, sir?"

"Forget about Assumption Day," the Patriarch muttered acidly. "Everyone else has."

"Yes, sir."

"You're a good man, Habrak. You are about to save the Empire. And his head. Save his head, too. Just like the Empire."

"Sir?"

"We'll need his head. For the pole."

"Yes, sir."

"You will not leave the Donjon without Caine's head. Give

him your key," the Patriarch said, indicating one of the Eyes. "The key to this gate."

Habrak dutifully removed it from his large iron ring and handed it through the bars to the Eye of God. The officer clutched it stiffly.

"The next thing to pass through this gateway will be Caine's head, do you understand?" the Patriarch said to the Eye. "No one enters. No one leaves. This gate will not be opened until someone comes up those stairs out of the Donjon and hands Caine's head to you. Do you understand?"

The officer said, "Yes, sir."

"If this gate opens for any other reason, all six of you will have *your* heads on poles instead. I don't care if Ma'elKoth Himself orders you to open this gate. He may punish you in your next life, but I can kill you in this one."

The officers eyed each other nervously.

He turned back to Habrak. "And do not hope that they will falter, or that some other may open this gate. I have dismissed the guards in the Courthouse above. They could not be trusted. Above you now there are only the Eyes of God. They will be watching."

The Patriarch nodded as though agreeing with some inaudible comment. "I'll be in the chapel."

Then he turned and limped back up the stairs.

Habrak stared after him for a moment, then for a moment longer he looked at the Eyes of God, who looked back at him and at each other, and who seemed decidedly frightened. He picked up his ring of keys in one hand, slung the thong of his iron-bound club around the other, and unlocked the iron-barred door that closed the stairway down to the Donjon.

"Hmp," he muttered under his breath. He'd almost left without a knife. *Can't cut somebody's head off with a club, can you?* From a drawer of his desk he got a large, single-edged dirk and stuck it behind the belt that girdled his armor.

Then he tromped down the stairs to kill Caine.

5

JEST HAD BEEN deep in the darkness for a long, long time.

By the time claws had finally reached out of the infinite

midnight of the caverns, seized him, and dragged him into this larger darkness, Jest knew exactly who he was and what he would do. He was a survivor. He would survive.

"I'm unarmed. I surrender," he repeated, as he had ever since he had escaped into the caverns a step ahead of the Eyes of God. He'd said it again and again, over and over, endlessly, for what must have been days, his throat dry, his lips cracking, his eyes so long benighted that he had lost the memory of light. "I'm unarmed, and I surrender."

He continued until his silence was invited by a cuff to the back of his head.

This darkness was textured with sound: shufflings and grunts and snorts and sniffles, the occasional metallic rustle of armor or the scrape of a blade on a stone.

His Grace the Honorable Toa-M'Jest, Duke of Public Order, would in similar circumstances have been inclined to bluster: to remind his captors of his importance, and hint at Imperial reprisals for any harm he might suffer. His Majesty the King of Cant would have been inclined to bargain: to invite his captors to set a price for his freedom, to negotiate a deal and then honor it or not, as suited his advantage. But both of those men had been eaten by the darkness.

Here there was only Jest, as his mother had named him: a cruel joke played on her by her body and the world.

"Welcome, Your Grace, to my humble home."

The voice was Kierendal's, though he wasn't sure that *voice* was the right word. It was curiously toneless, clear and soft, and sounded so near that he should have been able to feel her breath upon his neck. But he could feel only rough claws that dug into his arms and held him upright. He could see only the geometric flicker and amorphic pulse of his eyelights. And this place smelled like the fucking Shaft. "Kier—" he began.

"Hsst! Don't say that name! Don't *ever* say that name." The voice slid from cold panic to a cynical drawl. "It's bad luck to name the unquiet dead."

"Dead—?"

"Thrice dead. That feya died by her own hand: she drank poison. Then, some days later, she died of grief, at Commons' Beach. Finally, later still, she gave her life to protect her people, fighting the might of the Empire in the burning ruins of her own home."

"Three times dead and still kicking," Jest said softly, without mockery. "She must be tough."

"Once, perhaps. No more."

"If, ah, that lady is dead, then who am I talking to?"

The darkness replied, "I am that unhappy feya's vengeful corpse."

"Huh. I thought your voice sounded a little funny," he ventured, but received no answering chuckle.

"It is not my voice you hear."

"Yeah, all right," he said, thinking, *Fuck me, she's as crazy as Toa-Sytell*. But he had no other hope. "I want to make you an offer."

"Of course you do."

"I can tell you where the Cats, the Eyes, and the Thaumaturgic Corps are stationed—positions and numbers. I can tell you where our weapons and supplies are. I can map out our patrol routes through the caverns. I personally drew up the plans for the main assault—"

"And what good is this information to me?"

She couldn't be so crazy as that. Could she? "It'll win your war for you," he said patiently.

"There is no war."

"Lady, it sure as fuck looked like a war from our side."

Silence.

More shufflings and shiftings of weight.

Thick, wet drips and drops: perhaps the drool of something large and hungry.

"Your army—those human troops of whom you speak—" the voice finally said, dark and slow and empty, "have other concerns, more pressing than who might range these caverns. Your human city burns, and human ghouls stalk its ruin."

"Listen," Jest said, licking his lips. How much of this was madness? He didn't know how long he'd been down in the dark; Ankhana might as well have been on the far side of the world. Her raving could have truth in it, and he'd never know.

"Listen, the Patriarch's gone crazy. He thinks I'm a goddamn Cainist. I would have maybe stuck it out and fought back, but there's nobody I could really trust. Everybody's gone strange—and I mean *strange*." He softened his tone, made his voice warmer, more inviting. "You and I, what we had was never about trust. I help you; you help me. Favors given for favors received."

He took a deep breath. "I was thinking we could maybe work something out."

"Is that what you want? Is that what has brought you here? You are once again interested in my *favors*?"

"I, ah—" Damp as these goddamn caverns were, how could his lips be so fucking dry? He licked them again, and said, "Hey, I won't pretend I haven't missed you."

"Have you?"

"I mean, think about it: you and I? In some ways, we were made for each other."

"I remember . . ." that eerily toneless simulacrum of Kierendal's voice murmured. "I remember what it is to be desired."

"And I," Jest ventured, sensing an opening, "remember what it is to desire you. We were great together. You know we were. No other woman has ever made me feel—"

"I am not a woman."

"No female of any species," Jest amended smoothly. "No human, no primal or stonebender or whatever, has brought out of me what you did. I dream about you at night, and wake up in a sweat. I panic when I think I might never see you again."

"To see me? Is this your wish?"

"That, and more," he asserted. "I mean, we could turn all this around. There are still men loyal to me within the Eyes, and the Cats are mine to a man. Not only that, but I know where the Thaumaturgic Corps stockpiles their remaining griffinstones—"

"There is nothing to turn."

"Well, then . . ." Jest tried a smile. Could she see him that clearly? "Then maybe we can just . . . be together again. You know?"

"So." Her voice came back languid and earthy. "You wish once again to touch my breast, to lay your hand along my hip."

"More than anything else in the world," he said, thinking, *except maybe getting out of here alive*.

"Very well: I accept your devotion. Kiss me once, and it is done."

Hands like branches of a winter-killed tree seized his face and held him motionless. Something crusted and hard pressed against his mouth, oozing with a thick coppery goo like—no, not like anything; it *was*.

Half-clotted blood.

The crust parted into needle teeth that pierced his lower lip. A tongue like a bark-covered stump forced its way into his mouth, and it tasted like this cavern smelled: old meat, black and webbed with decay. The rough claws released him, and Jest sank to his knees, gagging, both hands at his throat.

"My kiss no longer wakes that familiar passion?" the voice asked with blank mockery.

"No, I ah . . ." Jest coughed, and coughed again. "No. You startled me, that's all. I was just startled. I didn't know you were already so, ah, close to me. I can't tell where your voice is coming from."

"This isn't my voice. It comes from inside your ear. I no longer speak."

"I don't understand."

"Of course you don't. Understanding is *my* curse. My gift."

A brighter patch gathered itself within the darkness: shapeless still, but slowly self-defining as the illumination grew.

"It was the gift of an old, old friend," the voice murmured. "He, too, once desired me. He gave me understanding at the same time he gifted me with death."

As it brightened, the shape seemed to resolve into a gruesomely mutilated spider: some sort of emaciated arachnoid creature with half its limbs cut off. The spider-shape's head tilted slowly, hypnotically, back and forth, as though it worked to swallow some half-choking chunk of meat.

"Can you imagine," the voice continued, "what it is to go mad, and to know you are going mad? Can you imagine understanding precisely what makes you want to murder your friends and eat their corpses—and yet to want it anyway?"

"No, I—ah, no."

"You will."

The pale glow from the mutilated spider increased until Jest could now make out her features: sunken, skeletal, skin of translucent parchment mottled with weeping sores, stretched over fleshless bones. Naked, sexless, a squirm of internal organs within the abdomen, pale mats of hair clotted across the scalp, blackened lips, cracked and oozing, that did not move though the voice went on. "I have shared this with you, Toa-M'Jest . . . Majesty . . . what you will. You'll become as I am."

"Yeah, all right," Jest said. She was beyond fucked, but maybe he could still manage to make enough of a deal to get himself away. "You've shared. I can tell you're a, yeah, a little under the weather, but that doesn't mean we have to lose the war."

She neither moved nor changed expression as that disembodied voice roared, *"There is no war!"*

"Then I guess I was wrong after all," Jest said with a small sad smile. He sagged back, losing hope. "I always said that every time Caine comes to town, we end up in a fucking war. Hah. I should be so lucky."

"Caine?"

The word was a hurricane blast, and with it exploded light so dazzling Jest cried out and covered his eyes with both hands.

"Caine is here? *Caine is here now?"*

Jest roasted in the savage glare. He couldn't take his hands away from his face. "I, ah—"

"Answer me!"

"Yeah," he said, flinching from the thunder in his ears. "The Monasteries caught him, and they delivered him to the Patriarch a couple days after the battle at Commons' Beach."

"It was him. All along. I knew, and yet I didn't know. It's so clear now. It's so obvious what we have to do."

Jest slowly managed to pull his hands down, and he squinted away from the light. The cavern was the size of the Great Hall, and it was filled with bodies.

Primals, stonebenders, ogrilloi, trolls and ogres and treetoppers, dressed in rags or wholly naked, sick, maybe dying, many already dead, vomit pooled in hollows of stone—and over them all rose Kierendal, naked and madder than the rest, the crippled spider queen. "Up, children! Awake and arm!—Do you not hear? This is our chance to revenge our own murders! We can kill the man who killed us!"

As her tattered rabble gathered themselves, her burning glare pinned Jest like a javelin through the eye. "You know where he is."

Jest licked his lips. He'd known Caine for twenty years. Caine had saved his life, had made him Duke. What he had said to Toa-Sytell was the truth: He loved the man like his own brother.

But . . .

Jest was who he was. He was a survivor.

He said simply, "He's in the Donjon."

With a shout, the darkness returned: darkness that clattered with boots and horn-soled feet, that snarled and shouted with fierce voices in unknown tongues, that clanged with weapons and rustled with armor. He was seized and dragged over stone, lifted and dropped and lifted again, passed up shafts from hand to hand and allowed to slide down steep bruising slopes.

And he knew: Darkness hides everything except who you really are.

6

THERE HAD BEEN a carefully orchestrated crescendo to the public clamor for Michaelson's rescue. When it reached its peak, Westfield Turner once again addressed the world, live on the net.

He explained that the Studio had spent these past days in frantic preparation for a rescue mission, but that Michaelson's position in the Donjon made direct action by Actors virtually impossible: the rock from which the Donjon is carved has a randomizing effect upon the Winston Transfer. Actors can neither be transferred in nor out.

A sizable minority of the concerned citizens found this difficulty puzzling. They had viewed, for example, *For Love of Pallas Ril,* and the rock had seemed to have no adverse effect on Caine's thoughtmitter transmissions during the rather extended action sequence inside the Donjon. On the other hand, the Studio people should know what they were talking about, shouldn't they? A few wondered if the Studio might be mistaken. Only the most paranoid of conspiracy theorists suspected that Turner's tale might be a direct lie.

But now, it seemed, some side-effect of the calamity overtaking Ankhana had cut the city off entirely from the Studio's technology. Sources across the net speculated that it might be related to the ongoing war in the caverns below the city. The Faces clearly had been able to strike back: the last images out of Ankhana had been of the whole city in flames. Now even those Actors with the ISP were off-line and in terrible danger. *"But don't lose hope,"* Westfield Turner told the world. *"As Caine himself once said: Never surrender.*

"We will not surrender. I ask you now to lend your support to my petition before the Leisure Congress. With the consent of the Congress, we can move combat troops into position for instant action. I ask for authorization to mount a full-scale military rescue, if need be. This may be Chairman Michaelson's only hope.

"He put himself on the line for us over and over again. Now it's our turn. We can't let him down.

"We won't let him down.

"We may not be able to save him, but we won't let him go without a fight."

President Turner failed to reveal that many of these preparations had begun days before, well in advance of the first confirmation that Caine was even alive.

At the very moment he made that speech, the first elements of Bauer Company of the Social Police 82nd Force Suppression Unit—a reinforced rifle battalion, accompanied by a number of Overworld-trained irregulars drawn from the ranks of the most reliable Actors worldwide—were already in inflatable boats, on their way down the Great Chambaygen into Ankhana.

7

HABRAK FOUND CAINE propped against the sweating limestone, legs splayed in the filth that slickened the step. He looked like a naked wooden puppet Habrak had found in an alley, once upon a wintertide many years ago. Some angry child had thrown it against a wall, and it had landed broken in a dungheap. Habrak had taken it home, cleaned it, and mended its broken back, and his daughter's eyes had glistened on her birthday morning—

The sergeant stood over him, scowling. Caine or no Caine, he didn't much like this idea of clubbing a helpless man to death. After twenty years in the army followed by seventeen years in the Donjon Guard—twelve of them as sergeant—he calculated that he had a clear idea of his duties. He was to see that prisoners in the Donjon stayed in the Donjon. That's all. He wasn't the bloody Imperial Executioner, was he?

No use trying to explain that to the bloody Patriarch.

But he couldn't duck or ditch, either. He sighed. He'd given this a fair think-on, and he couldn't get comfortable ordering any of his boys to do a job too dirty to do himself. Besides, he wasn't sure he could trust any of them to do it properly. Too many of them would make it personal. A lot of his boys had been in the Guard long enough to remember Caine's last visit.

It was on Habrak's watch that Caine had come, seven years

ago. It was the men of Habrak's watch who had been killed and maimed in the riot Caine had sparked to cover his escape.

The warm weight of his club brushed against his leg. He swung it by the leather loop around his wrist, spinning it up into killing position, then held it for a moment before his eyes: a rod of oak as long as his forearm, leather-wrapped butt, its business end knobbed with rings of iron. He paused for a moment, there in the Shaft, and the tip of his tongue stroked the inside of his cheek, following the thick rope of scar that connected the corner of his lip to the hinge of his jaw.

He could see it as though it happened again this instant: the Shaft door springing suddenly open, the black sparks of Caine's eyes, the white flash of his knife blade. In memory, the thrust came slow as a cloud across the summer sky; in reality, the blade had shattered his teeth and sliced through his cheek before he had even realized he was its target.

He had more reason to make this personal, maybe, than any of his boys. He had more reason to take his time, to hurt the man before he killed him. But he wouldn't.

The city might have burned down over his head—the whole bloody world might be going up in bloody smoke—but the bloody Donjon would stay in order, and Habrak and every man under him would do their bloody duty until ordered to do otherwise.

He swung the club back down to his side and jangled his keys where they dangled from their steel ring at his belt. He'd bash in Caine's head and feed him to the grinder. He didn't have to enjoy it. He just had to do it.

That's what being a soldier is.

Caine's eyes were open, glassy and staring; they remained still when Habrak passed his lamp before them. His pupils didn't react to the changing light.

Dead.

Habrak nodded to himself. Not too surprising, given the wet grey rot chewing away those legs. Looked like he'd scratched something in the wall before he died. Lot of Shafters did that kind of thing. Habrak always calculated these forgotten folks were just that desperate to leave some mark of their passing. Sometimes they wrote something interesting, or even funny.

Habrak squinted at the scratches, but he couldn't tell what Caine might have wanted to say. He seemed to recall that Caine was supposed to be Pathquan. Maybe that's what this was, something in Pathquan; maybe those Pathquans used a different alphabet or something. Couldn't even tell if these were supposed to be letters or numbers or some kind of picture writing.

He grunted to himself. So, sure, Caine left his last words engraved in stone—but there was nobody who could read them.

Just another deader, anonymous as the rest.

Well, that was a relief.

Still, dead or not, he had his orders.

One good overhand to the top of the skull. No point trying to smash the frontal bone—and besides, he didn't want to damage the man's face; he needed Caine recognizable to get himself out of here. He hooked a toe under one of Caine's knees and shoved it to the side, seeking better footing. Seemed a bit indecent, bashing a corpse like this—

Habrak frowned, squinting critically at Caine's head. Maybe he'd do better with a two-handed stroke. He turned and set the lamp down on the step behind him, and when he turned back he found that Caine's fixed stare had fixed on him.

"Hey," Habrak said uncertainly. "Are you alive, or what?"

Caine didn't answer. He didn't seem to be breathing.

The huge shadow Habrak cast on the wall shrank as the sergeant took a tentative step closer. He adjusted his grip on his club, to hold it with both hands before him, like a sword.

"Hey, you," he said. He nudged Caine's suppurating knee once more with the toe of his boot. "Hey, you *are* alive, aren't you?"

A slow stretch of Caine's lips showed teeth gleaming with the flame that shines in the eyes of wolves.

"Know what?" Caine said slowly. "When you kick me in the leg?"

His voice scraped like a handful of cinders.

"It *hurts*."

ON THE DAY the dead man named himself, the great stone that had sealed his tomb was shattered. Its shards were cast into the abyss, for what he breaks can never be mended, and what he opens can never be closed. This is the power of such naming.

He came forth from his tomb, glowing and strong as a morning sun that comes out of dark mountains.

TWENTY

THE CLUB COMES down from somewhere in the outer darkness: from the Oort Cloud of shadow behind and beyond the guard's head. It floats: a feather pillow dropped from the moon: the terminal velocity of a mother's kiss. It's a flash, a thunderbolt: the blast of a shotgun shoved in my face. It comes down cleanly, efficiently, professionally: a butcher's stroke, a guillotine's. The club comes down in every possible shade of lethal delight, and none of them matter one thin slice of goddamn.

Because when the club comes down, my leg moves.

Just a twitch, a sudden kink of the knee: no more than the reflexive spastic jerk of a dying man rattling his heels on the floor: but enough. That's the victory, right there. The rest is mop-up.

Because he steps into the stroke—in his solid, professional way—and puts his right ankle just inside my left knee, and when my left leg suddenly doubles it pulls him a bare two inches closer to me, so that the blow that should have splattered my brains into the shit on the floor instead slams the iron-ringed knob against the stone wall on which I rest my head, and stings the fucking club right out of his hands.

It also pulls him a trace off balance, a happy trend that I encourage: I take one of his wrists with my free hand and yank him down on top of me. His helmet and the head inside it hit the wall with a cartoon *ker-blank*, and before he quite understands what's happening I've turned his back to me and the chain that links my right wrist to the wall now wraps his throat.

He tries to shout, but the chain is tight. He tries to struggle, but I used to murder people for a living. Nothing in his professional experience has prepared him for someone like me.

While I throttle him, I consider if maybe somehow I can get away with letting him live. Maybe it was the mindview, I don't know, but . . . watching him come down the Shaft, I felt like I knew him. Like I could read him, somehow. I mean, I do know him, sort of secondhand—Habrak, I think his name is. A couple of Actors from the ISP have bumped into him now and again. He always seemed like a decent guy, and more than that: he seemed like the kind of guy who was doing what the gods intended for him when he was born. Maybe it's not a high destiny, being a sergeant in the Donjon Guard, but it's his.

I mean, how can you not like somebody who's so good at being exactly who he is?

I count the seconds after he goes limp. Too few, he'll wake right up; too many, he won't wake up at all. I make good use of this necessary pause by unbuckling the girdle that holds his hauberk close around his waist and getting my free hand on his ring of keys. I grip the chain with my right as I fit one key after another into the simple lock on my manacle: it takes only seconds to find the right one, and the manacle swings open.

Some ugly sores there, where the iron has scraped away skin. Yeah, big deal. The infections on my legs'll kill me before I have to worry about my wrist.

Pretty soon, I let up the pressure on the guard's throat. He's limp as a hunk of liver. Getting his hauberk off him is simple in concept, complex in practice, but I manage. I clip his wrist into the manacle before I slide his armor over my head.

It's a goddamn luxury to have clothes on after all this time, even if those clothes are made out of cold slimy iron links. I give the guard's ankle a grateful pat, and he stirs.

He's not awake yet, but he will be soon. So I'll let him wake up. So what? He's not going anywhere, and no Pit guard will hear his voice; anything he might yell will smother in this blanket of lunatic screams. They'll find him the next time they sweep the Shaft for corpses, but by then I'll be out of here, or dead. Call it my good deed for the day.

I don't think I'll manage another.

I lay the girdle out on the floor and roll myself onto it so I can buckle it around my waist. Huh. Nice knife. I tie the club to the girdle by its leather thong, and contemplate my next move.

I have no fucking clue how I'm going to get through the Shaft door, how I can get past the guards outside it, or what I can do out in the Pit, but:

First things first.

That Shaft door is a long hundred feet or more above me, up a slope of unevenly worn slick stairs, and a twitch or two of my no-longer-entirely-dead legs is a few damn miles short of an evening stroll.

Well, y'know: you have to crawl before you can walk.

I stick the sheathed dirk under the girdle at the small of my back, because I'm going up on my belly. Lamp in my left hand, keys in my right, I start pulling myself up the Shaft with my elbows.

I head for daylight, an inch at a time.

2

ORBEK RUBBED HIS stinging eyes with his free hand, then stared again at the jerky hook-and-pause of the point of light far below. He couldn't figure out what could be making it move like that; it looped and stopped and looped again, a stuttering spiral like the beckon-lamp of a hungry marshghoul.

The hot damp air of the Shaft became a snort of winter down his back.

He'd never heard of a marshghoul coming into a city. They stick to their swamps, where they can lure a guy off the road with their beckon-lamps till the unlucky bastard gets lost, then they suck out his eyeballs and all his juices and push his corpse down into the bogs and nobody ever sees them again, except maybe someday when somebody's cutting peat a hundred years later they find him, his skin gone to leather and his empty eye sockets slick and gummy, and if a marshghoul ever did come to a city, it'd sure as shit start in the Shaft, because the Shaft was as good as a bog and you can't get away and now it was coming for him like his dam always said it would—

And if he kept thinking about it, he would start to scream, and he didn't have much voice left anyway. He'd pretty well used it up a couple hours after they chained him here.

These other guys, though, their voices never did seem to go out. They were *still* screaming—and these screams and sobs and moans and shit were sounding different, now; not so hopeless, not so scared, not at all like he figured a guy'd howl when a marshghoul started sucking out his eyeball.

Orbek didn't really believe in marshghouls, anyway.

The light came closer, rising through the Shaft's murky gloom, and it *was* a lamp: a lamp in the hand of something that pulled itself up the steps of the Shaft with its elbows. And as it approached it might as goddamn well have been a marshghoul, considering the sizzle of superstitious terror it sent down Orbek's spine when he picked up the glint of its eyes and then the gleam of its teeth, and Orbek figured out what it was.

It was Caine.

And he was smiling.

Orbek had a fair amount of time to figure out what he would say, while he watched Caine inch his way up the Shaft. When Caine got close enough that he might be able to hear through the din of the Shafters' howls, Orbek hid his maimed hands behind him and said, "Hey."

Caine stopped. He twisted his head so he could look at Orbek past the flame of the lamp in his left hand. He set the lamp on the floor and slowly levered himself up to one elbow, and stared at Orbek for what felt like a couple of years.

Then he said, "Hey."

Only two things in the Shaft had reality for Orbek then. One was the look in Caine's eyes; the other was the iron ring of keys that he held in his left hand.

"Good to see you," Orbek said.

Caine said, "Yeah?"

"Yeah. Better, though: to see those keys."

"I'll bet." He grunted something that might have been a chuckle. "You don't ask how I got them. How I got loose."

Orbek shrugged. "Don't matter, hey?"

Caine nodded thoughtfully. "Y'know, Orbek, you and I, we're maybe a lot more alike than we are different."

"Maybe we are," Orbek said. "You gonna let me loose?"

"I'm thinking about it. What are you doing in the Shaft?"

"Sittin' on my fuck-me ass."

"You know what I mean."

Orbek shrugged. Now Caine's gaze became hard to bear; he had to look away, up into the darkness that shrouded the door. "That don't matter, either."

"Maybe not to you."

Orbek felt himself flush. He rattled his chain and coughed in his throat, and hoped Caine would let him off the hook, but the bastard just lay there staring until Orbek had to go on. "To explain ain't easy."

"Try."

"After they take you away . . . everything just goes to shit, hey? Thinkin' she's boss now, t'Passe orders everybody around, but nobody likes her, and everybody splits up into these little shitty groups that all kind of hate each other and, well, shit, I don't know. If you ain't come back, we all die anyway. So I figure I maybe chain my ass in here with you, so if you do come out, I can maybe help. Be your legs, like before."

Caine squinted at him. "Yeah?"

"So I throw shit at the guards. Whenever they come out on the catwalk. I lob a couple clods of shit, and here I am. I call you. I call your name and call again, but I don't hear no answer. Pretty soon, my voice gives out. You're dead, I figure. How come you don't answer?"

Caine said steadily, "I was busy."

"Yeah?"

"Yeah. I had my mind on other things. What about Deliann?"

"Dead, I guess."

"You guess?"

Orbek shrugged. "He's pretty sick when I come in here. That leg's bad. Don't think he's got a day left, and that's a while ago."

Caine stared down into the infinite black below.

"So," Orbek said after a while. "That's the story, hey? Unlock me, you gonna?"

Caine slowly drew back his gaze and met Orbek's eye. "Maybe I'm thinking you'd be safer down here."

"Don't do me no favor, Caine." Slowly, painfully, Orbek pulled his hands out from behind his back and showed Caine the crusted, filthy bandages around his wrists, where his fighting claws had once been. Where now there were only pus-weeping stumps.

Caine hissed through his teeth.

"More than I expect, they give me, hey?"

Caine murmured, "Holy shit."

"Boltcutters," Orbek said. "Click clack. Click fuck-me *clack*. You understand what they do to me? Do you?"

Caine's answer was a bleak stare.

"They do to me what you do to Black Knives those years ago: cut off what makes me *me*. Now I never get a bitch. Never get pups. What good's being safe? A good death is all I got left. A good death. Honor on my clan."

"I hear you," Caine said.

"Let me loose."

He didn't move. "Maybe *I'm* safer with you down here."

"Maybe you are." Orbek showed him his tusks. "What you gotta do, do."

Caine thought about it long enough to set Orbek's heart pounding against his ribs; then he shrugged. "Yeah, whatever," he said, and tossed Orbek the keys.

Orbek unlocked his manacle, and rose. He looked down on the crippled human at his feet. "Here we are again, Caine," he said.

"Yeah."

"I can kill you now."

Caine didn't answer.

"You know it's true," Orbek said. "You know that armor, that club, they don't help you. That wrestling you do, that don't help you either. Not this time. When you give me freedom, you give me your life. You understand what that means?"

"That I'm a goddamn idiot?"

"Maybe I die here in the Shaft. Maybe on the fire Assumption Day. But if I kill you now, I kill the man who cut off the Black Knives. Honor on me. Honor on my clan."

"So?" Caine said, flat and cold, waiting.

Orbek shrugged. "So maybe I got a better idea."

He knelt at Caine's side and stripped the bandage from his

right wrist. Its crust stuck to his infected stump. He ripped the bandage free, bringing an ooze of black blood, thick with pus.

"This is my battle wound," he said, and he laid his stump on one of the gangrenous sores on Caine's leg. "This is your battle wound. Our wounds are one. Our blood is one."

"What the fuck are you doing?"

Orbek's lips pulled back from his tusks. "I'm adopting you."

"The fuck you are."

"Black Knife, you are now. You give me your life. This is how I take it."

"Are you nuts? I'm the guy that—"

"I know who you are," Orbek said. "You remember who I am. Dishonor you put on the Black Knives. Now that dishonor, you share." He showed Caine his tusks. "Now what honor you win, you share that, too. Good deal for Black Knives, hey?"

"Why would I want to join your fucking clan?"

"What *you* want? Who cares?" Orbek rose, grinning. "You don't choose your clan, Caine. Born Black Knife, you're Black Knife. Born Hooked Arrow, you're Hooked Arrow. Now: Say that you are Black Knife, then let's go kill some guards, hey?"

Caine lay on the stone, silent.

Orbek growled, "Say it."

The lamp gave Caine's eyes a feral glitter.

"All right," he said at length. For all his tiny, mostly useless human teeth, he managed a surprisingly good mirror of Orbek's tusk display.

"Like you say: I am Black Knife."

3

DELIANN FELT, RATHER than saw, the slow amble of the drooling trusty who followed the arc of the balcony to the Shaft door, bearing his sack of hard bread and his jug of water.

Deliann's paste-colored head centered a dark stain of sweat, sweat that rolled down his face like tears and spread across a makeshift pallet of rolled shirts and ragged trousers and tattered robes layered over each other: clothing of dead prisoners. A few days ago, the Pit folk had begun stripping corpses before the guards could get down and pull the bodies out; now, most of the seriously ill prisoners possessed at least improvised, provisional beds on which to die. "Get them up," he whispered. "You don't have much time."

No answer came from the translucent shadows that crowded his uncertain vision. "T'Passe?" He forced his voice louder, trying for a shout. He managed a strangled croak. "T'Passe, are you there?"

A strong hand took his. "Deliann. I am beside you."

He rolled his head toward her voice. At his side crouched a slightly more substantial shadow; this shadow had a hint of solidity, half obscuring the twisting lattice of energy in motion that had washed away the reality of the Pit and all within it. Deliann frowned, and squinted.

"Night threads," he murmured. He had to make her understand. "Night threads draw shadows from the moon . . ." No, that wouldn't help; he lifted a weakly trembling hand and tried to massage his vision into focus. "Everything seems to be falling apart . . . ?"

T'Passe sighed and squatted beside him, lowering herself along with her voice. "Everything *is* falling apart," she said.

Deliann took her hand in his clammy, shaking fingers. "It *seems* like it's falling apart. But that's only seeming. It's falling *together*. It's gathering toward a center that isn't here yet."

The swelling on Deliann's thigh had risen and reddened and finally burst; its corrupt milk lent his makeshift pallet a fouler stench of rot. The abscess left behind was a crater lined with dead flesh, grey and slick and oozing, big enough that t'Passe could have put her fist inside it. Fever scattered his best attempts at coherence. "This is our chance," he said. "This is the blow we can strike in Hari's war."

"I don't understand."

"I can't help that," he sighed. Words were a microscope, the truth a planet. Even if he could describe the pale sliver of the shadow of the truth that he could see, could she understand? Indrawing concentric rings of force that shifted and flowed across two universes, narrowing and refining and focusing into a pinpoint star of *right now*, of *right here*; the scalar self-similarity of fractal reality from the interplay of quarks to the event horizons of all the universes—what words could make these comprehensible to a mind that had not experienced them directly?

He struggled to pull himself below the waves of fever, down into the calm depths of the here and now, down to where he could feel the gathering storm of violence that lowered upon the world, the Empire, the city, the Donjon. Violence swarmed the Courthouse like bees around his head; violence forced up the sump below the Shaft like rape. Violence shimmered toward existence on the Pit balcony: it gathered like pus within an abscess, stretching dying skin above. It grew where the trusty stood, waiting for the guards at the Shaft to open the door.

And on that same spot, a white flare of power sparked from outside the world. Knotted threads of black Flow streamed toward it, twisting themselves into strings, then ropes, then hawsers pulsing with furious energy. "Get them up," Deliann whispered. "Get everyone up. Get them on their feet. Just do it. This is your only chance."

"You heard him," t'Passe said roughly, speaking toward the shadows above. "What are you waiting for?"

Some of the translucent shadows moved away from him then, slipping past and through each other. Throughout the Pit, shadows overlapped and deepened as they came to their feet, and the sizzle of violence around was joined by one within.

T'Passe's shade leaned close. "What *are* we waiting for?"

"Not what, but who," Deliann whispered. A surge of energy hit him like nausea; he could barely choke out the words. "Caine is coming."

The guards unbarred the Shaft door.

"Deliann—" He heard the despair in her voice; she still didn't understand. She still didn't believe. "Deliann, Caine is dead."

"No," Deliann said.

"Yes. He's been in the Shaft for days. With open sores on his legs, deep ones. By now, he is certainly dead."

"No," Deliann said. "T'Passe, I was wrong. He isn't coming."

"I know," she said sadly.

The Shaft door swung open, and the trusty started to enter.

"He isn't coming," Deliann said. "He's here."

4

THE BAR SCRAPES across the outside of the Shaft door.

Orbek shows me his tusks and hefts the club. The hauberk fits him like the skin on an overcooked sausage. I'm naked again, but I don't mind. I've got the knife.

That's all the clothes I need.

Orbek wishes me luck: "Die fighting, Caine."

I raise the knife in salute. "Die fighting."

Then a crack of lamplight widens along one side of the Shaft door, and I tell him to *"Go goddamn go DO IT!"* because there is a time to be smart and careful and look before you leap, and there is a time to just rock and fucking roll.

Orbek plants a splay-clawed foot against the slats and gives the door a kick that could stagger a bull. The door booms open and the wetbrain is standing there with his mouth slack, one thin line of astonished drool stretching for the floor for maybe half a second until Orbek steps up and pegs him with the club. He falls, howling, and the doorway is clear, and Shafters pour out.

The guards to either side of the door don't even get a chance to unsling their clubs; Orbek and I found maybe eighteen or twenty Shafters—mostly human, but a couple primals and three or four 'rillos—who were still sane enough to give a coherent answer to the question: "You want to die down here in the dark, or up there in the light?"

The door guards go down under a howling tide of naked filth-crusted madmen. Guards pound around the balcony and across the catwalks, scrambling to get into position to fire their cross-bows without shooting each other. A pair of Shafters carry me out onto the balcony, holding my arms around their shoulders. Orbek and five or six Shafters sprint for the winch platform. The rest of them leave the door guards to bleed on the balcony and throw themselves onto the catwalks to intercept the fresh guards charging toward us.

"Put me right up to the rail," I tell the guys carrying me, and they stand me up against the low retaining wall around the balcony. Guards scream at me, at all of us, to put up our hands, surrender, there's nowhere for us to go, all that kind of shit, and there are a hell of a lot of crossbow quarrels aimed at my chest.

Everybody in the whole damn Pit is on their feet, staring, mouths birthing snarls: this place is a fucking live grenade, just waiting for somebody to twist the primer.

So I do.

"You said I was gonna die down there!" Thirty years of *ki-ai* have given me a voice that cuts through the shouting like a civil defense siren. *"I said I'd be back!"*

I give the Pit my wolf-grin and howl, *"What's Rule Two?"*

That brings them up like a storm surge in the Atlantic: they snarl and hoot and bunch toward me, shoulder to shoulder, a living mass of blood-hunger writhing and rippling as it shakes the sleep out of its joints.

The guards let fly, and quarrels chop into flesh. Blood sprays, skin and chunks of yellow bone flip through the air as Shafters fall; one of the Shafters at my side grunts and staggers back, a quarrel sticking out of the ragged hole it punched through his rib cage. Two-thirds of the way to the winch platform, Orbek takes one in the belly that doubles him over. A couple of the Shafters with him go down, but Orbek's up in an instant and running again.

Those armor-safe crossbows kinda suck when a prisoner has armor of his own.

Ten seconds to reload.

I'd had a vague plan to shout some kind of inspirational slogan, to get them all heated up and ready to charge the stairs, but I can't think of one goddamn inspirational word. Henry the vee I'm not. What I am, though, is a good enough Actor to know when to throw focus.

I point the dirk at Orbek and shout, *"Look!"*

He's left the Shafters behind. Two of the three guards from the winch platform run down the stairs to intercept, while the third stays back by the winch and cranks the crowsfoot on his bow. Orbek bulldozes the first one like a defensive end on a fistful of greens, and a roar goes up from the Pit.

Then he's past; the second guard whirls his club into a whistling overhand that Orbek deflects with a very professional roofblock—just like I taught him—before he counters with an *abneko* umbrella-strike that dents the guard's helmet and sends him staggering backward.

"It's not a fucking duel!" I shout. *"Just kill the sonofabitch!"*

Now the first guard is on his feet behind him, and he pegs Orbek a solid one in the floating rib; with no padding behind the chainmail, that shot folds him over like a broken doll, but he's moving sideways already and the guard's follow-up glances off his shoulder. Orbek turns into him and grabs him in a full clinch to tie up the guard's club. The guard clutches desperately at Orbek's weapon arm, gets it, and sets about working to free his own arm before he remembers that he's not fighting a man, here.

Ogrilloi have tusks.

The guard lets out a high, thin shriek that chokes to a muffled gargle as Orbek hooks a tusk under his chin that punches up through flesh to pin his tongue to his soft palate. Orbek has the neck muscle of a razorback boar; when he wrenches his head to the side, the guard's jaw dislocates and Orbek's tusk rips free, spraying blood that drenches the side of his face.

Orbek seizes the guard by collar and crotch, and lifts him over his head. *"I am Black Knife!"* he roars to the Pit. *"Orbek Black Knife!"*

They answer him with thunder.

And he tosses the guard over the balcony wall like a sack of meat into the lion cage. Prisoners swarm the fallen guard, and his shriek doesn't last long. He's no dummy, Orbek: that taste of blood whips them up more than any words I could possibly use.

When he turns his blood-drenched face on the guard with the dented helm, the guard suddenly remembers some urgent business he has on the far side of the Pit.

Quarrels zip past Orbek from the three or four guards with enough presence of mind to reload, but they don't come close enough to get his attention. The guy up on the winch platform gets off a shot as Orbek goes up the stairs, but that 'rillo has head movement like a middleweight; the quarrel just nicks his ear and glances off the shoulder of his hauberk. The guard drops his bow and unslings his club, and he's no dummy either—instead of coming to meet Orbek and giving the 'rillo a free shot at his feet and ankles from the stairs, he backs up warily and keeps the winch between them, dodging around it like a tower shield; all he really has to do is keep Orbek busy until reinforcements arrive.

Orbek, bright boy, doesn't bother to fight the guard at all, just feints him off the winch with a fake swing at his head and then spins the heavy club into an overhand that whangs into one of the ratchet pawls of the winch and snaps the fucking thing right in half. The guard shouts and comes back after him, but Orbek dodges away, grinning, and swings another overhand to snap the pawl on the other side of the winch.

The stairbridge comes down like the blade of a guillotine.

If I'd had a clue how smart that big bastard is, I would've picked on somebody else.

When the stairbridge hits the Pit floor, the guards up here stop thinking about regaining control of the situation and start thinking about getting the fuck out. Prisoners storm up the stairbridge in an endless snarling flood; there's more than a thousand people down there with nothing to lose, and the guards know it—they're not stupid enough to stick around.

Before any of the prisoners are even halfway up the stairs, most of the guards have broken for the steps on the far side of that brass-bound balcony door, heading for the Courthouse above.

The Donjon is ours.

No.

The Donjon is *mine*.

THE HERO RETURNED from the lands of the dead.

As true heroes always do, he returned with supernatural gifts: gifts that were already his nature, now transcending their mortal limits. He came forth as an infant: nameless, weak, and squalling. He faced the task of all returning heroes: to master the forces that had created him, and to reach atonement with his father.

In other words: to grow up.

TWENTY-ONE

WHEN HIS CONSCIOUSNESS intersected the world once more, he lay prone on dirty flagstones, his face turned to the left, rocks warm as blood digging into his cheek. Flame roared on all sides. Someone with agonizingly strong hands compressed his back to pump river water out of his lungs. He opened his mouth to speak, but instead retched forth a gout of water mixed with blood. It splashed across his right arm, his right hand, and he made a fist.

"I think he's awake," someone said.

For a gooey eternity, he could not recall who or where he was. He had dreamed of being Caine, of lying crippled in his own filth. The flame-streaked night offered no clue, and the feculent stench of the Donjon packed his head. Now, a bitter reek over-powered the outhouse smell: a sharp, throat-scorching tang not unlike the smoke from the Artan mining machines in Transdeia, when they chew away the mountainsides.

Those strong hands rolled him onto his back. He stared up past a pair of unfamiliar faces into billows of black smoke that smothered the stars. "Ambassador," someone said, his voice raised over the liquid roar of nearby flame. "Master Raithe—can you hear me? We must move you. How is your breathing?"

That's right, he thought. *Raithe. I am Raithe.*

He struggled for air, but he could not tell if this came of water still in his lungs or of the baking heat of the fire around him. A swamp belch of borrowed memory bubbled up from the quagmire of bruise inside his head, but it burst and vanished before he could fully grasp it.

"Raithe, you must speak now," a new voice said, a voice raw and ragged as though torn by screams.

A silhouette shambled into view above him, then squatted at his side. Scarlet firelight lit half this man's ravaged face from below and threw the rest into impenetrable shadow. Grey stubble prickled from his jaw, and his visible eye stared round and red as though he struggled never to blink. He wore the robes of a Monastic Ambassador, now stained and torn and streaked with filth. "I lost three friars to the burning oil when we pulled you from the river," he rasped. "Three good men. The last good men. The *last* men I could *trust.* Now I have you, and I will have my answer."

He leaned close and chewed at Raithe with starving eyes. "What is the significance of the sword? What did it *do* to you? What *are* you, and what have you done to the *city*?"

Raithe's mind stumbled spastically from word to word. He could make sense of none of this.

"Master Damon," a friar said warningly. "We must move. We must leave. Our lives are in danger here."

Damon's teeth showed yellow and savage as he turned on the man. "I will hear this! You can't stop me!"

"What he has to say won't mean much if we all burn to death," the friar retorted sullenly, and with an astonishing animal snarl, Damon sprang for his throat. The Acting Ambassador crashed into him and they tumbled out of Raithe's view. He couldn't seem to properly turn his head, but he could hear grunts and savage curses joined by the liquid smack of bone against muscle.

He tried to summon his mindeye, to look with his power

where he could not direct his eyes, but he saw only flames closing around him. He tried to lever himself up onto his elbows, to turn himself over or at least sit up. Tried, and failed.

His left arm did not work.

His exploring hand found a zone of numb flesh that bordered his pectoral muscle and grew outward to his shoulder, deepening until the arm itself was as dead as a steak in a smokehouse. He tried to call out, but all that could come from his throat was a strangled grunt; he tried to push himself away with his feet, scrabbling with his heel. But he pushed with only one heel; his left leg was as dead as his arm.

Help me was formed by his lips. *Please, someone—someone help me—*

Instead of flames charring his flesh, he now saw himself helpless under the knives and fingernails and teeth of men and women stripped of their humanity by Garrette's disease: demented homicidal bogeys with hearts empty of all save hunger and lust. He seemed to smell their slaughterhouse breath, seemed to feel the warm slide of their drool down his neck—

The sounds of fighting faded behind the roar of the surrounding flames. "There," Damon panted, out of sight. "There. *This* is the punishment for *treachery*. Does anyone else wish to *question* my *authority*?"

Raithe squinted against the sting of tears.

Damon reappeared at his side, and there was blood around his mouth. He sucked on a skinned knuckle for a moment before he spoke. "What is it?" he rasped. "I know you know, Raithe. *What has done this to us?*"

The only sound Raithe could summon was a thick, gargling "No—no—"

Damon drew close. "For *days*," he murmured, "I have awaited your rising. We are locked together, Raithe, you and I. This city has become a *madhouse*. You know why, and you know what I can do to save it. I have been patient, Raithe. My forbearance is at an end." A clawlike hand seized Raithe's dead left arm, and Damon lifted it with an expression mingled of lust and loathing. "I have become *hungry*."

His face spasmed, and he cast down Raithe's arm, pushing himself away like a man with vertigo retreating from the brink of a cliff. "Why won't you *help* me, Raithe? I know you can. I don't understand why you refuse . . ."

Refuse? Raithe raged inside his head. *Look at me! Will you look at me?* What exactly was he supposed to be able to *do*?

"Is it the water?" Damon asked softly, stroking Raithe's numb left cheek with his twisted clawlike hand. "I know we have been poisoned, but I must know where the good water can be found. It is our only hope, Raithe. It is the only hope of the city. Why won't you *tell* me?" Damon lowered his head and turned his face away. He whispered, "I am so *thirsty . . .*"

Raithe could only stare, gasping through the panic that crushed his chest.

"It's blood, isn't it?" Damon said suddenly. He turned back to Raithe. His eyes smoldered. "That is why you will not speak. I understand. Clean water avails nothing—it is too late for that. Our only hope is to find *blood. Clean* blood. Blood is life. Blood is what we must drink. We must sustain our lives with life itself."

Once more, Damon seized Raithe's dead arm. This time, he brought it close to his mouth, and his lips spasmed with tangled hunger and revulsion. "Is it *your* blood, Raithe? Is that what we must drink? The blood of a man become god? Is that why you will not speak? Is that why you want us all to die? Because you do not wish to share your blood?"

Blood, Raithe thought. *There is an answer in blood.* But he could not quite grasp the memory. He had learned something about blood, something important. From where?

The goddess.

From the goddess.

Close upon this realization came a heart-tearing burst of wonder: *When did she stop being the* Aktir *Queen to me, and become simply the goddess?*

There: it was *all* there, inside him. He could not contain all that she had shared with him, but he did not need it all: one small corner sufficed. Blood—

He remembered about blood.

Damon bit into Raithe's wrist, clamping down with a rending twist of the jaw, but Raithe barely noticed.

I can save him. I can save them all.

The tears that streamed now onto his cheeks were tears of gratitude.

Damon lifted his blood-smeared mouth from Raithe's wrist. "Does this hurt you? I am sorry for that, Raithe. Sorry—I truly am. But I *must* have your blood. Without your blood, I will *die,* and when I die the *embassy* will fall, and with it the Monasteries and the Empire, and my whole *life* will have been for nothing. For *nothing*, do you understand? Of course you don't; you are too young. You are too young and strong to comprehend the futility that *pursues* a man, gaining ground with the turn of each year, each month, each day—"

Raithe gathered his will and summoned his mindhand to work his body like a puppet. He shifted his lips and tongue to make himself say, "Nnno, Daaamon . . . I unnderrrstannn . . . I cannn hhh . . . hhhelllp you . . ."

"You can? You will?" The older man's staring eyes sparked with hope. "What must I do? What do you require?"

"Nnnot my bl . . ." Raithe forced out. He took a deep breath, and struggled to make his words clear. "Blood. To sssavve . . . you nnneed . . ." He summoned all his concentration, and sternly forced his lips and tongue to form distinctly the words he needed to save the world.

"Not my blood," he said, "but Caine's."

2

RAITHE HUNG FACEDOWN across a broad shoulder, and held on to consciousness by the clench of his teeth. With the winter-grey eyes of his body, he saw only oil-stained stone and the legs of the friar who carried him; with the invisible eyes of his mind, he could see everything.

Damon led the small group of Esoterics in erratic dashes from patch to patch of burned-out ground, sliding between walls of flame and slipping across oil-slicked cobbles. Behind them, at the dockside, buildings had started to collapse; now and then the friars were forced to fade into the dangerously narrow confines of alley mouths, to avoid the parties of bucket-armed soldiers who trotted past. The soldiers, and the civilian volunteers who worked beside them, no longer tried to save individual buildings, but rather tried to contain the fires; they struggled to build firebreaks of sand to smother the oil, but flame overleaped them, spreading from wall to wall and rooftop to rooftop, and soon the black oil soaked through the mounds of sand and began to burn anew.

Often the soldiers and the civilian volunteers fought not only the fires, but each other. The slightest disagreement might jump instantly to bloodshed, and the violence was more contagious than the disease that sparked it. Perhaps it does take two to fight—but it takes only one to attack. Only one to murder.

The winner, in such fights, was the fire.

In the dark depths of his heart, Raithe felt a shadow flow toward the city from far upstream, blank and faceless. With what sense he felt this he could not say—another revenant of the goddess and the god who had striven against one another within his brain—but he felt it with an acute certainty that left no room for doubt.

The Artans were coming.

The Esoterics dashed up Knights' Bridge, reaching the top of the arch; ahead, where it joined the end of the arching stone span, the massive timbers of the drawbridge's single-leaf bascule had become a towering forest of spider-branched oaks that seeped gleaming oil.

"We can make it," Damon decided, panting. "Here—" He turned to the men he led and pointed. "You—you're the strongest. Take the Ambassador on your shoulders. You, and you—your robes are wet. Strip and wrap him; the wet cloth will give some protection should the flames catch us still on the bridge."

And in that speech, Raithe heard an answer: For all his murderous dementia, Damon was still Damon. He summoned his mindhand to make himself speak once more. Exhaustion made moving his lips like juggling boulders. "Nnno."

Damon ignored him, studying the unnatural forest ahead. "Reese—scout along the left retaining wall. Rhoole, Cole, get a look to the right and in the middle. We must choose the clearest path, or none of us may survive."

"Nnno," Raithe repeated. "Leavvve me heere."

"We will not," Damon muttered distractedly. "You are a Monastic citizen in distress—"

"Leavvve mmme *here*," he said, louder. "Tha' . . . *that* is annn order."

Damon wheeled and seized the back of Raithe's neck in a crushing grip, straightening him one-handed across the friar's shoulder with lunatic strength. He leaned close enough to bite, and snarled, "Never give orders in my command! *Never! I* am in authority here! I! Do you *understand*?"

Raithe met Damon's snarl expressionlessly. "Nno," he said. "You arrre nnnot."

"I am invested by the Council of Brothers—"

"You arrre relievved."

"You have no authority!"

Raithe's command of his lips and tongue sharpened by the moment. He was able to say more strongly, "I amm . . . the Council's ch-chosen Ammmbassador . . . to the Arrrtans. T-to the *Ak-tiri*. Caine is Arr-tan. This—" He waved weakly with his good hand at the burning city around them. "—this is the w-work of *Aktiri*."

By extreme focus of his will, he forced the words to become perfectly distinct. "I amm vvested with fulll auth-thority in all dealings with Arta . . . annnd the *Aktiri*. I amm . . . in command, here."

Damon met his gaze squarely, pathetically dignified in his tattered filthy robes and the blood that streaked his face. "I shall protest," he said. "I shall protest to the Council."

"D-do ssso. Unn-til th-thenn, you arre rre-lieved."

Damon released Raithe's neck, and stepped away with lowered eyes. Raithe patted the flank of the friar who held him. "Ssset me downnn."

The friar obeyed, laying Raithe gently on the cold stone arch. Raithe said, "Daamonnn?"

The reply was half muffled, as though his mouth had difficulty forming the words, but was clear nonetheless.

"I am . . . at your orders. Sir."

3

RAITHE GAVE ORDERS as swiftly as his infirmity allowed, and the Esoterics sprinted away through the decaying trees of Knights' Bridge. He let his eyes drift almost closed; he had been through so much, and he was so tired—

Damon gazed longingly after his men. "And I still don't understand," he said, plaintive and puzzled, like a lost little boy. "How will this save us?"

"Hhhellp," Raithe said reluctantly. "Hellp mmme . . . up."

Damon knelt and slung Raithe's dead arm around his own neck. Slowly, working together, they managed to get Raithe to his feet. "What are we to do, now? Where are we to go?" Damon asked, his voice thickening with tears. "I fear—I fear I may not have the strength to carry you, Raithe. I'm sorry—I have not been well. Do you know I have not been well?"

"To th-the Courrthoussse," Raithe gasped. "Caine—Caine's blood—"

"But how will we even get in? The Courthouse will be sealed for the night—and it was built as a fortress! It would take a siege engine—"

"Th-thisss—" Raithe said. "This is hhhoww—"

He reached forth with his mindhand. No effort was required to find what he sought; the same odd, unexpected kinesthesia that enabled him to feel the cold approach of the Artans made this as natural as his one hand reaching for the other in the dark.

On the surface of the river beneath them, the flames leaped high, then parted. A circle of pure calm flattened the roiled water as though it were a mountain lake on a windless summer's day. Up from the center of that circle rose the Sword of Saint Berne.

Raithe drew the sword upward through the flame and smoke and darkness.

The blade sizzled to life as his fingers closed around it, and shot a bolt of power along his arm that blossomed into a fireball of acid within his left side—and he could *feel* it. The touch of Kosall's hilt had joined something that had been severed within him.

He pushed Damon aside, stood on his own two feet, and brandished Kosall at the sky; power shouted from the blade like lightning.

He thought, *Well. All right, then.*

He lowered the blade, and the glare around him faded. "No siege engine will be required," he said with grim satisfaction. "Come, Damon—"

Damon screamed: a raw, animal scream of agony and terror. He staggered away, clawing at his chest and shoulder, then fell to his knees. He tore at his clothing, his scream already ragged, hoarse, going choppy as he gasped for breath. Raithe was at his side in an instant.

A dripping patch of black oil the size of a fist stained Damon's robe; before Raithe could even wonder whence this oil might have come, flesh beneath the cloth began to smoke, and then to burn. As Damon tore at his clothing, the oil smeared across his hands, raising blisters so fast they burst before his skin could stretch over them, and his fingers began to swell, trailing streamers of acrid smoke.

Raithe grabbed a handful of Damon's robe and slashed it off with a swift stroke of Kosall, then ripped the rest of the robe free. He wadded it up and roughly scrubbed at Damon's chest and hands, wiping away as much oil as he could one-handed, since he dared not put down the sword.

At last Damon huddled on his side on the cold stone, crumpled fetally around the oil burns on his chest, shivering with pain, tears streaming from his eyes. Raithe stared numbly at the wadded cloth in his hand, unable to comprehend what he saw: the robe was nearly soaked through with oil, now, and oil dripped from its torn hem to stain the bridgestones at his feet.

He dropped the robe, and it landed with a sodden slap. He lifted his left hand, staring; he turned his hand this way and that, seeking some glimpse of human skin within a slick, wet-gleaming glove of jet.

He made a fist, and out through the pores of his skin flowed thick syrup ripples of the blind god's black oil.

4

IN A SHADOWED doorway of the Financial Block across Ten Street from the Courthouse, Raithe let Damon slide slowly to the doorstep. With an empty sigh, Damon settled onto the oil-slick stone and curled around the chemical burns on his chest. His eyes held the horizon-fixed glaze of the Control Disciplines. Raithe pressed back into the shadows, Kosall humming along his thigh.

Ten Street was choked with people: people with packs on their backs and bundles in their arms, people pushing carts and people pulling wagons, people who clutched the hands of children or the leashes of pets, people who sought this way and that in tears or red-faced rage, crying names indistinguishable from all the other shouts and screams.

With Fools' Bridge and Thieves' Bridge already in flames—as well as many of their homes and businesses—thousands had bundled whatever they could carry of their precious possessions and rushed to the west side of Old Town, only to find Knights' Bridge burning as well; the forest of oak that had sprung from its bascule had ignited only seconds after Raithe had carried Damon through. Now the only way off the island was the long arch of Kings' Bridge—and Kings' Bridge was held by a company of heavy infantry whose captain was grimly determined to keep this rabble of potential looters off the South Bank.

Flames slowly crept westward through twisting alleys and around rooftop peaks, behind water troughs and under boardwalks: anywhere the wind was broken. The whole city east of Rogues' Way burned, and the approach of the flames pushed more and more people into the Financial District. People were dying on the street already: now and again the press parted to reveal a body trampled or clubbed or surreptitiously knifed. The river itself stretched arms of flame around Old Town as oil flowed in from upstream, becoming a moat of fire.

Kosall hummed in Raithe's left hand, shedding tiny droplets of black oil in a continuous rain; Raithe watched them fall. He remembered, foggily, the agony he and the goddess had suffered when the black oil had first flowed forth; the right side of his body—the clean side—was blistered and scorched, and had the stiff swollen thickness of parboiled meat. Part of what frightened him was that he wasn't in much pain.

Far, far back behind his eyes, faint but persistent—a melody stuck in endless obsessive cycle within his brain—throbbed the lives of all within the river's bound: ghosts of the living. The clearest of them were the men and women who crowded the street around him; he could also feel men—soldiers, he presumed—within the Courthouse. He even got faint corner-of-the-eye afterimages of the confusion and anger among friars who struggled to arm themselves, blocks away at the embassy: fights broke out among them, and a number of the embassy's rooms held victims of virus-spawned murder.

He could feel other ghosts as well: terrified ghosts, cringing behind locked shutters; lunatic ghosts, giggling with gore-smeared mouths; even a few stolid, comfortably ignorant ghosts, snoring within bedlinens never tangled by any troubling dream, far from the fires and the madness that gripped the city.

And he could feel ghosts below him: unhuman ghosts that boiled through the caverns, terrified and savage; he felt their mad queen and heard the thump of her murderous command echo in the heart of ogre and primal, troll and treetopper. He could see the image of their destination and feel their bloody intention, and he knew that if he delayed, Caine might have no blood left with which to save the world.

Another part of what frightened him was what he saw across the street: The Courthouse doors were open, and on the verandah at the top of a broad sweep of stairs, two armored officers of the Eyes of God stood guard.

The facade of the Courthouse pulsed orange with reflected firelight and gleamed with black oil; the ivy that once had climbed its walls had become a jungle of knotted woody vines that now rotted and dripped oil that flowed across the broad railed verandah in syrupy waves. The Eyes of God officers shifted uncomfortably, trying to keep their boots out of the oil, and threw many nervously longing glances toward the crowded street, as though only fear of something worse than fire kept them at their posts.

The rest of what frightened Raithe was that he knew what frightened them. He could feel it.

With the same sense that tracked the approach of the Artan Guard along the river and through the outlying streets, he felt something huge and dark and rabid within the Courthouse: a wounded beast that licked itself in hungry silence. These Eyes of God feared this beast, not knowing that they themselves were parts of its limbs; Raithe feared the beast, for he knew that he was.

He felt the dark power's flow through the sword into his brain, and with his own powers of mind he seized upon it. *Power is power,* he thought. *I need all I can get.*

He felt the gate that the goddess had closed in his mind, the gate that his touch upon the sword had reopened. He turned his will upon that gate, and shattered it so that it would never close again. He would bear the ache, the legion of rats that chewed into his guts. He would bear the black-oil stigmatum.

Small enough penance, for his great sins.

He shifted his grip upon Kosall so that he held it by one quillon, and its eldritch hum died. He still could make a fist of his left hand, and his left leg still held his weight. Slowly, careful not to brush the sword's hilt, he slid the naked blade behind his belt. "Damon," he said. He yanked the semiconscious man to his feet and shook him roughly. "Damon, come up. Now. That's an order."

Slowly the Acting Ambassador's eyes drifted into focus.

"Yes." Damon's face was blank with returning pain. He

hugged his bare, burned chest as though he were chilled. He wore only his breeches and boots. "Yes—Raithe? Aren't you Raithe? What—what—? I'm hurt, Raithe," Damon said, blankly plaintive. "I must get to the embassy. I'm hurt, and they need me."

Raithe laced his fingers together into a specific knot, which tuned his mind in a specific way. The oil from his left hand made the skin of his right sizzle and smoke, but his mind was master of his flesh; he could accept this pain, too, and even welcome it, and in doing so he found he could accept his fear as well. His fear, like his pain, became a mere fact.

"You will stay here and await the embassy's soldiers," he said. "When they arrive, you will take command. Secure the Courthouse. Take it, and hold it. You will allow no one to enter until you are so ordered, by either myself or another who, to your certain knowledge, wields the full authority of the Council of Brothers. Do you understand these orders?"

"But—"

"Do you understand these orders?"

"Yes. Yes, sir. Yes. But—but—"

Raithe left him in the doorway and strode out into Ten Street. Most people in the crowds gave way before him; those who didn't, he brushed with a fingertip of his left hand. Their screams and the smoke that rose from their burns were more than enough to convince everyone else to let him pass.

"But—" Damon called after him. "What you have ordered— it's an act of war!"

"This is already a war," Raithe said softly, more to himself than to Damon. "And it is time for us to act."

He mounted the Courthouse steps, to face the Eyes of God.

5

As RAITHE CLIMBED the steps, one of the officers said, "You can't come up here."

Raithe reached the oil-stained verandah and stopped a nonthreatening five paces from the door. "Why not?" he asked mildly.

"Go on, back into the street, chummie," the other guard told him, pointing down into the mass of people with his sword. "Nobody's allowed on the steps."

"But I want to go in."

"Back on the *street*," the officer insisted. He took a step toward Raithe and lifted his sword. "Courthouse's been closed since dusk. Get moving."

"But the door is open."

"That's not your concern—" the officer began, but Raithe again knotted his fingers together, again ignored the sizzle of the skin on his fingers, and interrupted.

"Tell me why the door is open," he said.

"Because the Patriarch has a thing about doors, these days," the officer said. "He doesn't like doors closed on him when he's inside—"

His partner gaped at him. "Dorrie! Are you mad?"

The officer looked back, puzzled. "What?"

Raithe said, "The Patriarch?"

"Dorrie, shut up," the other officer said. He stepped in front of his partner and pointed his own sword at Raithe's belly. "And you, get out of here. You didn't hear *anything*, you understand? The Patriarch isn't anywhere *near* here, and if you say otherwise, I'll find you and kill you."

But he didn't sound as certain of that as he might, and his eyes were fixed upon Raithe's oil-covered left hand. "You—uh," he said, with a frown that was half a wince, "and you, you better wash your hands. I mean—don't you know that stuff is dangerous?"

Far better than you, Raithe thought. He reknotted his fingers. "I am Ambassador Raithe of the Monasteries. The Patriarch sent for me. You will direct me to him at once."

"I, uh, I uh . . ." the officer stammered. "Your Excellency, your clothes, I didn't—"

"At once," Raithe repeated. Without waiting for an answer, he swept past the officers and entered the darkened Courthouse.

"The chapel," the officer called from behind him. "He's in the chapel. I'd—uh, I have to stay on post, I'm—"

"I can find it," Raithe said, and strode into the darkness.

The atrium of the Courthouse was an immense vault of shadow, striped with dancing orange crosses cast through the cruciform slot-windows by the flames that approached outside. Raithe limped through the atrium, his boot heels clacking cavernously. He'd been inside the Courthouse dozens of times; in boyhood, he'd worked as a page for the *Imperial Messenger-News* to help his father pay for the cost of his education at the

embassy school. But seeing it gloomed in flame-tattered
shadow—and the smell—

The Courthouse had always had a peculiar odor of its own: the
colognes and powders and flower-oil sachets of the noble judges
half captured by the fear-sweat of guilty men, then soaked permanently into the limestone. That blend of perfume and guilt
had always been, for Raithe, the smell of justice.

Now the Courthouse smelled only of rotting plants and
burning oil.

The chapel had once been a shrine to Prorithun, the sky god
who was the keeper of men's oaths and the defender of
Ankhanan law. Here the judges would pray and purify themselves before presiding in court. A Prorithar priest had always
been present, empowered by the sky god to bestow upon the
judges His Blessing, to render them temporarily proof against
persuasive or compulsive magicks. Though Prorithun no longer
reigned in Ankhanan courts, the chapel remained. Now it was a
shrine to Ma'elKoth.

Here, too, the door stood open, flanked by Eyes of God.

"Hey, you," one of them said, intense but low, as though he
feared to be overheard. "I don't know how you got in here, but
you have to leave. Get out."

Raithe stopped in a column of firelight that painted half of
him scarlet and left the rest in black shadow. He knotted his fingers. "I am Ambassador—"

"I don't give a squirt who you are, pally." The officer paced
forward, stripes of firelight rippling over him as he approached
up the long dark hallway. "If you're still here when I count three,
I'll kill you. One."

Raithe frowned. Could some of Prorithun's influence still
linger? Again, he knotted his fingers. "Put away your sword,"
he said.

"Two."

"Go on, get out of here," the other officer said. "He means it."

Raithe settled into himself. He sighed, and shifted his balance
forward onto the balls of his feet. Reluctantly, he put his right
hand near the hilt of Kosall. "I don't want to fight."

"That makes one of us." The officer took another step; now
one long stride from Raithe, he said, "Three."

Yet he did not strike. Perhaps from this close, he could see
death in Raithe's sad, wintry eyes.

"Your Radiance?" Raithe called, pitching his voice to carry. "Your Radiance, it's Raithe—Ambassador Raithe."

"Sure you are," the officer said.

"Your Radiance, I must speak with you."

From beyond the chapel's open door came a sepulchral croak that hummed with the resonance of an empty room. "Go away."

"You heard the man, pally," the officer said, edging even closer. He raised his sword like a boy cocking a stick to threaten a strange dog.

"Your Radiance, it's about Caine," Raithe said. "I must speak with you about Caine."

For a long-stretched moment, no one moved.

"Let him pass."

The officer took a step back, and swung his sword to wave Raithe on. Raithe passed him without a glance, but as he did, he felt a shift of weight in that hungry wounded beast.

He said, "Don't."

He stopped, waiting. Oil from his left fist gathered into thick droplets that spattered on the floor.

The guard at his back slowly lowered the sword he had swiftly raised. "You can't scare me."

"No," Raithe agreed, without turning. "But I can kill you, though I would rather not."

He felt again the shift of that hungry wounded beast—this time a settling back, a slow uncoiling. He nodded to himself, and walked on.

6

THE HIGH VAULT of the chapel glowed with faint, reflected firelight; it leaked through the colored glass from the airshaft outside and rippled on the rows of padded knee-benches to either side of the aisle. The shift and pulse of the reflected light gave an eerie aspect of life to the stone Ma'elKoth that stood, double manheight, in the chancel. A bundle of filthy rags, stinking of oil and smoke, lay at the foot of the altar.

Raithe stood motionless in the transept, staring up at God.

A tear rolled from his right eye, tracing the fold beside his mouth to fall silently from his chin. Slowly, feeling suddenly old, ancient, Raithe dropped to one knee and lowered his head. He made a fist of his clean right hand. He struck himself on his chest, above his heart, and opened his palm toward the image of his god. *Father, forgive me,* he prayed. *I have no choice.*

More tears pricked his eyes.

Forgive me.

Yet somewhere in his heart, a secret flame burned. Even his tear felt forced—felt *performed*—as it rolled down his cheek. *What have I become?*

"Raithe . . ."

The voice came from the chancel. He lifted his head to find that the bundle of rags at the foot of the altar had opened to reveal a fatigue-seamed face smeared with muck. The rags shifted and moved in unpleasantly liquid ways, as though they covered some soft-boned sea creature that was barely more than a sac of jelly.

"Your Radiance," Raithe said. "Thank you for receiving me."

The bundle of rags shook itself and gradually unfolded to the height of a man. "I know why you're here."

I doubt it, Raithe thought. Remaining on one knee, he said, "I have come to save the city, and the Empire."

"Don't lie to me, Raithe." The rags shambled toward him along the nave. "Everyone *lies* to me. I can't understand why everyone thinks I don't already know the *truth*." A hand like that of a corpse in rigor extended from the rags, pointing with immobile fingers. "You've come for *Caine*. You were in this with him from the *beginning*."

"Your Radiance, I can help you. I have a cure. I can make you well."

"Don't lie to me!" The hand jerked at him as though casting a curse. "*You* came to me with this idea—this plan to bring him here. *You* came with him. You *inflicted* him upon me, and upon my *city*. All this—" The hand circled high, drawing in the boundless ravage of the city and the Empire around it. "All this is *your doing*. *You* made this happen, Raithe!" White flecks of spittle sprayed. "You! You! You!"

Each shout brought the swing of the accusing hand a step closer. Raithe could only lower his head once more; eyes directed at the ragged oil-stained hem that half masked a pair of cut and bleeding bare feet, he said, "Your Radiance, please—"

The shouts became a screech for the Eyes of God; a rattle of boots answered—many boots.

"Your Radiance, there is a cure. You can be saved. The Empire can be saved—"

The rigored hand swung down to point. "Arrest this man! Arrest him and *kill* him!"

Raithe finished softly, "Humanity can be saved . . ."

Now leather boots that sprouted leggings of chain shuffled into place around him. "All right, pally—that's it for you. Let's have that sword."

Raithe stood.

Five Eyes of God surrounded him, swords at the ready. Three more waited behind. The beast had him in its grasp. "The sword, pally. You can't fight all of us."

Raithe raised his black-gleaming left hand, and his right hovered an inch from Kosall's hilt. "Yes, I can."

"You'll lose."

Raithe flicked his left hand at the officer who had spoken, and droplets of the black oil spattered across his face; at the same moment he seized Kosall and turned the awakening blade so that it sliced instantly through his belt. One officer fell backward, howling as flames burst around his eyes; another stared dumbly at the stub of his sword, sheared off a finger's breadth above the guard.

But as they fell back, others came forward.

"I have your deaths on my conscience already," Raithe said. "Killing you all costs me nothing. But if you would live a little longer, leave now."

The voice of the beast spoke from the rags. "Any man who crosses that threshold while this traitor lives shall feel the full weight of Imperial justice."

"There is no Imperial justice," Raithe told them. "And this man will not live to see you punished. Go."

Their response was a single shared glance, to coordinate their rush.

As a swordsman, Raithe was only competent, but Kosall was a singularly forgiving weapon. Its irresistible edge took no account of shield or parrying blade, and armor provided only barely more resistance than naked flesh. His sense of the beast let Raithe meet attacks before they were even begun: in seconds the aisle around him was littered with bits of sliced-off swords and pieces of cloven shields. To pass within Kosall's reach on his right was to bleed; to close with Raithe from the left was to burn.

But he was one, and they were six. Raithe bled as well: from a long slash on his thigh and a deep stab below his ribs. Despite his words, he killed no one. These were the same men he was fighting to save—and he was uncertain what taking a life with Kosall might do to the goddess within its blade.

Now knives replaced broken swords, but the Eyes hesitated. To attack a sword-armed man with a knife is foolish; to do the same to a man armed with Kosall is suicidal.

A moment fell, and another, and another.

"Cowards!" hissed the beast. The rags shouldered through the officers. "Cowards! Traitors! Villains! Here is how We deal with traitors!" A pair of knives blossomed from tattered sleeves and swung wide, and the Patriarch sprang upon him.

Raithe's reaction had been trained into him by years in the abbey school, by hours on the diskmat and days spent hammering millions of punches into leather-wrapped bags of sand. Kosall shifted instantly from his right hand to his left; his left foot swung out a precise handspan, and his weight transferred smoothly onto it from his right while the knuckles of his right fist described an invisible wall exactly at the point of the Patriarch's chin. Chin met wall, bone to bone—

And Toa-Sytell collapsed.

I've knocked out the Patriarch, Raithe thought blankly.

The Eyes of God officers stared, uncomprehending; they could no more believe what Raithe had done than he could himself. He repeated silently, *I've knocked out the Patriarch,* as though thinking the words again could make the act more real.

What have I become?

He lifted his eyes to the Eyes of God.

"Run," he said.

They ran.

7

RAITHE STARED DOWN at the crumpled form of the unconscious Patriarch, terrified by how good he felt. Not happy—he could never be happy again—but calm. Centered. At peace.

In control.

As though his own chin had met the same wall his knuckles had described against Toa-Sytell's, a stunning impact had knocked things loose inside him, and now, for the first time, he began to understand—

Alone in the chapel, amid the dancing glass-stained firelight, Raithe turned once more to pray. But he did not pray from his knees, with bent neck and lowered eyes, as he had been taught. Instead he stood like a man and met the stone eyes of the icon of his god. He struck his breast again, and again opened his hand in offering.

But this was his left, and it opened upon the blind god's black venom.

I am Your Beloved Child, he thought. *I will always honor You. Now, and forever, you have my love, my devotion. My worship.*

But not my obedience.

I will always be Your Child, but I am a child no longer.

There are too many children; too many grow old but never grow up. I think I would have liked to be one of them, but that does not seem to be my fate. My destiny.

He allowed himself a bitter smile.

Father, forgive me, for I finally know what I'm doing.

8

THE CLAMOR FROM the guardroom reached Raithe even up in the broad hall outside the chapel: shouted threats and tearful pleas, roars of rage and shrieks of pain. In the stairwell, it was painfully loud. Kosall in one hand, leash in the other, Raithe rounded the last bend in the stairway.

In the small antechamber below, six men in chainmail that bore the emblem of the Eyes of God paced back and forth, gesturing as though they argued in voices that could not be heard above the clamor. The clamor rose from beyond the steel gate—within the guardroom itself—which was packed solid with desperate, panicked men in the gear of the Donjon Guard. The men of the Guard struggled and clawed and bit each other, fighting to get to the gate; an anemone-spray of arms waved between the bars, fingers clutching futilely toward the Eyes of God beyond.

Raithe watched for a moment, then he nodded to himself and thoughtfully brought Kosall's forte against the corner of stone beside him. Kosall bit into the stone with an earsplitting squeal. Below him, men jumped and flinched and covered their ears. He turned the blade slowly, carving a chunk from the wall as though the stone were hard cheese. The chunk rattled down the steps to the anteroom floor, skittered slowly across it with a fading *chikchikchik,* and then there was silence.

Raithe pointed Kosall at the Eyes of God. "You can go."

They stared at him, taking in his tattered clothes that dripped black oil down one side, while the other side hung thick and red, soaked in the blood that still pulsed from both the slice on his thigh and the stab wound below his ribs. One of the Eyes straightened and stepped forward. "We are ordered to hold this gate—"

"I don't care. Go."

"Toa-Sytell himself—"

Raithe drew on the leash in his other hand.

Around the bend of the stairway, leashed by the prisoner collar locked around his neck, hands bound and mouth gagged with strips torn from his own robes, came His Radiant Holiness Toa-Sytell, Steward of the Empire and Patriarch of the Church of the Beloved Children of Ma'elKoth.

His gaze was fixed, unseeing; as Raithe descended the last few steps to the anteroom, the Patriarch stumbled and half fell, striking his knees hard upon the stone floor. He knelt there abjectly, a low animal whine leaking around his gag. Tears rolled from his blankly staring eyes.

Kosall's whine hummed through the autumnal rustle of indrawn breath.

Raithe said, "Go."

The officers, with many an exchanged glance, slowly and carefully circled around him, then backed up the stairs.

"Hey," a Donjon Guard said from beyond the gate. "Hey, what about *us*? You can't leave us—you don't know what's going on down there—!"

"Enlighten me."

From many voices in conflicting babble, Raithe was able to piece together an impression of a riot in the Pit below. He thought, *Caine,* and remembered the boil of unhuman ghosts through the caverns: caverns that connect to the Donjon, through the Shaft.

He took a long stride forward and swung Kosall overhand. The men beyond shoved themselves frantically back from the bars. Sparks flew from the gate's lock as the blade sheared it through, and the gate swung open. Raithe stepped to one side,

shortening Toa-Sytell's leash as though the Patriarch were an unruly dog, and silently watched the rush of guards on their way up
and out.

The guardroom went quiet. The Donjon door stood open. The
stairwell beyond was dark as an open mouth. Raithe took one
deep breath, staring down, then shrugged. Drawing the Patriarch
after him, he went down.

As he descended, the living ghosts that had peopled the back
of his mind slowly faded; fading likewise was his sense of the
methodical approach of the Artan forces, both overland and
along the river. By the time he reached the lower landing he was,
for the first time in what could have been forever, alone inside
his head. Even Kosall's whine trailed away to silence.

He stopped, frowning.

If there was indeed a riot beyond these doors, he could not
hear it. The loudest sound in the stairwell was the shuffle of the
Patriarch's battered and bleeding feet. Scant light trickled from
the guardroom; Raithe could discern only the faintest gleam
from the studs that fastened the brass bindings on this door. He
glanced at the featureless silhouette of Toa-Sytell, and found no
advice in his silent shape.

He cautiously pulled the door handle. The doors were
locked—or possibly held from the far side. He pressed his ear
against the door. Now he could hear voices, many voices, from
the Pit beyond, though he could make out no words among the
general quiet murmur. He allowed himself a slow sigh, and
nodded to himself.

He breathed himself into his Control Discipline and built
within his mindeye an image of Caine as he had last seen him,
chained to the dungcart, drawn away in the processional while
the Imperial Army Band played "Justice of God." He detailed the
image with every scar he had seen in five days of study on
the barge, with every sweat streak that striped the travel dust on
his skin; he laid strands of grey along his temples, and imaged
perfectly the white-salted stubble that had coated his cheeks
and chin.

Now from this image he stripped away the sunlight and the
music; he erased the dungcart and the shackles; finally even the
tunic and pants of rough homespun evaporated from his consciousness. Then there was only Caine.

And Raithe saw him. Vaguely, blurrily, fading in and out of view, as if through a mist.

He sat upon a pile of rags and tattered clothing that somehow, beneath him, was a throne; he wore an age-greyed tunic, frayed at the hem and worn thin enough to be translucent, that became armor polished like the sun. At his feet lay a dying elf; at his side knelt a massively muscled ogrillo who tied strips of rag around Caine's raddled legs with hands that were themselves heavily bandaged; before him stood a thick-bodied woman, hands folded behind her like a student reciting in abbey school. Caine's hair had gone whiter than Raithe remembered it, and his beard had grown in full and shaggy; his cheeks had sunk close upon his teeth; hunger and illness had drawn his eyes deeper within his skull.

But those eyes still gleamed like embers at the back of a cave.

He shook his head to wipe the vision from his mind, and he passed the sleeve of his sword arm across his brow. Raithe had seen Caine not as he is, but as Raithe needed him to be: beclouded in a fog of legend. More than human: a hero: a myth.

Probably, he thought, *he is dead. Many will be dead, and many more injured. But: someone may have touched his blood. Someone may have tasted it, if it ran in the water, or was splashed from a wound. This may be enough.*

It will have to be.

He tried to summon the power of his mindhand, to manipulate the lock upon these doors as he had those in Garrette's office a lifetime ago, but his power had deserted him. He had a vague recollection—something about the rock from which the Donjon is carved—but he did not trouble to pursue it; he had another option.

He pushed Kosall's point between the doors and slid it downward until it met resistance. By extreme concentration, he was able to direct a shudder of power into the blade; it rattled to life, sank, then swung free before falling silent once more. Gasping, Raithe was forced to lean on the stone for a moment, to regather the shreds of his strength. When he pulled the door handle with the hand that held the Patriarch's leash, the door opened.

Framed in the stairshaft's shadow, Raithe found an array of crossbows centered upon his breast, held steadily by men and elves on the far side of the balcony, a hundred feet away. A voice closer at hand but out of sight said firmly, "Onto the balcony. Nice and slow."

Raithe moved into the light.

A few paces to his right, another small group of mingled species held cocked and leveled crossbows, near enough that the curve of the balcony's retaining wall could offer no protection. "Put down the sword," one of them ordered.

Raithe ignored them. He took one step closer to the retaining wall and looked down into the Pit. On a pile of rags and clothes become a throne, wearing a grey ragged tunic that should have been polished steel—

Gathered round him: elf, ogrillo, human—.

Gaze as solid as the Donjon stone: a state of being in which the unexpected receives barely a blink of recognition.

"Raithe."

Raithe said, "Caine."

A long, slow, measuring stare: a whole conversation passed in the meeting of eyes of grey ice with those of black fire. Raithe had to lower his head.

"Can you give me one reason," Caine said, "why I shouldn't have you shot where you stand?"

Raithe tugged on the leash, drawing Toa-Sytell to the retaining wall where Caine could see him. The Patriarch moaned into his gag.

Caine said, "Well."

He seemed to ponder this development for a moment; then he folded his arms and cocked his head fractionally to one side. "That," he said, "buys you a trip down here, to tell me what the fuck you're up to."

One of the crossbowmen on the balcony said, "He's armed."

Caine nodded, and spoke softly to the elf who seemed to be drowsing at his feet; the elf lifted his head and opened eyes so fever-shot that to Raithe, even dozens of yards away, they looked like bloody eggs. Those raw eyes swallowed Raithe whole.

He swayed.

The elf said something to Caine that Raithe could not hear, then laid his head upon his bed of rags and closed his eyes once more. Caine said to the crossbowmen, "Don't worry about it. Let him come."

Raithe led Toa-Sytell around the long curve of the balcony and down the straight span of the stairbridge. The mass of prisoners parted before him so that he could lead the Patriarch to Caine's feet.

He felt the pressure of their massed stare like a yoke across his shoulders, its weight compressing his spine, anchoring his feet to the stone. The ogrillo hulked nearby—closer to Raithe than to Caine—wearing a glare that invited violence. The woman mirrored him, saving only that her gaze was one of dispassionate measurement rather than threat. Blood trickled down his leg, and he could clearly hear the slow drop of the black oil from his left hand.

Caine said expressionlessly, "That's Kosall."

Raithe lifted the sword. The ogrillo shifted his weight onto his forepads.

"Yes."

"You've been using it."

Raithe looked at the slow pulse of blood soaking down his clothing. "Not well."

Caine did not respond.

"I have—" Raithe began weakly, then coughed, sighed a deep breath, and continued with more strength. "I have come to ask you to save the world."

9

CAINE OFFERED A smile that was cold, remote, and thin as the arc of a saber. "Yeah?"

"In your blood," Raithe said, "there is a, a *countervirus*—" He stumbled over the unfamiliar word. "—that is the cure for Garrette's disease."

"In *my* blood?"

Caine rocked back on his throne of rags, and his eyes fixed upon something that was not there.

"Yes," Raithe said.

"In my blood . . ." Caine repeated, but now with a tone of slow, wondering discovery, as though this explained some long-standing mystery.

"Yes," Raithe said again. "The tiniest drop will save a man, and then he himself will carry this cure, and can pass it on—"

"I know how it works," Caine said. The wonder drained from

his face, leaving only flat, cold stone. "What do you want me to do about it?"

Raithe stared.

Caine stared back.

Raithe gave his head a tiny disbelieving shake. He drew Toa-Sytell up beside him. "A drop of your blood, Caine. That's all I ask. One drop. You can save his life."

Caine lifted his right hand and examined it as though it were some piece of exotic machinery, unfamiliar in design and uncertain of use. He watched his knuckles as he made a fist; then he opened his fingers again. He met Raithe's gaze, shrugged, and turned his hand over, palm up. "What's in it for me?"

"Caine," Raithe said patiently, "he's the *Patriarch*. The Empire needs him."

"Fuck the Patriarch." Caine pushed himself forward and took his weight elbow-to-knee. "The last time I was this close to that little cocksucker, he *knifed* me. Fuck the Empire, too. And, while you're at it, fuck yourself."

Raithe knew better than to waste breath on argument or plea; he was, after all, the world's leading expert on Caine. "What do you want?"

Caine's smile sharpened. "First," he said with dark satisfaction, "though I know it's the worst kind of manners to mock a guy when he's down, I want to remind you: You told me that nothing, ever again, would be about *what I want*." He showed his teeth. "Shit, kid, thinking about that makes me all warm and fuzzy inside, like I just ate a kitten. Second?" He opened his other hand. "Make me an offer."

"Your freedom—" Raithe began, nodding back toward the Donjon stairway above.

That open hand waved a contemptuous dismissal. "My freedom has nothing to do with you."

Raithe swayed. The corners of the room dimmed, darkening into a tunnel that stretched ever longer, and the only light at the distant end was the face of Caine.

"Anything, then," he said tiredly. "Even my life."

"Your life? Look around you, pinhead." Five or six of the crossbowmen took more careful aim. "I have your life already. I just haven't decided what I want to do with it."

"Then what, Caine?" Raithe asked quietly, eyes drifting

closed, dizzy with blood loss and defeat. "What? Tell me. Say it, and if it is within my power—"

"When I make up my mind," he said, leaning back once more. "Start by telling me what the fuck happened to you."

Raithe stared at him blankly, uncomprehending. Words echoed along the dark tunnel in his head without releasing meaning.

"How'd you get *in* here?" Caine said, explaining. "Where'd you get those wounds? What happened to your face? You look like you got boiled in oil. How in hot staggering fuck did you get the Patriarch on a prisoner leash? And what's that shit all over your *hand*?"

Raithe lifted Kosall. The hanging lamps rippled orange light along its silver-painted design. He let the blade swing down by the quillon so that he could reverse it; he took again its hilt and spent the last of his strength to bring the blade to life, then drove its point into the stone. He let go and stepped back, leaving the sword to gently sway between them, and turned his hand as though to offer Caine its hilt.

"I—" His voice thickened, and he coughed apologetically to clear it; the pressure of his cough shot colored sparks curling through the tunnel that stretched ever farther, ever darker.

"I found out what those runes were for," he said, and fainted.

ON THE DAY the dead man named himself, that naming became a clarion, calling the heroes to battle. They came severally, one by one and together: the mad queen and the dead goddess, the faithful steward and the dark angel's spawn, the crooked knight, the dragoness, the child of the river, and the god who had been a man.

When the dead man named himself, that naming shredded all veils. None could now deny their natures; now was the test of their truths. They had come to fight the war between the dead man and the god of dust and ashes.

For the dead man's grave had been unsealed. From that mortal cocoon arose a butterfly; from that tomb of flesh, a dark angel, come with a flaming sword.

TWENTY-TWO

THAT FUCKING SWORD—

A steel crucifix, head wrapped in sweat-stained leather—

It swung like that—in exactly that gentle arc—through the waterfall's spray below Khryl's Saddle. Mist collected into droplets and trickled down the blade, and washed her staring eyes—

They wouldn't even let me wash off her blood . . .

I can still taste it.

I carry the countervirus. She must have created it in her own bloodstream. Shit, it makes sense. That's why nobody in the Pit has HRVP.

That changes things. That changes a lot of things.

Sitting around here waiting for somebody to come down and kill us is no longer an option.

"You." I jab a finger at Toa-Sytell, who's twitching like a panicked dog and whining through his gag. "Sit."

The stupid fuck looks for a chair.

"Right where you are, shithead. Sit. Dinnie, get the leash."

The nearest Serpent takes the prisoner leash, and Toa-Sytell lowers himself to the floor, slow and stiff like an arthritic old man. And who am I to criticize? He moves better than I do.

"Orbek."

"Little brother?"

"Take ten guys and reconnoiter upstairs. Nobody armed but you."

He looks a question at me. I answer, "You're not going up there to fight. You meet any resistance at all, get your ass back down here. If the place is empty, see what your boys can scrounge for weapons and armor. Take one of them along." I wave a hand at the six Donjon guards we captured, tied up near the foot of the stairbridge. "They'll know where the emergency shit is kept."

He nods. "Like you say, little brother."

I dismiss him. "T'Passe, see what you can do for Raithe. At least stop the bleeding."

She blinks at me, which is what passes on that bulldog face of hers for a gape of astonishment.

"Did I stutter? And be careful of that black shit on his hand—I don't like the looks of that at all. Some of those wounds could be chemical burns."

She nods, and kneels beside him, and her strong square hands go to work tearing the rags from my pallet into strips she can bind around his wounds.

"T'Passe—" She looks back at me. "Tie him up first," I tell her. "That fucker's dangerous."

"He's barely even breathing—"

"Do it."

She shrugs, and the first of her bandages goes instead to restrain his ankles; then she pauses to consider how she can tie his wrists without getting that oily stuff on her hands.

And I can't stop looking at the sword.

I keep seeing it sway above me in time with my breathing. I keep feeling its brain-freezing icicle spear me to the sand. I keep feeling it hum inside my spine while I pull Karl's neck against its edge—

"Deliann?"

He lies still at my side, eyes closed, breath hitching, face dry and corpse-pale. "Kris, come on, man. Stay with me. I need you."

His eyes don't open, exactly; it's more like they kind of roll forward from the back of his head. "Yes, Hari . . ." he murmurs. "I hear you."

"You got something off Raithe, right? You flashed on him?"

"Yes . . ."

"I need to know. He's out cold, Kris. I need to know what the hell is going on."

"I can't . . . It's too much," he says, faintly. "Words—I could . . . in the Meld, I could share—we can Meld—"

Christ, he's raving again. "Come *on*, Kris, snap out of it. You can't Meld with a human."

Now his eyes do open, and a distant smile creases his lips. "Hari, I *am* human."

Uh, right.

I roll my shoulders to untie the knots that are cramping all the way up the side of my neck. "Do it, then."

"You won't like it."

"Shit, Kris, it's a little late to start worrying about what I won't *like*."

"There are things—things about the goddess—"

"I'm not worried about the goddess. Shanna's dead."

His gaze drifts out of focus. "Mostly."

A thrill trickles down my spine and congeals into an iceball in my guts. "You better tell me what you mean by that."

"I can't." His voice is weakening; I can hear how much effort speaking costs him. "I can only show you."

"All right," I say solidly. "I'm ready."

"No, you're not. You cannot possibly be." He takes a deep breath, then another, and another, gathering his strength. "Find mindview."

It takes some doing, but in a few minutes I can pick out some of those black threads twisting insubstantially through the air; a few minutes after that, they solidify from mere imagining to actual hallucination. Another light gathers in the Pit, too, now: a soft but penetrating glow, like a full harvest moon. It draws in around us, until it seems to cradle Deliann's head. That soft glow wells into his face from some unimaginable spring, brims him full of moonlight, then reaches out and stabs me through the eye.

The light eggshells my head and blows out my brains.

Then, into where I used to be, he sluices Raithe's life.

Ah—

fuck—

fuck *me* . . .

. . . hhurrr . . .

2

A LOT OF it isn't so bad.

Toa-Sytell's chin against my knuckles . . . caustic oil leaching from the pores of my fist . . . flames on the dockside . . . drowning in Shanna . . . the logic of pain . . . the hum of Kosall, warm in my hand, there between the crates on the deck of the barge . . .

It's the other shit I can't take.

It's the—

What they did—

What they're doing—

I can't even think it; the briefest flash of the image rips me inside out and slams me to the cold stone of the Pit floor, puking.

"Caine?" This from t'Passe, close by. "Caine, do you need help?"

Vomit claws out of me, slashing at my throat, drenching my mouth with blood. It takes a long time. A lot longer than I would have guessed. Dry heaves keep twisting my guts, and that's okay.

Saves me from having to talk.

I manage to get my eyes open. The pool of my vomit spreads toward one of my hands. I don't move. Compared to my hands, my vomit is clean.

I force myself to examine the black crust along Kosall's blade. Dried blood. Her blood. Half of her falling away from the other half. The blade chopping into her face. That brief buzz as her life drains through the sword—

Drains into the sword.

I can handle this. I can take it. I'd rather look at these crusted remains of Shanna's life than think about what those soulless shitbag child molesters are doing to Faith.

My traitor heart ignores my desire. I can hear her scream. I can taste her tears. Faith—

My god, Faith—

Whack

A sharp sting from my right hand: I stare at it numbly, for it has become a fist, and a thin line of blood trickles from my knuckles, and only then do I understand that I have punched the stone floor beneath me.

This is the kind of pain I can handle.

This is the kind of pain I like.

So I do it again.

Whack

The calluses that once protected my knuckles faded years ago, but my bone density must still be good; my knuckles don't break. The flesh peels back over them, exposing red-streaked ivory like a pair of dice in sockets of raw meat.

"What is he doing?" t'Passe says. "Why is he doing that?"

Whack

"Hari, stop," Kris says from the floor beside me.

I turn my head and meet his eyes. They brim with compassion. So much compassion that there's no room for mercy. He won't spare me this. He'll hurt for me, hurt with me, but he won't spare me.

Whack

I leave a couple bone chips behind in the pool of vomit.

"There's something wrong with him," t'Passe says. "He needs help. Make him stop."

People come close, hands out to offer me aid, to offer me comfort. To offer me life. "Touch me," I force through my teeth, "and I'll kill you."

Everyone stares at me. I lift my fist, and shrug an apology. Blood trails down my forearm and drips from my elbow.

"My daughter," I say by way of explanation, and they seem, somehow, to understand. But they all keep staring; Deliann, t'Passe, the Cainists and Folk and Serpents, even Toa-Sytell— and slowly it gets through to me what they want.

They want me to be the guy who knows what to do next.

And I am.

I can see it: the smart move. The responsible thing. Slip away through the caverns. Run downstream. Defend the sword. Gather allies, fight a guerrilla war. Seek among the great mages of the Folk for a way to cleanse the blind god's taint from the sword and from the river. I can see it, but I can't say it. I can't put words to it and make it into a plan.

Because to do that would leave Faith in the hand of my enemy.

Whack

I stare at the chipped bone of my knuckles. It's starting to show hairline fractures of black scaling through the blood-washed ivory. It hurts. It hurts a lot.

Pain is a tool. Nature's tool. It's nature's way of saying *Don't do that, dumbshit.* My enemy is a universe away; I can't get to him. But now I know who he is. What he is. And I can make him come to me.

Then I'll let nature take its course.

Orbek and his detail tumble out of the Courthouse stairs onto the balcony in a Mack Sennett tangle. "Boss! Hey, *Boss!*" Orbek shouts. "Goddamn Courthouse's full of fuck-me *Monastics!*"

I lift my head. "I know."

The lunatic jumble Deliann poured into me clicks into place inside my head, faster and faster as I start to see how everything connects with each other and with itself: Shanna and Faith, Tan'elKoth and Kollberg, the Monastics who come at us from above and the Folk from below, the ring of Social Police troops that tightens around the city. Raithe. Deliann.

Me.

This has a shape.

Our lives ride an infernal tornado, a vortex that draws us, each and all, down to its single point of central calm. I can see it coming: the shape of the future. That shape gives me all the strength I need.

"All right," I say, my voice hoarse and thick. I say it again, louder. "All right. Shut up and listen. You want to know what we're gonna do? I'll fucking tell you what we're gonna do."

I look at t'Passe, and twitch my bloody fingers at Raithe. "Wake him up."

"Caine—"

"Wake him up," I repeat. "I have something he wants—" I lift my hand and watch the gather of scarlet become a drop that falls into the filth beneath me. "And there's something I want from him."

I make that hand into a fist, and squeeze out a thicker flow, rich and round and red. I can taste it.

"I'm gonna offer him a deal."

3

AT THE RECTUM of the Shaft, below the crusted gape of the sausage grinder, the iron grate that seals the sump is set into stone. A stonebender rockmagus did the work, under contract to the Imperial Constabulary. Her song had softened the stone to the consistency of warm tallow; once the grate had been pressed into place, the stone had closed around it like living lips, and the silent melody of the rockmagus had hardened the limestone to the solidity of granite.

In the Shaft, the human eye can find only darkness, but that is not because there is no light; eyes that see deeper into the lower frequencies of the spectrum might find the Shaft illumined with the dim thermal glow of living bodies, and the brighter plumes they exhale. Had such eyes looked upon the sump grate now, they would have seen stubby fingers wriggle upward through the bars like pale grubs twisting from black soil; had ears sharper than human listened, they would have heard a dark hum that pulsed with the millennial patience of the limestone itself. More fingers joined, and large hands pushed at the middle of the grate, and the iron squeezed free from the limestone's softened kiss.

The grate was passed silently from hand to hand down the sump all the way to the underground river below; an altered hum rehardened the stone lips of the sump, and two rockmagi climbed out. They were followed by a pair of hulking lambent-eyed trolls, then more stonebenders, some primals, more trolls, a few clumsy night-blind ogres, and even some treetoppers who had made the long climb up the sump with their birdlances strapped across their backs.

Many had armor; all had weapons. Each of the primals carried a small griffinstone, looted from the secret caches of the Thaumaturgic Corps, and many had magickal weapons to use the power the griffinstones provide. One of the ogres took a long whiff of the Shaft's wet stench and murmured that he was hungry; a troll replied that the place was usually lined with humans chained to the walls: a homophage's dream buffet.

But the Shaft was empty.

Up the long, long step-cut slope, there was nothing to be found save shackles left open, discarded, dangling by their chains from the thick bolts that anchored them to the limestone.

One of the rockmagi said grimly, "Might be trouble, this. Get moving." The rockmagus pointed the length of the Shaft. "Up there, have business, we."

But when they broke through the door into the Pit, the Donjon was as deserted as the Shaft had been.

Treetoppers, primals, ogres, trolls, stonebenders, and ogrilloi ranged throughout the concentric rings of tunnels lined with private cells, searching every one. The sole inhabitants of the Donjon were the corpses stacked at the downstream end of the Pit.

The doors that led toward the Courthouse above could not be forced, even by the strength of ogres. Someone suggested the doors might be magically held, and for a time there was debate whether the doors should be chopped through with axes, burned through by griffinstone-powered flame, or removed by a rockmagus softening the stone in which they were set. While this debate grew more and more heated, tangles of demented illogic twisting like threads drawing violence from thin air, Kierendal arrived.

She'd gotten the news by treetopper, and she came through the Shaft door cradled in the arms of Rugo the ogre, who peered around nervously, tongue shooting up along the curve of his tusks, because he had a sick suspicion that maybe that little fey fucker, that Changeling, had survived the battle on Commons' Beach, too, and he didn't want to get in trouble again with Kier for letting him live. He was pretty relieved to find the place as empty as the treetopper had said.

Alongside Rugo paced Jest, at heel like a dog, eagerly obedient to the prods and growled commands of the armored ogrillo, Tchako, who guarded him. Blood still beaded from the tooth punctures on his lower lip, and when he looked down from the balcony at the stack of bodies against one wall of the Pit, his mouth hurt worse. He thought his friend Caine's corpse was probably lying down there within that stack like a log in a rick of firewood, and reflected, *Better him than me.*

And when Kierendal and Rugo and Jest and Tchako came in, the primals and stonebenders and ogres and all started to jabber at once, everyone trying to explain why the doors should be broken this way, or that way, or some other way, and there came angry snarls, and shoving, and the rasp of steel on steel.

Some of the clouds of fever had begun to part within Kierendal's mind; in the hours since Jest's capture, she had even begun to doubt Caine's guilt. She was unaccountably relieved to find the Pit deserted. This relief troubled her more than her fever had, and sharpened the edge of her Fantasy-voice as she hissed inside all their heads. "He is not here. We are too late. To force the door is fruitless—we cannot fight the whole army above. We have lost him."

They fell silent while they considered the consequences of losing Caine.

As though the silence was itself a signal, the door to the Courthouse stairs swung open. In the doorway stood a huge, vicious-looking ogrillo with bandaged wrists, wearing a hauberk three sizes too small and carrying a Donjon guard's club. His lip flaps drew back in an approximation of a human's smile, and he waggled his tusks invitingly. "Hey, you fuckers," he said. "You looking for Caine? There's a party in the Hall of Justice, hey? Big party. Invites all around."

"What?" Kierendal rasped painfully, surprise drawing a word from her throat instead of her mind. "What?"

"Come on," he said, beckoning. "Don't be late. Everybody come."

Kierendal, naked and trembling, a half-dead, mutilated, spiderish *thing*, said, "Caine wants me to come to a party?"

"You gotta come, Kierendal," the ogrillo said seriously. "You're the guest of honor, hey?"

4

YOU GET INTO the Hall of Justice from the second floor of the Courthouse. It's a vaulted auditorium, where the King—later the Emperor, and until a couple days ago the Steward—of Ankhana sat to try cases that came before his personal judgment. Its design dates from the days when some civil cases were decided by combat; the circular expanse of floor where the litigants stand is still walled, still traditionally strewn with clean sand. Still called the arena. One thing I can say about arenas in general: Better to be up here looking down, than down there looking up.

Believe me.

On a broad dais above the arena stands the Ebony Throne, brother to the Oaken Throne in the Great Hall of the Colhari Palace. Since the Assumption of Ma'elkoth, though, the Patriarch has passed judgment from a smaller, unadorned, unassuming chair—the Steward's Seat—on a dais of its own, below and to the right: the proper place for he who is only a servant of the God above.

But the Ebony Throne has a better view.

It's pretty comfortable, too.

I sit with the blade of Kosall naked across my knees, and survey my new kingdom.

The seating sweeps upward in a steep bowl, broken by an imposing prow of limestone that rises behind the Ebony Throne fully to the vault overhead. This big-ass wedge had once been carved with the figure of Prorithun, but now bears the current face of Ankhanan Justice, such as it is: Ma'elKoth. Only Ma'elKoth can look over the shoulder of whatever judge might sit below.

Big bastard always did like to kibitz.

Row after row of those cut-stone benches are filled with my people, sitting, watching silently. Waiting for the show to begin. Almost two thousand, all told, human and primal and ogrillo, from the Pit and from the private cells. A few from the Shaft. Of those two thousand, maybe five hundred really feel like they owe me something, like they owe each other something. Of those five hundred, there's maybe fifty I can count on, when the shitstorm breaks. Maybe fifty, if I'm lucky.

Maybe twenty will actually fight.

The others just want to get the hell out of here. They want to live. I can't blame them. I don't blame them.

I don't need them.

For fighters, I've got those guys on the sand.

A hundred and fifty armed friars, at least a quarter of them Esoterics. They bristle with swords and spears and carry short compound-recurved bows, and who knows how many wands and magicked crystals and crap like that. Shit, I'd match them against the Cats, and put three-to-one on the friars.

Cash.

The guy that Raithe speaks quietly with, down there in the middle—Acting Ambassador Damon—is twitchy as a street

Temp on crank, but Raithe tells me he's solid. They all are. That's Monastic training for you: homicidal paranoia doesn't really get in the way. Might even be an advantage.

You have to be crazy, to fight the Social Police.

Raithe mounts the steps of the dais slowly, a little unsteadily. He's weak, shaky with blood loss, but his Control Disciplines keep him moving: biofeedback maintains his blood pressure, and he can mentally goose his endocrine system to release hormones that give him strength and suppress the pain. He can walk, talk, even fight, right up till he passes out again.

He gets close and nods to me. "They will perform as required," he says softly. "Damon is a good man. He knows how to follow orders."

I squint at him. "That's your definition of a good man?"

His wintry eyes meet mine steadily. "What is yours?"

Instead of answering, I look down into the five-gallon tureen somebody snagged from the commissary. It sits on the side table to my right, half full of water, warm as spit, in which my right hand soaks. I work my hand into a fist and out again. Ragged flaps of my knuckle skin drift like scraps of jellyfish, trailing straw-colored billows of blood.

"All right," I tell him, pulling my hand out. "Take it."

On the dais at my left side, I have Toa-Sytell, still chained, a huddled ball of feverish misery. Every once in a while he writhes, or makes a little whimpering noise; sometimes a tear or two trickles down his cheeks. Raithe makes a complicated gesture, knotting and unknotting his fingers like a cat's cradle of flesh and bone, and Toa-Sytell relaxes into unconsciousness.

Raithe unties the gag and gently frees it from Toa-Sytell's slack mouth; slowly, almost reverently, he rinses the rag in the blood-tinged water of the tureen, then wrings it out before retying it between the Patriarch's teeth.

I wave a hand at the tureen. "Here, take the soup down to your boys there. It's time for them to get to work."

Expressionlessly, he picks it up and carries it down to the arena. "Line up," he says. "By rank. Damon: you are first."

The Acting Ambassador steps up obediently. Slowly, with a kind of ritualistic solemnity, he cups some of the water in one hand and brings it to his lips, then steps aside to let the next friar come. Yeah, he'll take Raithe's orders.

Raithe will take mine.

Voluntarily.

Faithfully.

That's our deal: his obedience for my blood. And he is a man of honor. What does that say about me, if I can trust my enemies more than my friends?

Raithe sits on the dais below me, pressing a hand against the wound in his side. "It is done, then," he says, dark and doom-haunted. "It is done. I am yours."

"Relax, kid," I tell him. "It's not like you sold me your soul."

His gaze is bleak as tundra. "What is a soul?"

5

ORBEK COMES THROUGH the arch at the back of the Hall at the head of a gaggle of Folk. He flicks a tusk back toward the corridor behind and gives me a nod.

"Stay calm," I say generally. "Let them come."

Folk flood through the door: a spume of madness white-capped with the foam that trickles from their mouths. A lot of them are pretty far gone, so deep in the dementia that it's jangling their nerves, making them twitch and limp, stagger and spastically jerk. It's a testimonial to Kierendal's leadership that they haven't turned on each other; somehow she holds them together, somehow she directs their HRVP-spawned lunacy outside their group: toward the Imperials. Toward the humans.

Toward me.

And they smell: they carry a stink of bad meat and acid urine, of unwashed armpit and rotten teeth. It precedes them, an oily wave that flows into the Hall of Justice and fills it and closes over our heads. We could drown in this stench like rats in a rain barrel.

They smell like Dad.

Two weeks ago, that alone could have beaten me.

Funny how things change.

I lean to my right so I can see Kris in the Steward's Seat below, a step above and to the left of where Raithe sits. "Showtime."

He makes no answer. Only the irregular hitching of his breath shows he's alive. "Hey," I mutter. "Come on, Kris. The party's starting."

His eyes roll open, and he offers me a weak smile.

"How're you doing?"

His answer has the spooky distance of mindview. "Better. Much better, Hari. Up here—" A limp gesture takes in the whole world outside the Donjon. "—I can draw Flow to manage my fever. I am . . . grateful . . . that you brought me out of there."

"How's the leg?"

"It hurts," he admits with a wistful shrug, still smiling. "But only down in the bone, where it has always hurt. The flesh above . . . well—"

I get the picture. It's ugly. "Can you fix it?"

"You see here—" He lays a hand upon the pus-soaked rag that serves as a bandage over the gaping abscess on his thigh. "—the result of my healing skill."

"Hold your shit together. I need you lucid. None of this can work without you."

"Frankly, Hari—" He coughs, and turns up his palm in a shrug of apology. "—I don't see how it can work *with* me. You haven't even said what you want me to do—"

"Too late to argue about it now," I tell him, because here comes Kierendal, cradled like a bundle of sticks in an ogre's bridge-girder arms. She's naked, wasted, starved, smeared with filth. Her hair, her signature, that elaborate platinum coif, has become the straggled, finger-ripped wisps of a cartoon witch; what remains of it is plastered wet and greasy down the sides of her face. Her eyes like tarnished coins flick with foggy wariness. She didn't expect to find me waiting for her, and in her world, there's no such thing as a pleasant surprise.

Then I watch her eyes track the leash that stretches from the arm of the Ebony Throne to the prison collar, and I watch her squint, and blink, and bring a trembling skeletal hand to her eyes to see if she can wipe away the image of Toa-Sytell chained to my chair like a dog. Her whole body starts to shake.

That, right there, is a good sign: some rationality remains. She's sane enough to be freaked out by how crazy this all is.

At the ogre's heel comes Majesty, arms bound behind him, prodded along by an ogrillo bitch whose neck is bigger around than my thigh. Dried blood flakes across his chin. His eyes bulge and he mouths silently: *Caine. Hot staggering fuck.*

I acknowledge him with a glance, and squeeze my eyes into half a smile at Kierendal. "Have a seat, Kier," I say. "Tell your people to make themselves at home."

She glazes over like I hit her with a club. "Caine—" she croaks through the general rumble and mutter. "I don't—how did you—why have—I don't *understand*!"

"It's not that complicated," I tell her. "I'm doing some business in Ankhana right now, and I can't get it done with you trying to slip a knife in me every time you see my back. We need to reach an understanding."

I can read her lips. "You know—?" she breathes. "You know I came here to kill you?"

"You came to the Donjon to kill me. Here? You came because I *invited* you."

"I—I don't—"

"Look, it's simple," I tell her. "We're all here. We have maybe half an hour to settle this shit. Before anybody leaves this room, you and I need to be on the same side." I can't feel the Social Police closing in around the city—not like Raithe can—but I know they're there, closer every minute. Half an hour might be optimistic.

"You—you're asking me to *join* you?"

"Asking, shit. We need you. We need your people. I'd be on my knees begging, but you might have heard my legs don't work so well."

"You think I will accept this? Are you so naive?" Her voice has lost the croak, taking on instead a weird echoic nondirectional resonance, as though she's talking from inside my skull. She's recovering her self-possession in a hurry, and her eyes rake the room disdainfully. "To join you would make me an accomplice to your crimes."

"Let's not start about my crimes, huh?"

"Is that why you have brought me here?" she resonates acidly. "To protest your *innocence*?"

"Fuck my innocence." I'm losing patience with this; maybe I didn't have much to begin with. "Are you willing to stand and listen to what we're up against? Yes or no. That's all I need out of you right now. Yes or no or shut up and fight."

"Don't think you can bully me, Caine. I know what you are. Murderer. Liar. *Aktir*."

I can feel the blood coming up my neck. "As long as we're calling names, why don't you try *traitor* on for size, you fucking slag?"

This generates a warning rumble from the Folk she brought with her. "What are you talking about?"

"Treason," I say. "Your treason."

The rumble gets louder, but that weird voice of hers overrides it effortlessly. "Is treason really the word you want to use, Caine? When you have the Steward of the Empire chained like a dog?"

I shrug. "He's not *my* king. On the other hand—" I nod toward Kris in the Steward's Seat, who goggles back at me in open horror, mouthing *Hari, don't!* "—Deliann, here, is yours."

"You must be joking."

"Yeah, that's me: a laugh a minute. We could all use a chuckle. Go ahead and tell everybody how you tried to murder the Mithondionne."

That warning rumble from the Folk thickens, but it's met by a colder, darker growl from our guys, Folk and human alike: Kris is a popular guy. Kierendal's nonvoice overrides the swell of anger. "He is no king. He's a vile, murdering *Aktir*—as are you!"

"Yeah. So what? He's also the Youngest of the Twilight King, and you fucking know it. You knew it then. You knew he was the last Mithondionne, and you ordered him killed."

"He's not even primal," she snarls. "He's a human in disguise!"

"You've got it backwards," I tell her. "The human *is* the disguise."

Deliann crumples on the Steward's Seat as though something is eating his guts from the inside out and covers his face with his hands. "Hari," he murmurs, lost and empty and for my ears alone. "Hari, how can you do this to me?"

"It's midnight, Kris," I tell him simply. "That's all."

He lifts his head and shows me the question in his eyes.

I explain, "Take off your mask."

His eyes go wide and fill with sick pain. "They will never accept me."

"Who gives a rat's ass what they accept? You know what you are. Fucking act like it."

His gaze retreats inside his head, and I lift my eyes to meet Kierendal's disdainful stare. "I know you're not yourself these days, Kier. I know you've been sick, and it's hard for you to get shit straight in your head. This is your chance to make good. If you're willing to help, we can use you."

Her eyes shimmer like fish scales. "And what's in it for me?"

I shrug. "Your life."

"Is that all you have to offer?" she says with scalding contempt.

Raithe casts a surreptitious glance toward me from the arena floor. I give it back expressionlessly, then return to Kierendal. "I don't know what the penalty for attempted regicide is supposed to be among your people, but you're not among your people now. This is my court. You have a choice to make, Kier. Right now."

"My people are ready to die for me, Caine. How many of these . . . creatures . . . are ready to die for *you*?"

And that, I guess, pretty much says it all.

"There's one way to find out," I say evenly.

Her hands coil. "I do not bluff, Caine."

"Yeah, I've heard that about you." Then simply, coldly, finally, all I have to say is: "Raithe."

He claps his hands together as though he dusts sand from them in her direction. A spray of black droplets falls before him. Kierendal tries to speak, but her voice becomes a thick gargling roil of bodily sounds. She gapes at me for half of one blankly astonished second; then a rusty hinge-squeal hacking comes from her throat. Her sides heave, and she vomits blood down the legs of the ogre who holds her.

"You bazztidz!" the ogre cries as though its heart is breaking. "You bazztidz—whaddid you do to Kier?" It falls to its knees and cradles Kierendal like an infant to its breast.

Throughout the hall, my guys are on their feet. Below me, Raithe issues soft-voiced instructions to the friars; they spread out, closer to the cover of the arena wall, checking their weapons. He mutters at me over his shoulder, "Have you ever done anything that did not end in violent death?"

"Sure, lots of stuff," I tell him. "I just can't think of any right now."

This is gonna be one fucking ugly brawl. And maybe I knew it was gonna come to this. Maybe I was looking forward to it.

Maybe I am what they say I am.

But a new light grows within the Hall of Justice, paler, steadier than the lamp flames and the scarlet flicker of the fires outside: a softly penetrant moonglow that does not admit of shadow. It gathers strength, intensifies, and the hall falls quiet as it touches each and all among us here, and every eye turns to find its source.

It's coming from Deliann.

He rises from the Steward's Seat, slow with infirmity. In the throbbing quiet, his voice is soft enough to break my heart. "No. No fighting. Not among us. No killing. I can't stand it."

He sounds like he's standing at my shoulder. I have a feeling he sounds like he's standing at everybody's shoulder. The light gathers itself into a shining cloud around him and wreathes his brow with cold coronal flame. Then that light from his face flares out and grabs us all by the brain.

For one infinite second that light drowns me with everything everyone else is feeling: pain and fear and bloodlust and anguish and fierce fighting joy and everything else, and the light makes them feel what I'm feeling, and all of us feel the lives of each of us and together we make a world of pain that he somehow draws out and ties together into a giant ball of misery, and he hugs it and holds it and that doesn't make it okay—it's not like that, nothing could ever make all this okay—but somehow it's not so bad, now, because it's spread out a little, shared a little, and no matter how alone we all are he knows exactly, *exactly,* what we're going through, how scared and hurt we all are, and he kind of says—

All right, you're scared and hurt. It's okay to be scared, and it's okay to be hurt, because your life is a scary, painful place.

Deliann says softly, "Rugo."

The ogre lifts his head.

"She need not die," Deliann says. "But there is only one hope of life for her. She must be restrained from any interference in the battle to come. She must be taken into the Donjon, and placed in a cell, and kept there until what is to come has passed over us all. Will you do that?"

Rugo turns his face away. "I do thizz, she lives? You promizz?"

"I have said so."

Rugo's neck bends, and tears streak the globular surface of his eyes. "I guezz—she can't hate me more than zzhe doezz already."

Deliann searches the hall like he's expecting to see someone he can't find; after a second or two, he nods to himself. "Parkk," he says to a rugged-looking stonebender up in back, not far from where Majesty stands. "Save her. Stay with her in the Donjon, and tend her when she wakes."

The stonebender holds his place sullenly for a long moment like he's expecting a trick; then he shrugs and nods and makes his way to Kierendal's side. Stonebender magick should work even in the Donjon.

Deliann lowers his head like he can feel my disapproval against the back of his neck. "Is it so wrong," he says softly, "that I would not have my first act as king be the execution of a friend?"

"Did I say anything?"

"No," Deliann replied. "But you were thinking very loudly. What do you want me to do, now?"

All her people are still standing, staring, waiting. I can still use their help, if Deliann can get it for me. "You could start," I offer, "by telling everybody what the hell is going on."

"Tell—?" he murmurs faintly. "How can I possibly tell? It's so huge—there's too much. How can I know what's important, and what's just detail?"

"You don't have to know," I say. "Just decide."

His feathery brows pull together.

"I—" Pain twists his face, and it's not physical pain. "I think I see—"

"Go on, Kris. You've got the floor, man. Use it."

Suffering shines from him like the eldritch light from his face. He lowers his head, closing his eyes against his own light, and begins to speak.

6

HE STOOD IN the center of the arena. Fireglow that leaked down from the clerestory of the vaulted ceiling shaded his penetrant shine toward a pale peach. Though his voice had never been strong, and now was weaker still with his infirmity, all could hear—his meaning, if not his words.

All within that room were touched by his Meld.

The spider-tangle of black threads he could see flowing into Caine knotted together in a flare of white fire within Caine's chest—white fire that Deliann could touch, white fire from which Deliann had drawn the power to tune his Meld in a wholly new way. His shine resonated with the Shells of primals, gaining strength and the colors of life; it flowed into the Shells of stone-benders, and out again to blend into ogres and trolls; the shimmer of ogre brought it to frequencies that might touch the ogrilloi, and the ogrilloi shaded it enough to slide within the consciousness of Flowblind humanity.

He neither orated nor exhorted, but merely spoke. "This is the truth," he said, and through the Meld all knew it. He held on to what he knew was true, and let the story tell itself.

"Some of you," he said, "believe you are here because you were imprisoned for the crime of thinking for yourself; you are mistaken. Some of you believe you are here because you were falsely accused of treason; you, too, are mistaken. Some of you believe you are victims of political oppression, or official misconduct, or simple bad luck. Some of you think you came to revenge yourselves on your enemies, or to stand by your friends.

"You are all mistaken.

"What brings all of us here is not Cainism, or human prejudice; it is not greed, or lust for power, or blind chance.

"What brings all of us here is a war.

"This is a war that is fought every day in every land; this is a war that began with the birth of life itself. This is a war the best of us fight in our hearts: a war against *to get along, you go along*. A war against *us and them*. A war against *the herd*, against *the cause*. Against the weight of civilization itself.

"This war cannot be won.

"*Should* not be won.

"But it must be fought.

"Here is the truth: We are offered a gift.

"That we are here this night is the gift of T'nnalldion—what in the human tongue is *Home*, or *the World*. This is the great gift of Home: that once in an age, she brings forth this secret, silent war into the full light of day. This gift is the opportunity to stand as her shield; to see plain our enemy; to strike a blow face-to-face and hand-to-hand.

"She held out this gift to my grandfather Panchasell, more than a thousand years ago. In accepting, he named himself Luckless, for he knew the doom he chose.

"This was the first engagement in our theater of this war: when Panchasell Mithondionne closed the *dillin* that joined us to the Quiet Land. He fought the war in secret for two hundred years; when Home brought the war into the open day, Panchasell the Luckless and House Mithondionne took arms and led the Folk Alliance against the Feral Rebellion.

"Almost nine hundred years ago, barely a bowshot from where we now stand, Panchasell the Luckless fell in battle.

"On the day my grandfather was killed, Home held out this

gift to my father, T'farrell Ravenlock. My father refused, and named himself the Twilight King; he wished the bright day of the First Folk to draw slowly to a close, instead of suffering the sudden nightfall of extinction.

"He led our people away from the daylit war, ceding the open lands of Home to the enemy, and retired to the deepwood to preside over our long slow slide into history. This has come more swiftly than his darkest dream: We few, here today, may be the last of the Folk to stand together against our enemy.

"More than four hundred years were to pass before Home offered her gift again. This time it was to the race of the enemy, many of whom had come to love her as deeply as any of the Folk; this time the gift was offered to a human named Jereth of Tyrnall.

"Jereth Godslaughterer fought the enemy in each of its shadow-forms: as Rudukirisch and Dal'kannith, Prorithun and Kallaie, and in all the other names that humans give to the shared dreams that pool their collective desires. Like my grandfather, Jereth fell in battle—but it was a battle won: from it came the Covenant of Pirichanthe, which binds the human gods beyond the walls of time, and defends Home from their irrational whims of power.

"Now, five hundred years have come and gone since the days of the Godslaughterer, and Home once more offers her gift.

"Our enemy has struck already. He struck without challenge, as a poisoner strikes, against whom no armor may suffice. His blow has slain House Mithondionne, of whom I alone survive. Each of us in this room bears wounds from his hand. His weapon is madness, the same madness that some of us—here, tonight—feel coursing our veins. But against such an invisible sword, we now have a silent shield. T'Passe?"

T'Passe, pragmatic as a shovel, tromped down the aisle to the arena; Deliann gestured to Raithe, and Raithe put the tureen into her hands. T'Passe shrugged, and ducked her head toward the contents of the bowl. "A little drink, that's all," she said heavily. "Even a sip." She handed the bowl to a human, one of the Cainists who sat on the floor in the aisle. Though already carrying the countervirus as did all the former inmates of the Pit, she dipped her hand, and brought it cupped to her lips; like all Monastics, she had a profound respect for the power of ritual.

The Cainist who held the bowl scowled down into the straw-colored liquid within. "What is it?"

She looked at Deliann, who gravely inclined his head.

"Water," she said. "Water, with a little blood in it."

Again, she looked at Deliann; his expression never altered, nor did the angle of his nod. She shrugged.

"It's Caine's blood."

A general murmur stirred the room.

Deliann said, "Choose."

The Cainist still scowled, but he dipped his hand and drank, and held the bowl so that those beside him could do the same, before he passed it on to a nearby woman.

"In accepting the gift of Home, you bind yourself to fight in our war," Deliann said. "I know that many are without weapons, and more are without armor. Many—perhaps most—of you do not call yourselves warriors.

"But as Caine has said: There is fighting, and there is fighting.

"By this he means: It is not demanded of each of you that you take up a sword and slay. That is the task for warriors. Some may bind wounds, and comfort the injured. That is the task for healers. Some may cook food and carry water. Some may leave here this night, and never look behind.

"Let each of us fight in our own way, according to our own gifts. A cook who pretends to be a warrior endangers his comrades; a warrior who pretends to be a cook ruins food we need for the strength to fight on.

"Only this do I ask of you: I, not Home. Those of you who leave this place tonight, do not surrender to our enemy. Know that the shield of Home defends you, and can defend all whom you love. This shield does not move of its own. It does not grow unaided. It can truly defend only when passed from heart to heart, and flesh to flesh. To bring anyone or anything within the shield of Home requires only a kiss. Your choice can save more than you dream. It is the most important choice you will ever make.

"Some here do not have that choice."

A vague wave of his hand might have indicated the Patriarch, bound and leashed to the Ebony Throne, or the friars who stood on the arena sand, or both.

"But we do.

"We can choose to stand against the blind god.

"We can choose to stand for Home.

"We can—"

He broke off, and for a moment lowered his head; when he

looked up once more, he wore a small, melancholy smile, full of resigned self-knowledge.

"I should say, *you* can choose.

"My choice is made already. I have made the choice of Panchasell. The choice of the Godslaughterer.

"The choice of Caine.

"I am Deliann, the Mithondionne. Here I will stand. Here I will fall.

"I am Deliann, the Mithondionne. I set my name to this."

He fell silent, and his light faded, and with it the Meld; after a moment he lowered his head.

7

THEY'RE ALL FILING out, the Cainists and the Serpents and the Folk. After a minute, some clever guy gets a bright idea, and brings the tureen up to the arch where everybody can take a sip as they go out. Pretty soon somebody's at each of the other exits with a helmet upside down in their hands, holding a few cups scooped from the tureen, and the hall clears out faster. Most of them are heading for the Pit, where they'll go back the way they came: down the Shaft sump and out, to scatter across the Empire, and beyond. Stonebenders to the White Desert and the northern God's Teeth, ogrilloi to the Boedecken, treetoppers south to the jungles of lower Kor.

Primals to the deepwood, and whatever's left of Mithondion.

And that's it, then. Here, in this eerie muttering quiet, I'm looking at Shanna's victory. She and I and Deliann—and Raithe, too, can't leave that fucker out of it—we just beat HRVP.

Sure, the disease has a big lead, but it's slow, and random. The countervirus is fast, and will be purposeful: with a few hundred people fanning out of here, spreading Shanna's countervirus every time they sneeze, or piss in a river, or share a cup of wine, we'll overtake it.

Score one for the good guys.

Which is all the enthusiasm I can muster; it's kinda anticlimactic. I guess it's because HRVP was just for openers—just a light jab to probe our defenses, and it too fucking nearly punched our lights out. Like Tan'elKoth used to say: You can win every battle and still lose the war.

On the other hand, Kris' story was a good one; sometimes making a good story is winning, too. Spartacus. The knights of the Round Table. The Alamo. That's victory, of a sort.

Shit, I hope so. It's the only kind we're gonna get.

A couple of feys who used to do healing for the rough-trade girls at Alien Games work on my legs a little, scraping out the jelly of dead muscle and infected pus, and run some Flow in there to pump strength into the muscle.

About the time they finish up, Majesty threads his way down to the arena. Somebody cut him loose after that ogrillo bitch went off with the ogre and the dwarf to look after Kierendal. He rubs the rope burn on his wrists, and he's covered in filth, but he looks pretty cheerful: his smile cracks the dried blood on his chin, and it flakes away as he scrubs at it with the back of his hand.

"Damn, Caine," he says as he vaults into the arena. "Fuck a goat if you don't always find a way to come out on top." He bounces across the sand and climbs the dais, right up next to Toa-Sytell, and grins down at him. "Hey there, you shit-crazy cock," he says, and draws back his foot for a kick.

"Don't."

He looks at me and finds no room for argument in my eyes. He shrugs. "You're the boss, I guess," he says.

"Yeah."

The feys give him hard looks as they pack their shit and go. He ignores them. "What now, buddy? What's our next move?"

"My next move," I tell him heavily, "is to send those friars down there out to fight some troops that are coming after me. Troops from my world."

"Your world?" Majesty breathes. "Fuck *me*—it's *true*, then. It's true. It's always been true. You *are* an *Aktir*."

"Yeah."

"Fuck me," he repeats, but then he spreads his hands and smiles at me. "Hey, *Aktir* or not, you always knew who your friends were, right?"

"*Your* next move—" I nod toward the back of the hall. Toward the door. "—is to follow those guys up there. Clear your ass out of town."

"Huh?" Wariness sparks deep within his eyes. "I don't get you."

"You're not popular with the Folk, Majesty. I'd lay odds the only reason you're still alive is that most of them aren't quite sure who you are."

"Hey, c'mon, Caine. Aren't you the stag, here? You're saying you can't protect me?"

"No," I tell him. "I'm saying I won't."

His smile cracks like the blood on his chin. "Hey—hey, Caine, c'mon—"

"You're why Kierendal had to be locked up. You killed half her people. The only family she had. You and Toa-Sytell. Your fucking Caverns War."

"But, but, hey, I didn't have anything against her," he says, licking his lips. "Shit, Caine. This whole Caverns War—that was Toa-Sytell's thing. It was politics, that's all. Business. It wasn't personal—"

"It was for her." I nod toward the door one more time. "You better go now, while I still remember how much I used to like you."

He leans toward me confidentially. I can see sweat leaking out of his skin. "Come on, Caine. This is *me*. Even in the Donjon, didn't I help you out? Huh? Didn't I?" He reaches for my arm as though his touch will remind me of our friendship.

I brush Kosall's hilt with my fingers. Its blade buzzes a rattlesnake's warning against the arm of the throne. Majesty's hand freezes, and he takes a cautious step back down the dais stairs. "Yes," I say. "You did. That's what buys you the chance to walk out."

"But, but, hey, I mean, where am I supposed to go?" he says plaintively. If I didn't know him so well, I could almost feel sorry for him. Majesty's a weed; he'll flourish wherever he falls. "Where can I go? What am I supposed to *do*?"

"I don't care," I tell him, "so long as you don't do it here. Go."

He backs away one more step. "Caine—"

I point Kosall at him. The blade snarls. "Five seconds, Majesty."

He turns and scampers down the dais, across the sand. He forces his way into the outgoing stream of humans and Folk and exits the Hall of Justice without looking back. I watch him go, remembering all the good times we've had together, but they don't mean much to me right now. There was a time I considered him my best friend.

And I can't remember why.

Down on the sand, Raithe gives his instructions—my instructions—to the friars, detailing them in squads to intercept and harass the approaching Social Police: just my way of saying hello. Pretty soon the friars go, and t'Passe heads off to coordinate the Folk and Serpents and Cainists who want to stay here and fight; Orbek takes Toa-Sytell's leash and drags him off to keep his Patriarchal ass out of mischief, and in all the whole Hall of Justice it's now just Raithe, and Deliann, and me.

From the arena below, Raithe stares after Orbek and Toa-Sytell with those deep-winter eyes. He's wrapped pretty tight; he sizzles with the effort he's expending to hold himself still and silent. "What are you going to do with the Patriarch?"

"Nothing you need to know yet," I tell him. "Kris—?"

He stands in the center of the arena, lost in some infinite distance. "Kris—?" I say again, then more sharply, "Deliann."

Slowly, his gaze gathers focus and finds me. "Yes, Caine?"

"Let's do this thing."

"Here?"

I nod up toward the titanic figure of Ma'elKoth carved into the wedge of limestone towering over us. "You got a better place?"

He thinks about it, his face alien, unreadable. Then his eyes close and open again in a motion too slow and deliberate to be called a blink, and he says, "No. I suppose I don't."

"What do you need from me?"

"I'll explain as we go along," he says, mounting the dais to stand at my side. "Find mindview."

I breathe myself into it; it only takes a second or two, and then twisting corded nets of black ropes web the Hall of Justice like it's the lair of spiders the size of horses. "I can see it," I tell him, and I can. Even though I'm talking, I can hold the image.

"I know."

"It's easier now. Easier than it was even when I used to practice this. Back in school."

He offers me a smile of sad understanding. "Among the First Folk, we are taught that the path of power is measured by self-knowledge. To use magick, one must know oneself, and the world, and the identity they share."

I am at the center of that black and tangled web. It pulses into the base of my spine; strength and feeling swells in the muscles of my back and legs.

Deliann turns to Raithe. "Kneel here, facing him," he says, indicating a spot an arm's length in front of my knees.

Raithe looks at me.

"Do as he says," I tell him, and he does.

A different kind of glow surrounds Deliann now, a bluish Saint Elmo's fire kind of thing. That aura grows a limb—a pseudopod, an arm—and grabs on to something white in the middle of my guts. Lightning snaps back up that insubstantial blue and sparks it to a searing arc-welder blaze. It'd be painful, if I were seeing it with my eyes.

He reaches for Raithe, and Raithe gasps as the colors blossom around him.

"This will be a form of Meld," Deliann says. "It's a little like a Fantasy, except we will all be creating it together as we go along. Don't be alarmed at what you might see; none of us might look like we do now, but we'll know each other anyway. It's a . . . *metaphoric* level of consciousness, like a dream."

"And we can't lie," I murmur.

Deliann nods. "This is a state of consciousness where deception is impossible. Concealment, though, isn't difficult. It is simply a refusal to share. It is the same as you should do if any of these Powers tries to join with you, or enter your body. They cannot do so without your cooperation—but they can be very persuasive."

"Yeah."

"What Powers?" Raithe says, staring raptly at whatever Deliann's touch upon his mind is showing him. "You still haven't told me what we are doing."

I bare my teeth. "We're gonna have a little chat with Ma'elKoth."

8

A SOFT, HEARTH-WARM glow appeared, neither close nor distant, in no particular direction: near, far, before, behind, above, or below—

None have meaning in the infinite lack.

As patiently irresistible as gravity, the light drew her forward, or upward: in whatever direction from her that it lay. Without volition to resist its pull, she drifted toward it.

She came to understand that this light was the sun, and not the sun. It was a star, burning in the heavens of the lack, giving light and life and reason to the boundless nothing of her death—but it was also a man, with elven features and a mane of platinum hair that twisted outward in streamers of fire along the solar wind. The sun man held a bow of fusing hydrogen, and carried arrows of light.

Will gathered within her, strengthening with her approach as though she drew it from this man's light; she exerted this will to slow herself, gaining in caution as her awareness congealed. Somehow she knew: This was enemy territory.

She said to the sun: *I know you. You are Kris Hansen.*

The sun replied: *I am Deliann.*

Far, far above her—for now, imperceptibly, up and down had come to the lack—circled a bird of prey, soaring upon gleaming wings, proud and lonely. A falcon—perhaps an eagle—

Perhaps the phoenix.

It struggled toward the sun, drawn forever by light and warmth—only to fall forever back, crippled by a wound to its wing. Its cry echoed in her heart, for it was she who had given that wound. She could feel the wound herself—her arm burned as though she held it in a furnace—yet she knew it was his.

Within herself, she said, *You are the Caineslayer.*

The bird replied, *I am Raithe.*

Now on fields that rolled forever beneath that sun she found others: a great dire wolf with dewclaws cut, limping in pain but still fierce and deadly; a woman of volcanic basalt thrust freshly up from the earth, sharp edges not yet rounded by millennial erosion. She found trees and flowers and cats and mice, snakes and toads and fish—

And she found a man. He sat on a rock, elbows on knees, staring at her.

She knew every inch of him.

The glossy black hair, sprung grey at the temple above the salted black of his beard: her fingers knew that texture. His darkly gleaming eye, the slanted scar across his twice-broken nose—she had felt these with her lips. Those hard and lethal hands had cupped her breasts and stroked warmth along her thighs.

He wore a loose black leather tunic open in front, faded and cracked, white salt rings of ancient sweat circling the armpits. His soft black breeches were covered with cuts and tears crudely sewn. Coarse brown thread showed like old bloodstains against the leather.

Her heart sang, and she flew to him.

Slowly, deliberately, his right hand went inside his tunic, and when it came out again it held a long, keen fighting knife.

"That's close enough," he said.

She stopped, puzzled, hurt sparking somewhere behind what on a mortal body would have been her ribs. *Hari—*

"Hari's dead." He pointed the knife at her eye. "So are you. Let's skip the happy-to-see-you bullshit, huh?"

Hari, I don't understand—why won't you let me touch you?

He flicked the point of the knife toward the circling bird of prey. "Because I have too fucking good an idea what can happen if you do."

I only want to share with you. To join with you.

"No."

We can be one, here. We can truly share. We can love each other—

"Not like that."

All I want is to be together—

"Tough shit."

You treat me like an enemy.

His eyes glittered black and hard: chips of obsidian. "Yeah."

Hari—Caine— Her mental voice roughened, and deepened; she tried to cough it clear, but instead it swelled within her chest to Ma'elKoth's subterranean rumble. *Caine, I love you. We love you.*

"Hold out your hand."

She hesitated.

"Come on," he said. "We're a little past playing shy, huh? Your hand."

All right.

She reached out a hand that had the shape of her own, but the size of Ma'elKoth's—and had Kollberg's oiled-parchment skin and arthritis-knobbed joints. He shook his head and pointed to her left—her wounded, burning, all-too-human hand.

"That one."

She drew back.

"Don't you trust me?" His wolf-grin said he didn't really care about her answer.

She found, astonished, that she didn't—and at first she couldn't say why.

She didn't trust him; she *couldn't* trust him. She had been deceived by him before, hurt by him, destroyed by him. He had lied and lied and lied to her, and his lies had savaged her life; he was the source of all her unbearable suffering these long seven years. He had threatened her, and mocked their lawful caste relationship. He had *struck* her: he had broken her nose, had kicked her in the balls—

In the balls? she thought. *Hey, wait.*

Before the other two of the three she was could stop her, she put out her hand. Faster than their eyes could follow, his knife flashed underhand and drove up between the bones to jut through her palm: a conjured apparition of steel, welling black blood from its base.

The searing ice-steel spike turned to white-hot iron as he twisted it to wedge the blade against the bone; then he used the blade to wrench their hand over sideways and pull them off balance. They gasped in shock that was yet too fresh to be pain, and gaped in astonishment at the blood of black oil that rolled down the blade and dripped from the point.

Where the black oil touched, the grass beneath their feet curled and blackened and began to smoke.

What are you DOING?

His wolf-grin answered. "Holding you steady."

In the far black distance above, the sun drew an arrow of light back to his heart, and let it fly.

The arrow's meteor-streak drove through the injured wing of the phoenix and struck her on the hand, where Caine's knife had pierced her. It flashed into her and through her, through the god at her back and the god behind him, joining all of them with the phoenix along a dazzling line of blue-white Cerenkov radiation.

Power pulsed up the line toward the phoenix, and it gave a heartbreaking cry. From its injured wing, black blood sprayed like rain over all the world.

"This is a metaphor, you understand," Caine said. "I imagine if you concentrate, you can feel what's really happening."

She felt—

From the spring near the crest of Khryl's Saddle, a trickle of black oil joined the sewage runoff of the rail camp. In the great forest of the north, needles of spruce and aspen withered and blackened, and the amber that swelled from gaps in bark was black as onyx. In the Boedecken Waste, oil bubbled up out of the buried depths of the marshes and spread necrotic swathes through the living green.

Her horror spread to the others who shared her consciousness. *Stop it—you have to stop it!*

"No," Caine said. "I don't."

Hari—Caine, please! Stop it now!

"No."

She could feel the life draining from her already, deadness climbing her fingers like leprosy. *Caine—you'll kill me—*

His wolf-grin widened, and lost any trace of humor. "You're already dead. We're killing the *river*."

You can't! You can't do this!

"No?" He barked a harsh laugh. "Who are you talking to?"

Everyone—everything—will die! All of it—every living creature—

"That's right. Then what good does your fucking link do you? You'll have *nothing*. Shit, you'll have less than you started with. Think about it, Ma'elKoth: How many Beloved Children are gonna survive this? What happens to your precious godhood when all your worshipers are dead?"

And that was when Pallas Ril understood. Imaginary tears poured from her imaginary eyes. Her eyes said *Thank you,* but only her eyes.

His wolf-grin thawed a little. "I told you to trust me."

Other words held her lips. *This is a bluff.*

"Sure it is."

You'll kill yourself along with the river; this poison will slay you as surely as any salmon or hawk.

Caine's smile warmed even more. "Ever play Chicken?"

Outrage gathered within her, but the outrage was not hers. The voice from her lips said, *This is no game. Not when the stakes are the lives of all within the Chambaygen's bound.*

His smile went hot. "I wouldn't have come to the party if I didn't want to dance."

It seemed then that a long time passed, in which the only sound was the distant, thin sobs of a young girl. *We still have Faith.*

"Yeah?" His tone was square and warm, but ice in his eyes froze his smile into a mask. "And what can you do to her that's worse than what you're doing right now?"

You are beyond ruthless. You are beyond criminal. You are a monster—

Caine's presence solidified beyond his mask of ice: he became dark and gleaming, diorite in motion, absolute, unanswerable. "You should have thought of that before you hurt my daughter."

Stop this. You must stop this!

"Make me," he said, and vanished.

With him went the phoenix, and the sun, and the meadow, the world and all the stars.

She did not fall into the lack. The channel of venom pouring into the river was enough of a living connection to sustain her consciousness. She was herself the universe: vast and minute together, and empty of all save pain and creeping death.

And hope.

9

THE SOCIAL POLICE officer at the door to the surgery had stood so still for so long that when he finally moved, Avery Shanks flinched; a tingling shock from the middle of her back shot painfully out into her fingers and toes. She clenched her stinging fingers into fragile, futile fists and hunched her shoulders around the hammering of her heart. All this from the smallest gesture: the officer did no more than step to one side and open the door.

Through the door came Tan'elKoth, with two more officers behind.

Something—some subtle difference in his face, his bearing, something bleak and impersonal—brought a sick darkness to her chest. Her mouth tasted of tin. "Tan'elKoth," she said, still uncertain enough to hope that she was wrong. "Is it over? Is it finally over?"

He loomed over her like a granite cliff. "Gather your belongings. We leave within the hour."

"Leave?" she repeated stupidly. She made her aching joints move enough to let her sit up. "Tan'elKoth—?"

"Ma'elKoth," he corrected dispassionately.

Avery trembled. "I don't understand—"

He had already turned away. He stood beside the table to which Faith was bound, undoing her straps. A pair of Social Police officers pulled Faith's IV and catheter-line relief bags from their hooks on the table and hung them on an odd device nearby. This device looked rather like a levichair, but instead of magnetic suspensors, it rode on *wheels*: two large spoked wheels in back and a pair of smaller ones in front. Tan'elKoth lifted Faith from the table and began to strap her into the wheeled chair.

And that was the subtle change: she saw it now. He no longer seemed aware of the Social Police, nor they of him, but both worked with common purpose in mechanical coordination, requiring neither word nor gesture.

"What are you *doing*? Tan'elKoth—Ma'elKoth—she's too *weak*! You can't move her, she'll die!"

He reached her side in a single step, gathered her shirt into one hand, and lifted her to her feet, neither roughly nor gently—more with a kind of impersonal dispassion, as though she were so alien that he could not conceive what might cause her either pleasure or pain. "You will not let her die," he said. "You will provide whatever care she requires."

"I—I . . ." Tears gathered in her eyes, and she could not speak.

She was stretched too thin; she had lived in this tiny room before the silvered masks of the Social Police for too long; she had charred her heart with too many acid hours helplessly witnessing Faith's endless nightmare.

She longed for the bottle of Teravil that was still in her bag; chemical comfort was the only kind of which she could still dream. But she hated herself enough already. If she were to give herself rest while Faith stayed there, stayed strapped to that steel table, stayed in the twilight fever dream of the drugs that dripped into her arm, she could never live with herself.

Would never live with herself.

She had already decided that when she could no longer resist the pull of the sedatives, she would use them all. When she could find any way out from under the inhuman silver gaze of the Social Police, she would share them with Faith.

Because she could never leave her here alone.

She said, finally, softly, "Yes. Whatever she requires."

Behind him, the Social Police strapped a gleaming metallic harness over Faith's chest.

"But—but, where are we *going*?"

"Home," he said, and turned away once more to adjust the harness.

"Home?" she repeated, horrified. "*Overworld?* What has happened to you? Why are you acting like this? You can't just move her like furniture—she won't live a day!"

"A day," Ma'elKoth said distantly, "will be enough."

THE WAR OF the dark angel and the god of dust and ashes came to turn upon a question of battle.

Of the outcome, there could be little doubt.

The soldiers of the god of dust and ashes had weapons of unimaginable power. They were the best trained, most disciplined fighters this world had ever seen. Their officers were competent, and their morale was unbreakable.

The allies of the dark angel were starving and sick, wounded, disorganized, and distrustful of each other.

Yet there is fighting, and there is fighting: some weapons are more useful than others, and not all battles must be won.

TWENTY-THREE

THE FIRST AMBUSH was, in broad outline, representative of all the encounters between the friars of the Ankhanan Embassy and the Social Police. It came as the last boats of the Bauer Company of the 82nd Force Suppression Unit cleared Fools' Bridge.

The boats had proceeded without haste but steadily, threading their way through the dead and burning trees that studded the river; a man in the lead boat of each lashed-together triad held a large canister of pressurized foam that could be sprayed liberally onto any burning oil that came too close. The rest crouched watchfully, weapons at the ready.

The friars who lay in ambush had no time to make a concerted plan, but what they lacked in coordination they made up for in firepower. The men in the lead boats had no chance.

As the first triad of lashed-together boats hummed silently toward Knights' Bridge, close along the sheer Old Town wall, a shimmering blue-white plane of energy flared out from the dockside. This plane of energy fanned horizontally for barely a second, but in that time it sliced neatly through the heads and shoulders of several of the dozen riflemen in the first boat, and sheared exactly in half, just below the navel, the mage who guided the boat. His torso slid backward and toppled into the river, and the power he had been channeling through his staff exploded into a jagged ball of lightning that conducted well enough through wire-inlaid armor to roast several more riflemen.

Instantly the other three triads turned for the dockside, but the two remaining boats from the first triad drifted powerlessly while riflemen within them frantically pulled collapsible oars out from storage pockets. Before they could use them effectively, ionizing radiation made a laser-straight blue line from the arch of Knights' Bridge to the surface of the river.

Spreading in a fan upstream from where that line touched, the water instantly congealed to frosted glasslike solid that looked like ice, but was warm to the hand. The boats stuck fast within it, and now nut-sized pellets streaked toward them from several directions. These pellets stuck to what they struck, and an instant later they erupted in gouts of flame intense enough to melt the plastic components of the rifles, set fire to the ballistic cloth that covered the riflemen's armor, and ignite the flesh beneath it.

However, the thin line of radiation also marked its point of origin and gave the riflemen their first target.

Their reply was a stackfire volley from a double handful of Heckler-Colt MPAR-12 assault rifles. These rifles were a century and a half out of date, requiring manual sighting and carrying only sixteen stackfire cartridges in each of their dual magazines, but since a stackfire cartridge comprised a tube of eight 5.52 millimeter solid-block caseless rounds that fire sequentially in slightly more than a tenth of one second, a single volley proved adequate.

The friar who stood on Knights' Bridge, whose staff flamed with the power that had gelled the river, was exposed over the low retaining wall from his groin to the crown of his head. The exposed parts of him vanished into a spray of bloody mist and bone fragments, and his legs fell in opposite directions. The detonation of his staff bit a buckboard-sized chunk out of the stone arch; the river below melted into ordinary water and flowed once more.

Before the lead boat of the second trio could reach the bank, it was seized as though by a giant invisible hand and yanked into the air. The adept and most of the riflemen bailed out, but a few unfortunate soldiers had gotten their gear tangled in the boats' nylon-net storage pockets, or had foolishly chosen to hang on, and were hurled hundreds of yards up into the night sky.

As the boats fell, still lashed together, the rope that joined them caught on a bartizan of the Old Town wall; they swung down and slammed against the wall like clappers of a giant stone bell, crushing the men inside. Other men fell from the sky to their deaths on the streets; some landed on rooftops or in the branches of burning trees.

The Telekinesis that had seized the boat was invisible to ordinary eyes, but to an adept in mindview it blazed with furious light—as did the stream of Flow that poured through the hand sculpted of diamond that a friar, hidden around the corner of a warehouse, used to create it. The three surviving Artan adepts communicated his location, and a scant second later that location was the intersection of three expanding spheres, each comprising several thousand sewing-needle-sized flechettes, produced by three RG 2253A antipersonnel rifle grenades in simultaneous airbursts at an altitude of precisely 3.5 meters.

What remained of the friar was not recognizable as human.

The other two triads had reached the docks, and seventy riflemen fanned out among the burning trees that were the last of the unnatural jungle that still stood, here at the epicenter from which the fire had spread. Those riflemen who had bailed into the river were left to swim as best they could; they made inviting targets for the ambushers, and now each time magick flared the man who used it could be located and killed.

Bauer Company methodically and deliberately secured the dockside. They were in no particular hurry; they knew, as their opponents did not, that they were only the first of the 82nd's reinforced rifle companies to enter Ankhana. The whole of their job was to spring ambushes and probe the strength of resistance, and they had done it well.

The surviving friars fell back individually, winding through the streets and alleys toward the Courthouse, harassing the riflemen at every opportunity. They, too, had done their job well.

2

EARLY ENCOUNTERS BETWEEN Ankhanan citizenry and the advancing elements of the Social Police 82nd Force Suppression Unit were bloody. So many voices shouted in the streets that even the fluent Westerling commands and curses of the irregulars went unheeded, and the various companies of the 82nd were forced to resort to nonverbal means of clearing their respective paths.

On Earth, the hammer of automatic rifle fire aimed over the head is universally understood, but Ankhanan citizens, inexperienced with chemically propelled projectile weapons, could not interpret the loud but apparently harmless noise and flashes coming from these odd broken-crossbow-like devices. By lowering their point of aim a few degrees, the Social Police undertook to educate them.

But each lesson sufficed only upon those near enough to see the blood spurting from shattered limbs and riddled torsos, and to smell the voided bowels; thus, the lesson was regularly repeated as the Social Police advanced. Through the streets and along the gutters, blood and oil swirled red and black, immiscible, tracing fractal geometries of turbulence.

It was one of the irregulars who suggested the use of concussion grenades. This was more successful; not only does the airburst of such a device resemble a mage's fireball closely enough to send magick-leery Ankhanans diving for cover, these devices are *so* loud and *so* bright as to trigger the human animal's instinctive panic response: run and hide.

The 82nd now made better time.

The various companies converged, following the lead of one or more irregulars, each of whom carried some variety of seeking item: graven crystals and divining wands, runestaves and silver stilettos, needles that swung on balance points, pendula of crystal, copper, gold, and iron.

Some of these items were sensitive enough to trace the path of Kosall back to the mountains; some were sensitive enough to indicate the location of every hand that had ever touched its hilt. These items had been tuned, detuned, and retuned to filter out the mutilated barge that had been the blade's home, the rocks where it had rested on the river's bed, the headless corpse of a man who had once borne it, now buried in the potter's field southwest of the Cathedral of the Assumption.

Now, the seeking items all pointed toward the Courthouse.

3

ONLY MORGAN COMPANY—approaching from the southwest, through the stately homes of the South Bank—encountered resistance from the Ankhanan Army. When they reached the foot of Kings' Bridge, a mailed officer ordered them to halt; his order was backed up by a triple row of shoulder-to-shoulder pikemen supported by archers farther up the bridge's arch.

Invisible fingers poked dozens, then hundreds, of sudden holes in breastplates and helms, making a rattle like a bucket of stones emptied onto a griddle. Bloody wads of flesh burst from the Ankhanans as they danced to a clattered half rhythm of rifle fire. The survivors chose to allow Morgan Company to pass without further interference.

Once in Old Town, however, their progress became much more dangerous, as they came under magickal fire from a small contingent of friars who were somewhat more successful at keeping themselves under cover. Slowly, mechanically inexorable, Morgan Company beat back their attackers.

Morgan Company was the first unit to reach the Courthouse. Riflemen methodically began to disperse the crowds while the irregulars loudly announced that Kings' Bridge was now open, which produced a tidal surge toward the east and south. A hastily assembled column of Ankhanan infantry was scattered by two grenades and several well-aimed bursts that shredded their standard and their officers. The panic of fleeing men-at-arms was sufficient to awaken the caution of the other infantry columns; their commanders decided to delay engagement with these invaders until the situation could be investigated.

Shortly, the survivors of Bauer Company suppressed the

flames of Knights' Bridge with foam spewed from handheld canisters and marched across. No one challenged them.

The Social Police owned Ten Street, and the balance of the 82nd was mere minutes away.

Those friars who had been cut off on their retreat toward the Courthouse now slipped away into the flame-smeared night, descending the mucker shafts alongside each public pissoir. At the bottom, they were met by the Folk who had waited below, and were led swiftly through the caverns.

4

DESPITE THE URGINGS of caution from the irregulars attached to his command, the 82nd's brigadier ordered a standard attack.

Initially, all went as expected. A handheld launcher lobbed a shaped sticky-charge across Ten Street; the charge flattened against the Courthouse's bronze double doors, and three seconds later detonated with a resounding *whang!* that blew the doors into twisted hunks of fist-sized shrapnel.

It also managed to ignite the black oil that painted the building, and set the Courthouse on fire. Antipersonnel grenades arced up through the flames to explode above the roof.

Several canisters of airborne nerve agent sailed through the doorway, to finish up whatever hostiles the shrapnel may have missed. Chemically propelled grapnels shot toward the roof from the street, the Old Town wall behind, and the roof of the nearby Ankhanan officers' quarters. While their power-reels would not work in Overworld conditions, these soldiers were in superb physical condition, and teeth on their gloves meshed with the toothed cords to provide an effortless slip-proof grip. Hand over hand, they walked up the Courthouse wall at the speed of a moderate trot, while below fifty riflemen rushed the atrium.

This might have worked as a surprise attack; but the Social Police were part of the field of power that was the blind god, and Raithe of Ankhana could feel their every step.

They never had a chance.

The first hint that this operation may not go smoothly was the empty atrium itself. The riflemen found no bodies, no blood—only a stone floor littered with chunks of bronze, spent and flattened slugs, and chips of rock. The white vapor that served as a visual marker for the nerve agent hung in the air, swirling slowly; it had not dispersed farther into the Courthouse, nor did it eddy back toward the blown-open doorway.

The second hint was somewhat more dramatic.

As the riflemen who had reached the roof gathered themselves into order and approached the access stairs, some of the more sensitive among them noted a vibration—like a subaural hum—that seemed to come through their boots. Before they could call others' attention to this, the stone beneath their feet softened, and sagged, then bellied downward like an overloaded trampoline, sweeping the whole group off their feet into a muddled pile at the bottom; the stone then ruptured and dumped them in an unceremonious tangle on the floor of a small room below. The roof continued to collapse, pouring into the room like mud down a funnel.

As this mud fell upon the riflemen and oozed under and around them, the humming rose in both pitch and volume as the four stonebender rockmagi sang the mud back into stone once more. None of the riflemen managed to stand up before the stone closed over their faces; they barely had time to scream.

The riflemen in the atrium found all the doors to be closed, and sealed, by some invisible force that prevented them from even getting their hands within a span of the handles. Further, they found the blown-open doorway to be sealed by a similar force. The same inlay of silver wire that rendered them resistant to many forms of magick also rendered most magick quite invisible; they could not see the Shields that trapped them.

Most primals can make light: it's a simple enough conversion of Flow. As they become more skilled, they can make light in specific colors, from indigo far down into the reds; a mere extension of this ability enables them to produce electromagnetic radiation at a substantially lower frequency: that of microwaves.

Coherent beams of microwaves heated several earthenware pots that had been looted from the Courthouse's commissary. Within these pots was lamp oil. As the lamp oil boiled, it released a considerable amount of aromatic volatiles into the Shield-sealed atrium. The riflemen, wearing self-contained breathing apparatuses to protect them from the nerve agent, had no warning at all before the team of microwave-producing primals turned their attentions to a small piece of wood that lay on the floor near the center of the atrium. The wood caught, sparked

the oil vapor, and turned the atrium into a homemade, crude—
but effective—fuel-air bomb.

Bits and pieces of the riflemen returned to the street riding a
shattering blast of flame.

Having kept, as any good commander would, men in place to
observe the results of his probing attack, the brigadier now decided it was time to enlist local aid. He instructed his irregulars
to approach the officers of the encircling Ankhanan Army under
flag of truce.

He needed troops who had more experience with magick:
troops who had thaumaturges of their own.

5

FOR THE TABERNACLE: a Mylar dome tent of stainless white,
standing in the fireglow of the Financial Court, stretched over
gracefully arched poles of black graphite fiber.

For the congregation: the commanders of the Ankhanan army,
met under flag of truce with Artan officers.

For the priest: an Artan adept stripped of armor and cloaked in
cloth of gold, a bishop's vestments from the Church of the
Beloved Children of Ma'elKoth.

Within the tabernacle, the congregation knelt, for God was
among them.

Taller than the moon, He stood upon a sapphire sky, and the
stars played about His shoulders. His face was the sun: blindness
threatened any impertinent stare. His voice thrummed in their
blood; it spoke with their heartbeats; it was the voice of life itself.

LIVE EACH FOR ALL, His voice told them. EACH OF YOU
BELONGS TO ALL OF YOU. LOVE EACH OTHER, AND
AWAIT MY RETURN.

And His voice told each of them, severally and together:
THOU ART MY OWN BELOVED CHILD; IN THEE I AM
WELL PLEASED.

Within the tabernacle, Ankhanan commanders embraced officers of the Artan force that had invaded their city, that had
slaughtered their men and the citizens those men had been sworn
to defend. They received Artan embraces in return without
shame; were they not, in truth, Children of the same Father?

Were they not brothers?

6

A SHEET OF flame fills the window—the oil on the outside of the Courthouse still burns merrily—but one of the two feys sitting on clerks' stools has enough of a Shield going that the heat's no worse than the sunshine on a summer afternoon.

The window's tiny, not much bigger than a wallscreen. This drab little clerks' chamber is grey and airless, and I can imagine the drab little grey and airless men and women who have occupied it over the centuries, hunched over the copying table, the only music in their hearts the *scritch-scratch-scritch* of ink nibs on vellum.

Are people like that *born* soulless?

Christ, I hope so.

Otherwise, it'd be even worse.

We all have our chairs gathered around the window, despite the heat. For a long time, we sit and stare out into the flames.

It's what the fey on the other stool is doing that makes for such an interesting view.

Its name translates roughly as *firesight*; within the flames are red-gold shapes of buildings and soldiers and sundry weapons, from longbows to machine pistols; sometimes I can even see the Courthouse from the outside. It's a hell of a lot more efficient for reconnaisance than taking a physical look around; the last guy to stick his head above a windowsill took a bullet through the eye.

Say what you want about the Social Police, but don't ever try to tell me those fuckers can't shoot.

They don't seem too organized out there just yet; the fire shows me a lot of Ankhanan garrison troops holding off to either side of Soapy's perimeter, but they don't look like they're about to start killing each other. There's a couple squads on the wall already, too, and it looks like they've got RPGs on Two Tower as well as on the Knights' Bridge gatehouse.

Deliann's eyes open emptily, and he stares through the ceiling. He has to maintain mindview to keep our little game of Chicken going; he's holding himself in contact with the river. He lies on the writing table along one wall, Kosall across his lap. The same two feys who cleaned up my legs had tried to work on his, but when they put their hands on that abscess, black oil like from

Raithe's hand came bubbling out and burned the living shit out of them; now they're downstairs getting healing of their own.·

"Raithe?" I say.

"It's working," he answers. "The Social Police have made an alliance with the army."

"And?"

"Yes," he murmurs. "He's coming."

I nod. "Everybody here knows which *he* we're talking about, right?"

The grim looks I get from one and all tell me that seven years haven't done any harm to Ma'elKoth's reputation.

I lean back in my chair and fold my fingers over my stomach, and a contented sigh completes my portait of confidence. I meet their eyes one at a time: Raithe, Orbek, t'Passe, Dinnie the Serpent, and they all stare back, waiting, clearly calmed by my assurance. It's a fraud, but they don't know that: I'm showing them exactly who they need to see right now, and they're eating it up. "So," I start slowly, "here we are: in a natural castle closer to perfect than any in the history of warfare."

They favor me with the patiently blank stare people use while they're waiting for the punchline.

I'm pretty sure they won't be disappointed.

"Think about it," I tell them. "The Courthouse facade is our outer bailey. The inner offices and rooms are our killing ground—they have to come through there to get at us. With primals and rockmagi and a couple hours to prepare? Those poor bastards'll never know what hit them. Our keep is the Donjon: the only access to our position is down a single flight of stairs cut into the rock. But we have sally ports *everywhere*: every goddamn public pissoir in Ankhana, and not a few of the private ones. Through the Shaft sump, we can get into the caverns, out any pissoir—or two, or five—and hit the enemy anywhere in the city, with no warning at all. The Folk here have spent days underground already, fighting this Caverns War of yours. If they try to pursue us down through the caverns, we can fuck them till they never walk straight again.

"Between the primals, the rockmagi, and the human adepts, we have the greatest concentration of magickal power on this side of the God's Teeth. We have blooded fighters from the Pit, and we have over a hundred fully armed Monastics. Plus all the weapons and armor from the Donjon armory, food from the commissary, water from the Pit—

"We have everything we need to hold these fuckers off for a long, long time—and to chop them up every time they come for us. We can stand a long, bloody, expensive siege here, and still probably get away through the caverns when things finally go bad. I couldn't have set this up better if I'd planned it for years."

T'Passe nods. "A passive defense is a losing defense. To make this work, we should hit them now, before they're in battle order."

"No," I tell her. "Let's not."

"No?"

"No. We're not gonna fight them."

She looks at me like I'm crazy. "Why *not*?"

"These guys aren't the enemy. They just work for him."

"So? They are his soldiers."

"Yeah. But he has more. A lot more. We could kill a million of them, it wouldn't hurt him. It wouldn't give him a fucking *itch*."

"Then what are we doing here?" she asks. "Why aren't we running away?"

I fall back on good ol' reliable Sun Tzu. "The essence of victory is the unexpected. To win without fighting is the greatest skill."

Cryptic Chinese shit doesn't, apparently, go down too well with t'Passe. "What exactly do you have in mind?" she says sarcastically. "Surrender?"

"Well, sort of. Yeah. We're gonna surrender."

Now *everybody* looks at me like I'm crazy.

I nod. "Yes, we are."

7

JUST MORE THAN an hour before dawn, the flames that had enclosed the Courthouse finally flickered low enough that the 82nd could begin their final assault, in concert with the Ankhanan Thaumaturgic Corps. The brigadier turned to the commander of the city's Southwest Garrison—as the ranking Ankhanan officer present—and offered him the honor of giving the order himself.

Before the commander could speak, brilliant white light burst from every window of the Courthouse, and a voice great enough to make the streets tremble beneath their feet demanded, in the name of the Ascended Ma'elKoth, that they withhold their hand.

A moment later, Patriarch Toa-Sytell stepped through the shattered gap where the Courthouse doors had once been.

"Rejoice!" he proclaimed. "I am saved, and the traitors taken! A new day dawns upon Ankhana! Rejoice!"

In the confusion of spontaneous celebration that followed, the Social Police had some difficulty, initially, determining what had happened. The story, as they eventually pieced it together, was this: The Patriarch had been kidnapped by a rogue Monastic, one Raithe of Ankhana. This Monastic had held the Patriarch hostage, to drive away the Eyes of God, while his confederates arrived from the embassy. Then, they had all descended to the Donjon to free the prisoners.

But the threat to the Patriarch had been their fundamental miscalculation. Even the oppressed former denizens of Alientown had too much patriotism in their hearts to sanction such an act; they had poured up from their hiding places in the caverns below the city to slay the prisoners, capture the Monastics, and seize the two ringleaders, Raithe and Caine.

The brigadier did not find this tale fully satisfying. First, there were not nearly enough corpses. Well over a thousand human beings had been in the Pit; he suspected that the vast majority of them had somehow escaped the slaughter, perhaps through the caverns themselves, though he received sincere assurances from the subhumans that this was impossible.

Second, there was the matter of the sword.

The sword had been seen in the possession of this man Raithe—several of the Eyes of God confirmed it—but it was now nowhere to be found. Scouring the Courthouse turned up nothing, even when the irregulars attached to the 82nd consulted their bewildering array of graven crystals and divining wands, runestaves and silver stilettos, needles that swung on balance points, and pendula of crystal, copper, gold, and iron. Eventually, all agreed that whoever held the sword must have carried it off into the caverns beneath the Courthouse and the city, the rock of which is well known to baffle and defeat such magick. A good deal of their urgency could be relaxed, however; if someone did indeed hold the sword down there, it could not be used, and if this person or persons unknown brought the sword back up to the surface, the seeking items of the irregulars would locate it instantly.

With this the brigadier was forced to be satisfied, for a certain amount of protocol must be observed. As emissaries of the divine Ma'elKoth, the 82nd Force Suppression Unit would be expected to join with the army in receiving the blessing of the Patriarch from the Address Deck of the Temple of Prorithun, high above the Court of the Gods, as soon as the Patriarch had a chance to change his clothes and have some of the bruises of his ordeal treated by his healers.

One possibility disturbed him, however. It was brought to his attention by a particularly subtle thinker among his irregulars that an adept of sufficient skill might be able to have the sword above ground, and use his power to conceal not only himself and it, but also conceal the fact of his concealment. Such an adept might hide in plain sight: the sole method of detection might be the naked eye, as shielded by the silver-meshed helmets of the Social Police.

For example, the irregular pointed out with uncanny accidental accuracy, an adept could be holding that sword right behind the Ebony Throne in the Hall of Justice, and no one might ever know.

8

WITH THE REFINED sensitivity of a mewed falcon, Avery Shanks felt the attention of her captors shift away from her.

She could still see her face in their silver masks, stretched and half lit by the fleshy glow of bonfires outside, but she felt the eyes behind those masks follow the stare of Arturo Kollberg, who had his face pressed against the window, misting it with the slow grey-pulsing pseudopodia of the fog from his breath.

For indeterminate hours she had sat, silently patient, refusing thought. Her watch did not work, and the clouded night beyond the armorglass windows of the limousine gave no hint of time's passage. Her only clock was the occasional slow drizzle of urine down Faith's catheter tube. In the faint reflected firelight, she could see that Faith's relief bag was nearly half full.

She had hung that bag herself, a fresh and empty polyethylene sac, on its hook in front of one of the chair's large, incongruous wheels minutes before she and Faith and the Social Police and the Kollberg-thing and the whole limousine had gone through the mind-twisting silent roar of nonexplosion that had blown away the Studio's freemod dock and replaced it with the stinking gas-lit railyard. The limo's soundproofing had not sufficed to close out the appalling clatter of the enormous mechanized crane that had lifted the limo in a freight sling and lowered it onto a flatbed car of what Avery could only assume—from her limited exposure to historical dramas on the nets—to be a train.

Every few minutes for what seemed like hours, the train had chugged and clanked and jerked itself forward a few meters, only to stop again, perhaps as more cars were loaded behind her.

One of the couches had been ripped out of the limo's passenger lounge so that Faith's wheeled chair could be lashed to eyebolts screwed crudely through the carpeting. Avery knelt beside her, mopping fever-sweat from Faith's brow with a kerchief, giving the girl an occasional sip from a white plastic water bottle—a product of the SynTech subsidiary Petrocal—to moisten her mouth.

Finally the train had rattled out of the huge gas-lit dome of armorglass, through a forest of night-black buildings, under the startling walls of a medieval castle that had blossomed in moonlight through a chance break in the clouds, and finally up a long, long grade to stop here, in this meadow, overlooking a crater with five enormous bonfires spaced evenly about its rim.

Down in the crater, on a platform supported by spidery scaffolding, Ma'elKoth stood with arms upraised to the invisible stars. He was now Ma'elKoth unquestionably: the Ma'elKoth of old, the Ma'elKoth of *For Love of Pallas Ril*. His first act upon leaving the Railhead had been to summon the power of his Ascended Self, as he put it: his bruises shrank, and faded, and the stitched wounds across his brow and from the corners of his mouth consumed themselves and vanished. A beard of burnished bronze sprouted curling from his cheeks and jaw, and his eyes of mud brown became an astonishing emerald green. Now, in the crater, the air around him was the source of the new light: a globe half as large as the crater itself glowed with power, shimmering like a ghost-image of the moon in a rushing stream.

Deliberately, matter-of-factly, without any furtiveness of motion that might attract a suspicious silver-masked eye, Avery opened her shoulder bag and pulled out her bottle of Teravil caplets. She opened the bottle and shook three of them out into her palm.

But even that small motion was too much. "What is that?" a half-muffled voice hummed, sounding strange indeed without electronic digitization from the mask speaker—almost human.

The former Avery Shanks might have jerked guiltily; the former Avery Shanks might have ventured a bold lie. This Avery Shanks had been too far reduced. Instead, she extended them toward one of the Social Police officers at random, for she could not know which one had spoken, and she was not certain that it mattered. "Teravil," she said numbly. "My sedatives. I need to sleep."

"Very well."

She could feel the patient stare of the eyes behind the mask as she put the pills in her mouth, and she opened her hands to show them empty. She bit down, wincing slightly at their alkaline bitterness. She chewed them well, and held the gummy saliva-pudding they became under her tongue while she pretended to swallow.

She picked up the white plastic water bottle and pretended to sip from it, as though to wash down the pills, while she instead spat the wad of half-dissolved sedative back down the straw into the water inside. Then she did drink from it, to rinse her mouth; the fraction of a pill she would ingest from this wouldn't have the slightest effect on her high-tolerance system.

But combined with the hypnotics that dripped from the IV bag, a few mouthfuls of this poisoned water should more than suffice to kill Faith.

Sometime in this endless night, Avery had realized that she didn't need to kill herself. Once Faith was dead, the Social Police would take care of that small detail. Slowly, tenderly, she again moistened Faith's mouth with water from the bottle.

Outside, Ma'elKoth gestured, and the glowing sphere within the crater bulged and stretched forth an amorphous limb. When that haloed limb touched a vehicle on a flatbed railcar behind the limo, its running lights flared to life, and the vibration of its turbines hummed in her bones. Ma'elKoth's limb of light swept along the train, touching vehicle after vehicle, and one by one the bulky shapes of Social Police assault cars roared to life and lifted into a sky now clearing of clouds, high above the mountains, becoming blazing stars themselves as they climbed out of the horizon's shadow and met the first scarlet rays of the rising sun.

9

"HE COMES."

Raithe's voice is flat, and as chill as the chunk of blue ice that's pretending to be the sky. The season's changed overnight, and it's colder than a gravedigger's ass out here.

For a second or two I don't take his meaning; I'm thinking, *What is this, some kind of freaky sex joke?* because the *he* I think he's talking about is Toa-Sytell, who's standing up on the Address Deck of the Temple of Prorithun in his nice fresh clean Patriarchal robes with that big pointy hat, flanked by a couple Thaumaturgic Corps officers and a brigadier in the Social Police, giving his speech to the army, describing his rescue from the Enemy of God—that's me—and the evil conspirators of the Monasteries—that's Raithe, Damon, and the rest of the friars— by the astonishing heroism of the subhumans gathered below.

The blackened stonework of the Fountain of Prorithun against my back gives off some residual warmth from the overnight fires—like the bricks we used to heat on the woodstoves back at the abbey school, and put on our bedcovers to keep our feet warm in the wintertime—and the stone under my rapidly numbing ass is warmer than the air above. The closest we get to clouds today is the coils of smoke that still trail upward here and there across the city.

In the unforgiving dawn, Ankhana is a wasteland of blackened stone, charred giant's jackstraws of tree trunks and cornstalks and ashes and all kinds of shit everywhere. When the soldiers marched us here from the Courthouse—well, marched them, carried me—a lot of what people stepped on crackled like bone. Even from here, I can see six or seven bodies, curled into that burn-victim ball: the fetal contortion created by tendons shortening as they cook. Just across the street, beyond the Sen-Dannalin Wall around the Colhari Palace, the Temple of the Katherisi—once one of the jewels of Ankhanan architecture, its graceful spires topped with beaten gold, its high-vaulted walls supported by flying buttresses—is now a pile of smudge-blackened rock that half chokes Gods' Way.

It's hard on my eyes: they keep trying to see the city the way it was the first time I walked these streets, twenty-some years ago. I can only imagine what it must be doing to Raithe, who's lived here his whole life.

But if it bothers him, that desert-prophet face of his gives no sign. He sits impassively at my shoulder, staring into the sky, his legs folded in *seiza* beneath him, while Toa-Sytell rocks on through his speech.

Toa-Sytell gives an impressive performance; I guess being the Patriarch sharpens your public-speaking skills. He even manages to get a little weepy, nicely choked up, when he recounts all the abuse that the elves and dwarfs and the rest have taken at the hands of the Empire, the terrible oppression inflicted upon them, and how great and true their patriotism and love of the Empire must be, to have overcome their perfectly natural resentment and risked their lives to save the Patriarch yadda yadda yadda horseshit.

Down here in the Court of the Gods, I can't stop myself shivering, and the shackles on my wrists are burning me with cold. The friars around us look stoic, if not actually comfortable, huddled sullenly on the plaza flagstones—maybe they're in better practice with the Control Disciplines than I am. The Ankhanan regulars who guard us shift and stamp their feet, restlessly trying to keep their blood moving. The dawn is so bright that the glare off weapons and armor slices my eyes—but it brings only light today, not heat.

Raithe stares to the east, his bleached gaze seeking blindly somewhere near the rising sun. "So fast . . ." he murmurs. "Faster than the wind . . . faster than a falcon . . . faster than the noise of his passing. He comes with swiftness beyond imagining."

Now I finally understand who he's talking about. "You can feel it?"

He rattles his shackles, which shakes loose a few droplets of the black oil that continues to leak through the skin of his left hand; his sleeve is black with it up above the elbow, and I can see a splotch soaking through at the shoulder.

I wince. "Doesn't that hurt?"

"Yes," he says expressionlessly. "It does."

Fast. Faster than a falcon, he says. A fact floats up from the cesspit buried in the part of my brain where I leave useless trivia.

A peregrine falcon can dive at something over three hundred kilometers per hour.

Oh, crap.

If Tan'elKoth's got a way to make cars work in Overworld physics, this is gonna get ugly. I don't even want to think about the other shit he might be able to make work. "How long do we have?"

Raithe shakes his head distantly. "I cannot say. They move with speed that baffles my judgment. They are so far—days away—yet they come so quickly that I cannot believe they are not already here."

A second later, I remember that I'm supposed to be the confident one. "We'll deal," I tell him. "Somehow, we'll deal."

"Or we'll die."

"Yeah. Probably both."

Toa-Sytell goes on, "And because these Folk—the folk we call *sub*human—could so give of themselves as to accomplish what even the great warriors sent to us by Ma'elKoth from beyond the world—" A gesture toward the soapy brigadier at his side. "—could not: to save not only me, but *through* me the Imperial Church itself, I declare here, on this Assumption Day morning, the word *subhuman* to be banished from Ankhanan tongues. There shall be no more elves, but primals; no more dwarfs, but stonebenders; no sprites or goblins, but treetoppers and ogrilloi. Henceforward, these heroes of the Empire shall be known by the name they call themselves: the Folk. Hear me, Ankhana! Today, the Folk become our brothers, and we theirs: citizens all, Ankhanans all, equal before the law and in the eyes of God Himself."

That part was my idea: a little nod toward Deliann, a seed for the future. If any of us have a future.

But—

"It's Assumption Day?" I mutter at Raithe out of the side of my mouth. "Today?"

He shakes his head slowly. "I do not know. I have been further removed from the normal calendar than even a prisoner in the Shaft. But, if it isn't—"

He turns his leather-colored face toward me, and his ice-pale eyes see me all the way down to the crud between my toes.

"If it isn't Assumption Day," he says, "it ought to be."

Yeah.

Seven years ago today—

Seven years ago right now, I was asleep at the bottom of the la-
trine in the old gladiator pens at Victory Stadium. I remember
opening my eyes in the gloom, down there in the fecal dust and
petrified turds; I remember the toilet-shaped hole of daylight
overhead. I remember monologuing, as I went up, that I seem to
spend most of my life climbing out of other people's shit.

Not today.

Today, it's *my* shit. That's progress, I guess.

I guess.

Christ, has it really been seven years? So much has changed,
and so little; I can't decide if it feels like yesterday or ten life-
times ago.

Toa-Sytell's winding up his speech: heading for the punchline
of our little prank.

"And we have been tried, as our city has been tried, in the crucible of faith, tested by the Enemy of God, and by traitors from
within—and we have not been found wanting."

A chuckle sneaks past my lips before I know it's coming. Raithe
gives me a look of wintry astonishment, and I shrug at him.

"Toa-Sytell wanted an Assumption Day that Ankhana would
never forget." My nod takes in the blackened ruins of the city.
"And this is how he thanks us."

Raithe's expression stays as cold and disbelieving as before.
Some people have no sense of humor.

"And now, in gratitude to the divine Ma'elKoth for our deliverance," Toa-Sytell proclaims, "let us now join together in one
voice, one Folk, Ankhanans all, in the Imperial anthem."

Here's the payoff: he reaches up, and takes off his hat.

What puts the punch in our punchline is that he's the Patriarch; as soon as his hat comes off, every single Ankhanan soldier
is obliged to uncover his head in respect. They unstrap their
helms and tuck them under their left arms, and everybody takes
a deep breath while they wait for Toa-Sytell to begin the hymn.

Toa-Sytell, though, holds his tongue—he's staring at the
Social Police brigadier next to him. Expectantly. The brigadier,
after all, is an "emissary of the divine Ma'elKoth."

Slowly, with obvious reluctance, the brigadier takes off his
silver-wire-inlaid helmet.

A brigadier of the Social Police—

Exposing his face—

Christ, I can't look. I can't *not* look—

He's got kind of a moon face, large protuberant eyes, thinning mouse-colored hair, and I get a sick feeling from looking at him, as he blinks and squints and tries to shade his eyes against the dawn glare, which must be blinding, absent the smoked armor-glass face shield.

He's so ordinary. It's shameful.

I can't look away.

A humiliated fascination has me hooked through the jaw. It's like seeing your father naked for the first time—*Jeez, he's flabby, and he's got a little knobby dick, and his chest sags, and what are these tufts of hair in embarrassing places?*—and he's not really much like a father at all anymore. There is something so *peeled* about the brigadier: now that he's lost the power of his soapy anonymity, he's been shucked like a fucking oyster.

It's like the Patriarch said *Shazam!* and Captain Marvel vanished, leaving a middle-aged bookkeeper in his place.

The whole battalion follows suit—and now, as their helmets come off and they stand before us all with naked faces, they're not Social Police anymore. They're just a bunch of guys in armor with guns.

So the Patriarch starts in on the opening bars of "King of Kings," and the army joins in, and up on the Address Deck, the brigadier decides to lie on the floor and have a little nap. Below, all the soapies yawn, set down their rifles, curl up on the ground, and fall right to sleep.

They do this because the adepts of the Thaumaturgic Corps, good as they are, can't read Toa-Sytell's Shell. They can't read his Shell because a couple of primal mages—who have the advantage of a few hundred years' experience apiece—built a Fantasy that the Patriarch's Shell was 100 percent A-OK normal. They had to do this, because it's not.

This Fantasy is powered by a little chip of griffinstone, in a technique once used by Kierendal to get the whole Kingdom of Cant into Victory Stadium. This means not only that their Fantasy pulls no perceptible Flow, but that it'll keep right on going even if the adepts cover the Patriarch with a silver net or examine him using griffinstones of their own in a magick-negative room—both of which we guessed they might try, since Thaumaturgic Corps adepts are nasty and suspicious by nature—

because the griffinstone in question is secreted on the Patriarch's person.

We had some discussion on where to put the stone. My own suggestion was vetoed on the grounds that the Patriarch might have an unexpected bowel movement and give away our plan.

So he swallowed it.

He swallowed it because that chip of griffinstone is also powering another effect, and the action of that effect, roughly speaking, is to make Toa-Sytell willing to do just about anything—even swallow a griffinstone, even accept the Folk as full citizens of Ankhana, even get a whole rifle battalion of Social Police to take off their magick-resistant helmets so that a hundred-odd primals could hit them all with a shot of mental fairy dust—to please his new best friend.

While the whole Ankhanan army looks dumbly at the snoozing Social Police, Toa-Sytell beams a smile down toward us and gives Raithe a little wave.

I nudge him with an elbow. "Congratulations, kid. You just took over the Empire."

"I have taken over nothing," Raithe says. "We have accomplished nothing."

His voice is bleak and fatal, so empty that the orders bawled by the Patriarch—*bind these Aktiri traitors; disarm them; bind them hand and foot*—fade into a background wash of white noise; while the astonished Ankhanan soldiers gradually bestir themselves to comply, I'm lost in the vast echoic hollow of Raithe's stare.

"I wouldn't call this nothing, kid. We took the city . . ." But the forced whistling-in-the-dark tone of my own voice muzzles me, and the words trickle away.

"Did you think He wouldn't know?" Raithe asks. "Did you think we could surprise Him?"

"I have before."

"No," Raithe says, "you haven't."

Dark thunder rumbles in the east and becomes a buzzing whine that threatens a roar.

"He is no longer the man you defeated," Raithe says, his voice mirroring the rising howl that curdles my stomach, because I know the sound, a sound I never dreamed could shimmer Ankhanan air.

Turbocells.

"He is no longer a man at all."

He lifts his eyes to the east, and I follow his gaze, and the howl of turbocells becomes a shattering roar.

The sun weeps lethal titanium tears.

ALL TRUE STORIES end in death.

This is the end of the tale of the crooked knight.

TWENTY-FOUR

DELIANN SAT UPON the Ebony Throne, the blade of Kosall rough-crusted and cold across his knees, and the Hall of Justice throbbed with pain.

Pain shimmered starkly in the brilliant sunbeams that struck like spears through the clerestory; pain sizzled in the black oil that seeped from the abcess on his thigh and burned the flesh of his leg to the smoking bone. The granite countenance of the giant carven Ma'elKoth had gone blank with agony, and the sand on the arena floor below the dais stung as though it had been rubbed into an open wound. The air itself snarled and snapped and bit at his flesh, and his every breath inhaled white flame.

The hall was empty, ring upon ring of vacant gaping benches climbing the sides of the bowl; Deliann was alone with the pain. But the pain was not alone with Deliann. With the pain, threading among and through its every splinter, came terror and panic, despair and the bleak surrender that is the bottomless abyss of death.

Some small portion of this pain and terror and despair and

death was Deliann's; the rest came from outside. It rode the river's pulse into his heart from the brilliant sunlit morning, in the crisp autumn air, where assault cars swooped and spun and spat fire.

Deliann had less than nine minutes to live.

2

THOSE SUN-TEARS BLOSSOM in four petal-perfect wingovers, and laser-straight lines of tracers from their gatling cannon stitch geometric gouts of exploding stone into the streets below. They claw pyrotechnically along Gods' Way toward us, and the air hums with shrapnel, and I—

I can only sit and watch.

The assault cars sweep overhead, spraying missiles and HEAP rounds. The western curve of the Sen-Dannalin Wall shrugs like it's tired after standing five hundred years; it decides to sit down in a landslide of masonry and limestone dust. The cannon rounds hit the street like grenades with splintered flagstones for shrapnel. They shred the army, the primals, the soapies indiscriminately: shrapnel has no friends.

I still don't move.

I am paralyzed by how badly I have miscalculated.

Up on the Address Deck, Toa-Sytell stretches his hands toward the assault cars. He could be ecstatic at the power of his returning god, or begging for mercy, or panicked and crapping his robe. Nobody will ever know, because a missile takes him right through the chest—an eyeblink of astonishment at the gape of his guts to the morning sky—before it detonates against the wall at his back. The Patriarch, the soapy brigadier, the Household Knights, and most of the wall of the Temple of Prorithun vanish in a fireball that spits blood and bone fragments and chunks of stone into the sky.

And that's it, right there: that's what Raithe was talking about. Tan'elKoth wouldn't do this. He loves this city more than the world.

He would never do this.

Pieces of the Patriarch and the Temple and the rest rain over us in clatters and liquid plops, and I can't really hear anything anymore except a general roaring in my ears and I know the assault cars are banking around for another pass, and now some riot vans swing into view over Six Tower and settle toward the middle of the far end of Gods' Way, seeking solid earth beneath them to absorb the recoil of the heavy artillery that sprouts from their turrets.

The riot vans open up with their twin forward-mount fifties, taking chunks out of the stonework along the whole street, enfilading the fuck out of us—the heavy slugs popping through plate mail sound like God's shaking a tin can full of rocks—and somehow that finally gets my attention. I twist around so my shackled hands can grab the lip of the Fountain of Prorithun behind me, and I drag myself over into the bowl, leaving skin behind on the smog-corroded limestone. I fall into the shallow fountain water that's now turbid with dirt and blood, and—

Oh—

Oh, my good and gracious motherfucking *god*.

I get it now.

He can make the cars work, he can fucking well make *anything* work—

The Courthouse—maybe Deliann—maybe if I can—

Christ, my legs, I'll never make it—

I could be wrong. I have to be wrong.

Jesus—Tyshalle—anybody who's listening: Please, please, please let me be wrong.

3

FROM DEEP WITHIN the oceanic boil of pain and fear, using the whole of the river for his senses, Deliann watched the slaughter. It became for him an ebb and flow and tangle of conflicting energies, an abstract action-painting come to life. The sky erupted incarnadine and amethyst that swept against the sunflower, azure, and viridian of the lives in the city below. The colors met and mixed, broke apart and blended together again in a *rith* dream of astonishing beauty: a living Mandelbrot set spiraling into itself and out again: a spray of wildflowers springing fresh and lovely from a shitpile of ugly, desperate brutality.

For all its terror and savagery, for all its howled agony and whimpered despair, the flesh that bruised and bled was only shadow: translucent, incorporeal, more rhythm than reality, a semivisible expression of energy at play. That energy followed laws of its own making, in a system as ordered as a galaxy and as random as a throw of dice, an ever-shifting balance of the elegant with the raw.

For the first time, he understood Hari. He understood his passion for violence. He could see how Hari could love it so.

It was beautiful.

But it's his eyes that see that beauty, Deliann thought. *Not mine.*

Because with the sense of the river, Deliann felt each slash and smack of bullet and shrapnel into flesh; he saw through the eyes of men and women who clutched futilely at the spurt of blood from their own wounds and the wounds of their friends, who tried to stuff spilled guts back into the gape of ripped-open bellies, who tried to kiss life back into staring dust-coated eyes; he felt their terror, and their despair, and he decided that he was going to have to do something about this.

It was this decision that killed him.

He had six minutes to live.

4

I PULL MYSELF up to the lip of the fountain, and the limestone shivers with impacts of fragments and slugs and the air is alive with zips and zings and shrieks of jagged shrapnel and the hand-clap hypersonic pops of 50-caliber slugs: the open space above the fountain's lip is itself a predator and it's got my scent. I have looked death in the eye plenty of times, but this is different: it's random, unconscious. Unintentional.

Impersonal.

This is *not* my kind of fight.

Poking my head up to get a peek over the rim is the hardest goddamn thing I've ever done in my life.

Pretty much everybody who can still move has cleared the plaza by now; a few scarlet-smeared shapes of anonymous flesh drag themselves inch by shivering inch toward any shadow that might promise cover. At the far end of Gods' Way the main cannon of the riot vans *ca-rump* whistling shells that blast house-sized chunks out of the row of temples and government buildings lining the Way; the East Tower of the Colhari Palace overlooks the massacre with a lopsided face of gaping ragged empty eyes and smoke-drooling idiot's mouth before one more shell blasts out the cheek and the whole damn thing topples sideways and collapses in a mushroom cloud of masonry dust to the courtyard nine stories below.

The Folk are starting to fight back now, with the kind of heroism that would be inspiring if it wasn't so pathetic: firebolts splash harmlessly off the radically sloped ceramic armor of the riot vans, and some ogrilloi have figured out how to shoot the soapies' assault rifles. They'd do more damage with harsh language and a stern look.

One lone treetopper flutters up into the path of an assault car, and she and her birdlance get sucked into one of the turbocells. What's left of her sprays out the back in a crimson mist, but that birdlance was steel. The turbocell chews itself into a metal-screaming burst of junk, and the assault car slews sideways and dips and hits the street and bounces, skipping up over my head in a thundering meteor-trail of flame that skips one more time before it slams into the Financial Block and explodes, which takes out the whole building, and the damn thing just keeps on exploding as its munitions pop off like a full-scale fireworks display: rockets and starshells and mortar bombs and showers of flame.

And fucking Raithe is still sitting where I left him: in *seiza* right in front of the fountain, calmly picking the locks on his shackles while he stares at the carnage around us with a dreamy smile on his face. The next assault car swoops toward us and strafes a line of cannonfire that's gonna go right up his nose, so I reach over and grab the back of his collar and haul his ass into the fountain next to me.

He still has that dreamy smile after I dunk us both in the water and three or four 25-millimeter rounds blow chunks out of the fountain's bowl but somehow manage to miss our tender flesh. He lies on his back, the dirty water swirling bloody mud clouds around him as it drains out from the fractured bowl. He says something—the roar of turbines and artillery fire blows it away, but I can read his lips.

You saved my life.

I give him a shake that bounces his skull off the limestone. *"Where's Ma'elKoth?"* I shout against the roar-walled air. "Can you still feel him? Is he still coming—or did he *stop*?"

"You said you'd kill me if you ever got the chance," he shouts back, *"but you saved me, instead!"*

"I *changed* my fucking *mind*, all *right*? Don't make me regret it. *Where is he?*"

His eyes glaze, fixing on some quiet distance where the blood and smoke and howl of combat is not even a dream. "Stopped," he says, voice dropping. "He's stopped. Half a day's walk, almost."

Ah, god.

I let go of his shoulders and bury my head in my hands.

I never dreamed I could be so utterly outfought.

A day's walk, to a friar on a decent road, is about thirty miles. I know why he has stopped, fifteen miles outside the city.

I know what he's waiting for.

Ah, god.

I prayed I was wrong, and this is Your answer.

5

DELIANN SIGHED.

He lifted Kosall by the quillons, and discovered that he was afraid. He remembered too well the excruciating rip of his mind stretching beyond its tolerance, when he had only flashed upon the goddess; he feared that to touch her directly, mind to mind, would burn his brain in an instant.

Rather than put his hand upon the hilt and confront her, he sought within himself the chain of energy he had created, to bind the gods to the river and the river to the gods. When he found it, he visualized it as a channel, rather than a chain; a long narrow sluice through which flowed the river's pain. Along that channel he sent forth a tendril of consciousness—gingerly, almost tenderly, attempting only to brush her uttermost periphery.

In a vast darkness of doubt and horror, he found her: clothed in sunlight, weeping tears of blood.

She lifted her head and regarded him. He could not guess what it was she might see; he had no sense of a body, or a face. To himself, he seemed only a disembodied spark of awareness.

I know you. She extended a hand, pierced through the palm, as though offering a kiss of the wound's bloodless lips. Her other hand she placed upon her breast, above her heart. *Have you come to hurt me again?*

I hope not, he replied.

My daughter, she said tragically, grey winter closing down upon her robe of light. *My daughter is dying.*

He thought of Demeter and Persephone, and could not know if that thought was his, or if it had come from her. *Many others live. You must save those who can still be saved.*

Once I styled myself a savior, she replied. *Now I am only the image of a dead woman. Saving is beyond me.*

I will not argue. You must act.

How can I? With no body—with no will—

I have a body. Take me as you would have taken Raithe. What you lack, I will provide.

Fresh tears of blood coiled down her cheeks. *You do not know what you are offering—*

I do not offer. I demand: Take me. Save these people.

He opened his mind to the wounded goddess.

She drifted toward him helplessly.

It will kill you, she wept.

He replied, *I know.*

He drew her to him, and then she was around him, and she was within him, and she was him. He made her pain his, and he made his intention hers. She reached through him to the river, and the Song of Chambaraya swelled within his heart from a single thin chime of welcome to a titanic symphony of power.

Five minutes.

6

THE GOD FELT the questing tendrils of a mind colored in the shades of the goddess touch briefly upon its inmost nature—

And just as suddenly fade.

The creature that had been Kollberg felt the ghost-echo of the goddess' pain vanish from its collective consciousness; an instant later, Faith's silent weeping stilled, and it knew it had been betrayed.

The girl was unconscious, and the link was broken.

A sunburst of rage flashed through him, its glare wiping away the grassy meadow on the bank of the Great Chambaygen, wiping away Ma'elKoth who paced on the grassy verge in his stylish suit, wiping away the limousine, the Social Police, Avery

Shanks—wiping away, for one instant, even the power of the god he was.

For that instant, he was again Arturo Kollberg, once an Administrator, once again betrayed.

By a Michaelson.

With a snarl, he lunged across the passenger lounge and grabbed the collar of Faith's white cotton shift. His arthritic fingers twisted into a fist—and his arm was seized by the impersonal gauntlet of a Social Police officer. He tried to yank himself free, but he might as well have tried to shift a mountain with his wasted arm.

Futility flashed in where his rage had been. He hung, helpless—but that helplessness, so long familiar, brought him back to himself. He was once again the god, and he was happy.

The god understood that the girl had been poisoned; it could feel her slow slide down to death through Ma'elKoth's magickal perception. The god also knew, now, that the sword was in the Hall of Justice in the Ankhanan Courthouse.

In the same instant that knowledge had been acquired, an impulse had formed itself somewhere in the unimaginable vastness of ten billion subconsciously linked minds. It may have come from Ma'elKoth, or from Kollberg, or from Marc Vilo, or from any of the other mutually anonymous members of the Board of Governors; it may have come from a SynTech chemical engineer, or an undercover operative of the Social Police at an illegally clandestine Labor gathering, from a housewife in Belgrade or a janitor in New Delhi. Perhaps it originated in all of them together; it was another way of sharing guilt. One ten-billionth of the responsibility for this was a light enough burden for even the most sensitive to bear.

The bodies that had once housed Arturo Kollberg and Ma'elKoth shared a single identical smile.

Five minutes from now, the girl would be irrelevant.

Twenty thousand meters above Ankhana, a Bell & Howell AAV-24 Deva completed a long dive-curve, released a MEFNW blast-negative HEW, then generated maximum thrust as it sped away toward the east.

7

MY MOUTH IS numb; my lips barely work. I shout in Raithe's ear to be heard above the shatter of cannonfire. "Can you talk to him?"

"What?"

I dig one hand hard into his shoulder. "Can you *talk* to Ma'elKoth? You're aware of him—is he aware of *you*? Can you *communicate*?"

His eyes are still lost in the heavens. "One vehicle—one Bell & Howell AAV-24 Deva, crew of four, effective ceiling twenty-five thousand meters, top speed Mach two-point-one, armament—"

"Stay with me, goddammit!" I give him another shake. "You have to talk to Ma'elKoth—you have to *tell* him—"

"It dives, falling like a falcon—"

All I can think about for one endless second is how fucking cold the water is as it trickles away around us; I'm freezing in here, my hands are numb and my whole body shakes, and my voice fades in and out behind a roaring in my ears that's even louder than the battle around us. Because I knew that car would be up there. One, all alone.

One is all it takes.

I want to look up, absurdly, to hunt the sky for the pinprick of titanium that I know will be invisible. I want to look, but I can't.

I'm afraid.

My mind smokes with cinematically vivid recollection of file footage from Indonesia. Inside my head, that titanium teardrop lays a tiny silver egg before it speeds away toward the rising sun—

"Tell him we *surrender*!" I snarl. "Goddammit, Raithe, you have to tell him we surrender! *Tell him I give up!* I'll give him the sword—whatever he wants—just tell him *don't do it*!"

The funny thing is, I'm the one who gave him the idea.

"Shit, they'd nuke the city."

"One city is a small price to pay for an entire world."

"Yeah? What if it's your *city?"*

"I am willing to take that risk."

He's trumped us. Called my bluff.

It'll kill every single one of the former inmates of the Pit who carry Shanna's countervirus. It'll kill every single one of us.

Raithe.

Deliann.

T'Passe.

Orbek.

Dinnie, Fletcher, Arken, Gropaz—

Damon. Majesty. The Faces. The Serpents. The Subjects of Cant.

Me.

One single flash of invisible light will burn our bones, and Ma'elKoth walks in here whenever he feels like it and picks up the sword, and game fucking over. I thought I was hard-core. I thought I was ruthless.

Shit.

I didn't even know what ruthless *looks* like.

"Does he hear you? Raithe, goddammit, does he *hear* you?"

Raithe's gaze returns from heaven and meets mine. "No," he says. "No, He doesn't. I can no longer feel Him. Any of them."

An ice dagger slips in between my ribs. I make myself ask, "Faith—?"

He gives his head a tiny shake. "Unconscious, at the very least. Possibly dead."

My head lowers: my neck bending under the brutal weight of the futility of existence.

Before the astonishing pain can take full hold of me, a new thunder blossoms in the sky. I wrench myself over beside Raithe and look up. Above us a coruscant aster of flame spreads its tendrils for an instant, then vanishes into a jellyfish spray of black smoke and falling bits of metal. Even as I watch, another assault car detonates the same way, and another.

Raithe speaks my guess, but in his voice is certain knowledge. "Deliann has joined the battle."

"You can feel him?" I seize Raithe's shoulders and bounce his head off the stone. "You have to talk to him! You have to tell him to get the fuck out of here—"

A grin blossoms on his face, the only honestly happy smile I've ever seen there. "No."

"Raithe, you have to *tell* him! The caverns—he can still make it to the caverns! He can live—he can defend the sword! You have to tell him to *defend the sword*!"

"No, I don't," he says serenely, lying back as though the puddled water is a comfortable bed. "I don't have to do anything."

My vision hazes red and the next thing I know I have my
hands on his collar, twisting it into a strangle with tension
against the chains that connect my shackles. But he's a trained
Esoteric, and he breaks my hold with a leverage move of his left
hand against my right wrist—and the oil from his skin burns me
like acid. My hand springs open, and he shoves me away.

"I'm free," he says. "Free."

Christ, he's raving. "You're free to fucking *die*," I tell him.
"You don't know what's coming—"

"I don't care what's coming."

That assault car dives above my head and inside my skull simultaneously; I don't have time to waste on Raithe right now.

Guess I'm gonna have to do this the hard way.

I leave him lying on the wet stone aiming his idiot's grin at the
sky, and drag myself toward the western edge of the fountain's
bowl, hoping the fountain's superstructure will give me at least a
shadow of cover.

It takes me a long time to get into mindview.

I know I'm there when I don't care anymore about getting
shot or shredded or flash-roasted to death; I only care about getting to the Courthouse. Getting to Deliann. To Kris. Slowly, unsteadily, I climb out of the bowl and stand.

Bullets and shrapnel fan me with turbulence-swirled breeze.

I lean forward, and one of my legs swings ahead to stop me
from falling. I keep leaning, and my legs keep swinging, and I
don't fall yet.

I'm on my way.

8

HEW STANDS FOR High Energy Weapon, a centuries-old desig-
nation for offensive devices that rely primarily upon nuclear fis-
sion, nuclear fusion, or some combination of the two for their
destructive effect.

Blast-negative is a somewhat misleading appellation created
by the weapon's design team, reflecting their successful tamping
of energetic photon—gamma and hot X-ray—emissions, thus
reducing the blast and thermal effects of the individual fireballs
to roughly .1 kiloton apiece: a mere hundred times as powerful
as a large chemical high-explosive bomb.

MEFNW stands for Multiple Enhanced-Fast-Neutron Warheads. Fast neutron radiation decreases by a factor of ten for every five hundred meters from the detonation point, due to atmospheric absorption; the weapon's design team countered this effect by using a large number of very small individual warheads that automatically deploy during system activation, spreading a nuclear umbrella over the entire target area that delivers an average of ten thousand rads of prompt radiation to all targets within the deployment radius. Fast neutrons are extremely penetrating; even heavy shielding may only reduce this exposure by two to five thousand rads. A dose of eight thousand rads is instantly incapacitating and fatal; five thousand induces incapacitation within five minutes of exposure, and death within two days.

Enhanced-Fast-Neutron weapons also produce strong secondary radiation, as neutrons striking atomic nuclei in the ground and surviving structures create a broad array of extremely unstable isotopes. Neutron-induced secondary radiation decays by 90 percent within seven hours, but it can still kill; total exposure rises with time. The passage of forty-eight hours reduces radiation to a nonhazardous level, but by this time, any living material that might have survived the initial prompt radiation has suffered mortal damage from the secondary radiation.

This is, in fact, the use for which this particular weapon was designed: to sterilize localized HRVP outbreaks. Part of the rationale for the blast-negative feature of this weapon is that it, unlike conventional thermonuclear weapons, does not generate powerful Mach waves that might scatter viral proteins beyond the lethal radiation zone.

As it fell, the HEW deployed computer-controlled warpable airfoils to control its path and counteract the vagaries of high-altitude winds, and began to shed bomblets with airfoil vanes of their own. Each bomblet carried its own targeting system, comparing the radar signature of the central device against the infrared image of the city below. Cities are always hotter than the surrounding countryside, and this one in particular blazed like a beacon.

Radar-altimeters ticked off the fall of the warheads. Drag created by the airfoils stabilized their terminal velocity at 97.3 meters per second after approximately nine seconds, continually adjusting for increasing air pressure as they fell.

Optimal detonation altitude is two kilometers.
One hundred seventy-six seconds to go.

9

RAITHE LAY ON his back in the fountain's bowl, savoring the chill
of the wet rough limestone against his back. The sky above him
was full of lead and steel, smoke and flames, the howls of
Boeing VT-17 Air Superiors and the shrieks of the dying. The intimacy of his connection to the waiting god lent him a curiously
doubled perspective: his Overworld eyes saw armored giants
hurling fireballs at the city while his Earthly knowledge showed
him RV-101 Jackson MAATTs—Mobile Armored Artillery
and Troop Transports—dug into the street with their recoil-
absorbing mounting screws, firing their 122-millimeter main
guns; the Air Superiors that strafed the city looked to him like
flaming chariots of minor sun gods, though he could at will
quote the specifications of their powerplants, armament, speed,
and range. At need, he felt sure he could summon the name of
each individual crewman. But it was not this that brought the
bliss to his thin lips.

He smiled because he could die here.

He had realized it even as he knelt at Caine's side and watched
the first strangely beautiful arc of swooping assault cars. Caine
had scrambled for cover, and Raithe had not moved. He didn't
have to. He had answered all his destinies.

He was free.

For more than ten years he had sought only to discover what
his destiny required. He had never even asked himself what he
wanted. *I may not master my destiny, but I don't have to let my
destiny master me.*

Raithe smiled up into the infinite sky.

And it took Caine to teach me that.

He rolled over and crawled to the lip of the fountain's bowl to
peer out. Through the smoke and flame and the sizzling death
songs of slugs and shrapnel that ripped the air of the plaza, Caine
staggered like a zombie that decomposed with every step,
heading for the far curve of the Sen-Dannalin Wall. He'd never
make it.

Raithe said, "All right, then."

He gathered himself, and sprang.

Machine-gun fire tracked him as he sprinted across the plaza, the air solid with howling bullets that he knew, abstractly, were 12.5-millimeter armor-piercing rounds tipped with depleted uranium traveling at an average of 423 meters per second. He fully appreciated the reality of these slugs only after one punched through his thigh—a crisp impact like being hit by a rattan practice sword, leaving two thumbnail-sized holes on opposite sides of his leg but missing the bone and not even breaking his stride. Another took him low in the back as he tried to jink and skidded on a puddle of blood; an instant later his foot tangled in loops of intestine that spilled from half a corpse. He fell, and a third round drilled a neat hole in his shoulder blade before exiting an inch below his collarbone.

He rolled with the impact, his shoulder spreading numb fire through his chest—the bone shot would be excruciating, once feeling returned—and came to his feet as a shell whistled overhead and blasted a huge chunk from the Sen-Dannalin Wall just as Caine reached it. Raithe lunged, throwing himself through the air, and his wounded shoulder slammed into the small of Caine's back, the impact carrying them both out from under a hail of head-sized masonry.

They lay on the ground together for a few seconds, panting air back into their lungs, as more shells boomed and blasted all around.

Raithe struggled to his hands and knees. "Come on," he said, beckoning. Slowly, still gasping, Caine pulled himself onto Raithe's back, looping his shackled arms around Raithe's shoulders. When he was finally able to speak, he said breathlessly, "What the fuck?"

Raithe allowed himself a smile as warm as the blood that ran down his legs. "I changed my mind."

10

HE CARRIES ME through the twisting backstreets and alleys with artillery blowing everything to shit all around us. Blood pumps out of him at a pretty good rate, but none of it's spurting— probably missed the arteries. He might live through this.

That is, if he doesn't do anything stupid, like haul a crippled old man around on his fucking back.

He's wheezing already, staggering drunkenly. No chance we'll get to the Courthouse. No chance we'll get to a pissoir and make it into the caverns—the pissoirs around the fountain are shattered and choked with rubble, and the next nearest is at the foot of Knights' Bridge, right by the Courthouse. I shout in his ear, "We're not gonna make it! Tell Deliann to get his ass down into the Pit!"

He stumbles on, grimly desperate. "I . . . can't communicate . . . and run . . . at the same time. Without Faith . . . there is only the link . . . that Deliann himself created . . ."

Up ahead I see a storefront that looks like it took a direct hit: a jagged gape invites us into darkness. "In there! Go on: maybe they have a cellar!" He shakes his head and tries to keep going, but I wrap my arms around his neck in a modified sleeper. "Do it, or I'll choke you out and we'll both die in the street."

He sags, surrendering, and carries me into the ruined building. It looks like it might once have been some kind of apothecary shop. There is a man-sized wad of bloody flesh just inside the door, and a trail of blood into the back hallway ends with the body of an old woman, dead. Looks like she had tried to drag herself toward the apartment whose door stands open at the end of the hall.

"Put me down."

Raithe stares at the blood-streaked floor. "Here?"

"Yeah. It's just blood, kid."

He nods, and lowers me to the floor so that I can put my back against the wall. He looks like he wants to say something, but a second later he just collapses against the wall and slides down beside me.

"Now," I tell him. "Talk to Deliann. Tell him to quit fucking around with the goddamn assault cars and get his ass into the caverns."

Raithe's eyes defocus for a moment, and when his gaze returns he shakes his head. "He won't."

"He has to! Tell him he fucking *has* to—"

"He won't. The power of the goddess is upon him, and he fights to save us all. In the caverns, he would be powerless."

"Tell him about the bomb!" I snarl, sinking my fingers into Raithe's shoulder. He tries to yank free—fat fucking chance.

The rest of me might be out of shape, but I've still got a grip like a bench vise. "It's a fucking *neutron bomb*! If he stays up here, it's all for nothing—we should have just handed over the fucking sword in the first place and everybody goes home. What the fuck does he think the goddess can do about a *fucking neutron bomb*?"

"He says . . ." Raithe murmurs thickly, his voice trailing away. "He says . . ." His face twitches spastically, and his eyes glaze over entirely. I shake him, hard, then again; I grab his face with my other hand and turn him toward me.

"Tell him, Raithe! Fucking *tell* him—tell him—" But I can see he no longer hears me. My hands fall to my lap, limp, useless, and the chain that links the manacles clatters like distant mechanical laughter. "Tell him that one goddamn person I love has to live through this," I finish softly.

But Raithe only stares, unseeing, into the invisible distance.

11

FIFTEEN MILES AWAY, senses that belonged to the body of Ma'elKoth showed the blind god a sudden current in the Flow, a trickle that became a tide that swelled to a maelstrom the size of the sky.

The blind god sent Ma'elKoth's body lunging for the limousine, hammering upon its silvered windows; it could not wait for this knowledge to trickle along the involute pathways of its aggregate mind. "The child! Stimulants—injections—shake her! *Slap* her!" the blind god roared through Ma'elKoth's mouth. "Wake the child!"

12

THE GODDESS FELT the downward sweep of the hundreds of bomblets, already below the highest-flying eagles that cruised her skies. She had no leisure for subtlety, or for configuring Deliann's body as she had Raithe's; she could use only the sort of skills he already had.

She poured the power of Chambaraya into Deliann's Shell; she expanded it beyond the Courthouse, beyond Ankhana, beyond the matrix of golden force that sealed the city against the

Winston Transfer; she made of it a rising dome that compassed all the land for miles about, and swallowed every individual falling bomblet.

She felt each of them—and each of the assault cars, and the riot vans that rained death on a smaller scale upon the city. She felt even the limousine on that distant grassy riverbank, where a Social Police medical officer had produced an evacuant syringe and forced its flexible plastic tube down Faith's throat, and now methodically pumped the water and digestive acids that were the only contents of her stomach into a stinking puddle on the limo's carpet, while another officer injected a stimulant mixture into her IV drip.

The goddess felt the energy that surrounded each bomblet, each vehicle: the crackling power of transmutative force that enclosed each of them within a bubble of local physics like those of Earth. She spent precious seconds examining that energy, letting it speak to her mind. What she must do, she could do only once, and all in an instant: too slowly, and the randomizing boundary effect might bring about the detonation she sought to prevent.

Then she tuned Deliann's Shell in the same way he had done, those long weeks ago in the white room at Alien Games, when he had tapped into the power of Kierendal's griffinstone. She touched that energy, all of it. Then she took it.

She drained every joule, every erg, every electron volt.

This was energy that Ma'elKoth—himself a transhuman creature specifically designed to channel energies that would incinerate any mortal frame—had spent many hours summoning and channeling piecemeal; to have done it any faster might have destroyed even him. This unimaginable energy, she drained in an unmeasurable fraction of a second. All that energy had to go somewhere.

And to get there, it had to pass through Deliann.

13

DELIANN WAS CONSCIOUS. More than conscious. More than superhumanly conscious. Transcendently conscious. He had not surrendered to the lack; he had let the goddess flow through him. He remained aware.

He felt his brain begin to boil.

This boiling was the effect of a burst of gamma and hard X-ray radiation originating in his pineal gland; it superheated his cerebrospinal fluid, and in approximately 10^{-4} seconds, his brain, his skull, and the rest of his body would vaporize into a cloud of plasma as high-energy photons ionized his tissues.

He could feel this happen because he was thinking, roughly speaking, at the speed of light.

In his next-to-final ten-thousandth of a second, he used the river's power to find Raithe, where he leaned against a wall in a darkened building ripe with the stench of blood. Deliann took some of the energy that screamed into him and used it to join that place to this, warping reality and space so that for just a ten-thousandth of a second, he could reach into that dark, gore-smeared hallway.

There, he dropped the sword.

In his final ten-thousandth of a second, he thought of his father, back in Malmo, of his mother, dead these many years. Of his human brothers and his sister. Of T'farrell Ravenlock and the Living Palace, of Kierendal and Tup.

Of Torronell, and Caine.

He said good-bye, and used his last instant of will to transform the radiation that killed him.

He made himself into light.

14

THE SOCIAL POLICE officer who flew the lead car had only an eyeblink to comprehend that his computer-controlled flight surfaces no longer responded to his commands before every molecular logic circuit in the vehicle underwent spontaneous quantum decay and the car tumbled like a wad of paper and crashed into the Old Town wall just below One Tower. The wall held. The car didn't.

Beside the Great Chambaygen, Ma'elKoth fulminated as the limo's idling turbines whined down to silence.

The crew of the AAV-24 Deva had several minutes to watch the ground fall up toward them.

Assault cars rained out of the Ankhanan sky one after another, crashing into buildings and streets and the river. The riot vans simply settled into themselves as their electronics shut down: their screens went dark and their turrets froze in place.

And all the surviving soldiers in Old Town, Social Police and Ankhanan regular alike, all the primals and the treetoppers, the stonebenders and ogrilloi and trolls and ogres—every creature that still lived—stopped and stared in awe.

The roof of the Courthouse peeled back like a rose opening toward the sun.

From it burst a vertical shaft of pure white light as big around as the Colhari Palace. It roared into the sky louder than thunder, expanding as air ionized to incandescence along its path; the sheath of burning air concealed the shaft's killing glare, saving the onlookers from flashburns and blindness.

The Courthouse melted like a snow castle in an oven.

A few seconds later, several hundred depleted-uranium canisters sprouting immobile airfoils fell—in a still fairly precise pattern—across more than a hundred square kilometers, hit the earth, and bounced.

15

CHRIST, IT STINKS in here.

One of my feet trails in a puddle that has the coffee-grounds texture of clotted blood. I'd ask Raithe to move it, but why bother? I roll my head to the side and look at him. He sits with his knees drawn up, hugging them and staring at the wall.

Kosall lies on the cold filthy floor between us.

Raithe isn't the person I had in mind to spend my last few seconds with, but then nobody ever promised me I'd have a choice. So I'll stay here, in this anonymous hallway with its anonymous corpses. Here is good enough. Right here, next to the sword. Because if I'm about to die, I want to do it beside my wife.

Or something.

What a thing this sword is. I can still feel it sliding in below my navel. I can still feel the buzzing hum in my teeth when it severed my spine. Berne's sword. Lamorak's sword.

I wonder where Lamorak got it, all those years ago. I wonder if he ever felt the weight of its future dragging at his arm. This sword killed my career; this sword took Shanna's life. Kosall is all that's left of her.

All that's left of all of us.

It passed from Lamorak to Berne to Raithe to Deliann—

To me.

To each of us, it's been something different, yet somehow all the same. Like what Kris said about that whole Blade of Tyshalle bullshit: it's the knife that cuts everything. It lies on the splintered hardwood between me and Raithe, and that's where it should be. It's where we should be: on opposite sides of the blade that cuts everything, waiting for the end of the world.

So much pain—

So much hatred—

Everything between us cuts like this sword, but here we are anyway, together. Pretty much all either one of us has left is each other. There is no one else I could share this moment with. There is no one else with whom I could simply wait, and have it be all right.

"It's so quiet out there," I murmur. "Think it's over?"

Raithe shrugs, and turns his face away.

Yeah.

I look down at the sword. I'm afraid to touch it. I guess I knew what it meant when the sword fell out of nothingness and landed right between us.

That was Kris, saying good-bye.

First time I saw him, in that goddamn mad-scientist mask of his, standing over me in the weight room, I knew he was gonna be trouble. How astonished I felt, how *bereft*, when I came back to Earth after my freemod, and they told me Kris hadn't made it—

I guess I went through my grieving then, because right now, all I can feel is grateful. All I can feel is how lucky I have been, to know a man like him. One Kris Hansen makes up for a shitload of Kollbergs, and Marc Vilos, a shitload of Majesties and Lamoraks and all the other fucking scum that swim in the pool where I live. I wish Shanna could have met him—really met him, when they were both human. I think she would have liked him.

More than that: She would have *admired* him.

I think I'll just sit here for a while, and tell myself some of the stories I know about him. I can tell myself about that cold courage of his, where he could just stand there and do what had to be done.

I guess that's how *I* say good-bye.

Tell myself? Shit.

"Raithe?" I say softly. "Let me tell you a story, huh?"

16

THE BODY OF Ma'elKoth rested upon the riverbank, arms en-wrapping knees, as though it were a boulder exposed by eonic erosion of the grassy meadow behind. A Social Police officer approached uncertainly, unsure of his balance on this alien ground.

"Stimulants have been administered. She'll wake soon," the officer said. "But not for long."

"I know," the blind god replied with Ma'elKoth's voice.

"She's very weak," the officer said. "The strain on her heart— I don't think she'll live out the afternoon."

The body continued to stare downriver. "Get in the limo."

The officer retreated. The blind god caused Ma'elKoth's body to follow. It stood outside, still staring toward distant Ankhana. The part of the blind god that was Ma'elKoth could feel what had happened there through the senses of its worshipers: only Beloved Children are permitted to serve in the Imperial military. "Seal the door," it said.

Without power, the officer had to manually drag the gullwing door down and latch it into place.

The part of the blind god that was Ma'elKoth now touched the power of His divine Self: the incorporeal image to which His worshipers prayed. He conjoined that power with his physical form and drew upon it to telekinetically anchor himself to the bedrock beneath the meadow, and to bring him strength.

"Wait for me in the car," he said. Then he picked up the limo and threw it in the river.

The limo—airtight, and constructed of modern titanium alloy—bobbed like a cork, spinning slowly as it drifted downstream. He could have pushed the car into the river with a mere shrug of his power, but some things, as Caine once notably observed, cry out to be done by hand.

He reached into the clay of the riverbank with his mind and drew forth a hundred kilos. The knife of his mind carved it into shape: a medium-sized man with the build of a boxer, somewhat tall for his weight, gone now perhaps a bit to seed—a thickening of the waist, a suggestion of jowls along the jawline—but with eyes penetrating and cold, and a slant of scar across a twice-broken nose.

He summoned his will, and he Spoke.

"Caine."

And as he Spoke, he thought: *Some things cry out to be done by hand.*

17

A WHITE THUNDERBOLT blasts though my brain in the middle of telling Raithe about Ballinger, and for one nerveless second I think the bomb's gone off after all. But the shattering agony goes on and on in a ringing and a roaring that's splitting my fucking head, and it gathers itself into a voice. A Voice. I know that Voice.

It's calling my name.

"Caine—what's wrong?" Raithe reaches for me, but I hold him off with one hand while the other presses against my temple to keep my brain from exploding.

"I hear you," I answer.

I AM COMING FOR THE SWORD. I AM COMING FOR YOU, CAINE.

"I knew you would."

AND I, TOO, KNEW THAT YOU WOULD BE THERE TO MEET ME.

"Yeah, you're a fucking genius."

Raithe stares at me like I've gone completely shit-swallowing loopy.

I CAN BRING MORE TROOPS. I CAN BRING MORE VEHICLES. I CAN BRING MORE BOMBS.

"Don't bother. I give."

Silence inside my head.

"You hear me, you bastard? I said I *give*. I surrender. Bring whatever you want. I'll give myself up. The sword's yours."

Raithe's expression transforms into understanding tinged with awe, and then gathers dismay.

AND IN RETURN?

"Faith," I tell him. "I want my daughter. Alive."

Silence.

"And while we're talking deal, there are a lot of innocent people still on this island, and in the city. Let them go, huh?"

WHY SHOULD I?

"Because that's the deal, motherfucker. Your word: I get Faith, and everybody else walks. You get the sword, and you get me. Otherwise, I run. It'll take you a long time to catch me."

Silence.

"The longer you wait, the more expensive this is gonna get."

VERY WELL. I ACCEPT YOUR TERMS.

"Your word on it."

YOU HAVE IT.

Then the Presence is gone from the inside of my skull, and I sag back against the damp stone.

Raithe is no waster of words. "Ma'elKoth?"

"The blind god. Same thing."

He scowls doubtfully. "You think his word is good?"

I pick up the sword, and it snarls to life in my hand. I squeeze its hilt until its hum matches my memory: it buzzes in my teeth.

"Who gives a shit?" I turn Kosall so that its blade catches sunlight along the edge. "Mine isn't."

ON THAT DAY of prophecy fulfilled and transformed, the plain of Megiddo has become a cobbled street, and the Fimbulwinter a firestorm, and all the echoes and shadows of truth were gathered: Ahura-Mazda and Ahriman, Satan and Yahweh El Sabaoth, Thor and Jorgmandr, the Prince of Chaos and the Ascended Ma'elKoth.

It was the hour of battle for the dark angel and the god of dust and ashes. The heavens would break, and the earth be torn asunder, and their pieces cast into the winds of the abyss. On what new shape the universal shards might find when they came once more together, every prophecy, tale, and legend disagreed.

And all of them were wrong.

TWENTY-FIVE

HE COMES OUT of the clouds, down from a line of thunderheads that advance from the east: clouds that keep on rolling right into the teeth of this wind that blows on the back of my neck.

First comes a glossy black-and-chrome meteor—a Mercedes stretch, bigger than the apartment where I grew up. It comes down with a rumbling growl like distant turbines, but it's not turbines. It's thunder.

That sonofabitch rolls thunder the way other guys clear their throats.

The limo settles into place between the two dead riot vans down where Gods' and Rogues' Ways intersect. Then the clouds swell until they swallow the sky, and a darkness falls upon the ruins; a single rift parts to admit a golden shaft of autumn sunshine.

Down through that rift, riding that clean light, comes Ma'el-Koth, glowing with power: Superman in an Italian suit.

He trails streamers of black Flow—he is the center of a tangle of pulsing night-threads that twist into massive cables before they vanish in a direction my eyes can't follow.

Some of them I *can* follow, though. Some of the biggest cables connect to me.

My own tangle makes a fantastical rats' nest around me, dense and interwoven, impenetrably opaque, yet somehow it doesn't obstruct my vision, which I guess makes sense because I'm not seeing it with my eyes.

He touches down like a dancer, light and perfectly balanced, posing in his sunlight halo. The warm taupe of his Armani suit complements the tumbled char-blackened blocks of limestone that choke the street. Huh. He's let his beard grow.

Yeah, well, so have I.

His eyes find me at this end of Gods' Way, and his electric stare surges through me like an amphetamine bloom: waves of tingling start at the back of my neck and jangle all the way out the ends of my fingers and toes.

He smiles vividly.

He reaches behind his head and unbinds his hair, shaking it free in sun-streaked waves. He rotates his shoulders like a wrestler loosening up, and the clouds part: above him, infinite blue opens like a flower. The clouds retreat in all directions, flowing out from the city as they flee the center of all things that are Ma'elKoth.

He's brought his own kind of spring, drawing life from the city's fallow earth: the ruins sprout cardinal-red, maroon and gold, scarlet-streaked saplings that uncoil toward his solar presence: Social Police and Household Knights and good old Ankhanan regular infantry digging themselves out of their burrows of rubble, helping each other up, even the wounded, even the dying, so that all can rise in respect, then kneel in reverence, at the arrival of God.

And it's weird.

Weird is the only word for it.

Not in the debased and degraded sense of the mere peculiar. Weird in the old sense. The Scottish sense. The Old English root.

Wyrd.

Because somehow I have always been here.

I have always sat in the rubble of the Financial Block, facing down the length of Gods' Way over the carnage and ruin of Old Town, perched on a blast-folded curve of assault-car hull with Kosall's cold steel across my lap. The rumpled and torn titanium wreckage permanently ticks and pings as it eternally cools under my ass. A few hundred yards to my left, there has always been a smoldering gap where the Courthouse once stood, surrounded by a toothed meteor-crater slag of melted buildings; even the millennial Cyclopean stone of the Old Town wall sags and bows outward over the river, a thermal catenary like the softened rim of a wax block-candle.

It's from that direction that the shade of Kris Hansen whispers, in a voice compounded of memories and grief.

I have always been here because there is no past: all that exists of the past is the web of Flow whose black knots are the structure of the present. I will always be here because there is no future: everything that is about to happen never will.

Now is all there is.

There is a folktale—I can't dignify it with the name prophecy, or even legend—that's popular with the common mass of uneducated elKothans; true believers are all pretty much of a type, I guess, no matter what they believe. They've been telling each other for seven years that the Prince of Chaos will return from beyond the world, to face the Ascended Ma'elKoth in a final battle.

On Assumption Day.

I used to get a chuckle out of that every time one of my ISP Actors heard it. I'd shake my head and laugh. Those poor ignorant bastards—if they could only see me and Tan'elKoth going out for a drink at Por L'Oeil. If they could only see me in my wheelchair; if they could see Tan'elKoth at the Studio Curioseum, jazzing the tourists with his fucking party tricks, two shows a day. Poor ignorant bastards.

I say that, and I can't tell if I'm talking about them, or us. Because I should have known. Shit, I *did* know.

Dad said it to my face: A powerful enough metaphor grows its own truth.

So those poor ignorant bastards ended up closer to right than us smug cognoscentic motherfuckers who used to laugh at them. This eternal now in the ruins of Ankhana, facing the god across the wreckage of his city and the corpses of his followers—

Impossible. And inevitable.

At the same time.

I touch one of the black threads, a simple one, almost straight: that's Deliann, dropping Kosall into the shattered hall-way betweeen me and Raithe. That thread is tied to an infinite number of others, progressively more tangled: that's me, screen-ing Shanna to summon her back from Fancon. Here is Raithe, shaking hands with Vinson Garrette, which is tied to me stand-ing over Creele's body at the Monastic Embassy, which is tied to me giving Shanna a battered black-market copy of a Heinlein novel, which connects to Shanna standing over me in an alley, staring at Toa-Phelathon's head lying on the shitstained cobbles, but all these strings are tied to many others, and the others to others still, some of which splice back in closed loops, some of which curl outward into the invisible distance.

A lot of them trail back to the Language Arts shitter, but even that one is a tangle of Toothpick and Dad, and a kid named Nielson hitting me in the head with a brick, and somebody knocking over a vial of HRVP two hundred years ago and Abraham Lincoln and Nietzsche and Locke and Epikuros and Lao-Tzu—

Sure looks like destiny from here.

Try and tell me that Dad could have had the faintest fucking clue I would end up here when he wrote the passages on the Blind God in *Tales of the First Folk*. Try and tell me I should have seen this coming when I brained Toothpick with that length of pipe, or when I proposed to Shanna, or when I lay chained on dark stone in a puddle of my own shit and thought life back into my legs. Destiny is bullshit.

Your life only looks like fate when you see it in reverse.

The universe is a structure of coincidence, Kris told me, and he was right. But that doesn't make it random. It only feels that way. The structure is real: strange attractors ordering arrays of quantum probabilities. I can *see* them.

I can see the threads of black Flow that bloom and curl out-ward in time, connecting every event to every other, each acting upon every other in a matrix of force so complex that there is no such thing as a simple progression from one to the next—but even when the whole structure of reality is laid bare, all you can see is the outline of the past.

The future cannot be predicted. It can only be experienced.

Because one single thread as infinitesimal as what some lab tech had for breakfast one morning two hundred years ago exerts enough pressure to have bent all of Earth toward the Plague Years and the Studio; because the Butterfly Effect of a thirteen-year-old boy named Hari deciding that he wasn't gonna live in fear has tied the history of two worlds into the knot that is today.

And that, when you come right down to nuts and guts, is the most infinitely fucked-up part of this infinite fucked-up now: They finally got me. In the final minute of my life, I've become a Cainist.

Christ.

All right. Enough.

I'm ready for this to be over.

Mortality is a gift: It's never a question of whether you'll die. It's just a question of how.

2

FOUR STRAIGHT BLACK lines crossed by a succession of shorter lines—like dead centipedes with their legs smashed flat—pointed into the ring of light from the darkness around it. They did not quite meet in the center, but it was clear where they would, if extended: in that center-point was Ma'elKoth's right eye.

Orbek slipped the yellow hooked talon of his right index finger through the trigger guard.

This weapon was not designed for ogrilloi; his fingers were too thick to squeeze the trigger properly, and to use the aiming tube mounted above the grip required him to crick his neck in a very uncomfortable way: his right tusk came hard up against the weapon's stock. But ogrilloi are gifted with weapons, and this was not so different from a crossbow. Orbek could make the necessary adjustments.

Sunlight shining through the blown-open roof above warmed his legs; he lay prone on the rubble of what once had been priests' quarters, on an upper floor of a temple to Urimash, a minor god of good fortune. The shell that had destroyed the roof had taken a substantial chunk out of the third-floor facade but had left some of the walls intact, providing stark shadow to conceal his head and the barrel of his weapon.

It had taken him a good long time to haul his ass up here, with his leg half dead—goddamn fuck-me chunk of pavement came outa nowhere while he was diving around a corner when everything blew up, slammed his thigh like a fuck-me morningstar. It took most of the battle for him to crawl out of the street. Everybody else—pretty much all the Folk, the prisoners, probably all the fuck-me Monastics as well—they took off, scattering over the bridges and into the caverns, getting the fuck out of here while they had the chance.

Orbek had never been one for running.

Besides: with this leg, he could barely walk.

Then he'd found this weapon clutched in a dead human hand, pried it out, and decided the best way he could be a real Black Knife was to find a quiet spot where he could shoot some humans before they killed him.

That shimmer in the air—fuck-me Ma'elKoth had a fuck-me Shield going. Orbek didn't know how to tell how many shots he would have with this weapon, but he calculated that even if he couldn't overload the Shield, he should be able to knock the fuck-me bastard down.

That counts for something.

His talon tightened against the trigger, and the aiming tube went suddenly black, and a soft human voice said, "Don't."

Orbek froze—except for his left eyelid, which popped open; with that eye he could see a dark-skinned hand covering the far end of the aiming tube.

"Fuck *me*," he breathed.

He lifted his head, and found himself staring into eyes the color of ice.

His mouth worked soundlessly for a second or two before words could force their way out. "How do you get up here? No, fuck that—how do you even *find* me?"

Raithe said, "I have a message from Caine."

3

MA'ELKOTH, THOUGH—HE'S been waiting for this moment for a long, long time, and he intends to savor it.

He walks toward me, between the broken rows of kneeling Household Knights and Social Police and Ankhanan infantry, swinging his ass, as arrogantly loose-jointed as a tiger. Air shimmers around him: a Shield. He knows we captured some rifles and shit, and he doesn't want a sniper to ruin his party.

He strolls along about a third of Gods' Way; then he stops and opens his arms as if to say *Behold!*

"You said I would never see My city again, Caine," he says with a smile a lot warmer than the sun overhead. "Yet here I am."

He speaks in a casual, human tone, which I can hear perfectly from hundreds of yards away. "No answer? Nothing to say, after all this time, old friend?"

I have a fucking answer for him.

In my mind, I create an image of a white stream of power coming out of the middle of my guts and vanishing into Kosall's hilt. A second or two later I can *see* it, in mindview: twisting and sparking, coruscating, an electric gap-spark thicker than my wrist: a spark that is the path of all the power from every single black thread that is tied to my life. It hums in my subconscious as I anchor it, good and tight, to Kosall.

Not to Shanna, not to Pallas, not to the goddess, not to the wife I have loved and the woman who bore the child I call my daughter, not to the woman I watched die below Khryl's Saddle. I can look at her image in my heart, but I had better keep it out of mindview, or I'll give the fucking game away.

He eyes me closely, cycling through levels of mindview, looking for some kind of Flow current—looking to see what kind of power I might be pulling from the river.

But I'm not pulling. I'm feeding.

"Ah, David, My David," he says, shaking his head in what looks like honest remorse. "Where is thy sling?"

The white gap-spark sizzles. He can't see it.

This might work.

"I am not a vengeful god, Caine. And I know that you have not been brought to bay: that you have chosen to surrender, when you could flee. I would be remiss, not to reply in kind. Thus, I have brought gifts."

His only visible gesture is a slight widening of his smile. Far behind him, the door of the limo swings up: a crocodile jaw opening a mouth of shaded darkness. In that rectangular shadow I can just make out an odd, irregularly globular particolored shape. Ma'elKoth smiles indulgently, and the shape materializes out of sunbeams and dust motes right in front of me, and I still can't make my eyes see what it really is—

My brain unties an invisible knot, and that lumpy black-and-white blob of Ma'elKoth's Fantasy suddenly resolves into a tiny crumple of tragedy. It's Faith: wrapped in a stained and filthy hospital gown, strapped in a wheelchair.

Strapped in *my* wheelchair.

So real—

If I put out my hand, would I feel her hair? Could I bend close for a kiss, and catch the scent of her skin? If I cry over this Fantasy, will she feel my tears?

Faith—

Christ—how can I—

Watching Shanna die was only a warm-up.

"A small enough return, I suppose," Ma'elKoth says. "But one, I think, that you may value as much as I value your surrender. I give you: your family—"

His hand pauses in midgesture, as though to rest a moment on Faith's matted hair, and I don't understand why the rolling boil in my brain doesn't burst my skull, and then he nods and tilts his palm toward Rover.

"—and a place to sit."

4

RAITHE LIMPED OUT from the shadow of a half-crumbled wall, squinting against the harsh sun-glare. The silence was infinite as the sky: the only sound within the ruined city was the slow scrape-crunch of his footsteps. He left a trail of blood, swirling with black oil. The Artans—the Social Police—turned to stare, as he slowly, painfully scraped along the middle of Rogues' Way, to the intersection with Gods' Way.

Far down that broad avenue, he could see the back of the man he had once worshiped. Beyond, at the opposite end of the street, his personal demon sat on a crumple of steel. The air was so clear Raithe could read the look on his face. He nodded slightly.

Caine nodded back.

Raithe turned toward the powerless vehicle that sat, lifeless, between the pair of equally dead riot vans. Artan helmets tracked him. Ankhanan soldiers watched him silently, fingering their weapons.

Raithe smiled to himself. He wondered if this was how Caine had felt, as he paced across the sand in the arena at Victory Stadium. He wondered if Caine had felt this strong, this happy.

This free.

Back in the apothecary shop on Crooked Way, Raithe had risen to leave while Caine was still using Kosall to carve away his shackles, one careful stroke at a time. Raithe had looked at the dead woman nearby in the hallway, remembering: He had been in this shop many times, first as a child, later as a Courthouse page, then as a novice at the embassy. He had known of this old couple for as long as he could remember; he recalled now that they had a son, somewhere, but that was the only detail he could summon. They had been the old apothecary and his wife. He could not recall their names.

His head had swum, and he'd sagged against the wall, gasping. Caine had looked up from his cutting. "You better sit down again."

"No," Raithe had said, shaking his head, dizzy. "No. Just . . . catch my breath—"

"You're gonna catch a bad case of dead, you don't take it easy."

"No. This is where our paths diverge, Caine. I don't imagine I'll be seeing you again."

"Raithe—"

"I would like to—" He'd stopped himself, shaken his head, started again. "If I could find some way, without being disloyal to the memory of my parents, and to the memory of Master Creele—I would . . . I wish I could say I'm sorry. I wish I could say thanks. But I can't."

"Kid—"

"I cannot undo the damage I have done."

"None of us can."

To that, Raithe had only nodded and turned once more to leave.

Caine had caught his clean arm. "I'm not done with you, kid." When Raithe went to yank free, Caine had wrapped his wrist with the chain from his shackle, holding him fast.

"Let me *go*—" He had swung his left hand toward Caine to threaten him with the black oil.

Caine had snorted at him. "Go ahead. You just got done saving my life, now you're gonna kill me? Sure."

"What do you want?"

"We'll probably both be dead in a few minutes, anyway," Caine had said. "But if you're not, I'm gonna need you."

"Need me for what?" Raithe had said, surprised at the strange sound of his own voice: he'd been trying for scorn, but a little bit of hope had worked its way in, instead.

"There's a little girl. A little six-year-old girl with golden hair, who used to smile a lot. She likes pretty clothes, and nursery rhymes, and going to school with the big kids—"

"You're talking about Faith."

"Yeah. Ma'elKoth's bringing her. I need you to take her away. Find someone to look after her." He had shrugged and looked away, his mouth taking on a bitter twist. "Save her."

"Me? Save your daughter?" Raithe had been sure he must have misunderstood. "Where will *you* be?"

Caine had lifted Kosall and sighted along its shimmering blade. "I'll be dead." He let the chain slip free from around Raithe's wrist, releasing him. "That's why I need you."

"I am no longer subject to your orders, Caine—"

"Yeah. That's why it's not an order. I'm asking."

Raithe had only been able to shake his head in wonder. "And why would I do this for you?"

"You won't be doing it for me. You'll be doing it for her. You know what they've done to her. You know what they'll keep doing. You'll be doing it because if you don't, you'll have to live with the memory of letting an innocent little girl be raped to death."

Raithe's breath had come hot and harsh. He had leaned against the wall once more, gasping, his hand leaving a splotch of black oil smearing down the paint. "But why me?" he'd asked. "I'm the one who put her there, as much as anyone else. I killed her *mother*. How can you entrust your daughter's life to *me*?"

Caine's stare had been level, steady and without fear. "Who else is there?"

Who else is there? Raithe thought as he limped toward the open hatchway of the vehicle. In the shade of the hatch door, the child was strapped in a wheeled chair. Beside it, two burly Artans in helmets polished like mirrors restrained a screaming, sobbing old woman with short-cut hair the color of steel. She thrashed in their grip, begging and threatening in a language Raithe could not understand.

Deeper within the vehicle, almost lost within the shadows, was a creature Raithe recognized; a skeletal, eroded caricature of famine. He had felt this creature within his heart. Their eyes met, and they knew each other.

In the creature's eye was hunger. In Raithe's, only ice.

One of the mirror-masked Artans silently showed Raithe how to unlock the chair's wheels. He took it by the handles at the top of the seatback, then turned and pushed Caine's daughter out into the sunlight.

5

I WATCH THEM go: Raithe, wheeling her up Rogues' Way, pauses at the last moment before he disappears around the corner of the temple to Shentralle the Messenger, meets my eye one last time, and nods good-bye.

He and my daughter vanish from my sight.

I wish I could have said good-bye to Faith.

"So, you have your daughter, and you have the lives of your followers. Yet these are not the greatest of My gifts to you," Ma'elKoth booms expansively. He extends an open hand in my direction. "The greatest gift I give is this: that I *buy* your surrender. That I allow you to come to Me with your dignity as well as your life. This is less a surrender than it is a contract: value given for value received. Thus do I demonstrate to all history the love I bear you, Caine; thus shall it be written in every—"

I send a little trickle of black Flow threading through my bypass, and stand up.

He pauses, and his eyes narrow.

"You've learned a new trick," he murmurs appreciatively. "Come, then: Let us meet as men, standing face-to-face, for the surrender of the sword. I applaud your sense of ceremony: Grant and Lee at Appomattox Courthouse, rather than Brutus at the feet of Ant—"

I point Kosall at him. "You talk too fucking much."

He stops, making a face like he tastes something sour; he hates interruptions when he's being clever.

I show him my teeth. "You and me, we both know what's going on here, and it has nothing to do with surrender."

His smile settles in, fading from that big theatrical grin to a half curve of honest satisfaction; his feet settle in, spreading to a wider, stronger stance as he squares up to me; his shoulders settle in, dropping half an inch and seeming to spread and swell like boulders under his suit.

The Fantasy image of Faith strapped in Rover's seat dissolves back into a swirl of dust sparkles in the sun.

He says, "Yes."

"So shut the fuck up. Let's just do it."

He opens his hands. "Come on, then."

"Yeah."

6

RAITHE PUSHED THE girl's chair swiftly into the first alley north of Gods' Way and then began to jog, bouncing her along as fast as he dared on the uneven surface. The girl lolled bonelessly, semiconscious. Though he weakened swiftly, he could keep moving by leaning on the chair himself for support, and they didn't have far to go.

The shattered building sagged in the sunlight; its drooping second floor provided deep shade where Orbek waited with the two primals, the healers from Alien Games. Raithe pushed the chair up to them, stumbling, gasping for breath.

"Did they . . . agree?" he rasped at Orbek. The primals had not trusted him at all, naturally, and for good reason, given the history between the First Folk and the Monasteries; he had barely managed to convince them to wait and speak with Orbek. "Will they help? Did they send—"

"Like you say, friar," Orbek said, grinning around his tusks. *Friar* came out like a curse.

Raithe ignored it. "And the net?"

Orbek nodded. "On its way."

The primal healers crouched near Faith, examining her without touching her, their faces shining with the blank, impersonal pain that a man might show when he finds a dying puppy.

"There's no time," Raithe said, sagging. Only the chair kept him upright. "It's happening now—right now. It's happening."

"Yeah." Orbek's grin widened, and he twitched a tusk to point along the alley: four treetoppers flew toward them swift as sparrows, sharing the burden of one of Kierendal's silver antimagick nets. "It sure as fuck-me is."

7

WE FACE EACH other in the infinite now.

Down the long street lined with people, squinting against the noon-day sun.

We both know how this is supposed to play out. Our parts have been carved in legend's stone for centuries. The gunfighters. The samurai. Zorro and the Governor. Robin Hood and Sir Guy de Guisborne.

No: more accurately, Leonidas at Thermopylae.

Roland at Roncesvalles.

Because Ma'elKoth is the face of ten billion people come to crush me, and here I stand, at the head of my Companions: Raithe; Faith; Shanna and Pallas Ril and the goddess; Hari and all the men I have ever been. They put me here, to be their champion.

Deliann and Kris both stand behind one shoulder.

Dad stands behind the other.

They made me possible.

Relaxed and ready, Ma'elKoth waits for me to start the Walk: the long slow measuring stroll where we both psych ourselves into the killing zone. He knows there has to be a Walk; he knows I have a profound respect for tradition.

He's expecting a trick: he's waiting for me to commit before he makes his move. I caught him off guard last time, and he won't make that mistake again. From a hundred yards away, I can only hit him with magick or a gun, and his Shield can handle either.

A shimmer starts in the nerves of my hand that holds Kosall, and with it an aching sense of loss creeps through my veins. Ma'elKoth's eyes widen, then narrow, and he nods, offering me an appreciative smile.

"What was it?" he asks casually, as though his interest is entirely academic. "How have you broken our link? Did you put one of those silver nets of yours on Faith? Like the one you used on me last time?"

I don't answer, but I don't have to.

Power flares around him.

Now Pallas and I, together, have all the might of the river. Ma'elKoth has all the power of millions more worshipers than he had last time, plus whatever it is the blind god pumps into him.

Head to head, him against me—

We can tear the planet in half.

Armageddon. Ragnarok: the Twilight of the Gods.

He's looking forward to it.

He was always into that Wagnerian shit.

He's spent seven years studying me. Studying Pallas. He's had plenty of time to cycle that superhuman intelligence of his through every possible combination of her powers, my skills, our tactics. I know he's watching in mindview, waiting for any hint of what kind of power I'm going to draw and what I might want to do with it. I can't possibly take him by surprise.

So I don't even try.

I lift Kosall to vertical, turning the flat of the blade toward him in a fencer's salute. He replies with an ironic bow. "I have always known we would come to this, Caine. We are natural enemies, you and I; this is why I have loved you so."

Instead of sweeping the blade down to my right—the traditional acknowledgment of the returned salute—I lift it, swiftly but without haste, above my head.

There is a principle in some of the Japanese fighting arts that translates as *appropriate speed*. It's one of the most difficult elements to master. To move with appropriate speed is to act slowly enough that you don't trigger your opponent's defensive reflexes, so that he doesn't *feel* like he's being attacked: so that he doesn't flinch, or even feel threatened. We are all conditioned by a bazillion years of Darwinian heredity to interpret sudden movement as a possible threat. On the flip side, you can't give him time to think *Hey wait—if that hand gets any closer he could hurt me with it*. It's a delicate balance; appropriate speed varies according to the situation, and to the psychology of your opponent.

Screwing it up is a short trip to the land of the seriously dead.

So while he's still a hundred yards away, watching that sword shine in the sunlight over my head, still talking, still saying, "I have always been fortunate in my—" I twist the black Flow that I've been feeding into the sword in a way that will make my right foot swing forward in one long step.

Which is the signal to the ghost of my dead wife in the sword to use the energy I've been channeling into it to warp space in that seven-league-boots way of hers, and bring the rubble where I stand and the cobbles in front of Ma'elKoth within one step of each other so that the foot I picked up from Nobles' Way comes down a little less than a meter from Ma'elKoth's Gucci Imperiales, and the sword I had lifted over my head comes down at his collarbone, edge striking his Shield as my weight falls forward.

Ma'elKoth finishes blankly, "—enemies—" as we both discover that, in fact, its edge powered by black Flow, Kosall can indeed cut through anything, including Shields.

Including gods in Armani suits.

8

MA'ELKOTH'S EYES GO wide and his mouth works silently, and I let my weight carry the stroke all the way down till the blade comes free somewhere around his hip bone.

I stagger—goddamn bypass, goddamn *legs*—but manage to catch my balance and step back. I want to watch this part.

In a kind of Alpine-avalanche ponderously majestic natural slow motion, his head and his right arm and about half his torso slide off the other half down a fountaining scarlet slope. His legs stand there for a second or two, empty bowels and quivering organs half unrecognizable from this high-side view, and y'know what?

He doesn't stink.

The smell is like ground beef, fresh from your local butcher. I never realized: Since he hasn't eaten for something like fifteen years, I have misjudged him ever since we first met.

He's not full of shit after all.

I have maybe two more seconds before Soapy shoots my ass off. I make good use of those seconds. I lift Kosall again, but this time let the blade swing down, hanging vertically below my clasped hands upon its hilt.

Ma'elKoth looks up at me. His mouth makes empty popping noises; he's left most of his lungs in his other half.

At the speed of thought in the permanent now, I bring an image of Shanna to the front of my mind—a vision of Pallas Ril, a ghost-shadow of the goddess shining and strong upon a field of night. The dash of sunlight off a rippling stream comes from Her eyes, and the hand She extends to me is the color of a peach in leaf shade. *Is it time?* She murmurs within my heart.

I reply, *Take my hand.*

Her ghost hand touches mine, and our flesh flows together; Her warm summer skin shades sun dew into my Donjon-bleached arm, and my death-sealed heart draws Her season down to skeletal autumn. We mingle and swirl, surface tension and turbulence, touching at every geometrically infinite point but forever apart.

Because everyone lives together, and everyone dies alone.

In that single second, when We join in a union of which Our marriage had been only a pale time-reversed ripple of echo, We regard Ourselves and say—

Oh. I understand, now.

One instant of searing melancholy—

If only I could have been the man you needed me to be.

If only I could have accepted the man you are.

—then the river blossoms inside me, from the trickling sewage runoff at Khryl's Saddle to the mighty fan of half-salt flow where We join the ocean beyond the Teranese Delta—

—and my heart cracks because my only wish is that I could stay here with them forever, but as infinite as now might be its end still comes when Shanna says—

Good-bye, Hari.

—and I cannot even reply.

Instead, I give farewell to the man trapped within the dying god at my feet.

"Happy Assumption Day, fucker."

Then I fall to one knee and let my weight drive Kosall's rune-painted blade through his forehead into his brain.

Right between the eyes.

And power blasts back up through the blade, through my fists, my arms, my shoulders—it hits my heart, slams up my neck, and blows away the world.

A TALE IS told of twin boys born to different mothers.

One is a dark angel of slaughter and destruction, a death's-head moth arising from mortal cocoon; one is a crooked knight of flame, a heart of ashes thunderstruck and smoldering.

They each live without ever knowing that they are brothers.

They each die fighting the blind god.

They are tethered by moon threads, woven of love and hate, the stronger for their invisibility: tied to the god who had been a man and to the dark angel's spawn, to the dragoness and to the child of the river, to the dead goddess and to each other.

Where these threads spin a single weave, they knit the ravell'd fate of worlds.

TWENTY-SIX

I DON'T REMEMBER being dead.

I remember some of the dreams that flitted in and out of my slowly reassembling mind as I woke, though, and what I remember of them seems to be about drowning, or being strangled by hands of inhuman strength, or having my head stuck inside a plastic bag. Trying to scream, but without enough breath to give sound to my voice—

Perhaps that should be taken as a hopeful sign about the afterlife. It must be lovely, if I was so reluctant to leave.

I suppose I'll never know.

I'd like to keep this roughly chronological, if I can. It's not easy; there are connections here more subtle than simple sequence. And I'm not always sure in what order everything happened, and I'm not sure it's always important. Somebody wrote once that the direction of time is irrelevant to physics. I'm sure this half-remembered physicist would be pleased to know that my story only makes sense when it's told backwards.

That seems much more profound when you have a fever.

I sometimes catch myself thinking that life is a fever: that the universe fell ill two or three billion years ago, and life in all its fantastic improbability is the universe's fever dream. That the harsh intractability of the inanimate is the immune system of reality, attempting to cure it of life. That when life is extinguished, the universe will awaken, yawn and stretch, and shake its metaphoric head at its bizarre imagination, to have produced such an unlikely dream.

But I get over it when I cheer up.

It's not always easy to distinguish between existentialism and a bad mood.

One might suppose that I would now be immune to melancholy, but that is not so; I seem to be immune only to senescence, and to death. It's better thus—to be eternally happy would deprive me of the bulk of human experience. And, for all else, I am still human.

More or less.

But to give the story a moral before I recount its events will rob the moral of meaning. Meaning is the goal. I sometimes think the greatest danger of immortality is the infinite leisure to digress.

So:

I could write page after page on the process of waking up that very first time in my new life. I could string together fading details of dreams with the incredibly soft warmth of the wool-felt blankets and the fine-woven linen of the sheets, and shuffle the bracing sting of sunlight through closed eyelids with the faintly animal musk of the goosedown that filled the feather bed on which I lay. It's a powerful urge to recount these things, because each individual sensation of living has become indescribably precious to me; though each breath is as sweet as the last, there comes always something wistful, because I cannot forget that this breath is a single thing, as discrete as I am, and no matter how wonderful the next will be, this will never come again.

I was lucky, though: the antidote for such wistfulness was waiting for me beside my bed, grinning like a wolf.

When I opened my eyes, he said, "Hey."

I smiled, and thus discovered I had lips; I squeezed his hand, and thus discovered I had arms. A moment later, I found my voice. "I'm not dead, then?"

"Not anymore."

"Oh, that's good," I said with a feeble chuckle.

"What's funny?"

"Well—finding you here, I was pretty sure this can't be heaven."

His wolf-grin widened: his substitute for a laugh. "It's close enough for me."

I thought about that for a while, while I watched dust motes drift through slanting sunbeams. The window was enormous, nearly the size of the titanic eight-poster bed. Lamps of gleaming brass topped each of the posts—which were ornately carved from some luminous stone like translucent rose marble, and slowly the name for this stone surfaced inside my head: *thierril*.

That was when I understood that we were on Overworld.

"Caine?"

"Yeah?"

"I was wrong," I said. "This is close enough to heaven for me, too." Closer than I deserve, I finished silently.

He heaved himself to his feet and walked to the window, his gait only slightly unsteady. The window faced west, and the afternoon sun painted him with scarlet and gold.

"I'm glad you feel that way, Kris," he said, "because this is as close as you're ever gonna get."

"I don't understand."

He stared beyond the sunset. "Let me tell you a story."

2

IT REALLY WAS the end of the world.

In less than an eyeblink, the world as it had known itself had been destroyed and replaced with a new world, a different world, so like unto its predecessor that a man might fool himself into believing the two were one. The time of nonexistence that separated the two was itself nonexistent; no one saw or heard or even felt the interval, but everyone knew.

Things were different, now.

I understood well enough what had happened, as Caine explained it, at the instant when the world became new: The spell painted in runes upon Kosall's blade had captured Ma'elKoth's pattern of consciousness even as it had that of the goddess—but because the goddess had, in that moment, been touching the river's Song through Hari, the Ma'elKoth-pattern had been channeled through them both. That pattern, that shade, that consciousness would have dispersed like smoke before a wind, sunk back within the Song, save for the idea of the Ascended Ma'elKoth: the image to which millions of Beloved Children pray every day: the Power they endow with the energy of their devotion. That Power was so nearly co-resonant with the pattern of Ma'elKoth that harmonic entrainment caused them to merge in an instant—and through Hari and the goddess, they touched the Song of Chambaraya.

At that moment, He became both a god of humanity, and a limb of the Worldmind: a power which had no precedent in all the aeonic history of Home. Given that place to stand, He moved the world.

He became the world.

But not the world that the Blind God had desired.

The Blind God's grip upon Ma'elKoth was physical: a function of the physical thoughtmitter implanted within Ma'elKoth's physical skull—left behind in Ma'elKoth's physical corpse. And though in one sense Ma'elKoth is as much an agglomerate entity as is the Blind God, in a greater sense He has always been an individual; that individual is, above all else, an artist, and He could not bear to destroy a thing of beauty.

With the conjoined power of his human worshipers and Chambaraya, he could pattern himself even to the matrix of the Worldmind. He flowed outward from the river, and sent His will into the great symphony that is T'nnalldion—Home—itself.

His stroke had been elegant: He had taken the transfer shield—the patterning of force that blocked the Winston Transfer from Ankhana—and extended it over the world entire. In that fraction of a second, every transmission from every Actor on Overworld had ceased.

In the next fraction of a second, He had sung a new note in the Song of Home. Neither Caine nor I have a very clear way to describe its effect. It was, one might say, a minor alteration of local physics.

He made the Blind God improbable.

Extremely improbable: down to the quantum level.

The small segment of the Blind God that had stretched to Overworld disintegrated, and its remnants burst into a scattering flight of night-black shards. The rest recoiled like a knife-cut worm, back to its nest, to lick its wound and brood.

The Social Police in Ankhana felt the difference as a sudden surge of panic, real panic, the ancient panic: the unreasoning terror of being lost and lone in the deep forest of night, in the grip of its unhuman god. Many screamed; all twisted and staggered; most ran; and some fired their weapons into the air, or at each other.

Some turned their weapons upon Caine, where he knelt on Gods' Way; some upon the limousine; some upon any targets they could find. All who did so died before they could squeeze their triggers.

Some of the Social Police still live. I have not yet decided what to do with them.

For now, they are in the Pit.

I wondered at the irony of it, when Caine had finished describing the end of the world: "You made him a god. You transfigured him, and he ascended. On Assumption Day."

"Yeah."

"You took the fiction of Caine and Ma'elKoth, and made it truth."

"Fiction," Caine said, "is a slippery concept."

"You defeated your enemy by granting his fondest wish."

He shrugged. "I'm not sure *enemy* is the right word," he sighed. "Our relationship is . . . complicated."

"But I don't understand," I said. "How did *I* get here? Why am I alive? What does all this have to do with me?"

His smile faded then, and he looked down at his hands. He laced his fingers together and cracked his knuckles in swift succession. "That's a different story," he said.

3

His NEW STORY began some few days after the end of the world: after the dead had been collected, in their hundreds and their thousands, after graves had been dug and pyres lit. It began at the prow of Old Town: a jumble of rock that once had been Six Tower, overlooking a blunt spit of river sand. Caine stood upon the sand, his daughter riding his hip, while from the broken rocks above watched an honor guard comprising the whole of the surviving Household Knights.

But I will not transcribe the story he told; the story I care most about is my own. His gift to me, of the device he calls the Caine Mirror, later let me see for myself the events that he then described. Though I saw them through his eyes, what's important, to me, is how I tell the story.

It begins:

One arm about Faith's shoulders. Her hands locked around his neck and her forehead tucked into the hollow beneath his jaw. Faith in the white-tasseled shawl of Ankhanan mourning; Caine in a tunic and pants of new black leather, belted with a thin cord, and low soft boots.

He held the blade of Kosall so that it reflected the rising sun, while he said good-bye to his wife.

I will not recount what passed between the three of them there. The device—which sits on my desk as I write this—shows me less than all, but more than I can bear to know. I will say only that their good-byes were private, and brief. The details are Caine's story to tell, if he chooses; any who might wish to know them will have to ask him.

I will say this: Pallas Ril chose to pass on.

She could not be both goddess and woman; though she could build a mortal body for herself once more, she could not make herself wholly woman. To have been a god is to be forever less than human, but to be wholly goddess was within her grasp.

And she had no better way to keep her family safe.

When their good-byes were done, Caine drove Kosall into the stone before him until the hilt alone projected.

"Faith, honey, get down for a minute," he said, lowering her to the sand. She dutifully found her feet and took a step away from him.

He said, murmuring as though to himself, "Let's do it."

And the power to which he spoke answered him with fire.

He extended his hands, and from his palms burst flame like the surface of the sun; all had to shield their faces, and even Caine was forced to close his eyes. When the flames died, the great stone block had been reduced to a pool of slag, and Kosall was no more.

Pallas Ril had gone to join the river forever.

That was her happy ending.

The only music that marked her passing was the splash of the Great Chambaygen, the chatter of a pair of foraging squirrels, and the scream of a lone eagle, far, far above.

After a moment, Caine looked down at Faith. "You ready?"

She nodded solemnly.

He held out his arm to help her back up onto his hip, but instead she took his hand. "I'm big enough to walk," she said.

"Yeah," he agreed, slowly and with some reluctance. "Yeah, I guess you are."

As the two of them helped each other negotiate the tumble of rock, a dry voice spoke within Caine's mind. *Touching.*

"Have some respect," he muttered.

Ironic: that the man least likely to show respect is the first to ask for it.

"Shut the fuck up."

Faith blinked up at him owlishly. "Are you talking to God again?"

Caine said, "Yeah."

She nodded, solemnly understanding. "God can be a *mean bastard* sometimes."

"You got that right."

4

THEY THREADED BETWEEN the ranks of Household Knights, who stood at attention with weapons at port arms and standards lowered. Alone at the end of the ranks, shivering despite being half buried in an enormous raccoon coat, stood Avery Shanks.

Caine and Faith stopped before her.

She matched his level stare.

"Faith?" Caine said, releasing her hand and placing his own on the middle of her back. "Go with Grandmaman back to the palace."

Faith's eyes had the otherworldly half emptiness of the river's Song within her head. "All right." She held him with her gaze. "I love you, Daddy."

"I love you too, honey. I just—I have some things I have to do by myself. I'll be there in time for supper."

"Promise?"

"Promise," he replied, and the memory of his last promise to her, and how badly he had failed it, ripped him like fishhooks dragged across his heart.

Reluctantly, Faith joined her grandmother and took her hand. Caine once again met Shanks' gaze. "Take care of her."

She snorted. "Better than you ever did," she said. "Better than you ever will."

As he watched them walk away, hand in hand, picking along the winding pathways that had been cleared through the debris-choked streets, he murmured, "I have always been fortunate in my enemies."

Mm, flattery, the voice within him hummed dryly.

Caine opened his mouth as though he might reply, but instead he grimaced and shook his head in silence. He swung his legs into motion, climbing over a crumbled wall, heading toward Rogues' Way, toward Fools' Bridge. When he told me this story, he said that he simply needed to move, that he wanted to get off the island for a little while; the Caine Mirror confirms this, but I think it is not the whole of the truth. I believe he wanted to go into the Warrens to see what was left of his old neighborhood.

To see what was left of himself.

5

THE GAP IN Fools' Bridge where the timbers of the bascule had burned away was spanned by temporary planking supported by ropes of knotted hemp. On that morning, workers trundled barrows of brick and salvaged limestone blocks across, and so Caine took the catwalk on the upstream side: a pair of taut ropes, one above the other. He did not pause over the river—he kept moving, sliding one foot ahead of the other along the lower rope while he slid hands along the upper—but his wife was much on his mind as the water rolled beneath him. He thought, so his Soliloquy claims, of what she had shown him, in that infinite instant when he had joined with the river: how the river was everything within its bound, and everything within its bound was the river.

He thought of so many men and women and children on Earth, for whom a river is a natural toilet, suitable only for flushing away their waste. In a distant, abstract, impersonal way, he felt sorry for them. But not too sorry. If they wanted their world to be different, they could change it.

It wasn't his problem, not anymore.

Just so. But this begs the question: What, then, is your problem?

Caine left the bridge and wandered at length upon the north bank of the river. From the Warrens to the ruins of Alientown and back again, the streets were filled with people clearing away debris, separating what could be salvaged and used again from what would be suitable only for landfill. Nearly all the corpses had been cleared away and burned days before, and there was a certain grim cheerfulness among the townsfolk, a camaraderie in adversity, that bespoke their shared determination to rebuild their home.

Much of the rebuilt Ankhana will be constructed of timber from the goddess' unnatural spring: young and sap-filled, many of the tree trunks had burned only on the surface, where the oil had oozed through their bark. Their hearts are sound, and will form the skeleton of the city that will rise from this waste of ash and rubble.

Everywhere Caine went, he was greeted with nods of recognition. It was a strange feeling: Everyone knew who he was, and no one feared him. The greetings he got were instead respectful, and that respect was tinged with awe. Most of the citizens of Ankhana were Beloved Children of Ma'elKoth, and each of these had awakened to the new world with an eldritch knowledge in their hearts of what Caine had done for them, and for their world.

Even more strange for him, I think, was to walk, and walk, and continue to walk with no particular place to go; to return nodded greetings in a friendly way, to listen to the breeze and the conversations, smell the old char on the wind and feel the crunch of gravel beneath his boots—

And find nothing he had to do.

I cannot be certain—the device records no commentary—but I believe he took some comfort from this. These few days were the closest he had ever come to a respite from the struggles of his permanent war. In all his life as Caine, there had always been someone he had to kill, or someone who sought to kill him; always treasure to be searched out, or adventure to be pursued; there had always been the pressure to keep his audience entertained.

Now he was the audience, and he found that the path of a cloud across an autumn sky had an unexpectedly great entertainment value of its own.

Whenever his wandering turned him back toward the Warrens, he found himself staring at the vast hulk of the Brass Stadium. The lone structure of stone in all the Warrens, it towered above the remnants of burnt-out buildings around. In years before, Caine had been an honorary Baron of the Subjects of Cant, the Warrengang that had used the abandoned stadium as their headquarters. In those years, the Subjects had been his family. He had left his family on Earth—his father—for the family of the Monasteries; he had left the Monasteries for the Subjects of Cant; and he had left them in turn to make his own family with Pallas Ril—

But once again, the device records no commentary. And perhaps I am not telling his story here, so much as I am my own.

Sometimes I have difficulty telling the two apart.

I can say for certain that he spent much time staring at the Brass Stadium, and twice made halfhearted attempts to pry off the boards nailed across the street entrances as though to slip inside, and twice changed his mind. Here I do have his words, in Soliloquy: *I'm breaking into the wrong stadium.*

With that, he turned once more to the west, walking with purpose now, following the dockside to Knights' Bridge. On the Old Town side, he passed the crater where the Courthouse once stood with barely a glance.

I suppose Caine and justice have always had little to do with each other.

For me, though—my heart clenches whenever I review this part of the recording. That crater, that slag-crusted gap in the city, is a scene of personal destruction: I did that.

I died there, doing that.

It's not easy to look at.

I've had, as of this writing, some few weeks to brood on the experience of being dead. It's not easy to think about.

Caine had seven years.

The recording admits only of a stew of emotions, cycling and shifting and mixing until all that is definite is their overwhelming power; I will not venture a guess as to what Caine might have been thinking as he crossed Kings' Bridge and saw, for the first time with his own eyes, the Cathedral of the Assumption.

6

HE'D SEEN IT hundreds of times, if not thousands, through the eyes of his Studio's Actors, but to be there in the flesh makes it immediate in a way that a simichair can't duplicate. It towers overhead, looming until it eclipses half the sky: a titanic arc of snow-white marble, the tallest structure in Ankhana, overtopping even the surviving spire of the Colhari Palace. There are no straight lines or hard angles here; the facade curves away in an eye-fooling trick of perspective, to seem even larger than it is, its true dimensions unguessable. Its appearance dwarfs even its reality, and it is fiercely blank: no decoration or detail gives it human scale.

It stands unscathed by fire and battle. No living thing grows upon or within it; no ivy scales its pristine walls. Its floors are stone, its doors iron, and its ceilings brass. The Cathedral of the Assumption transcends mere intimidation; to enter is to be crushed by one's personal insignificance.

Caine barely noticed.

He walked up to it, whistling tunelessly, absently: a whisper that carried only a ghost of music. Teams of acolytes swung from ropes moored to the roof, scrubbing the facade; though none of the black oil had fouled it, smoke from the fires had stained its gleaming surface.

"I suppose you'll be shutting this place down," he muttered.

Why should I? the voice within him replied. *Ma'elKoth yet exists—still the patron of the Ankhanan Empire, still the grantor of His Children's petitions. Though He is only part of what I Am, the name Ma'elKoth still compasses what He is.*

There are many such: I am an entire pantheon. Did you not

understand this? Pallas Ril is part of Me, now, even as is Ma'elKoth; she shall be the patron of the wild places that she loves, and also the defender of the weak and oppressed, even as the wilds shelter those who must flee—

"Christ, shut up, will you? If I'd known I'd have to listen to you yap for the rest of my fucking life, I would have let you kill me."

He went to the gate, and a priest wearing white robes under a mantle of maroon and gold opened it for him. "In the name of the Ascended Ma'elKoth, this humble Child bids the Lord Caine welcome."

Caine made a face and brushed past the priest's deep bow with a bare nod of acknowledgment. The priest called after him, "Would the Lord Caine desire an escort? A guide, perhaps? Can this humble Child direct him in any way?"

"I can find it," Caine said, and kept walking.

He had no difficulty making his way to the sanctum. Seven years is not so long a time that any detail of this place was less than fresh in his memory. He knew the sanctum well: he had died there.

The Cathedral of the Assumption had been built around Victory Stadium.

He came out a long dark gangway into blinding sun: the interior of the stadium was still open to the sky, and virtually unchanged since that original Assumption Day. He descended the shallow steps toward the retaining wall around the arena, and every time I review the recording I think he's about to vault the rail and alight upon the sand.

But he never does.

Instead he sighs, and I feel a grim set fix itself on his face. He looks about, and finally moves along the rows until he sits in one of the Ducal Boxes—the one that had belonged, in fact, to the late Toa-Sytell. He leans forward, supporting his weight with his elbows upon his knees, and stares out across the sand.

For a long, long time.

Again, the recording offers no Soliloquy, no clue to his thoughts, save only the occasional adrenal race of his pulse, and once or twice the hot sting of incipient tears.

Finally, he mutters, "The problem with happy endings is, nothing's ever really over."

Amen.

Another long, long silence, while he searches the sky as though he seeks there the clashing eidolons of the goddess and the god; then he fixes his gaze on one spot of sand, far out near the center. Near the altar.

"And Lamorak?" he says, at length. "That shitbag's a god now, too?"

Of course.

"Christ."

No. Say rather: Judas. Lamorak shall be the god of traitors, of jealous lovers, of all who plot harm in their hearts, and seek to carry it out in secret. Poisoners.

Assassins.

"Great," Caine grunts, his mouth a bitter twist. "That's like a little gift just for me, huh?"

No reply comes.

"What about Berne?"

Alas, no. I do not carry Berne within Me. A pity; he would have made a lovely god of war, don't you think? Very Arean, in so many ways."

Now it is Caine who does not answer.

A bit later, he mumbles pensively, "What about Hannto the Scythe? He—you—started out as a necromancer, right? God of death?"

Beauty.

Caine snorts.

Ironic, yes? A man so ugly I could not bear to be him—yet his sole passion was the beautiful. Even now, it is only this for which He truly cares.

Caine shakes his head. "Seems kind of a pissant job. I mean, he's the original You, right?"

And that is why He is chief among Us, Caine.

"Chief? The god of beauty?"

If you'll permit, I believe Keats put it well:

Beauty is truth, truth beauty;
That is all ye know on Earth,
And all ye need to know.

This sets Caine to leaning back, staring into the sky to consider; I think he might sleep for a time, here; there comes a point when he closes his eyes, and when he opens them again, the shadow of the cathedral wall seems to have climbed the eastern grandstand.

He seems calmer, when he speaks again, almost—almost—at peace.

"What's with this *Lord Caine* shit?" he says slowly.

The dry voice replies without hesitation, as though for it no interval has passed. *Only the smallest gesture of My gratitude. My Children will address you so, and will do you honor every day of your life.*

"Well, fucking cut it out. I don't want to be Lord anything. I'm Caine. That's enough."

There comes a pause.

Then: *Perhaps it is. But how then am I to express how deeply I value you, and what you have done for Me? What reward could possibly suffice?*

"You could leave me the fuck alone."

Ah, Caine, has either of us ever been able to do that?

Caine does not answer.

Can I offer you a job?

"A job?"

Would you like to be, say, Emperor?

"Good Christ, no!" Caine says, and actually bursts out laughing. "Call that a reward?"

But the Empire needs a ruler, and many men would consider nearly unlimited power—

"I have plenty of power," Caine says. "Remember?"

After a pause: *Just so.*

"Stick me with a job I'd suck at? Yeah, that'll cheer me up. Shit. And working for you doesn't always turn out so well for either of us, you know?"

Again: Just so.

How about eternal youth?

Caine blinks, startled by the idea. "You can do that?"

I can. In the moment when you and Pallas Ril joined Me to the river, I knew you utterly. I know you to the molecule, Caine; to the atom. I can make a new body for you, just as Pallas Ril began to make one for herself. I can make you twenty-five again—twenty-five forever. Think of it: no pain in the hip and shoulder, muscles with the supple flexibility of youth . . . And I can do better: I can give you superhuman strength, and speed, make your flesh regenerate wounds—

"You can stop there; I've heard enough. No thanks."

This would not be some simulacrum, Caine: You would be you. The nervous system of the new body would receive your consciousness every bit as well as the one that channels it now, and probably better.

"And that's it. That's exactly it: that part about *better*."

Why would you turn down a perfect body?

He says through his teeth, "Because I can't fucking *trust* you."

Caine, you have My word—

"Yeah, we both know how much that's worth," he says. "And we both know that while you're building me a new body, and you're already in there tinkering around, you'd start to get the itch to perfect my mind, too. Erase a couple of those bad habits that nobody likes about me—cussing too much, scratching in public, whatever—it'd start with minor shit like that, and end up with some of my other bad habits. Like kicking your ass every once in a while."

A long interval passes in silence.

At least let me fix your legs.

"They work all right, these days."

Their use remains a chancy proposition, Caine. You may live to regret declining this offer.

"I'm living to regret plenty of things," he says with a deep sigh.

Here I flatter myself: I believe he might possibly be thinking that he is the sum of his scars.

7

HOW, THEN, MAY I show My gratitude? How may I show the world how much I value you, My friend?

Here Caine takes a long, slow breath and speaks in tones deliberately flattened, to rob them of any suggestion that some emotion might color his words: a judge issuing final instructions to a jury. "We," he says, "are not friends."

Caine—

"No," Caine says with inarguable finality. "I had a sort of friendship, once, with a man named Tan'elKoth. He's dead now. You—I don't even know what you are, but you're no fucking friend of mine."

You know what I am: I am as you have made Me, Caine.

I am Home.

And I am your friend.

"Well, I'm not yours. You killed my wife, you sack of shit. You hurt my *daughter*."

And from those crimes, you and I saved the world.

"Fuck saving the world. You could save ten worlds. You could save the motherfucking *universe* and it won't get you off the hook with me. I don't care if you are God. Someday, somehow, I'm gonna fuck you up."

We were at war, Caine. We both fought for what we most loved.

"So what?"

Sacrifices had to be made to defeat our common enemy.

"Yeah? What did *you* sacrifice?"

Apparently, your friendship.

Caine spends a long, long time staring at his hands, making fists and opening them again, watching them transform from tools to weapons and back to tools once more.

"I saw that statue," he says finally. "The night of the fire. *David the King*. It was a good likeness. A good statue. Your best work. But it's not me."

I disagree.

"I'm not your David."

Oh, that—yes. You are correct, however much I would wish that you were wrong. Where I disagree is this: David the King *is not My best work. You are.*

"Shit."

I see a man who was shattered more thoroughly than that block of marble—who has been reassembled into something greater than the sum of his parts. The artist in Me will always take pride from My participation in that reconstruction. If you and I must be enemies, so be it.

It has been said that the true measure of greatness is the quality of one's enemies. If this be so, then I am proud to be yours, Caine.

Caine?

"Hmn?" Caine grunts. "Were you talking?"

You weren't listening.

He shrugs. "When you start to drone on like that, it makes my eyes glaze over. I was thinking: That new body trick—you can do that for anyone who was joined to the river?"

I can.

Caine ignites his wolf-grin. "Then I think I've got an Emperor for you."

And that's where I come into the story once again.

8

I CONFESS TO watching my resurrection many times. I find it fascinating, and not only for the impressive ceremony, which took place at the Cathedral of the Assumption a few weeks later. It involved the great brass icon of Ma'elKoth in the midst of the temple statues of every god in Ankhana, a Great Choir of elKothan priests, all the nobility and most of the gentry of the Empire, a tremendous amount of chanting and singing and incense and fireworks, and every possible kind of symbolic pinch of this and trace of that: sand from the Teranese Delta, a cup of Tinnaran brandy, an apple from a Kaarnan orchard, et cetera ad infinitum. It was the culmination of a weeklong festival throughout the Empire and was, in Caine's words, "the biggest fucking dog-and-pony show in the history of the human race."

Part of what I find fascinating is the way my body seems to assemble itself from the mound of symbolic bric-a-brac, and how when it's done, it's me.

It's me the way I always thought of myself, when my body allowed me to forget the approach of middle age: young, smooth of face, a corona of platinum hair around golden night-hunter eyes.

A primal mage.

I'm sure this came as rather a rude surprise to many of the nobility's more hardened bigots. But even they can't object too loudly: the whole capital garrison of the Imperial Army heard Toa-Sytell proclaim all the Folk as citizens of the Empire, with the full complement of rights and duties. And for now, anyway, even the bigots carry the certainty of God Himself within their hearts: that this slim ageless fey is their new Emperor.

I say again: That would be me.

Someday, perhaps, if I say this often enough, it will no longer sound so strange, or so awful.

And so I watch it happen again and again: I watch God Himself, through His faithful priests, carve me out of a mound of dead things and breathe life into my nostrils, and it still seems entirely wonderful, and entirely terrifying.

That is not the only portion of the recording within the Caine Mirror that I watch again and again; I further confess that I spend much of my time reviewing Caine's talks with me, and our first meeting in the Pit, and every other time he and I were together.

What a gift he has given me—

For this is the one seeing my flash can never offer: to see myself through another's eyes. It is altogether humbling, and exalting, and to precisely the same degree.

Not too dissimilar, in that respect, to being Emperor.

9

I LAY UPON the bed where one ruler of Ankhana had died, and one had awakened from death, and stared numbly at the man responsible for both.

"I don't understand," I said. "Why me? It doesn't make any sense."

He replied through half a smile. "You just haven't had time to think about it yet."

He came back from the window and pulled the high-backed laquered chair from the vanity table. He reversed and straddled it, reminding me for one instant so strongly of Tommie that sudden tears stung my eyes.

"The new Empire can't just be for humans, not anymore," he said. "Everybody's gonna have to work together. You're already the Mithondionne. The Folk will follow you. But you were born human, so the nobility can accept you—reluctantly, sure, but remember, God's on your side. *Their* god. And you'll need him: the Blind God's still out there, and we both know it can't give up."

He leaned forward as though sharing a confidence. "The task of the Empire will be the defense of Overworld. You were born on Earth. You know what we're up against. Part of what makes a great Emperor is the ability to choose people who are responsible, capable, and honest enough to administrate the business of the realm. Who better than you? Who better than you to mediate disputes and disagreements between provincial Barons? Who better than you to negotiate alliances? Who's gonna work harder? Who's gonna care more? Shit, Kris—who better than you for *anything*?"

"But, Hari—" I brought fingertips to my eyes to hold back tears. "But everything I do, it turns out *wrong*."

He shrugged this off as irrelevant—and perhaps he was right. "Sure, shit doesn't turn out how you expect—or how you hope—but wrong?" He grinned at me. "You'll have to take that one up with t'Passe."

"T'Passe . . ." I murmured. "How is she?"

"She's alive. Took a bullet and an assload of shrapnel out on Gods' Way, but she made it. That's a tough broad, no mistake. But this whole thing has flipped her lid a little—I guess she's decided I am some kind of god after all, and she's my prophet. She's been running around trying to start up a church for me. Every time I tell her to cut it out, she just shrugs and tells me she respects my wishes," he said sardonically, "but she is not *compelled* to *comply*."

"T'Passe liked to say that people are either sheep or wolves," I said wistfully, watching a cloud billow past the window. "Which am I, Hari?"

"Well, you know what I always say: There's two kinds of people in the world: the kind who say things like 'There's two kinds of people in the world,' and the kind who know that the first kind are full of shit."

He waits while I parse this, and I give him a smile to let him know I've gotten the joke.

"But that's serious, too," he said. "Two-valued systems break down in contact with the real world. True or false, right or wrong, good or evil: those are for mathematicians and philosophers. Theologians. Out here in the real world? Sure, there are sheep, and there are wolves—and there are also shepherds."

"Shepherds," I echoed.

Hari nodded. "Yeah. Maybe your real job is to protect people like them—" A jerk of his head indicated the world beyond the bedchamber's window. "—from people like me."

I thought about that for a long time, and I have to admit I liked the sound of it.

I am always mildly astonished when such things come out of his mouth; it's so easy to forget that he was raised by a former university professor—by the author of *Tales of the First Folk*, no less. And that is, itself, a reminder of how shallow and caste-biased I remain, even after all these years: my need to explain his gifts according to his bloodline. Perhaps, immortal, I can someday outgrow myself; for this I maintain some hope.

"But what about the other way around?" I asked. "Who will protect the people like you?"

"Wolves don't need protecting," he said. "All we need is some open country—without too many fences, or too much concrete—and we can take care of ourselves."

"Sheep, and wolves, and shepherds," I murmured. I sat up in bed, and Caine handed me a robe of such silken liquid softness it was barely even there. I wrapped it about my shoulders and wandered to the window, marveling at my straight, strong, painless legs.

I looked out over the city, watching the people slowly bring it back up from the ashes. "And so there must also be ants and eagles, trees and flowers and fish. Each to its own nature—and the more there are, the more beauty in the world."

"Butchers and bakers and candlestick makers," Caine snorted. "It's just a fucking metaphor. Don't beat it to death, huh?"

I nodded. "And Emperors. Do you really think I can do this, Hari?" I turned to face him. "Do you?"

He squinted at me against the light from the setting sun. "In my whole life, there are only three people I've ever really trusted," he said. "One of them was my father. The other two are you."

This burns me every time I watch this scene in the Caine Mirror; it wounds me with a pity I can never share with him. I can never tell him how sorry I am that he could not include his wife in that small company. I know too well how deeply it wounds him.

Through his eyes I watch myself say, "All right. I can try. I just . . . need time to get used to the idea."

"Not too much time," he tells me. "Your fucking coronation's in less than an hour. Come on. Let's get you ready."

"Yes," I see myself tell him. "Let's."

10

MY CORONATION WAS very grand, in a disconnected, slightly nightmarish way. I lack sufficient interest in pageantry to spend much ink upon the details. In the vast stark shell of the Great

Hall of the Colhari Palace, I accepted personal fealty from hundreds of nobles and from the lords of the Folk. I sat upon the venom-stained bulk of the Oaken Throne and watched myself receive the diadem in that dreamlike dissociative state where I was and was not myself: an experience both terrifyingly immediate and as familiarly comforting as the hundredth hearing of a favorite bedtime story.

I still could not make myself believe it was happening.

It finally became real when Querrisynne Massall approached through the assembled ranks and climbed the steps to the dais, to kneel and offer me the *mithondion* that had been borne by the Twilight King. I took it from his hand, and received his embrace, and neither shrieked my pain nor collapsed upon the throne.

The Massall is father to Finnall: brave, lovely Finnall, my comrade, whom I stabbed on the precipice above the mines of Transdeia. Father to Quelliar: the murdered chief of the legates to Thorncleft. That the Massall was here told me all I could bear to know of the fate of my family, and my people.

Yet I took the symbol of my House from his hand with no feeling other than a grave respect for what was offered and for what I then accepted. This was how it first became real to me: At that moment, I understood how different I am from what I had thought to become.

Caine had tried to make me understand, while he helped me layer myseif with ceremonial dress.

"The real problem with monarchy as a system of government," he'd said, "is that virtue is not hereditary. So I guess the Big Guy decided he had a better plan."

I have been improved.

I am immortal.

Immune to illness, to age, to every infirmity that afflicts mortal kind. It may be possible to kill me, though Caine tells me that if I should, by some fluke, be destroyed, the power that I call T'nnalldion—Home—can create me again as I am at this moment.

I don't think it's changed me too much; to alter my essential nature would defeat the purpose of having a living ruler at all. One might as well cede authority to a book of bloodless law; one might as well have a robot for a judge, dispensing justice according to its programming, unable to mitigate, unable to abrogate—which of course is not justice at all.

Justice is just only when it is specific.

It seems I am myself, saving only a subterranean connection to the pulse of Home: a constant wellspring of strength. It is strength I cannot live without. Only by touching that living world within myself can I bear the pain of all the lives that come before me. Without it, their pain would overwhelm me; I have no doubt I would go mad, banish the sorrowful from my presence, and end up a Fool King in a court of happy idiots. Provided a court full of such folk could be found.

There are so few happy people in the world.

11 .

MANY CAME BEFORE me in my Audience the next day; I will mention only those who are part of this story. Nor will I make any attempt to preserve the order of their coming; I find I cannot even recall who was first, and who came after.

Kierendal came to plead the case of the former Duke Toa-M'Jest in absentia; the former Duke himself had not been seen since he left the Courthouse on the night before the battle. I had confirmed the decision of the late Patriarch to strip him of his title, though I rescinded the order for his arrest and execution, and sentenced him only to banishment. As Tommie had said, the only reason to kill a man is for something he's going to do. His threat to the Empire is mostly symbolic: the resentment of the Folk he had persecuted in the name of the Church, and the vendettas of victim's families. The Empire cannot be perceived to condone his actions.

"But this is the only home he has ever known," Kierendal pleaded, kneeling on the steps below the Oaken Throne. She wore the white of Ankhanan mourning, and her face was smeared with black ash. "Banishment might as well be a sentence of death. He is not a bad man—"

"Bad or good is irrelevant," I said gently. "And this sentence is kinder than he deserves."

"But the amnesty—"

"Does not apply." I'd decreed a general amnesty for crimes committed during the height of the outbreak; it would have been impossible to sort out who was responsible for what, when so few could be considered responsible at all. "The crimes for which Jest is banished occurred before the disease took hold."

"He is a friend to Caine—he helped Caine, freed him from his cell—" Her voice dropped to a bare whisper.

"And it is Caine who spares him execution. Caine has done what Jest himself refused: argued for the life of his friend. That is why the sentence is banishment, not death."

She lowered her head and flooded my chest with her pain. I understood her too well. She pleaded for him not because he deserved such support, but because he was familiar. Jest was the only remnant of her former life that she could still hope to salvage; she hoped for a rock to anchor her in the empty ocean of her life, even if it was itself the rock that had battered her to pieces.

I have never been able to decide if it might be kinder to allow such false hopes to survive.

"And what of my punishment?" she said.

Without my flash to show me her heart, I might have been confused by this, for—far from punishing her—I had declared her a Friend to the Throne; she is one of the few true heroes of this story, pure-hearted and strong, and fierce in her defense of her people. I knew what she wanted, and I knew what she needed, and I knew that these two things only loosely resembled each other.

"Kierendal, this is the punishment I decree for you: to live without those whom you could not save. I further sentence you to bear this punishment with dignity, and never to disgrace their memories by claiming guilt which is not yours. Let it be so."

She wept as a steward led her away.

Acting Ambassador Damon came before me, to make the traditional refusal of the honor I had, in respect to that same tradition, offered: a title and lands on the borders of the Empire. He desired only to stay within the Monasteries. He had already resigned his post, though his resignation had not yet been officially accepted by the Council of Brothers. Despite the amnesty, despite all arguments to the contrary, he held himself responsible for the destruction of the embassy. He put it thus: "This happened on my watch. There is no possible mitigation."

I suppose it is a function of conscience, to insist upon our fair share of guilt.

T'Passe as well came before me. To her, I offered the only reward she would accept: a proclamation rescinding Toa-Sytell's criminalization of the Disciples of Caine.

"The Disciples of Caine, as a group, are under no obligation to you for this," she reminded me stiffly.

"I thought the Disciples of Caine, as a group, don't believe in groups."

This sparked a tiny smile. "I personally, however," she said, "am in your debt."

"If you would repay that debt, visit me on occasion," I told her. "I value your insight, and would welcome your conversation."

This seemed to both startle and please her greatly, and she promised to comply.

And I remember Faith Michaelson, brought before me by Businessman Shanks. I remember how pale and serious she looked, how her eyes had retreated into black hollows, and I remember the slight tremble of her hand as she reached for the hem of her dress to perform a curtsy. Her voice was thin, fluting like a rabbit's whimper. "Your Imperial Majesty . . ." she said.

"I am so very pleased to meet you, Faith," I told her. "I hope that we may someday become friends."

"Mm-hm," she hummed faintly. Avery Shanks squeezed her hand and murmured, "Yes, sir."

Faith repeated, "Yes, sir."

"And I hope," I said to her there, "that someday you will feel free to call me Uncle Kris."

Her expression did not change. "Yes, sir."

This child was so profoundly wounded by the unspeakable crime she had suffered—

More: she had been ripped entirely from the world she knew.

The best I could offer was some stability, and the hope of comfort. For her services to the Empire and the world, I created her Marchioness of Harrakha, giving her title to Imperial lands where the Transdeian railway comes down from the God's Teeth, and to the river town nearby.

Avery Shanks regarded me with eyes that glittered like a falcon's. "I'm told you're Gunnar Hansen's youngest son," she said, speaking the English that was her sole tongue.

"I was," I admitted.

"I know your father." Her gaze judged my robes and my diadem, the *mithondion* in my hand and the vertical pupils of my eyes. She said coldly, "I can just imagine what he would think if he saw you now."

"Then your imagination far outstrips my own," I replied.

"I don't suppose a man like you truly understands the importance of family—"

"And you may perhaps be correct."

"—but I am the only real family this child has. You must not take me from her."

"I had no intention of doing so."

At this she looked startled. "But Michaelson—"

"I know no one by that name."

She shut her mouth so abruptly that her teeth clicked together.

A formidable woman: even more so than she had been on Earth. The new world had been transformative for her, as well. In that instant when the world had become new, and the Social Police officers who had restrained her had fled in terror, she had found herself alone with the creature that had been Arturo Kollberg. Mad with rage and loss, it had leaped upon her, knocking her down, kicking her, clawing at her, and the totality of her universe underwent an instant skew-flip.

She had suddenly, instantly, passionately comprehended that despite being fifteen years her junior, and male, and the aspect of some unimaginable creature of nearly limitless power, physically he was a small, frail, malnourished little man—

Who had hurt her granddaughter.

For the creature that had been Arturo Kollberg, I can only imagine that the new world was equally transformative. It must have found itself entirely astonished to be pummeled and clawed and kneed and kicked by Avery Shanks. How could it have possibly guessed that such a beaten, broken old woman could have become so instantly fierce? It couldn't have guessed how much hand and arm and leg strength Avery Shanks had, even at seventy, from her five weekly sets of tennis. It could never have anticipated that this woman had spent thousands of hours reviewing the recorded Adventures of not only her son, but also of Caine, her dearest enemy. While her body might not have the trained reflexes of a warrior, she had gleaned considerable theoretical knowledge of personal combat, and she had long ago overcome the sort of squeamishness that stops ordinary folk short of savage murder.

It could not have guessed that, in fact, Avery Shanks rather enjoys the taste of blood.

And so when her sharp teeth latched into the side of its neck, sawing through skin to rip its jugular, she still didn't let go as blood poured across them both, but kept biting deeper and deeper, and chewed through muscle to sever its carotid artery.

It must have still been entirely surprised when it died.

All this I got in the instant's flash. I regarded her with the same wary respect I offer Caine: the recognition of being in the presence of a natural killer.

"All who know your granddaughter desire nothing beyond her welfare," I told her. "We are agreed that she can do no better than to remain in your care; and it is for this reason that I now create you Countess of Lyrissan—which you will hold in fief from Lady Faith—and further name you Steward of all the lands and holdings of the Marchionness until she reaches her majority."

"Countess?" she said. I watched her try the title on and discover that she liked its fit.

Which was as well. She cannot be returned to Earth, and she is an aristocrat to the bone. I confess that I had the interests of the Empire in mind: Placing a ruthless and frighteningly capable Businessman in control, for the next fifteen years, of what was sure to become our primary overland trade route would certainly redound to the Empire's benefit.

I had thought to make her title conditional—to make her swear to give over her vendetta against Caine—but Hari himself had earlier persuaded me otherwise. "Let her be who she is," he'd said. "You put a rule on her like that, she'll just start trying to figure out ways around it. And in the meantime, she'll be pissed at you for making her go to the trouble. Avery Shanks is a bad enemy to have. Let me worry about her. In the end, she'll understand that hurting me hurts Faith; she'd chew off her own arm first."

This might have been my first true lesson in governance: Sometimes, to accomplish more, do less.

And then, inevitably, there was Raithe.

I think of him often, now, and when I think of him, I see him as he was before me in that Audience: kneeling upon the steps below the Oaken Throne. He kept his head lowered, refusing to meet my eye. His left hand he had held as a fist before him, wrapped in layer after layer of linen to the size of a white fabric boxing glove. While he knelt, the oil from his hand had slowly soaked out through the linen, until it dripped upon the steps before him like black tears.

He had come in search of a doom. He wished his tale to end
with punishment for his crimes.

I didn't want to judge him. I had seen all that he has suffered,
all he has done, and all that has been done to him. He is a very
lonely, very troubled young man.

Caine and I had discussed Raithe, as well, for I had anticipated this moment.

"Better keep him close," Caine had advised. "That fucker's
dangerous. He's only gonna get more dangerous as he goes
along. You need him where you can keep an eye on him."

"What do you have in mind?"

"I was thinking," Caine had said, a wicked glint sharpening
his smile, "that he'd make a pretty good Ambassador to the Infinite Court."

I thought about that for a while.

While I was thinking, Caine had gone on: "Get Raithe installed here, and I'm pretty sure between the two of you, you
could get Damon on the Council of Brothers. That's the place for
him: making policy."

"You could be right," I admitted.

"You're better off with Raithe. You need somebody who isn't
afraid to break a rule here and there."

"Like you."

"Me?" He laughed. "I don't break rules. I don't even notice
them."

I remember musing how alike Raithe and Hari were, in so
many ways, and I made mention of this. "In a sense, you're almost like father and son."

"Yeah," he grunted. "Not in a good sense."

"Have you ever wondered if you might *be* his father? You told
me he's illegitimate—that his mother was a prostitute in
Ankhana—and his age would be about right. You said you were
pretty wild, in those days."

"Nah, he's not my son," he said carelessly. "Might be yours,
though."

I stared, drop-jawed and blinking. "You must be joking."

"No, I'm not. That's what makes it so funny. His mother was a
Korish whore at the Exotic Love; I didn't hang out at the Exotic
in those days—I couldn't afford to look through the goddamn
doors, let alone buy a girl. My place was Fader's, over in the
Warrens."

"Fader's," I said hollowly, caught in memories a quarter century old. "I remember Fader."

"Yeah, well, she's dead now. You used to work at the Exotic, right?"

I nodded, numb.

"You remember a girl named Marte? Dark skinned, tiny?"

"Marte—I do, I think."

"Ever bang her?"

"Caine—"

"Come on, you can tell me. Did you?"

"I—I'm not sure. I might have. I had a lot of sex in those days, Hari, and I wasn't often sober."

"Well, he's got your build. I don't know what color your eyes were, before the surgeries—"

"Blue."

He shrugged. "And he's got all these mind powers and shit, and you're the bust-ass thaumaturge, right? You gotta admit it's possible."

"Yes," I murmured slowly. "I suppose I do."

All this swirled through my mind as I looked down upon him in the Great Hall. I tried to persuade him to drop his request; he is not, after all, my subject. Any punishment for his crimes must come from the Council of Brothers, for he retains his rank of Ambassador, with its attendant diplomatic immunity. "Don't preach law to me," he said there. "I don't need law. I need justice."

His plea moved me, and so I reluctantly consented.

"This, then, is your doom, Raithe of Ankhana." I pointed down at the pool of oil collecting on the step. "You are now the chokepoint of the Blind God's ambitions for this world; it is through you its power will still seek to poison us. Your doom is to resist the Blind God with every breath, and to struggle every day to repair the damage he has done through you."

He said, "How can I—?"

"You cannot. You will strive without respite until the day of your death, always knowing that you will ultimately fail. Always knowing that the instant you surrender, things you love will begin to die."

For a long moment he knelt there, his head lowered; and then without a word he slowly and deliberately used the hem of his robe to mop up the oil that had dripped from his hand. Then he touched his forehead to the stain, rose, and backed out of my presence.

I watched him go in silence.

"That's kinda harsh."

There is a small alcove behind the Oaken Throne. Within the alcove, there is a chair, set so that its occupant can peer out an unobtrusive spygate concealed within the ornate carvings of the wall; it was through this spygate that the dark, dry voice came.

"You think so? What I gave him wasn't punishment, it was a gift," I said softly. "I gave his life purpose. Meaning."

"Some gift. Next Christmas? Cards only, huh?"

I allowed myself a gentle chuckle. "I still wish you'd let me give you a title."

"Forget it. I have other plans." Hari had, over the past day, dropped veiled hints that he and the god had reached some sort of rapprochement. "There are some places," he'd admitted, "where our interests coincide."

"Hari—"

"Drop it, Kris. Like I told you the first time—" When he had turned down my every offer, from Duke of Public Order down to what he called Baronet of Buttfuck Nowhere. "—if I hold a title from you, some people are gonna hold the Empire accountable for shit I do. Believe me, Kris, you don't want that. Believe me."

I found I did believe him.

"And what is it you're going to do?"

His voice warmed with that familiar wicked grin. "Make trouble."

12

HOURS BECAME DAYS that turned to weeks. I kept myself buried in work—which was primarily discovering whom among the nobility I could trust to administrate the Empire's business. I also helped Lady Avery and Lady Faith establish their household; Francis Rossi, the unfortunate Actor Kier and I had kidnapped so long ago, became Lady Faith's aide. Caine trusts him, and the new Marchioness needs someone who can not only protect and defend her person, but can translate her English into Westerling. Lady Avery has already gathered a substantial cadre of former Actors to be her agents. I saw little of Caine during those weeks, by my choice.

I could not face him.

I had made one dreadful mistake, a mistake that haunted me, poisoning my every waking moment, until the only answer my horror would allow was the distraction of constant work.

I had looked into the abyss.

This was how I did it:

"I need to know, Hari," I said one day. "I need to know how you knew it would work. When you killed Ma'elKoth. How could you have possibly known? How did you know he was not wholly the blind god? How did you know he would turn upon his master once you joined him with the river? How did you know you weren't handing the enemy the exact victory it most desired?"

Finally I came to the real question, which I barely dared to ask. "How did you know you weren't destroying the world, instead of saving it?"

"Ma'elKoth asked me the same thing,"

"And?"

He shrugged. "I didn't."

I stared, speechless.

"I thought I was dead, Kris," he said. "There was no way Kollberg and the Social Police were gonna let me walk out of there. All I could do was try to save Faith."

My mouth opened, and a chill coiled within my guts. "You . . . all you could—"

"I didn't even know that killing Ma'elKoth with Kosall would channel him into the river. Didn't have a clue. How could I? All I knew was that he was the one who had the hold on Faith. She was the link to the river, but he was the link to her. So I killed him. He's dead; she's off the hook. Then Soapy shoots my ass off, and I'm dead, too. The blind god gets the sword—it doesn't need her anymore. Raithe was gonna leave her with the elves. They'd have looked after her, healed her as best they could. She might have had some kind of life." He shrugged again. "It was the best I could do."

Still half dumbstruck, I stammered, "Then—then your plan— you didn't—all this—?"

"That *was* the plan. The only plan I had."

"From the beginning . . ." I murmured.

"Yeah. From as soon as I understood what was going on."

"All this—the prisoners, the Faces, the Monastics. The destruction of the city. Raithe. Me. You used us all."

"Yeah."

"You made all this happen just to save one little girl."

He nodded. "And to take a chunk out of Ma'elKoth. Leave the world something to remember me by."

He spread his hands as though offering a hug to my horrified stare. "Hey, what can I say? I am who I am."

"Yes," I agreed numbly. "Yes, you are."

"You never know how things'll play out. You can't. The universe doesn't work that way." He grinned at me. "So cheer the fuck up, huh?"

"No, I—no, I mean . . ." I shook my head, trying to fit all this into my reality. "You found yourself on a precipice, in the dark. So you jumped."

"Every day, Kris. Every fucking day."

And he sounded *happy* about it.

I can't be happy about it. I can barely even think about it. It makes me feel empty: hollow, fragile, broken inside.

It's all so *meaningless*—

I have been judged with every judgment I have pronounced. Like t'Passe, I represent a people suddenly granted the full rights of Ankhanan citizens, whether we want them or not. Like Kierendal, I am sentenced to live without those I could not save. Like Faith, I must take comfort from a title and power bestowed—inflicted—upon me without my desire or my consent. Like Raithe, I have been given the thorny gift of purpose.

Like Caine, the world now asks of me only that I be who I am.

What have I done to deserve this?

Hari likes to quote Nietzsche: "And when you gaze into the abyss, remember that the abyss gazes also into you."

My only reply is the mantra of Conrad's Kurtz.

I am aware that this is yet another failure of character, that other, stronger men do not suffer from the nausea of the void. I am also aware of the gape of hell beneath my feet. The history of both my worlds is replete with monsters called kings, and demons called emperors.

In every case, they became so simply because, in a universe without meaning, there was no reason not to.

And here is another gift I have been given, far greater than I can possibly deserve: When the horror overwhelms me, I have someone to whom I can always turn, who will always save my life.

13

CAINE TOOK ANOTHER long, slow sip of the hundred-year-old Tinnaran in his snifter and made a face. "Know what really sucks?" he said. "On this whole fucking planet, nobody makes a decent scotch."

We sat together in the palace library, long after midnight. I sat at this very table, near the warmth of a slowly wavering lamp flame. Caine sprawled across an overstuffed chair upholstered in glistening crushed velvet the color of black cherries, while we shared a cask of the palace cellar's finest brandy. "There are worse problems," I said.

"For you, maybe. How am I supposed to face old age without Laphroaig?"

"Hari—"

He waved his snifter at me. "Pour me some more of this nasty shit, huh? It's hard enough to be serious when I'm sober; it's impossible when I'm only half drunk."

I tipped another splash of brandy into his glass, and he swirled it while he waited for it to warm to his hand. After I refilled his, I added a splash to my own. I took a long drink and replenished again before I replied. "Do you remember the last time we sat and drank together like this?"

He lifted his glass and stared at the lamp flame through the warm amber transparency of the brandy. "Last time, it was retsina. Remember?"

"Vividly."

"Twenty-five—no, twenty-seven, twenty-eight years ago, it must be. Yeah, I was thinking of that. You were pretty down that night, too."

"Too?"

He gave me a knowing *Oh, come on, now* look. "Shit, Kris, if we were on Earth, I'd be taking you to an emergency room somewhere to get your serotonin balance adjusted."

I suddenly found my brandy much more interesting than I did his face.

"Hey," he said, "you want to talk about it, we'll talk. You don't want to talk, we'll drink. I'm easy."

For a time, we did just that: sat, and drank. He seemed to enjoy the quiet; for me, the silence rang with anomie, and I felt as though my chair were made of knives.

At length, I made a try. "I only—" I began. "I remember, a few days before I left on freemod, I wrote the story of what happened to us at the Conservatory, and what we did. I remember wondering what our lives would be like, twenty or thirty years from then. How we might meet again."

"You didn't come close to this, huh?"

"Not really."

"Is that a problem?"

"Maybe. Maybe that's part of it."

"How come?"

"I just can't make myself understand, Hari," I said helplessly. "I can't figure out what I did right, and what I did wrong. Here I am: Emperor of Ankhana. Power. Limitless wealth. Eternal youth. And I can't even decide if this is a reward or a punishment."

"I might not be the right guy to be having this conversation with," Caine said, chuckling. "For me, breathing is its own reward."

"How can you *laugh*?"

"What, should I cry? Would that make more sense?"

"I don't know, Hari." I set down my glass and turned away from him. "I don't even know what sense is, anymore."

Suddenly my face was in my hands.

"Hey—hey, come on, Kris." He'd lost his bantering tone, and his hand was warm on my shoulder.

"Maybe laughter is the only answer," I said, rubbing my burning eyes. "It's all so . . . ridiculous, you know? How could these things have happened to me? How can I possibly be who I have become? I don't understand, you see? I need to understand, and I *can't*. Everything is so . . . *random*. I can't make it make *sense*."

"Yeah, no shit. What did you expect?"

Slowly, I raised my head once more. "I don't know. Maybe—maybe I expected that I would have *learned* something. That I'd have an idea what it all meant."

"The meaning of life? Shit, Kris, I can help you there."

"You can?"

"Sure. It doesn't mean anything."

Now I did laugh—bitterly, hopelessly. "Some help."

"It is what it is, Kris. One day you're alive. One day you're dead. One day you're a loser. One day you're king of the fucking world. No reason. It doesn't mean anything. It just *is*."

"I don't accept that. I can't accept that."

He shrugged. "Everybody spends their whole lives pretending that shit isn't random. We trace connections between events, and we invest those connections with meaning. That's why we all make stories out of our lives. That's what stories are: ways of pretending that things happen for a reason."

"I keep thinking of my father—of the Ravenlock. Of my brother Torronell. What did they do to deserve such horrible deaths? How is it that I live to rule, and they died in agony?"

"How should I know? Those aren't my stories."

"Are they mine?"

"Maybe you shouldn't worry so much about their stories. Maybe you should just pay attention to their roles in *your* story. Let *them* worry about what they deserved or didn't deserve."

"Let the dead bury the dead," I said.

"Yeah. What you're gonna do about it, that's *your* story. You might find things make a little more sense."

"What kind of story can possibly make sense of that? What about all the innocent citizens of Ankhana who murdered each other in the plague? What about all the ones who burned to death? What about all the cowards who ran and hid and let others die, and now walk free in the sunlight?"

He took a slow, meditative draft of brandy and let it rest in his mouth while he considered.

"I had a lot of time to myself to think shit over not too long ago," he said at length, holding up his right hand so that the lamplight fell upon the scars the Shaft shackle had left on his wrist. "I'll tell you what I think. I think capital-L Life has no meaning in a human sense—it is what it is, like a rock, or the sun, or anything else. It means itself, and that's all. But that doesn't mean our *lives* have no meaning, you follow? Life might not have a meaning of its own, but the stories we tell about it do. You told me once that the universe is a structure of coincidence. It means whatever you decide it means. Which is another way of saying: What your life means depends on how you tell the story."

"That's not good enough," I said. Like all words of wisdom,

those had been much easier to say than to accept. "What meaning can I possibly give a story like mine?"

"How the fuck should I know? Maybe if you just tell it the best you can, it'll grow its own meaning."

And that is what I hold on to, now. That is how he saved me, yet again.

It's my life.

What it means depends on how I tell the story.

14

I SAID GOOD-BYE to Caine in a grey dawn at the dockside, lashed by spits of winter rain. Lady Avery was already bundled into her cabin within the riverbarge, and the crew stood at ready, waiting for Caine.

Past his shoulder, as we embraced, I saw Lady Faith, still on deck, watching with wide, solemn eyes—making sure that her father was not going to leave her again. Beside her, Orbek stood in motionless guard, an assault rifle cradled in his massive arms.

I was at the dockside incognito, dressed in a commoner's tunic and pants, covered only by a woolen cloak that hung heavy and wet about my shoulders. I do not fear to walk unguarded among my subjects; I still have skills of hand and mind to defend myself at need, and the word of T'nnalldion that the Empire will not go untended should I fall.

Caine wore no cloak of his own, only a tunic and pants of black leather that seemed to bristle with knives at every angle. These made embracing him an uncomfortable business—

But I suppose it would have been so, regardless.

"What will you do, now?"

He smiled at me from under hair plastered flat by the freezing rain. "After I get Faith and Shanks settled in? Maybe it's better you shouldn't know. I don't want you to worry."

"I'm not your mother." I fisted him in the ribs and tried for a tone of cheerful banter. "I'm your king."

"Yeah, well, let's keep that just between us, huh?" Then he shrugged, and grinned at me. "It's occurred to me that if I'm gonna be raising a daughter on this world, I'm gonna want this to be a decent world to raise her on. So I'll be heading southwest—

down into warm weather. There's a place in northern Kor I need to visit. Chanazta'atsi."

"Chanazta'atsi?" The name was familiar, and after only a moment I remembered why. "There's a *dil* in Chanazta'atsi."

His grin spread. "I know."

Before I could pursue this further, his eyes shifted toward something over my shoulder and his smile faded. His face hardened to stone.

I followed his gaze. Toward us through the rain came a man dressed as I was, though the hood of his cloak was drawn up until it occulted his face. He carried a large black valise in his right hand, and only when I saw the bulge of white linen around his left did I realize who he was.

A twist of motion in my peripheral vision: Orbek adjusting his grip on the rifle to hold it at low-ready.

Caine stepped away from me and moved to intercept Raithe. He stopped midway, and his hand went beneath the hem of his tunic at the small of his back; it came out with a large, matte black automatic pistol, which he held against the back of his thigh, where Raithe could not see it. He waited, motionless, as Raithe approached. He said something that I did not hear, and Raithe replied by lifting the valise and offering it to Caine.

"It is the only gift I can offer that might have meaning," I heard him say. "And the greatest gift you can give in return is to accept it from my hand."

They spoke together then for some little time, while I watched.

As did Orbek.

As did Faith.

What they said to each other is not part of my story, but it was not long before Caine shrugged, showed Raithe the gun he held—and then put it away.

Raithe departed with a bare nod in my direction. Caine returned to my side and handed the valise to me. "You might find this useful," he said; then he explained to me what it was, and how it is used, and left me there on the dockside in the rain holding the Caine Mirror in its case.

"See you around," he said as the poleboys unmoored the barge and shoved it away from the dockside.

I could only wave.

He returned my wave with a nod; then as the freezing rain thickened toward sleet, shading the barge and all upon it to grey silhouettes, I saw his dim ghost place an arm around the blur of his daughter's shoulders, and they turned and went into the wash of firelight through the cabin door.

Orbek stood in the rain for a moment longer. He gave me one solemn nod, then followed them within.

I stood in the sleet until the barge could no longer be seen.

Then I came back here, to my writing table in the library, and poured myself more of this fine Tinnaran, and finally—hours or days later—summoned the courage to use Caine's gift to me.

15

SOME MONTHS AFTER the battle was over, war was finally declared. I wasn't there—I don't know the details—but I have a powerful and detailed imagination, which has proved accurate in the past.

I see it like this:

The members of the Board of Governors are summoned to an emergency plenary session; their personal implants—similar to thoughtmitters—alert them to the emergency, and each of them hurries to find a private place where they can activate without fear of discovery or interruption.

For Leisureman Marc Vilo, the alert comes while he's sitting on the toilet, off the master bedroom of his sprawling estate in the Sangre de Cristo Mountains. This being already more than private enough for his purposes, he speaks the required code phrase, then sighs as the reality of the bathroom around him thins to translucency; his final independent thought, as his consciousness melds with the electronic group mind that is the Bog, is that this business of being on the Board—far from the huge accession of power it had seemed to him as an outsider—is really kind of a pain in the ass. Especially now that the entire Studio system has been shut down for more than a month. What he finds, though, is electrifying.

Every POV screen in every Studio on Earth has suddenly come back to life, and they all show the same thing.

Caine.

He squats on his heels in some kind of desert setting: a rock outcropping at his back, scraps of scrub like sagebrush around his feet. He wears his familiar costume of black leather, and his familiar wolf-grin. His hair is a bit more grey than some of the Bog recall, and his waist a trace thicker, but there is nothing about him that looks the faintest bit old, or soft.

He bears no resemblance to the former Chairman of the San Francisco Studio.

Shortly thereafter, telemetry confirms from whom the POV is being transmitted: an Actor named Francis Rossi, aka J'Than. Several of the Bog comment that this seems ironic—wasn't J'Than the Actor who had been used as a camera some months ago, when all this began? A lightning consult of the Studio's on-line data files confirms that he is.

Caine, meanwhile, seems to understand that his audience is now assembled. "Hi there," he says, darkly cheerful. "You fuckers know who I am, so I'll bite right to the gristle."

He stands. "I know there are people over there who are thinking, Yeah, big deal, we'll reopen the colonies. Yeah, we'll find a way around this transfer shield, and then we'll send Actors and tanks and guns and all the rest of that shit. I know people are thinking that. I know I'm talking to some of those people right now.

"I know you're thinking: In the end, numbers and technology let you do whatever you want. You're thinking there really isn't dick we can do about it. Well, guess what?

"I'm here to tell you that you're wrong.

"We can hurt you."

He walks away, around the outcrop of wind-eroded sandstone, and J'Than follows. Caine stares off, far down a long, sloping hill; several buildings cluster in the twilit distance, window lights winking on as the sun gives way to night. "Sure, you can probably find a technological answer that'll get you back to Overworld. I just wanted to let you know that we can get to Earth."

He points down at those buildings. "See? You know what that is?"

Marc Vilo, alone among the Board of Governors, does.

Holy crap, he thinks. *That's my house.*

Something seizes J'Than from behind—possibly Caine himself—and he seems to fly through the air: desert rolls beneath him, and the complex soars to meet him with terrifying speed.

In his bathroom, Marc Vilo's hand finds a hazily translucent key on the pad beside the toilet, and alarm klaxons blare.

They land on the pool deck, beside an artificial waterfall, and the shriek of sirens seems to please Caine in some darkly savage place. "Think about it," he says. "All of you. Okay, you can get at us. Now we can get at you. We know what your tanks can do to our cities. Imagine what a dragon can do to New York. Imagine being in a skyscraper in downtown Chicago while rockmagi liquefy its foundation.

"Imagine."

The general consensus of the Board is that Caine must be bluffing. Dwarfs? Dragons? Magick on that scale cannot be done on Earth—

As if in answer, Caine turns away from J'Than. "Ma'elKoth?"

A shaft of crimson flame bursts from his outstretched hands, and the building he faces explodes.

He watches it burn, grinning.

He turns back to J'Than and leans close, his face demon-lit by flames behind. "Marc? You home, old buddy? Knock fucking knock."

The Vilo Intercontinental secmen who guard the estate barely have a chance to prime their weapons before Caine scatters them with a tidal bore of fire. He strides among the buildings, and his merest glance strikes ablaze even the brick of the walls.

When he reaches the main house, he batters through the carbon-fiber-reinforced ceramic armor of the front door with his bare hands. Brick and stone shatter under his fists, and he disappears within, leaving the Actor staring helplessly after him.

He disappears from the view of the Bog. But Marc Vilo sees him when Caine rips the bathroom door from its hinges. To Marc—half his consciousness subsumed in the Board—Caine seems translucent, only partially there, but his half reality is doubly terrifying.

"Never expected you'd die on the toilet, huh?"

"Hari—" he says. "Hari, for the love of God, please—"

"Which god?"

"Hari, I'm begging you, please—c'mon, kid, all the stuff I've done for you—I *made* you. Please, you can't—"

Caine shakes his head. "You of all people, Marc. Of all the people in the world—in *any* world—"

His lips stretch open over his teeth, feral and cold. "You should have known better than to fuck with my family."

That is the last Vilo sees: his eyeballs boil and burst in the first wash of flame. He does, however, have time to hear himself scream.

To the Bog, watching through J'Than's eyes, it seems the house detonates like a fuel-air bomb. J'Than himself is hurled tumbling through the air by the force of it, and lands gasping and stunned upon the lush green grass that defines this desert home's front lawn. For several seconds, the Bog allows itself to believe that Caine might have perished in the explosion, but then he walks out of the flames. Unhurt.

Not even singed.

"You want a war?" he says with that same dark and savage cheer. "Bring it on."

He leans so close to J'Than that his teeth fill the world. "As of right now, the Studio is out of business. So is the Overworld Company.

"Overworld is *closed*."

He puts his hands on J'Than's face.

"Thank you, and good night."

The light from the last Actor's eyes contracts to a point, and winks out.

16

So:

Here I am.

At my desk, my head full of stories.

There are so many heroes in these stories: Hari, and Caine; Raithe, and the Caineslayer; Avery Shanks and Kierendal and Damon of Jhanthogen Bluff—

Tan'elKoth, of course.

And, I suppose—in my backward way—even me.

I remember reading somewhere that the name for how we structure reality is myth: that myths are stories that offer a perception of order within the chaos of existence.

I'm still not sure I will ever understand, but I think I see how to survive without understanding. I will tell the story as best I can, and let it grow its own meaning. And if I can't find myths that properly order the chaos of my life, I'll make up some of my own.

My story begins:

A tale is told of twin boys born to different mothers.

One is dark by nature, the other light. One is rich, the other poor. One is harsh, the other gentle. One is forever youthful, the other old before his time.

One is mortal.

They share no bond of blood or sympathy, but they are twins nonetheless.

They each live without ever knowing that they are brothers.

They each die fighting the blind god.

THERE ARE SOME who say that Time is itself a hammer: that each slow second marks another tap that makes big rocks into little rocks, waterfalls into canyons, cliffs into beaches.

There are some who say that Time is instead a blade. They see the dance of its razored tip, poised like a venomous snake, forever ready to slay faster than the eye can see.

And there are some who say that Time is both hammer and blade.

They say the hammer is a sculptor's mallet, and the blade is a sculptor's chisel: that each stroke is a refinement, a perfecting, a discovery of truth and beauty within what would otherwise be blank and lifeless stone.

And I name this saying wisdom.

ALL ACTORS HAVE A PRECISELY
DEFINED ROLE—
to risk their lives on Overworld
in interesting ways.
It's not personal; it's just market share.

Caine has long been the best of the best.
A generation grew up watching the
superstar's every adventure.
Now he's chairman of the world's largest
studio and he's making changes.

Higher powers of Overworld and Earth don't
approve. It's just business.

But for Caine, it's his wife, their daughter,
his invalid father, his status, his home.

And it's always personal.

HEROES DIE

by Matthew Woodring Stover

Published by Del Rey Books.
Available at bookstores everywhere.

Visit Del Rey Books online and learn more about your favorite authors

There are many ways to visit Del Rey online:

The Del Rey Internet Newsletter (DRIN)
A free monthly publication e-mailed to subscribers.
It features descriptions of new and upcoming books,
essays and interviews with authors and editors,
announcements and news, special promotional offers,
signing/convention calendar for our authors and
editors, and much more.

To subscribe to the DRIN: send a blank e-mail to
join-ibd-dist@list.randomhouse.com
or you can sign up on Del Rey's Web site.

The DRIN is also available for your PDA devices—
go to www.randomhouse.com/partners/avantgo for
more information, or visit http://www.avantgo.com
and search for the Books@Random channel.

Del Rey Digital (www.delreydigital.com)
This is the portal to all the information and
resources available from Del Rey online including:

• Del Rey Books' Web site, including sample chapters
of every new book, a complete online catalog, special
features on selected authors and books, news and
announcements, readers' reviews and more

• Del Rey Digital Writers' Workshop, a members-only,
FREE writers' workshop

Questions? E-mail us...
at delrey@randomhouse.com